THE WESTERN WIZARD

Also in Millennium

THE LAST OF THE RENSHAI

THE
WESTERN
WIZARD

Mickey Zucker Reichert

MILLENNIUM
An Orion Book
LONDON

Copyright © Mickey Zucker Reichert 1992

All rights reserved

The right of Mickey Zucker Reichert to be identified as the author of
this work has been asserted by her in accordance with the
Copyright, Designs and Patents Act 1988

Interior map by Michael Gilbert

This edition first published
in Great Britain in 1993 by
Millennium
An imprint of Orion Books Ltd
Orion House, 5 Upper St Martin's Lane
London WC2H 9EA

First published by DAW Books, USA in 1992

A CIP catalogue record for this book is available from the British Library

ISBN: (Csd) 1 85798 108 1
(Ppr) 1 85798 070 0

Millennium
Book Eighteen

Typeset at The Spartan Press Ltd,
Lymington, Hants
Printed and bound in Great Britain by Clays Ltd. St Ives plc

To Mark Moore
for listening
(and much more).

Acknowledgments

I would like to thank the following people:

Sheila Gilbert, Jonathan Matson, Jody Lee, Mikie Gilbert, and D. Allan Drummond.

Also my 'evil stepsons': Benjamin Jordan Moore & Jonathan Lager Moore, with love.

Contents

'We . . . were by nature the children of wrath.'
– Ephesians 2:3

Prologue

For centuries, the Amirannak Sea had kicked spindrift on the ragged Northland shores, but the Northern Sorceress, Trilless, watched waters glazed with calm. Perched upon a seaside cliff in the country of Asci, she stared into the fjord, watching wind scarcely ruffle ocean the color of steel. The tide tugged so gently that the waters barely seemed to pulse in time with her heartbeat.

Trilless had come to this unpopulated shoreline for the quiet solace it offered, yet the ancient champion of all goodness found no peace within or without. For all its stillness, the ocean seemed coiled and restless, locked into the dark instant of lull that preceded the most violent storms. As if in answer, the memories and surviving slivers of identity from Trilless' eighteen predecessors seemed to writhe within her. Always before, they had remained quiescent, a conglomerate of experiences and references she called upon in time of need. Now, they heaved and fidgeted like tempest-wracked waves, while the ocean itself remained uncharacteristically stagnant.

More than four centuries ago, the ceremony that had established Trilless as the Northern Sorceress, one of the four Cardinal Wizards, had also, by necessity, claimed the life of her direct predecessor. Trilless knew that the pool of knowledge granted to her by that ceremony made her the most powerful of her line, just as her own successor would gain the benefit of her lore and become even more wise, knowledgeable, and skilled. The first four Cardinal Wizards established by Odin, including the original Northern Sorceress, had no magical powers. Haunted by dreams and images, they had written or spoken their prophecies, leaving them for later, more adept successors to fulfil. Now, Trilless found herself haunted by the first prediction of the first Northern Sorceress:

In an age of change
When Chaos shatters Odin's ward
And the Cardinal Wizards forsake their vows
A Renshai shall come forward.

Hero of the Great War
He will hold legend and destiny in his hand
And wield them like a sword.
Too late shall he be known unto you:

The Golden Prince of Demons.

Clearly, that promised age of change had come. Trilless knew a tense expectancy that seemed to follow her, an inescapable current that suffused the world and all the creatures in it. Some of the tenets had already come to pass. Goaded by Carcophan, who was the current Southern Wizard, King Siderin of the Eastlands had launched the Great War against the mixed races of the Westlands.

Trilless' brow knit. A scowl formed naturally on her creased features at the thought of Carcophan, her evil opposite. Law and propriety had barred her from directly observing or taking part in this war. But, through magic, she had glimpsed those parts which involved Northmen. Only one of the eighteen Northern tribes had chosen to aid the Westerners in the War; the Vikerians had gone, allied to the Town of Santagithi. Their second-in-command, a lieutenant called Valr Kirin, showed promise as a warrior and as a possible champion of goodness. But, despite his competence, the hero of the Great War was not Kirin 'The Slayer.'

Trilless' thoughts flowed naturally to the Renshai who had earned the title 'Golden Prince of Demons,' Colbey Calistinsson. She saw his cold blue-gray eyes in a hard face scarcely beginning to show age. He kept his mixed gold and white locks hacked short, a style that looked out of place amid the other Northmen's war braids. Though relatively small, he moved with a strength and agility she had never seen matched in any warrior or acrobat. At sixty-five, Colbey was older than any Renshai in history, except for the ancient Episte who had died a decade and a half ago. Enamored with war, Renshai rarely lived through their thirties, and inbreeding had fostered a racial feature that made them seem younger than their actual ages. This, combined with a custom of naming infants for brave warriors slain in battle, had given rise to rumors that Renshai drank blood to remain eternally young.

Trilless sighed, missing the connection between Colbey and the doom suggested by the first Northern Sorceress' forecast. So far, the Renshai's actions fell well within the tenets of Northern honor. She found him as predictable as any of her own followers, though he had chosen neutrality over goodness. She doubted any mortal could challenge the Cardinal Wizards, let alone begin the *Ragnarok*, the great war destined to destroy the gods. Still, the prophecy implied that he would have some connection to the primordial chaos that Odin had banished to create the world.

Below Trilless, the ocean remained gray and still. The presences of her predecessors shifted fretfully, reminding her that the poem never stated that Colbey would directly cause the Wizards' broken vows, the change, or the rise of chaos. Yet just the linking of his name with those events made their imminence loom. *How many more years can a sixty-five-year-old mortal have?* Trilless answered her own question. *At most, a decade.* To a sorceress nearly five centuries old, it seemed like an eye blink.

Trilless rose, her wrinkled features lost in the shadow of her hood. She wore a white cloak over robes so light they enhanced an otherwise nearly invisible tinge of pink in her ivory-pale Northern skin. To the Northmen, white symbolized purity. And, though no law of gods or Wizards made her dress the part of goodness to the point of caricature, she chose to do so anyway. It reminded her always of her job and her vows, and it gave added credence to her station. Odin's constraints against direct interference kept her contacts with mankind rare and brief. Few enough men believed in Wizards anymore.

Other concerns touched Trilless then. The Southern Wizard had disappeared even before the Great War had begun. Surely, he knew that his champion had been defeated; yet he had chosen not to acknowledge the loss or the rout of his followers. The experiences of Trilless' predecessors led her to believe that he had retired to a private haven to sulk. It was not uncommon for a Cardinal Wizard to withdraw for decades, returning only when large-scale events made a swift or strong defense necessary.

Yet Trilless knew her opposite too well. Despite two centuries as a Cardinal Wizard, Carcophan had scarcely more patience than a mortal. She could not help but admire his dedication to his cause though it stood in direct opposition to her own. She guessed Carcophan had left to plot in quiet; and when he struck, she knew it would be with sudden and unexpected competence and efficiency. His predecessors had relied on subtlety, insidiously infusing the followers of neutrality and goodness with his evil. Trilless and her predecessors had done much the same thing with their goodness. Over the millennia, this had led to a balance and a blurring of the boundaries and definitions of their causes. But Carcophan tended to choose warrior's tactics: abrupt, committed strategies that resulted either in massive victories, or, as in the Great War, in wholesale defeat. *I need to know what he's planning.*

And Trilless faced one more urgent worry. Odin had decreed that the number of Cardinal Wizards should always remain four; yet she had not heard from Tokar, the Western Wizard, in nearly half a century. Ordinarily, this would not have bothered her; the actions and locations of the paired champions of neutrality, the Eastern and

Western Wizards, meant little to her. But when she had last seen Tokar, he had just chosen his apprentice, which meant that his time of passing was imminent. As well, the attack by Carcophan's champion should have brought the Western Wizard into the foreground. But it had not.

Shadimar, the Eastern Wizard, had taken over the tasks the Western Wizard had been destined to fulfill. While Odin's Law allowed this, the Eastern Wizard was always the weaker of the two and far less capable of handling his stronger compatriot's duties in addition to his own. Odin's laws stated that if a Wizard was destroyed, the others must band together to replace him; but strict protocol regulated who could initiate the proceedings. Neither Trilless nor Carcophan benefited from neutrality, and their causes could only strengthen without the Western Wizard to oppose them. Had Shadimar requested their aid, Trilless and Carcophan would have had no choice but to give it. There could be only two reasons why Shadimar had chosen not to do so. Either the Western Wizard still lived, or Shadimar was as uncertain as she of the fate of the Western Wizard. Until Shadimar could prove his partner's death, revealing his need to work alone could only make him vulnerable.

Trilless wrestled with the problem. She knew there were only two ways to discover the fate of the Western Wizard, and both seemed frighteningly dangerous and difficult. The first involved trying to link minds with the missing Wizard. This had its practical difficulties. Although the Wizards could touch thoughts, to do so uninvited was considered a rudeness bordering on attack; and it required knowledge of the other Wizard's location. That could only be achieved by physical means, and Tokar had not deigned to answer the messages she had sent him. The second means of gaining knowledge involved summoning. The idea sent a shiver of dread through her. Several Cardinal Wizards, including some of the Northern Wizards, had called forth creatures called demons from the magical plane of Odin's banished Chaos. But Trilless had never done so.

Trilless looked out over the Amirannak Sea, her legs braced and her focus distant. Clearly she had no choice. Given his recent defeat, Carcophan could not afford the risk of a summoning. Weak and burdened with the tasks of two Wizards, Shadimar could hardly be expected to accept the peril either. Of the three Cardinal Wizards who had been killed unexpectedly, two of them had been slaughtered by demons, and both slain in such a manner had been Eastern Wizards. Though knowledge of the Western Wizard would serve Shadimar best, Trilless could understand his hesitation. Still, this ignorance could not continue. Someone had to determine the fate of the Western Wizard. Clearly that someone would have to be Trilless.

The memories of the previous Northern Wizards fluttered, some in agreement and a few in opposition to the decision. Then, as Trilless came to her conclusion, the suggestions disappeared beneath a rush of unified support. Those few who had summoned demons came to the forefront with solid advice and the words of the necessary incantation.

Trilless closed her eyes, blanking her mind except for the guidance of her predecessors. Slowly, cautious to the point of paranoia with every syllable, she began the incantation that would call the weakest of demons to her.

Gradually, a dark shape formed above the glass-still waters. Horror shivered through Trilless from a source unlike any she had known before. The familiar tingle of magic strengthened to a stabbing rumble that tore through her like pain. Space and time upended, physical concepts that lost all meaning. She gritted her teeth, not daring to cry out and lose the steady, unwavering cadence of her incantation. She grounded her reason on the constancy of Odin's world and the necessary constraints of his laws. The collective consciousness of her predecessors began a low, changeless chant that gave her focus.

As the creature's presence strengthened, Trilless shifted her spell, weaving tangles of enchantment about the hazy shadow. She worked with methodical efficiency, winding webs that shimmered white against the shapeless, sable bulk of the demon she had summoned.

'Lady.' The demon's voice made the threatening hiss of a viper seem benign. 'You called me to your world. You will pay with the lives of followers, and perhaps with your own. You had best hope your wards can bind me.'

Trilless tossed her hooded head without reply, keeping her attention fully focused. She knew that when the time came to return the demon it would demand payment in blood. But the amount it took would depend upon the quickness and competence of her craft. *Dismiss it, distract it, and slay it.* Trilless let the process cycle through her mind, hoping the knowledge of her predecessors would enhance the procedures while she concentrated on more immediate matters. *Stay alert*, she reminded herself. *To lose even one life to this abomination would be a travesty.*

Demons cared nothing for good or evil. They followed no masters and obeyed no laws. The only feature about it on which Trilless could rely was its certain and violent inconsistency. And the longer she kept it here, the stronger it would grow. 'By Odin's law I have called you here. You must answer my questions and perform a service to the best of your knowledge and abilities.' Trilless hated wasting time with formality and information she believed they both already understood, but her predecessors assured her of the necessity. Unlike men the demons had no natural constraints. They were bound only by the laws thrust upon them and then only when on the world Odin created.

Wound with enchantments, the demon assumed a vague man-shape. Its eyes looked like points of fire in a bed of dying embers. 'Ask, then, Wizard. But hope your answers are worth the blood I shall claim in return.' A glob of spittle fell from his mouth and struck the ocean with a hiss. Smoke curled from the water as its surface broke in widening rings.

Trilless raised her arms to a sky gone dull as slate. She knew that the demon, though forced to answer with truth, could deceive to the limits of that boundary. Clearly, it would reveal more of the information that it wanted her to have, skewed in the direction of primordial chaos. She would need to phrase her questions carefully. 'At this time, is there a living Western Wizard?'

The demon faded into the gloom. Its semisolid form oozed beneath Trilless' wards. Abruptly, wind chopped the jeweled calm of the sea, took down the hood of the sorceress' cloak, and spilled her white hair into her face. But the demon's bonds held. The gale withered and dropped. The demon's eyes gleamed, and its jaws parted to reveal pointed teeth as dark as its form. 'Lady, I do not know.'

Trilless gritted her teeth, prodded by frustration and rage. She dared not believe she had taken such a risk for nothing. 'Who does know?' She tried to keep her mood hidden, but her question emerged like a shout.

'More powerful demons,' it suggested, then laughed. 'Perhaps.' Its features contorted to a blur, then returned to a facelike configuration. 'Though one of your own did witness the ceremony.'

Trilless considered. The demon had volunteered the information; apparently, it had more to say on this topic, and that intrigued her. Its words gave her two courses to follow, and she chose the more promising one. 'By ceremony, do you mean Tokar's ceremony of passage?'

'Yes.'

'So Tokar is dead?'

'As dead as any Cardinal Wizard can be. His being, as such, was utterly destroyed.'

Trilless concentrated on the demon's explanation. A Wizard's ceremony of passage did result in the utter destruction of body and soul, leaving only memories, including misconceptions and weaknesses, that joined the collective consciousness and became a part of his apprentice. 'What happened to Tokar's successor?'

'I do not know.'

'Is he alive?'

'I do not know.'

'Is he dead?'

'I do not know.'

Trilless abandoned this line of questioning, following the other path instead. 'You said that one of my own witnessed the ceremony.'

The bulk of the demon darkened until it seemed less a being and more the absence of being, a dense hole in the cosmos. 'I said this.'

'Who?' Trilless asked. Then, realizing she had left the question far too vague, she clarified. 'Who witnessed the Western Wizard's ceremony of passage?'

'Many birds.'

The answer seemed obvious. The Western Wizard had an empathic link with birds similar to the Eastern Wizard's connection to land animals and her own with denizens of the ocean. The Southern Wizard could command the creatures of transition, those that lived part of their life cycle on land and part in water or those land creatures that laid eggs. Recognizing the demon's answer as delay, Trilless pressed. 'Who is the "one of my own" who witnessed the ceremony?'

'Carcophan.'

Trilless' eyes narrowed. The response seemed unlikely. 'The Western Wizard witnessed Tokar's ceremony of passage?'

'No.'

Trilless froze at the seeming contradiction, retracing her thoughts for the mistake. She rephrased the question more carefully. 'Was there a mortal or a Wizard present at the Western Wizard's ceremony of passage who was not Tokar or his apprentice?'

'Yes,' the demon said, supplying nothing more.

'Name all the mortals or Wizards present at the Western Wizard's ceremony of passage.'

The demon's face became manlike enough to reveal a toothy grin. 'That, Lady, was not a question.'

Near-immortality had bestowed patience on Trilless. She did not allow the demon's stalling to fluster her. 'Who is the "one of my own" who witnessed the Western Wizard's ceremony of passage? And what makes you refer to him as "one of my own"?'

The demon chose to answer both questions at once. 'He is a Northman, Wizard. Men call him Deathseeker. The gods use the title Kyndig.' He used the Northern pronunciation *Kawn*-dee, which translated to 'Skilled One.' The demon's features achieved a near-human sneer. 'You call him the Golden Prince of Demons.'

Trilless recoiled as if slapped. Immediately sensing the new weakness in her wards, the demon thrust at the enchantments that held it. Hurriedly, Trilless fought vulnerability, plugging the gap with webs of utter purity. Her magic burned it. Screaming, the demon struggled backward, deeper into the sorceress' wards.

Annoyance made Trilless' head throb. Pain was a tool of evil, not

7

good. Despite the nature of the demon, she had no wish to torture it. She softened the magics of her bindings, and the demon's shrieks changed pitch to the deep rumble of laughter.

Trilless spoke in a controlled monotone. Over time, her magic was losing power while the demon gained more. She could not afford to keep it much longer. Yet, one question still begged asking. 'I know Carcophan is plotting against us already. Who is the Southern Wizard's new champion?'

The demon writhed in its bonds. It waved one splay-clawed hand and spoke in a voice that could quail a brave warrior. 'Carcophan has no champion yet.' The hand dissipated. Though not bound to say more, the demon chose to continue, perhaps hoping to further rattle its keeper. 'But it is fated. Carcophan shall command a swordsman unmatched by any other mortal.'

Trilless paled, but this time she retained control. 'Who is this mortal?'

'I do not know.'

'What more do you know about Carcophan's champion?'

'Only what I've told you.'

Another dead end. Trilless hesitated. There were more questions she would have liked to ask, but none seemed worth the risk. Clearly unless Colbey died before Carcophan selected his champion, he was the only mortal who answered the demon's description. That, combined with the early prophecy that linked the Golden Prince of Demons with *Ragnarok* left her little choice. Her course of action seemed clear. First, Colbey must be questioned about the ceremony he had witnessed. A Wizard's passage required the use of magics more potent than the sum of all the spells used throughout the centuries of his reign. Any interference could cause consequences she could only begin to contemplate. Since Colbey had become a follower of neutrality, his interrogation could only be carried out by Shadimar. Afterward, Trilless had no choice but to see to Colbey's death.

Odin's laws bound the Wizards to see that their predecessors' prophecies were fulfilled; yet, as far as she knew, no Wizard had been specifically assigned to instigate the *Ragnarok*. In fact, it would stand against the survival of nearly all of the gods, the Wizards, and the world to assign anyone to such a task. Fortunately, without a Wizard to back it, the prophecy had little chance of coming to fruition, and Trilless saw no reason why she should not oppose it. Still, it went against her many oaths to confront any mortal directly or to suggest that another Wizard do such a thing. Even if she did, Shadimar might mistrust her intentions. Their causes did, at times, come head to head. She could only choose her own champion, send him or her after Colbey, and hope that Shadimar did not step in the way. To let Carcophan's champion skew the balance toward evil meant a fate nearly as ugly to Trilless as the *Ragnarok*. And there was only one way to even the odds between Colbey and whatever champion she chose to send against him, *Ristoril, the White Sword of Power*. The calmness that accompanied this decision felt as right as the eternity she had dedicated herself to preserve. Many Northern Wizards before her had placed the Great Sword in a champion's hands.

'Demon,' Trilless said softly, her mind made up. 'You still owe me a service. I would have you retrieve the White Sword of Power.'

This once, the demon had no taunts. 'I shall fulfill your request, though it is folly. Should Carcophan recall the Dark Blade, his champion would still best yours by skill. You take an unnecessary risk with lives you claim to protect. Including your own.'

Trilless stood statue still. She knew the demon spoke truth. Another prophecy claimed that the *Ragnarok* would occur when all three Swords of Power existed in Odin's world of law at once. Previous mages had already crafted two of the Swords, storing them on the plane of magic when not in a champion's hands. Yet the third Sword had not yet been crafted, and Trilless believed it would require a joint effort of Eastern and Western Wizards to create it. So long as the Western Wizard did not exist, she was taking no risk. Without Ristoril, her champion had no chance at all against Carcophan's chosen one. Surely Carcophan knew this, too. He would have to guess that Trilless might call the White Sword against Colbey. After all, the Southern Wizard had been wise enough to withhold the Dark Sword from Siderin. 'You cannot defy me.'

'As you wish, Lady.'

Trilless tightened her control on the snarled webs of warding as the demon bellowed harsh, vulgar syllables that made her ears ache. Yet the result of his ravings was beautiful to behold. The sun shouldered through a crack in the clouds, as golden and bright as the elves who dwelt far north of the Amirannak Sea. Gradually, light emerged from the globe, streaming tendrils of sun that dropped from the sky and merged at Trilless' feet as a starry burst of energy.

Its brilliance obscured the demon who summoned it. Within the light, a shape took form. Silently, the Sorceress watched as the sun streamers guttered and sank, leaving only a great Sword sheathed in a worn leather scabbard. Despite its imposing size, the plain steel hilt suggested nothing of the Sword's power. Yet Trilless knew the Sword of Tranquillity as a mother knows her child.

Lightning flared, breaking the peace of the union between mistress and treasure. The demon's obligations finished, Trilless could no longer hold it. Enchanted fetters fell from it with a sound like breaking harp strings. The demon howled its challenge, each word louder than the one before. 'I've served you, Lady. *Now, I'll claim my BLOOD!*'

'No!' Trilless screamed. Breakers frothed against the cliffs as the sorceress pictured the demon ravaging innocents as the price for her knowledge. Tapped of power by the summons and wards, Trilless struggled to gather strength to call magics of slaying upon the demon. Yet, constrained by Odin's laws to never directly harm men or Wizards, Trilless had no practice with such spells. She had carefully drawn the sequence to the forefront of memory before summoning the creature, and she mouthed the syllables from rote. But now, her concentration seemed scattered, and the hubbub of internal suggestions only added to the confusion.

Vibrant sparks of sorcery flashed from Trilless, their glow rivaling the sun. They struck the dark shape of the demon, spattering harmlessly to stone. The demon laughed, huge, serrated wings unfurling from its dark formlessness. Blood-flecked saliva oozed from its mouth.

Despite her weakness and confusion, Trilless held her voice steady and raised one arm. The sleeve slid back, revealing pale, wrinkled flesh. 'Take my blood, Vile One. You shall have no other!'

Bound by the sacrifice, the demon sprang with a wavering howl. His wail filled Trilless' head, drawing and tugging, as if to pull out her soul. Claws tore her forearm like knives. She retreated, protective incantations burning her throat. Nothing of flesh or law could harm her, but she had dared to call a creature who could. Agony scattered her wits, and she called upon the memories of her predecessors for strength.

The sea surged and boiled. Trilless fell to her knees, drawing strength from the ocean's perfect basic power. She recovered her senses quickly and, with them, confidence. Her shouted sorceries regained their rhythm. Light flashed, blindingly brilliant against the demon's darkness, and the creature vanished before the spell sequence ended.

Trilless whispered the last few syllables from the deep-seated need for completeness. The demon's claw strikes trailed blood, four ugly gashes only magic could heal. Had she still been mortal, each would have stolen a decade from her time left to live; but this meant little to one who had survived four centuries and who would choose her own time of passing. She guessed this incident would have a profound significance when passed, with her soul, to her successor.

The tide accepted Trilless' blood and swirled it to the sea. Quietly, she began the sequence of magics that would restore the skin of her arm. The pain was not so easily banished, but she turned her concentration to the Sword for which she had paid. It lay so still, yet to her trained eyes so alive with magic. And, with that glance, came the memory of runes carved upon a tablet-shaped stone in the ocean, attributed to the early mages, though no Cardinal Wizard could trace the author through his memories:

A Sword of Gray,
A Sword of White,
A Sword of Black and chill as night.
Each one forged,
Its craftsman a Mage;
The three Blades together shall close the age.

When their oath of peace
The Wizards forsake,
Their own destruction they undertake.
Only these Swords
Their craftsmen can slay.
Each Sword shall be blooded the same rueful day.

When that fateful day comes
The Wolf's Age has begun.
Hati swallows the moon, and Sköll tears up the sun.

If, indeed, Odin had crafted those phrases, he foretold his own doom. By legend, the Wolf's Age began the *Ragnarok*, when the earth and heavens would run with the blood of men and gods.

Trilless retrieved the sword. It lay heavy in her hands. Summoning Ristoril to this world formed the first leg of a perilous tripod, and she had to believe that Carcophan would prove wise enough to keep his impatience and pride from doubling the danger.

The sorceress reminded herself of her own bold words. The Gray Sword had yet to be forged. Without the Western Wizard, she guessed it would be impossible. Lulled by this thought, Trilless rose and headed toward the Northland cities, trying to ignore the dark, forgotten chaos that hovered over the artifact. An aura of dread darkened her features and those of the sea.

Part I
Béarn's Return

1 Pudar's Homecoming

A half moon glazed light across the farm fields and forests of the central Westlands, and the sky seemed gorged with more stars than Colbey Calistinsson ever remembered seeing. Soldiers from a dozen different cities sprawled on grimy blankets or beds of piled leaves. Others gathered to talk or to play games with cards, stones, or dice, their laughter booming over the chorus of insects, the whirring calls of foxes, wolf howls, and the shy chitter of *wisules*. A general aura of fatigue still enwrapped the armies, even though three weeks had passed since the Great War ended, but triumph sweetened the exhaustion, tempering complaints and easing the grief over lost companions. Siderin had been defeated. The Eastlands had taken thousands of casualties; a long time would pass before they threatened the West again. And soon enough all the Westerners would be home.

Home. The word held little meaning for Colbey. Born during the Renshai's hundred-year exile from the Northlands, he had spent his childhood rushing from battle to battle with his tribe, conquering, gathering food and plunder, celebrating those lucky enough to die in the glory of battle, mourning those who lost their lives to lingering injury or infection, and then charging into war again. When not engaged in battle, he practiced for it or taught the techniques to others. To Colbey, violence was simply a way of life. He knew no other.

Yet, in a matter of days or weeks, that would change. Rache had died in the Great War, leaving Colbey as the only full-blooded Renshai in existence. And Colbey knew from experience that he could sire no children, even had there still been a Renshai woman with whom to try.

These thoughts made Colbey frown. Standing just beyond the protecting canvas of the officers' quarters, he stared out over fields so fertile they seemed to flow into one another like a vast green ocean. Fifty years ago, he had stood in this same location, looking out over Westerners' crops in the moonlight. Then, as always, his people had won the battle, but they had been the invaders not the defenders. Now, Colbey looked out over the campsites of five thousand men, nearly thirty-five hundred of them under his direct command, including the organized military of the great trading city of Pudar and the mustered farmers of dozens of tiny towns. *Colbey Calistinsson, the highest officer of the Westland's largest army. The last of the Renshai led Westerners to war.* The irony gnawed at him, quickly replaced by a sense of obligation. *But I'm not really the only Renshai.*

Colbey knew that bloodline meant little. By their own ancient laws, sword skill, not breeding, defined the Renshai. Rache's long-held belief that he was the last of the tribe had given him the right to teach the Renshai combat maneuvers to another. He had chosen Mitrian, the daughter of a town leader named Santagithi, who was the general of the remaining soldiers in the camp and the West's master strategist.

A good choice. Mitrian had a natural grace and dedication to the art; logically, Colbey supported Rache's decision. Yet deep within, he could not help wondering if it would have been better to let the Renshai remain dead in the eyes of the world after the bloody slaughter by neighboring Northmen that had destroyed all of the Renshai except Rache and himself. He thought of the red harvest of violence that the Renshai had once casually reaped across the world, spurring a hatred so deep that, in some countries, simply speaking the name was cause for execution. *Better for all, perhaps, if the 'Golden-Haired Devils from the North' remained the corpses everyone believed them to be.*

Still, Colbey did not brood long over lost possibilities. Rache had fathered a son whom he would never see. The toddler lived with his mother in Santagithi's Town. Mitrian and her husband Garn had left their only child, an infant boy, with a friend in Pudar during the war. Soon, Colbey and Santagithi would arrive in Pudar along with its army. They would retrieve Mitrian's son, now called Rache in the Renshai tradition of naming children for warriors slain in battle. Once Santagithi and his guard force returned to their town, Colbey's training of the two boys would commence. And, in a few months or years, when Mitrian and Garn returned from restoring the king of Béarn to his throne, the Renshai would be united once again.

United. An army of four, two of them babies. And all facing the enmity of nearly the entire world. The odds against Colbey seemed enormous, yet he did not flinch from the responsibility. His loyalty to the Renshai never faltered, though his understanding of their purposes did. *Obviously, we can't ever again become the wanton killers we once embodied as a tribe.* Colbey recalled stories of the gory border skirmishes between the eighteen Northern tribes, battles in which the Renshai had committed the worst sin any Northman could imagine. To destroy morale, the Renshai had sliced body parts from their enemies, thereby barring the dead from the rewards of Valhalla's afterlife. Despite minor disputes over territory, the Northern tribes believed themselves a brotherhood, and the crimes of the Renshai had resulted in their banishment from the North.

Colbey leaned against a withered oak, the bark gouging into the light fabric of his tunic. Though he moved with a casual ease that seemed to border on carelessness, every sense remained alert. A part of his mind assessed the location of every soldier and, seeing no threat, discarded the information. Movement inside the tent told Colbey that General Santagithi, too, was still awake.

Colbey knew that the Renshai's century without a homeland had been spent gleaning the most elite battle techniques from every culture in existence. Driven first by bitterness and blood lust and later by blood lust alone, the Renshai had blended philosophy and skill into the most successful combat system in existence. Rumors told how the least competent Renshai could fight three of any country's best warriors and win, and Colbey had never found reason to doubt the veracity of the statement.

Still, the Renshai's single-minded devotion to war had goaded them to answer every problem with violence. Renshai rarely lived past their early thirties; the youthful exuberance and vigor of the tribe only fed the cycle. Colbey mulled the situation, forming no judgments. In his time, he had been as eager for combat as any other. A scene emerged from deeply rooted memory. He recalled when the Renshai had finally returned to the North after their hundred years of wandering. The tribal area which had once served as home to the Renshai had become a part of Thortire. So the Renshai spokesman had asked the high king in Nordmir for an icy, barren island that was then called Ti. The king's reply remained vivid in Colbey's memory, 'Pick a champion from among your people. If he can best my champion, the island is yours. So long as you don't threaten other tribes, you may live your days in peace.' A strange smile had touched the king's features then, 'But should my man win, your tribe must leave the Northlands and never return.'

At twenty-nine, Colbey had already been the Renshai's most accomplished sword master for fifteen years. Yet their spokesman had chosen a challenger from the ranks at random with a bored nonchalance that enraged the king. A young woman faced and defeated the king's champion. Then, in an ugly gesture of defiance that had galled even Colbey, she had lopped the head from the king's warrior, stealing from him the glory that came with death. The Renshai had won a homeland that never again bore any name but Devil's Island. And twenty years later, when the massed armies of the North slaughtered the Renshai, they never truly broke the king's promise. General/King Siderin of the Eastlands had steered the Northern king to the loophole in his vow. By attacking at night, the Northmen had allowed the Renshai to live their '*days* in peace.'

Colbey drew a long sword from each hip sheath, watching the familiar glow of starlight on the blades. Even after sixty-five years, the beauty of the sight never dimmed, nor the excitement that thrilled through him at the melody of steel rasping from its sheath. But the joy of other things had disappeared. Thoughts of some of the Renshai's actions sickened him, especially the ritual mutilations that had led to their exile. Yet there was a beauty and integrity to the Renshai that outsiders rarely understood. They remained loyal to one another to the extreme of cutting down one of their own from behind to prevent his dying of illness or infection, for a coward's death would doom a warrior to Hel. Their honor forbade them from using anything but their own individual, physical skills in war; therefore, they shunned armor, group strategies, and any weapon that did not require a direct, hand-to-hand technique. Rache had died of King Siderin's poison. And that, Colbey had found the most distasteful weapon of all.

Still, despite the many laws that bound the Renshai, they never expected their enemies to follow the same code of ethics. *A man who dies fighting with his principles intact dies in glory. To expect enemies to follow the same code of honor defiles that honor, reducing it to a set of arbitrary rules.*

With that thought, Colbey launched into a *svergelse*, a series of sword maneuvers practiced alone. Though swifter than his heartbeats, the perfect, committed figures came easily, along with a memory that, to his mind, defined the Renshai's creed. Before Colbey's birth, the tribe had worshiped the god Odin as their patron. Then, one day, Colbey's elders swore that Thor's wife Sif appeared before them, promising that a child born that day would become the most skilled sword master in history. Three babies joined the tribe that day. The first, a boy, barely met the Renshai's definition of average before his death in a childhood combat. The second, a girl called Kelrhyne, was hardy and robust. Clearly the object of Sif's promise, she perfected her first sword maneuver before the other two pulled to a stand. She had breezed through the Renshai training as though it was created solely for her. The third child born had been Colbey.

The swords whirled about Colbey, veering with a speed that kept them invisible. Even the flashes of starlight shifted too quickly to betray their positions. He recalled how, at five years old, he had been told about Sif's promise. Immediately, he had made a vow. If Kelrhyne was destined by gods to become the most skilled sword master in history, then, by setting his goal to best her, he would become the finest swordsman possible, constrained only by time. Now, remembering, Colbey smiled, spinning into a complicated kata designed for battling hordes of enemies at once. From that day, he had forsaken everything but his swords. He had spent every moment of every day drilling sword maneuvers until exhaustion battered him into unconsciousness. Over time, his parents discovered that no promise of reward nor threat of punishment could drive Colbey to fulfill the mundane duties of life. He would rather practice than eat, would rather hold his sword than another person, and would rather train than sleep.

By the time Kelrhyne died in brazen glory, Colbey had become the best. Therein, Colbey knew, lay the fundamental difference between Renshai and other men. For, where others would simply say that Colbey had been Sif's Chosen One all along, the Renshai still believed Sif had specified Kelrhyne; and they revered the dedication that had allowed Colbey to thwart a god-voiced prophecy.

Colbey plunged into a wild flurry of strike and parry, both arms arching and driving with equal mastery, his body weaving in a finely coordinated dance. His thoughts jarred back to the present. The responsibility of recreating the greatest of all tribes from a Western townswoman and two young boys gnawed at him. The honor, glory, and skill of the Renshai must live on. Fifty years of training the world's best swordsmen had made him confident of his abilities. That he could make them competent, he harbored no doubts. The uncertainty came with thoughts of what philosophies to instill, what purpose the Renshai would have in the new order of the world. The only possibility that made any sense at all to Colbey was to have the Renshai become soldiers for hire, to fight for money or glory, but only where the cause was right. And to make allies where before they had only enemies.

As easily as the idea came to Colbey, it brought with it no fanfares or certainties. Logic told him the decision was right, yet he wanted something more, approval from a deeper portion of his being or from the golden-haired goddess who guided the Renshai. Colbey whipped his swords into a forward cross block, then whirled, slicing opposite loops to meet imaginary opponents beside and behind him. Faster than thought, he spun again, gliding the blades through controlled, committed arcs. Like all of the Northern deities, Sif took her sacrifices on the battlefield, and Colbey had delivered hundreds of Easterners to her in the Great War. Afterward, he had recited his quieter, more personal prayers alone beside a campfire. Now, seeking guidance, Colbey dedicated his practice to Sif, sincerely trying, as always, to make it his finest effort. The elderly Renshai twirled and lunged, his swords carving the air in flawless arcs, lines, and ovals, a lethal whirlwind of flashing gold and silver.

Sif never directly answered Colbey. He sought only the peace of mind that he had always truly believed came from the goddess, though he had no proof but faith. Now, a pinpoint of light sparked before him. Gradually, it grew and spread, widening to a vast, shapeless glimmer. Colbey continued his practice, creating a grand new sword maneuver in his exuberance. He kept his attention partially on the glowing object, uncertain whether to attack or painstakingly avoid it. Never once did he question its presence. That his goddess would send him such a sign was an honor he dared not belittle with doubts. Other realities touched his subconscious. He knew that Santagithi had emerged from the tent and sat watching Colbey's prayer, deferentially silent and still. A few of the Pudarian soldiers stopped to stare from a distance, nudging one another and passing whispered comments. Yet these things seemed of so little consequence, Colbey ignored them.

The light surged and sputtered before Colbey. Still uncertain of his role, he finally decided to bring a sword stroke through the image. As tentative as the decision seemed, Colbey never jabbed or cut without a full commitment to the blow and its consequences. The blade cleaved the glow. Fully powered, it met no resistance. A gold-white star flashed from the steel like a highlight, then disappeared, and the glimmer flared suddenly into the form of a woman in black leather.

The functional battle garb detracted nothing from a face and figure that redefined Colbey's feminine ideal. Long blonde hair spilled free in the spring wind, so thick and saffron that it seemed like strands of spun, metallic gold. She clutched a gleaming broadsword that lashed abruptly for Colbey's head.

For a fraction of a heartbeat, Colbey hesitated. The lack of reaction from the spectators told him that he alone saw the image. If she did not exist, he had nothing to fear from her attack. If she was a manifestation of his goddess, then he would die on her sword with honor. *But not without a bold and glorious fight! She deserves that much. And so do I.*

Colbey flicked his left sword into a block, boring in rather than retreating or dodging. Her blow crashed against his left blade with an unexpected strength. His right sword swept beneath her guard. She leapt backward into a crouched defense, her blue eyes sparkling with pleasure over features that clearly revealed surprise. She skipped to the left, as light and quick as an animal and with a grace that might have sent a practiced dancer into a jealous rage. Colbey did not press his offensive, instead using the instant to assess her potential. Already, he could tell that she would prove the most potent threat he had ever faced. And the challenge thrilled him.

The woman remained crouched, patient as eternity. Colbey waited, too, content to enjoy the fatal beauty of even her slightest movements. He made an almost imperceptible gesture, indicating that she should take the next attack.

The woman laughed, the sound deep and resonant yet still somehow feminine. Suddenly, she lunged. Colbey sidestepped the jab, then returned a double stroke of his own. She met the attack with a snaking parry that redirected both of his blades.

Now, Colbey laughed, too, feeling carefree and as vibrant as a child. More than fifty years had passed since any opponent could meet him stroke for stroke. Even the next best Renshai had never returned more than one attack for every two. He rescued his left sword from her maneuver, using what little remained of its momentum to catch the knurling of her hilt near her fingers. Torn from her hands, the sword pinwheeled between them. Colbey's other blade, driven toward her abdomen, seemed certain to land.

Horror flashed through Colbey's mind as her sword neared the ground. By Renshai tradition, a sword was the most important and deeply personal part of a warrior; to let an honored opponent's sword touch the ground was considered the basest insult. Instantly, he whisked his right sword into its sheath. He dove for the falling weapon, catching the hilt a finger's breadth before it hit the grass.

Colbey's gaze lost his opponent for only the barest fraction of time. Yet, when he looked up, a sword clenched triumphantly in each hand, three cold steel blades in the hands of three identical women slammed down toward him.

'Modi.' Colbey called to Sif's son, the god of battle wrath. From infancy, he had been taught to shout the name whenever he or his people needed an extra burst of blood lust. Decades of training responded to Colbey's need. Rage surged through him, bringing strength like a second wind. He rolled, parrying despite the awkwardness of his position. He felt the blades scratch down the two in his fists, felt the swishing pass of the third as it missed his skull by a finger's breadth. He spun to his feet, slashing a furious barrier of metal between him and his three opponents.

'General Colbey!' The cry seemed distant and unimportant, yet it jarred Colbey's concentration. The triple images of the woman blurred.

No! Colbey forced his attention back, needing this fight which was the greatest challenge of his life.

'General Colbey!' The Pudarian voice grew louder, followed by Santagithi's sour reprimand.

'Be still soldier. It's not polite to interrupt a man's prayer. Nor wise, if his gods hold him in half the regard that I do.'

'Prayer.' The Pudarian snorted. 'He's just practicing.'

The woman faded to oblivion, leaving only a pale outline of light. The sword that had been hers disappeared from Colbey's hand. *Three women. Three sparring partners. Three other Renshai.* Colbey pounced on the significance of the number, narrowing his concentration, trying to recreate the phantom that must have come from his imagination. Still, he could not let go of the possibility that his sparring partner had been a divine manifestation of Sif.

Santagithi continued in his usual gently authoritative manner. 'He is a Northman. To them, war *is* religion.'

The Pudarian's tone went icy. 'With all respect, General, I need to speak with the other general, not with you. Prince Verrall wishes Colbey now. His grace must not be left waiting.'

The light winked out. Annoyance suffused Colbey, and he glanced directly at the speakers for the first time. Santagithi stood with one foot propped on a weathered stump. Dark blond hair flecked with gray fringed features just beginning to wrinkle. Tall and broad, he towered over the darker Pudarian soldier, yet the smaller man glared back with a look of controlled defiance. Colbey, not Santagithi, was the leader of Pudar's army, and the man seemed determined to make that point clear.

Colbey jabbed his remaining sword into its sheath. 'Prince Verrall will not wait for a man to finish his prayers? Then "your grace" has none. What does he want?' Colbey did not mince words, nor question semantics. King Gasir of Pudar had died in the war, leaving no direct heir. Of his four nephews from two brothers, Verrall had legal claim to the throne. Until his coronation, however, he could not use the title 'king,' so he had chosen 'prince.'

The Pudarian blanched beneath Colbey's intense scrutiny. 'He . . . his grace wants to speak with you as soon as possible.'

'About what?'

'I don't know, sir.'

'Very well,' Colbey sighed in resignation, the conversation sounding almost too vivid and real in the wake of his holy experience. 'Take me to him, then.' Colbey had no interest in politics, and royalty meant little to him. The other seventeen Northern tribes, and most of the West's largest cities, were separate monarchies, each country organized under a high king. But the Renshai had never had a government. For the rare matters of diplomacy, they had chosen whoever seemed the best speaker for the occasion.

'This way, sir.' The Pudarian turned, relaxing as he no longer had to confront Colbey's cruel features and hard blue-gray eyes. He headed toward the center of the camp.

Colbey followed, and Santagithi joined him. The broadboned Westerner dwarfed the slight Renshai.

Colbey smiled. 'You would join me?' They wound between trees and tent.

'I think it would be best.'

'Your company is always a pleasure, but you don't often offer it.' Colbey could not help asking, 'Do you think I'm in danger?'

'Do I think *you* are in danger?' Santagithi's mouth twitched upward. He cleared his throat, as if to make one of his ringing diplomatic or strategic announcements. 'Isn't that rather like worrying about a wolf being attacked by a flock of starving hens?'

Colbey chuckled, watching the back of the Pudarian's shaking head. It went against Santagithi's usual tactful finesse to insult anyone, especially within earshot of a soldier so closely linked to the prince of the West's largest city. He tried to guess the reason as they finished the trip in silence, and he believed he understood. For Santagithi, the war had proven taxing – physically, mentally, and emotionally. He had lost both of his captains to death. Despite being Renshai and a cripple, Rache had been like a son. The second had been Santagithi's confidant. His only daughter had run away from home with Garn, the gladiator who had paralyzed Rache. Nearly a year later, the Great War reunited father and daughter, only to reveal that she had borne him a grandson, married Garn, and, taught by Colbey, she had become as skilled at war as any of his soldiers. Named the West's prime strategist, Santagithi had had to orchestrate the Great War, coordinating armies of mixed backgrounds and even a single tribe of Northmen. The lives of thousands of men, and ultimately of their wives and children, had lain in his hands. Even the kings and generals had pinned their hopes on the man that the Eastern Wizard had called their finest strategist. Now, Colbey suspected, Santagithi simply needed a chance to shake off the lead weight of responsibility heaped upon him.

The Pudarian came to halt before a huge, enclosed tent in the center of the camp. Four Pudarian guardsmen stood watch at the corners, each clutching a bladed pole arm that Colbey's sword-skewed education did not allow him to identify by name. The Pudarian escort nodded to his on-duty companions, then addressed Colbey and Santagithi. 'One moment, please, sirs.' Raising one folded tent flap, he disappeared inside. The canvas flopped back into place behind him.

Thoughts wafted to Colbey from the nearest sentry. Bored, he explored them, finding the man unusually alert and restless for a soldier on a routine watch. Curious, Colbey probed, discovering an awe that bordered on fear; he, it seemed, was the source of the sentry's discomfort. The Renshai suppressed a smile of amusement. He held a neutral stance, defensible, yet in no way coiled or threatening, hoping to put the man at ease.

The mind-reading ability had come to Colbey eleven years past. Shortly after the Western Wizard had informed him that the tribe of Renshai had been massacred five years earlier, a madness had descended upon Colbey. It had taken the form of driving obsessions, voices in his head, and glimpses into the past and future. One by one, he had crushed the intruders and the seeds of insanity they represented, systematically destroying them with the same competence and control he used on the battlefield. At first, he had believed that the madness itself caused him to accidentally catch stray thoughts of people around him, ideas that he later discovered he had read verbatim. Since every voice had disappeared, he realized that each winning war had honed his mind in the same way every battle enhanced his skills. Now, he was just beginning to explore the possibilities of a mental tactic that went far beyond the philosophy and mind over body mastery he had learned since infancy.

The guards stood in stony silence. The one Colbey had studied shifted uncomfortably beneath his scrutiny. Santagithi stood with his head raised, his gaze following the sweep of stars across the heavens.

Shortly, the tent flap jiggled, then folded aside. The Pudarian who had escorted Colbey and Santagithi peeked through the opening. 'General Colbey, Prince Verrall will see you now.' He gave Santagithi an apologetic glance. 'Sir, he asked for the general alone. He would be happy to meet with you later if you feel the need.'

Colbey glanced at Santagithi. The Western general's expression did not change, but Colbey sensed discomfort in his companion's demeanor. Though he had no reason to think the prince meant him any harm, the decision to meet after dark and Santagithi's casual insistence on accompanying Colbey made him careful. He trusted Santagithi's instincts.

Inexperienced in affairs of state, Colbey chose his words cautiously and kept his tone respectful. 'Please thank his grace for seeing me.' Since the prince had called for him, Colbey guessed his gratitude was unnecessary, but it helped him lead into his request. 'Please also inform him that Santagithi has come along as my . . . as my . . . ' The idea of Colbey needing a bodyguard seemed ludicrous. Unable to think of a better word, Colbey found an equally absurd one. ' . . . my retinue. Anything the prince can say in my presence, he can say in front of Santagithi.'

The Pudarian stared, as if waiting for Colbey to admit he was joking.

Colbey made an exaggerated gesture of dismissal. 'Go on. Tell him.'

Reluctantly, the Pudarian retreated.

Colbey glanced at Santagithi, hoping he had not offended the general. Though they had become fast friends, they had only known one another since the war. And, where Colbey's title was wholly military, Santagithi was leader of a country as well. 'Sorry about the retinue thing,' Colbey whispered.

A tight-lipped smile ruined Santagithi's otherwise somber expression. He spoke as softly, 'You must think much of my abilities to consider me an entire retinue.'

Colbey suppressed a chuckle. In his attempt to sound as respectful as possible, he had not realized he had used the plural.

The Pudarian's head again appeared through the slit. 'His grace again asked to see *his* general alone. He has promised to tend any business with the other general afterward.' He addressed Santagithi directly. 'Or before, if you prefer, sir.'

'With all due respect . . . ' At the moment, Colbey estimated the amount due as a spoonful. ' . . . you know Santagithi has no business with the heir. He came with me. Verrall can see me with my retinue or not at all.'

Apparently briefed for this contingency, the Pudarian did not bother to consult the prince again. He sighed in resignation. 'Very well, then. Both of you come inside.' He exited, holding aside the flap.

Santagithi and Colbey entered together. The spacious area enclosed by the canvas surprised Colbey. Prince Verrall sat in a crude, wooden chair in the center. Behind him, straw and blankets lay neatly spread as bedding. To his left stood a pile of supply crates. To his right, a series of crates surrounded a huge stump that served as a table. A dozen Pudarian soldiers armed with swords were positioned around the prince, and two boys in peasant garb waited behind the chair.

Colbey lowered his head respectfully. Santagithi bowed, and the prince answered with the same courtesy. 'I didn't expect the pleasure of your company, too, Santagithi. Please, accept my hospitality. My business is with my general.' He waved toward the table and crates. The boys scurried in the indicated direction to tend to Santagithi even before he arrived.

Colbey opened his mouth to protest again, but Santagithi squeezed his arm in warning. 'Let it lie, friend,' he hissed, barely audibly. There's something to be said for compromise.' He spoke aloud, 'Thank you, Verrall.' Without further comment, he took the seat closest to the prince and facing Colbey.

The peasant boys talked softly with Santagithi, then trotted off to attend some request. The prince turned his attention fully on Colbey. 'First, General, I and all of Pudar would like to thank you for your leadership and your dedication to our effort in the war.'

Colbey glanced toward Santagithi, seeking clues to the proper formalities. But the town leader slouched with his head resting on a hand propped on the table. Legs crossed, he watched the proceedings with mild curiosity. As Colbey's delay stretched past politeness, Santagithi raised his brows.

You bastard. Colbey knew Santagithi was gleaning some amusement from the situation. 'You're welcome.' Colbey could think of nothing better to say, but the ensuing hush encouraged him to continue. 'Your uncle, King Gasir, was a good man and a decent soldier. He died bravely. It was my pleasure to honor his only request to me, that, in the event of his death, I lead his army in the war.' Colbey stopped, hoping he had said enough.

'Sire,' the nearest Pudarian hissed at Colbey.

Surprised by the address, Colbey glanced at his escort.

Prince Verrall continued, apparently unaware of the exchange. 'As you know, King Gasir had four nephews. Though I am the second in age, my father was the king's next eldest brother, while my cousin was born of Gasir's youngest brother. I am, by law, the heir.' He studied Colbey with an intensity that seemed to bear no relation to his words.

Colbey nodded, rapidly losing interest.

'I am concerned my cousin may try to claim the Pudarian throne.'

Again Colbey nodded. He watched one of the peasant boys thread through the prince's entourage with a mug of wine for Santagithi.

'Do you understand the situation, General?'

Colbey's brows knit in a mixture of confusion and annoyance. The situation seemed obvious enough for a senile street beggar to grasp, and he wondered if he should take offense at the question. 'It seems terribly clear, yes.'

'Sire,' the Pudarian guard whispered more forcefully.

'What?' Colbey hissed back.

The soldier emphasized his point with an abrupt gesture with both open hands. 'Sire. Call the prince "sire."'

'Why?'

'Why?' The guard's voice rose an octave, serving as both outraged repetition and query.

'Why?' Colbey repeated with vexing calm.

The guard wore a bemused expression somewhere between shock and horror. His cheeks looked aflame. 'Because. Because that's what you call him.'

Colbey saw no reason to further antagonize the sentry, aside from a mild curiosity about whether the man could become so enraged that he ruptured the vessels in his face. 'Sire,' he added, the belated title lost beneath the king's next words, which was just as well. Frustrated at being drawn from his prayers for matters that held no interest for him, Colbey had muttered the word with a disgust that even his melodious Northern accent could not soften.

'As commander of my troops, you will, of course, see that any rebellion Bacshas might instigate is quickly laid to rest.'

'Bacshas is your cousin,' Colbey guessed.

The Pudarian guardsman's face flared to purple. As he opened his mouth, Colbey said simultaneously, 'Sire.'

Santagithi uncrossed his legs, sitting straight in his chair. He seemed as interested in the exchange as the prince.

'Yes,' Verrall confirmed. 'Bacshas is my cousin.'

'Thank you for the opportunity, Sire,' Colbey said politely. 'But I'm not interested.'

The room quieted.

The prince seemed to have difficulty finding words. 'You would not put down a Bacshas-backed rebellion?'

'No, Sire.'

The hush deepened. Even the rare click of the guards' armor disappeared.

Prince Verrall's features flushed, nearly to the color of his sentry's. He leaned forward in his chair. 'General, are you aware your words are treasonous?'

The hands of the prince's guards inched toward their sword hilts. This did not escape Colbey's notice, nor did he miss the growing expressions of fear on several faces. All of Verrall's men had seen Colbey in battle.

Colbey remained calm, seeing no significant threat from only a dozen Pudarian soldiers. 'Sire, I admit that the Trading tongue is not my first language, but I believe I do know the definition of treason. I've not raised a hand against you. Surely, there's nothing treasonous about resigning my command.'

The sentries fidgeted. Santagithi sat with the mug clasped between his palms; he had not yet taken a single sip. The prince looked stricken. 'So you would resign your command and lead Bacshas' forces against me?'

'No.' Colbey corrected the misconception. 'I am resigning my command so I can go to Santagithi's Town. Pudar's politics are not my concern.'

A glimmer of hope appeared on Verrall's face. 'You're not going to back my cousin?'

'No.' Colbey glared at his Pudarian escort, pronouncing the next word distinctly for his benefit. 'Sire.'

'Then you will back me.'

'No.'

The prince lapsed into a frustrated silence. Though bored and impatient to return to his practice, Colbey waited to be dismissed.

'Why not?' Verrall asked, at length.

Colbey glanced at each of the dozen guards in turn. Not one held his gaze. This time, the Renshai thought it best to begin with the title of respect. 'Sire, I've already told you I plan to return to Santagithi's Town with him.'

The prince leaned forward, guarded hope again showing in his bearing. 'Santagithi and his soldiers would be shown the hospitality due visiting dignitaries. They've been away from home several months already. A week or two, even a month or two, longer won't make much difference. And the trading city will give them a well-deserved vacation and a place to buy presents for their wives and families.' He glanced in Santagithi's direction as if to confirm the invitation. It had become common knowledge that, when Santagithi sent his yearly trading party to Pudar, the guards clamored for the opportunity to go.

Santagithi continued to cradle his drink. Apparently not wishing to interfere with Colbey's decision nor insult Prince Verrall, he gave only a brief, noncommittal nod.

Colbey ignored the nonverbal communication. 'With all respect, Sire, that's not the issue.'

'And the issue is?' Verrall encouraged. Thick brows arched over dark eyes, smoothing the middle-aged features.

'That I'm not involving myself in Pudar's politics. May I go now, Sire?' Colbey clamped the sentences together so quickly, it took the remainder of the men in the tent a moment to recognize his sudden shift of topic.

'No.' Prince Verrall made a crisp gesture to his men. The two nearest Colbey shifted inconspicuously behind him to block the exit.

Colbey followed the men's passage by sound. Until they drew weapons, they would prove no danger to him. He left their presence and movements to his subconscious, which had already processed and chronicled the skill of each soldier by his stance and his gait.

'Colbey, I'm no fool . . . '

Colbey stared in stony silence, believing that any man who needed to say such a thing obviously was precisely that which he denied.

' . . . You're a Northman fighting for the West. Obviously, politics alone don't concern you. You willingly pledged yourself to my uncle. I'm his heir. Why do you refuse me?'

Colbey lowered his head in consideration, but found no words to soften the blow. 'Sire, it would be best if I didn't say.'

'But you will.'

'Will I?'

'I think we would both find it preferable to sitting here staring at one another all night.'

Colbey frowned. What kept him in the prince's tent was not force or threat of violence, but protocol. He considered leaving, aware he could probably move quickly enough to forestall any immediate retaliation. But Santagithi had more ground to cover, and it seemed unfair to put a friend in danger in the name of simple defiance. Besides, Colbey had just committed the Renshai to finding allies and to a future as swordsmen for hire. Antagonizing the king of the Westlands' largest city did not seem prudent, yet Colbey saw no way to avoid it.

Unwilling to lie, Colbey ran the risk of offending with words or with silence, and he chose the former, hoping that it would save time and that the prince would remember he had pressed Colbey to speak. 'Sire, if you don't have the power to claim your throne without me, what makes you think you can keep it after I'm gone?'

The guards exchanged nervous glances. Santagithi frowned, suddenly intent on the conversation.

Prince Verrall recoiled as if struck. Then his features creased in outrage. 'You think I'm weak.'

Having spoken freely, Colbey saw no reason to back down now. 'I've seen you fight. You're not King Gasir.'

'You think I'm weak?' The prince seemed locked on the phrase.

Though he had little experience with smoothing strained relations, Colbey tried. 'I don't mean to be offensive. It's probably just my upbringing. Northmen revere heroes. Kings nearly always serve as their own generals. Those who don't run the risk of losing their followers to their generals. It's not malicious,' Colbey added quickly. 'It's just that good people tend to reward competence, in war and in leadership.'

Colbey paused, distracted by a realizaton that he had never before considered. The Northmen were, by definition, the followers of good and the Easterners followers of evil. Yet though their motivations always clashed, often the end results were similar. The Eastern cities banded beneath a single king who, if not a skilled warrior as well as a powerful presence, could lose his throne to a stronger soldier. Self-motivated, the Renshai had paid little attention to the divisions. And though a tent in the Westlands seemed an odd place to consider philosophy, Colbey could not help noting that pure good and evil, like genius and madness, might prove so opposite as to become too alike.

Prince Verrall pounded a fist on the arm of his chair. 'And you? I imagine you believe you would be powerful enough to rule Pudar.'

Colbey hesitated, the concept so foreign he had never considered it. The answer was obvious. 'Certainly, Sire. But I have no inter . . .'

'You arrogant *wisule*!' Verrall leapt to his feet, using the vilest insult Colbey knew. By calling him after a rodent so skittish it would abandon its young rather than face a threat, the prince had accused Colbey of cowardice. 'Do you think I'm stupid?'

Even had Colbey deigned to grace the rhetorical question with an answer, the prince did not give him the opportunity.

'You speak of might. You talk about generals usurping kings. You won't support the rightful heir to Pudar, nor even his conniving cousin. Clearly, what you plan *is* treason! You want the throne for yourself!'

The accusation seemed too ridiculous to answer. Tossing his hands in exasperation, Colbey turned to leave. Even as he moved, he caught a glimpse of the prince beginning a gesture to his guards. His other hand fell to the hilt of his sword.

Colbey spun back to face the threat.

Santagithi hurled the contents of his mug. Wine splattered over the Prince of Pudar, staining his silks and leathers. Purple droplets wound across features that went nearly as dark. His hand whipped from his hilt, waving in flustered outrage. Sputtering, he turned on Santagithi. 'Why? How dare . . . !' Apparently remembering he was addressing a man with as high a rank as himself, he kept accusation from his voice. 'Why?'

The guards formed a circle around Colbey, but they kept their distance and did not pull weapons.

Santagithi stood, large and dangerous even when compared to a tent full of soldiers. His voice sounded more booming than usual in the stunned hush that fell over Verrall's warriors. 'I apologize for the soaking, but I found it necessary to rescue a dozen innocent men from death, and you, too.'

'From death?' Verrall shook off wine by snapping his arms through the air. 'What death?'

Colbey folded his arms across his chest, awaiting Santagithi's explanation with bland curiosity. Around him the guards squirmed, obviously unnerved by his casual disinterest in them.

'If anyone in this tent had drawn a weapon, Colbey would have had no choice but to take it from him. I doubt he would have sheathed his unblooded.' Santagithi's level tone surely did more to dispel tension than his words.

But Verrall took offense. 'So you think I'm weak, too.'

'No.' Though he addressed the prince, Santagithi's attention strayed to the soldiers as he assessed a threat Colbey had naturally considered from the moment he had entered the tent. 'I'm not a Northman. I can see strengths Colbey would never understand. What you lack in sword skill, you make up in wisdom and diplomacy. And I know you're shrewd enough to realize that nothing good could come of attacking the hero of the Great War.'

The prince's eyes narrowed. Wine dribbled to the floor, leaving purple rings on the dirt as Verrall sought the words to end the conflict and still keep face.

Colbey remained silent, allowing Verrall the courtesy of space and time. Santagithi also said nothing, presumably for similar reasons.

At last, Prince Verrall spoke, 'Very well. Colbey, you're dismissed. As to you,' he sat, twisting his head toward Santagithi, 'I want you to gather your men and head home. I don't want you or your people in my city.'

Santagithi grimaced. Knowing the cause, Colbey tried to explain without sounding as if he was undermining the prince's decision. 'Sire, we'll be gone as soon as we can. But Santagithi's baby grandson is in your city. Surely, you'll let us retrieve him before we leave.'

The pause that followed seemed to span eternities. Until now, Colbey had tried to avoid violence. But the idea that Verrall might try to prevent him from gathering one of the three remaining Renshai raised his ire. For this cause, Colbey would fight until either he or every last Pudarian lay dead.

'Very well,' Prince Verrall said calmly, though runnels of wine stole all dignity from his bearing. He strode the fine line between compromise and surrender. The first would make him seem a diplomat, the second as weak as Colbey had implied. 'But Santagithi's army stays outside the walls. And you stay only long enough to get the child. If you cause any disturbances, I will see you punished to the fullest extent of the law.'

Santagithi pursed his lips, unaccustomed to allowing others to speak to him in this fashion. Still, for the sake of peace, he allowed the pronouncement to go unchallenged. 'It will be as you say.' He threaded past the guards to Colbey's side. 'Let's go.'

Nodding, Colbey turned to leave.

The prince called after him. 'Oh, and General.'

Colbey and Santagithi both looked back.

'Colbey, you're relieved of your command as of this moment. I can lead my own forces, thank you.'

Colbey nodded once, barely managing to make it through the tent flap without grinning. He whispered to Santagithi. 'With such leadership, let the Pudarian army hope that we meet no enemies en route.'

Santagithi's answering laugh was strained.

2 The Night Stalker

Weeks later, the fields just outside the walled city of Pudar became a crowded chaos of jubilant soldiers and civilians. Wives and children clutched husbands and fathers in grips that seemed unyielding, tear-streaked faces buried in war- and travel-stained leather. Others wove frantically through the masses, seeking one face among four thousand soldiers, while a few stood in huddled misery, knowing they would never see a loved one again. Among so many, these last seemed terribly alone.

Arduwyn paused just outside the open, bronze gates, unable to take another step. The strings of his eyepatch crushed his spiky red hair in crisscrossing lines. His bow lay slung across one shoulder. His quiver held half a dozen arrows, each crafted on the return trip, and each decorated with his crest: two gold rings and one of royal blue. He studied the crowd through his single dark eye. Hope blurred every woman to the plump, beautiful shape of his wife, Bel. Every child seemed to be one of the three she had borne her first husband who had also been Arduwyn's closest friend, children who had become the little hunter's own by right of marriage. Yet, clearly, Bel had not come.

Grief crushed Arduwyn, and he clutched the irregular blocks of stone composing Pudar's wall. For hours he stood, watching couples and families sort from the hubbub and disappear through the gates. Some of the citizens slunk back into the confines, empty-handed. Yet no soldier returned alone. No soldier except Arduwyn.

A long, staring vigil blurred Arduwyn's vision, until the people became milling outlines. In the fields, fires sprouted, red against dusk, as Santagithi's army prepared their camps outside the gates. Beyond their campsite, forest loomed, and evening turned the trees into tall, brooding shapes, dark except for a tinge of green. Despite its murky appearance, the forest beckoned Arduwyn like a mistress. He had spent most of his childhood in the wilds surrounding the city of Erythane. There, his father had taught him the ways, habits, and haunts of the animals and the finest points of bowmanship. There also, Arduwyn had learned to hide in times of stress, sadness, and joy.

Despite his sorrow, the thought made Arduwyn smile. He thought of the cool kiss of night air winding through the trees, heavy with the scent of pine, elm, and moss. He heard the click of needles and the rattle of leaves in the limbs above him, knew the branch-snapping footfalls of deer as they brushed through copses, nostrils twitching to catch his scent. Foxes whirred and yelped in the night, their sound easily identified over the constant chitter of *wisules*, and the rumble of night insects.

Arduwyn had taken two steps toward the woodlands before he realized he had moved. A thought arrested him. He pictured Bel, her huge, brown eyes sparkling in the candlelight after the children lay in bed, blonde streaks sending shimmering highlights through her long, brown hair. He imagined the warmth of her body pressed against him, a soft presence full of beauty and grace. The picture filled him with a desire he had not satisfied in longer than a month, but it also stirred something deep, a love that, until recently, he never thought he would experience. For Arduwyn, there could be no other woman.

Yet Bel had not come. Reality intruded, souring Arduwyn's daydream. The grin wilted from his face, and his fingers cinched about folds of extra fabric in his pants. He had always been too scrawny; the excitement and horrors of the war had claimed the last of his weight. His clothing hung loose, hiding a skeletal frame. His cheeks had gone gaunt, a thin layer of skin wrapped tightly over jutting bone. His flame red hair stuck out in unruly spikes, no matter how he wet or combed it, and he had lost an eye to the battle. *Bel probably did come. She took one look through the opened gates, saw what was coming back to her, and turned away. And how could I blame her?*

Arduwyn shuffled a pace closer to the woods. There a man was not judged by his appearance or by his words, only by his ability to survive. There the gods had placed the greatest of the world's beauty, its fastest and quietest movement, its most consistent and emotionlessly logical behavior. So many times in the past, Arduwyn had used the forest's cycle of death, birth, and self-protective illusions to put his problems into clear perspective, if only for a time. And the forest gave him so much more. Every time he entered its haven, he discovered more of its secrets, and he hungered for the knowledge every exploration revealed.

The train of thought sparked memories of the day he had returned to Pudar accompanied by Mitrian, her ex-gladiator husband, Garn, and a massive, childishly simple hermit called Sterrane, who had turned out to be the rightful heir to Béarn's high throne. Then, Bel had refused Arduwyn's advances. 'When you wander,' she had said, 'you're not really looking for adventure, you're running from responsibility. Always, you believe you're seeking something more, something you think is special out there, maybe over the next hill, something other men can't find. You spend so much time looking, you're blinded to the small pleasures that you have. You'll die searching for something that doesn't exist, never having recognized or enjoyed what you had.' Later, she had given him an ultimatum, 'Choose. Me or the forest. You can't have both.'

Now, Arduwyn winced at the recollection, Bel's voice like harp chords in his ears. The deliberation had taken weeks, but he had chosen the woman he loved and never believed he regretted the decision. He had agreed to return home every night. And he had done so, until circumstances had sent him, Garn, and Sterrane to rescue Mitrian. Soon after, he had been sucked into the Great War like so many others. Bel had opposed his departure, even to rescue Mitrian, and leaving Mitrian's and Garn's baby in her care was not enough to allay her fears of permanently losing Arduwyn.

'And she was right, too.' Colbey's voice came suddenly, from too close.

Startled, Arduwyn whirled to face the Renshai. He had always felt a natural awe of Colbey, but an equally natural aversion to his cold and casual cruelty. Now the Northman stood before Arduwyn with his legs braced and his hands light on his sword belt. Beyond him, the darkness of evening huddled like a giant shadow, disrupted by the scattered camps of Santagithi's soldiers. Arduwyn's thoughts had blinded and deafened him. Now, he could hear the rumbles of men forced to remain outside a city of plentiful inns and taverns. Apparently, someone had managed to obtain supplies because the odors of ale and fresh roasting beef perfumed the air.

Arduwyn ran a hand through his hair, his thoughts scattering into incoherency. While readjusting his bearings, he had completely forgotten Colbey's words. 'Huh?' was all he managed.

Colbey smiled, amusement seeming out of place on his flint-hard features. 'I said she was right, too.'

Arduwyn shook his head, not comprehending.

'Bel. When she worried that you wouldn't return.'

Though familiar with Colbey always seeming to have information he had no right or means of knowing, Arduwyn dared not believe the old Renshai had read his mind. 'What are you tallking about?'

Colbey remained still, a statue draped in shadow. 'I saw you edging toward the forest. Don't tell me you weren't thinking of running. I know you too well, archer.'

'Archer?' Arduwyn repeated, insulted. 'If you knew me well, you'd know I prefer the term "hunter." I kill game, not men.'

The corners of Colbey's mouth twitched upward again. 'You killed your share of men a few days ago.'

Arduwyn scowled, hating the reminder, wondering why Colbey

always seemed to find it necessary to bait him. 'The war is over.'

'Yes. But not forgotten. Nor should it be. Distraction is not a substitute for learning to deal with reality.'

Arduwyn glanced toward the two guardsmen at the gates, aware that, as night fell, they would pull closed the panels. Once that happened, he would lose all chance of seeing Bel until the morning. Then he would have to explain not only why he had stayed away so long, but also why he had not returned to Bel the moment he had arrived in Pudar. *She'll think I don't love her.* Arduwyn grimaced, hating the concept. *And nothing could be further from the truth.* Still stalling, he confronted Colbey. 'And I suppose you remember every battle you've fought and every man you've killed.' He met Colbey's gaze, doubting the possibility. Surely no one could remember fifty years of war.

'Every man who faced death bravely, I remember,' Colbey replied. 'I pray daily for the ones who gave their all to a noble fight. The others have no significance to me, to the gods, or to themselves.' The matter-of-factness with which Colbey spoke of the value of men's lives made Arduwyn shiver. 'As to the battles, the larger causes may fade with time, but the details remain. Every sword stroke and its result changes the style of my combat. Every competent maneuver used against me remains vivid in my memory. And that's the way it should be.'

Arduwyn recalled the wild blur of battle when Siderin's men had rushed the Western archers. Blades had seemed to leap and slash from all directions, a crazed, lethal creature with a thousand arms. He had ducked and run, trusting luck and gods' will to keep him safe, anticipating the agony of sharpened steel plunged through his back. As the archers nearest to him had fallen, he had whirled to fight. He had never seen the blow that claimed his eye, had never felt it land; yet its momentum had sent him tumbling down the dune to the feet of the Western forces and had probably saved his life. The idea of sorting individual sword strokes from the chaos seemed madness. For Arduwyn, war meant shooting enemies from a distance. When circumstances required hand-to-hand combat, he believed most men simply swung and thrust toward the enemy, dodging ripostes and praying that one of their own blows landed first. Yet clearly there were dimensions of skill that went far beyond his comprehension.

Santagithi strode toward Colbey and Arduwyn from the direction of the camps. The little hunter watched the West's prime strategist approach. Had he not known that Colbey had two decades on Santagithi, he would have been hard pressed to guess which warrior was older. Silver streaked both men's hair, but it seemed less conspicuous amid the Northman's yellow-white locks than the Westerner's darker blond. Years of tending to the welfare of two thousand citizens had etched lines onto Santagithi's features. In addition, he had a wife and daughter to attend to and the elaborate strategies that kept his small army honed while larger ones withered and grew decadent in times of peace.

Colbey turned to face the approaching general.

Santagithi stopped directly before Colbey and Arduwyn, rearranging his hair with a battered, callused hand. 'The men are settled. Can we fetch my grandson?'

Arduwyn froze, filled with guilt that quickly turned to terror. Caught up in his own concerns, he had nearly forgotten that Santagithi and Colbey had come for Mitrian's child. *Had I slipped off into the forest, not only would I have been cruel and irresponsible to Bel, I probably would have had Santagithi's army on my heels. Or Colbey.* The last thought seemed even more horrifying. He smiled weakly, hoping Santagithi had not read his ideas of escape as easily as Colbey. 'Of course, sir. Let's go.' Arduwyn trotted through the gates.

Colbey and Santagithi followed.

Arduwyn led them down the familiar roadways, past long chains of selling stands closed early in honor of the returning soldiers. Jubilant whoops and friendly howls replaced the usual screamed promises of merchants that rose above the constant hum of softer-voiced salesmen and the conversations of the masses. Arduwyn knew that in the morning the stands would open with renewed enthusiasm, as merchants hawked wares to warriors who had gone too long without luxuries and personal toys.

Off and on, Arduwyn had been a part of the noise and bustle of the trading city of Pudar, working for merchants as a clever salesman. Yet now the city that had become his home seemed foreign and forbidding, a world full of ghosts. His mind conjured images of Garn, Sterrane, and Mitrian gawking like children at the wonders of a city larger than any of them had ever imagined. He tried to picture Sterrane as the king of Béarn, but the image of the massive, lumbering simpleton sitting on the high king's throne would not come. He knew that, for them, the war had scarcely begun. He also believed that he belonged at their side. They would have little need of a hunter though, and he belonged with Bel even more.

Colbey and Santagithi took the sights in stride; they had obviously traveled through Pudar before. Their silence pleased Arduwyn, leaving him to tangle with memories he dared not verbalize. Excitement thrilled through him, tempered by fear. He hungered for a glimpse of the woman he loved, to feel her body against his, to hear her voice ring in his ears. But the promise he had broken could never be forgiven. She had agreed to marry him based on his vow to return home every night, to see to it that she and the children never wanted for food or protection. Now she would be far more likely to drive him off than to greet him, and Arduwyn was uncertain whether his heart could stand the rejection.

Colbey's voice broke through Arduwyn's self-imposed agony. 'If you were moving any slower, you'd be walking backward.'

Arduwyn spun to face the old Renshai. Santagithi watched quizzically as Arduwyn regained his bearings. Habit had taken him directly home, and they now stood before the cabin next door, where Garn and Mitrian had lived. It lay dark and abandoned. Beside it, candlelight filtered through the main windows of his own home, a single glow also flickering from the loft bedrooms. 'This is it.' Arduwyn said, his words referring as much to the coming events as the location. 'We're here.'

Colbey made a throwaway gesture toward the house. 'You first.' Arduwyn shuffled forward, unable to delay any longer. He steeled himself for the coming rebuff, trying to cling to one last illusion that everything would be all right. Then, before he knew it, he had stepped up to the door and his fist tapped the oaken panel as if on its own accord. Santagithi and Colbey took positions on either side of him.

A moment passed, during which Arduwyn felt his heart rate double. Then the door creaked open, and Bel stood framed in the doorway. She wore a simple house dress of her own making that hung loose over her plump curves; her dark hair fell to her shoulders in disarray. No woman had ever seemed so beautiful to Arduwyn. 'Bel,' was all he managed to say.

Bel's gaze roved over Arduwyn's scrawny frame, then fixed on the eyepatch. A look of horror glazed her features. Before she could speak, her younger daughter shoved between her mother and the door, hurling her three-year-old body into Arduwyn's arms with a force that drove him back a step. 'Uncle 'dune! Uncle 'dune's back!'

Footsteps pattered across the floorboards as the elder two children approached, peeking at the newcomers. On tiptoes, the elder girl looked over her mother's shoulder. The boy, Effer, stared from beneath Bel's arm.

'What's this?' Rusha, the child in Arduwyn's arms, reached for the eyepatch.

Not wanting to upset Bel and afraid the sight might frighten the girl, Arduwyn caught Rusha's hands and spun her until she collapsed into a giggling heap. Trying to salvage the situation, he began the introduction, counting on the presence of important strangers to give him a reprieve from Bel's wrath or rejection. 'Bel, this is Mitrian's father, Santagithi.' He indicated the leader, who nodded a greeting. 'And this is Colbey, once general of the Pudarian army.' He indicated the children in order of age. 'Jani, Effer, and Rusha.'

The color returned to Bel's face, along with her manners. 'Please, come in. We've eaten, but I'm sure I can find more food.' She turned, heading back into the cottage, though only Arduwyn followed her. 'Of course, you'll stay the night.' She turned. Then, realizing the two guests had not entered, she raised her brows in curiosity. 'Please come in.'

Santagithi shook his head. 'Madam, thank you so much for the invitation, but we can't stay.' He glanced at Colbey, who formed a tight-lipped half smile at some private joke. 'We've just come for Rache.'

'Rache?' Bel glanced at Arduwyn.

'Rusha seized Arduwyn's hand, swinging it with childish excitement. The hunter gave the girl's hand a loving squeeze. 'That's Kinesthe's new name. It's a cultural thing.' He did not explain further. The information that Kinesthe was a Renshai might prove the final shock that drove Bel over the boundary into madness. In Pudar, mentioning the name of the tribe of rampant murderers was considered rude. In other towns and cities, it was a crime punishable by death.

Bel turned to her oldest child, a girl of thirteen. 'Jani, honey. Get the baby and his things. And as much milk as we have around.'

Santagithi went suddenly rigid. Apparently, it had just struck him that the infant would require special care that a lot of dirty, foul-mouthed soldiers might not be able to deliver. Surely, his wife had provided most of the feeding and care during Mitrian's infancy, so that her husband could focus on the needs of the town.

Jani headed into the room to obey. She clomped up the loft ladder.

Rusha headed into the main room, dragging at Arduwyn's arm. 'Sit! Sit!' she insisted.

The main room looked exactly as Arduwyn remembered. The single couch sat beneath the eastern window. Crates that served as chairs lay scattered about. Beyond the couch, a ladder led to the loft bedrooms. A doorway opened into the kitchen. Arduwyn hooked a crate with his toes, drawing it over to where the others stood. Removing his bow and quiver from his shoulder, he tossed them on the couch then sat on the crate.

Effer pulled up a crate beside Arduwyn. Rusha plunked into her stepfather's lap. Again, she reached for the eyepatch.

Arduwyn caught her hand. 'No, sweetheart, you don't want to touch that.'

'What's it for?' Obediently, she withdrew, but her gaze remained fixed on it.

Bel, Santagithi, and Colbey remained silent, clearly interested in Arduwyn's response. Embarrassed at being placed on stage, Arduwyn stammered. 'W-well. It's . . . it's like a bandage.'

'Did you get a oopey?' she asked, using the child's euphemism for injury.

'Something like that.' Arduwyn smiled at the girl, her calm innocence strangely soothing.

'Can I see it?'

Arduwyn hesitated. *She's going to see it eventually. Better not to make it into something awful.* 'Sure.' He looked at Bel, who seemed abruptly agitated. 'But it's real ugly. You see, I met this man who didn't have any eyes. So I gave him one of mine.'

'Really?' Rusha looked awed.

Effer stood, balancing a hand on Arduwyn's knee. 'Nah, he's just foolin' you. You can't give away a eye. He got in a great sword fight.' The boy danced around, simulating combat. 'An' it got poked out. But I'll bet Ardy chopped out both the other man's eyes. Didn't you, Ardy?' Effer remained standing directly in front of Arduwyn, apparently also wanting a peek beneath the patch.

Arduwyn coughed, rescued from answering by Colbey's hearty laugh and, a moment later, by Jani's appearance with the baby and a loaded sack. She dropped the baby's paraphernalia in front of Santagithi, then handed Rache to her mother.

Bel cradled the child so tightly that Arduwyn feared she would refuse to relinquish Rache to his grandfther. 'He's only got a few teeth, so you'll need to keep lumps out of his food. Everything he eats should be finely ground, his milk should be fresh, and he needs to be kept warm . . .'

Her instructions droned on. For a few moments, Arduwyn enjoyed watching the West's master strategist, the man who had commanded thousands in war, squirm over details of diapering and burping.

Yet, although the presence of the baby spared Arduwyn the need to address Effer's question, Colbey chose to do so anyway. 'As far as I know, Arduwyn didn't chop anybody's eyes out. But he did kill the Eastern king.'

The towheaded boy studied his new father with a respect bordering on hero worship, while Rusha repeatedly flipped the eyepatch up and down, alternately recoiling from the empty socket with a squeal, then needing to peek again. Effer's interest in the injury disappeared as his imagination was caught by this new piece of information. 'A king? You killed their king?'

Arduwyn glanced over Rusha's head to Colbey, trying to read his intention. In some ways, the Renshai had spoken truth. Toward the end of the war, Arduwyn had caught a distant glimpse of Colbey and Siderin embroiled in battle in the midst of a galloping stampede of horses. Finding an opening, Arduwyn had fired an arrow through a gap in Siderin's armor, killing him in the instant before Colbey landed what would have been a fatal blow.

Guilt mingled inseparably with fear. At the time, Arduwyn could not explain why he had attempted such a distant shot, especially knowing that a miss might have taken the life of the West's hero and seen to Siderin's escape. Arduwyn had needed to restore the confidence that he had lost with his eye, had felt a pounding, driving need to know if he could still shoot with the accuracy it had taken him nearly thirty years to perfect. And pride had goaded him as well. Raised to loathe even the term 'Renshai' and all it represented, Arduwyn had, at first, tried to oppose Colbey, a task of monumental proportions. Later, both intimidated and awed, Arduwyn had found himself inexplicably drawn to Colbey's golden courage with the fatal devotion of a moth to flame. It had inspired a wary friendship which allowed them to exchange gibes that always seemed on the verge of degenerating into warfare.

Arduwyn caught Effer's hands. 'No. Colbey's just teasing. He killed the Eastern king.'

Colbey's face acquired an expression just shy of levity, and he returned Arduwyn's stare with chilling ferocity. He pulled a broken piece of arrow from his pocket, the fletches crusted with blood, the blue and gold rings about the shaft unmistakable. 'Whoever fired this killed King Siderin of the East. If it wasn't you, Arduwyn, you'd better find out who's stealing your arrows.' He tossed the fragment. It struck the floor with a click that was nearly lost beneath Bel's instructions, then it skittered across the boards.

'Whoo-ah!' Effer chased the war toy, pinning it to the floor with his hand. He picked it up and returned to Arduwyn, examining the broken shaft with amazement. 'You really killed the enemy's king?'

Arduwyn fidgeted, afraid of the penalty of stealing a kill from a Renshai, especially after a long and glorious battle. 'We'll talk about this later, Eff.'

'When?'

'Later tonight.'

'Now,' Effer pleaded.

Bel jumped into the exchange. 'Tomorrow. I want the three of you in bed now.'

Jani looked stricken. 'But it's just getting dark.'

Bel whirled to face her daughter. Something in her face must have conveyed rage, because a moment later Jani was herding her complaining siblings up the loft ladder. No longer pinned beneath Rusha, Arduwyn rose.

Bel passed Rache to his grandfather, the sluggishness of her movements betraying reluctance. The infant looked tiny cradled in one of Santagithi's massive arms. Yet, clearly, the general knew how to hold babies. With this, at least, he seemed comfortable.

'Thank you for all you've done for Rache.' Santagithi shifted the child to his other arm, dipping his hand into his pocket. He emerged with a fistful of coins, which he pressed into Bel's palm.

'This is unnecessary,' Bel said, reaching out to return the money. 'I loved taking care of him, and I'll miss him.' She flushed at the confession. 'I almost hoped Mitrian wouldn't come back for him, but it all evens out, I suppose. In a few months, I'll have a baby of my own.' She patted her abdomen.

Arduwyn dropped back down, missed the crate, and crashed to the floor. His hip brushed a corner of the box, sending it tumbling end over end.

'Congratulations,' Santagithi called, somehow managing to lock his face into a serious expression, though one cheek twitched and he did turn away more quickly than decorum demanded.

Colbey laughed unabashedly. 'When our heroes show such grace and artistry, is it any wonder we won the war?' He was still chuckling as he closed the door, leaving Bel and Arduwyn in an abruptly choked silence.

Arduwyn clambered to his feet, dreading the coming storm. In the presence of Santagithi and Colbey, Bel had had to pretend. Now he was about to discover whether he had anything left with the woman and family he could not bear to lose. He sought the words to make up for his lapse, but found none. Years as a salesman had taught him to read people and their motives. Clearly, any attempt to salvage their marriage had to focus on the new baby.

Before he could say a word, Bel's arms encircled his waist, and she crushed him against her.

Surprised, Arduwyn clutched Bel as tightly. He savored as many hushed moments as he dared before speaking. 'Bel, I'm sorry. I'm so sorry. I meant to come home sooner, but the war . . . and I couldn't stand the thought of the Easterners taking you and the children . . . and . . . '

Bel's grip tightened still more. Her tears soaked through the shoulder of Arduwyn's tunic, warm and wet. 'For days I cursed you, hating Garn and Mitrian, and even Sterrane.' She shivered, the latter seeming almost evil. Disliking Sterrane's simple innocence was like despising a child or a puppy. 'Then the army left suddenly, and I guessed what must have happened. But I just couldn't be sure.'

Arduwyn knew Bel well enough to guess the rest. 'That's why you didn't come to the gates to meet me. Isn't it?'

'If you weren't there, the soldiers would have told me whether or not you fought with them. If I never went, I could always believe you died in the battle. No one could tell me that you had just chosen to abandon us and returned to the woods instead.'

Arduwyn closed his eye, nearly suffocated with the guilt of how, outside the Pudarian gates, he had nearly run again. He would see to it Bel never knew how close she had come to losing him for no better reason than his own uncertainty. 'Are you . . . are we really going to have a . . . a baby?'

Bel nodded, the movement clear against Arduwyn's neck. 'Just promise me our child won't grow up without a father. Promise me you'll never leave again, for any reason.'

Arduwyn knew the danger of making such a vow, yet, at that moment, he would have promised Bel anything. And he did.

Garn rose to a crouch after hours of crawling across jagged rock that Sterrane had dared to call a road. A faintly glowing circle traced the outline of the new moon. Stars burned through a veil of clouds, scarcely revealing the trees, carts, and cottages surrounding Béarn's streets in rows and clusters. Other shapes towered darkly, unidentifiable to Garn, apparently devices used for breaking or collecting the famed Béarnian building stone or for carving the magnificent statues he had seen for sale in the Pudarian market. Ahead, surrounded by peasant cottages and shops, a wall protruded directly from the mountain. Beyond it, Morhane's castle loomed gray against the blackened sky, carved, like its curtain wall, from the granite of the Southern Weathered Range.

Garn ran for a gnarled pine growing within the boundaries of the mountain city, and cramps ached through his heavily-muscled chest and legs. Huddled behind the tree, he worked knots from his muscles, using a rag to stem the flow of blood from his tattered knees. He shook back bronze-colored hair, now entwined in a long snarl. From long habit, he readjusted his tunic and breeks to cover the whip, blade, and shackle scars left from his eight years as a gladiator. A metallic rattle caught his attention, and he trained his green eyes on the ramparts.

A tall silhouette paced the top of the wall. Links of mail clicked beneath his cloak, and his bootfalls added a hollow, clomping harmony. Garn watched the sentry march across the back wall. The Béarnide walked with a stiff precision that radiated professionalism and training. A tabard flapped through the open front of his cloak. Darkness robbed Garn of his color vision and distance did not allow him to perceive details, but he could make out a lighter patch against a dark background. Months of preparation by Sterrane and Shadimar, the Eastern Wizard, gave Garn reason to guess that the sentry wore the tan rearing bear on a blue background that was Béarn's symbol.

The man passed around a bend in the wall. A moment later, another guard appeared from the far side. Garn frowned, hand falling naturally to his hilt. His fingers curled around empty air, and a sudden jolt of panic shot through him in the instant it took to remember that he carried no sword. It would hinder the many maneuvers he would need to perform to enter Béarn's castle, add bulk to a stocky frame that might already wedge him into the tighter corners, and would be impossible to explain should his mission fail. Feeling naked, he curled his hand to the inner pocket that held his dagger and the bladder of wine, laced with a mild poison, which he would use to incapacitate the king. He also carried a tinderbox and two wax-coated torches.

Garn's painful crawl had raised irritation, and he forced it away. He had no need for nor right to bitterness. When the time had come for a volunteer for this responsibility, he had all but stolen the opportunity. Clearly, the heir to Béarn's throne could not have gone. Even ignoring the unacceptable risk, childlike Sterrane had no experience with subterfuge or guile. The Eastern Wizard would not or could not directly interfere in the affairs of mortals. Of the two remaining possibilities, Mitrian seemed best suited. Trained by Colbey to Renshai sword mastery, she might fight her way free if subtlety failed. But Garn had argued against the choice, phrasing his points carefully to mask his fears and protectiveness behind the guise of logic. His heart fluttered at the thought of Mitrian killed or jailed, guards' grimy hands fouling the companion he had won only with battles of conscience and honor over instinct. He loved her too much. Instead, he pointed out that he had more experience with stealth, theft, and escape. And though Mitrian's morality would not tolerate deceit, Garn could distort the facts, if necessary.

The second sentry passed around the bend, and another appeared as he did, their succession impeccable. Garn frowned, aware he would need to call upon the same timing and intuition that had kept him alive in the gladiator pit. At first, he cursed the guards' fastidiousness. Then, almost as quickly, he realized it would make their patterns predictable which might work to his advantage.

A moist breeze blew wisps of fog across the stars, obscuring them. All but blinded by darkness, Garn edged closer, counting footsteps as the sentries made each pass. He watched, assessing with a hunter's patience, as the clouds thickened in the heavens. Lightning flared, revealing the nearest sentry. Thunder boomed between the granite crags. Suddenly, rain pelted from the heavens, soaking Garn. He welcomed the storm's cover. *One, two, now.* Garn sprinted for the wall. A second flash sputtered, then lit the sky like day, revealing him. *Damn!* Garn ran on, head low. As he came to the wall, he skidded to a stop, whirling and pressing his back to the stone. Beneath his own stifled panting, he heard the uninterrupted slap of feet above his head.

As the sentry passed, Garn turned, seeking irregularities in the wall that could serve as handholds. Finding many, he climbed, fully attuned to the positions of the sentries. One retreated toward the bend, and another approached. Hugging the wall, Garn kept his face buried in the stone to muffle his breathing, tasting mossy dampness. Cold seemed to penetrate his hands, making them ache. Rain slicked the granite, forcing him to gouge his fingers into stone. Again, lightning split the clouds. Garn held his breath. He had given up on gods and prayer as his months in cages and pits stretched to years. Now fully displayed by the storm, he placed his faith in luck; and, apparently, it did not fail him. A booted foot touched the wall a hand's breadth from his nose. When it passed, Garn flung himself across and over the ramparts, prepared to roll on the ground below. He plummeted.

Garn snapped off a gasp, nearly biting through his tongue. Thorns clawed his face. A branch pierced his arm and splintered. He landed hard in a tangle of shrubs, wood snapping in a widening path beneath him. Incensed by pain, Garn gritted his teeth and lay motionless, preferring the stab of limbs to a guard's spear.

A sentry shouted from above in Béarnese. 'Who's there?'

Raised on the Western trading tongue, Garn had only learned a spattering of Béarnese in the last few months. This challenge, he understood. He dared not move.

'Who's there?' The voice became gruffer with repetition. Footfalls thumped in the courtyard, and another guard answered from the ground. 'What's the problem?'

'Thein!' called the sentry on the wall.

A third sentry answered from the ground, a few yards to Garn's right. 'You call me?'

'There's something in those bushes. Something big.'

Garn pursed his lips, tasting blood.

Boughs crackled. A spear darted toward him. He shied back as far as he dared, and the point became tangled in the brush. The guard tugged, sending the branches into a rattling dance. He pulled harder, and the tip came free in a wash of leaves and twigs. Suddenly, a cat burst from the shrubs, howling in rage as it raced into the night.

Startled, Garn stiffened, his sinews clamping into a rigid, painful spasm that, mercifully, passed quickly. Thein shouted words Garn did not understand, clearly profanities by his tone. Apparently, either Garn's fall had stunned the cat or fear had held it immobile until the spear had shaken it free. For the first time in more than a decade, Garn seriously contemplated the existence of gods.

'Thein?' The sentry on the wall prodded his companion.

'One of the princess' stupid cats,' Thein yelled back.

'You sure?' The wall guard sounded skeptical.

'I know what a cat looks like.' Lightning flashed, revealing a burly guard in Béarnian blue, staring at his hand, his shield propped against his hip. 'Damn animal clawed me.' Spear butt dragging in the mud, Thein shuffled back to his post.

Thunder slammed against Garn's ears, then faded into a rolling grumble. Apparently, the wall guard could not see through the twined branches that had closed over Garn. The gentle splash of his feet signaled that he, too, had resumed his vigil.

Garn sagged, waiting until his heart rate slowed and the sentries had fully turned their attention from the brush. Then, he freed himself from the jabbing branches, using thunder to hide the rustle of his movements. In the flashes of lightning, he glimpsed trees and outbuildings that did not fit Sterrane's description. Distant spying had already revealed that the crafted castle grounds had grown, the old wall had been dismantled and a new one carved to enclose more of the surrounding valley. In the nearly two decades since Béarn's heir had escaped his uncle's purgings, details of the castle and its courtyard had changed as well. Garn hoped desperately that Sterrane's escape passage had survived, though its exit now lay within the repositioned and restructured fortifications.

Once free of the bushes, Garn followed them and the wall eastward, skirting the castle's few lit windows. Wind stung, numbingly cold against his sodden tunic. He used each branching bolt of lightning to define the location of the sentries and tried to spot the ancient ash that Sterrane had called the 'tree of life.'

The brush grew denser until, at length, Garn was forced to crawl. Mud and thorns stung his cut knees, but the thick brambles hid him from the courtyard guards, and the springy green vines made little noise with movement. Bruised and wet, Garn cursed Sterrane. From the courtyard, the new wall towered higher than they had anticipated. He saw little chance of slipping past the wall sentries a second time to escape, and too many battles lay ahead. The steady pattern of rain seemed to mock him, a lone soldier against the defenses of the West's high kingdom.

It never occurred to Garn to surrender. Time and again, Santagithi's guards had shoved him into the gladiator pit to face adversaries who, under other circumstances, would have been strangers, acquaintances, or friends. Then, he had focused on the freedom that would one day become his and the woman whom he would one day marry. Survival had become his religion. And, once too familiar, despair became a stranger.

Lightning arched above the castle spires, etching a dark ash tree from the gloom, less than a yard ahead. Irrationally afraid he might lose it in the blackness, Garn sprang for it. Bark scraped skin from his fingers. A low moan of thunder sputtered and died.

Garn groped along the weathered trunk. His palm calluses grated against bark, then caught on the rim of a small hole. His fingers sank into wood chips and fur. Lightning flared. Fully revealed, Garn bit off an oath and dug furiously through the burrow, seeking some sign of the promised door, secured by inner hinges. A fingernail snapped against metal. Garn sucked air through his teeth. It required effort to shift the ancient, rusted latch, but the door yielded with a creak of corroded hinges. Swiftly, Garn ducked into the opening and pulled it closed behind him.

Blindly, Garn drew the tinderbox and dagger from his pockets and a torch from his belt. He slashed the dagger across flint, scattering sparks. These met the wet torch and died. *Damn!* Garn used the unsharpened edge of his dagger to scratch wax from the torch head and then tried again. This time, the pitch sputtered feebly, then lit. The wax made a soft hiss. Garn headed down the passageway.

Rats fled like shadows before the torchlight. The semi-circle of light revealed intricate carvings on the walls, blackened in patches from dampness and partially obscured by moss. Masters of stone craft, the Béarnides had sculpted the castle and its city from the mountain. Yet, despite their skill and the solidity of their materials, Garn wondered if a path so old could withstand time. He tried to imagine innocent, naive Sterrane as a child, fleeing through a damp, rat-infested tunnel with the screams of his mother, six siblings, and the most loyal guards and servants echoing behind him. Garn shivered at the pictures his mind conjured, marveling at how Sterrane had remained so innocent and gentle after such a tragedy.

Garn continued, the dense silence of the tunnel revising his conception of Sterrane's escape. More likely, buried beneath thicknesses of stone, he had heard nothing of the battle. Still, regardless of how much or little Sterrane had directly witnessed, the fact remained that he had lost his family, all of them at once. At one time, before the birth of Garn's own child, the significance of such a disaster would have been lost on him. His own father was a skilled gladiator who, offered freedom, had chosen the pit and died there. A scullery maid beaten and abandoned by her own parents, Garn's mother paid him little heed. At the request of Garn's father, Captain Rache had raised Garn, though little more than a child himself. But that relationship had degenerated into hatred the day Rache had helped capture Garn so that Santagithi could sentence him to life in a cage.

As always, bitterness welled up in Garn, accompanied by rage. He suppressed his wrath with the mental control to which Colbey had steered him more than a year ago. His thoughts returned to Sterrane, and he could not help but wonder how Béarn's heir had managed to escape the hot, vengeful malice that had at times driven Garn to madness and volcanic violence, even against his friends. With Rache's death had come a control, though not for the reasons Garn had expected. Now, Garn sincerely hoped he could fulfill Rache's dying request, wished that he could raise Rache's child better than Rache had raised Garn.

The passage ended abruptly. With a vicious curse, Garn threw back his dark, dripping hair and assessed the presumed cave-in he would need to clear to complete his journey. Wedging the torch in the crevice of a carving, he drew his dagger and chopped at the moss. Dirt peeled from the surface, then the dagger rasped against rocks, uncovering an etching of a spitted deer. Rather than a collapsed barricade of rubble, Garn had discovered the far wall of the tunnel. Replacing the dagger, he grabbed the torch, raising it to the ceiling. Cracks formed a square hatchway, with a central hole. Once, Garn guessed, a rope had graced the middle section, the hemp now rotted away.

Garn extinguished his torch, groping for the hatch in darkness. Sterrane's description and Shadimar's magic had revealed that the doorway would open into the room of a young girl who Sterrane could not identify. The brief research they had managed to do suggested that the child was Morhane's granddaughter.

Sterrane had also warned Garn that the closed hatch fell flush with the floor and could not be pried open from inside the castle, thwarting pursuit. Decades ago, Sterrane's eldest brother had slept in this room, with the panel wedged open but hidden. Sterrane had come upon the hatch by accident. Unable to justify his jaunt into his brother's room and fearing the elder boy's wrath, he had never mentioned his find. On the day of Morhane's attack, Béarn's oldest prince had been away from his room. Sterrane alone had escaped, pulling the hatch closed so that Morhane's men could not have followed, even had they known of the tunnel's existence. At that time, the ash tree exit had stood just outside the castle wall. Now, the damp, rodent-filled darkness confirmed Shadimar's claim that only the king, his heir, his most trusted bodyguard, and the Eastern Wizard knew about the route.

Light diffused through the crack. Hearing nothing, Garn poked his head into a room dimly illuminated by a single candle. Despite the gloom, rich furnishings struck a vivid contrast to the moldering plainness of the hidden tunnel. Multihued streamers dangled from the ceiling. Across the room, a simplistic pastel rendition of an animal-crowded forest encompassed an entire wall. To Garn's right, a shelf held a line of thin books with Bearnese titles and a silver mug. On a bed to his left, a child huddled beneath a finely-woven blanket. Wisps of sable hair spread across the pillow.

From long years of habit, Garn listened to the child's breathing, hearing the deep, slow regularity that indicated sleep. No other sound reached him. Quietly, Garn hooked his fingers through the crack and hoisted himself through the hatch, using his shoulders and back to support the door. As he eeled his legs through the opening, he twisted to catch a grip on the panel. The wood-lined stone slipped beneath his breeks. His grab fell short. Fear touched Garn as the hatchway slammed toward closing. Desperate, he thrust his left hand for the opening. The door crashed onto his knuckles, causing pain that momentarily incapacitated him. Garn hissed, choking off a cry.

The sleeper stirred. Her breaths quickened and went shallow.

Grasping his spent torch, Garn worked an end beneath the hatch, levering it open far enough to free his fingers. He left the torch in place to brace the hatch. Redness washed across his fingers, threatening a long, ugly bruise. He bit his lip, waiting for the agony to ebb.

The child rolled toward him. Black hair framed a round, olive-skinned face.

Garn froze, shielding the entryway with his body. Seeing no place to hide, he chose silence instead. The knife slid into his hand.

The girl's lids parted to reveal dark eyes. They rolled briefly, then she looked directly at Garn. '*Noca?*' She used the Béarnese word for 'grandfather.' She sat up, the fur trim of her sleeping gown ending in a jumble at her thighs. She looked no more than five or six years old.

The ache in Garn's fingers receded enough for him to drive it from his mind. He knew pain too well to let it steal his concentration when matters of consequence needed handling. It joined the background throb of his knees and the branch-stabbed bruises that peppered his body. He rose from his crouch, the dagger hidden, couched against his wrist. The steel felt cold and solid on his flesh, and the child looked small, no threat to his venture. Still, she only needed to cry out once to bring Morhane's guards, to cause Garn's execution, and to see to it that Sterrane never returned to his throne. Garn had hated the murder that Santagithi's guards had forced him to commit in the pit, and the idea of harming a child seemed an evil too repulsive to contemplate. *What must be done must be done.* Garn grimaced at the thought. *Damn! Why did she have to wake so easily.* Stalling the inevitable, he spoke. 'Hello,' he said in his best Béarnese, his voice sounding thick after the long silence. 'Who are you?'

The girl yawned. 'Miyaga,' she said in a tone that implied he should not have needed to ask.

Miyaga's confident fearlessness, despite the wary stranger in her bedchamber, aroused Garn's suspicions. He studied the room by the rapidly dimming candlelight. Nothing moved. He heard no breathing other than his own and the girl's. Satisfied they were alone, he dried moist palms on his tunic and headed to her bedside with the assurance of a man in a place where he belonged. 'Is King Morhane your *noca?*'

He guessed that her bravado stemmed from years of exposure to foreign courtiers. She had little to fear in a heavily guarded castle.

Miyaga hugged her knees to her chest, giggling. 'You talk funny.'

Garn fought impatience, kneading his fingers to restore the circulation and to work away tension and pain. He supposed his Béarnese must sound as imperfect as Sterrane's broken rendition of the trading tongue. 'So, is he your grandfather?'

Still snickering, she nodded assent.

Garn threw up his hands in an exaggerated gesture of sudden understanding. 'Then I'm your uncle, Garn.'

'Uncle . . . Garn?' She examined Garn, apparently uncertain of the significance of the title, but intuitively understanding it meant family.

'Which is *Noca*'s room?' Garn dropped his voice to a soft, conspiratorial whisper. 'I've got a surprise for him.'

Miyaga's eyes fairly danced. 'Can I see?'

'Not yet. First tell me where his room is.'

'Down there.' Miyaga pointed to the left of the door to her room, stretched the trim of her robe to her knees, and smiled. 'Two down. Are you really my uncle? What's the surprise?'

Garn fingered his dagger, the child's coy innocence like a lead weight in his chest. Miyaga's description only confirmed the location of Morhane's chambers, and Garn recognized his discussion with the child as a delaying tactic. No doubt she had to die; Garn dared not take a chance with his own life, the safety of his wife, and Sterrane's kingdom. But the idea of killing a child awakened a deep-seated ache of guilt he never knew he could feel. Sorrow descended like a storm. His own son, Rache, might be nearly as old as Miyaga before Garn held him again.

Memories surfaced in a hot rush, of the baby's near weightlessness against his chest and the joy that lit Mitrian's eyes whenever Rache had smiled. Yearning formed a hard knot in Garn's stomach. While his parents tended politics in a distant kingdom, Rache lived with the grandfather who had kept Garn a slave. While Garn attempted to usurp the mountain king with only a dagger and a flask of drugged wine, Rache was learning combat from the master of all swordsmen, adopting a reckless, savage heritage that might turn the world against him. Garn tried to picture his child, now a little more than two years old, but he could only visualize the baby he had not held for longer than a year. He knew that, in his place, Mitrian could not have slaughtered this little girl. *And neither can I.*

Garn slid the dagger back into his pocket. As he did, his arm brushed the bulge of the drugged wine, and it gave him an idea. Surely, the Wizard had left a margin of error on the amount of wine he would need for Morhane. *Even if there's not enough for both, I'd rather put the girl to sleep and kill the usurper than the other way around.* 'This is the surprise.' Crossing the room, he plucked the silver mug from her book shelf. 'I brought a special drink for your *noca*. But because you're so beautiful, I'd like you to taste it first.' He removed the bladder of wine, returned to Miyaga's side, and perched on the edge of her bed. 'You'll try it for me?'

Miyaga stared into his green eyes. She wrapped a hand about his well-muscled arm as he filled the mug with wine. 'I like you, Uncle Garn.'

'I like you, too.' *Obviously.* Garn handed her the cup, doubting Shadimar had given him enough of the sleeping poison for two, even if one was a child. Still, Garn did not brood. Getting Morhane to drink the drug-laced wine had always seemed the weak link in an otherwise reasonable plan. Shadimar had insisted that Garn take Morhane alive, leaving the pronouncement of punishment to the true king. When the time came, Garn hoped he would find some way to incapacitate Béarn's usurper king.

Miyaga took it from him, sniffing doubtfully at the sweet, red vintage. With Garn's encouragement, she took a mouthful and swallowed with a grimace. 'Oh, it's wine. Mother won't let me drink it, but she's dead and *Noca* doesn't care if I . . . '

Garn waved her silent. 'It's good. Finish.'

Obligingly, Miyaga took another swallow. Garn welcomed the reassuring return of caution that memory had dispersed. He placed his hand lightly on Miyaga's knee as she drank, but his senses were focused beyond the door. His eyes riveted on the exit, alert to any subtle movements. He listened for the gentle tap of footsteps or the soft hiss of voices.

Miyaga shook Garn's arm. 'Can I have more?' She raised the empty mug.

Garn frowned. Shadimar had said the poison worked quickly and that it was reasonably safe, but he did not want to give the child too much. 'Rest,' he said. Limited by time and the language barrier, he said nothing more.

Thankfully, that seemed enough for Miyaga. She yawned, crawling beneath the blanket. 'You'll be here in the morning?' She took his hand, her warm and sticky fingers nearly lost in his callused palm. Her squeeze, though feeble, reawakened the ache in his fingers.

'Yes,' Garn lied, uncertain what the morning would bring yet believing Miyaga would sleep through it anyway. With his other hand, he returned the wine pouch to his pocket. He remained at her side until her grip went lax and he recognized the familiar pattern of slumber that years caged beside other gladiators had taught him. He had learned to sleep on the barest edge of awakening, aware of every movement of his neighbors and their relation to himself, his food, and the tattered, foul-smelling rag that served as his only blanket.

Garn disengaged his hand, rose, and crept to the door. Back pressed to the wall, he clasped the hilt of his dagger and eased the door open a crack. The dimly lit corridor seemed deserted. Apparently, Morhane believed his outer gates impenetrable, and he saw no need for sentries in the inner bedchambers. At least, not in the hallways, which explained why the falling of the hatch had awakened Miyaga so easily. A child accustomed to booted footfalls marching outside her door all night would have slept through the noise.

Garn stepped into the corridor and pulled the door shut behind him. Many torches had burned to ashes in their wall sconces. Others guttered in a draft that swept the hall, creating a wave of flickering shadows. Anticipation tightened in Garn's chest. As he crept down the passage, he cringed at the faint scrape of his sandals against stone. He passed a bronze-bound teak door with only a casual glance and stopped before a set of metal doors emblazoned with the royal crest, a rearing bear beside a crown. He smeared sweat from his palms across his tunic, then pushed on the door. It opened on well-oiled hinges, without a sound.

Finery dazzled Garn as he slipped inside Morhane's room and eased the door closed behind him. In each corner of the room, hooks of gold and ivory supported hooded lanterns. A wardrobe crafted from silver lined one wall. Three chairs and a divan stood in a neat array, all padded with blue silk that matched the sapphires circling the lock of a chest beside the couch. In the center of the room, a curtain trimmed with lace partially hid a dais.

Sinews taut, Garn studied the room, gaze playing across the ornate furnishings. Snoring obscured any other noises in the chamber, but instincts nurtured by years of living like an animal alerted Garn to a movement in the shadow of the wardrobe.

Garn crouched, dagger whipping free. A smoke-colored hound advanced toward him, stiff-legged. A ridge of fur rose along its back. Head low, the dog curled its upper lip to expose wickedly sharp teeth. It growled.

A single snort sounded from the dais, then the snoring disappeared.

Garn's fingers locked on his dagger. His other hand hovered protectively near his throat. 'Call off your dog.'

No answer came from the bed, but Garn knew whoever lay there had awakened. The dog continued toward him.

'Call off your dog. Or Miyaga dies.' Garn had no intention of carrying out his threat. Unsure whether the king would even care about the girl's life, Garn waited, tense as a coiled spring.

No reply. The dog's legs bunched beneath it. Its hackles spread.

Sweat broke out on Garn's skin, but his voice remained steady. 'So be it.'

A rumbling, Western voice came from beyond the curtain. 'Bosh.'

The dog paused.

'If you're dead, you can't hurt Miyaga.'

Garn's attention remained on the dog. 'I've given her a slow poison. Only I know the antidote. She has until morning.'

'You're lying.' Anger entered the other's tone, but Garn believed he heard doubt as well.

'Would you risk Miyaga's life on that hunch?' Cautiously, Garn reached for the wine, uncertain where to take the stalemate. To spirit Morhane from his room to show him Miyaga's abnormally deep sleep meant risking the king shouting for his guards.

A hand slithered through a slit in the silks. Its next to last finger bore the king's signet ring that Sterrane had described. On it, an exquisitely detailed gold bear clutched a milky gemstone with a black center, a unique pearl discovered in a monstrous, ancient oyster that must have engulfed a smaller one. The hand parted the curtain, revealing a dark eye fringed by a black brow as thick as Garn's thumb. The other man studied Garn. Then, apparently noting the lack of an obvious weapon, he poked a bearded face through the slit. Curly black hair sprinkled with gray formed a coarse mane about craggy features. A medallion with the Béarnian royal crest nestled against his beard. 'You're lying,' he repeated.

The dog stalked forward again, now dangerously close to Garn. 'Six elephants around a tree. A giraffe with its head wrapped in vines . . . ' Garn began a calm recitation of Miyaga's mural to prove that he had just come from her room. He broke off suddenly, finishing with a command. 'Call . . . it . . . off!'

'Bosh, here!' the man said.

The dog sidled to its master. Its ears twitched toward Garn, and its thick tail fell in supplication.

Though relieved, Garn did not drop his guard. He studied the man before him. His sleeping robe shimmered purple in the veiled lamplight. His figure and features reminded Garn of Sterrane, though this man held himself with far more grace and confidence. The black locks, liberally flecked with gray, fell past his shoulders. His wide girth proclaimed wealth. The signet ring made the identification certain. Clearly, Garn had found the king.

'Who are you?' Morhane asked. 'How did you get past the guards?'

'Sit here.' Garn indicated the jeweled chest.

Morhane hesitated a moment, then strode from the dais without a hint of fear, purple robe swirling about his ankles. He paused before the chest.

'Sit.' Driven to paranoia by the king's composure, Garn swept the room with his gaze. Stepping cautiously around the king, he tore open the curtain. A metal-framed bed sat upon the dais, empty except for a rumpled pile of furs. For an instant, Garn thought he saw movement further in the room. His head jerked toward it, but he saw nothing out of place.

The dog growled. Morhane took a seat on the chest, tapping it with both hands. 'This box holds more gold than you could carry.'

'I don't want your money.'

A faint noise scraped beneath Garn's words. He spun toward the sound, seeing nothing.

Morhane made a sudden noise. The dog launched itself at Garn.

Garn whirled to meet the attack, slammed suddenly by a beast that weighed nearly as much as he did. Teeth gashed his right forearm, then clamped onto flesh. Garn turned a pained scream into a gasp, the dagger thudding to the ground. He staggered, jerking the dog off-balance. He lashed his left hand up to its throat and strained against it. His foot lurched against the knife, sending it skidding across the planks.

The dog bore in, its teeth crushing through muscle, seeking bone. Agony roused anger, and Garn drew on the strength that Colbey had taught him to find within himself. He kicked, driving his foot into the beast's gut. Garn's flesh tore. The dog hurtled through the air, crashing into the wall. Bone snapped, and it slid to the floor, limp.

Blood trickled from Garn's arm with a heat that only fueled his rage. The battle had placed him between Morhane and the only door, and he remained there, green gaze boring into the king. 'You idiot. Is this how little you care about your granddaughter?'

Morhane's mouth split into a cruel grin of triumph that seemed horribly inappropriate. An instant later, Garn knew without the need to look that someone stood behind him. The tip of a blade gouged his spine. 'Don't move.' The speaker radiated a confidence Garn dared not challenge. He froze.

'Put your hands behind your back.' The bodyguard spoke fluent Béarnese, yet his accent reminded Garn of the dialect used by the regular citizens of the trading city of Pudar.

Garn hesitated less than a second, yet that was too long.

'Now!' the man said. He did not shout, yet the authority in his voice became nearly irresistible. Clearly, he was the thing that had twice flitted across Garn's peripheral vision, using Morhane and the dog to mask his progress.

Garn searched for his dagger. It lay on the planks, halfway between him and the king.

Morhane laughed. 'What took you so long, Mar Lon?'

Almost instantly, cold steel jabbed Garn's back, a grim, nonverbal warning from a guard forced to address his king instead of reinforcing his threat. 'Sire, I timed it as well as I could. Are you displeased?'

Garn dove, rolling for the dagger. Scooping it into his hand, he spun into a crouch, the movement splashing blood from the dog's bite on his arm.

Mar Lon charged, meeting Garn as he rose. The sword tip poked the base of Garn's throat. Even as Garn whipped up the dagger to meet the attack, his mind registered the grim certainty of death. The world's slowest warrior could bury the blade into his windpipe before he could complete his defensive strike. Still, he finished the arc from momentum and habit. Years in the pit had taught him not to consider the consequences of defeat. Death only meant an end to the cycle of hunger, chains, and forced murders, the slashing agony of whips and the pounding bruises or stinging blade cuts inflicted by enemies. Day after day, battle after battle, he fought for no better reason than survival, to continue a life he hated because he had no other.

For reasons Garn could not fathom, Mar Lon hesitated. Garn's dagger rang against the sword hard enough to jerk it sideways. The tip raked Garn's throat, drawing blood. *I should be dead. He could have killed me. And he should have.* Mar Lon ripped the sword from Garn's block, reversing into an arching upstroke. Garn met the attack with a brutal twist, parrying it harmlessly aside. Mar Lon feigned a long sweep to Garn's head, changing to a sudden jab for his abdomen. An abrupt dodge and lunge was all that saved Garn. He did not press his advantage, instead risking a sideways glance at Morhane. The king still sat on the chest, watching, fully trusting the ability of his guard.

Garn assessed his opponent. Mar Lon stood half a head taller than Garn, about average for a central Westerner though small for a Béarnide. He wore leather gauntlets molded to his fingers, designed to protect his hands without hampering his agility. His quick responses and movements revealed sword mastery, but his hesitant, not quite committed style betrayed inexperience. *Well trained and naturally agile, but mostly untried.* Garn filed the information away. *Surely I can use that against him.* Garn tensed, aware Mar Lon had every other advantage: familiarity, support, and a longer weapon that would soon tip the odds completely in his favor. *I have to move fast. Have to do something unexpected or I'm dead for sure.*

Mar Lon slashed for Garn's chest. Garn shuffled backward. Risking his fingers, he surged in with the dagger. His shorter blade scratched down the longer one, locking the sword against his cross guard. Twisting, Garn threw off the weapon, driving a foot into Mar Lon's leg.

Mar Lon dodged, saving his knee. For an instant, he lost control of the sword's direction.

Garn seized the moment. Flipping the dagger to his left hand, he sprang into extension, reversing his direction. The knife hovered at Morhane's throat. 'Don't move.' He used the trading tongue, gaze flicking from Morhane to Mar Lon.

The king went rigid.

Mar Lon regained control of his weapon, then stopped. Sweat trailed strands of dark hair across his forehead. Hazel eyes swiveled to the king, requesting guidance and receiving none. He lowered the sword but did not sheathe it.

Garn knew he stood in a tenuous stalemate. Clearly, his capturing King Morhane was no longer a possibility. His options had narrowed to three. He could try to use Morhane as a hostage to slip from the castle, though he doubted he would get far, considering Morhane's retinue of guards. He could surrender and hope curiosity or cruelty would goad the king to keep him alive for information or torture. The third possibility seemed the most useful to Garn, one he once would have chosen without the need to consider. With a single stab, he could kill King Morhane, opening the way for Sterrane's rule, but guaranteeing his own death on Mar Lon's sword. Only one dagger cut lay between Garn and completing his mission, if not in the most ideal fashion, at least in a successful one.

Garn choked on the irony. Now that he had a wife he loved, a child that was a part of him, and a safe haven in a town that had once kept him a slave, he was about to die for a king who had, so far, shown little interest in reclaiming his throne. Garn recalled sitting before a campfire at the end of the Great War, remembered Shadimar telling Sterrane that the time had come. He recalled how a look of terror had crossed the heir's gigantic features and how he had refused the Wizard like a child on the verge of a tantrum.

Mar Lon shifted ever so slightly, studying Garn, seeking an opening.

'Be still.' Garn's grip tightened, and he despised his own pause. The dagger poked Morhane's flesh, indenting the swarthy flesh. Rache had taught Garn never to hesitate, that battlefield decisions should be instantly made and executed as quickly as the thought rose to mind. But Garn had little experience with strategy. Always before, his only decision had been to kill or to be killed. Never had he held so much more than his life at stake. He pictured Mitrian, large-boned, with masculine hands and feet, yet beautifully slender and graceful. The Renshai sword maneuvers that Colbey and the elder Rache had taught had granted her a skill any warrior would envy, but it had only enhanced the arcs and curves that, to Garn, made the female body seem so perfect. Mitrian had paid a price for her skill. Since Garn had gained control of the temper that had committed him to life as a gladiator, he noticed that the Renshai training had claimed Mitrian's gentleness, replacing it with a savagery that Garn hoped she would learn to control, as he had.

Suddenly, Morhane stiffened.

Cued, Garn whipped his attention to the king, too late. Steel flashed from the king's sleeve. A needle sharp blade gashed Garn's wrist, severing part of the muscle. The knife toppled from his hand. Pain spread through his arm, sparking rage. The familiar primal desperation overcame him, throwing him into blind, murderous rage. He slammed his fist into the king's head, feeling flesh give beneath his knuckles. Morhane slumped. Garn whirled to face Mar Lon.

The bodyguard's sword cut a gleaming arc. Garn lurched toward it, prepared to duck under and bolt for the door. The blade curved abruptly inward, slapping into Mar Lon's gauntlet. The last thing Garn expected was for the guard to hit himself. Surprise stole his timing. And, when Mar Lon grasped the blade, lashing the hilt in a full stroke for Garn's head, it caught him fully off his guard. Steel crashed against Garn's temple. White light exploded in Garn's head, stealing thought and vision. A sensation of falling trickled through to him. Then darkness pounded him into oblivion.

3 Béarn's Justice

Garn awakened to an agony that throbbed through his head and the significant, but lesser pains of his injured arm, wrist, and fingers. Not daring to move, he assessed his surroundings through closed eyes. He lay on a stone floor warm from his body, and he recognized the linen touch of his tunic and breeks against his skin. He felt the familiar, heavy pinch of shackles around his wrists and ankles. He tensed at the restraints, even that simple movement flashing pain through his head. Nearby, he heard another man breathing. Other noises wafted to him as well, distant and muffled by stone: an intermittent, wailing moan; clanking metal; and garbled voices with Béarnian accents.

Cautiously, Garn opened his eyes. His blurry gaze found bare stone walls and a single oak door, bound with brass. Between him and the exit, Mar Lon crouched with his sword drawn. He met Garn's stare, saying nothing.

Garn struggled to a sitting position, hindered by dizziness as much as by the fetters that clamped his hands together behind him and the shackles that encircled his ankles. He exaggerated the difficulty these gave him, using the time and movement to test their strength. The bonds would hinder escape, but they could not prevent it. He had worn manacles the day he broke Captain Rache's back, and the weighted steel had only added power to his blow. The memory of that incident remained vivid in Garn's mind, though the rabid sense of triumph that had accompanied it had soured. Then, they had fastened his arms before rather than behind him. And Rache had hurled himself in front of the strike to protect Santagithi's other captain, believing himself quick enough to avoid Garn's hammering fists. It was the only time that Garn knew Rache to misjudge an opponent, and it had cost the Renshai the use of his legs. Now, in a dark, squalid corner of Béarn's castle, Garn hoped Morhane's personal guard would also underestimate him.

'Who do you serve that Morhane's gold can't buy you?' Mar Lon studied Garn intently, and Garn returned the scrutiny. The guard wore mail beneath a tunic of blue decorated with the tan bear that was Béarn's symbol. A cap with a royal blue plume identified him as an officer, and he still wore the leather gauntlets. Garn could see why a man who wielded his sword by the blade might need to protect his hands. The thought made him frown, the facial movement causing another wave of pain. The ex-gladiator had raised dirty fighting to an art form, yet he had never seen such a technique, not even from the master swordsman, Colbey. *And why should I have? Like me, Colbey fights to kill. What possible purpose could this guard have for hitting me with the hilt instead of the blade?* Garn tried to assign reason to action, but the blow to his head muddled his thoughts.

Little experienced with conversational conventions, Garn let the pause hang long beyond propriety before answering. He spoke in the same tongue Mar Lon had used, the Trading language. 'I don't *serve* anyone. And I never will.'

Mar Lon looked perplexed. He kept his sword drawn, the blade resting across one knee. 'What's your name?'

Garn declined to answer.

Mar Lon's face creased further. He tried a different tack. 'I'm Mar Lon. I'm the current bard.'

Garn said nothing, unfamiliar with the term 'bard' and confused by the guard's decision to volunteer information to one he should have been questioning. The oddities of the man's manner made Garn cautious, and the fog that hazed his mind made even simple concepts difficult to grasp.

Mar Lon pressed. 'Does that mean anything to you?'

Garn shook his head and immediately wished he had not. The throb intensified. He winced.

Mar Lon flinched in a response Garn could only interpret as sympathetic. 'Hundreds of years ago, my forefather angered the gods with his curiosity. In punishment, Odin cursed him with a driving need to know everything, yet to pass the knowledge on only in song. We're musicians.' He paused, one brow cocked, awaiting some comment from Garn.

Long years of listening without speaking made Garn a poor conversationalist. Uncertain what Mar Lon expected from him, he remained insolently silent. He noted that the need to play an instrument might explain Mar Lon's caution with his fingers, but he saw no reason to announce this observation aloud. Surely, Mar Lon already knew his reason for using gauntlets.

When he received no response, Mar Lon kept his gaze locked on Garn as he spoke, as if to gauge the response to each word. 'Odin also saw to it that the current bard, male or female, became the closest personal bodyguard of the king of Béarn.'

Garn returned Mar Lon's attention stare for stare, though the effort dulled his vision. Garn had no idea why Mar Lon continued to talk about himself, but he feigned interest. Behind his back, his fingers explored the fetters, the attempt reawakening the pains in his arm, wrist, and the fingers bruised by the trapdoor. For an instant, their sharpness stole his attention from the pounding in his head and the dense fog that smothered his thoughts. Someone had tied bandages across the dog bite as well as the gash the king's stiletto had raked across his wrist. The cloth added bulk to Garn's meaty forearms, making the shackles unnaturally tight. His tactile exploration told him that the weakest point was the chain between the cuffs, yet breaking even that would require a burst of mentally-enhanced physical strength. He lowered his head, trying to dredge power from his innermost core, as Colbey had taught him.

Mar Lon continued, 'My grandfather served King Buirane, then his son Valar. My father protected Valar, even through Morhane's coup. But once the fighting was over and Morhane proved the survivor, he had no choice but to guard the new king, no matter how Morhane came to power. Had Valar survived, it would have become my lot to serve his heir. And I would have done so with honor.' He fell silent.

Garn raised his head to Mar Lon's earnest and somewhat urgent glance. Though inexperienced with puzzles, Garn was gradually placing inconsistencies together and trying to find sense in them. *He could have killed me, but he didn't.* Garn concentrated on the grinding in his head, aware Mar Lon must have pulled the blow that grounded him. *He could have killed me twice, at least.* For the moment, Garn put escaping on hold. *He's volunteered useful information without pressure. And he's all but pledged his services to Sterrane.* Two possibilities seeped sluggishly into Garn's concussion-slowed mind. *Either he's guessed who I'm working for and he's trying to join our cause, or he's trying to get me to trust him so I accidentally betray my friends.* Preparation for breaking his bonds was forgotten as Garn struggled with a decision he felt ill-equipped to make. To keep Mitrian safe, he knew he would do better not to place faith in the goodwill of a stranger, especially one so obviously trusted by an enemy. Yet to pass up the opportunity to have an ally inside the castle seemed folly, especially with his own wits blunted. 'My name is Garn,' he said, uncertain where to go from there.

Mar Lon sheathed his sword. He avoided Garn's gaze, apparently forced into a decision of his own. He opened his mouth as if to speak, then closed it. He opened and closed his mouth again. Suddenly, he rose, moving swiftly toward Garn.

Garn held his ground, studying angles. The shackles gave him scant space to maneuver.

Mar Lon pulled a key from his pocket, displaying it for Garn. He inched closer, reaching for Garn's legs. Carefully, he inserted the key into the lock of the shackles, twisting until it clicked. The metal cuffs fell free.

Garn glanced from shackles to Mar Lon, not bothering to remove his ankles from the opened bands. He found himself completely incapable of fathoming the other's motivation. 'Why would you do that?'

Mar Lon twirled a finger, indicating that Garn should turn around so that he could work on the wrist fetters. 'Because I need you to trust me. It's nearly sunup, and we just don't have time to go through all the preliminaries.' He repeated the gesture. 'Turn around.'

Garn obeyed, watching the bard from over his shoulder. 'Why should it matter if I trust you?'

The lock on the fetters snapped open, and they fell from Garn's wrists. Mar Lon answered indirectly, 'According to the songs I learned from my father who learned them from his mother and on back through the centuries, there was a time when the terms "lie" and "traitor" had no meaning. In the beginning of time, Odin banished all chaos, including dishonor, disorder, and immorality, creating our world and its beings only from law. A Cardinal Wizard once accused me of harboring chaos. If that means I might turn against the false king who had my father executed and slaughtered his own twin to gain the throne, then so be it.' He broke off somewhat abruptly.

Rubbing at his arms, Garn turned back to face Mar Lon. The bard stared at the ceiling as if expecting divine retribution, if not for his claim of harboring chaos, then for violating the restriction against the bard teaching in any way but song.

There was nothing subtle about Mar Lon's proclamation, yet still Garn hesitated.

Mar Lon's gaze flitted to Garn, awaiting some response he did not get. He pulled Garn's knife from his pocket and offered the hilt.

Shocked, Garn took the dagger, no longer able to really doubt Mar Lon's good intentions. 'What makes you think I have some connection to Valar's heir?'

Mar Lon flashed a weary smile, the expression making him appear ten years older. 'You didn't harm any of the palace guards. I checked. To avoid all of them, you have to be the quietest sneak thief in the kingdom. Or else you came through the tunnel.'

Garn fingered his dagger, confused. He could not help wondering why, if Morhane's men knew about the secret entrance, they did not keep it guarded.

That thought was answered by the rest of Mar Lon's words. He broke into song, his voice beginning as a mellow tenor, then crossing three octaves without a break or quaver:

'Prophecies are only words until
A Wizard chooses to fulfill
The forecast his predecessor spoke
From the strongest magic he could invoke.

'Long ago, it was decreed
That a Béarnian heir would find the need
Of a secret tunnel through the stone
That to all but a few must remain unknown.

'So the Eastern Wizard carved a route,
And being magically astute,
Told of it only to the kings,
Their eldest sons, and the guard who sings.

'Although it seemed cruel and stark,
The queen and heir's siblings were left in the dark.
For the Wizard feared rightly the king's own seed
Might turn against brother, driven by greed.'

Mar Lon finished, lapsing back into his normal speaking voice. 'Sorry about the rhyme scheme, but I improvised. Obviously, there's not a standing song about such a thing.'

Garn did not know whether to laugh or back carefully away. 'Do you always do that?'

'Do what?'

'Just start singing for no good reason. It's like having a conversation with a bird.'

Mar Lon shrugged. 'It goes with the title, I'm afraid. Odin's curse. If I say too much in normal words, I risk the wrath of gods.'

Garn questioned the guard's sanity. He had seen some strange rituals in the name of religion, but this went beyond Colbey's battle cries, the ululating chants of Santagithi's people beseeching the faceless god of winter to allow spring to come, or the unison storytelling of the idol worshiping cult at Corpa Leukenya. 'I see,' Garn said, though he did not.

'It only becomes a problem when I have to teach.' Wisely, Mar Lon dropped the conversation. 'Forget about that for the moment. All I'm trying to say is that, besides me, the only people who could know about that tunnel are a Cardinal Wizard and Valar's heir. If either of them sent you, I have to support you. Perhaps I'm misinterpreting my position, but I have to believe my loyalties lie with Valar's heir and not with Valar's brother.'

Garn could not wholly drop his skepticism, even with his muddled sensorium. 'If you don't like Morhane, why do you serve him? And, if you're so willing to turn against him, why does he trust you?'

'Garn, neither of us has time for a seventy verse aria. The simplest way I can think to say it: When the father of all gods tells you that your line must faithfully serve the king, you do it to the best of your abilities, no matter how repulsive that king might seem. Until now, I had no choice of king but Morhane. Your presence suggests otherwise. My loyalty to Valar's heir cannot and will not falter so long as he lives.' He turned a hopeful look on Garn. Having told all, he could not afford to have made a mistake. 'As to Morhane, he knows Odin's curse on the bards as well; always my ancestors have served the ruling king. But he doesn't know about the tunnel. Nor that I would place the true heir's needs over his. He has every reason to trust me implicitly.'

Garn mulled the information, understanding the importance of time. To deny the existence of gods meant rejecting all of the supernatural phenomena that accompanied faith. Though Shadimar bore the title Eastern Wizard, Garn had seen nothing to prove Shadimar was anything more than a learned old man who tended to talk with a confusing and cryptic subtlety that annoyed Garn. Shadimar's claim that Odin's laws bound him too tightly to squander magic seemed more like an excuse. Still, it did not matter if Garn believed in gods, Wizards, or bards and their vows. If Mar Lon and Morhane believed the bodyguard had a divine bond to the king of Béarn, the truth did not matter.

Mar Lon fidgeted. 'You did use the tunnel?'

'Yes.' Garn chose to put Mar Lon at ease by proving his knowledge. 'From the ash tree to Miyaga's room.'

Mar Lon smiled. Tension seemed to flow from his limbs, and it made him look boneless in comparison to his previous alertness. He leaned forward conspiratorially. 'We're in the deepest part of the dungeon now. The exit leads just outside the wall.' He amended, 'The new wall. The way the escape tunnel once did. That way, if a dangerous enemy ever escaped, he wouldn't get loose on the castle grounds. Be careful. You'll still have to get past the guard on watch, and there's always a good one selected for that sector. I'll tell the king not to say anything about your break-in because I think you must have had help from within the guard force and I don't want the traitor to know of our suspicions until we catch him. Morhane will believe that.'

Mar Lon began to pace, scratching at the stubble on his chin. 'Later, I'll tell him that things have gotten too dangerous. I'm not sure who to trust, and I need to secrete him from the castle with one or two of his most faithful while I work on the problem.' He stopped short, directly before Garn. 'I can't go myself. Directly leading the king into a trap would violate my vows for sure, and I think I can help your cause more here at the castle. I'll have these others slip him from the castle tonight. Where do you want them to take him?'

Again, Garn hesitated at the thought of revealing his friends' location to Morhane's bodyguard. Then, darkness hovered, and he feared for his consciousness. He desperately needed sleep, an escape from the throbbing and some quiet stillness for his body to heal the damage. Having chosen to trust Mar Lon, he had little choice but to place as much responsibility as possible into the other's hands. 'Lead him to the woods on the northern border of town. Continue as if on the second street to the east of the main road. Take him to the first clearing.' Garn chose a random location a short distance from Sterrane's current camp. 'We'll find him.'

Mar Lon resumed pacing. 'Please, try not to hurt whoever I send with Morhane. I'll try to pick guards likely to shift their loyalties to Valar's heir without arousing Morhane's suspicions, but he may insist on those he trusts most. Here, at the castle, I believe your worst threat will be Morhane's captain, Rathelon. He's the king's illegitimate son and every bit as evil as his father. Under ordinary circumstances, he'd become regent until Miyaga grew old enough to take the throne.' He stopped before Garn again. 'The less blood shed, the better. I know how to fight. It's part of my training. But my cause is, and always has been, peace. I've never killed a man. I would do so in the cause of my king.' He smiled, looking at Garn. 'My *real* king.' He savored the words, then shifted back to his more sobering point. 'But I'd rather not be placed in a position where I have to.' Moving to the door, he opened it a crack and peeked through it. A moment later, he opened it fully, exited, and motioned for Garn to follow.

Garn rose, still clutching the knife, and slipped through the door after Mar Lon. Light from the room diffused into a black hallway, revealing unadorned stone walls. Reluctant to stumble through darkness, Garn addressed the bard. 'Should I take the torch?'

'It's probably safer in the dark.'

Garn did not agree, but he trusted his instincts and hearing. So long as he followed in Mar Lon's footsteps, he doubted he would fall prey to a trick, trap, or ambush.

'It's a dismal maze from here, completely empty of implements for light or marking. If you don't know your way, you might never get out. Stay close.'

Garn had no intention of doing otherwise. He followed the light, steady scuff of Mar Lon's boots against granite through a series of winds and turns, trying to concentrate on the specifics of the route, though with little success. His bruised mind seemed incapable of clinging to details. Breezes and occasional touches to the walls revealed cross corridors that Mar Lon avoided.

Either because he needed to concentrate himself or to avoid distracting Garn, Mar Lon did not speak until he came to a sudden stop in the middle of a hallway. 'There.' Taking Garn's hand, he raised it to the ceiling, guiding his fingers to the outline of an ironbound trapdoor. Mar Lon released Garn. Keys clinked, followed by the snap of an opening lock. 'I'm going to need some help. It's heavy.'

Garn placed his hands on the hatch near Mar Lon's.

'Ready. Push.'

Garn strained, hearing the rush of air as Mar Lon assisted. The panel shifted.

'Careful,' Mar Lon hissed, stepping aside. Rubble funneled through the opening, moist soil mixed with weeds and small stones. First light filtered through behind the avalanche, dim yet blinding after the total darkness of the labyrinth. Dawn wove pink between layers of pale blue clouds, igniting chips of pyrite in the Béarnian roadway. Garn could see the castle wall to his left. On the far side of a cleared area with only a few trees, a scraggly, mountain forest stretched into the distance. To his right lay the gray blocks of Béarn's city. 'Go,' Mar Lon said. 'Quickly and carefully. Good luck.'

Garn scampered through the hole. The instant he stood on high ground, the panel winched closed, disappearing into the granite of the roadway. Again, Garn marveled at the intricacies of Béarnian masonry. Excitement thrilled through him. After so many near mistakes, he had set the stage for a coup more thoroughly than Shadimar had any right to hope. *Morhane delivered to us. An ally in the castle.* It seemed too right to be real, and that concerned Garn. His intuition told him to trust Mar Lon. But though those same instincts had saved him from maiming or death in the gladiator pit, they had not served him so faithfully when it came to judging people and their intentions. His upbringing gave him little basis for understanding deceit.

I need to get back to the others as quickly as possible. Let them judge Mar Lon's words. Garn gave the territory around him only a cursory glance, crouching and waiting behind a tended hedge. Time trickled past, during which Garn let his mind lapse into the void it sought. Finally, just when he feared he might have dozed off and missed the sentry's passage, footsteps crunched over the rocky roadway. Garn saw flashes of blue between the branches, the movement of a guard wearing Béarn's colors. The man marched by without pausing. Clearly, he had not seen Garn's still form, and his assigned route would now take him into the thickest quarter of the royal city.

Garn followed the sounds of the sentry's movements until they faded. He knew he should remain still, seeking others, tracking every noise. But, muddled by his head wound and believing himself safe now, he chose speed over caution and made a dash for the woodlands.

Trees whirled past, and the town of Béarn became a blur of dark and light patches in the dawn light. As Garn whisked past a twisted copse of vines, he saw sudden movement. A stranger's voice broke the early morning hush, speaking Béarnese in deep, strident bellows. 'Hey! Hey, you there! Stop!' Footfalls chased him.

Garn lowered his head and ran on. The other lunged toward him, quick despite his tremendous size. He jabbed a spear haft at Garn's feet.

Garn swerved, but not far enough. Wood crashed against his ankle, sparking pain. A sweep of the pole stole his balance. He teetered momentarily, then fell, rolling from habit. Pain slammed his head, masking his lesser pains. He had just worked his way to a crouch when he found himself staring at the business end of the spear. The guard held the weapon just far enough above him to gather the momentum he would need to kill Garn, yet just close enough to strike before he could move. Certain he faced a trained warrior, Garn froze. *Mar Lon told me only one guard would be here.* Though he felt misled, Garn doubted Mar Lon had done so on purpose. He let the deeper portions of his mind worry the inconsistency while he struggled to focus more intense concentration on the threat.

The spearman towered over Garn, large even for a Béarnide. Muscle packed his tall, huge-boned frame. Black hair and a beard framed a meaty face with small, deep-set eyes. He wore the chain mail, tunic, and tabbard of Béarn's on-duty guards and the plumed cap of an officer. A sword hung in a scabbard at his hip. 'Who are you?'

Garn saw no reason to withhold the information; this man would have no cause to know his name. 'Garn.' *A commander. Why would a commander be here?* Garn drew upon his own brief experiences as a Pudarian town guard.

'Where were you going?'

Cautiously, Garn raised a hand, pointing toward the woodlands. The fall had dizzied him again, and he did not yet trust himself to speak.

The officer watched Garn's hand rather than the direction indicated by the gesture. 'Where did you come from?'

Garn shifted his arm, now pointing toward the town.

The guardsman frowned. He had received fair answers to his questions, yet they told him nothing. 'Why were you running?'

Dazed and inexperienced with alibis, Garn found no clever responses. Believing any answer less incriminating than hesitation or silence, he spoke the first words that came to his mind, using the trading tongue. 'I was told running makes a man healthier.'

The guard's craggy features crunched in doubt. He switched to the

trading tongue as well, though far less gracefully than most Westerners. 'Did you hear me chasing you?'

It seemed pointless to lie. 'Yes.'

'Why didn't you stop?'

'I . . . ' Garn started, seeing only one way to go with the query, yet
knowing it might antagonize the guard. Still, any answer seemed
better than a guilty pause. 'I thought, perhaps, someone told you the
same thing about running.'

The guardsman frowned. Still, he chose to talk rather than act, and
Garn could only presume that, until he admitted to some crime, the
man could not legally harm or arrest him. 'You're injured.'

Naturally, Garn glanced to the bandages on his left wrist and right
forearm. Mar Lon had done a careful job, yet the fall had reopened
Morhane's knife slash and blood drew a red smear across the rag. The
wounds being self-evident, Garn saw no reason to reply. Yet from his
years of freedom, he had learned that most people expected a response
to anything they said, no matter how obvious. Silence might seem
insolent, so he replied. 'Yes.'

'How?'

'Work accident.' Garn could think of nothing more specific or
cunning. 'It was healing fine until you tripped me.'

The officer abandoned that line of questioning for now. 'You're no
Béarnide.'

Again, Garn saw no reason to respond. He felt queasy with pain,
and the guardsman's comments seemed pointless. But he forced an
answer. 'True, I'm no Béarnide. I'm just visiting. Could you please
remove the spear?'

'Who?'

'You. Could you please remove . . . '

The guard waved him silent. 'I meant "who" as in *who* are you
visiting?' The spear remained in place.

Now, Garn could not help but hesitate. He knew no individual
Béarnides, except Sterrane, Miyaga, Morhane, and Mar Lon. None of
those seemed appropriate. Memory brought one other name to mind,
a man Mar Lon had mentioned. He hoped he had the name's
pronunciation correct. 'Rathelon. The guard captain.' Garn fairly
grinned at his cleverness. Surely this lesser officer would not risk
offending a guest of his commander.

'Yes,' the Béarnide said. 'That's me.' He relaxed slightly, apparently
put at ease by Garn's knowledge. 'Now, who are you visiting?'

It took Garn a moment to understand what had just transpired.
Trapped, he knew he had to divert Rathelon without arousing more
suspicion. He considered inventing a name that sounded Béarnian, but
he knew that would be folly. Surely, Rathelon knew every citizen of

the mountain city. 'May I go now? Or is there some law against running in Béarn?'

'There is if you're running because you stole something.'

'I didn't.'

'How do I know that?'

'Is anyone missing anything?'

The spear continued to hover. 'Not that I know of. Yet.'

Garn considered the objects on his person. Rathelon would not be able to tell the wine was poisoned unless he drank it, an action which would, by itself, solve the problem. Surely many people carried a knife and a tinderbox. Impatient to return to Mitrian, Sterrane, and Shadimar, Garn grew sarcastic. 'You're welcome to search me for . . . um . . . whatever it is that's not missing yet.' He opened his guard fully, hoping Rathelon would take the challenge. If the captain came close enough to touch Garn, the spear and sword would become useless. Even as large and sinewy as Rathelon was, Garn guessed he would prove stronger, and his shorter limbs would gain him leverage.

Apparently deciding that a man who would offer him an open search could be hiding nothing, Rathelon did not bother. 'We do have a curfew.'

Garn glanced into the sky where the golden glow of morning crept over the background of forest. 'You have a curfew against being out after *sunup?*' Garn's words reminded him of the passage of time, and urgency kept him from measuring his words or his tone. Rathelon's stalling made it clear that he held no true charges against Garn.

Rathelon studied Garn through slitted, black eyes as emotionless as marbles. 'Clearly, you were out before sunup.'

'Clearly to who? Did you see me then? I didn't leave the indoors until dawn.' Garn spoke honestly, though it did not matter. Truth or lie, Rathelon could not prove otherwise. 'Now, I'm honored to have met the captain of the guard, but I really do have to go.' Cautiously, he rose. This time, luck had worked against him. Probably, he had come upon Rathelon coincidentally, while the captain was making routine rounds to check his sentries.

Rathelon frowned, keeping the spear on Garn, though he did not stop the ex-gladiator from standing. 'You still haven't told me who you're visiting.'

No longer able to avoid the question, Garn chose insolence, seeing a personal affront as the only sure way to divert the guard. 'Your wife.'

'What?'

'I was visiting your wife.' Garn knew that, as the captain of the guard, Rathelon would have a full and unwavering faith in the law. Trusting in that, Garn pressed, hoping his effrontery would pass for understandable, self-righteous annoyance at being inappropriately detained. 'You won't recognize her, though. I shaved her beard.'

Rathelon's nostrils flared. His hands blanched on the spear haft.

Garn held his ground. 'May I go now?'

Reluctantly, Rathelon withdrew the spear. 'Go. But I warn you. If I find out you've done anything, no matter what it is, I'll find a way to get you executed. And I'll do it with my own hands.' He glowered. 'I'm forbidden to challenge on duty; but if I ever see you when I'm not working, you had best hope your sword is at least half as sharp as your tongue.'

Fighting words Garn knew. Many retorts sprang to his mind, the least of which would have goaded Rathelon into immediate combat. But Garn wisely kept these to himself. Instead, he walked away, careful to move out of spear range before turning his back on the captain.

Rathelon's grumbled words reached him, garbled but understandable. 'Stupid *wisule's* bastard.'

Garn scowled at the insult but continued on, certain he would see the captain again. When he did, he doubted he could avoid a real fight. And he was not at all sure he wanted to.

4 The High King's Heir

Sterrane sat on a weathered stump in the sparse, mountain forests of Béarn, watching the sky dull to pewter as the sun sank below the line of trees. His war ax lay propped against a deadfall near his feet. The last rays of sunlight gathered on the blade, making it seem to glow, a strange, metallic presence amid nature's softer colors and less angular shapes. Shadimar sat in the center of the clearing that now served as a camp, stirring ashes from the dying campfire with a stick. Wrinkled flesh hugged arms so thin they seemed to lack muscle or fat, yet the ease of his movements kept him from looking frail. White hair cascaded from his head to meet a full beard. Though age had changed the color, the strands maintained their youthful thickness. He had not changed in the eighteen years since he had met six-year-old Sterrane and spirited the heir to his storm-warded ruins near the Town of Santagithi.

The wolf, Secodon, sat before Shadimar, gaze following the repetitive circles of the Wizard's arm. Sterrane knew that Garn and Mitrian crouched in the trees beyond the clearing, awaiting the arrival of Morhane and his promised escort. Yet, for once, the closeness of friends failed to soothe Béarn's heir. Always before, Sterrane had broken circumstances down to their simplest components. Always, it came down to integrity. All promises, whether stated or implied must be honored, and he trusted all men to follow the natural candor and order imposed by the world Odin had created from law. When men forgot their vows, Sterrane presumed it was by accident, and he saw to placing them back on the proper path, whatever it took. The struggle between good and evil was not his concern.

This philosophy, instilled in him by Shadimar, had served Sterrane well through his twenty-four years. *Trust all; help all.* Those four words had brought him through a lifetime of friendships and gained him no enemies. Yet, on the issue of his uncle, King Morhane, Sterrane found himself wrestling with his conscience for the first time in his life. Shadimar had insisted that the traitor must die, yet Sterrane could not see the method or the cause. Grimly, he shook his head. Noticing that Shadimar had turned his attention at this movement, Sterrane addressed the Wizard. He used the trading tongue, though he seemed doomed never to learn its rules or complexities. 'No.'

Shadimar snapped the twig between his fingers, tossing the halves into the smoldering coals. He trained eyes as gray and timeless as mountains directly on Sterrane. 'What do you mean "no?"'

Sterrane met the Wizard's warning glare. 'Not kill family. It wrong.'

'Sterrane, we've already been through this.' Shadimar's voice lacked its usual, near-immortal's patience. 'Morhane cannot be forgiven nor trusted. If you leave him alive, he will find a way to kill you and retake the throne.' Secodon whined, cringing from Shadimar. Empathetically linked to his master, he could surely read the anger and disappointment that the Wizard's tone conveyed to Sterrane.

'He family. Me talk. He learn. He change.'

'No.' Shadimar rose, his cloak falling in folds and wrinkles about a body nearly as narrow as a staff. 'I see things you can't. Morhane cannot be changed, and your mercy will only assure your death.'

Sterrane pouted, his face childlike despite the dense black mane of hair and beard and a massive frame packed with fat and sinew. 'We both live.'

Shadimar shook his head, denying the possibility. 'For you to reclaim your throne, one of you must die.'

'Then me not reclaim throne.'

'What!' Shadimar sounded shocked for the first time since Sterrane had met him. He covered the ground between himself and Béarn's heir in an instant, the wolf skittering aside to save its paws from a trampling. 'That's nonsense.'

Sterrane stuck with the easy solution. 'If not be king, not need kill family.'

'Damn it, Sterrane.' Shadimar stomped his foot, kicking up a divot of dirt. 'I thought this was settled. We haven't time for this madness now.'

Sterrane shrugged noncommittally.

'Prophecies aren't random; I thought you understood that. They don't just happen because they fit the whim of fate or the cosmos.' Shadimar made a broad gesture, encompassing the horizons. 'Millennia ago, the first Eastern Wizard determined that you would take back the high kingdom. Since then, twenty-three Eastern Wizards have worked to see to your ascension. Jalona talked Odin into giving the bards the job of king's personal bodyguard in addition to entertainer. Drero built the underground tunnel that saved your life. Seeing you back on your throne is one of the primary reasons for my existence.'

Sterrane stared in silence, uncertain how to respond to the Eastern Wizard's revelations. Since the day of his escape, Shadimar had taken a personal interest in him. The Wizard had raised Sterrane for two years before turning him over to Rache and Santagithi for a year, in the belief that Rache, not Mitrian, was the Renshai destined to help Sterrane retake the throne. Shadimar had then claimed the job of guardian until Sterrane was old enough to strike out on his own. Yet, the Béarnide would never have guessed Shadimar's life or the integrity of Wizards hung in the balance. 'If me give up throne, *you* die?'

Shadimar frowned, considering Sterrane's broken rendition of the trading tongue, apparently wanting to answer the correct question. 'No,' he admitted, his demeanor calmer. 'I can't die until I choose to do so.'

Sterrane nodded, his view of reality restored. He knew that Shadimar's life already spanned more than two centuries, and, from experience, he had noticed that no object seemed capable of harming him, accidentally or by intention.

As if to reinforce the point, Shadimar hefted Sterrane's ax, carelessly clamping his fingers along the blade. 'Sterrane, Béarn is as much your child as baby Rache is Mitrian's. Your decisions, no matter their content or reason, no longer affect only you.'

Shadimar's words confused Sterrane. 'Not understand.'

Brush rattled behind Sterrane, followed by Mitrian's voice. 'They're coming. Morhane and two very alert guards. Garn's preparing.' Without awaiting a reply, Mitrian disappeared back into the forest, the swish of branches and vines defining her route. Unlike Garn and Arduwyn, she had little experience creeping through woodlands. The harder she tried to move silently, the louder she became.

Sterrane turned back to Shadimar. Sorrow made the old gray eyes seem liquid, and the Wizard's stance was resigned. 'Do what you feel you have to do, Sterrane. It's your world and your kingdom.' Without another word, he turned and headed back to the fire. He sat cross-legged before it, stirring a finger through the coals. Secodon walked a narrow circle, then lay down at Sterrane's feet, his busy tail covering his nose.

Sterrane swallowed hard. Forbidden from harming mortals by Odin's law, Shadimar could do nothing but goad and observe. And Sterrane found himself in the same position as before their talk, torn between correcting an old sin and committing one of his own. Teachings from his childhood rumbled to the forefront, little more comprehensible now than then. But one thing did seem clear. The high king in Béarn held the task of keeping a balance he did not understand, of dedicating himself to enforcing Odin's law and codes of honor, no matter the price in morality. Sterrane could not begin to explain his uncle's willingness to abandon honor and slaughter family, but his self-interested need to place his own person and line on the high throne was clearly evil. And evil, like goodness, did not have a place in Béarn's rule. Clearly Morhane had to die, yet Sterrane wanted no hand in his murder.

Leaves and twigs crunched and snapped as Morhane and his escort approached the clearing. Sterrane used the haft of his ax like a crutch, grinding the base into the dirt. He rose, unprepared to meet his uncle, but knowing that, one way or another, he must.

Suddenly, a burly figure in Béarn's blue and tan stepped into view from behind a cluster of trees. Seeing Sterrane and Shadimar, he stopped short, briskly gesturing someone behind him still, presumably Morhane. A moment later, another guard stepped up beside the first, slightly smaller, but equally Béarnian dark. 'Who are you?' the first guard demanded. His blanched fingers kneaded the hilt of his sword.

The Eastern Wizard removed his hands from the coals, silently deferring to Sterrane. He had nothing to fear from mortal weapons, nor could he take an active part in the conflict. The wolf looked from Wizard to heir to guards.

'Who are you?' the guard said again. He focused directly on Sterrane, apparently having assessed the unarmed, scrawny elder as the lesser threat. But his gaze did stray to the wolf.

'Me – ' Sterrane started, but Shadimar cut him off.

'Use native,' he said softly, yet with authority. He modulated his voice perfectly to command without undermining.

Sterrane switched to Béarnese. In his youth, the Wizard had always encouraged him to use the trading tongue for the practice. For reasons he could not explain, Sterrane had a clumsiness for learning languages that did not seem to improve with time or exposure. 'My name is Sterrane.'

Abruptly, Morhane's bearded face appeared from behind the trees, his sudden lack of caution rattling the guards. He studied Sterrane in the gray haze of evening, surprise darkening his swarthy, bearded features. The royal crest swung from a chain around his neck, the rearing bear medallion resting in his speckled beard.

Sterrane recognized his uncle at once by his uncanny resemblance to Sterrane's father and, more recently, to Sterrane himself. A mixed swirl of emotion assailed him: the crushing heaviness of grief, a hatred so pure it seemed to burn, and an unconditional love that honor decreed must come with shared blood. 'You killed your brother, Morhane. My father. You murdered my brothers and sisters and Béarn's most faithful guards.' Sterrane's gentle features twisted with anguish, and his eyes grew moist. But his tone betrayed nothing. 'Why?'

The guards shifted restlessly, awaiting a command. One politely motioned Morhane back behind him, though the king ignored the gesture.

A noise above Morhane and his escort drew Sterrane's attention. His gaze drifted to an ancient oak as Garn settled into the branches. He did not see Mitrian, and he guessed that her inexperience with scouting forced her to move intolerably slowly. Still, when he listened carefully, he thought he could discern the noises of distant motion.

Morhane and his guardsmen seemed to take no notice of the rustling leaves above them, apparently either attributing the sound to wind or distracted by the danger Sterrane posed to their king.

Morhane circled around his bodyguards and approached Sterrane with his empty hands displayed in a gesture of welcome. A huge, gilded ax lay strapped across his back, and a jewel-encrusted sword hilt jutted from a tooled, leather-wrapped scabbard at his waist. He made no move to draw either weapon. 'Sterrane?' His voice went thick with guarded hope. 'Nephew? Is that really you?'

The guardsmen's shock reflected clearly on their faces. They strode hesitantly after their king, obviously wishing they could retake their positions in front of him, yet knowing better than to challenge his intentions.

Sterrane remained standing in place, unsure how to react. Of all the possibilities that had played through his mind, he had never expected a heartfelt greeting from Morhane. In response, he nodded. His own repertoire of thoughts and emotions did not include deceit, and, since childhood, he had known nothing but friends who coddled and protected his innocence like a toddler's.

Morhane twisted his head to his escort. 'Flent. Koska. Do you see? My nephew Sterrane is alive!'

Despite the sincerity in Morhane's voice, the guards seemed uncertain whether to celebrate the circumstance or to remedy it. In the tree, Garn froze, watchful. Mitrian remained out of sight.

Still, despite his naïveté, Sterrane was not stupid. Though he trusted his uncle's candor, he had not received a satisfactory answer to his question. 'Why?' he repeated. 'Why did you kill my family?'

Morhane's grin wilted, replaced by an expression of pained sorrow. 'You think I killed your family?' Incredulity radiated from him. 'My own brother? My nieces and nephews? No, it's not true, I fought by their side against the invaders, and I worried when I found you missing. Who told you such a horrible lie?'

The Béarnian bodyguards exchanged glances, seeming as surprised as Sterrane by the king's words and manner.

Sterrane glanced toward Shadimar, both in answer and to solicit advice. As his attention shifted, he caught a glimpse of Mitrian moving up behind Koska. Garn remained in the tree, no longer above Morhane, though a leap could still carry him to either of the guardsmen.

Morhane followed Sterrane's dark gaze with his own, locking on Shadimar. 'Old man, you told Sterrane that I killed our family?'

Addressed directly, Shadimar rose, unfolding his long, lean frame. The wolf remained, quiet but alert, at his feet. 'I saw no reason to keep the truth from him.'

Morhane's eyes went as flat and dull as the spent coals. 'How dare you make such an accusation. How could you claim to know? You weren't there.'

'When the mouse is missing and the snake has a bulge in its belly, I do not need to see the consuming.'

Sterrane thought he heard a horse whinny. He dismissed the sound as a phantom creation of his own discomfort. His nerves had gone taut as bowstrings.

Apparently also cued by a noise, Koska whirled to face Mitrian. He crouched, eyes flicking from her obviously feminine features to the incongruity of her readied stance and the sword at her hip. Flent turned, too, placing his person between Morhane and this new threat. 'Caution, Highness. He has allies.'

'Ah.' Morhane ignored his guards, still studying Shadimar, and his eyes flashed with an emotion Sterrane could not place. 'So you admit your evidence is circumstantial. And you would condemn a man and destroy a family bond based on empty guesses?' Passing off the Wizard as beneath his dignity, Morhane turned back to Sterrane. 'I have nothing to fear from my nephew, and he has nothing to fear from me.' Despite his reassurances, Morhane glanced briefly at Mitrian before returning his attention to Sterrane. He wore a broad smile, and the light in his eyes became an excited twinkle. 'I can't believe you're alive. All these years lost, and now we're together again.' He lowered his head. 'Of course, these are yours.' He seized the medallion by its chain, levering the Béarnian crest over his shaggy head. He handed it to Sterrane along with the signet. 'Your Majesty.'

Sterrane could hear other things now, leaves jostling, heavy footfalls against dirt, a mass of movement headed toward the clearing. A horse snorted, the sound explosive in the sudden hush. Shocked and deeply moved by Morhane's graciousness, Sterrane paid these others no more heed than his uncle did. Words failed him. His fingers closed over metal warmed by Morhane's body, and he met his uncle's flinty gaze. All his doubts fled. He did not see Shadimar's agonized frown, the strained glances passed between Garn and Mitrian, or the vigorous shaking of the woman's head. Nor did he notice that Morhane's guards had relaxed slightly as a semicircle of mounted men partially surrounded the campsite behind Mitrian. Sterrane flung his arms around Morhane's massive waist, feeling the king's strong arms encircle him as well.

A touch of air on his back was Sterrane's only warning. He tensed as a razor-sharp stiletto gouged through the muscle of his lower back. Though slight, his movement saved his spine. Instinctively, he staggered aside. Flesh sliced open, lancing agony through him. Then Morhane leapt back, clutching a knife smeared with Sterrane's blood, his brown eyes now rabid with rage.

The horsemen held their ranks. Flent froze. Koska sprang to assist his king, and was instantly cut off by Mitrian. Garn jumped from the tree, committed to his attack. But, still dizzy from his head wound and unused to striking from above, he miscalculated. The side of his sword caught the guard a glancing blow. Garn overbalanced, collapsing into an uncontrolled roll. The guard stumbled to one knee. Garn plowed into Mitrian.

The wound in Sterrane's back ached, but the realization of his uncle's treachery hurt worse. He dropped the crest and signet, catching the haft of his ax, and he launched a powerful upstroke for Morhane's face. Morhane back-stepped, freeing his own ax. His riposte slammed onto Sterrane's blade, meeting resistance solid as a mountain. Sterrane bore in, driving the older man back a step.

A stranger's voice cut through the din. 'Flent! Koska, be still! It's not your fight.'

'Majesty!' Pain filled Koska's cry. Ignoring the command, he lurched for the king and heir while Garn and Mitrian untangled themselves. Accustomed to quick and dirty fighting, Garn made a desperate grab, catching the guard's ankle. He pulled, sending the bodyguard crashing to the ground, then leapt bodily upon him.

The realization of betrayal turned to cold anger. Abruptly, Sterrane tugged his ax loose. Unexpectedly freed from opposing pressure, Morhane pitched forward, baring his head to Sterrane's next strike. Sterrane hesitated, momentarily undecided as he whipped his blade into position. He knew what had to be done. And, once he admitted it, he did not falter. An expression of terror crossed Morhane's features. Then Sterrane's blade cleaved his uncle's neck. Morhane's dark eyes glazed, and he collapsed to the dirt beside Béarn's royal crest.

Koska squirmed, twisting to reverse Garn's hold. His gaze found the king, and he went still. 'Gods!' He made a gesture of surrender.

Only then did Sterrane register the presence of strangers at the clearing's entrance. Six white horses fanned into a perfect semicircle, their manes braided and wound through with the gold and blue ribbons that identified them as the steeds of Erythanian knights. Their riders sat, rigidly attentive. They clutched pikes in a rest position, helmets covered their heads, and their swords remained sheathed. Each of their tabards displayed the Béarnian symbol. In the center of their arc, a stomping bay mare and a chestnut gelding completed the formation. The men perched on these horses were large-boned, one black-haired and the other white-haired, clearly Béarnides. The younger wore the colors of Béarn's royal guard and a blue plume of office; clearly he was the one who had commanded Flent and Koska from the battle. At his side, the richly dressed elder carried no weapon. Surely sent by Mar Lon, these men were no threat to Sterrane, nor would he have cared if they were. Grief stole all concern for his safety.

Sterrane's ax fell from his fingers. His eyes went as vacant as his uncle's, with no sparkle of triumph. No wicked grin of vengeance crossed his face. The pain in his back seemed unimportant, and he scarcely felt the steady trickle of blood along his spine. He sank down on the nearby stump, his back to his companions and the Knights of Erythane. His shoulders shook rhythmically as he cried.

Sunlight angled through the tallest branches of the pine and elm forest near the Town of Santagithi, lighting the teaching clearing. Colbey steadied Rache, readjusting his grip on a sword that, though crafted short and light for a child, still maintained perfect, proportional balance. Two years old, Rache understood little of Colbey's teachings; but he seemed to have an intuitive grasp of their importance. His pudgy hands clutched the hilt, fingers remaining where Colbey had placed them. Beneath a mop of sandy hair, eyes as green as his father's fixed on his teacher, desperately seeking approval.

'That's the way, Rache.' Familiar with a child's short attention span, Colbey gave praise freely. Over time, that honor would become increasingly more difficult to earn. Seizing Rache's arms, he raised the child's sword above his head. The movement gained him a glimpse of his other student. Four-year-old Episte knelt before a meandering line of wild flowers, his sword dangling from his hand.

Rage suffused Colbey. Forgetting Rache, he cleared the distance to Episte in a single bound. Drawing his sword as he moved, he hammered the blade up against Episte's crossguard. The underhand stroke slapped the sword from the child's grip, sending it spinning into the air.

Episte gasped, whirling to meet the attack. He clamped his aching sword hand to his chest, yet still managed to catch the hilt in his left hand before the blade struck the ground.

Pleased with Episte's honoring his sword and by the boy's agility, Colbey found it difficult to scold. Yet, disrespect for a sword master was a crime that could not go unpunished. 'Didn't I tell you to practice *odelhurtig?*'

Episte nodded, moisture welling in his eyes. Still clutching the sword, he rubbed his right hand with the knuckles of his left.

'And what were you doing?'

'Picking flowers for Mama, *torke*.' A tear rolled down Episte's face. Though only half Renshai, he had inherited the racial feature that made him look younger than his age. Already, Rache was the larger of the two. Episte had also acquired his father's golden hair and blue eyes, though his skin bore the darker, rosier hue of the Westerners. Still holding his sword, Episte crouched, scooping up a handful of purple blossoms. 'These would look pretty in her hair.'

Colbey stared, with a look of withering disdain. 'Is this how you would meet an enemy? With a bouquet and a dragging sword?'

The flowers fell from Episte's fingers, gliding to the dirt. 'No, *torke*, I–'

'You are always a warrior first, Episte. You are Renshai.'

'I wasn't going to . . . I wouldn't . . . '

Wanting no excuses, Colbey made a sudden lunge with his sword for Episte's abdomen. Episte tensed, whipping his smaller weapon to block. Steel rang against steel. Colbey threw only enough power into the blow to hone Episte without hurting him. Episte riposted with a flawless *odelhurtig*.

'Good.' Colbey redirected the strike with an easy, snaking parry, glad for the opportunity to temper anger with praise. He feigned another jab, at the last moment turning it into a high cut that swept harmlessly over Episte's head.

An instant later, Episte ducked to avoid a blow that, if real, would already have landed.

'A little too slow.' Colbey circled his sword back into a reverse cut, trapping Episte's blade against his own knee. 'Now, I'm going to take Rache home. I want you to stay here and practice *odelhurtig*. I'm going to return quietly and unseen. If I find you doing anything but training, you're not going home. You're going to work all night, and I'm going to sit here and see that you do. Understand?'

Episte nodded, tears again welling in his eyes.

Colbey freed the boy's blade, frowning at the tears though he did not chastise Episte for them. With time, Colbey hoped, Episte would find that crying gained him nothing, and the tears would disappear. He turned his attention to Rache.

The younger boy still stood exactly as Colbey had left him, in a defensive crouch with the sword raised above his head. His hands had blanched, his arms had gone rigid with strain, and sweat trickled from his brow.

Rache's dedication surprised Colbey nearly as much as Episte's natural skill, and he doubted most adults would have had the stamina to hold a raised sword so long. Wanting to keep the eagerness to please as natural as possible, Colbey kept his expression and tone neutral.

'Rache, you're done for the day.'

Rache sheathed his sword. He shook his arms against the ache of returning blood flow, but he did not complain.

Colbey motioned to Episte, waiting until the older boy started his practice before turning back to Rache. Then, tousling the sandy hair, Colbey steered Mitrian's and Garn's son from the clearing.

That night, Colbey hacked through a wild flurry of slash, thrust, and pary, his sword bounding and arching about the practice room near the southern corner of Santagithi's estate. Once, this plain room and its blade-scarred walls had served as the gladiator training quarters. Here, Episte's father had taught Rache's father the tricks and skill that had kept him alive in the pit. Here, too, a hatred had grown between the two men, fueled by Garn's savage temper and Rache's unyielding need to make his charge into a survivor.

The windowless room was now an indoor practice area. Its only door, currently closed, led into a hallway that ended in a door to the outside. Near this larger exit, a chamber filled with pegs and shelves held swords, shields, axes, maces, bows, and spears of sturdy design; these replaced the fighting gauntlets, wooden practice blades, and ancient, notched and battered swords that once served the fighting slaves. Outside, the cages that used to hold wary killers more like animals than men now contained only Santagithi's dogs. Those gladiators too unstable to free had been presented to King Tenja of the Northern tribe of Vikerin to join his troupe. Santagithi had seen to it that, when Garn returned, he would find no sign of the life he had once been forced to lead.

Colbey's blade moved in a silver blur, stopping only when he paused to assess a killing blow, and his thoughts moved with equal speed. As before, he dedicated his session to Sif, requesting the support that would reassure him that he had chosen his methods of instruction well. He had trained Renshai for fifty years, yet it never seemed to get easier. And, in the nearly two decade gap since the Renshai had been all but annihilated, Colbey had trained no one but Mitrian and himself. He knew that the fine line between driving a swordsman to his best effort and discouraging him must not be broached, especially with the two boys who were nearly all that remained of the once great Renshai.

Colbey switched to techniques designed to use against mounted opponents, committed leaps and spinning back-kicks that violated the rules of keeping both feet on the ground for stability and ease of movement. Filled with prancing jumps and spirals, the Renshai maneuvers seemed more like dance than combat; but the punctuating sword jabs and sweeps added the deadliness stolen by the limitation to rapid changes of direction. His specialty, Colbey had created most of the Renshai's horseback techniques, as well as those designed to meet mounted enemies when on foot.

A knock on the door disrupted Colbey's practice. He landed in a defensive crouch, the single sword angled before him. Despite hours of continuous *svergelse*, his voice emerged barely winded. 'Who is it?'

A female voice wafted from beyond the portal. 'It's Emerald.'

Episte's mother. Colbey sheathed the sword, surprised by the visit. Since he had begun his daily teaching sessions with Episte, she had only deigned to speak with him once. 'Please. Come in.'

The door creaked open, and Emerald stepped into the training room. Her oval face supported plain features framed by dark hair. Her cheeks looked hollowed, as if she had once weighed much more than her slender figure indicated. She wore a blue dress belted at the waist; and, though thin, she sported none of a warrior woman's firm musculature. Her brown eyes seemed soft, but her pursed lips and tenseness betrayed anger. And her tone matched her manner. 'Episte says you hit him today.'

Colbey remained calm. 'Hitting is not part of my teaching.'

Emerald hurled the door. It slammed closed with a bang that echoed through the room. 'Are you calling my son a liar?'

'Did I say that?'

'Did you hit him?'

'No.'

Emerald glared. 'You say you didn't hit him. He says you did. So you *are* calling him a liar.'

The situation had come full circle. Colbey stared. 'Did I say that?'

Emerald tossed up her hands in disgust. 'You didn't have to say it. Either you hit him or you didn't. One of you is lying.'

'Or one of us misinterpreted what happened.' Colbey continued to study Emerald, wondering why she bothered him with trivial matters that did not concern her. He did not interfere with the foods she chose to offer Episte nor the way she tucked him into his bed at night. And she had no right to intrude on his training. 'I knocked a sword from his hands. Perhaps the only word he could find for that in your language was "hit."'

'Well, perhaps he could speak *my* language better if you didn't confuse him with your foreign tongue.' Emerald's volume rose to a shout. 'And, by the way, it's not *my* language, it's the language of this town and this part of the world. What need does he have for a weird tongue spoken by a bunch of barbarians he'll never meet?'

'It's part of the training.' Colbey saw no reason to continue the conversation. He had a practice to finish, and this woman had passed beyond polite composure. 'If you'll excuse me.' He waved his fingers at the door.

Emerald ignored the hint. 'And I suppose it's also part of his training to teach him about pagan gods? I've spent too much time giving him a proper, religious upbringing to let you ruin it with savage, tribal mythology.'

Colbey's arms tensed, hovering near his sword hilts, and his blue-gray eyes went nearly as dark as Emerald's own. He battered down fury, maintaining the perfect self-control and discipline derived from years of training. *To strike in anger means to strike without mastery.* 'I think it would be best if you left now.'

'No,' Emerald said, though she did take several backward steps, nearly pressing her back to the door. 'No! I've had enough! Episte is my son, not yours.'

'That's true, though he means as much to me.'

'No! I love him. I'm his mother, by Suman. I love him in a way no one else but his father possibly could. And his father is dead.'

Colbey folded his arms across his chest. 'Bloodline and love are unrelated. To love someone only because he shares your blood is as hollow and meaningless as loving someone only because he's young and beautiful. To a Northman, an unrelated blood brother becomes more important than kin, since the bond is based on honor and merit, not inescapable coincidence.'

Colbey's words inflamed Emerald. 'Don't preach at me! I'm not one of your students. *I am Episte's mother.* I decide what Episte does or doesn't do. And his time with you is finished.'

'What?' Colbey hoped he had misinterpreted her intentions.

'Perhaps *you're* having trouble with the language?' Emerald's tone became sarcastic. 'Let me say it in words you can understand.' She adopted a parody of the melodious Northern accent, speaking the trading tongue with the loud, emphasized pronunciation she might use with the near-deaf. 'You are no longer Episte's teacher.'

'You don't mean that.'

'I not only mean it, I should have said it a long time ago.'

Colbey sighed, sizing the woman up from habit. 'Then you leave me no choice but to kill you.' Despite his words, he made no motion toward his swords.

All color drained from Emerald, leaving her as pale as any Northman. 'What?'

'I'm going to kill you now.'

Emerald shivered back against the door. 'You can't . . . You wouldn't . . . '

Colbey continued to study Emerald calmly. 'I can run you through in one stroke. I could decapitate you as quickly, if you prefer, but I see no reason for the dishonor. Or the mess.'

Emerald found her voice, though it emerged as a pinched whisper. 'I'm a woman.'

'That means nothing.' Colbey remained in place, annoyed by Emerald's change. Clearly, all of her shouting and threats had been false bravado and bluff, easily called. 'Half of the finest warriors in my tribe were women.'

'But this isn't your tribe.' Emerald crushed her spine against the door, cowering behind one raised arm. 'I'm unarmed.'

'I have an extra sword.'

'I don't know how to fight!' Hysteria flooded Emerald's voice. She burst into tears, sliding to the floor. 'Don't hurt me. Please don't hurt me. Please don't hurt me.'

Colbey watched the groveling woman in silence, and her cowardice disgusted him.

'I didn't mean it.' Emerald fixed glazed, pleading eyes on Colbey, cringing behind her hands. 'You can train Episte. I won't do anything about it. I won't say anything about it again. I promise.'

'Stand up,' Colbey said.

'What?'

'Stand up,' Colbey repeated.

Reluctantly, Emerald obeyed, still hiding behind her arms.

'Is this what you want for your son?' Colbey pointed to the place on the floor where Emerald had cowered.

'I – I don't understand,' Emerald said. When no further threats came from Colbey, physically or verbally, she seemed to relax a bit.

'Is that how you want your son to meet his enemies? They won't show him the mercy I showed you. They'll hack him to pieces and revel in the slaughter.'

'Enemies?' Emerald straightened as she realized Colbey had no intention of harming her. The first tinge of color returned to her features, though tears still rolled down her cheeks. 'Episte is barely four years old! How many enemies could he have?'

'Hundreds.' Colbey remained unmoving. He hated the limitations placed on him and his charges by living among a culture that worshiped gods who allowed cowardice, that treated children like simpletons, and that allowed its women to grow soft and weak. 'Whether you like it or not, the man you slept with was Renshai. And, whether I like it or not, most people find bloodline as important as you do. Just the fact that my people were Renshai was considered ample reason for the Northmen to murder them and the Westerners to rejoice in the killing. When his enemies come for Episte because he is Renshai, it will not be enough for him to know how to fight. He must know how to fight like a Renshai.'

'No one needs to know.' Emerald spoke cautiously, her tone pitched to placate.

Colbey frowned. 'Several people know already. Secrets spread; they don't die. It can only help Episte to be the best warrior posible. Why would you want anything less?' Colbey did not add that the Renshai needed Episte even more than he needed them. He doubted that saving the dwindling tribe would concern or interest Emerald.

'Because I don't like your methods.' Emerald looked up quickly, apparently fearing for the consequences of her boldness.

Colbey gave a casual wave to indicate that she should speak freely.

'And I don't like what you're turning my child into.'

Colbey's pale brows rose, smoothing his forehead. 'I'm turning him into a competent swordsman.'

Emerald brushed strands of hair from her face with nervous strokes. 'You're turning him into a Renshai.'

'No.' Colbey's features lapsed back to normal. 'Episte is already Renshai. His father determined his bloodline, and you chose his father. I'm simply helping him become a *competent* Renshai.' It was an oversimplification. By Renshai law, sword skill, not blood, determined who became a member of the tribe. Yet, for purposes of solidarity and identification, the decision of who could learn the Renshai maneuvers was based on family. All full-blooded Renshai qualified for the privilege. Only the last Renshai could teach the maneuvers to outsiders, who then became full members of the tribe. From that time, all offspring of Renshai, no matter their blood, could learn the sword skills. 'If it makes you feel better,' Colbey added, not really caring whether his words soothed, 'I trained Episte's father as a boy. You must have found something attractive about him that you chose to bear his child.'

Emerald took the words as a challenge. 'I *loved* Rache,' she fairly hissed. 'He was the most beautiful man I ever met.'

Colbey stared expectantly, certain Emerald did not love on this basis alone. Clearly, she had sought out the one quality for which Colbey could take no credit.

Emerald continued, though whether to prove her depth or from honesty, Colbey could not guess. 'He was graceful and agile. Just watching him move was a pleasure. He was afraid of nothing, and he was always eager for battle. Without Rache's teaching, Santagithi's guards would be half as able and his gladiators would have died.' She sighed. 'Rache's coldness and mystery only made him more desirable.'

Colbey smiled, believing he had won the argument. Surely even a woman with no weapons training could understand that Rache's early training had established his dexterity, courage, and his method of instruction.

Emerald fiddled with the door's knob, glancing sidelong at Colbey to see if he would stop her.

Colbey remained still.

Emboldened, Emerald opened the door, but she remained in the room, facing Colbey. 'And all of those qualities killed him: pride and skill and courage. Without them, he would never have been crippled. He wouldn't have charged into war with no concern for his own welfare. He would still be alive.'

'Dying young and with honor is part of being Renshai,' Colbey said. It was a fact, not an admission.

'And you wonder why I don't want it for my son!'

'But,' Colbey continued as if Emerald had never interrupted. 'It was a consequence of a lifestyle the Renshai can no longer afford to live. We can't charge recklessly into war any more. I'm sixty-six, and I was as eager as any Renshai for battle. More so, because I joined other Northern tribes in pirating raids and border skirmishes when the Renshai were at peace. Skill kept me alive.'

'And modesty,' Emerald added, her voice just shy of sarcasm. She smiled nervously to indicate that she meant no offense, though obviously she meant exactly that. 'Skill and modesty.'

'Modesty has no place in a warrior's training. If he is not the best, he should force himself to drill until he becomes so.' Colbey fidgeted. To his mind, the discussion had ended, and he wished to return to his *svergelse*.

'What does your age and skill have to do with Episte?' Emerald stood in the doorway, her gaze trained on the elderly Renshai.

'Only this.' Colbey's hands slid to his hilts as he considered his practice, and the gesture sent Emerald skittering just outside the door. 'Episte has a natural grace his father did not. He's quick, and his movements are smooth. He has more innate potential than any student I've ever trained.

Emerald managed a nervous smile at the compliment. Like all mothers, she knew her child was special. Apparently, the competence of her boy did not surprise her, only the length of time it had taken for others to notice.

Colbey delivered the end-all. '*If* I can get him to take his lessons seriously. *If* I can get Episte to learn some control and dedication, he could, by the time he reaches my age, nearly equal my skill.

Emerald went still, silent for several moments.

Colbey waited. 'But he needs your full support.'

Gradually, Emerald came around. First, she blinked several times, then she shifted back three steps. 'You can force me to let you train my only child. You can steal the time I would use to teach the things I feel are important to him and to me. But not at any price will I let Episte become as cruel and single-minded as you.' Whirling, she stormed down the hallway. Her footfalls thundered along the passageway, then disappeared. The outer door slammed.

Colbey laughed. *Teach Episte that belligerence, rather than the tears, and he'll do well.* It pained Colbey to see a child with such potential reined, yet he saw no solution. He never truly considered slaughtering Emerald, though not from any respect for the woman. He knew it would hurt Episte and his relationship with the only other person with significant Renshai blood. *If I can't make him the best, at least I can train him to the limits of his upbringing.* With that thought, Colbey closed the door and continued his practice.

5 The King's Return

Smoke from Morhane's pyre curled through Béarn's forest, rising above the trees to become lost among the wispy clouds. Morning sunlight glazed the sky a nearly uniform yellow-white. Standing in the clearing with Mitrian, the Béarnian lieutenant, Morhane's body-guards, and one of the six Knights of Erythane, Garn thought little of Sterrane's insistence that his uncle receive an honorable send-off. To him, a dead body was simply dead, not worthy of time, prayers, or effort. And a dead traitor seemed the perfect food for *wisules*, rats, and vultures. Lack of sleep and pain made Garn even more cranky, though the seriousness of their mission left him alert and on his guard. At least, his head seemed to have mostly cleared.

Two of the Erythanian knights had ridden back to the city, with the elder, to announce Morhane's death and the arrival of the new king. Shadimar and three knights attended Sterrane in the fashioning of Morhane's pyre. The last knight stood at attention in the clearing, guarding Koska and Flent. He also watched over the horses, four white and one chestnut, while they grazed branches and the stubbly patches of weeds that managed to twist upward through the mountain soil. The lieutenant, Baran, spoke earnestly with Mitrian, their conversation floating clearly to Garn, though the ex-gladiator felt too tired and irritable to participate in the exchange.

Baran's brown eyes sparkled with all the excitement Sterrane's had not shown. Dark curls tumbled about youthful features, and he wore the standard Béarnian beard, well-trimmed. A bastard sword hung from his belt, its leather grip black with use. 'I can't believe Sterrane's returned,' he said, animated as a child with a new toy.

Garn believed he had counted eleven times that the lieutenant had spoken those same words. Though his friendship with Sterrane made him hope that all of Béarn's guard would prove as loyal, Garn could do without the repetition. It seemed out of place for an officer, even one scarcely older than himself, to sacrifice dignity for joy. In the company of the stoic knights he currently commanded, the Béarnian lieutenant seemed silly.

The knight nodded politely, clearly more interested in guarding than listening. Garn recalled the tales of valor he had heard about the Knights of Erythane. Their strict code of honor and prowess as warriors had made them famous throughout the Westlands. Based in Béarn's sister city of Erythane, they wore the orange circle pierced by a black sword that served as the symbol of their home city on the backs of their tabards. Ultimately, they served the Westlands' high kingdom of Béarn, and the fronts of their tabards bore its tan bear on blue. In peacetime, the main body trained and served in Erythane while a small, rotating contingent served the high king.

Mitrian encouraged Baran. 'You've waited a long time for Sterrane's return.' Though statements, not question, her words encouraged explanation.

Baran took the bait eagerly. 'Eighteen years. Since the purge.' He lowered his head in solemn remembrance, his brief, mournful silence obviously ingrained habit. 'Morhane and his men slaughtered Valar, his family, and all of his majesty's most loyal soldiers, including my father.' He turned his gaze toward the distant castle. All of the giddiness left him, and Garn caught his first glimpse of the serious and commanding nature that allowed the sizable Béarnide to lead men. 'I don't think anyone was supposed to know that one of Valar's children wasn't found or slain. I don't know who leaked the information. Some say there is no surviving prince, that the Western Wizard created the legends only to keep hope alive among Béarn's peasants. But I knew from the start that Sterrane was the one. And that he would return.'

'Were you there?' Mitrian asked incredulously. Sterrane had been six years old when the coup occurred, and it seemed unlikely that Baran carried many more years than Béarn's heir. Still, Mitrian and Garn had grown up around Rache Kallmirsson and the Renshai racial feature that had made him seem much younger than his age. At his death, at the age of twenty-six, Rache had barely begun to shave.

'There? Me?' Baran laughed bitterly. 'Sterrane and I were young children then.' The smile returned to his face, apparently in response to some happy memory. 'Best friends. I remember playing with him. I always pretended I was a court guard, like my father. When we'd romp through the castle corridors, I'd charge ahead to make the way safe for my liege.' Baran laughed again, this time joyfully. 'Sterrane hated that. He always wanted *me* to play the king so *he* could guard *me*.' Baran explained further. 'Sterrane was the middle child of seven. He had two older brothers and one sister, too far from the crown to ever expect to wear it. We always hoped we'd grow up to become court guards together.'

Even Garn had to grin at the irony.

Mitrian clarified. 'So when you say you knew Sterrane lived . . . ' She trailed off, letting the guardsman finish.

Baran obliged. 'I knew the way a child knows. With unshakable certainty and no need for proof. Of course, the legends supported me.'

Childhood memories meant nothing to Garn. Although born free, he had spent too much of his youth locked in a cage to find details of boys' play moving. 'The more important question is, how're the town and the guards going to react to all this? Are we going to have to fight wars a hand against hundreds?'

Baran and Mitrian turned to Garn at once, both suddenly somber. The lieutenant threw a brief glance at the knight and Morhane's bodyguards, then gestured Garn over.

Garn rose. His muscles ached from overuse. Movement pulled at a myriad of bruises, the dog bite, and the healing knife wound. Exhaustion swam down on him, making him wish he had not bothered to enter the conversation. Still, he knew he had asked a valid and important question. He needed answers, no matter his mood. Walking to Baran and Mitrian, he leaned against a tree, careful that his view included the dead king's bodyguards, though the knight seemed properly alert and watchful.

Though several moments had passed, Baran addressed Garn's question as though he had just spoken it. 'I think the citizens will revel in the king's return. Morhane didn't make any friends among Béarn's people. He raised taxes against incoming merchants, which drove many to other markets. That meant imposing taxes on the citizens to make up for the loss. As you'll see, the castle hardly needed the additional revenue. Kings don't make friends when they garishly display their own wealth and indulgences to a starving populace. The courtyard boundaries expanded at the expense of the town.'

Garn liked Baran's answers, which were direct and uncluttered by detail. 'You're saying the people will gladly follow Sterrane.'

'I'm saying . . . ' Baran kicked at the deadfall that Shadimar had used as a seat, rolling it back and forth beneath his boot. ' . . . that it shouldn't take much to rally the citizenry to support Sterrane. Few liked Morhane. His twin, Valar, was a better king; and death has a way of taking away people's memory of the few faults a man might have had. Many clung to the legends as their last chance for happiness. They served Morhane out of duty and the law. But, like the knights, their loyalty is to the kingdom not the king.' Baran brushed back the plume of office, and the pinions flared. 'King Orlis of Erythane is bound by oath to support the Béarnian king, but he didn't care much for Morhane's greedy and overbearing politics. It didn't take much to convince the knights not to interfere in a battle between the true heir and his father's usurper. And, once finished, they owe their allegiance to the new king.'

The political details confused Garn, but he believed he had caught the essentials. 'So we have the people's support, so long as we rally it. How do we rally it?'

Mitrian took Garn's hand, squeezing lovingly, accidentally sending spasms through his bruised fingers.

'The stage is being set.' Baran's foot stilled on the log. 'Mar Lon sent Nifthelan and me along with the knights for a reason.'

Guessing Nifthelan was the older Béarnide, Garn nodded for Baran to continue.

'He's our master mason, an elder well-respected and trusted by the townsfolk. Mar Lon sent him along to witness the exchange of power. Of course, the knights' presences alone will appease most of those who aren't already so devoted to the legends they don't even need proof.'

The information pleased Garn. 'So the people hated Morhane. They've eagerly awaited Sterrane's return. This'll be easy.'

Lieutenant Baran stared, clearly wondering if Garn was as simple as his understanding of politics. 'Not that easy. No one's universally hated, and Morhane wasn't an idiot. He had his allies, mostly those who benefited from his reign. And, from court to outer to militia, Morhane treated his guards well. To do otherwise would be folly.'

Sterrane emerged from the forest, the medallion's chain disappearing beneath his loose traveling shirt, hiding the royal crest. He wore the signet on his smallest finger. Shadimar and the three knights trailed him, their stances tight and their expressions grim. 'We go now,' Sterrane said, his voice gravelly from crying.

Garn smiled, pleased by a decision that he felt should have been made long ago. Baran hastily removed his foot from the log. He executed a deep and graceful bow. 'Your Majesty, welcome home. My sword is in the service of Béarn and yourself until the end of time. May your reign prove long and . . . ' Baran paused, his somber confidence dissolving into a cautious playfulness. ' . . . beautiful.'

Apparently, Baran had mangled the pledge. The knights tensed as one, every gaze straying to the lieutenant. Even Koska and Flent seemed surprised.

Sterrane studied the lieutenant through red-rimmed eyes. His lips bowed into the first smile Garn had seen on his face since just after the Great War. A moment later, the huge king caught his massive lieutenant into a bear hug large enough for the two of them. 'That's *fruitful*, Baran,' Sterrane managed through a lungful of laughter. 'Fruit-i-ful.'

The origin of the error seemed obvious to Garn, and he guessed it had triggered Sterrane's recognition of a friend he had not seen since early childhood. Most likely the proper greeting had become trite and standard formality, passed from subjects to king a dozen times a day. Too familiar with it, few took care to enunciate. It only made sense that children might misinterpret a word or phrase. For the longest time, Garn himself had believed Santagithi's archers greeted one another with, 'Good eating.' Only as a teenager had he noticed the similarity between the terms 'fafra,' to eat, and 'feflin,' to hunt.

The lips of several knights twitched, but every one managed to contain a smile. Mitrian grinned. Koska buried his face in his hands, his eyes as swollen as Sterrane's. Flent remained still.

King and guardsman separated, but the smile seemed permanently pasted to Sterrane's face. He exchanged a few words with Baran in rapid Béarnese, none of which Garn understood. A moment later, Baran caught his horse, raised its head, and bridled it. Dry grasses jutted from either side of the bit, and the gelding pawed its irritation at the interruption of its meal. All of the knights, except for the one standing sentry over Morhane's bodyguards, prepared their mounts as well. The muscled white chargers obeyed every touch and word, standing as attentively as their masters while the men prepared and mounted.

Baran shouted a few commands, and the knights responded immediately. All of the childish excitement left the lieutenant, and Garn grudgingly admitted that he had misjudged the other's competence. When it mattered, Baran became as serious and businesslike as any of the knights. The lieutenant held the chestnut while Sterrane mounted, and two of the knights positioned their horses in front of the heir.

Baran shifted to the common trading tongue for Mitrian's and Garn's benefit. 'Mitrian, Shadimar. I'd like to place you behind the king. Then Koska and Flent, with Garn and myself behind them.

Mitrian and Shadimar moved into position, Secodon at his master's heels. The Erythanian sentry ordered Morhane's bodyguards to stand. As one, they rose. When the knight maneuvered him past Garn and Baran, Flent stopped and addressed the lieutenant. 'What's our status, sir? Are we in trouble for doing our job?'

'Not yet,' Baran said.

'Not yet, sir?' Flent turned the commander's words into a question. 'What does that mean?'

'You'll need to be tried.'

Koska glanced up quickly, then lowered his head again, staring at the ground. All color drained from Flent's face. 'Tried? Why? We were just following orders.'

'Morhane chose the two of you for a reason.' Baran instinctively inserted himself between Garn and the bodyguards, and his manner softened. 'I doubt you'll find Sterrane's justice as ugly as Morhane's. So long as you're honest and pledge your loyalty, I don't believe you'll be punished. Just keep in mind that your service is to the reigning king.

From what I remember about Sterrane and from what Mitrian told me, I'm certain he'll prove fair.'

The knight nudged Flent, encouraging him to keep moving.

Flent squared his jaw. 'The king is dead. Long live the king.' He headed for his indicated position, Koska quiet at his side.

'Long live the king,' Baran repeated formally, then turned his attention to the knight sentry. 'Garn and I can watch these two.' He indicated Flent and Koska. 'Take your position.'

The knight acknowledged the command with a nod, then hurried to obey. Garn turned his attention to Koska. The larger bodyguard's attempt to attack had already singled him out as the more dangerous, and his silence during the recent exchange only reinforced Garn's impression.

Baran waited until every person had taken his or her position. 'To Béarn,' he said.

With two Knights of Erythane in the lead, they marched from the sheltering forest toward the city. Koska walked with his head low and his shoulders slumped, Flent restive at his side. Garn believed the smaller guard's disquiet represented concern for his own welfare rather than preparation for an attack. In front of the bodyguards, Mitrian remained alert, her fingers resting on her crossguard. Beside her, Shadimar strode grimly. Garn always found the Wizard's moods difficult to judge. Instead, he watched the wolf at his master's side. For reasons Garn could not explain, its manner always seemed to reflect the Eastern Wizard's attitude. Now, it trotted with its ears pricked forward and its tail waving like a flag.

Even from a distance, Béarn appeared far different by day, and Garn scarcely recognized the cottages, trees, and boulders that had served as his cover the previous night. A mass of hardy, olive-skinned Béarnides waited at the border. Several raised their arms and gestured at the approaching procession. Their voices wafted to Garn as a distant, indecipherable hum.

Perched upon a carved stone speaking dais, Nifthelan watched the approaching group, seeming as interested as the other citizens. His two-knight escort threaded through the throng, opening a path for Sterrane and his entourage. Though the Béarnides politely moved aside for the Erythanians, they huddled at the edges of the pathway. Sheer numbers caused them to compress the pathway by increments, and the knights had to continuously redefine the boundaries. The knights leading the procession dropped back, guarding Sterrane from the sides as well as the fore.

The irregular stones of the roadway, which had torn Garn's knees the previous night, now crunched beneath his feet. He remained wary, nearly to an extreme. Trusting Baran to watch Koska, he studied the

Béarnian citizens. Though work-hardened and gigantically boned, the women as well as the men, they seemed mostly gaunt. The previous night, Garn had simply assumed that he had taken the shortest route through the town. Now he could see that Béarn spanned less than a sixth of Pudar's size. The finding surprised him enough to question, despite the potential threat of the citizenry. 'Is this all?'

Baran kept his gaze fixed on the bodyguards. 'Isn't it enough? I think every man, woman, and child in Béarn is here. Except the courtiers and guards, of course.'

'I've seen bigger crowds in the Pudarian market on an off day.' Garn conceded slightly. 'Though not usually this tightly packed.'

'Pudar's the trading city.'

Baran's explanation did not appease Garn. 'And this is the king's city.'

The noise of the crowd swelled as they came closer, though their words still remained garbled. Baran fairly shouted to be heard. 'So?'

Baran's glib dismissal gave Garn pause. He did not know why he had expected grandeur to radiate outward from the palace and encompass the entire town; it had just seemed to follow naturally from the high king's presence. 'I thought there'd be more.'

'Most people do. I have to assume our distant ancestors placed the town here for security. There's not a lot of unnecessary travel to a mountain city, by tradesmen or by tourists. More recently, Morhane's tax drove most of the wealthier merchants away. That meant less money for the stone masons, craftsmen, and inns. Used to be, anyone with spare floor space could make a few coins putting up visitors for the night. But people came to see the statues and stone carvings; and most of Béarn's citizens had to sell their treasures for food. The masons have to market every piece of artwork to the traders to make ends meet, so there's no place to go anymore to see shops filled with samples and works in progress.'

'Oh.' Garn remembered the rampant displays of wealth in Béarn's castle corridors, wondering how much food Morhane's bedroom furnishings alone might buy.

'Since Morhane came, the most lucrative job has become court guard, followed by military service. Nifthelan has done well because the townsfolk see to it that he wants for nothing. But the other artists get far too little, in pay or credit, for their talents.'

Despite his curiosity, Garn focused in on the more important matter raised by the lieutenant's words. 'So if the guards are well-paid, they may stay loyal to Morhane's memory.' His voice was all but swallowed beneath the hubbub.

The wild clamor of Béarnian voices finally became decipherable. 'Sterrane! Sterrane!' The cliffs seemed to quiver to the vibrations of their chant.

Apparently tired of shouting to be heard, Baran dismissed the concern with a wave. 'It's more complicated than that. We'll see how things stand when we get to the castle.' He added something more, but the chant swelled to a peak, drowning his words.

The two Erythanian knights already in the town joined with the pair at Sterrane's side. Together, they managed to open the way to the base of the dais steps. Baran nudged Garn, putting his mouth close to the ex-gladiator's ear. 'Can you take care of the guards?' He pointed at Flent and Koska. 'I'm going up with the king.'

Garn nodded vigorously. He doubted the bodyguards would cause trouble with Sterrane beyond their reach, and he preferred a position that kept him away from the center of attention. Crowds reminded him of the gladiator fights, especially crowds screaming names and encouragements.

Sterrane mounted the dais in the company of Baran, Shadimar and Mitrian. Secodon remained with Garn and his two charges, and the Erythanian knights fanned into formation behind them, a wedge between the king's retinue and the crowd. Garn could see Baran's lips moving as he coached Sterrane, and the king's shaggy head bobbing in response, but his ears rang with the villagers' seeemingly tireless chant.

As they joined Nifthelan, Baran raised his hands. Spreading his fingers, he jerked his hands apart, a signal for silence. In response, the crowd quieted. Only whispers touched Garn's ears, the last tiny hisses of judgment prior to the unofficial pronouncement of the new king. Baran executed a stiff bow, then began his speech. 'Fellow Béarnides, as our esteemed mason has told you, King Morhane is dead.'

Koska looked up then for the first time since the clearing. His hands balled to fists at his sides, though the Knights of Erythane had relieved him of his weapons.

The crowd remained silent, more interested in the information that followed.

Baran did not disappoint them. 'As the last surviving heir of King Valar, it's Sterrane's right to take the throne.'

Support rose from the citizenry. It started as a dull rumble, then again flared to a chant. 'Sterrane! Sterrane! Sterrane!'

As the voices died to allow the heir to speak, Koska shouted his disapproval. 'Stop it!' He flung an arm into the air for emphasis. 'Fools! Stop it at once!'

'Quiet!' Garn swore viciously at his charge. He grabbed Koska's arm, wrenching it back to his side.

Koska twisted free with a hiss, making a crazed dash for the dais stairs.

Garn dove on Koska. He caught the Béarnide around the waist, and they crashed to the ground together.

Flent staggered aside, giving the combatants room. Secodon crouched, ears twitching to catch his master's command. The chestnut sidestepped nervously.

Koska writhed like an eel. His fist caught Garn with a blow to the head that flashed white light across Garn's vision. His belt raked the bruises mottling Garn's side. Stung to fury by the pain, Garn wrapped his fingers around Koska's throat, driving his thumbs into the guard's windpipe. Koska thrashed frantically beneath him, skittering half free of Garn's pinning weight. His own hands locked on Garn's wrists. He gouged his nails beneath the bandage, tearing at the gash from Morhane's stiletto.

'Garn, stop! Let go!' Sterrane's voice rang out, and his agitation indicated that he had shouted more than once before blood rage had receded enough to allow Garn to hear. A furry blur sailed over Koska, catching Garn full in the chest with his weight. Bowled over, Garn lost his grip. He rolled, raising to a crouch, and found himself staring into Secodon's bared teeth and a warning growl. He froze.

Sterrane was still talking, but he changed to the Béarnian tongue, presumably at Shadimar's prompting. The difference in the formality, timbre, and competence of his speech surprised Garn. If not for the complete familiarity of the voice, he would have searched for the speaker. 'My first act as king will be to pass the following law: All citizens may express themselves freely before me, no matter the subject. While I'll keep the right of final decision regarding Béarn's fate, I will take counsel from any citizen.'

The crowd became motionlessly expectant. By convention, king's proclamations were always decided before advisors or the gentry first, in the safety of chambers or the courtroom. Not only had Sterrane broken the ritual even before his coronation; he had preached a policy that, Garn believed, no man could deem anything less than just.

'Rise, Koska.' Sterrane indicated the platform of the dais. 'Approach and speak your mind.'

Certain Secodon would not harm him, Garn ignored the wolf. Blood flowed freely, staining his bandage, and every injury he had taken in Morhane's castle ached. Sullenly, he tended to the open wound, leaving Koska to Mitrian's and Baran's guarding. Flent wrung his hands. He seemed to have no intention of starting a row. If he tried to run, he would not get far through the press of the crowd.

Given free rein, Koska seemed less sure of himself. He mounted the stairs slowly, glancing first at Sterrane, who gave him a warm smile of welcome. Baran stepped between guard and king, his features crinkled in warning. Mitrian watched Garn, obviously concerned by the blood. Shadimar stood in silence beside Nifthelan, looking unperturbed, as usual.

The crowd remained quiet but restless.

Koska cleared his throat. Then, apparently taking Sterrane at his word, he raised his voice in opposition. 'Fellow Béarnides, have you all gone mad? How can you fawn like jackals over the man who murdered our king!'

Many answers rose from the audience, yet they all blended into an indecipherable outcry. When the din died again, it was Nifthelan's reply that cut above the others. 'You know the legends promised the return of Valar's son, accompanied by the Western Wizard.' He gestured at Shadimar, who frowned. Garn knew Shadimar called himself the Eastern Wizard, but his presence could serve legend equally well. Few enough believed in any of the Cardinal Wizards any more. 'You may be too young, Koska, but I still remember Valar: regal, fair, proud and strong! Béarn flourished under his rule, as it will in the reign of his son. Hail, King Sterrane!'

The crowd answered with a resounding cheer.

Koska's mouth opened and closed, but his words were drowned beneath the roar. At length, when no one gave him an opening to speak, he descended from the dais in defeat.

Having staunched the bleeding, Garn wrapped a new bandage about the wound. Grudgingly, he stepped back to let Koska and the others retake their positions in the processional, soothed by mental images of his own sword thrust through Koska's back. Apparently aware of Garn's gaze drilling into his spine, the bodyguard glanced behind him several times. They headed for the castle, the citizenry following in a tumultuous mass. Despite the obvious victory, Garn did not allow himself to drop his guard. Buoyed by myth and the promise of a better life, they had understandably given their support to the new king. The palace guards and militia, Garn guessed, would not prove so easily swayed.

Apparently, the noise in Béarn's streets had alerted the castle sentries. As Sterrane's processional reached the walls, Garn discovered a half dozen guards in mail perched upon the ramparts with readied bows. Five men stood before the gate, each clutching the leashes of several gray war dogs like the one Garn had fought in Morhane's bedroom. The mongrels growled at the crowd of peasants, some of whom had armed themselves with axes, staves, or shovels.

In the courtyard beyond the gates, Rathelon was poised before a small army dressed in Béarn's blue. Sunlight flashed from his helmet, and his black eyes seemed to burn as brightly. The blue plume of office waved in a mild breeze. 'What is this?' he demanded as Sterrane and the others approached.

Sterrane cleared his throat, speaking in crisp Béarnese. 'I'm

Sterrane, Valar's son, and rightful king of Béarn.' Sweat trickled from his brow, and Garn's anger receded slightly. Usually, words of any kind came only with difficulty to his childlike friend. Despite his bold oratory before Béarn's citizenry, Sterrane still despised confrontation.

The crowd shouted unintelligible support. The knights formed a semicircle behind Sterrane and his entourage. Garn kept his gaze locked on the captain.

Rathelon glowered. His men remained still. 'We have a king, and we're faithful to him. Go away!'

'Morhane is dead!' Baran shouted from Sterrane's side. He said something to the heir that Garn could not hear. 'All these and the master mason stand in witness.' He made a sweeping gesture to include the knights and all of the people enclosed by their formation. Nifthelan had left the entourage to stand among the craftsmen.

Sterrane drew the royal crest from beneath his shirt and ducked through the chain. He raised the medallion, letting the links dangle from his fist.

Rathelon's gaze found Baran, and he squinted in rage. 'If the king is dead, then Miyaga is queen. Long live the queen! And as her regent, I demand that you surrender the crest and signet.'

Baran shouted back. 'Valar's line, not Morhane's, has birthright to the throne.'

Rathelon did not give the claim a moment's consideration. 'The law states that in the event of the king's demise, right of ascension goes first to his queen, then to his legitimate offspring in order of age, then to his grandchildren, beginning with the offspring of the king's oldest child.' Rathelon kept his voice in monotone to indicate a direct quotation of the law. 'It goes on from there, but there's no need in this case. By right, the throne belongs to Miyaga. And King Morhane, may he sleep in Dakoi's loving arms, designated me as regent.'

The crowd dropped to tense whispers. Baran went rigid. His uncertainty bristled warning through Garn. Clearly, Baran had not considered semantics. Legend and loyalty had blinded him to detail. 'But Valar's line is the true king's line.'

Rathelon grinned, now fully in control. 'The law implies otherwise.'

Apparently knowing Rathelon was wrong, in theory if not by the specific wording of the law, Baran rolled a desperate gaze to Shadimar. Clearly, he hoped the Wizard would have the eloquence and knowledge to make the point the lieutenant could not. Though every eye had shifted to Baran, awaiting the reply that would turn the tables on Rathelon, it was Mitrian who answered Rathelon's challenge. She gestured one of the Erythanian knights forward.

The knight first looked to Baran, who nodded his approval. The white charger threaded calmly to Mitrian's side. Garn folded his arms across his chest, tired, aching, and irritable; but still curious about his consort's approach. Apparently, her years as a strategist's daughter had not wholly gone to waste.

'I'm a stranger to Béarn,' Mitrian started. Although she did not shout like the others, interest and need held the citizens quiet. Her steady voice thundered over the whispers. 'I don't expect you to listen to me. But will everyone here trust the words of this man?' She indicated the Erythanian knight.

Heads bobbed along the line of peasants, and many of the guards added their agreement. Garn eyed the guards, trying to sort Rathelon's followers from those more likely to join Sterrane, with little success. He could measure bulk and potential weapon skill, but not intention.

The knight removed his helmet, spilling straight brown hair to his shoulders. His dark eyes sought and held Mitrian's. He kept his shoulders back and his head high. Above all else, he would not betray his honor.

Mitrian eased into the questioning. 'Your name?'

The knight responded from long rote. 'Sir Kakkanoch Larrinsson, Knight of the Erythanian and Béarnian kings: King Orlis and his majesty— ' He broke off there, suddenly recognizing his quandary. He grinned sheepishly, obviously with more humility than most of his fellows. 'I guess we're here to decide that.'

Twitters ruffled the crowd. The other knights frowned.

Bothered by the distraction, Garn crouched.

Mitrian continued her questioning. 'Sir Kakkanoch, if a living king specifies an heir other than the one who fulfills the standing law, who would become his successor?'

Kakkanoch considered briefly. Then a smile touched his lips as he recognized the purpose of Mitrian's tactic. He kept his answer straightforward. 'So long as the king designated his successor freely and without duress, his word would overrule the law.'

Rathelon remained still, glaring at Garn. Surely, he could not believe that Rathelon would have given away Miyaga's right to the throne, yet Mitrian's calm presentation had to whittle away at his confidence.

Mitrian elicited the coup de grace. 'Did you hear Morhane do this?'

Kakkanoch gave the question a moment's consideration, apparently needing to get the facts right. 'King Morhane acknowledged Sterrane as his nephew. Following that identification, he said 'Of course, these are yours.' At that time, he gave Sterrane the symbols of his office: the royal crest and the king's signet.'

Rathelon went still as a statue. Then rage shivered through him, and he hollered in defense, 'Of course his majesty gave over his badges of office to assassins who cornered him. Who among us wouldn't have done the same?'

It was a rhetorical question, yet Garn wished he could have answered. Even he would sacrifice his life before handing power and the lives of his subjects to an enemy.

Mitrian had an answer for Rathelon's charge. 'Sir Kakkanoch, in your opinion, did King Morhane face any threat when he gave his throne to Sterrane?'

The silence intensified until Garn could hear his own heartbeat. It seemed impossible for such a huge crowd to fall into a hush that deep.

The Erythanian knight spoke cleanly, his voice plainly audible over the silence. 'No weapons had been bared and no threats exchanged. The king had declared, 'I have nothing to fear from my nephew, and he has nothing to fear from me.' In my opinion, King Morhane passed his title to his nephew, Sterrane, Valar's son, of his own free will.'

The crowd erupted into a frenzied cacophony.

'Lies!' Rathelon shouted. 'All lies! My father would never steal the birthright from his own.'

Even Garn could see the error in this argument. Fired to recklessness by his own impatience, he shouted. 'Morhane murdered his own brother for a title. Did you think he would hesitate to betray you and Miyaga as quickly?'

For the first time, Rathelon's attention snapped to Garn, and his brows beetled so low that his eyes all but disappeared. 'You! I knew you were causing trouble. I should have killed you when I had you groveling at my mercy.'

Mitrian headed toward Garn, intending to calm him before his mouth caused more trouble than it had already. But Garn had heard enough. His wounds throbbed, his head had started to pound again, and he had tired of fools' games. 'Open the damned gates, Rathelon, unless you're too much of a coward to face my sword.'

Rathelon howled a command. One of the guards before the gate released his dogs, and the beasts leapt at the crowd.

Screaming, the villagers broke and fled. One dog sped for Garn. He dropped to one knee, drawing and slashing in the same motion. His sword opened its belly, and the beast collapsed in a scarlet pool. Secodon sped from Shadimar's side to hold two dogs at bay. A fourth writhed in Sterrane's beefy fist by the loose folds at the back of its neck. The last sprang forward, impaling itself on Baran's blade.

Rathelon's hands knotted into fists. He shouted again, pointing angrily at Garn and his companions. At his gesture, the other guards released their dogs.

Ten mongrels charged Béarn's heir and his entourage. Garn bit his lip and tensed to meet the assault, his arm still burning from the previous bite.

Shadimar lowered his head, muttering something Garn did not try to understand.

'Back! DondRondBiffBorkBouncerBonnieKrimKramLosMorst! Heee-al!' Despite the length of the list, the names slid gracefully from the speaker's tongue, and the tone still managed to retain enough authority to stop the dogs in their tracks, perhaps with Shadimar's aid. Whoever had spoken was a master with words and voice, and Garn guessed the identity of the newcomer at once.

Mar Lon. As the hounds fell back, Garn jerked his head toward the man on the wall who had given the command. Mar Lon still wore his uniform and plume of office, and his sword dangled from his hip, sheathed. He carried a tear-shaped, ten-stringed instrument with a long neck, strapped across his chest.

Finally. Relief dulled the edges of Garn's rage, but not for long. *What in hell took him so long?* He had forgotten the patient timing that Mar Lon had used to his advantage in Morhane's bedroom.

Rathelon looked shocked. As the dogs cowered at the sentries' feet, their captain reddened.

Mar Lon rested a hand on his musical instrument, well away from his sword. 'This is the man who should have been king.' He indicated Sterrane. 'He deserves to take back his throne without bloodshed.'

Shadimar grinned. 'Mar Lon, I presume?' He did not await confirmation. 'I had expected Davrin. Last I heard, you were an infant.'

Mar Lon took the insult in stride, though the Wizard's casual attitude cheapened his entrance. 'How easily immortals lose track of time. My father is dead. An "accident" that conveniently occurred right after he suggested that Béarn help the cities of its own kingdom in the Great War.'

The Knights of Erythane exchanged glances over this revelation. It was the first time Garn had seen them react to anything other than a direct command.

Mar Lon bowed. 'And you, of course, must be Tokar.' He used the Western Wizard's name.

Shadimar winced. Before he could correct the misconception, Rathelon bellowed.

'Mar Lon, damn you, traitor! I delegate command!'

The bard laughed. 'You may still lead the men, Rathelon. But obviously the dogs obey me.'

Garn did not understand Rathelon's next harsh words, but the townsfolk recoiled in fear. And Garn had no trouble translating the command that followed. 'Kill them!'

The archers on the walls nocked arrows. The swordsmen pressed forward, and two soldiers among Rathelon's ranks worked to open the gates. Shadimar raised his arm, though Garn knew the Wizard would not harm mortals. Mitrian's sword rasped from its sheath.

Garn strode forward, coming so close to the gate that the archers could only shoot him if they leaned over the ramparts. 'So my impression was correct, Rathelon, you coward. Send your men to fight your battles now that your mother's too old!'

Rathelon howled wordlessly. Muddled by this unrecognizable command, the guards hesitated. Many turned their heads, awaiting a definite order from their captain, unwilling to fire upon a crowd until directly instructed to do so. Others shifted nervously, their loyalties torn. To pledge service to the losing faction, whichever that might turn out to be, meant certain condemnation: imprisonment, banishment, or death.

Garn stared into Rathelon's rabid eyes, seeing the same uncontrollable rage he had fought so hard to overcome in himself. He forced away a smile. Anger would make Rathelon careless.

On the ramparts, Mar Lon tuned each string of his instrument individually, not needing to compare their pitches. He seemed to take no notice of the threat beneath him. Shadimar lowered his head, his voice emerging as a dull, senseless rumble. He raised both arms, as if to indicate Mar Lon, but his gaze did not follow his own motion. He still studied the ground.

Mar Lon's unpolished poetry in the dungeon maze did not prepare Garn for the perfection of his talent. The first few notes that blossomed from the *lonriset* drew the anger out of Garn, their pitch flowing about him in a golden wave of sound. Then Mar Lon sang, his voice as deep and resonant as eternity. His verses wove a story more intricate than any tapestry, conjuring images of silver-colored cliffs carved to a castle's spires and a hero king of the mountain, named Valar. Mar Lon's description of the king made Garn swell with a power that seemed real and personal.

Even as the description left the bard's lips, the clouds pinwheeled, as if sucked into a central vortex, then stretched into streamers above his head. Sunlight spilled through the opening, and the sky turned as blue as the ocean's depths.

Crowd and guards alike gasped in wonder.

A moment later, the wispy tendrils reshaped, taking the form and figure of a thickly-muscled and heavily-bellied man. Features swirled into place: piercing eyes, rugged brows and forehead, and a solid chin. It could have passed for Sterrane, though silver streaks of cloud colored the temples, giving an impression of age. Clearly, the vision represented Sterrane's father.

Still, the bard sang. His voice became deep and solemn as he described Morhane's spree of slaughter. The sky picture went fuzzy, striped suddenly with dawnlike stretches of red. Shadows seemed to crowd upon Garn in a whisper of song that left an impression of evil in its wake. The clouds, too, darkened, bunching into a solid mass that blotted the sun and made the day seem more like night. Then Mar Lon performed Sterrane's return, a simple melody as straightforward and natural as the break of waves upon the shore. The clouds lightened to a neutral slate, drawing and twisting into a more normal configuration. He concluded with the imminent beauty of peace foretold by the legends. Normal colors and patterns returned to the horizon, though it seemed distinctly brighter to Garn, the sun sharper, the clouds whiter, and the blue blush of its background more uniform.

Buoyed by hope, Béarn's citizens stood in the vacuum of the bard's final note, and Garn knew they all longed for more music. Most moved in a dream whose silence was broken only by the last fading notes of the *lonriset*. Though grounded in reality, even Garn paused, enmeshed in that tranquil web of sound. Though it was the music that had spellbound him, the sky images seemed less explicable. Never before had he seen Shadimar use magic that could not pass for coincidence, yet Garn could think of no other source. But when he finally thought to turn his attention to the Eastern Wizard, Shadimar stood in place, looking as moved by Mar Lon's performance as anyone.

Rage accentuated the rise and fall of Rathelon's chest with every breath, and the rearing bear symbol seemed to twitch with a life of its own.

Baran accepted the necessary burden of first words in the wake of Mar Lon's song. The bard's harmonics made the guard's voice sound tough and gravelly. 'Lay down your arms, Rathelon. For the kingdom as well as your cause, it would be best if you do so peaceably. I would suggest you remand yourself to the custody of the Knights of Erythane.' The lieutenant hesitated a moment, as if hoping someone else would also jump rank and share the burden of degrading a superior officer. When no one did, he continued. 'You'll be temporarily relieved of your duties as captain until a swift and fair hearing.'

Garn remained in place at the gate, and Baran stepped up beside him.

Rathelon's gaze flicked to the archers, who had lowered their bows. As his attention shifted to the swordsmen in his ranks, they looked away, not daring to meet his fiery stare. Gingerly, he removed his sword and dagger from their sheaths and stepped forward. Though Baran had spoken, Rathelon passed his weapons to Garn through the space between the bars of the gate. He spoke so softly, his words did not travel to the crowd. 'I await the day I can deliver these to you again, *point first*.' Head high, will unbowed, he motioned for the gates to be opened.

6 A Call to Home

Garn awakened on a yielding surface that seemed to mold to his body and felt smooth as silk against his skin. He lay still, savoring the security and downy comfort, hoping the dream would never end. An instant later, the dull ache of his wounds returned in a rush; and his thoughts flashed back to the morning after a pit fight that had nearly killed him. Enraged by the agony of a sword cut that had all but disemboweled him, he had attacked a guard. The bruises and slashes that the other guards' whips had stamped into Garn's flesh felt hauntingly similar to the injuries he had sustained during his break-in to Béarn's castle.

Garn pushed pain aside, concentrating on the heat of sun rays magnified through glass. He opened his lids. Late morning sunlight glared into his eyes, slanting through a window set over the head of his silk-sheeted bed. *Bed?* The image did not fit into Garn's view of the world. He shook his head, trying to clear a sensation he had known only a few times before: morning confusion. Usually, he slept on the barest edge of waking, alert to every sound and movement around him. This time, two days without sleep and his body's need to heal had driven him into the darkest depths of unconsciousness. He lay still, seeking clues to time and place by the flickering shadows on the ceiling. A wall sconce studded with pearls supported a lantern above his head, and the image snapped the last piece into place.

Garn recalled trailing Sterrane, Baran, and Mar Lon through the courtyard, across the planking that bridged the shallow moat, and through great, iron doors festooned with the royal crest. They had entered a hallway broad enough to hold a small war. Brackets of bronze held burning torches carved into the shapes of every animal Garn had ever seen, and some unfamiliar ones as well. Bears, deer, cats, horses, and foxes clutched the flaming rods, each etched in intricate detail. Precious gems hung in strings from each bracket, swaying slightly in the breeze of his passage.

There, Garn's memory ended. He furrowed his brow, delving into his mind for clues, but the lost time would not come. Concerned, he crawled across the bed. It gave, pliant to his every movement, and he clambered to the floor amid the grind and ache of his injuries. The room had no other furnishings. A niche in the wall supported a bar, a fresh tunic, a pair of breeks, and a matched set of white wraps draped across it. Beneath it, a pan held a pitcher of tepid water.

Garn glanced at his own tattered clothing. His shirt clung like a moth-eaten rag, and the knees of his britches had nearly disappeared. Bruises mottled his arms, knees, and calves. Old blood discolored the bandage on his wrist, and the cut itched mercilessly. Quickly, he washed and changed, rewrapping the dog bite and the slash across his wrist. He saw no evidence of infection, and both had already begun to heal.

As Garn buckled his sword belt into place over his new breeks, a knock rattled the door to his room, the sound reverberating through the confines.

Unfamiliar with the proper conventions and hating to shout at someone he could not see, Garn pulled the panel open. A burly guard in Béarn's colors appeared startled at the swiftness of Garn's answer. For a moment he froze in place. Then, restoring formality, he bowed. 'Sir, I was told to escort you to the feast and coronation.'

Garn had no idea what the last word meant, but feast he understood only too well. He scarcely remembered his last meal, meager fare before a campfire at a time when anticipation and excitement had held hunger mostly at bay. Assuming he had slept through the night and nearly to midday, a full day's cycle had passed since he had last eaten. Nevertheless, his first thought was for his wife and friends. 'Where's Mitrian?'

The Béarnide ushered Garn out into the corridor. 'The king and your friends will meet you there.' Without another word, he headed up the hallway. Garn trotted after him, fascinated by the walls' ornamentation. Where they were not carved and painted, spotless tapestries told stories, scene by scene. Some depicted tales of the world's creation, equally split between the religions of the Westerners, the Easterners, and the Northmen. Garn recognized the lore from his companions' prayers, though he believed none of it. Other tapestries showed gruesome slaughters at the swords of golden-haired reavers who, he supposed, were Renshai. Several particularly intricate weavings displayed mages, always in a cluster of four and surrounded by beasts of earth, sea, and air.

Garn's previous short excursion through the hallways, and even into Morhane's bedchamber, had not prepared him for the finery of the West's high kingdom. Even the castle in Pudar, which he had seen in the days when he served as a guard, held only a fraction of Béarn's grandeur. The guard led Garn down a cross corridor, while the ex-gladiator savored the creative beauty of the halls. Soon, the gild on the torch holders became simple, a blue brocade, but that did not detract from the dazzling display of Béarn's wealth.

The hallway ended at a double set of teak doors emblazoned with the royal crest, outlined in fire opals. A pair of guards stood at attention just outside, their glaives crossed over the entrance. As Garn and his escort came up to them, the glaives snapped down to the guards' sides, butts smacking the stone simultaneously. Together, they turned, pushing aside the teak doors.

Loud, tinny music escaped from the growing crack between the doors. When they opened fully, Garn first noticed a rough-coated bear capering at the end of a chain. His gaze went naturally to the man at the other end, a tall, lean Westerner dressed in a multicoloured tunic. The music came from a line of minstrels playing mandolins, their harmony competent but disappointing in the wake of Mar Lon's talent. Beyond the entertainment, four rows of tables filled the dining hall, each with a central candelabra made of silver and a lace cloth covered with steaming dishes. At the farthest end of the room, Sterrane sat at the head table, Mar Lon and Mitrian at either hand. Shadimar and Baran sat across from the king, an empty chair between them. The lieutenant wore a casual black tunic and britches, the castle colors conspicuously absent, especially so near Mar Lon's ever present uniform. Courtiers and visiting dignitaries occupied the other fifteen tables, and servants wound along the aisles, refilling wine glasses and collecting discards.

Garn's escort led him on a winding course between the tables, then gestured him to the seat beside Shadimar and directly across from Sterrane. Garn took it gladly, unable to resist the allure of roast fowl, thick cream soup, and an array of vegetables.

Baran greeted Garn cheerily. 'Ah. The sleeper awakens at last. You missed the action.'

'What happened?' Garn asked, more interested in the huge portions of food a servant dolloped onto his plate. Though he had meant his query to refer directly to Baran's comment Mitrian apparently misinterpreted. She addressed his other unanswered question.

'You collapsed in front of the court.' Mitrian studied Garn with her soft blue eyes. 'Are you well?'

'Fine now,' Garn hoped to steer the conversation away from his welfare. The bruises from his crawl, climb, and fall began to ache again, and he shifted restlessly to find a comfortable position on the hard wooden chair. 'Just needed some sleep, I guess. I'd stayed awake for a day, a night, and another day.'

Mar Lon smiled, aware, as no one else in the room was, of what had kept Garn awake through the previous night. Sterrane remained silent, obviously still somewhat dazed by the circumstances and proceedings.

Shadimar's silence seemed natural and familiar. Garn could feel the wolf stirring beneath the table when his own fidgeting caused him to poke a furry side. Now that sleep no longer remained his top priority, the throb of his many wounds had become more noticeable.

As the server wandered away to tend another latecomer, Garn ate ravenously, more than his share of the finest food he had ever tasted. Sterrane feasted with the same exuberance, but Shadimar passed food to Secodon beneath the table and seemed not to consume anything himself.

When Sterrane had eaten his fill, and even Garn debated over a last serving of corn, a guard approached Mar Lon. They spoke in earnest tones for some time. Then the bard excused himself, leaving Sterrane in Mitrian's care. The guard who had approached Mar Lon dismissed the musicians and the bear. At first, Garn thought the bard would sing again, and he smiled at the memory of Mar Lon's previous concert. Yet the bard did not carry his instrument. Instead, he waved his fingers at one of the tables, and the Knights of Erythane joined him on the entertainment platform.

Baran groaned.

Garn turned his attention to the lieutenant. 'What's wrong?'

Baran kept his voice low, pitched only for Garn to hear. 'If the knights take part in the coronation, it'll last halfway to the harvest. They'll invoke every convention since the first king crawled from his mother's womb.'

'What's coronation?' Garn watched as the servants cleared food away, rearranging tables and their occupants to open a lane from door to platform. Soon, only the head table remained in the way.

Baran watched the servants work. 'That's when they give Sterrane his crown, and he officially becomes Béarn's king.'

'Oh.' Garn pondered. It seemed a simple enough feat to place a crown on a man's head, even a man as large and tall as Sterrane. Though Santagithi had demanded obedience to himself and to his officers, the general cared little for formality and not at all for pomp. Not until Garn had become a Pudarian guard had he discovered that kingdoms tended to turn even the simplest tasks into stilted, rehearsed exchanges or hours of ceremony.

One of the servants approached Sterrane, nudged from behind by his fellows. As he reached Mar Lon's vacated chair, he prostrated himself on the floor at Sterrane's feet. Accustomed to the dignified bows of the courtiers, Garn was wholly surprised by the maneuver. At first, he believed the servant had fainted. Apparently thinking the same, Sterrane leapt from his seat to the servant's aid. Concern drove him to slip back into the language he had used almost exclusively for the past eighteen years, though badly. 'You well?'

The servant rolled his eyes to Sterrane, the nearness of the king sending him into shivering spasms of fear. 'Majesty . . . I,' he stammered. 'I just . . . ' He froze there, avoiding Sterrane's eyes, his own gaze measuring the distance back to his peers.

Garn felt certain that Morhane had made the servants' jobs difficult. The man's terror made it clear that, not long ago, coming so near the king would have guaranteed punishment.

Many silent moments passed. Finding Béarn's heir on the floor, the courtiers and guards froze.

Sterrane rose first, offering a hand to the servant for support. When the man remained in place, Sterrane seized an arm and hoisted him gently to his feet. The servant went rigid, eyes wide and jaw set, obviously torn between respect and the need to run.

Garn exchanged a smile with Mitrian. They had for too long thought of Sterrane as a giant, harmless idiot to imagine men paralyzed with fear in his presence. A full night of sleep and the three glasses of wine Garn had downed with dinner allowed him to see the humor in the situation.

Sterrane clapped his other huge hand to the servant's back, continuing to support the man's arm. He returned to Béarnese. 'What can I do for you?'

'Do for me, Sire?' The servant squeaked. 'For me, Sire? Nothing for me. We just wondered . . . ' He trailed off, glancing toward his peers for support. They shifted nervously, saying nothing.

Many of the courtiers and dignitaries rose, politely craning to see the spectacle.

'Wondered?' Sterrane repeated.

' . . . wondered, Sire, if we could move your table a little to open the way for your coronation.'

Sterrane's brow furrowed. He glanced from the head table to the platform. The servant trembled in his grip. 'You need my permission to move a table?'

The servant flushed, his voice clear in the quiet that had descended over the dining hall in the wake of the entertainment. Even the conversations ceased as the court watched curiously to see how the new king handled the lowest of his subjects. 'Well, Sire. That's your decision, Sire. Usually not, but this move required you to stand, Sire.'

Warmed by the wine, Garn nudged Baran and mimicked in a whisper, 'Usually not, Sire, but this move required you to fling yourself on the floor, Sire.'

Baran snorted, but he regained his composure before he laughed outright. Garn decided to make it his mission to provoke Baran back into the wild excitement that had made him seem silly back in the clearing. 'You're obviously feeling better,' Baran returned.

'Sleep helped. And I don't ache as much as I did.'

'That's the wine.'

'Where?'

Baran chuckled softly. 'I meant the wine took some of the pain away. Where'd you get those wounds from anyway?'

Garn thought it wiser not to reveal the treachery. 'Sometime when we're alone and we have a lot of time, I'll tell you.'

'I'll take that as a promise.' Baran turned his attention back to the exchange between Sterrane and the servant.

Garn followed the lieutenant's gaze in time to see the servant trotting back to his fellows. Shadimar and Mitrian had risen. Baran and Garn did the same. Seizing a lip of the table, Sterrane personally dragged it into position. As its wooden legs skidded across the floor, the edge of the overly long cloth bunched on a lumpy object that had lain beneath the table, and fur poked between the weave. As the lace fluttered back into position, Secodon was revealed. The wolf slithered back beneath the table, the diners readjusted their chairs, sat back in place, and resumed their conversations.

Baran motioned one of the servants over. He spoke rapidly in Béarnese. As the servant trotted off to attend to the lieutenant's request, Mar Lon raised his hands for attention. The bard remained on the platform, and the Erythanian Knights fanned into a symmetrical formation. Each held a pike. Those to Mar Lon's left clutched the half in their right fist, and those to his right directly mirrored their partners. Helmets covered their heads, polished to a brightness that reflected the torchlight; but their stillness kept those highlights in position. Their pressed tabards covered dress tunics without a wrinkle, though they looked bulky over mail.

Mar Lon cleared his throat, and the room fell silent. He lowered his hands. 'As you know, we have gathered to . . .' The remainder of the speech strained Garn's knowledge of Béarnese, and he abandoned attempts to follow the proceedings. Instead, he allowed Mar Lon's pleasant voice to flow around him, comfortable with its pitch and tempo and not needing to understand individual words.

'Do you see what I mean?' Baran whispered.

'It's not so bad,' Garn hissed back. 'I like listening to Mar Lon.'

'That's because you haven't heard the "responsibility of the high king of Béarn" speech ninety times. And just wait. The knights will have their chance. Then you'll wish you hadn't awakened yet.'

The servant who had chatted with Baran slipped up to his side, clearly nervous about disrupting the ceremony. He placed an un-opened flask of wine on the table. Through the irregular thickness of glass, it looked nearly black.

'Thank you,' Baran said.

'Here.' The servant pulled a second flask from his shirt and set it beside the first. 'Once the carpet goes down, I'm not bringing more.' He added in after thought, 'Sir.'

Baran smiled. 'This'll do fine. Thank you.'

The servant scuttled back the way he had come.

Baran turned back to Garn, speaking just loudly enough to be heard by Garn without disrupting the ceremony. 'The "sir" was for your sake, you know. Yernya and I have known one another forever.'

'What's this?' Garn indicated the flasks.

'Medicine.'

'Medicine?' Garn glanced over at Mitrian, knowing she would not approve of his inattentiveness. But she sat in a thoughtful silence, her eyes riveted on Mar Lon. Shadimar seemed equally engrossed. Sterrane shifted restlessly, his gaze circumscribing the room before returning to Mar Lon. He stifled a yawn with great dignity.

'It's an import from the East. It'll take away the pain of your wounds completely.' Uncorking the flask, he filled Garn's glass as well as his own. 'As a lucky side effect, it takes away the pain of sitting through long-winded speeches.'

Mar Lon indicated the dining room doors, and they opened as one. Two sentries unrolled a thick yellow carpet that spanned the lane between the tables and ended at the platform. A dozen guards took paired positions beside it, their castle uniforms thinner and more crisply pleated than the military tan and blue worn by the soldiers in the courtyard.

Garn stared at the glass Baran had poured for himself. 'Aren't you on duty?'

Baran grinned at a private joke, then explained it. 'Yesterday and last night I was. This morning Mar Lon commanded me . . . ' He stiffened, imitating the Pudarian accent of the king's personal bodyguard with impressive accuracy, ' . . . Lieutenant, you're officially off duty now. You can remove your court colors and relax for the day. Or you can walk the south grounds for six consecutive nights followed by a beating, a bludgeoning, and a month-long fast. I may add your execution for good measure. Make your choice.'

Only two years after the Great War, Garn still held an aversion to anything Eastern, but he tasted the wine out of politeness. It had a sweet, comfortable flavor, enhanced by a brace of unfamiliar spices. 'That seems a bit extreme.' Enjoying the wine, he drained the glass.

'In all fairness, I got rather insistent. But I'd been on patrol the night before Mar Lon sent me to you. Excitement kept me going in the clearing. And, of course, I couldn't go to bed until the trials finished, which wasn't until this morning and –'

'Trials?' Garn lowered his empty glass.

'Trials, yes. Did you think we'd crown Sterrane without removing his enemies first?'

'You mean Rathelon and Koska?'

'And a few others. Yes. We also freed a handful of political prisoners left by Morhane. There weren't many. Morhane believed in removing his dissenters more permanently.' Baran sipped at his own wine.

The news hardly surprised Garn. 'His family, too, apparently.'

Baran took a longer pull, shrugging to obviate the need to talk with his mouth full. He swallowed. 'My father died in that coup, and I hate even the memory of it. Morhane had no right to be king. I despise his decision to slaughter so many every bit as much as I treasure Sterrane's escape. But taking a throne does require ending the previous line. Eventually, Sterrane's going to have to terminate Morhane's descendants. Luckily, he only has to deal with one. I don't envy his need to kill a child, but to do otherwise would be folly. It would mean making the same mistake as Morhane: leaving an enemy and a figurehead alive.'

The turn of the conversaton saddened and unnerved Garn. While Baran refilled the glasses, Garn recalled the moments when he had believed Miyaga's death necessary. He wished he had gathered the coldness and courage to perform the deed. Her slaying might have become just one more murder plaguing his conscience, and he would have done his part to protect innocent Sterrane from suffering the guilt. 'So Rathelon's already been handled?'

'Depends on what you mean by "handled."' Baran took another sip. 'He was banished, along with Koska and the others.' Obviously bothered by the king's decision, Baran nearly emptied his second glass in one gulp.

Dizzied by the speed with which he'd consumed his own last drink, Garn savored the Eastern wine more slowly. 'You would have had Rathelon executed, wouldn't you?' Garn knew he would have seen to Rathelon's death in Sterrane's place. Something about the banished captain reminded him distinctly of the Eastern enemies he had battled on the Western Plains.

'I won't question the king's judgment.' Baran dodged the inquiry.

'Fine. Don't question. Just tell me what you would have done if you were Sterrane.'

'I'm not Sterrane. And it's not for me to imagine such a thing.' Baran took another huge sip. He looked past Garn, suddenly intent on the proceedings he had dismissed moments ago.

Garn smiled, feeling contented, despite the topic. As Baran had promised, the wine did ease most of the pain. What remained scarcely bothered him. The razor edge of alertness had disappeared from his consciousness; and, for once, he did not miss it. He trusted Mar Lon to roust every potential Morhane supporter. With Rathelon and the other enemies dispatched, Sterrane and his companions had nothing to fear. 'Just pretend you're six again. It's your turn to play king and Sterrane's to play court guard.'

Baran returned his gaze to Garn. 'You're not going to let this go, are you?'

Garn finished the last swallow. 'No.'

'Very well.' Baran lowered his voice further, though the booming speeches of knights and bard already fully drowned their exchange. 'I'd have killed Rathelon. Given the chance, I'd have done it with my own hands.' Baran poured Garn another drink, then emptied the flask into his own glass. He stiffened, abruptly realizing his mistake. 'Not that I think Sterrane should have done it himself. Zera'im's blessing.' He invoked the Western god of honor. 'That's the price you pay for a fair king. I'd rather a few sentences that seem too light than Morhane's standard beheadings and hangings.'

Garn looked at Baran, and both men smiled. Garn had seen and heard enough to know that he liked Sterrane's lieutenant. When he worked, he worked with full dedication. And, apparently, he became equally committed to his play. Garn liked the balance every bit as much as the deep-seated loyalty he knew Baran held for his king. The aftereffects of the wine also left him feeling happy, frivolous, and benevolent at once. He wanted to tell the guard how good he felt about leaving a close friend in his hands, wanted to encourage the responsibility that Baran had already taken upon himself.

But before Garn could find the words, he found the need for another drink. This time, he poured.

The coronation lasted longer than Garn's patience, and he quickly tired of the politics. To him, even the finery and indulgences were not worth the tedium of becoming a king. The wine kept his pain at bay, but it also spurred a need to urinate that became nearly irresistible. It seemed to Garn as if his bladder might burst before a change in Mar Lon's tone drew even his eye to the ceremony. A moment later, he realized that everyone else, including Mar Lon, had his or her attention fixed on the door. Garn followed their gazes to a boy who traveled the length of the walkway. A satin pillow balanced on his forearms, cradling a gold circlet. The light of myriad torches winked and sparked from its surface; apparently the page was quivering. As he arrived before the platform, Mar Lon gestured to Sterrane.

Sterrane glanced briefly at Garn, and his eyes betrayed uncertainty. Baran reached across the table and gave the heir's hand an encouraging squeeze, knocking over a salt bowl with a clumsiness attributable to the wine. Shadimar nodded in encouragement, saying nothing.

The instant Sterrane's foot sank into the carpet, the room fell completely silent. The guards shifted, falling into a well-rehearsed backup pattern around the platform and along the walkway. Sterrane moved up between Mar Lon and the page. The boy knelt, head bowed, circlet offered to the massive new king.

Mar Lon spoke directly to Sterrane, but his voice remained clearly audible. 'Sterrane Valar's son, your majesty, welcome home. Our swords are in the service of Béarn and yourself. May your reign prove long and . . .'

' . . . beautiful,' Garn and Baran whispered simultaneously. Both men buried their faces in their hands to suppress their laughter. For quite some time, Garn studiously glanced at every other person in the room, knowing a single glimpse of Baran's face would send them both over the edge into hysteria. His view gve him an interesting perspective of the room. Despite the solemnity of the knights and guards on duty, the courtiers and off-duty guards smiled and drank at least as much as the lieutenant and himself.

Insight blossomed slowly; but when it did, it seemed like the wisest revelation that had ever come to a man. *Of course they're celebrating. Sterrane's return is a happy occasion, not something to suffocate in solemnness.* The joy seemed tangible. And though Garn reveled in it, he also appreciated the decorum and good sense that those on duty displayed. Should a threat arise, the guards would meet it. *Not me though.* Garn rolled his gaze back to Baran as the lieutenant did the same. They stifled laughter again, though one snort broke through.

Mitrian glared at her husband, and her disapproval stole Garn's mirth in an instant.

Sterrane plucked the circlet from the pillow, placing it, as was the custom, on his own head. 'Thank you,' he told the boy.

The page seemed at a loss for a response. 'Thank you more, Sire.' He rose. Turning elegantly, he walked from the room at a pace faster than formality dictated.

Sterrane faced the crowd, about to speak his first words before an inner court audience. The suspense grew tangible. Though well-liquored, the nobles waited like carvings, unspeaking for fear they might miss a single syllable.

Sterrane wiped his palms on his breeks. 'Friends, I made my first proclamation on Béarn's streets, so this will have to be my second.' His gaze shifted in Garn's direction, and the ex-gladiator suddenly wished his vision less blurry. 'I would like to name my new captain of the guard: Baran Barder's son. Rise, Captain.'

'Gods' mercy.' Baran froze in his seat, shaking his head as if to clear hours worth of wine in an instant. Tears sprang to his eyes, and he stood with a grace that belied his state of near-inebriation. He pronounced each word cautiously to avoid slurring, and that made his speech as ponderous as that of the knights. 'I don't believe it's possible for any man to be happier than I am right now. I can think of no-one I'd rather serve and no title I'd rather hold.' He considered a long time, his mind slowed. Only the fact that he remained standing clued Garn that Baran had more to say. 'By morning, I hope, I'll be worthy of serving you again.'

Laughter ruffled through the audience, and it felt comfortable after hours of ostentation. Mar Lon cringed, his sympathy for Baran obvious. If not for his insistence, Baran would still be at Sterrane's side, with his dignity and sobriety intact. Garn felt proud of his drinking partner, certain his own mind and mouth could not have risen to the occasion at all.

'Welcome home,' Baran finished. May your reign prove long and . . . ' His lips twitched as he tried valiantly not to laugh. Garn suffocated his own amusement with a hand clamped over his lips.

'Beautiful,' Sterrane finished. 'Beautiful, Captain Baran.' Hopping down from the platform, he caught his childhood friend into a hearty, masculine embrace that surprised his escort. The guards hastily scrambled to follow their king. Garn felt tears welling in his own eyes. His labor in Béarn was finally finished, and none of it had been in vain. Though Garn would miss his guileless companion, Sterrane belonged here in Béarn, where he could speak the language with competence and the people loved him. It reminded Garn that he still had a long way to go before he found his own niche, with his wife and his son in a town that had once kept him enslaved. Sterrane's battles had ended, Garn's had not yet begun.

The dancing bear and the mandolinists amused the feasters as dinner dishes replaced the ones from lunch. Garn left the dining hall to empty his bladder. By the time he returned, the excitement and thrill had disappeared, exchanged for a snug, wine-induced stupor. His eyelids glided repeatedly and irresistibly closed. He vaguely recalled an orange that Sterrane had chosen for dessert rolling twice from the table before the king imprisoned it with his crown. Garn's mind remained attuned enough to register the conversations of the courtiers as normal and ascertain that there was no threat to himself or to his friends. Then sleep overtook him again.

The dining room door burst open. Garn snapped awake, spinning toward the sound. Everything remained as he last recalled, except for six guards standing in the doorway. One approached Sterrane. 'Sire, a falcon flew into the castle, and we haven't managed to catch it. It has something tied to its leg.' He added cautiously, as if fearing ridicule. 'A message, perhaps, Sire.' It seemed an odd or impossible use for a bird of prey. 'Sire, should we . . . '

A shout from the doorway interrupted him. Garn's attention whipped back to the entry. A red hawk wound through the press of guardsmen, dodging the flailing wave of arms that tried to intercept it.

'Close the door!' The guard who had addressed Sterrane sprinted for the oaken panels, just as the bird cleared the last of his companions. It glided over his head. He ducked, then sprang, missing it by fingers' breadths. He cursed, reversing his direction so quickly, he skidded to the floor at Sterrane's feet.

The falcon flew straight for the royal table. Candlelight illuminated flecks of gold and ebony in its plumage.

Mar Lon sprang between his king and the falcon. The bird swerved as it reached the table, fixing amber eyes on the bard.

The guards charged.

Delicately, the falcon glided around Mar Lon and lowered itself to Shadimar's bare forearm. Surely its long, daggerlike nails gouged his flesh, yet Garn saw no blood and the Wizard seemed oblivious.

The guards checked their rush, but not quickly enough. They crashed into a tangle. The first went down to his knees. Another tumbled over him, rolling beneath the head table, dragging the leader with him. The others managed to backpedal, saving themselves and the royal table. Garn jumped out of the way, Secodon lurched from beneath the table, toenails scrabbling on stone floor.

Only Shadimar seemed undisturbed. He slid two fingers along the falcon's wing. The bird cocked its flinty head and regarded the Eastern Wizard through one golden eye. Chuckling noises issued from deep in its chest.

The guards disengaged. Discovering the falcon in Shadimar's control, they brushed off their uniforms and tried to look dignified, though they had already lost the battle.

Garn watched as Shadimar plucked a strip of parchment from the bird's scaly leg. As the Wizard unrolled and read it, the hawk bounced to his robed shoulder. A frown puckered Shadimar's lips, and he crumpled the note in his fingers.

'What does it say?' the leader of the guard unit asked.

Shadimar shook his head. 'It is of significance only to me.'

Conversations had ceased at the other tables, and all eyes remained on the Wizard and the falcon. Secodon whined, pacing like a caged animal, though the Wizard echoed none of his pet's consternation.

The guard glanced at Sterrane but continued to address the Wizard. 'Your pardon, sir. But the king has the right to read any message delivered to Béarn.' He reached for the falcon.

The bird waited until the Béarnide closed, then flapped to

Shadimar's other shoulder. 'This matter does not concern the king,' Shadimar replied with equal authority, still without a hint of emotion.

Sterrane waved the guard away. The man obeyed, though he shuffled backward only a few steps, still obviously concerned for Sterrane's welfare. Garn knew Shadimar's falcon could mean Sterrane no harm, but he did not fault the guards for becoming overprotective of a king so long awaited.

Mitrian watched in silence. Mar Lon looked at Shadimar, brows raised expectantly. Garn remained where he stood. 'Bad news, Shadimar?' Mar Lon inquired carefully, his gaze on the agitated wolf. Garn realized the Eastern Wizard must have corrected the bard's misconception about his name sometime during the sorting of politics.

Shadimar followed the bard's attention. Scowling, he snapped his fingers, and Secodon wriggled back beneath the table. 'Neutral, really. Though its source is the greatest good of our world.'

Awakened from sleep, Garn found the Wizard's cryptic pronouncement annoying. 'What do you mean; and why didn't you say it?'

Shadimar swung his head around to face Garn directly, but he did not grace the impertinence with a response. Instead, he chose to put the guard commander at ease. 'The message was for me, and Swiftwing only delivered it to Béarn's castle because here is where I am.' He smoothed the wrinkled parchment between his fingers.

The bard addressed the guard's leader. 'Escort Swiftwing outside.'

The Béarnide led his men from the room, the last pulling the panel toward closing. The falcon soared through the narrowing crack before the door shut behind them.

Once the commotion died away, and the courtiers returned to their own concerns, Mar Lon pressed Shadimar, 'So what did the Northern Sorceress have to say?'

Again, Shadimar wadded the parchment between his fingers. 'She claims Colbey witnessed Tokar's ceremony of passage.'

'Ceremony of passage?' Mar Lon's eyes widened at a danger only he and the Eastern Wizard could understand. 'Then Tokar is . . .'

Shadimar's scowl silenced Mar Lon.

Less easily appeased, Mitrian pressed. 'What does that mean for us?'

'It means,' Shadimar started, obviously rattled by the message, 'that we're leaving tomorrow.'

'No!' Sterrane's fist crashed against the table, sending utensils and dishes into a rattling dance. A wine glass overbalanced, and Mitrian caught the candelabra before it fell. Guards recoiled from the king's wrath.

Mitrian rose and stood before Sterrane. She rested her hands on his shoulders. 'Sterrane . . .'

'No,' Sterrane repeated, this time more sullen than angry.

'Let's talk elsewhere.' Shadimar motioned them toward the door.

Sterrane hesitated like a petulant child. Then he stood and headed for the door. Shadimar, Mitrian, Garn, and Mar Lon followed. To Garn's relief, Shadimar held the door for the three, though he closed it before anyone else could trail through behind them.

As they entered the corridor, Shadimar slipped past Garn to place an arm around Sterrane's shoulders. 'We have to go now.'

'Not leave.' Sterrane pulled free of the Wizard's grip, pressing his spine to the wall. 'Promise with me when me need you.'

'And I was.'

'Still need,' Sterrane insisted.

Mitrian's face crinkled sympathetically. Garn placed a warning hand on her shoulder before she could volunteer to stay longer. They had gone long enough without seeing their son.

Shadimar sighed. 'Mar Lon will see that you want for nothing. You'll never find a better adviser. And you've shown you can make a good decision with your captain as well.'

Mar Lon nodded solemn agreement.

Sterrane bit his lip. 'You say when king, me can do whatever want.'

Shadimar nodded.

'Me want make you stay.' Sterrane gave Shadimar an off-center stare, as if he doubted but hoped the argument would pass unchallenged.

The Eastern Wizard shook his head impatiently. 'You can't do that.'

'Then me not king anymore. Me quit.'

Garn started to laugh. Mitrian gave him a warning squeeze.

'Stop that.' Shadimar went from comforting to stern. 'We already discussed this. You can't do that either.' Sterrane looked away. 'So what can me do?'

Shadimar gestured impatiently. 'You can understand. Garn and Mitrian have a son they haven't seen in more than a year. I have important business. The time has come for us to leave.'

Huge tears rolled down Sterrane's cheeks.

Mitrian, too, began to cry. Before Garn could stop her, she tossed Sterrane's raven hair playfully. 'We can . . . '

Certain she would delay their trip longer, Garn cringed.

Mitrian continued, ' . . . stop in Pudar on the way home and send Arduwyn and his family to Béarn. He let you live in his cottage for months. You could pay back the favor; you've got plenty of room.'

The king's face brightened. 'That good idea.' He smiled. 'That great idea.' Then the grin wilted as swiftly as it had come. 'You think he come? You think Bel go from Pudar?'

Garn recalled the distant look and the bittersweet smile that crossed

Arduwyn's features whenever he spoke of the city of his childhood, Erythane, Béarn's neighbor. 'Hmmm,' he said with good-natured sarcasm. 'Do I think Arduwyn would come to live near the forests he never stops talking about? Do I think Bel would give up a crowded, tiny cottage to live with a king? Certainly not. Who'd want to –'

Mitrian interrupted, apparently afraid Sterrane would take Garn's joking seriously. 'I think, Sterrane, that you can count on it.'

7 Havlar's Prophecy

The Southern Wizard, Carcophan, paced around the single tower he had built near the Eastern city of LaZar, his salt and pepper hair streaming in a mane behind him. He had made no attempt to hide the location of the structure, yet its placement on a barren plot of ground had discouraged visitors. Once, fields of wheat and corn had stretched from this location to as far as the eye could see, but greed had caused the farmers to cultivate the last shred of fertility from the soil. Precedent dictated that a city would soon sprawl onto the pale ghost that the land had become, yet the tremendous loss of life during the Great War had delayed the inevitable. So Carcophan had appropriated the territory for himself, a place to hide, from view and from Wizards' contacts, until he discovered a new strategy and a new champion.

Eventually, Carcophan decided, *this place will have to be rebuilt in a more mundane fashion, with a courtyard and a curtain wall.* Thoughts spun through his mind, and he sought to recapture the confident arrogance that had come naturally before the Great War had crushed centuries of planning and whittled the ranks of his followers. It had become his way to champion his cause with grand acts of slaughter, rather than the slow, subtle trickle of evil his forebears had inflicted on the Northern Wizards' people. *Trilless will expect me to strike swiftly and boldly again. Which is why I have to find something more discreet, something she will overlook until it's too late and too overwhelming to stop.*

Carcophan halted before the double doors to his tower, his green-yellow eyes missing nothing. Many ideas sprang to his mind, not the least of which was a personal spree of murder. A few well-placed spells could decimate the followers of goodness, yet Odin's laws forbade such an action, even on a small scale. Carcophan knew he must not kill a single mortal, and he understood and respected the reasons. He could destroy all of Trilless' Northmen, and she could inflict nearly as many casualties upon his Easterners. *Nearly.* Carcophan could not allow himself to believe her power could equal his; he had always trusted himself to be stronger and a superior tactician. Within days, he knew all of the Northmen and Eastlanders could lie dead, and most of the neutral Westerners would die in the fallouts and backlashes.

The idea of wholesale destruction drove a shiver through Carcophan. Without mortals, there could be no Cardinal Wizards. Odin had created the system of Wizards to modulate the forces of the world and their impact on his men and women. The Southern Wizard stood, his hand poised on the latch. Sometimes, it helped to study the big picture; at the least, it reinforced the necessity of Odin's laws whenever frustration drove Carcophan to doubt the AllFather's intentions. The Cardinal Wizards stood as a buffer between gods and mortals. Once mortal themselves, the Wizards maintained a unique outlook that the gods could never have, yet their near immortality gave them a glimpse of the other side as well.

The system of the Cardinal Wizards saved the gods from needing to regulate mortals and the morals that directed them. The few times Carcophan had heard of gods interacting with men had resulted in profound shakings of the foundations of mortality, and the ripples stretched far beyond the gods' intentions. It was easier and safer for the gods to keep their distance, to worry only about the grandest issues of reality: creation, death, nature, and the cosmos. Even the fact that mankind had invented false gods and pantheons did not faze the gods; they found their fulfillment from sources other than peasants' adulation. And they understood the limitations of the mortals they had made.

Carcophan pulled open the tower doors, exposing a dry, winding staircase. The breach in the otherwise solid structure caused magic to shimmer and flash through the stone, and alarm shivered through him. Carcophan paused, frowning. Crafted from the Chaos that Odin had banished, magic was unpredictable, even in a Cardinal Wizard's hands. Illusion and fleeting intangibles posed little threat; but magic instilled into objects opened a portal for Chaos and its creatures, the demons. Because of this, the Great Swords and the Pica Stone were, at most times, the world's only significant magic items. Shadimar kept the Pica; it was felt to be of least danger in the weakest Wizard's hands. The swords were stored on the plain of Chaos, except in times of need.

Carcophan knew he was taking a risk by placing such a huge volume of sorcery at one site, yet he had a need and a plan for his tower. First, it gave him a protected fortress other than the underground labyrinth that usually served as the Southern Wizard's home. The other Cardinal Wizards had no right to enter his territory. Law forbade them from locating him by spying, and they could contact him only by the messenger falcon, Swiftwing. Even then, they would need to direct the bird to the proper location. For now, Carcophan wanted to plot and study in solitude; he would not be disturbed, for any reason, until he found the champion to replace dead King Siderin. Still, the Southern Wizard had another reason for constructing his magical tower. He was going to summon a demon more powerful than any he had called before. And he needed to contain it.

Carcophan entered the tower, closing the doors behind him. As the panels fell flush with the building, closing the breach, the sense of warning disappeared. Turning, the Southern Wizard touched the tower with magic sense. He felt the smooth sheet of magic coating the inner walls, humming like a trapped insect, a force unused to order or containment. The cold, still seams of the door felt thin as string, surely not a significant hole in his defenses. Yet the Southern Wizard chose to take no chances. Tracing the outline of the portals with a finger, he sealed the gap with sorcery as rough and strong as solder. Satisfied, he trotted up the steps.

Carcophan passed a dozen doors as he wound his way up the tower. Moans wafted softly beneath the cracks, interspersed with an occasional delirious soliloquy or scream. Though the voices belonged to followers of his own evil, their wails had become too familiar to bother Carcophan any longer. After the Eastern healers had plied their craft with as much aid as he could give them, Carcophan had collected those men too injured to steal from death. With magic, he had kept them alive longer than nature could allow, ignoring their suffering for the greater cause they had all once served, though not wholly certain of his purposes. Later, he had collected those men who had developed incurable wound infections and added them to the horde. Now, Carcophan smiled, hating to lose any of his followers, yet glad their deaths could serve the cause of evil for which they had already given their lives.

Carcophan ducked through the opening to a room at the top of the staircase. Magical light diffused through the room, creating no shadows. A ladder led to the highest level of the tower. Bookshelves lined the walls, crammed full with historical texts, some of which he had written. A table in the center of the room held an ancient volume, crumbling with age despite the care it had received over the millennia. The dangers of magicking tangible objects forced the Wizards to restore at least some of their texts every few centuries, which was just as well. Rewriting the books forced Carcophan to give them a thorough reading and allowed him to translate some of the events and phrases into less archaic, more solid terminology.

Carcophan wandered to the ancient book on the table, placing a finger on the line that had caught his attention, and decided his next course of action. Buried amidst a pedantic litany on how the Cardinal Wizards fulfill the prophecies of their predecessors had come the following words: ' . . . it is this wryter's opinyon that the gods favor neutralitee. Therefor, it seems unlikelee that Havlar's first divinatyon, of the eyghteenth Southern Wizard's superlative champyon will ever come to pass. This wryter believes wee should take the prophesee of the Grayt War to be Havlar's first real prophesee and the other as wishful thinking.'

Carcophan tapped his finger on the page thoughtfully. He had never before heard even casual mention of a prophecy spoken by the first Southern Wizard predating the ones concerning the Great War. Carcophan had found no further references in this tome or, so far, in any other. A mental search of predecessors' memories had drawn a blank. The seventh Wizard in the Southern line had died, run through by the White Sword of Power in the hands of a Northern Wizard's champion, and all of the previous Southern Wizards' memories had died with him. The thought made Carcophan shiver. The gap was frightening enough, but the idea of a Cardinal Wizard's death made him ill. Successful completion of Odin's seven tasks of wizardry made a Cardinal Wizard impervious to any creation of law; only demons or the Great Swords could slay him before his time.

Demons had killed two of the East Wizards, but the double system for neutrality had allowed the Western Wizards to keep the world in line until new Eastern Wizards were established. Luckily, when the seventh Southern Wizard had been killed, he had a trained apprentice who had already completed the tasks and stepped into his place. Carcophan shuddered to think of the damage and power the Northern Wizard would have achieved had he gone long unopposed. And that thought reminded Carcophan of the Western Wizard.

Carcophan had noted Tokar's disappearance even before the Great War. It was not uncommon for Wizards to get caught up in rescribing texts or in research and lose centuries that passed more like days. But for Tokar to worry about such tasks when he had prophecies to fulfill concerning the war made no sense. That in itself might hold the answer. The ninth Western Wizard, Niejal the Mad, had been clearly psychotic. The fourteenth in the line, Sudyar, had never once contacted the other Wizards, and many hypothesized this antisocial behavior came as a direct result of Niejal's influence. Clearly, the negative aspects of misconception and personality accompanied the power and knowledge inherent in a collective consciousness. In that respect, Carcophan felt lucky that his line had been broken, despite the information this lost him.

Carcophan closed the book on the table, recognizing his thoughts as a distraction. He had slaved over his defenses, tending them to the minutest detail. There was nothing left to do, except the summoning. Anything else was only delay.

Carcophan raised his head, gathering strength and reveling in the singly-focused support of his mental retinue. He crossed the room, centering his thoughts on the emotional motivations he had used to prepare himself for battle in his mortal years, and his predecessors worked to strengthen his mind-set. In his time, Carcophan had been a warrior of reasonable skill, unlike his colleagues and predecessors, most of whom had chosen more spiritual pursuits.

The ladder rungs felt solid beneath Carcophan's feet. He climbed to the upper story, a narrow chamber, wholly empty. He did not bother to close the hatch. The simple wooden door would not contain the creature, should it escape his bonds. He could only hope that the magical wards with which he had coated the tower would not fail.

Twice before, Carcophan had summoned demons for information. The magics he called forth for personal protection came easily. He felt the tingle of sorcery enwrapping him, felt the same sense of balanced comfort that accompanied sitting in a well-braced saddle. He chanted the familiar syllables that opened a demon-sized pathway to the plain of chaos.

Almost immediately, dread enveloped Carcophan, its source external. Gradually, it took a visible form, a tarry stream, like smoke but more solid, an oily, shapeless blackness. Carcophan snapped the gateway shut with a word, then shaped bands of binding magics that looped around a figure more perception than reality. Each coil brought the darkness further into detail, defining a grainy, shimmering substance unlike anything on Odin's world. Carcophan felt his magic pulse as the demon struggled, and pain hammered through his head, nearly breaking his concentration. He balled his hands to fists, tightening the web of magics until each individual band glowed red against the blackness.

The demon ceased its fight. It took the shape of a massive serpent, its neck covered with spines, its pointed yellow teeth surrounding a forked tongue the color of blood. It spanned nearly the entire room. Its closeness gave Carcophan chills, yet he did not move. The wards would prevent it from touching him. Giving ground would only allow it more space to expand until it crushed him into a corner. The constraint might hinder his magic and, should the demon break free, it would assure his death.

The demon spoke, though its serpent jaws did not move. 'Wizard, you called me to your world at the cost of your followers, who will die in an agony you cannot imagine. Your wards are trifling. When I shatter them, I will joyfully slaughter you first.'

Carcophan ignored the taunts, recognizing them as bluff. 'By Odin's Law I have called you here. You must answer my questions and perform a service to the best of your knowledge and ability.' Having spoken the necessary words, Carcophan bound the creature to truth, an entity the Wizard knew exclusively and the demon not at all. 'Demon, you underestimate my power and my imagination. I've dealt with your kind before, and I will do so again.'

The demon writhed and twisted over itself, its neck spines cutting a line across its empty darkness that did not leave a mark. It said nothing, only obliged to answer questions.

Carcophan went directly to his interrogation. Time would only weaken him and strengthen the demon. Familiar with the creatures' deviousness, he phrased his query fully and carefully. 'What was the first actual prophecy spoken by the first Southern Wizard, prior to his forecast of the Great War?'

The serpent head extricated from beneath a coil. It whipped around suddenly, its gaping jaws and razor teeth a finger's breadth in front of the Wizard.

Despite himself, Carcophan recoiled; yet training caused him to tighten his wards along with his sinews. The bonds burned red indentations into the demon.

The creature made a noise of pain.

Regaining his composure, Carcophan hid a smile. Trying to unsettle the Southern Wizard, the demon had only succeeded in hurting itself.

Its reptilian expression never changed, and it answered the question as if no time had passed. 'The eighteenth Southern Wizard will train a champion of more competence than any before him. This champion will be a swordsman unmatched by any other mortal.' Its voice faded into silence.

Straining to catch every word, it took Carcophan several seconds to realize that the demon had finished. Excitement thrilled through the Wizard, but he kept it in check. As long as he lacked the knowledge to carry out such a prophecy, it could not occur. 'Is there more to Havlar's first prophecy than you told me?'

'No.' Despite the demon's concise, clear answer, something in its tone indicated that it had not yet finished.

Carcophan waited, aware he could not allow too much time to pass. He had called up a demon more powerful than he had ever dared before, and each passing moment increased its danger. His eyes blazed with the excitement of the demon's revelation, yet he kept his attention on the wards. The prophecy of a champion would do him little good if he lay dead at the feet of a demon.

The demon's form warped into a blur, the wards still clearly visible looped around it. 'Consider this information a gift for the feast you prepared for me downstairs.'

Carcophan shivered, now glad the creature could have no expression. To betray loyal followers went beyond the self-interest that was evil to the chaos that was the realm of demons. He reminded himself that the men he had gathered were beyond salvaging, that they would have died long ago had he not preserved them. Now their deaths could and would serve the cause to which they had pledged. Yet he could not help feeling touched by cold, demon chaos.

'You will not need to seek this champion out. He will come to you, betrayed by one he considers kin, and he will turn traitor to his people.' A face appeared from the black formlessness, followed by two thick arms and legs as it assumed the form of a womanlike parody. 'And do not become complacent. The Northern and Eastern Wizards will also have powerful champions. A lucky stroke could kill even the best. If you truly wish to serve your cause to your best ability, your champion will need an edge against his enemies.'

'An edge,' Carcophan repeated, his discomfort barely tempering the wild joy possessing him. His followers' ranks badly whittled, he could not afford to lose another battle, to have evil vanquished from the world. He knew that his wards bound the demon to truth, yet it would skew the picture by choosing what information it volunteered. Carcophan did not know why it had chosen to assist him with facts about which he would never have known to ask, but he could only use them as efficiently as possible and remember their source. *At a time like this, after a vicious defeat, it only makes sense that I should have the advantage.*

'I believe we both know what that entails.'

Carcophan frowned, aware the demon referred to Morshoch, the Black Sword of Power. The danger seemed too significant to contemplate. He had not called up the Sword for his last champion, and that might have been the cause of his defeat.

'I owe you a service,' the demon reminded. 'Shall I bring the Sword?'

'No.' Carcophan was too shrewd to let elation overcome common sense. 'I'm not finished with my questions.'

A smile filled the demon's face, over bulbous breasts as large as its head. The wards enwrapped its finger-thin waist like belts. 'I am in no hurry.'

The comment reminded Carcophan of the urgency of releasing the summoning. He had gained himself some time with the dying followers. The demon would need to slaughter and devour them before he could attack Carcophan directly. By then, the Southern Wizard hoped, he would have his defenses fully reinforced. 'You spoke of the champions of the Northern and Eastern Wizards. Will the Western Wizard have a champion?'

'No.' This time the answer came as a definitive end.

Carcophan thrust for the loophole. 'So the Western Wizard is alive.'

Though not obligated to answer the statement that was not quite a question, the demon chose to do so. 'I didn't say that.'

'So the Western Wizard is dead.'

'I didn't say that either.'

Carcophan zeroed in on the question. 'Is the Western Wizard alive?'

'I can't answer that.'

As the demon danced around the question, frustration plied Carcophan. 'Why can't you tell me whether a Western Wizard lives?'

'Because the way you phrased the question, I would have to go into more explanation than your binding necessitates.'

'But it's a simple "yes" or "no" question.'

The demon said nothing.

'I thought you were grateful for the feast.'

'Not that grateful. Rephrase your question to ask what you really want to know.'

Carcophan considered. Before the Great War, he had sought the Renshai destined to become the Golden Prince of Demons, hoping to remove the threat to his own champion. Then, too, he had called a demon. Clued by the knowledge that the prophesied Renshai would meet his tribe's definition of Renshai, he had overspecified his question so that it excluded Mitrian and Colbey, leaving only Rache. Yet, Carcophan realized, there had been more to the problem than too narrow a definition. He had asked for the names of all the surviving, full-blooded Renshai, and nothing about that restriction should have eliminated Colbey from the list. Although the demons could not lie while bound, they were still constrained by their own base of knowledge. Carcophan could only guess that either that particular demon had been ignorant of Colbey or that he had bound it incorrectly.

Carcophan reworked the current question in a way he considered fail-safe. 'Does the collective consciousness of the Western Wizard exist?' If Tokar still lived, so would the memory of his predecessors. And, if his ceremony of passage had succeeded, the line would have passed to his successor.

The demon considered for a brief moment. 'No. It does not.'

Dead. The information did not surprise Carcophan. Odin's vows constrained all of the Cardinal Wizards into working together to replace Tokar. First, they would need to find a likely candidate. Then they would send him or her through the god-mediated tasks of Wizardry. If he survived, he would have proved his worth and become as immune to objects of law as demons and Wizards. But Shadimar was the one who had to set the process in motion. And, apparently, he still did not know the fate of the Western Wizard for certain. *Surely, the weakest of the Cardinal Wizards would not risk summoning demons. Which means he has to find out by slower, more routine methods.* Carcophan knew that eventually he would have to help replace the missing Wizard, but not until Shadimar contacted him. *And I can't receive word unless and until he finds me.*

Carcophan stared at the demon, attentive to the necessary question. 'Is it true that the creation of the Gray Sword would require the presence of both Eastern and Western Wizards?'

Now the demon hesitated longer, apparently lost in thought. It assumed a more familiar demon shape, an angular horse body with splayed, catlike claws, a barbed tail, and a serpent's head. 'That was Odin's intention. I have no reason to believe it would work otherwise.' It grinned, displaying a mouthful of black teeth, as sharp as daggers. 'But you know as well as I that magic can never be fully predictable.'

Carcophan dared not hold the demon any longer. He turned his mind back to the service it owed him. 'I don't want you to retrieve the Sword of Power. But I want you to place it where I can call it without bringing one of your kind here.'

The demon laughed. 'My kind will be grateful.' It lowered its head, black lids closing over huge, red eyes.

Carcophan shifted his focus from the binding wards to his own self-protection. The red bands began to fade, even before they burst, splattering magic into multicolored sparks. A high-pitched shrill rang through the room, like the scream of a dying rodent amplified to an ear-splitting volume. The demon spun, whisking through the opening.

Human cries revealed its passage, echoing up the stairwell and throbbing through Carcophan's head with a pain he knew might last for days. Tears washed to his eyes and he swore, not for the first time, that he would never summon such an abomination again. Then he set to his own defenses. And hoped that his magic would prove strong enough to contain it.

Béarn's royal nursemaid, Dorina, perched on the ledge of Miyaga's bed, mesmerized by the stirring coverlet that matched the rise and fall of the girl's every breath. The elderly Béarnide lowered her head, ignoring the thin, gray curtain of hair that fell into her eyes. Her mind continued to count in the rhythm of the child's breathing, though she could no longer see the bed. Soon enough, Dorina knew, she would bury the child she had nurtured since birth, just as she had reared and lost Miyaga's mother. But, at least, Morhane's daughter had died of illness. Miyaga would be slaughtered to end the line, a child's life stolen to satisfy custom.

A knock on the door disturbed Dorina's lengthy vigil. She cringed, having dreaded this moment from the instant she had learned of Sterrane's return. Miyaga stirred but did not awaken. 'Who is it?' Dorina called softly.

In response, the door swung open, and Mar Lon entered. 'The king will see Miyaga now. You need to come take him to her. It's your job.'

'No.' Dorina crouched like a mother wolf. She stroked the girl's hair protectively, unconsciously matching the cadence of her breaths. 'He'll kill her.'

Mar Lon met Dorina's eyes directly, his dark gaze sympathetic but unyielding. 'It's his right. Don't make this harder than it is already.'

Dorina hissed, tears filling her eyes. She glared back into Mar Lon's eyes, so gentle for one who had just condemned a child. 'You're inhuman.'

Miyaga rolled, murmuring something unintelligible.

Mar Lon jerked his head toward the hallway, indicating Dorina should follow.

The nursemaid hesitated. As much as she needed to protect, it seemed cruel to discuss the child's fate in her presence. Rising, Dorina walked slowly from the room, but only far enough for Mar Lon to slip outside with her and close the panel.

Once in the corridor, Mar Lon addressed Dorina's comment as if no time had passed. 'Inhuman? Me? Morhane tortured citizens for trespassing. He killed his brother and all but destroyed the true king's line. He put his son-in-law to death because Miyaga was a girl, not a grandson. That, Dorina, is inhuman.'

The hot tears stung Dorina's eyes, and she stared at her feet. She harbored no love for Morhane, but Miyaga had become the focus of her life. The young princess seemed more daughter than charge. 'She's only a child. An orphan.'

'Which makes his majesty's unpleasant task mercifully easier. Any of Morhane's line left alive menaces his security. Surely even you can see that Béarn needs Sterrane and his descendants on the throne. You can't thwart two decades of legend. If you'd troubled to come meet him like the rest of the staff, you'd see just how lucky we are that he came home.'

Dorina sobbed, her resolve shattered.

Mar Lon took her hand. 'Come on. It's time to meet the king.'

Dorina went, lost in a spinning maelstrom of grief. After a walk that seemed far too short, Mar Lon halted outside a game room door to brush the last tears from her eyes and smooth her disheveled, gray hair. 'It has to be this way, Dorina.'

Dorina heard nothing. She stared at her feet until Mar Lon opened the door, revealing Sterrane. The king had risen to meet them and waited by the door. Though startled by the sudden and close presence of the king, Dorina remembered her manners. She curtsied mechanically, not daring to lift her eyes to his face. 'You would see the child, Sire?'

When she received no reply, Dorina looked up, just in time to catch the end of Sterrane's silent nod. The misery on his features, from his own recent loss, seemed nearly as intense as her own.

'Certainly, Sire.' Dorina spoke in a dead monotone. Memories of the vibrant girl whose fate rested in Sterrane's hands reawakened waves of anguish. 'Come with me, please, Sire.' She led the new king through corridors of carved granite, haunted by thoughts of Miyaga at play. Though she knew what she had to do, she considered leading Sterrane on a long, tortuous route. She discarded the idea as quickly as it formed. Born and raised to Miyaga's age in the castle, Sterrane surely knew the location of its bedrooms.

The torch-lined halls seemed unusually bleak and unfriendly. Dorina stared without seeing the steel-smoothed walls nor the fine oak door, with its tiny replica of the royal crest. One day, Dorina hoped, Sterrane's children would sleep in that room in her charge, and the cycle could begin again. Much as she tried, that promise could not displace her sorrow. Every child was special, but no one could ever replace Miyaga.

When Dorina did not open the door, Sterrane admitted himself, shutting the panel behind him.

Outside, Dorina paced fretfully, hoping death would come quickly and without pain. She could not understand why Sterrane had chosen to perform the deed himself when so many guards would have had no choice but to do it at his command. Perhaps the new king had inherited some of the cold bloodthirstiness that his uncle had embraced. Still, in some ways, Dorina admired the decision. Miyaga had become Sterrane's problem. To relegate such ugliness to another would be cruel.

Dorina let the tears drip from her eyes, collapsing helplessly against the wall to Miyaga's room. For half an hour, she remained unmoving, oblivious to the crampy ache of tense muscles left too long in one position. Finally, gingerly, she climbed to legs that tingled from the restoration of blood flow, steadying herself against the door. Through the ironbound wood, she heard high-pitched giggling. She froze, pressing her ear to the door. Again, she heard childish laughter. At least, it seemed Sterrane intended a merciful execution. Dorina relaxed slightly, straining to hear the verbal exchange that followed. Though she could easily discern Sterrane's gruff voice from Miyaga's lilt, Dorina could not make out a word of the conversation.

More giggling wafted from beyond the door, followed by a crash so loud it ached through Dorina's ear. A scream welled up in her throat, and she stifled it so abruptly she bit her tongue. Heart racing, she waited. Violent pounding shattered her composure and sent her scuttling halfway down the hall. As her wits returned, she became furious. Even Morhane would not kill a child in such a brutal fashion.

Drawing a resigned breath she believed might be her last, she paraded to the door. She grasped its handle, and the door swung open before she could pull. She found herself staring into the thick chest of the king.

Dorina stumbled backward and fell, eyes wide in terror. Only then did she notice the grinning child on Sterrane's shoulders. 'Nanna!' Miyaga shouted a greeting. 'Have you met my new papa, Sterrane the Bear?'

The image proved too much for Dorina, and she lapsed into hysterical laughter. The solution seemed too simple and obvious for her to have missed, though panic had stripped her of logic. Raised as Sterrane's daughter, Miyaga would become sister to his line. Suddenly, Dorina found herself liking the new king with all her heart, and she made herself a solemn vow to instill the morals and loyalty to blood that Miyaga's grandfather had lacked. She owed Sterrane that much for his mercy.

A moment later, the king and his adopted daughter joined Dorina's mirth. The three laughed until the hallways rang.

8 Vendor of Lies

Two weeks of travel through fertile fields and woodlands brought Mitrian, Garn, Shadimar, and their escort of two Béarnian guardsmen to the plains before Pudar. Daily, they had overtaken merchants with heavily-loaded horses, mules, or covered carts. Their dusty party had earned glares and challenges from merchants suspicious of their unburdened horses and obvious weaponry, but the letter they carried, stamped with the high king's seal, brought them safely through the lands between Béarn and Pudar.

The sun raised a scarlet glare in the dust swirling from the trail. It cast spears of light between the trees, accentuating every leaf and reddening the foam that bubbled on the horses' chests. The wolf padded at the heels of Shadimar's horse. Cottages lined their way, placed conveniently near the fields yet within sight of the city's defenses. A merchant spoke with one of the guards at the gate, while his entourage prodded a string of stocky pack beasts through the entrance. Children stood beside piles of fresh vegetables, bowls of butter, and handmade crafts, their parents unable to afford stands in the marketplace.

Mitrian followed the merchant's pack line through the gates, ignoring a young man who thrust a piece of parchment at her. She had little interest in the myriad religious and secular causes touted by the masses outside Pudar. The constant buzz of conversation drowned the cries of vendors lauding their wares. Merchants in gaudy robes tended stands covered with every item Mitrian could conceive of, and some she had never before seen. Sweet spices, meats, and fresh breads mingled their odors, reminding Mitrian of the savory meal Bel would serve when they arrived. Arduwyn's wife had worked in a tavern frequented by Pudarian locals because of its food. The transients and businessfolk tended to go to *The Dun Stag*, a tavern/inn combination famous for its ale. Freed of the need to work outside her home, Bel had turned her creative cooking efforts to meals well worth the trip.

Mitrian dismounted, passing the reins of her horse to one of the Béarnides. The animals would become dangerous amid the milling crowds in Pudar's market. 'We'll meet you in the morning at *The Dun*

Stag with the family you're to escort back to Béarn.'

'Thank you.' the guard smiled. He had talked about his craving for *Dun Stag* ale for days.

Garn and Shadimar alighted, handing their reins to the other guard. The two Béarnides headed from the market, chatting animatedly in their native tongue.

Mitrian stood indecisively in the road. Despite months of living in the trading city, she had never tired of its market. Each day brought new wares and bargains, and she had even begun to learn the art of haggling. Still, she had come for a purpose, and Shadimar seemed anxious to continue home. Always introspective, the Wizard had become even quieter. Usually patient to a fault, he had begun to fidget, and he read or wandered while the others slept. Surely, he could travel faster alone. But he had promised Santagithi he would accompany Mitrian and Garn home; and, apparently, he would not break that vow. 'I suppose we should go straight to Arduwyn's and Bel's cottage. I presume they live in the same place.'

'It's day,' Garn addressed Mitrian, though his gaze remained fixed on the market. 'He'll be working, either out in the forest hunting or maybe selling.' He added the last, clearly as an excuse to browse the marketplace. 'That merchant he used to work for seemed to think Arduwyn was a pretty good salesman. Maybe he's back and hired him again.'

Mitrian had some difficulty following Garn's pronouns, but she translated his intentions easily enough. Arduwyn was a competent salesman. She had seen him twist a patron's emotions until the man essentially wound up buying his own dagger. But she guessed Garn's underlying motive for searching for Arduwyn there was to give him a chance to shop. Sterrane had handed them each a pocketful of gold that begged spending. And Mitrian still had one gem left from the collection she had amassed from the war spoils her father had given her, piece by piece, each bauble won in a different foray.

Garn took Mitrian's hand, his strong, callused fingers warm in her grip. 'If Brugon's back, he probably set his table in the same place as last year.'

Mitrian turned a questioning look at Shadimar.

The Eastern Wizard shrugged. 'It makes no difference. Whether you find Arduwyn now or at sundown, we still can't leave until morning. You might as well let Garn look at the weapons.' He smiled ever so slightly. 'I wouldn't want him to die for lack of gawking.' Without awaiting a response, Shadimar strode off into the crowd, Secodon trotting after him.

'Wait!' Mitrian started after the Wizard, but Garn caught her arm. 'Where are you going?'

Mitrian pointed in the direction Shadimar had taken. 'We forgot to decide where and when to meet.'

Garn chuckled, jingling the gold in his pocket, his attention already straying to the glimmer of armor and shields on a nearby table. 'Do you think for a moment that he'll have difficulty finding us?'

Mitrian recalled how she had first met the Eastern Wizard. She had fallen asleep while daydreaming about a sword the blacksmith's son promised to forge for her as a birthday present. The Wizard's magic had spirited her to his storm-wracked ruins where he had given her a pair of topaz stones to place in the hilt of her sword in exchange for the largest gem in her collection, a sapphire he had called the Pica. She had awakened in her bed, with the yellow gems present and the sapphire gone. Her hand went naturally to the wolf's head that formed the pommel of her sword, running her finger over its topaz eyes, feeling the winding flaw that she had broken in one of them during the Great War. Now, in Pudar's market, Garn's words made her laugh. 'No, I don't suppose Shadimar would have any trouble finding us.' By the time she finished speaking, Garn had already drifted to the stand.

While Garn browsed among protections that Renshai dismissed as cowards' crutches, Mitrian glided from tables of artistically wrought silver to bowls of gems.

Shadimar had little interest in the material wonders of Pudar, yet he meandered through the crowd, hoping to distract himself from the burden of his thoughts, if only for a time. He pulled his travel-stained cloak taut about his skinny frame, scanning stands of exotic vegetables, toys, and tools, the teeming masses of locals and foreigners that filled the square, and the entertainers who hawked their talents for the spare change of the shoppers. For a time, Shadimar managed to shed his mental burdens for the rich baritone of a musician who accompanied himself with a battered lute; but even that peace did not last long. Before the singer reached his final notes, thoughts of the Western Wizard again invaded Shadimar's mind.

Colbey witnessed Tokar's ceremony of passage. Shadimar reviewed Trilless' message, aware he needed to act, and soon. *If he initiated his ceremony of passage, then Tokar is clearly dead.* The conclusion did not surprise Shadimar; more than forty years ago, Tokar's apprentice, Haim, had successfully completed the Tasks of Wizardry. Since the apprentices did not achieve near-immortality until after their predecessor's ceremony of passage, a Wizard did not take an apprentice until his time had neared. And Tokar's failure to complete the many prophecies set for him during and after the Great War had caused Shadimar to become alarmed. It had been the Western Wizard's duty to gather most of the armies of the Westlands; instead, Colbey had done so, instructed by a note from Shadimar that he had received in Tokar's absence. It had been the Western Wizard's job to find the Renshai who would become the Golden Prince of Demons, keep him safe, and guide him to the Great War. Instead, while Shadimar had concentrated on Mitrian and Carcophan on Rache, Colbey had found his own way to the war. And the Western Wizard, not Shadimar, should have accompanied Sterrane to his throne.

The crowd split around Shadimar and his wolf, some muttering rude comments as they passed. Blinded by the intensity of his thoughts, the Wizard ignored them. He pictured Haim as he had looked after the Tasks, a gawky, Pudarian youth with shaken features and undisguised insecurity and fear. To Shadimar, Haim had seemed a poor choice; yet his questioning had only earned him Tokar's wrath. For whatever reason, the eldest and most powerful of the Wizards had selected a weak successor. And now, Shadimar feared, the transfer of the Western Wizard's lineage might have proven too much for Haim.

It killed him. Shadimar clenched his hands, assailed by grief and rage. A worse thought struck him. *What if Haim isn't dead? What if the process drove him mad?* The possibilities seemed endless, ranging from tragic to dire. *He might be cowering in a cave somewhere, paralyzed by the responsibilities thrust upon him.* Shadimar had never heard of such a thing happening, yet he also knew how cautiously the previous Wizards had chosen their apprentices. The memories of his own predecssors shifted through him, sifting out instances where Wizards had reacted poorly to their power. Most brought forth stories of the ninth Western Wizard, Niejal the Mad. Prone to violent outbursts and prolonged periods of sulking, Niejal had also suffered from episodes of sudden, complete memory failure. He had attempted suicide multiple times with knives, falls, and hanging, apparently forgetting that objects of law could not harm him.

There had been others. The fourteenth Western Wizard had contacted his peers only once, when he had sent his chosen apprentice to the Tasks of Wizardry. The eighteenth Eastern Wizard had become obsessed with summoning and dispelling demons, making five successful contacts before one killed him. And even Tokar had stayed mostly a loner. One of Shadimar's forefathers hypothesized that the collective consciousness itself had driven Niejal mad, overwhelming him with the need to consult and understand a vast myriad of strong personalities of both sexes. Following that logic, Shadimar had to guess that the longest uninterrupted line, that of the Western Wizards, might become particularly vulnerable to insanity, especially with a known lunatic already ingrained in its perceptions.

In that respect, the eighteenth Eastern Wizard's death had given Shadimar an advantage he had always before seen as a lapse. He carried the memories of only five predecessors compared to Tokar's nineteen, Trilless' eighteen, and Carcophan's ten. Still, at this time in history, the world could not afford to lose the collective consciousness of the Western Wizard. The power and knowledge that it had amassed through the millennia would prove absolutely necessary to prevent the doom forecast to occur during Shadimar's own reign as Eastern Wizard. *Haim must be alive; the future of all men, Wizards, and gods depends on it. I have to find him, rebuild his character, and train him to use the powers of his inheritance.*

Secodon whined. Pained by the depth of his master's concerns, he sat, flopping a huge paw onto Shadimar's knee. The touch drew Shadimar from his contemplations, and he tried to console himself with information that raised more questions than it solved. *Colbey watched the ceremony of passage. He may have answers.* Yet Shadimar knew Trilless had to have a more personal reason for sending the message. She would not have done so simply to point out Haim's failing; a weak or absent Western Wizard unbalanced the world to her advantage as well as to Carcophan's. For some reason, she wanted Shadimar to confront Colbey. *Danger there.* Shadimar felt certain, though the details of that menace eluded him. He had nothing to fear from the old Renshai who had joined with him in a blood brotherhood. Shadimar patted Secodon's head, and the paw withdraw. The wolf's plumed tail waved.

Absently, Shadimar drew a silver *chroam* from his pocket and tossed the coin at the musician's feet. Without awaiting a 'thank you,' he turned and headed into the crowd, the wolf again trailing after him. He tried to focus his attention on the lines of stands, forcing himself to assess the quality of silks, gems, and brass trinkets to keep from falling back into musing. One thought kept trailing back. *Colbey saw the ceremony. What was an old Renshai doing at such a private affair? Did he do something to spoil the ceremony? Could he have harmed Haim?* This last speculation raised ire as well as curiosity. *Colbey swore a blood oath with me at the Great War. So why did he keep this information from me?*

Shadimar's annoyance rapidly turned to anger. Ignorance made him irritable; until he knew the Western Wizard's fate for certain, he had no right to call a Wizards' meeting. Even the best of the possibilities scared him. He seemed unable to escape thoughts that he had too long worried like a dog with a bone, and he still harbored outrage over Morhane's treachery in the Béarnian clearing. *There was a time, not so long ago, when no one lied, cheated, or stole; and a man's word was as unwavering as the cycle of day and night.*

A nearby hiss shocked Shadimar from the thoughts that had again overtaken him. He spun to face a muddy-eyed merchant in a robe, woven through with shimmering fabrics, and a matching skullcap. 'Wizzzzard,' he said.

Accustomed to being addressed by this name, if not in this manner, Shadimar naturally surrendered his attention. Ordinarily, he would have found the man's dress humorous, but drawing a Cardinal Wizard from deep mental consideration of the world's fate seemed intolerable, no matter how much he had been trying to do so himself. The dark scowl he assumed should have left no question of his displeasure.

The merchant paid no heed to the Wizard's expression, apparently too pleased by Shadimar's attention to care. His mouth twitched into a grim smile. He adopted a tone of consequence, attempting to use an ancient dialect that sounded like a crude parody to one old enough to remember when such formality was standard. 'My instincts fail me not. I recognize ye as of the true order, not the scoundrel lot of mages and quacks.' He closed one eye, cocking his head sideways conspiratorially. 'Ye carry an aura of power.'

Shadimar glared, uncertain what to expect yet doubting it would do anything more than fuel his temper. One lie would damn his control. 'I warn you. I have no mercy for rogues who waste my time. What do you want?'

The merchant continued in a dramatic singsong. 'I've many magics to interest one so powerful. The sovereigns of a dozen mighty kingdoms journey far ways to me to supply their wizards: Erythane, Bruen, Loven. I alone sell true magic.' He waved a hand with a grand flourish. 'Even the high magistrate of Béarn comes to me, and the Western Wizard descends from the mountains each month to purchase . . . '

Inflamed by the mention of the Western Wizard, Shadimar crooked a bony finger at the blue-cloaked merchant. 'You've nothing but bottles filled with as many tricks and lies as your mouth.' Secodon punctuated the words with a warning growl. 'I am the only sorcerer Béarn has. The Western Wizard had no need for your false potions, and neither do I.' He tossed his head with all the fury of the tempests that surrounded his ruins. 'A man who deals with Wizards would know that they cannot lie and that they deplore mortals so touched by chaos that they cannot be trusted. Speak one more word to me, and you will regret it.' He spun to leave.

'Wait!' The vendor reached for Shadimar's shoulder.

Secodon lunged for the offending arm. With a cry, the merchant recoiled. The wolf's fangs ripped cloth. As his paws touched the ground, he crouched, dark gaze fixed on the merchant.

The merchant's face went deathly white. 'Can't . . . can't blame a . . . merchant trying to sell his wares.'

Shadimar reined his anger, and the wolf's sinews uncoiled. The man's voice grew more steady. 'Please, allow me just one demonstration to prove that my goods are real.' He wound his fingers in the tear in his sleeve.

Shadimar stopped, knowing that it was folly. Rather than distracting him, the merchant's false promises only reinforced the many breaches chaos had found in the world of mortals. Still, he waited, hoping that Secodon's attack had shocked the man back within the confines of Odin's law.

Color crept back into the merchant's cheeks, and he hefted a jar half-filled with sorrel dust. He fell back into the ancient rhythm. 'Know ye, O mage, that contained in this crusted phial is solid fire.' The merchant's voice trailed off as he assumed a dramatic stance.

Shadimar bit his lip, shaking his head in warning. Secodon growled.

But the merchant had fallen into a well-rehearsed patter and seemed oblivious to the threat. 'Not,' he continued suddenly, 'not the soot of coals spent nor the flickering orange of a normal campfire. Trapped within this phial, I have the incandescent whirlwind of magical fire, the kind that blazes emerald and lavender.'

A cluster of curious Pudarians gathered, attracted both by the theatrics of the merchant and the statuesque Wizard. The merchant's strategy became clear. Just Shadimar's presence before his stand was enough to draw attention. It was not the Eastern Wizard he was trying to attract, but a horde of customers lured by Shadimar's apparent interest.

Used, Shadimar reddened, further enraged by the merchant's obvious disregard of his warnings. Clearly, like most men of his era, the merchant did not believe in the Cardinal Wizards and, thus, saw no threat in anything except the wolf.

The vendor uncorked the flask, dumping powder into his right hand. He made grand gestures with it that attracted every eye, except Shadimar's, who focused on the lump of flint concealed in the man's left hand. With grossly exaggerated eloquence, the merchant pulled both arms to his body. A flick of his wrist scratched the flint across his buckle, and he used the spark this caused to ignite the powder. He tossed the flaming chemical in a wide, turquoise arc that landed at Shadimar's feet, sputtered, and died there. Head thrown back and arms wide, the merchant reveled in the crowd's gasps of amazement.

Furious at the charade, Shadimar spoke a single harsh syllable.

From the charred pile of ash, flames shot toward the sky in deep olive, indigo, and dappled cream, as strong and wild as a living thing. Its heat darkened the wooden stand. The crowd scurried, and the merchant leapt for cover as his wares burst into varicolored fires.

Quietly, Shadimar left Pudar's market. And the wolf padded calmly in his wake.

*

Shields covered a wooden tabletop like scales, scattering sun glare in a spray of colored highlights. Garn stared, captivated by an iron buckler, while Mitrian paced an impatient circle around him. 'You don't even wear armor,' she reminded.

The crowd surged and parted around them, a ceaseless tide that had grown familiar. Mitrian no longer found herself concentrating on conversations that disappeared a moment later. Strangers' chatter ceased to distract or interest her.

'Maybe I'll start wearing armor.' Garn reached for an ornate shield.

'Colbey calls armor the bane of swordsmen.' Mitrian placed a hand on Garn's solid shoulder. 'And we came to find Arduwyn. Remember?'

'Colbey moves faster than weapons and doesn't need armor.' Garn ran his finger along a gilded edge of the finely polished steel. 'Arduwyn'll be working till sundown. Why hurry? How often do I get a chance to examine fine merchandise or have enough gold to buy it?'

Garn hefted the shield. Then, seeing one with a reinforced steel edge, he lost all interest in the piece he held.

Mitrian sighed. The Renshai shunned shields and armor as cowards' defenses, but she could not begrudge Garn these things. Colbey had not allowed Garn even to watch her practices. As a gladiator, he had been given only the occasional, crude shield. Mail was reserved for Santagithi's officers, and the gladiators had no access to anything more than secondhand helmets and gauntlets. Personally tired of staring at metal, Mitrian tapped Garn on the shoulder. 'I'm going where Brugon's stand was last year. I'll meet you there.'

Garn mumbled an incoherent reply that Mitrian accepted as an affirmative answer. She continued along the cobbled walkway, attentive to the collage of sight and sound surrounding her. Merchants spewed limitless promises to snag naive foreigners or to reaffirm the trust and optimism of citizens who had gotten the worst of previous bargains. More experienced shoppers prepared rhetoric as loud and convincing as that of the salesmen, the most challenging and difficult customers for the merchants.

After a time, even Mitrian fell prey to a fast talker who pressed a gold necklace into her hand. Yellow gems in its center sparkled, a perfect match to the topaz stones set as wolf's eyes in her sword hilt. She studied the merchant from the corner of her eyes, unable to fully remove her attention from the trinket. Silks of rich design dangled from a narrow, angular frame. His dark eyes flashed as he moved in for the sure sale.

Suddenly Brugon's familiar baritone cut over the normal sounds of the market, accentuated by nervous excitement or fear. ' . . . have a gripe with my salesman, we can . . . ' A short scream snapped through a shrill shatter of metal and glass.

Arduwyn's voice was unmistakable. 'Wait! Stop! We can talk . . . '

Mitrian dropped the necklace, not caring where it landed. She ran toward the voices, plowing through the milling horde. People leapt or staggered out of her way, some cursing her as she passed, though she heard none of it. She collided with a child, and they both fell. Leaving the wailing boy to the ministrations of his mother, she scrambled to her feet and continued toward Brugon's stand, brutally shoving customers aside.

The few wares remaining on Brugon's stand lay tipped or broken. A bronze teapot balanced on its open lid in a sea of glass chips near the back half of what had been a horse-shaped statuette. Most of the merchandise lay scattered over the road. In the center of the mess, Brugon sat with his hands clasped to his jaw. To his right, a burly Pudarian pinned Arduwyn against a tree with the point of a bronze short sword. Flattened against the tree with the blade at his throat, the little, flame-haired hunter scarcely dared to breathe. His eyepatch hung askew. His hands crept, almost imperceptibly, toward the dagger at his belt.

'I gave you my last two *chroams*,' the man shouted, spit spraying into his captive's face as he spoke.

'Give it time,' Arduwyn replied hoarsely. 'Nothing grows overnight.' He tried to soothe, but his words seemed to have the opposite effect.

The burly man jabbed the point of his sword until it indented the skin at Arduwyn's neck. Fear swam through Arduwyn's remaining eye, and the movement for his weapon turned into a sudden grab.

Afraid for Arduwyn's life, Mitrian ran to the stranger and touched his arm. 'Here's your gold. Now leave him alone.' She plucked coins from the handful in her pocket. They were Béarnian gold, not *chroams*, but worth at least as much.

The man glanced at Mitrian, scowl deepening, and he shook off her arm. 'Get away from me, wench. This doesn't concern you. I've got a lesson to teach this cheat.' His blade remained in place, and he turned back toward Arduwyn.

Mitrian's hand whipped to her hilt, and anger tightened her grip. She flicked the sword from its sheath, cut air, and struck in silent fury. Bronze shattered beneath steel, the broken sword raking a line across Arduwyn's chin. The hunter clamped a hand to the wound.

The burly man staggered, still clutching his useless hilt.

The blood trickling between Arduwyn's fingers incited Mitrian to war frenzy, but she fought the Renshai blood wrath nearly as easily as Garn controlled his killing rages. She flung the two gold coins at the stranger. 'Go away!'

The man stared.

Mitrian tossed him three more coins. 'And buy yourself a real sword.'

The man retreated, then whirled and disappeared into the crowd.

Arduwyn brushed himself clean and readjusted his eyepatch. Clamping a handkerchief to his chin, he greeted Mitrian with a welcoming smile and an embrace. 'You still have impeccable timing.'

A piece of glass crunched beneath Mitrian's boot, and she frowned at the compliment. If she had truly timed things well, Arduwyn would not have gotten hurt.

Arduwyn stepped back, examining Mitrian. 'Where's the wild man?'

Mitrian grinned. 'Have you forgotten his name already?' She laughed. 'Garn'll be here soon. He dawdled, figuring you'd work till sundown.'

Brugon limped from the shambles of his stand, clutching a brass candle holder that seemed to have survived the fall. The left side of his face had begun to swell, and spices smeared the right side of his cloak from armpit to hip. Apparently, the disgruntled patron had landed a punch that sent the merchant sliding across his table. 'Ardy won't be working. He's done for the day. It'll take me all afternoon to clean up this mess.'

Sheathing her sword, Mitrian placed a hand in her pocket and fondled the last remaining gem from her collection, a large, uncut diamond. She pulled it out and pressed it into Brugon's hand. 'You shouldn't have to take this loss,' she said.

Brugon glanced from gem to woman in astonishment. 'Neither should you. I can't take this.'

'Consider it payment for something I'm going to take from you.' Mitrian winked at Arduwyn.

Brugon glanced over the mangled clutter of objects, most broken and bruised, but several that could be sorted, intact, from the wreckage. 'My entire inventory isn't worth this gem.'

'I'm taking your salesman.'

'After what just happened, that might be a blessing.' Despite his words, Brugon closed his fingers around the diamond.

Arduwyn removed the cloth. Dried blood caked his flesh, but the bleeding had stopped.

Mitrian continued, trying to sound solemn. 'He has business with the king of Béarn.'

Arduwyn made a brisk gesture of triumph. 'That's the best news I've ever heard.' He caught Mitrian and danced a small circle. 'I was afraid to ask. I thought if things went well you would have told me right away.'

Mitrian extracted herself from Arduwyn's grip. 'Sorry. Strange as it may seem, I thought I'd save your life before chatting.'

Brugon tried to return Mitrian's diamond, but she refused him with a wave. 'What's this?' the merchant said. 'I thought the king of Béarn liked Ardy about as much as *he* did.' He gestured in the direction that the enraged patron had taken. 'Something about you selling him forged documents.'

Arduwyn laughed. 'I just made up that story to get this job.'

Mitrian chuckled at the memory of Arduwyn speaking faster than she could think, making random statements designed to keep the merchant responding with 'yes' until Arduwyn had his job.

'Besides,' Arduwyn continued, 'this is a different king. Do you remember Sterrane?' He hefted a pewter mug from the grass and returned it to the table.

'Brawny fellow. Quiet. Kind of slow. Worked at the docks.'

Arduwyn smiled at Mitrian. 'He's king of Béarn.'

'Of course.' Brugon did not miss a beat. 'And I'm the god of merchants.'

Mitrian took the writ from her pocket, handing it to Brugon. 'He's telling the truth.'

Brugon perused the letter, and his face alternately assumed varying shades of red and white. 'Well . . . I,' he stammered. Then the truth struck him. 'The king of Béarn hauled cargo for me?' Brugon stared at the smashed chaos of his wares and chuckled.

Soon, all three were laughing as they gathered together the surviving goods.

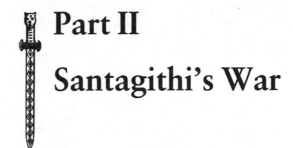

Part II

Santagithi's War

9 Checkmate

The gentle, rhythmical breathing of Santagithi and Colbey broke the otherwise total silence of Santagithi's strategy room. Maps decorated the plain gray walls, fusing into one another until the world seemed to form an infinite circle around them. The two men sat on opposite sides of the long table, a chessboard between them. The general stared at the strategic jumble of pieces on the board, as always cautious to paranoia over his next move. Politely, Colbey did not make a sound.

A knock echoed through the confines. Santagithi frowned, ignoring the noise.

Despite the lack of acknowledgement, a guard tapped open the door. He wore Santagithi's black and silver, the uniform crisply ironed, his hair cropped short. 'Sir?' he said.

Santagithi's pale eyes remained fixed on the pieces. He made no reply. Colbey glanced at the newcomer, but propriety demanded that he let the general answer his guard's summons. In deference, he said nothing.

'Sir,' the guard repeated, a little louder.

Santagithi sat immobile, though surely he had heard, and the guard fell silent. Deliberately, the general pinched a white rook and sidled it four spaces to the right. He pursed his lips grimly. 'Check.' Only then did he turn to face the guard. 'I told you I didn't want to be disturbed. I *am* going to beat this Northman.'

'Not this time.' Colbey tapped the black queen to the square beside the white king. 'Mate. I was hoping you'd do that.'

'Damn!' Santaghiti slammed his fist on the table, sending the pieces toppling. A pawn rolled across the table, and Colbey caught it before it hit the floor. 'You'll get careless eventually. Set a new game.'

Smiling, Colbey gathered the game pieces while the guard shifted nervously from foot to foot.

'Sir,' the guard began again. 'I'm sorry to interrupt, but I think you should know that your daughter and her husband have arrived.'

Santagithi remained silent, but Colbey could see the huge, work-hardened hands begin to shake. The old Renshai had little room in his fierce heart for pity. Throughout his adolescence, the world had been prey to take or spare as it pleased the whims of the Renshai leaders. After the Renshai were slaughtered, Colbey had lived for years in a land of enemies, with only his swords as companions. Still, he could not help but be moved by Santagithi's plight. They had not seen Mitrian for two years, not since the Great War. Santagithi's wife had died a year ago, leaving Mitrian and her son as all the family he had. And Colbey did not envy his need to make peace with Garn.

Santagithi rose, following his guard from the room and down the unadorned corridor of the guard quarters. Trailing, Colbey recognized the general's stalwart manner as a facade. As they filed past the closed doors of the guards' personal quarters, Santagithi glanced neither right nor left. Even when he reached the room that his dead captains, Rache and Nantel, had shared for sixteen years, he did not flinch at the memories he could not quite seem to shake. In his two years in Santagithi's Town, Colbey had never before seen the general fail to pause in quiet sadness or bow his head. Now Santagithi whisked past without a glance, and Colbey realized just how deeply the coming promise of reuniting with Mitrian and Garn affected him. The guard opened the outer door, ushering Santagithi and Colbey onto the grass.

The last streaks of sunlight carved over the horizon, striping Santagithi's citadel. Walled defenses enclosed the hill, surrounding the main dwelling, the guard quarters, the stable, and the buildings in the southern quarter that had once served for gladiator fights and training. A gate in the eastern wall led down the hill to the town below, a series of roads and cottages rimmed by forest to the north and east and by fire-cleared plains to the south. The Great Frenum Mountains formed a hazy gray barrier to the east, the northern and southern Weathered Ranges filling the horizon to the north and south. Westward, the smaller Granite Hills barely rose above the distant trees. The setting sun backlit the shadowy forms of sentries pacing their watches.

Santagithi's long strides set a pace that quickly brought them to the main house, Colbey following at a graceful trot and the guard jogging to beat Santagithi to the door. Colbey smiled at the picture. Whatever his trepidations, Santagithi would meet the situation with the same eagerness Colbey admired in the man in battle. The general saw everything quickly and competently executed no matter the emotional cost.

The guard opened the door to Santagithi's citadel, waved Santagithi and Colbey through it, then closed it behind them. Inside, Santagithi stopped before the first door, the one to his court. Though trained to notice such subtleties, even Colbey almost missed the hesitancy of the general's hand on the ring and the not quite careless toss of his gray-streaked hair that was, if only for a fraction of an instant, delay. Then the door swung open to reveal four of Santagithi's guards surrounding

Mitrian and Garn, Shadimar, and his wolf.

Emotion radiated from Santagithi, too strong for Colbey to miss, though he felt rude for his intrusion. He could sense the raw clash of joy and grim sorrow as well as an uncertainty that seemed jarringly out of place. Never again would Mitrian crawl into her father's lap and beg for stories of war or adventure; she had experienced too many of her own. Her lean white legs had tanned and grown firm and knotted. The leather scabbard that swung from her sword belt was blackened from nights in the elements, but Colbey knew the weapon it shielded must gleam, as sharp as the day it was forged. If not, her first new lesson would become a lecture she never forgot.

Colbey grinned as his own concerns mingled and became lost in the thoughts so clearly radiating from Santagithi.

'Welcome home, all of you.' Santagithi caught Mitrian into an embrace, and she returned his greeting with equal fervor. Then, as they both pulled free, Santagithi turned to Garn.

The tension rose even further. Colbey saw the guards exchange uncomfortable looks. Surely, they could not imagine that any words could seal the chasm of bitterness that had grown between father and son-in-law. Yet Colbey knew that the hatred Garn had held for Rache made this dispute seem small; and those two had found their peace.

Santagithi wrapped his arms around Garn briefly. 'I'm glad you chose to come. You won't regret that decision.' He released Garn.

Colbey stood by aloofly, pleased by Santagithi's greeting. The general had a talent for reading people, and much of his strategic success same from a sensitive understanding of human nature. Clearly a short, to-the-point message would work best with Garn. Santagithi had made the ex-gladiator feel valuable and welcome, without gushing or the kind of sentimentality that could only have looked false.

Garn nodded his thanks.

While Colbey played judgmental observer, Shadimar strode up beside him and reached to seize his arm. Sensing something alarming in the Wizard's bearing, Colbey instinctively avoided the touch with an agile sidestep. Then, feeling guilty for mistrusting, he smiled a welcome.

Shadimar's face drew into a stony pall of unreadable emotion. 'You and I have things to discuss.'

Struck by the anger and insolence in his blood brother's tone, Colbey replied stiffly. 'Things to discuss, my friend?'

The Eastern Wizard spoke softly, but his voice held the uncontrolled power of a rock slide. 'The Northern Sorceress claims you know things about the Western Wizard that only his successor should know.'

Shadimar's words baffled Colbey. 'No, friend. I've never even heard of this sorceress, and I don't know much about the Western Wizard either.' Colbey met Shadimar's hard gaze with his own. 'Stay the night in Santagithi's guest chamber, and we'll talk then. I'm afraid it might not be until late if Santagithi insists on losing another game of chess.'

Shadimar's mask dissolved to a twisted frown of surprise. 'You've beaten Santagithi at chess?'

'Fifty-three games.'

'Clever as well as skilled.' Shadimar laced thin fingers through his beard. 'Few men could outthink the West's prime strategist. We'll have to discuss your other talents as well.'

Santagithi called across the chamber. 'Colbey. I thought you should be the one to take Mitrian and Garn to their son. Shadimar, you'll stay the night, of course?' The question emerged more like a command.

But the Wizard handled it good-naturedly. 'Of course.'

'Come with me, then. I'll take you personally.'

Shadimar glanced at Colbey, silently confirming their meeting that night, then headed for Santagithi, the wolf at his heels. The guards shuffled after him.

Colbey watched general and Wizard leave, certain of Santagithi's motivations. He would get as much as he could of the story of Sterrane's return through the impartial Wizard before plying Mitrian and Garn. Shocking news or impropriety could be better handled coming from an acquaintance rather than family. The old Renshai turned his attention to Garn and Mitrian, remembering the grueling sword practice he had put the boys through that evening. 'Rache's asleep.' He studied Garn as he spoke, watching for the father's reaction to his child's name. Garn and Mitrian had not seen their son since he had ceased to be called Kinesthe.

Garn returned Colbey's stare without flinching or scowling. Apparently, even without the boy's presence, he had come to grips with the change.

Mitrian looked at the floor as she replied. 'I know he's sleeping. I just want to look at him before he starts looking back with hostility. I left him too long for others to raise. I couldn't blame him for hating his parents.'

'Come on.' Colbey led Garn and Mitrian through the court door and into the main corridor. 'That's ludicrous, Mitrian. Rache doesn't hate you. He asks about you every day, and his grandfather has made you both sound like gods. A year from now, he won't even remember the gap of time when he didn't have his parents.'

Colbey in the lead, they strode through the half-lighted gloom of Santagithi's austere hallways, which had to seem eerily plain after Béarn's finery.

'What did Santagithi tell Rache about me?' Garn asked, trying to sound diplomatic, though the nature of the question could not wholly keep bitterness at bay.

Mitrian winced.

Colbey made a vague gesture as they passed the room that had once belonged to Mitrian to indicate that the couple would stay there. 'Actually, he's played up your heroics in the war. He's talked of your courage and your battle skills.' He turned a corner, aware Garn wanted a more specific answer. 'As far as I can tell, he hasn't said a word about you having once been a gladiator, and the guards have respected his silence.'

'Good.' Garn smiled, obviously pleased by Santagithi's decision.

Before the door to Rache's room, Colbey stopped, spinning to face his charges. 'Garn, normally I wouldn't interfere with a parental thing, but I think you know how important Rache is to me, too.' He reached behind him, catching the latch without bothering to look. 'I think it would be better if you explained things to Rache in a calm, rational manner, before some ill-mannered townsfolk or guardsman makes a rude comment.'

Garn scowled, his first hint of remaining enmity. 'When the time comes, I'll tell him. He's my son, and I'll decide when that time has come.'

Colbey shrugged. 'If you don't feel you have the words, you need only ask Santagithi to speak for you, Rache respects him, and he's had more practice discussing delicate matters.'

Garn's scowled deepened. 'When the time comes,' he repeated, 'I will tell him.'

Colbey turned back to the door, only partially displeased by Garn's reply. Though he worried for Rache, he knew the boy was strong. Had Garn displayed no cynicism at all, Colbey would have fretted more. A complete shift from violent hatred to apathy would have been unnatural, a painted facade hiding a volcano. 'Fine. But I can't control what Emerald tells Episte. And if Rache asks me directly, I won't lie to him.'

Mitrian jumped in, apparently concerned about Garn's possible reply. 'We don't expect you to.' She changed the subject too abruptly. 'Episte? Isn't that a Renshai name? I presume he's Rache's son?' She clarified quickly. 'I mean the other Rache, the one Rache's named after.' Her brow furrowed as she recognized a contradiction. Since the elder Rache had not known of his child until he lay dying on the battlefield, it made no sense that the boy had a Renshai name.

'It's Rache's son,' Colbey confirmed, addressing the unspoken question as well. 'His mother named him. A seventy-six-year-old Renshai named Episte completed Rache's training after the mass slaughter of our people, though the old man's dedication meant that he died of age rather than in battle. Apparently, Episte's sacrificing Valhalla to train the last young Renshai impressed Rache. He must have spoken Episte's name with reverence around Emerald. And she remembered it.' Colbey lifted the latch, but he finished before opening the door. 'She knew Rache never wanted to have children. I think she hoped that naming the boy for Rache's hero would bring him closer to his child. Of course, it never became an issue.'

Colbey did not await a reply. Instead, he pulled open the panel. Light from the corridor fell across Rache's small figure huddled beneath a sheepskin. He breathed evenly, his head framed by sandy blond hair. His features resembled Santagithi's more than either of his parents.

Colbey remained in the doorway as Mitrian and Garn walked silently to the child. As if she feared Rache might break, Mitrian hesitantly lowered a hand to his head.

Rache's breathing changed slightly, and he lay unnaturally still. Garn stiffened, then apparently dismissed his concern as foolish. Mitrian leaned closer to kiss the child, and Colbey detected an all but invisible movement.

'Rache, no!' Colbey cried.

Rache stirred, then went still.

Mitrian froze. 'What happened?' she whispered.

Colbey and Garn joined her at the bedside. The old Renshai peeled the sheepskin from the child, revealing a knife nestled in his hand. He opened eyes like his sire's, dark pupils rimmed with green. '*Torke?*'

Aware how narrowly Mitrian had escaped getting maimed by her wary child, Colbey explained. 'Rache, these are your parents.'

The boy sat up and studied Mitrian and Garn. He said nothing, but a smile split his face, and he laughed with excitement.

Colbey knew his presence was no longer necessary, so he bowed out graciously. 'If you need me, I sleep in the tan room.' *When generals are not begging for chess games and Wizards are not demanding counsel.* Colbey closed the door and headed back down the corridor, moving with the lithe confidence of one whose mastery has kept him alive past his time. He suffered from none of the stiffness nature normally inflicted on men approaching seventy.

Colbey negotiated the sequence of corridors that took him to the guest chambers, hoping to find Santagithi as well as Shadimar. He knocked at the closed door.

Within moments, it opened, and Santagithi stood there, framed in the doorway. Time had not been quite as kind to the general. Twenty years younger, he moved as easily as Colbey, yet his face bore the haggard lines of responsibility. He placed a hand on Colbey's forearm. 'Good, you're here. We'll save our game till tomorrow. It's late and

Shadimar wants to talk to you.' He pushed past Colbey into the hallway. 'See you both in the morning.' He strode down the corridor, then stopped, turning. 'Did Mitrian ask about her mother?'

Colbey shook his head. 'She had so many questions and concerns, I'm not sure she knew which ones to ask first.' He considered the many situations that Mitrian would need to sort out, nearly all the same ones bothering Santagithi: reuniting with the family, friends, guards, and acquaintances after she had changed so much; regaining her son's trust; meeting Episte, who would need to become like a second son; and finding a way to fit Garn into a society he had so long seen as an enemy. Though horrible and traumatic, the pain of her mother's death in a late life childbirth had to blend into the many other adjustments.

Santagithi sighed, obviously tired. 'After her son, her mother will be the first thing on Mitrian's mind. I think it's only wise to tell her tonight.'

Colbey nodded his agreement, though his input only confirmed the course Santagithi already knew was right.

Turning, Santagithi headed down the hallway in his usual stalwart manner.

Colbey entered the guest chamber, his mind shifting to his own problems. Shadimar sat on the straw-ticked mattress, stately as a tree trunk against the leaf-green walls. The Pica Stone lay beside him, the huge sapphire indenting the covers. The room also contained a desk with a matching wooden chair. Secodon lay on the floor, attentive at the Wizard's feet.

Colbey closed the door, crossed the room, and sat in the chair.

For several seconds, neither man spoke. It was Shadimar who broke the silence. 'You haven't forgotten our vows on the battlefield.'

Colby blinked. At the end of the Great War, he had found Shadimar with the sapphire that had once been a symbol of the Renshai. Reminded by Shadimar that the gem had belonged to his own people, the Myrcidians, before the Renshai decimated the town and took its treasures, Colbey chose to swear an oath of fealty with the Wizard rather than fight him. He had let the Wizard keep the Pica. 'I haven't forgotten. We're blood brothers. What's bothering you?'

'Who is the Western Wizard?'

Colbey licked his lips thoughtfully, but answered with wild incaution. 'Has age addled your wits? I told you he died. If you're asking what he became afterward, you would know his religion better than I would. If he was a Northman, I'm afraid he would not have found Valhalla.'

Shadimar traced a line across his beard, obviously unamused. 'Who replaced Tokar?'

Colbey could make no sense from the question. Shadimar's question seemed more like an attack than coversation. 'Do I look omniscient to you? I don't know a damned thing about Wizards, despite what this Northern Sorceress told you.' He smiled, trying to lighten the mood for them both. 'Men have called me a demon, but they've never asked me to summon one.'

Shadimar leaned forward and struck with verbal fury. 'Trilless cannot lie. She says you witnessed Tokar's ceremony of passage.'

Irritated by Shadimar's vague accusations, but still in control of his temper, Colbey sighed. 'I don't lie either. I don't know this Trilless. And I don't know what a ceremony of passage is. I only spent a few days with the Western Wizard before he died, and, if you don't mind, I'd like to forget what happened there.'

'Mind?' Shadimar's face crushed into deep wrinkles, and his voice gained volume. 'Those events might affect the entire course of the world, for Wizards as well as mortals. I should let your fear of a memory damn us all? *Of course, I mind.*'

Shadimar's words outraged Colbey, yet confusion and friendship softened his mood. All Northmen held a blood brotherhood sacred. Colbey would have made any other man pay for his accusation, but he accepted insult from Shadimar with only a warning. 'I don't *fear* anything, and I can't imagine why my words or silence could damn anyone. We're brothers. If you want to know something, just ask.' Colbey sat up straighter in his chair, his left hand resting casually on the sword hilt at the opposite hip. 'You claim I can't hurt you. If you push me too hard, you may find that I can.'

A fleeting smile flashed across Shadimar's lips and disappeared. Clearly he doubted Colbey's threat, yet his tone did grow less violent. 'Forgive me. Sometimes I forget that mortals don't always see significances that seem obvious to Wizards. Please. Tell me about your time with the Western Wizard.' Coming from anyone else's mouth, the words would have sounded stilted; but they seemed right from the Eastern Wizard.

Colbey studied his blood brother in the light of the room's single candle. Blue robes of an old-fashioned cut draped over his narrow shoulders, and a black cloak enwrapped his skeletal frame. The old gray eyes seemed unnaturally watchful in a face that betrayed great age. Renshai rarely lived to their mid-thirties, so Colbey had little early experience with judging maturity. Estimating from his own features, Colbey guessed that the Wizard was some two decades older; but he could not be certain. Renshai appeared younger than other mortals, and Colbey supposed Shadimar might be the same age as himself. Yet the Wizard had mastered the art of looking as ancient and mysterious as carvings from previous generations, and his claims of immortality and invincibility added to the aura. Colbey had seen nothing of consequence from the Western or Eastern Wizards, nothing he could not explain by clever sleight of hand or illusion.

Shadimar waited for Colbey's reply as if no time had passed. At his feet, the wolf rolled to his back, his paws curled to his belly.

Colbey closed his eyes, allowing recollection to flood back into conscious memory, bringing physical pain. Fire seared his fingers, flashing up his arm to engulf his body like an inferno. He crinkled his face, trying to remember the incidents without reawakening the agony, only to find them inextricably linked. It seemed odd to the verge of impossibility. In fifty years of combat, Colbey had felt the grazing slam of war hammers, the biting gash of pole arms, axes, and swords, and the sting of whips. He could remember the incidents behind the wounds and the extent of the torment, but he could not relive the actual pain. Somehow, though, the suffering that accompanied his memories of the Western Wizard could not be banished.

Still, Shadimar waited patiently.

Driving, through pain, Colbey opened his mind to the shadows of past years. Shifting backward, he found memories that swirled like fragments of a dream, then merged into a cold, gray reality. 'Nearly twenty years ago, the Western Wizard summoned me to his cave with a message sent to the island of the Renshai.'

'He asked for you by name?'

Colbey shook his head. 'No, he asked for the most competent sword master.' Colbey looked up. Among his people, to claim such a truth only meant risking challenges from those who thought themselves more skilled. Here, it was considered immodest to the point of vanity.

Shadimar nodded knowingly, lips pursed.

Colbey awaited the Wizard's comment. The moment stretched into a long silence.

At length, Shadimar prodded, 'Go on.'

Colbey cleared his throat. 'I take it that . . .' He imitated Shadimar's head bobbing. '. . . means you know why Tokar summoned me.'

'I can guess.'

'Would you mind telling me?'

'I would mind.'

Colbey stared, his expression growing increasingly grim. 'And I already told you that I mind telling you this story. But I'm doing it.'

'Yes.'

Another long pause.

Exasperated, Colbey stood. 'In my life, I have taken exactly three blood brothers. One was Renshai, a cousin of mine and a good warrior. Another was the captain of a ship of pirates, one of the fiercest Northern warriors I ever met. With you, I believe I may have made a mistake.' He turned to leave.

'Wait.'

Colbey whirled back to face Shadimar.

The Wizard's gaze flicked over the furnishings, then stopped on the hilt of Colbey's left sword. 'Do you know those swords you carry?'

'Better than most men know their children. Why do you ask?'

Shadimar sat up straighter on the bed. Secodon rolled to his side, twisting his head to look at Colbey. 'Those swords are like mortals, capable of great tasks yet needing the guidance of a warrior. Gods and Wizards can wield mortals with the skill of Renshai or the awkwardness of untrained children. Or we can stand back and let you wield yourselves.'

Colbey blinked, the analogy lost on him. 'What are you trying to say? That you can't share your thoughts because I'm as stupid as a piece of steel? I've heard men say that the more skillfully a man swings a sword, the less ably he spells it. They also say strength makes men slow. I've seen more than one idiot lose his life to that fallacy. I would have thought you had lived long enough to see through the lie.'

'That's not my point, Colbey,' Shadimar snapped back. 'I wasn't commenting on you. I was just trying to establish the differences between affairs of mortals and those of Wizards. We tend to matters that take centuries or millennia to come to fruition. Ultimately, though, those efforts always come back to you.' He amended quickly, 'By "you," I mean you in mass. Mankind.'

Colbey put the Eastern Wizard's point together, though he did not like it any better. 'You believe that your concerns and problems would be more than I could handle.'

'My concerns and problems may be more than *I* can handle. And the more I tell you, the more I draw you into affairs that are way over your head.' Again, Shadimar tried to soften his words. 'Not because you're Colbey, but because you're *not* a Wizard.'

Colbey returned to the chair. 'Which gives me a perspective you might find useful.'

'What are you saying?'

Now Colbey smiled, hardly daring to believe he had become too obtuse for a Wizard. It felt good to put Shadimar on the receiving end for a moment. 'Brotherhood works in several directions. I can be there for you when you need me, like now. But I can't *not* be there when you *don't* need me or when you think it's too dangerous for me.' Colbey sat, still grinning. 'You accepted that brotherhood. I'm afraid you're stuck with me.'

Despite the disagreement, Shadimar seemed more comfortable than he had when the discussion had started. Whatever bothered him about the Western Wizard apparently transcended arguments about power and control. It pleased Colbey that he had distracted Shadimar from the topic for the time being, even at the risk of the Wizard's wrath.

Secodon sat up, whining softly. Shadimar's hand dropped absently to the wolf's head. 'You can't force your help on me. I can tell or withhold whatever information I wish.'

Colbey's grin broadened. 'And so can I.'

The stalemate clearly rattled Shadimar. His fists opened and closed in a rhythmical cadence. 'Involving oneself in the affairs of Wizards is not something to be done in blithe ignorance.'

'Exactly. Which is why I'm trying to get you to share your thoughts.'

'Magic and demons make war look trifling.'

'Good.' Colbey never flinched. 'No mortal war has given me what I've searched for all my life.'

'Death,' Shadimar guessed.

'Death in glory,' Colbey clarified. 'Maybe your magic will prove more of a challenge.'

'Colbey.' Shadimar sighed, obviously wanting to say many things, yet pressed for time. 'I can't teach you in a night what it took me centuries and my predecessors millennia to learn.'

'I don't have to learn everything to help you.'

'And I don't need your help.'

'Clearly, you do. You called this meeting, not me.'

Shadimar frowned, saying nothing.

'Surely, I'm not the first mortal to help a Wizard.'

Shadimar's look turned from annoyed to pensive. 'Odin's laws constrain us tightly. The influence a Wizard can use over individuals is minimal. We can't harm or force. We can only suggest courses of action. And we can be as wrong as anyone.'

Colbey remained silent, certain the Eastern Wizard had something more to say.

'Each Cardinal Wizard can take a champion.'

'What does that entail?'

Shadimar turned his hard gray eyes on Colbey. 'Much thought and a cautious choice. The man or woman I choose represents me, to mortals and to the other Wizards. On different levels, we work together on the same causes, and my champion would have to believe and trust in me implicitly. I can tell him or her things I can't mention to other mortals.'

Colbey awaited the unfavorable aspects. So far, the position seemed ideally suited to him.

'The other Wizards are forbidden to harm a colleague's champion to the same degree that we cannot harm one another.' Shadimar curled his legs beneath him. Secodon circled, then lay down, head on his paws, facing Colbey. 'That law is understandably far stricter than the one barring us from killing mortals.' Shadimar fixed a piercing, narrow-eyed stare on Colbey. 'The actions of a champion reflect directly on the Wizard. Therefore, it is within a Wizard's right to use magic to destroy his own champion.'

Colbey met Shadimar's gaze mildly. He saw no need to mention that slaying the eldest Renshai would not prove easy, even with magic. But he did see one flaw in the picture of himself as Shadimar's champion. 'Does this champion have to stay with the Wizard? Would he have to give up his own goals and concerns?'

'For the most part, a champion can live as he pleases. His goals become a problem only if they directly clash with the Wizard's cause.'

'And the Renshai?'

'What of them?'

'Do they clash with your cause?'

'No.' Shadimar raked long, age-spotted fingers through his beard. 'By that question, should I guess that you're volunteering to become my champion?'

That seeming self-evident, Colbey was taken aback. 'Isn't that why you mentioned it?'

'No.'

Uncertain how deep Shadimar's negative response went, Colbey sought an answer. 'No, that's not why you mentioned it; or no, you don't want me as a champion?'

'Both.'

Though Colbey had more than enough of his own concerns, Shadimar's rejection stung. 'Oh.' He did not request explanation.

But Shadimar felt obligated to give one. 'It takes time to work with a champion.'

'I have to teach, and I have to practice. But I still have time to play chess with Santagithi. It might do Santagithi's competitive spirit some good if I gave that time to you instead.'

Shadimar straightened, sitting on the edge of the bed, with his feet on the floor near Secodon's rump. 'I'm not talking about time during any given day. For months or years, sometimes decades, a Wizard may speak to his champion a thousand times, once, or not at all.'

Colbey considered. Realization dawned slowly. 'You're saying I'm too old.'

Shadimar looked away.

The concept had no solidity in Colbey's mind. From childhood, he had accepted death as a daily certainty. Age had only given him more time to learn technique, human nature, and strategy. Never having seen an aged man until his own adulthood, Colbey had no idea that growing older, in and of itself, could cause degeneration. His own eyes worked as well as ever. His hearing had not diminished. At no previous point in his life had he ever been so skilled or knowledgeable;

his reflexes had become honed to a perfection few men could understand. 'I am more capable today than yesterday.'

'Mortals' years are numbered.' Shadimar spoke softly. 'That's what makes them mortal. Someday, like it or not, Colbey, you will die.'

Amazement trickled through Colbey, and he could not believe Shadimar's words. 'I'm not afraid of death, Shadimar, and I certainly don't deny my own. Remember, I'm the one the Pudarians call "The Deathseeker."'

Shadimar relented. 'You're right, Colbey. I didn't word that well. I'm just upset. And you have to understand something. Age takes every mortal that fate doesn't. Whether or not you find the death in glorious combat that you've been seeking, your years are numbered. Experience tells me that number is less than ten.'

A chill shivered through Colbey. The idea of dying outside of battle had always bothered him, but a new idea rattled him until he could barely stand to think. *Is it possible to become too skilled to die in glory?* Colbey had driven himself into a personal paradox. To give anything less than his best in battle meant damning his soul to Hel as surely as death on a sickbed. Yet by dedicating his all to the fight, he had become too proficient to die of anything but age.

Unaware of Colbey's inner turmoil, Shadimar only added to the pain. 'And I don't need a champion eager to commit suicide.'

'Odin damn you to Hel!' Colbey leapt to his feet, so swift and light that even the wolf did not think to move until the Renshai was finished. 'If I simply wanted to die, I'm quite capable of inflicting fatal wounds on myself or anyone else.' He glared, his words verging on threat. 'I've been plunging into every war I could find since I was born. Death has eluded me so far. What makes you so sure it'll happen if you take me as a champion?' Another thought dashed over the first, and it emerged before Colbey had a chance to consider it. 'And if I did die? What would it hurt? You could always get yourself another champion.'

'And waste the time I took to train you.'

Colbey shrugged. 'Train me to what? I already know how to fight. I'm no more afraid to die than you, and I'll gladly give my life for anything I believe in.' It occurred to Colbey to question why he felt so strongly about the matter. Two reasons came to the forefront. With blood brotherhood came responsibility, and the Wizard's cause might give him powerful enough enemies to find the death in battle he sought.

Shadimar laced his fingers through his beard. 'Colbey, sit.'

Colbey sat.

'I've been a Cardinal Wizard for longer than two hundred years.'

Colbey raised his brows, wondering how the Wizard dared to call

Colbey old.

'And I've never chosen a champion before. That should tell you how carefully and slowly I make such a decision.'

'Ah.' A light dawned for Colbey. 'So slow decision-making is your weakness, too.'

'Too?' Shadimar's hands fell into his lap. 'Surely you don't mean you.'

'No, I mean Haim. Tokar's apprentice. Slow decision-making killed him; and, perhaps, the Western Wizard as well.'

Shadimar looked hopeful as the conversation returned to the matter for which he had summoned Colbey. 'You'll tell me the story?'

'You'll answer my questions about some of the things that happened that I didn't understand?'

'To the best of my ability, your knowledge, and the limits of my vows.'

It seemed fair to Colbey. 'I can't ask for more than that. And the champion thing?'

'I'll consider it with the seriousness that you and it deserve. But I can't guarantee I'll come to the decision you want.'

'And I can't guarantee that I won't get offended.'

Shadimar's lips twitched upward into less of a frown, but not quite a smile. He borrowed Colbey's words. 'I can't ask for more than that.'

Having come to a tentative agreement, both men nodded. Colbey prepared to launch into his story.

10 Colbey's Story

Darkness enfolded the forest north of Santagithi's Town, and stars speckled the gaps between the branches. Moonlight slashed a line through the practice clearing, dwarfing the light from a candle jutting out of a bronze holder in Emerald's hand. She balanced it on a deadfall, the circle of light it shed glazing into and heightening the celestial glow trapped beneath the canopy of leaves.

Beginning at one end of the fallen trunk, Emerald examined the length of it by finger's breadths. Each crevice, every rotting piece of bark fell under her scrutiny, and she shifted the candle as she moved to highlight each new area she searched. Episte had told her that Colbey had nicked young Rache with a sword blade in spar. Propriety did not allow her to remove the shirt from another woman's child to expose the injury; but if she could find the bloodstain that Episte had mentioned, she might gather enough proof to convince Mitrian and Santagithi that Colbey was a danger to the children.

A danger. Emerald snorted, enraged by the understatement. That Colbey hit and cut her son seemed ugly enough. Worse, each night, she found herself dealing with issues of philosophy and concepts too adult for a four-year-old mind, concepts like death, glory, war, and the value of others' lives. She hated to think of the emotional damage Colbey had inflicted upon her only child, whom she dearly loved, her only remaining link to the man she had loved as well. *And I'm powerless to stop Colbey from destroying my child.*

Tears welled in Emerald's eyes, blurring the clearing. She halted her search, no longer able to distinguish dappled shadows from stains. A glimpse of movement caught the edge of her vision. Startled, she whirled toward it.

A man stood at the end of the clearing. Moonlight sent white accents shimmering through a golden hair. A dark leather jerkin and breeks covered a slender figure and sinews honed by battle. A sword hung at his hip. His pale Northern skin was clearly visible against the night's pitch.

Rache? Emerald froze, uncertain whether to enfold him in her arms or run screaming in terror. Eyes locked on the figure, she made a religious gesture warding against evil spirits, her fingers tracing the form repeatedly and mindlessly. Hope trickled through her, then widened to a torrent that nearly overwhelmed her. The soldiers had told her that Rache had died in the Great War, yet she had never seen his body. *They could have lied.* Need overcame all caution, and desire made her sure of things that could not be possible. *It* is *Rache. Rache's alive! Alive!* She took a sudden step toward him, arms raised in greeting.

'Hello,' the man said in the trading tongue, his Northern accent a heavy singsong. The voice was a stranger's.

Emerald stopped, blinking rapidly. Tears stretched into colored streamers across her lashes, then her vision cleared and she could see the man's face was not Rache's. He wore a short, stiff beard, while Rache had always shaved cleanly. Her arms fell to her side. *A Northman? Why? How? Northmen don't come here.* In her twenty-seven years in Santagithi's Town, she had seen no Northmen except Rache and Colbey. Sudden fear dried her mouth, and she backstepped abruptly, forgetting the deadfall. Her calf struck wood, knocking the candle to the ground. The flame drew a spiral through the darkness, then sputtered out.

'Hello,' the man repeated, taking a cautious step further into the clearing, his hands outstretched in a gesture of peace. 'I-eh won't-eh hurt you.' His voice rose on every second syllable, and he seemed determined to ascertain that every word contained a second sound, even if he had to create it.

'Who are you?' Emerald continued to inch backward until she bunched tightly against the deadfall.

'My-eh name-is Ivhar Ingharrson of Vikerin.' He pronounced it EEV-har, with the nearly silent 'r' sounding like an afterthought.

Emerald recognized the tribal name, Vikerin. The soldiers who had fought in the Great War spoke of the single Northern tribe that had banded with Santagithi's army and its Western cause. Faced by an ally, she relaxed slightly and sat on the trunk. His presence still alarmed her. Northern xenophobia had become legendary; and she knew most Northmen never crossed the barriers that divided West from North: the Granite Hills and the Weathered Mountains. The rare times they did, it was to trade in Pudar. 'What do you want here?'

'I-eh come for een-fra ma-sheen.'

'Information?' Emerald repeated, as much to clarify the Northman's pronunciation as to confirm his intention. In the sixteen years that Rache had lived in Santagithi's Town, she had concentrated on his speech patterns enough to catch most of the nuances of his accent. But Rache had come to them as a child. Over time, Western phrases and pronunciations had colored his speech until even he abandoned the

Northern 'Ra-keh' for the Westerners' 'Rack-ee' when it came to saying his own name.

'A-bout one-called Cull-bay.'

Emerald's blood seemed to ice over in her veins. 'Colbey?' she said, realizing that, so far, she had managed to do little more than repeat the final word of each of Ivhar's questions.

'*You* do *know* him?' Ivhar shuffled forward to normal speaking distance.

To Emerald, the Northman seemed far too close. 'I know him,' she said. It seemed pointless and rude to lie. 'Why?'

Ivhar shifted from foot to foot, clearly uncomfortable. Moonlight shifted white highlights through his hair as he moved. 'Lady, I-eh don't mean to alarum you.'

Emerald looked up, meeting sincere blue eyes, so like Rache's.

'We-eh fear he might be Renshai.'

Emerald opened her mouth, but her tongue seemed paralyzed. 'Renshai,' she managed. She turned her gaze to the deadfall, no longer able to meet his eyes.

'We-eh have reason to believe he was involved in killing Northmen without honor. He-eh is old enough to have had a hand in the slaughter of Westerners.'

Emerald became more engrossed in the bark on her seat.

Apparently wanting Emerald's attention, Ivhar moved closer and placed a booted foot on the deadfall. 'Lady, if he is-eh Renshai, he-eh is-eh danger to you all-eh. They-eh train to kill many with few. And-they don't spare women or-eh children since they teach their own to fight-eh.'

Emerald continued to study the wood, her gaze tracing a dark, irregular stain. Realization struck with sudden and vivid clarity. *The blood. I've found it.* Anger accompanied the discovery. She reached out a finger and touched it, her attention swiveling to Ivhar Ingharrson. 'What is it you want to know?'

'I-eh need to know for certain. It would-eh not-eh do to harm a man for being-eh Renshai he is not.' Ivhar raised his brows, apparently realizing his construction was not quite right, yet hoping Emerald had understood.

Emerald remained silent, deeply thoughtful. She could not help but realize the significance of the Northmen's hatred for Renshai that one had traveled so far on rumor. Colbey's life meant less than nothing to her. Yet she had to consider the risk to the Town of Santagithi, and to her own son, of revealing the information.

'If-eh he is Renshai, he-eh must be executed.'

'How?'

Ivhar seemed confused by the question. 'Legally, of course. Is that-eh what you mean?'

Emerald nodded absently, aware Ivhar could have no way of understanding the minutiae of the question she wanted to ask. She knew it would take more than one man and a vast score of dedication to kill Colbey, and she needed to understand the danger to the boys. Her gaze strayed back to the bloodstain. Now that she knew its location and shape, it seemed huge, a cruel and ugly testament to one who murdered strangers and mutilated children he claimed to love. She looked at Ivhar again, fire in her eyes. 'For the price of a promise, I will tell you anything about Colbey you wish to know.'

Ivhar's expression mixed hope and doubt. Clearly, he feared Emerald might ask a price he could not afford. 'What-eh is the promise?'

Emerald held the Northman's gaze, her finger tracing the stain repeatedly, from memory. 'Whatever happens and whatever you learn, my four-year-old son will not be harmed.'

Ivhar relaxed visibly, a smile crossing war-hardened features. Surely, he never doubted that Emerald's request stemmed only from a mother's natural protective instincts. 'Fate works in-eh strange ways, and I-eh would never-eh make a vow I could not keep. But I-eh can promise that we will do our best to keep him safe. It is not our wish to hurt anyone innocent. Will that do?'

'That will do.'

'And Colbey?'

'He is Renshai,' Emerald said. 'And he is every bit the killer you claim him to be.'

Colbey Calistinsson felt fatigue grow strong enough to dull his reflexes. Idly, it occurred to him to tap his mind for strength and clarity, yet he let the tiredness touch him instead. He had nothing to fear from Shadimar, and the story he had promised to tell would surely seem less painful when drowsiness took the edge from the memory.

Shadimar lounged on his side, his back pressed to the chamber wall, his feet stretched across the coverlet. Despite his reclining position, he still seemed dignified. He kept his attention locked on Colbey. The wolf remained curled on the floor by the bedside, nose tucked beneath his tail.

Resigned to a sleepless night, Colbey brushed wisps of gray-flecked hair from his eyes. 'Having crossed the Northlands, I arrived at the Western Wizard's cave in the Weathered Mountains early one morning. Actually, I was lucky to find it. It didn't seem like the kind of place I could have stumbled upon blindly. Sunlight reflecting from the cliffs seemed to form a curtain in front of the entrance, and I felt rather than saw the opening.' He glanced at Shadimar.

The Wizard's head bobbed almost imperceptibly. Otherwise, he gave no response to Colbey's revelation.

'I was staring at the entrance, when Tokar spoke to me from inside. His voice was light and free as a breeze yet powerful as a gale. He asked for my name, and I gave it. He invited me inside. I went.' Colbey continued to stare at Shadimar for clues as to whether his story contained too few details or too many.

The Wizard nodded ever so slightly.

Taking this as encouragement, Colbey continued, 'That was when he told me that the Northmen had annihilated the Renshai six years past. He told me I was the only survivor.' His focus on Shadimar grew even more intense as he considered a fact he had not placed into this context before. 'He was wrong.' Colbey's forehead crinkled. 'I thought you Wizards have magic that makes you right all the time.' *At least, you always talk as if every word that comes from your lips is indisputable fact*. He kept the idea to himself.

'Usually we are.' Shadimar did not apologize for his comrade's mistake. 'Under the circumstances, he had reason to believe you were the last.'

'Why wouldn't he make certain?'

'It's not pertinent. Continue.'

Colbey kept his gaze locked on Shadimar, gradually raising his brows to remind the Wizard of his agreement to keep Colbey informed.

Shadimar sighed. 'If you keep interrupting yourself, we'll be here all night.'

Colbey did not budge. 'If you keep resisting my questions, we'll be here into next week.' He smiled. 'Surprise. I can be as patient and stubborn as you.'

Shadimar returned a grudging smile. 'That's not a thing on which to pride yourself.' He sighed again. 'Very well, it's already cost me too many words. I might as well try to appease you. To confirm facts, a Wizard has to summon a creature of magic. We call them demons. Grossly understated, that would be dangerous. Since you lived only because he called you away, and the Northmen seemed certain they had slain every Renshai on Devil's Island, Tokar had good reason to believe you were the last Renshai.'

Shadimar's explanation reminded Colbey of their first conversation on the battlefield after the Great War. 'You once said that the Southern Wizard probably consorted with demons to find me.'

'True.'

'Yet he only found Rache.'

Shadimar nodded.

Colbey pressed, recalling the conversation vividly, though years had passed since that time. 'You told me that this Wizard missed Mitrian because early Wizards named the Golden Prince of Demons a man. But this wouldn't have kept him from finding me. Then you said that this Carcophan probably only asked about full-blooded Renshai to sort out the children of conquerors.'

Again, Shadimar confirmed Colbey's memory with a nod.

'You questioned my parentage.' Colbey's eyes narrowed, still angered by the offense. His mother and father had both died in battle, heroes, as Renshai had been meant to die. Neither line held a trace of foreign blood.

'Clearly a mistake,' Shadimar said.

'You said there were other possible reasons why the "sources of magic" did not identify me.'

'A few, yes.'

'And those are?'

'Technical reasons that have to do with the proper way of calling, binding, and questioning demons.'

Colbey said nothing, awaiting more details.

'Will that do?' Shadimar prompted.

Colbey considered. He realized that, if he were explaining a combat to Shadimar, he would use the vague term 'sword stroke' rather than specifying the mechanics of the maneuver. He nodded. 'I'll continue my story.'

'Please do.'

Colbey rested a heel against the leg of his chair. 'After Tokar told me about the slaughter of the Renshai, I vowed vengeance against every member of every one of the seventeen tribes that had united against one people. Eventually, they would have slain me, but I would have left many corpses in my wake.'

'What stopped you?'

'Tokar. First, he tried to convince me to stay. He said he had summoned me for a purpose that went far beyond vengeance. That didn't convince me to stay. Then he lapsed into a coughing fit that did.' Colbey explained. 'To a Northman, and especially to a Renshai, nothing is worse than illness. It robs all glory from death and assures an eternity in Hel. I've studied herbal lore; at times my knowledge has bought me a welcome in Western farm towns that would otherwise have spurned or attacked me. I believed I could help Tokar's malady.'

'There was nothing you could do, you know.' Shadimar smiled knowingly.

'I know that now. He was preparing for some kind of magical death. But, at the time, I decided to delay my revenge a few days longer. And Tokar didn't try to convince me otherwise.'

Shadimar yawned, dismissing his rudeness with an apologetic wave.

'Did you meet Tokar's apprentice?'

'Haim. Yes.'

'What did you think of him?'

'Quite frankly, not much.' Colbey looked at Shadimar for clues to his response. He did not want to offend. Colbey considered trying to read the Wizard's thoughts, but dismissed this as rude. Yet just the idea of trying brought him the faintest trace of Shadimar's derisive mood. Encouraged by Shadimar's own apparent scorn, Colbey continued. 'He seemed frail and uncertain. He had that high-strung manner of a man who always anticipates failure, no matter how careful his preparations. He talked often, yet it rarely seemed of consequence. I don't remember much of what he said.'

'And Tokar? What did you think of him?'

Colbey considered a moment, then answered honestly. 'He seemed a man of great consequence, yet deeply troubled. And, of course, he killed himself before I got to know him well.' Colbey cringed. To a Northman, suicide was a grave and cowardly dishonor, assuring a place in Hel. Though he knew other cultures did not view self-slaying as heinous, that some even considered it an act of courage, Colbey could not help feeling as if he had affronted Shadimar and his colleague.

Again, Shadimar combed his fingers through his beard. 'Tell me about the ceremony of passage.'

The terminology confused Colbey. 'You mean Tokar's death rite?'

Shadimar nodded. 'You witnessed it?'

'I watched the whole thing.'

'A rare honor indeed. I'm not certain any mortal has ever done so before you.'

'Strange.' Colbey drew his other foot to the chair. 'As insistent as Tokar was that Haim and I come along, I just assumed mortals were necessary.'

'A mortal, yes. His apprentice.' Shadimar spoke calmly, but the fingers twisting in his beard betrayed distress. 'Tokar *asked* you to watch the ceremony?'

'I was all ready to leave.' Despite the years, Colbey could feel rage and anguish rising. 'Had my people simply died in a brave combat, their bodies intact and their souls in Valhalla, I would have rejoiced and held no grudge. But the Western Wizard confirmed my worst fears. The Northmen had come at night, unannounced, like a pack of slinking curs. And they had mutilated the bodies so no Renshai could reach Valhalla, no matter how bravely he had fought.' Colbey scowled, gaze distant, arms crossed over his sword belt.

Shadimar's hands stilled in his beard. 'Just like the Renshai once did to their people.'

Anger seared Colbey. 'Never,' he said through gritted teeth. 'Never once did Renshai attack at night or without fair warning.'

'Perhaps not.' Shadimar bore in. 'But they did hack apart enemies. You know that's how they became an exiled tribe.' A sibilance entered his voice as he added, 'And though Renshai did declare war before attacking, sometimes *they declared war on cities at peace so long they had no army.*'

Colbey drew breath to defend the Renshai, to remind Shadimar that the tribe had always accepted an enemy's surrender. But the grief in Shadimar's usually empty eyes unsettled Colbey, and he remembered the Renshai's attack against the so-called 'mages' of the town of Myrcidë. They had fought back valiantly, despite having no army, yet their visual trickery had proven no match for sharpened steel. He knew that Shadimar still lived in the ruins of that city, which had once been his own.

From deference to his blood brother, Colbey softened his rationalization. 'I admit that, sometimes, the Renshai's exuberance for war overcame their common sense. I'm sorry about what happened to Myrcidë. That was clearly wrong, and I hope it won't come between our friendship.'

Shadimar's face returned to its usual, placid configuration. 'When I became a Wizard, I gave up my mortal ties. Always, Colbey, the tasks and causes of Cardinal Wizards come before anything and anyone that might have seemed important to me when my life had a visible end.' His fingers fell from his beard. 'And even if I could still hold the offense against Renshai, how could I hold it against a man who was only a child then, following the ways of his elders?'

Colbey did not tell Shadimar that, in the Renshai culture, a child became an adult the day he first blooded his sword nor that he had found the same thrill in the war against Myrcidë as his elders. Only as he had aged did he see the folly in the Renshai's war indiscretions, and he did not mean to push Shadimar's forgiveness too far. 'I appreciate your benevolence. Many men would hold such a grudge. That's one of the things that made me choose your cause over that of most Northmen. To the good, evil must be destroyed, and life is simple. They see the world in absolutes: good and evil, right and wrong, white and black. They miss all the shades of color in between. That which doesn't conform exactly to the concepts they see as right, like the Renshai, must be destroyed.' He looked directly at Shadimar, finding an expression of surprise. 'The Myrcidians were too different. They could never have survived in the Northlands.'

Shadimar studied Colbey as if seeing him for the first time. 'I'm impressed.'

Colbey smiled insolently. 'I can spell "sword," too. Now, do you think I'd make a suitable champion?'

Shadimar sucked in a deep breath, then exhaled slowly. 'Yes. And no. The age thing is still a problem, and remember what I said about giving up mortal concerns. Since you'd be a Wizard's champion, not a Wizard, you wouldn't have to surrender your ties. Currently, they're not a problem. But if for any reason the Renshai turned against neutrality, you would have to work against them. Could you do that?'

Colbey did not hesitate. 'No.' He added, 'But I can't possibly see that as even a potential problem. I'm training all of the Renshai with the same loyalty to one another as I have to them. And they're all Westerners, which gives them a natural bent toward neutrality.'

'Likely or not, it's still something to think about.'

Colbey nodded, having serious doubts about this offer, despite the bond he had willingly formed with the Wizard. He hoped Shadimar did not see something he had missed. From birth, his loyalty to the Renshai had never wavered or faltered, and he would rather die in withering agony, his soul condemned to Hel, than bring ruin upon his own. *If it became a problem, I could kill myself.* The idea seemed foreign, so against the tenets he had lived for so long, the glory in battle he had sought above all other things. Yet, if it became necessary, Colbey knew he could force his hand.

Shadimar's voice penetrated Colbey's brooding, seeming horribly misplaced. 'You were about to tell me about Tokar's ceremony of passage.'

Colbey felt as if he were awakening slowly from a nightmare and tumbling into a second, equally vivid. With effort, he drove his mind backward, to a day a decade past that he would as soon forget but remembered as clearly as yesterday. 'You want details, I presume?'

'As many as you can remember.'

'I agreed to watch the Wizard's ceremony with the condition that, when it finished, Tokar would let me treat his illness.' Colbey cringed at the memory of the old Wizard's hacking cough and the blood that stained his teeth and beard. 'So, late that evening, Tokar led Haim and me along a rocky trail in the Weathered Mountains. The sky had gone gray, yet there was not a hint of rain. It seemed more as if the clouds had drawn together to form a veil. I felt a sensation I can't describe well, a certainty of impending crisis, as if gods struggled beyond the curtain of clouds. Silence seemed to hang, more like a void than an absence of sound, and only bird trills broke it on occasion. I remember wondering why birds were out in the gloom. As to us, we made no conversation. Tokar's face held a look of pain, which seemed natural because of his illness. But he also looked uncertain.'

Shadimar's expression turned dubious, his features nearly matching Tokar's though surely for different reasons. 'Uncertainty? Purpose, perhaps.'

'Uncertainty,' Colbey clung to his description. 'I sensed it, though I spent most of the walk gathering herbs. Haim was sweating so badly, his clothes were soaked. I thought he might have wet . . . '

'Uncertainty?' Shadimar clung to the question.

Colbey laughed at Shadimar's tenaciousness. 'I was absolutely certain. So I asked if something troubled him. And if I could help.'

'What did Tokar say? Exactly.'

'Exactly?'

'If you can remember.'

Though ten years had passed, Colbey recalled every word. 'He said, "Renshai, the most important decision I will ever make confronts me at a time when I thought I had already made my final choices."' Colbey assumed the Western Wizard's graveled tone. '"And I have only moments to make it." Then he turned to Haim. "How do you make a decision?"' Colbey paused, his memory failing here. 'I'm sorry, Shadimar. I can't remember Haim's reply.'

'Paraphrase.'

Colbey cleared his throat, though he felt no need. It was a delaying tactic. 'Haim went into a long explanation that sounded like a well-learned lecture. He talked about gathering every shred of evidence, considering every alternative, and exploring each possible outcome. I remember him saying that the process could take months or years and that the more difficult and important the decision, the more patience a man must have. He said that this method rarely failed him.' Colbey chuckled.

'Did you laugh *then*, too?'

'Yes,' Colbey admitted.

'You disagree with Haim's method?'

Colbey laughed again. 'That's precisely what Tokar asked me.'

'What did you say?'

Colbey considered. 'I said, "My method is the same. The difference is time. I make my decisions as quickly as an eye blink, and the more important the decision, the faster I have to make it. I make my choices on the battlefield. Since I'm still alive, I've obviously never once made a mistake."'

Shadimar sat up. 'What did Tokar say to that?'

'Nothing. He fell into a troubled silence. We'd been walking for the entire conversation, and we entered a lush valley deep in the mountains. The clouds had stretched apart, and rainbows arched from peak to peak. Streaks of light slithered like snakes between the bands, but they weren't lightning. I still smelled no rain. Clearly, Tokar had made his decision, because his aura had changed to one of utter tranquility.'

Shadimar leaned so far toward Colbey he seemed on the verge of falling from the bed. Secodon sat up, ears pricked forward.

'Haim sat on a rock, wringing his hands. I waited nearby, clutching the herbs I hoped to use on the ailing Wizard. Tokar stood on a knoll, his stance as open as a Western preacher at a ceremony.' Colbey paused, hoping Shadimar would stop him. He waited for the Eastern Wizard to claim he had heard enough and to let Colbey drop the memory before the pain returned, still excruciating despite being dulled by time. But when Shadimar said nothing, Colbey continued dutifully. 'The old Wizard chanted strange words in a language I didn't recognize. Visions appeared – '

'The beings that represent great good and great evil in your mind.'

'Baldur, the most beautiful of the gods,' Colbey confirmed. 'And Mana-garmr, the wolf destined to extinguish the sun with the blood of men at the world's end. These came together, warping into a shapeless, gray cloud that floated into the sky. Then streaks of crimson slid from the heavens, forming into the shapes of long, lean men.' The first stirrings of agony lanced through Colbey's chest, and he caught his breath. 'True to my word, I made a decision instantly. Drawing my sword, I sprang to pull Tokar from the path of the creatures.'

'Gods.' Shadimar's usually unperturbable features etched into a warped caricature of horror. 'You didn't touch him.'

'I caught his shoulder.' Pain speared through Colbey, and he broke off with an involuntary gasp.

Secodon whined.

'Gods,' Shadimar repeated. 'What happened?'

'Pain,' Colbey said, breaths quickening against the memory. 'The worst I've known and the longest.' He kept the description as succinct as possible, needing to get past the moments of suffering that had passed like weeks. 'I consider myself a strong man, not the least tolerant of pain. Yet even as the price for ultimate power and knowledge, I would not relive that moment.' A chill traversed him from head to toe, convulsive in its intensity, then the pain disappeared.

Shadimar studied Colbey quizzically. 'What happened next?'

Colbey wiped beads of sweat from his forehead with his sleeve. 'I don't know. Oblivion finally found me. And, for the only time in my life, loss of control became a welcome friend.'

'What about Tokar?'

'I found him dead.'

'And Haim?'

'Dead, too.'

Anguish twisted Shadimar's face. 'Are you certain?'

The question seemed absurd. 'I'm a warrior. I know "dead."'

'You were in a weakened state. Perhaps you only thought Haim was dead.'

Colbey shook his head, positive. 'It hardly matters now. I put them both to pyre.'

'And they both burned?'

'Yes.'

'Then they were dead.'

'Yes,' Colbey confirmed, his tone becoming sarcastic. 'For one who claims to know the wisdom of the ages, that should seem obvious enough that it doesn't need to be said.'

Shadimar frowned, his features still tensely bunched. 'Had they been alive, fire could not have harmed them.' For a long time, Shadimar stared at the wall in silence. Secodon paced, revealing the agitation that his master hid.

Colbey settled more comfortably in his chair. 'Did I tell you what you wanted to hear?'

Shadimar sat bolt upright and stiffly, considering a question that, in Colbey's mind, seemed simple. 'You did tell me the part of the story I needed to hear. But you could not have given me worse news.'

Colbey wanted to apologize for dropping the death of two friends so suddenly on Shadimar, but he could not forget that the Wizard had pressed him to the tale. And the rigidness in Shadimar's manner told him that something far more serious than a colleague's demise troubled the Eastern Wizard. 'Should I have kept my silence?'

'No.' Shadimar heaved a deep sigh and relaxed slightly, his first movement for quite some time. 'I cannot work without facts. Like it or not, I need the bad news more than the good.'

Colbey tried to understand the problem. 'There is no Western Wizard anymore.'

'Apparently.'

'Is that bad?' Beginning to find patterns in the Wizard's replies, Colbey beat Shadimar to the answer. 'And if you just answer "yes" without explaining, I'll put so many holes in your mattress it'll be good for nothing but horses.' He jabbed a foot toward the straw ticking.

A ghost of a smile touched Shadimar's lips, then was lost beneath the burdens that crushed in on him. 'The Western and Eastern Wizards champion neutrality the same way the Southern Wizard spreads evil and the Northern Sorceress goodness. Neutrality requires more than just staying aloof from others' battles. It isn't just a wall between them, and the Westlands is more than a no-man's-land separating North from East. Without neutrality, the world would exist, as you aptly said before, only in extremes. As it is, for all the pride Carcophan and Trilless take in their accomplishments, by sneaking their own cause into one another's followers, they've mostly made all mortals essentially neutral. It's a matter of degree.'

Colbey suspected it wiser not to question a system about which he knew only a few tenets, but he could not help asking. 'If the result of good and evil trying to take over is mostly neutrality, why do we need a Western Wizard?'

'Because neutrality is a force all its own. Without it, men could only be good or evil, not a combination of both. Besides . . . ' The contemplation invoked by Colbey's questioning seemed to banish Shadimar's other concerns, at least for a time. ' . . . I only said that neutrality results so long as the Southern and Northern Wizards sneak their causes into mortals, using subtle techniques. More than any Wizard before him, Carcophan likes grand war tactics. Had he goaded Siderin and his army against the North rather than the Westlands, the war would still be raging. And there'd be few survivors.'

Colbey tried another tack. 'You represent neutrality, right?'

'Right.'

'And the Western Wizard?'

'Also champions neutrality.'

'But only one Wizard represents good and one represents evil.'

Shadimar said nothing, clearly awaiting a point that seemed obvious to Colbey.

'If neutrality is an entity like good and evil, why do you need two Wizards for it?'

The wolf stopped pacing. Instead it walked a tight circle and curled up on the floor. Shadimar watched Secodon position himself. 'Odin made it so.'

Colbey clung to the point, thinking of the stories he had heard as a boy of the three fates and the three women Heimdall slept with to create the different races of men. 'But the gods always seem to like the number three. Why four when three will do?'

'It's a child's question, Colbey. The gods have reasons even Cardinal Wizards don't understand. Perhaps Odin believed that two Wizards could more easily stand between the others, and he saw the ultimate necessity of and balance inherent in neutrality.'

Colbey chose not to take offense. 'So the Western Wizard and his apprentice are dead. Does that mean there can't ever be another Western Wizard?'

Shadimar frowned, shaking his head. 'Now that I have proof that there is no Western Wizard, the Southern and Northern Wizards have no choice but to help me find a replacement and to help put him or her in power.'

'Then what's the problem?'

Shadimar sagged to the bed again, the intensity of his thoughts keeping exhaustion at bay. 'I need to find a mortal who embraces neutrality and is competent, honorable, and skilled enough to survive the tasks of Wizardry with little or no training. Without the collective consciousness of the previous Western Wizards to guide him, he will need to be self-confident and rock stable. A man or woman who passes that description will not be easily found. And I can't afford to compromise. Until I have that person, I can't gather my colleagues.'

'Do you have anyone in mind?'

Shadimar fidgeted, avoiding Colbey's gaze. 'I know of only one man who fills enough of that description to consider. But I'm not completely certain of his loyalties, and I think he might refuse me.'

'Who?'

Shadimar met Colbey's fierce blue-gray eyes with gray ones equally as hard. 'You.'

Colbey could not have been more surprised had Shadimar named Secodon. 'I'm flattered, really. But I have no interest in immortality or guiding anyone's life except my own and the Renshai. And I have no experience with magic at all.' Colbey did not feel wholly certain his last comment was truth. He did not know what magic entailed, but he had seen nothing to make him believe it was anything more than trickery, illusion, and mind over body control. All Renshai learned meditation techniques; it was part of their training. Colbey knew his own ability to catch radiating emotions and occasional verbatim thoughts was unique.

'I thought not,' Shadimar said. 'And it's probably just as well. Despite all of your age and ability, you would make a strange Wizard indeed.' He glanced sideways at Colbey, apparently trying to lighten the mood. 'You may go now.'

Colbey rose. 'Sometime, you'll have to tell me about returning Sterrane to his throne.'

'Sometime soon,' the Eastern Wizard promised. 'I will.'

11 The Wizard's Advice

Wisps of smoke twined from braziers on either side of the chessboard and hung like a cloud above Garn's and Colbey's heads. In the two weeks since his return from Béarn, Garn had seen the pieces set up in Santagithi's game room, and he had needed to understand the allure of the game. So far, it still escaped him. He watched, annoyed, as Colbey took his ninth white piece from the board with a black knight. 'You can't take my queen!'

Colbey cradled the ivory piece in his hand. 'Why not?'

Garn squeezed the edge of the table so tightly, his knuckles blanched. His gaze ranged from pillows tossed carelessly across wooden couches lining the walls to the simple chairs and tables spread in a random arrangement about the room. A keg of ale sat in one corner. 'My queen is three times bigger than your . . . ' Unable to recall the name of the piece, Garn tapped a finger on the black knight, sending it sliding several squares to the right.

Colbey laughed as he repositioned the black knight and placed Garn's queen next to the board, with the other captured pieces, all white. 'In chess, the largest and strongest don't always win. The shape decides movement and – '

'Let's say – ' Garn interrupted and was in turn cut short by the creak of the opening door.

Both men turned toward the sound. Shadimar and Santagithi stepped through the portal, and the general closed it behind them. Smoke eddied in the breeze, winding between the pieces.

'Let's say,' Garn started again, attempting to complete his war analogy about mailed generals against farmers armed with shovels.

But Colbey would not allow it. 'Let's say you made a foolish mistake and lost your queen. Can we continue?' He turned his attention to Santagithi. 'Do you mind if we finish, sir?' He smiled maddeningly. 'It shouldn't take but a move or two.'

Santagithi waved the Renshai off, shaking his head vigorously. 'No. Not at all. Finish your game, please. I'd love to watch you beat someone else for a change.' He winked at Garn to indicate that he meant no offense.

Garn stared at the board in sullen silence, disappointed that no one felt he could compete with Colbey, yet knowing they were right. He had chosen the game mostly from boredom; Santagithi's people treated him with a respect that kept him at a distance. Most still remembered the volcanic temper that had driven him to kill a playmate as a child and had committed him to life in a cage. Many feared him. Others gave him tolerant greetings, then turned to grumble beneath their breath, as if he could not tell. And, while ordinarily peasants' antics would not bother Garn, the huge amount of time his wife and son spent in lessons and practice made him long for a friend or, at least, a companion. Now Garn's gaze followed Shadimar as the Wizard moved behind Colbey to examine the arrangement on the chessboard. Santagithi sat in a chair, a polite distance behind Garn.

Delicately, Garn moved his bishop two spaces, then a third. He kept his finger on the piece, staring into Colbey's eyes. Finding them cold and gleaming, Garn returned the bishop. 'You'd like me to do that, wouldn't you?'

Colbey smiled in amusement but said nothing.

Garn's hand drifted, then settled on a white rook. He sat still for several moments while smoke rolled about them like fog. What little he understood of rules and strategy suggested that he move the bishop. Slowly, he took that piece in hand again. His gaze swept past Colbey to Shadimar, and the approving smile on the Eastern Wizard's face gave him confidence. He inched the piece in a diagonal, stopping at the first square.

Shadimar shook his head, frowning.

Garn pushed the bishop another block.

Again Shadimar shook his head.

Garn moved the piece one more space.

Shadimar's scowl became a smile, and he nodded his agreement.

Garn tapped the bishop's head with his index finger, leaning back in his chair with a smirk.

Colbey stared at the board. 'Is that your move?'

'It is.' Garn folded heavily-muscled arms across his chest.

'Interesting.' Colbey removed Garn's bishop, replacing it with the black queen. 'Checkmate.'

Garn grasped the end of the table with enough force to send the pieces tumbling. He glared, first at the shambles of the game in disbelief, then at Shadimar. 'For one who pretends to be so vast and mighty, you don't play very well.'

Calmly, Colbey reset the board without bothering to look at Garn's coconspirator. 'You're assuming, Garn, that Shadimar wanted *you* to win.'

Garn rose, grumbling, but not too self-absorbed to note how the color drained from the Wizard's narrow features. Apparently, Colbey had spoken Shadimar's mind verbatim and, unlike Garn, the Eastern Wizard did not have enough experience with Colbey to have grown accustomed to his strange talent. Visibly shaken, Shadimar swept silently from the room. As Santagithi took Garn's vacated seat, the ex-gladiator headed for the door as well.

Still with his back to the door and the exiting Wizard, Colbey called after Garn. 'Tell Mitrian, Episte, and Rache we'll practice after this game.'

Garn nodded. Though Colbey could not see him, Garn felt certain the old Renshai had received his message.

Within a dozen moves, Santagithi had lost both rooks and both bishops to Colbey. The general's pieces stood in random formations, without semblance of strategy.

Seeing no reason to continue the game, Colbey swept the cheesmen from the board.

Santagithi did not flinch, which only made Colbey more sure of his decision to cut short their play. Usually, the general was nearly as cautious with the positions of his chessmen as with his soldiers. At times, he set the pieces into stalemates that he pondered for days, obsessing over the slightest movements of any one in his absence.

Colbey looked at Santagithi. 'Your mind is elsewhere. We'll play when it comes back. What's bothering you?'

Santagithi stared into one of the braziers, composing his thoughts.

Colbey leaned back, folded his hands on the chessboard, and waited. For all his years of moderating guards' disputes, Santagithi had only rarely allowed others to share his own doubts. According to the guards, Santagithi had confided in the archer captain, Nantel, now dead, but even those exchanges had been uncommon. Gradually, Colbey's forthrightness and ability to see the world from a general's perspective was making him as much Santagithi's friend as his citizen. Though he knew he could probably search Santagithi's mind for answers, Colbey refrained. It was a discourtesy he did not use on enemies and would not inflict on friends. Except on rare occasions, the only thoughts Colbey read had wafted to him without intention or warning.

'I've spent a lifetime guessing men's moods. I know when my soldiers are working too hard and need some time for play. I know when they're playing too much and have lost the fine edge that comes with practice.'

Colbey nodded to indicate that he understood Santagithi's point and concurred.

Santagithi returned Colbey's stare, coming to the point. 'Garn's bored. He's not happy here. And if he chooses to leave, my daughter and grandson will follow him.' He did not need to add how deeply losing Rache would hurt him. Captain Jakot had told Colbey how Santagithi had sunk into the depths of grief when he believed he would never see his daughter again. His wife's death had hit him hard, and Colbey guessed that this final loss would plunge Santagithi into a despair so deep he would simply die.

Yet the solution seemed simple to Colbey. 'Why don't you give Garn something to do that he enjoys?'

'Like what?'

'I hardly need to be the West's top strategist to know that Garn appreciates a good fight as much as any warrior, and your army wouldn't suffer from having another skilled swordsman. Why not ask him to join the guard force?'

Santagithi rested his elbows on the table, his chin sinking into his palms. 'How can I ask Garn to fight for me after so many years in the gladiator pit?'

Colbey laughed. 'I don't think it'll be as difficult as you think. Garn's a born slayer. If he had stayed a free man and you had asked him to fight in the pit for the glory and honor of this town, he might very well have done it. He only hated not having a choice. If you asked him, I think he'd become a guard. A fish needs little excuse to swim.'

Santagithi's fingers drummed his cheeks, and his gaze went distant as he turned his thoughts inward.

Colbey continued, 'Garn's fascinated by weapons of every kind, and I've seen him stare at Jakot's armor long past the point of politeness. He still tries to refine the techniques Rache taught him, and with some success. I can't help Garn. First, I have too many training responsibilities of my own. Second, I know almost nothing about many of the weapons he chooses. A little guidance and discipline could turn him into one of the best soldiers you've ever had. And into a good teacher as well.'

All of Santagithi's fingers stilled, except one. The last tapped his jawbone with all the speed and force the others had lost. 'But can I trust him? One wrong word could reawaken all that I've fought to put behind us both. And what if something triggers that god-given savagery of his?'

Colbey gathered the chess pieces, placing them on the board without bothering to sort color or location. 'Garn's worked hard to control that temper of his. He hates it as much as you do, not only for what it's made him do, but because it destroyed his life.' He placed the last piece on the board and sat back. 'Let's face it, Santagithi. Is he really that much more savage than either of us? Most stable

Westerners think of war as a necessary evil that disrupts their jobs, not *as* a job.'

Santagithi took the bait without thinking. Idly, he sorted chessmen, placing them in their proper starting positions on the board.

Colbey smiled, pleased by the normality of the general's routine. Deep consideration bothered him far less than the disruption of procedure by an obsessive planner. 'There's always danger in saying the wrong thing to a strong man, especially one in whom you have so much emotion invested. But you've been pacifying personality conflicts for decades. If you say the right things, you have much to gain. Would you rather lose Garn to an accidental offense or from boredom? It's hard to imagine you being unwilling to take a chance with – '

The game room door swung open suddenly, and a young, on-duty guardsman, named Kloras, appeared in the doorway. 'Sir?'

Immediately, Santagithi's confusion cleared, and his posture returned to its usual, dignified configuration. 'Yes?'

'A courier from Vikerin requests an audience, sir.'

'Vikerin?' Santagithi's brow furrowed. Colbey knew that the general had not heard from the Northern tribe in the year and half since they had exchanged congratulations and compliments at the conclusion of the Great War and their joint victory on the battlefield. Santagithi waved. 'Have him wait in my court. I'll be right there.'

The guardsman backed from the room, closing the door behind him.

Santagithi glanced at Colbey, presumably for advice on the Vikerians' possible motives or on procedure. Few Westerners had any political dealings with the Northlands, and Colbey's background gave him knowledge others would not have.

Colbey shrugged to indicate ignorance. He had no way of knowing the Vikerians' reasons, but the sending of a messenger did not sound hostile. Usually, Northmen declared war by charging a city with drawn weapons and in full battle regalia, howling like wolves.

'Would you like to come along?'

Colbey tried to find a polite way to bow out of the responsibility. Without threat of violence, he had no interest in politics. Still, he owed Santagithi a debt of friendship. 'Do you want me to come?'

Apparently some of Colbey's reluctance came through, because Santagithi looked surprised. He pushed his chair back, legs scraping wood floor with a grinding noise.

Colbey explained. 'I just sent Garn to gather my students. I'm not good with diplomacy, as you know.' He smiled at the memory of the discussion in the tent of Prince Verrall of Pudar. 'And I don't think the Vikerian king's lieutenant cares much for me.' Colbey pictured Valr

Kirin, his hawklike nose jutting from a rugged face that looked as if it never smiled. The lieutenant had proven a superior warrior, one of the finest non-Renshai Colbey had ever seen. The Vikerians had claimed Kirin the Slayer as the greatest hero of all time, until Colbey had joined the nearby combats. Then their allegiances had shifted to the old Renshai, prompting an animosity and competition between the two leaders that had threatened to erupt into violence.

Colbey still recalled Arduwyn taking him aside to chastise him for the Renshai tradition of calling upon Modi, the god named 'wrath,' when wounded or when the battle tide had turned against them. From infancy, all Renshai were trained to respond to the shout with renewed vigor, to fight not through pain but because of it. Valr Kirin had fought in the war that devastated the Renshai. Nowhere, Colbey guessed, had the Renshai's battle cry been voiced with more frequency or fervor. Arduwyn's words struck home: 'Choose the gods you call on with care. Kirin suspects you're Renshai or I'm the worst archer in camp.'

'Very well.' Santagithi rose, his tone calm and reassuring. His voice made it clear that he did not consider Colbey's refusal in the least offensive. Had he felt strongly about Colbey's presence, he would have commanded, not asked. He leaned his head toward the chessboard. 'We'll play in earnest tonight. Remember this day, Colbey, because you've won your last game.'

Colbey met the taunt with one of his own. 'Battles are won by deeds, not words.' He raised the black queen. 'She may not look strong, but this woman is quite the warrior. Do you think you can handle her?'

Santagithi took the piece from Colbey's hand, examining the stone from all angles with a frown of concentration. Suddenly, he flung the queen across the room. It struck the far wall, ricocheted to the floor, and skidded under the table at Colbey's feet. 'No problem.' He headed for the door.

Santagithi hurried through the familiar, unadorned hallways of his citadel and toward the courtroom. He could still feel the impression of the smoothed stone queen against his fingers, and the idea that he had thrown it both bothered and pleased him. His rigid personality obsessed over the concept of hurling a piece that he had protected for so long and leaving it on the floor where it might get stepped on or lost, yet the strategist in him clung to the image of Colbey's open-mouthed expression. Surprising the old Renshai did not come easily; it might affect his play that evening. And Santagithi trusted Colbey to replace the queen in her proper position on the board.

As Santagithi whisked past familiar doors, his mind released thoughts of chess strategies for the more urgent matter of a Vikerian visitor. He could not guess King Tenja's intentions, so he did not try.

Speculation could only send his thoughts spinning off on inappropriate tangents. When he discovered the message, he would deal with it as necessary.

By the time Santagithi stopped before the courtroom door, chess and the thrown queen had fully disappeared from his mind. The guard captain, Jakot, awaited him at the door. He wore the mail shirt that Santagithi accorded his on-duty officers under the black and silver tunic and black breeks that formed their uniform. A sword girded his hip. Gray sprinkled the sandy hair at the captain's temples, and his beard had turned mostly white. He stood as tall as Santagithi. Heredity and hard work had graced him with bulk. His dark eyes seemed weary, his face permanently etched into an expression of somber competence. Jakot had found it difficult enough to fill the position that Rache had held for eleven years. The depth of Santagithi's depression between the time of his daughter's disappearance and the start of the Great War had heaped more responsibilities onto Jakot. At thirty-four years old, he appeared nearer to fifty, and he had surrendered any semblance of a social life to dedicate himself to his position and to his leader. He snapped to attention as Santagithi halted. 'May I accompany you, sir?'

'Of course.' Santagithi placed his hand on the doorknob, but paused before turning it. His brow furrowed. 'Are you expecting trouble?'

'No, sir.' Jakot stepped to his general's side. 'But I've never heard of Northmen coming south before, except Rache, of course. Better to prepare for trouble and meet none than to let it catch you unaware.'

So long as preparation doesn't make you twitchy and quick to resort to violence. Santagithi kept the thought to himself, trusting his captain's judgment and not wishing to lecture. For all his size, the sandy-haired captain was slow to anger. The general pulled open the door, gesturing Jakot inside before him.

A matched pair of tapestries depicting both sides of a war were tacked to the back wall, the colorful interweave seeming out of place on the otherwise bleak stone walls. Santagithi's guards had brought them as a present from a highly successful trading session in the city of Pudar. Just in front of the tapestries, Santagithi's chair perched upon a wide, low box that served as a dais. Three similar chairs formed a semicircle before it. Currently, a lone Northman stood near the center seat, clutching a rawhide cylinder bound with brass. He watched Santagithi. Six guardsmen waited, three along each side wall. Though armed with individual weapons of preference – four longswords, an ax, and a scimitar – they did not crowd or threaten the Vikerian. Whenever possible, Santagithi tried to keep his courtroom comfortable, despite its plainness.

Santagithi traversed the room swiftly, with dignity but without formality. Jakot accompanied his general most of the way, stopping at the chairs, a polite distance from their guest. Santagithi mounted his dais.

The Northern messenger remained motionless, though he watched Santagithi's every movement.

'Good morning and welcome,' Santagithi said, using the West's common trading tongue.

Apparently accustomed to the decorum of Northern royalty, the Vikerian knelt, his head bowed.

The gesture embarrassed Santagithi. He considered himself a leader, not a superior. 'Please. Sit, my friend.'

The Vikerian stood. 'Si-re, my-eh name is Ivhar Ingharrson, and I-eh bring two messages from King Tenja of Vikerin.'

Though so thick it sounded like a parody, the Northman's accent was pleasing to Santagithi. Rache had been like a son to him, and too many years had passed since he had heard the melodious intonation of the North in a young man's voice. 'Please, speak freely, Ivhar. And there's no need to call me "sire." I'm not a king.'

Ivhar seemed confused. The leader of each of the seventeen Northern tribes was called a king, regardless of his wealth or power. 'King Tenja sends his deepest and-eh sincere wishes for your realm to flourish beneath your most-eh just and noble rule . . . '

Santagithi forced himself to concentrate on the Vikerian's stilted speech, aware how much more difficult court formality must become in a foreign tongue. Ivhar's grip on the rawhide case made it clear that he carried the more important message, and Santagithi remembered the verbosity of Northern scouts from the Great War.

After a few moments that seemed twice as long, Ivhar finished. 'I-eh must deliver this.' To Santagithi's relief, the Vikerian stepped forward and placed the container into his hand.

Santagithi peeled wax from the end of the cylinder, undid the catch, and withdrew the parchment. He read silently, careful not to disclose any expression:

Lord Santagithi:

Years have passed since we fought side by side in the Westland marches. Our skjalds still sing of Santagithi's wise heart and strong arm around Vikerian fires. The bonds between men who have warred as allies are not easily broken. I have torn at my beard many nights rather than tell you of the hurt you inflict upon us. The time has come.

You are harboring one who would call you friend, then slit the throats of your children in their sleep. Stories of Renshai are never spoken at night and, in daylight, only whispered, for their dishonor is too great. We no longer have any doubt that the man you call Colbey is Renshai. Slay him or deliver him to us. Act quickly, or his deceit will ruin both of our peoples.

I trust you will take the appropriate action.
King Tenja of Vikerin

Santagithi's face grew hot, and he struggled to control his rage, keeping his features a tense, but blank, mask. He sat for several moments without moving or speaking, until he felt certain he seemed outwardly composed. He gestured to the young guard who had informed him of the Vikerian's arrival. 'Kloras, take Ivhar to the dining hall and show him the hospitality befitting a king's messenger.'

Kloras snapped to attention. 'Come with me.' He motioned to the Northman, then headed for the exit. Ivhar trotted after him.

Santagithi waited until the door banged closed behind them before confronting Jakot. 'Find Shadimar and tell him to meet me in the strategy room at once. Alone.'

'Yes, sir.' Jakot prepared to leave, but Santagithi beckoned him close. Obediently, Jakot approached.

Santagithi lowered his voice to a whisper. 'See to it Colbey and the Vikerian don't see one another.'

Jakot's brows rose in question, but he did not speak. When Santagithi did not clarify his odd request, Jakot did not press. With a shrug, he headed for the exit.

Santagithi allowed anger to swarm down on him. That the Northmen would still hold a grudge against the Renshai for events that had occurred decades ago made them seem ridiculously petty. But the idea of an ally trying to dictate who could live in Santagithi's citadel enraged him. Despite the flowery wording, Santagithi sensed threat beneath Tenja's request, and he knew without the need to consider that it would leave no room for discussion or compromise. Waiting long enough for the messenger to pass well beyond sight, Santagithi stormed from his court, hearing the guards erupt into whispers behind him. He slammed the door closed.

It would serve the bastards right if I did give them Colbey. Still clutching the message and its container, Santagithi stomped down the corridor toward the entrance to his citadel. *At the head of a legion of my finest.* Although the image of Vikerin razed and Tenja fleeing, half-naked, through the snow seemed pleasant now, Santagithi would never react in his current mood. And he saw the danger in any action but compliance. *Tenja will settle for nothing short of Colbey's life. If I refuse him, there will be a war. We may be able to best Vikerin, but we can't vanquish the entire Northlands.*

Outrage gave way to brooding. Santagithi left through the front door, carefully closing the thick, oak panel. The autumn breeze felt unseasonably cold against his flushed skin. A group of guardsmen practiced pole arm maneuvers in the grass. In the distance, Santagithi could hear the thunk of arrows hitting the rotting stumps the archers used as targets. He ignored the sounds, passing the sparring guards with a grunted greeting. He tore open the door to the guards' quarters with a violence that loosened the hinges, then let it crash shut behind him.

Voices echoed along the hallway. A door opened to Santagithi's left, and a guard stood framed in the doorway. Startled to find Santagithi so close, he hesitated before opening his mouth. By the time he prepared to call a greeting, Santagithi had passed beyond the range of anything short of a shout.

Within a dozen strides, Santagithi came upon the door to the room that had once belonged to Rache and Nantel. As always, he stopped. More than a year had passed since he had bothered to open the door. This time, he felt an urge to go inside, and the need to wait for Kloras to deliver his message and for Shadimar to arrive supported the decision. Without hesitation he entered, using his foot to snap the door closed behind him.

Most of the objects Santagithi found belonged to Nantel. After his crippling, Rache had been moved to a cottage in the village, to recover under Emerald's care. The main room held a table with two chairs. A hearth formed an opening in one wall, an empty pot swinging from the spit. Cupboards filled the area above and to either side of the fireplace, the rancid odor wafting from them convincing Santagithi that the time had come to clean the room. An old keg sat near the doorway into the second room. A layer of dust covered the table. Through it, Santagithi could see a wine stain. A crack spidered along the upper surface of oak, a remnant from an angry blow with a sword hilt or a heavy mug, almost certainly Nantel's work. The archer captain had always had a volatile temper.

A pair of carefully hammered nails supported the hilt of a sword and a hand's length of broken blade. Santagithi crossed the room to examine the odd decoration. Brown blood still etched the crack where the blade met the crosspiece. A curled shred of parchment balanced on the hilt, words scrawled across the surface in Rache's fine hand: 'Why Nantel will let Rache choose his swords from this day forth.'

The familiarity of the writing and the choice of words cut through Santagithi's rage, allowing bittersweet memory in. Clearly, Nantel's sword had broken because he had bought an inferior weapon, at least in Rache's opinion. Santagithi remembered the blacksmith's complaints that it cost him three times more in materials and time than he got paid to craft swords that met Rache's demanding specifications. Santagithi pictured his young sword master, his golden hair flying, since he had always refused the helmet his rank accorded him. The black jerkin he wore instead of the officers' mail had become more familiar and right than the routine black and silver uniforms of the remainder of the army. An emptiness filled Santagithi. Though years had passed, he could not suppress a tear. He thought of the respect Rache had always held for the greatest of all sword masters, Colbey, the man who had trained him as a child. Over the years, Rache had become as much a son to Santagithi as Mitrian was his daughter. *I can't do anything more for Rache, except to keep true to his memory. I will not betray his teacher.*

Santagithi rubbed away the tear dribbling across his cheek, holding back the ones that tried to follow. Turning, he left the room. He closed the door and continued toward the strategy chamber.

When Santagithi entered, he found Shadimar sitting in one of the ten high-backed chairs set around the table. Flicking the door closed, Santagithi passed his usual seat at the head of the table, choosing one beside the Wizard. He tossed the Vikerian's message in front of Shadimar before he could speak. 'Read this.' Santagithi sat.

Shadimar uncurled the parchment and read. Long after he must have finished, he stared at the page, thinking or rereading.

Santagithi's fists clenched while he waited.

At length, Shadimar rerolled the message. 'Santagithi, you have a decision to make.' He offered no counsel.

Nor did Santagithi request any. 'I wish I did have a decision. But I'm afraid King Tenja made it for me when he wrote this letter. I won't give him Colbey. Even if I were base enough to betray a friend, how long would it be before the Northmen demanded my daughter, Rache's son, and my grandson?' He met Shadimar's stony eyes. 'I'll send every Northman to their Hel by my own hand before I'll turn over my family.' He slammed his fist on the tabletop, the blow quivering through fingers that, clenched too long, had fallen asleep.

'You still have a decision.' Shadimar stroked his beard, his voice calm despite Santagithi's pounding. 'How will you answer King Tenja's letter? I suggest you choose your words with care.'

Santagithi slid back his chair.

'You could still avoid a war.'

Santagithi rose, head shaking. 'I'm afraid that, at this juncture, I can do little more than delay it. Unless you have the words I can't seem to find.'

'I'm afraid I don't.' Shadimar's gaze followed Santagithi's movement. 'But I don't think I have to tell the West's prime strategist that, as much as Northmen war against one another, when one tribe fights an outside enemy, they all band together. If you start a war, you will not fight Vikerin. You will fight the Northlands.'

Santagithi walked to his seat at the head of the table. Opening a drawer in the table that he knew well, he withdrew several sheets of parchment, a quill, a bottle of ink, and sealing wax. Closing the drawer, he sat in his usual seat. Nothing the Wizard had said came as a surprise to him.

'You have no nearby allies. I'm afraid the armies of the civilized West may not help you. I heard things that make me believe that the new king in Pudar doesn't like Colbey. Or you, for that matter.'

Santagithi's elbows bored into the tabletop, and he wished Colbey's audience in Prince Verrall's tent had progressed more smoothly.

'I believe Sterrane would assist you. But his kingdom is at the exact opposite end of the Westlands. It would take months to send an army. And I believe he'll find himself beset with troubles of his own.'

'As a new king restoring an old line, he may still have his own battles to fight.' Santagithi took the quill in hand. 'I understand that.'

'There is one other thing to consider.' The Eastern Wizard paused for some time.

Santagithi turned his gaze, as well as his attention to Shadimar.

'Colbey is old. And he would love to die fighting Northmen. If you showed this note to him, he might make the decision to leave. Surely, King Tenja could not hold it against you if Colbey attacked on his own initiative.'

'No!' Santagithi refused to consider such an option. Colbey came to me to give him a safe place to train his people. Right or wrong, directly or indirectly, every one of his people is related to me. And I still believe that, after Colbey's death, the Northmen will come for Mitrian and the boys. The Renshai need Colbey to teach them to defend themselves against Northmen.' He tapped the quill against the parchment, considering. 'I can't let myself or this town get bullied by Northmen holding a stupid grudge that lost pertinence long ago.' Without awaiting a reply, Santigithi wrote:

> *King Tenja:*
>
> *I received your note and have shown your messenger the courtesy a valued ally deserves. Your words recalled memories of the Great War, where both of our armies fought side by side, neither giving ground.*
>
> *It pains me to think any action of mine might have earned your disfavor. You may rest peacefully, knowing that no threat against my house will go unavenged; and I will deal with Colbey as he deserves.*
>
> *Santagithi*

Santagithi passed the note to Shadimar, waiting while the Eastern Wizard perused it. 'And I believe Colbey deserves to be treated as any trusted friend.' He added, 'Would you translate to Northern?'

'Of course.' Shadimar nodded. 'I don't envy your position. If it makes you feel any better, I believe your stand is sound and honorable, though it may kill you. I hope things go well.'

Santagithi picked up the ink, parchment, and sealing wax, carrying them to Shadimar. 'I only ask that you don't mention Tenja's letter to anyone. Especially not to Colbey.'

'I will do as you ask.' Shadimar smoothed a blank piece of parchment on the tabletop. 'When I'm finished rewriting, I have to go home. I have business to attend. I can't help you in battle; but if you send for me, I will come.'

'Thank you.' Santagithi's gaze played over the many maps that papered his walls, coming to rest on the area north of the Granite Hills. The few passes through the miniature but rugged mountains gave him a million ideas for strategy. And he hoped he would need to use none of them.

12 Mind Powers

Rain spilled from the autumn sky, drummed against the canopy of leaves, and dribbled into the practice clearing. Droplets trickled clumps of gold-white hair into Colbey's face, plastering it to his cheeks and forehead, but he paid this discomfort no heed. His attention remained on his three students and the maneuvers he had given each one. Mitrian performed long, intricate katas with a smoothness and skill that proved she had drilled in her absence. Rache kept his sword sheathed, repeating a dodge that formed the basis for one of the first Renshai maneuvers. Episte executed a choreographed strike with a grace that made it seem as if the move had been created for him.

Colbey smiled, pleasure spiraling through him, certain that this mixed band could form a tribe. Each had his or her own strengths, and each would bring his talent to the reformation of the Renshai. Mitrian knew a dedication and agility few could match. Rache threw his all into every lesson, needing to oblige his *torke* with the same exuberance as the original Renshai. Episte had talents that came so easily and naturally that, even when the boys became old enough that the two years between them made little difference, Episte would always remain a step ahead of Rache. Colbey hoped Rache's determination would stimulate him to work even harder to try to best his near-sibling. Perhaps the competitive spirit would touch even Episte.

Damp tinged the air, keeping the clearing close but cool. Episte performed another perfect sequence, then sheathed his sword. He headed for a deadfall at the clearing's edge.

Surprised by the boy's bold defiance, Colbey stepped directly into Episte's path. 'Where are you going?' He used the Renshai tongue.

Episte looked up at his teacher, yellow hair falling into his eyes, the rivulets twining across his face mingling rain and sweat. 'There.' He pointed to the log.

'Have you performed *hastivillr* a million times?'

'At least, *torke*.' Episte sounded sincere. 'Maybe two million.' He pawed hair from his face.

To Colbey's count, it was closer to ten, but he did believe the child needed to move on to something more difficult. 'Then I will teach you another.'

'In a little while, *torke*.'

Colbey did not give ground. Endurance was as much a part of his teachings as swiftness and strength. 'Now.'

'No!' Episte stomped his foot. His voice turned to a whine, and he slipped back into the Western trading language. 'I practiced five million billion times and – '

Colbey cut him off. 'Use Renshai.'

Episte's speech slowed. 'I'm sleep almost. And not thirsty. Too not thirsty. The day is rabbit.'

'Stop.' Colbey remained between Episte and the log, trying to meet the child's eyes. Though on the shorter side of average, Colbey stood twice the boy's height. 'You're not making sense. Slow down. Tell me what you're trying to say, and I'll translate for you.'

Episte whined. 'I'm tired. I want to rest. I'm cold and wet.'

Enraged by the child's complaints, Colbey snapped his mouth closed.

Episte glanced up, studied the anger on Colbey's face, and returned his gaze to his feet.

Colbey spoke slowly, emphasizing each word, though he kept his voice too soft for the others to hear. 'I will not translate that into Renshai, because no Renshai would say such a thing.' He studied the boy's tiny hands, already a man's fist, scarred with calluses. 'Is this what you would tell your enemies?' He simulated Episte's whimpering. 'I can't fight back anymore because it's raining and I'm tired.'

Episte fixed eyes as blue and deep as the Amirannak Sea on Colbey. 'My mommy says that when I'm tired, I should rest. I'm just a little boy.'

Colbey felt a hot flush of fury, which he quickly controlled. 'Your mother, gods love her, has never been in combat, and I hope she never is. If you learn to quit when you get tired, you will die when you get tired. You're not a little boy; you're a Renshai. Soon enough, you'll become a man.'

Episte's face screwed into an indignant knot.

Recognizing the first signs of a rising tantrum, Colbey distracted the boy. He whipped his left sword from its sheath, jabbing it so close to Episte's side that it pressed his tunic against his skin.

Though the killing thrust would already have landed, Episte sprang backward, pulling his own weapon free. Colbey swept high, and Episte met the stroke with a block. Immediately, Colbey reversed the direction of his cut. The tip of his blade licked under Episte's grip, catching one of the protrusions of the cross guard. He jerked back, sending the weapon spinning from the boy's hand. Episte retreated defensively.

Colbey caught the hilt of Episte's sword in midair. In the same motion, he tossed it back to its wielder. 'Now – '

Episte caught the leather-wrapped hilt effortlessly. The instant his fingers curled around the grip, he charged his teacher in anger.

Pleased by his student's sudden exuberance, Colbey laughed. He parried aside Episte's sword. The commitment of the boy's attack sent him skidding past his target. He spun, but not quickly enough. The flat of Colbey's sword slapped his back twice before he came fully around.

Despite his attention to Episte, Colbey noted a movement at the corner of his vision. Shadimar stepped into the clearing, his long, lean form unmistakable.

Episte slashed, his strokes powerful. Temper stole precision from the techniques, and Colbey dodged the deadly cuts easily. He had taught his students to treat every spar with him as a real combat, trusting his own skill to keep any blade from landing. In fifty years, no student had so much as scratched him. 'Hold.' Attention turned toward Shadimar, Colbey met Episte's frantic upstroke. He parried it in a circle, stepping beneath the crossed blades. Casually catching Episte's hilt, he wrested it from the child's hand.

Shadimar approached, Secodon padding silently through the clearing behind him.

'What can I do for you?' Annoyance colored Colbey's politeness. Strangers observing a Renshai practice session disturbed him. Interrupting one verged on criminal.

Shadimar's expression seemed even more serious then usual. 'We need to talk.'

'Fine. I'll see you tonight, after I've trained my students and finished my own practice.'

'We need to talk now.'

Colbey frowned. He would not have wasted a moment considering such a demand from anyone else. *Shadimar is my brother*, he reminded himself. 'It can't wait?'

Shadimar dodged the question. 'I'm leaving for home immediately after our talk. I have research and work I need to do. The longer I wait to talk, the angrier I'll get.'

Already prepared to give one student a lecture on controlling his temper, Colbey interrupted. 'The angrier you get, the longer you'll wait.'

'You *won't* like facing an angry Wizard.' Shadimar's quiet threat made it clear he would not banter words.

Colbey kept his irritation in check. He returned Episte's sword, offering it hilt first.

Episte accepted the weapon, clutching it, waiting for Colbey to finish.

The elder Renshai sheathed his own blade. 'Very well.' He called to Mitrian. 'Show Episte *ulvstikk*, and keep him working until I get back.' He turned to Shadimar, his words meant more for the Eastern Wizard than for Mitrian. 'This *won't* take long.'

Without replying, Shadimar turned, headed into the woods and back toward town. Colbey trailed after, the wolf at his side. Secodon's ears were swept back to his head, and his hackles spread stiffly. Apparently something had upset the wolf, or else it just echoed the Wizard's mood.

Shadimar stopped at the edge of the woods. The sparser arrangement of trees allowed glimpses of cottages between the trunks. Rain pounded through the thinner interlace of branches, soaking Wizard, wolf, and Renshai. Colbey's tunic clung wetly to his skin.

Shadimar leaned against a trunk. His gray eyes studied Colbey coldly.

In no mood for another battle of words, Colbey went right to the point. 'What can I do for you, Brother?'

'There's something you're not telling me.'

Annoyed by the vagueness of the statement, Colbey counted to three before replying. 'I would venture to guess there are an unlimited number of things I'm not telling you. Could you be specific, please? I have better things to do than to try to guess your mind.' Colbey seriously considered invading the Eastern Wizard's thoughts to save time, but he resisted the urge. Even aggravation could not drive him to mistreat a blood brother, and he had to guess that the Wizard would judge such an intrusion as an attack.

'You have mind powers.'

Colbey stared, not daring to believe the Wizard had dragged him away from a training session for such a thing. 'I have mind powers,' he repeated. 'Fine, I've told you. Is that what you wanted to hear?'

'Why didn't you tell me before?'

'You didn't ask.'

'I shouldn't have to ask.'

Colbey snorted. 'Shadimar, there're more than a few things you've never told me. Without knowing what you want from me, how can I guess which things to tell you?'

Shadimar's voice rose nearly to a shout. 'You had to know that a thing so powerful would be of importance to me!'

'No.' Colbey kept his tone paradoxically calm. 'I don't have to know anything. What's important to you isn't always what's important to me. If it was, you would have asked me to detail sword maneuvers.' He added carefully, 'Which I couldn't, of course. Blood brother or not, you're no Renshai. Now, what is it you want to know?'

Shadimar dropped his offended expression for one of eager interest. 'Where did you get these powers? When did they start?'

'Childhood.' Colbey leaned against an elm. 'It's part of the Renshai training to learn to control the body with the mind.'

'But not to read minds.'

'True.'

'Yet you stole my words.'

Colbey had done this to people for so long he hated the need to explain it now. 'I steal everyone's words.'

'You do?' Shadimar seemed shocked.

'I do.'

'That makes no sense.'

The comment seemed even sillier than the previous one. 'Which word didn't you understand? "I" or "do"?' Colbey glowered. 'If you're going to question my integrity, don't bother to talk to me. There's little honor more consistent or treasured than that of Renshai. How many races do you know who would rather face extinction than loss of principle? Even the Northmen who massacred the Renshai admitted that none ran from them. Not one Renshai wore armor or hid behind a shield of any kind. No Renshai hurled rocks, arrows, nor any other cowards' weapons. No Renshai – '

'I'm not questioning your integrity!' Shadimar roared. Though not loud, the words carried a depth that silenced Colbey's defense. 'I've been a Cardinal Wizard for over two centuries, and I've read more history than men know exists. In all that time, I have never personally, or through reading, discovered any man nor even any Wizard who could read mortals' minds.'

The revelation held Colbey quiet.

'Now can you understand when I say it makes no sense?'

Colbey nodded, too many questions occurring to him to ask them all at once. He cleared his throat. 'I don't know if this makes a difference, but I don't actually read minds. More often, people's thoughts come to me, and I speak them. Sometimes the meaning of the thought is obvious. Occasionally, it comes to me with enough emotion and detail that I can figure it out. Other times, the thought or emotion comes alone, and I don't understand it.'

Shadimar's brows dropped suddenly, turning his eyes into narrow slits. 'So you can't actually read minds?'

' "Can't" may be too strong.'

'What do you mean?'

Colbey fidgeted, torn between his needs to work with the other Renshai and to understand his gift. 'It just feels wrong invading other people's minds, so I don't do it.'

'Yet you have no compunction about speaking the thoughts that come to you.'

Colbey shrugged. It had taken him time to test and to believe that the thoughts had come from others, not from his own conjecture. By the time he had learned the truth, it seemed too late to concern himself with propriety. 'I also have no compunction about guessing men's moods from their faces, their next attack by shifts in position, or their intentions by the tone of their voices.' He shrugged again. 'Anything that a man gives me to work with, I will. I draw the line when it comes to me consciously invading his privacy.'

Shadimar nodded, apparently accepting that explanation.

Colbey had to laugh. 'When you have a talent that neither mortal nor Wizard has ever shared, you have to make up the rules.'

Secodon snuffled amongst the roots of an elm, and Shadimar leaned against the trunk. 'Actually, there is one precedent.'

Colbey raised his brows.

'The Cardinal Wizards can communicate with one another through their minds.' Shadimar sighed deeply. 'We rarely do, though. To do so uninvited would be like drawing your sword in another man's house in the presence of his wife and children.'

Colbey winced at the analogy, even more certain of his decision to stay clear of friends' thoughts whenever possible.

Shadimar laughed, the sound out of place in a conversation of consequence.

'What's so funny?'

'I think I finally figured out how you've been beating Santagithi at chess.'

Colbey laughed, too. 'I've never met anyone who could put a full war strategy into one or two sentences before. He's good. The Renshai were never much for strategy, but I've learned a lot just being around Santagithi for a few years.'

'Now you know why the larger Western kingdoms deferred to his judgment in the Great War. And why a tiny town has managed to survive for so long so near the Northlands.'

Something in Shadimar's voice cued Colbey to a deeper issue hidden beneath the statement, but he did not pry. 'Are we finished?'

'No.' Shadimar's features again grew somber, and the wolf abandoned his search to stand at his master's side. 'I need to understand just how much magic you know.'

'Magic?' Colbey shook his head. 'Less than none. Unless you count the mind thing.'

'Concentrate.' Shadimar raised his arms, chanting strange, harsh syllables in a language Colbey did not recognize. He lowered his right arm, extending his hand toward Colbey. A flame danced on his palm, tiny and insignificant.

Colbey blinked, certain he witnessed an illusion of sunlight. Raindrops sprinkled to the Wizard's fingers, but they had no effect on the wisp of fire.

Shadimar stopped speaking suddenly, eyes eager, left hand still hovering above his head. The flame sputtered. 'Colbey, try to finish the incantation.'

Colbey obediently searched his mind for a thread of knowledge. He discovered nothing but his own neatly filed memories of thrust, parry, and dodge, the mental strength to convert idea instantly into movement, and the control of personal thought and action. Opening his eyes, he shook his head.

The flame shrank nearly to nothing. 'Quickly, now,' Shadimar said.

Again, Colbey tried to find a hint of the arcane tongue Shadimar had used to create the flame. Nothing came. Wishing to please his blood brother, Colbey tried to keep the flame aloft by directing his concentration on it.

The fire winked out.

Shadimar lowered both hands. 'Nothing?'

'Not a whisper.' Despite his hurry, Colbey could not help asking. 'Do you think that mind thing of mine is magic? Is that why you believe I know more?'

Shadimar shook his head in a bobbing, half-committed manner, as if to indicate that Colbey's guess was only part of the explanation. Apparently, he also took the blood brotherhood seriously, because he explained rather than dodging the situation with his usual self-absorption. 'This may sound impossible to you, even crazy. But, for a time, I actually wondered if you might not already be the Western Wizard.'

'What?' The question was startled from Colbey. 'That's absurd.'

'Not really. I considered you as a possible replacement for Tokar. Why shouldn't I wonder if he had the same thought?'

'I'm no Wizard. I have no interest in becoming a Wizard. And, had Tokar asked, I would have refused.'

Shadimar accepted Colbey's insistence, but he did not drop the thought. 'You have to admit, there's evidence for the assumption. Tokar asked, nay practically forced, you to come to his ceremony of passage. He talked about making a significant decision that he should have already made.' Shadimar flipped both palms up in a gesture that implied an obvious conclusion. 'The choosing of his successor. Haim. An apprentice who always seemed a weak and poor choice to us all. Tokar giving each of you a chance to answer a significant question, the one about decision-making, fairly clinches it.'

Even Colbey could not help considering the possibility. 'But could he make me into a Wizard against my will? Without even asking?'

'I don't know,' Shadimar admitted. 'I'd tend to doubt it. I've never heard of such a thing. From all recorded history, it's never happened before.' Shadimar threw up his hands. 'And why should it? Why would a Wizard train an apprentice for decades, only to take another successor at the last moment?'

'Because,' Colbey said, trying not to sound too immodest, 'he found a better replacement, worth the risks.' He thought of combats in which he planned a specific maneuver to use against an enemy's known weakness, only to discover a better killing stroke during the actual battle.

Shadimar frowned dubiously. 'That's not the nature of Wizards. Still, it no longer matters. If you were the Western Wizard, you would have been able to finish that incantation.'

'Magic comes naturally to Wizards?'

'No, they must be trained.' Shadimar plucked bark from the tree with a long fingernail. 'But if you were Tokar's chosen successor, you would carry the memories of every Western Wizard before you. And any one of them could have directed you to finish my spell.'

'Oh.' Colbey's mind slipped backward, to the madness that had afflicted him for years following the Western Wizard's death. Colbey had attributed it to the agony that had accompanied touching Tokar, to the ceremony, or to the shock of discovering his entire tribe had been killed in his absence. He shivered at the memory of the foreign voices and obsessions that had driven him. He had faced and destroyed the insanity with the same directed skill he used in combat, obliterating the presences one by one until nothing remained but his own clear consciousness. Colbey had always believed that this battle had won him the mind strength that he now possessed. 'Would it be possible for a Wizard to get rid of these others' memories?'

'Certainly not.' Shadimar sounded offended and horrified. 'A Wizard's mind becomes linked into the chain. It would be impossible to do so without suicide.' Shadimar froze, the significance of Colbey's question finally absorbed. 'Why do you ask?'

Colbey kept his response vague. 'After the ceremony, I was haunted by voices in my head for a time. They're gone now.'

Shadimar shook his head, dismissing the importance of Colbey's revelation. 'I doubt that means much. After such a trauma, any mortal could go temporarily insane, especially one so linked with his mind.'

Colbey doubted the possibility. His mind link involved control, not simply an emphasis on calculation over action. Wanting to return to his practice, he did not start an argument.

But, even without Colbey's direction, Shadimar saw the flaw in his suggestion. 'There's no way to know exactly how your touch disrupted the ceremony. Possibly, sensing imminent destruction, one or two of the Wizards' consciousnesses grasped hold of the only living mind in the vicinity. Yours. If your mental powers are astoundingly strong, I suppose you might have suppressed those presences. *But no mortal in existence has the power to control or destroy millennia of Western Wizards.*' Shadimar continued, obviously thinking aloud. 'Or perhaps, since the ceremony was disrupted, a bit of magic was never dispelled. If an entity of that magic remained . . . ' Shadimar trailed off, eyes widening. The stiffness of his demeanor told Colbey that the Eastern Wizard wished he had kept the thought to himself.

'What?' Colbey pressed.

'Never mind.' Shadimar clipped each word, making it clear that no bond or promise would make him continue.

Colbey followed the natural line of thought. 'A magical entity could have entered my mind?' The idea made him laugh. 'I really could be the Golden Prince of Demons?'

'Stop!' Shadimar's voice rang out. Though he remained outwardly calm, Colbey sensed concern and perhaps, a faint hint of dread. 'I must consult my books. I won't speculate further in ignorance.'

Amused by the Wizard's dramatics, Colbey laughed again.

The wolf threw back its head, loosing a deep howl, full of ancient pain. Discomfort wafted from the Wizard, thick with consideration and ideas Colbey could not begin to decipher.

At least, Colbey guessed the source of Shadimar's fear. *He thinks I'm reading his mind. And there's something there he doesn't want me to know.* Colbey attempted to soothe. 'Shadimar, don't worry, I'm not reading – '

Colbey's words only further agitated Shadimar. The old Wizard whirled, heading toward the town at a dignified pace that bordered on a run.

Too late, Colbey realized his mistake. By claiming not to be reading the Wizard's mind, he had again identified Shadimar's thought nearly verbatim, thereby practically proving that he was, in fact, intruding. Though a logical guess on Colbey's part, its accuracy made it seem sinister. 'Shadimar, wait!'

Branches snapped closed behind the Wizard's passage, flinging droplets from the wet branches. Soon, the rustles gave way to a silence broken only by the patter of rain on the leaves.

Thinking it better not to pursue, Colbey turned and headed back to his students.

13 Preparations

Deep in the ruins that served as his home, Shadimar paced the library floor until his tracks seemed to wear an impression in the stone. A lantern on the desktop cast his shadow upon the opposite wall, and it spun back and forth, keeping perfect time with his movements. Secodon lay beneath the reading table, his head cradled between his paws, whining frequently at his master's consternation.

At length, Shadimar again sat before an opened book, the lamplight glazing the page he had stared at too many times and for too long. The seventh Eastern Wizard, Benghta, had originally inscribed the paragraph, her expertise understandable since her own predecessor had lost his life to a summoned demon. Yet the text told Shadimar nothing he did not already know:

'. . . Should a Cardinal Wizard pass before his chosen time, it is the responsibility of every other Wizard to fill the gap. In this matter, thoughtful consideration should take precedence over speed. This is true particularly in the case of an Eastern or Western Wizard, since each of these has one of equal bent who can cover his responsibilities for a time. To act too quickly risks an incompetent, weak, or poorly trained replacement at a time when strength and ability become most necessary. It should be kept in mind that this new Wizard would have no access to the collective consciousness and would, therefore, already hold a disadvantage.

'In the case of an Eastern or Western Wizard's passing, it would naturally fall upon the other to find a successor, then to call the Wizards' Isle meeting. While he could elicit aid from the Northern or Southern Wizard in finding said successor, such a request would seem unlikely to prove advantageous. Since forces work in opposition, either of these others might profit from finding a weak replacement. In the event of a Northern or Southern Wizard's unexpected passage, responsibility would fall to the Western Wizard to call counsel and find a replacement. This task could be willingly shared, or even passed, to the Eastern Wizard. Again, to place the responsibility into the hands of one of the champions of the "extreme forces," that is good or evil, would introduce bias. It would, however, be in the best interests of neutrality to balance Northern and Southern forces.

'It should also be realized that Odin has placed many protections into his system, through law and propriety. Any Wizard "passing" due to anything other than his chosen ceremony should prove a rare occurrence over the millennia. Therefore, it becomes incumbent on the responsible party to ascertain that "passing" without a doubt. Attempting to establish another Wizard while there are already Four would result in the death of the subject as well as a shaking of the foundations of law. It might open the way for chaos and, ultimately, begin the *Ragnarok*. . . . '

From there, the tome turned to other topics, and Shadimar gave it a mild shove. Its edge struck the lantern's base, jiggling it. Light whirled over the crude stone ceiling, then went still as the lantern came to rest in its new position. Pain speared through Shadimar's head at the intensity of his concentration. The book fell short of addressing the intricacies and details that he needed to make a decision. When Tokar's apprentice, Haim, had undergone the Seven Tasks of Wizardry, the powers in charge had told him that the 'Age of Change' that heralded the *Ragnarok* would come during Shadimar's time as a Wizard. That prophecy haunted him now, and he would do nothing without massive research, profound thought, and cautious consideration.

Shadimar clamped his fingers to his temples, massaging away the throbbing in his head, his elbows propped on either side of the book so as not to damage the pages. Colbey's story seemed conclusive. The Western Wizard was dead, and the ceremony had taken his apprentice's life as well. Surely, that was enough proof for Shadimar to start the search for a successor. Yet two ideas would not leave his mind. First, he had already found the most competent replacement for the Western Wizard, and his demanding standards would not allow him to settle for less. He would need to convince Colbey to take the position, hampered by the understanding that most of the qualities that made the Renshai most suited for the honor also made him willful and difficult to lead. The title could not be forced upon him, and wearing down Colbey's objections would take patience and time.

Second, Colbey's mind powers fit no plan, pattern, or source that Shadimar could fathom. The possibilities seemed endless, few of them positive. If a fragment of the collective consciousness had entered Colbey, it did not behave like any predecessor to whom Shadimar had access. More likely, a stray spark of magic had altered the makeup and basic functioning of Colbey's mind. If so, his jest that he had become a 'demon' was not entirely ludicrous. Clearly, nothing could transform law's tangibles, such as men, directly into creatures of chaos. But chaos, in the guise of magic, could have perverted Colbey's mind. In that case, he posed an incalculable threat to the world, Wizards, and gods; and he would need to be utterly destroyed.

Shadimar scowled at the irony. Depending on what his research uncovered, his necessary course of action could fall to either extreme, or anywhere between. And other questions still begged answering. He had never heard of anyone disrupting a ceremony of passage since the beginning of time, though the earliest Wizards predicted vague but ominous horrors would result. Composed of chaos, even channeled magic nearly always had unexpected results. When it came to the disruption of a ceremony that required the most powerful sorcery of all, the consequences seemed impossible to determine or even to guess. Perhaps the Western Wizard did exist, the collective consciousness transferred to some unsuspecting innocent who had not yet come to grips with the position or the power.

Shadimar's fingers stilled, and he clapped his hands over his white hair in frustration. His beard had settled over the tome, obscuring the writing. Secodon rose, stretched, and sat, resting his chin on Shadimar's knee. Shadimar stroked one of the wolf's ears absently. The plumed tail struck the floor once, and Secodon cocked his head as if to understand concepts far beyond his ability to reason.

The Eastern Wizard's library had fallen short. Shadimar knew he had only two more places to turn, and he discarded the first out of hand. He had never found the need to summon demons before, and he could not risk neutrality's only remaining champion now. Of all of the Cardinal Wizards, the Western Wizard's library was the most complete. There, if he found no answers, at least he might gather enough information to guide his thoughts to more limited possibilities. Perhaps, too, in Tokar's cave, he might discover more clues to the Western Wizard's intentions, fate, or whereabouts.

Odin's Laws did not allow the Cardinal Wizards to intrude upon one another's quarters uninvited, except with the messenger falcon, Swiftwing. This once, Shadimar felt certain, the Western Wizard would not protest.

Santagithi sat at the head of his strategy table, looking down the double line of men and the lone woman who was his daughter, assessing each commander's ability for the thousandth time. To his right, the archer's captain, Bromdun, waited attentively, his arms folded across his chest and his expression grim. Mouse brown hair hacked short fringed hard, well-defined features. Quiet nearly to a fault, perhaps because of his large size, Bromdun spoke only when he had a message of consequence, and his followers clung to his every word.

Santagithi's gaze rolled from Bromdun to his warrior captain, Jakot, who had proven his worth repeatedly. Though he lacked Rache's skill, Jakot had taken the dead Renshai's position with faultless commitment and honor. Now, he plucked at his wiry, sand-colored beard in silence, the movement betraying his impatience.

Across from Bromdun, Mitrian laced her fingers on the tabletop, her hands as large and callused as any guardsman's. A thong tied her dark hair neatly back from her face. No matter how many times Santagithi watched her perform a kata with an agility and skill that matched Rache's, he could not imagine her in war. He had dug through his mind for the memory of Mitrian at the Great War, riding at Rache's side, the two forming a wall of flashing steel that sent more than their share of Easterners to their deaths. Yet Santagithi's mind created defenses, substituting another face for his daughter's in the memory. Still, as a commander, she had inherited her father's thoroughness, if not the strategic expertise that came with experience. And then there was Garn.

Santagithi rolled his eyes to his son-in-law, careful not to stare too long. Garn fidgeted like a child forced to attend a ceremony that had dragged on forever. His wild, bronze hair hung in his face, and he had worn his jerkin at least one day too many. Sweat stains marred leather stretched taut over muscles so defined they made Bromdun and Jakot look fat. What he lacked in guile, Garn made up for in ferocity and strength, yet Santagithi had second thoughts about naming Garn as a secondary leader. Still, working in concert with Mitrian, Garn might make a reasonable half of a commander.

Santagithi's eyes strayed naturally to the empty chair beyond Garn, where Colbey should sit. Of his leaders, only the old Renshai was excused from strategy sessions; and then only to train the boys.

Santagithi cleared his throat, as always beginning with a rallying speech that gave his leaders a reason to fight. 'For years, the Northmen remained content warring among themselves. Now they're looking southward. If we want to keep our homes, our women, and our children safe, we must be ready to fight! And we must be ready to win!' This deceit scarred the old general deeply, but he saw no recourse. Since its founding, the town had treasured equality and the worth of every citizen. Though not an original member, Colbey had dedicated his time and ability to the Westlands and this town, in its Great War, through training guardsmen, and by counseling and honing its general. *My citizenry is not for Northmen to dictate about. I would not give up Colbey any quicker than I would Jakot, our women, or my grandson.* He knew his men would see the wisdom in his decision, that they would gladly fight for Colbey; but Colbey would never allow them. If he knew the truth, the Renshai would ride north to kill Vikerians and die in glory. And Mitrian would follow.

Jakot frowned, clearly skeptical of the explanation, yet he did not question. Only once, he had inquired about the contents of King Tenja's note. He had accepted his general's silence as an explanation, apparently placing his full trust in his leader's judgment. Now Santagithi motioned to his captain, and Jakot produced and unrolled a map that detailed the Granite Hills. Though Santagithi had memorized the terrain, he stared with the same interest as his officers. Another piece of intelligence had surfaced. Though the Vikerians had, so far, done nothing to indicate that they planned an attack, one of Santigithi's scouts had reported a doubling of sentries at the border. That boded ill, and Santagithi needed his leaders alert and attuned to every update. He considered the posibility that the Vikerians had increased their security in response to his own caution, yet discarded it almost instantly. It had been common knowledge for decades that Santagithi kept his army in fighting trim, even in times of peace.

Santagithi trapped the nearest edge of the map beneath his massive hands, studying the hash marks that defined each mountain. Located at the tail of the Northern Weathered Range and the head of the Great Frenum Mountains, the Granite Hills had been misnamed by explorers who noted only that the peaks, though snow-capped, stood smaller than their towering neighbors. The barren valleys, jagged slopes, and narrow mountain ledges limited passage to the North to a single safe pass and a few branches that might prove too precarious for more than a handful of infantry.

Apparently tired of the silence, Garn revived an argument that he had been bandying with Jakot for days. 'I still think slashing works better than jabbing. You can't take a man's head off with a stab.'

Santagithi frowned, but he did not interfere. He did not mind if his leaders chatted while he gathered his thoughts, so long as they kept their minds on combat.

When his commander did not reprimand Garn's outburst, Jakot accurately read Santagithi's silence. The captain replied, 'Taking off a man's head isn't the ultimate goal in battle. Hel, most soldiers don't have the power to do that, even if they had a sharp enough blade. All you have to do is stop him.'

Garn leaned across the table, with an exuberant interest that pleased Santagithi, even though the ex-gladiator was wrong, as usual. 'A slash'll take him down faster. It covers more area.'

'More *nonvital* area,' Jakot insisted. 'A jab takes the weapon deeper. It's quicker. With a lunge, you've got further range and expose yourself less. And even if your enemy survives the initial combat, a puncture is far less likely to heal — '

A tap sounded on the door, and though muffled by the thickness of oak, it halted the conversation. Nearest the door, Santagithi leapt to his feet before any of his commanders could respond. Unlatching the bolt, he pulled open the panel to reveal a guardsman named Harrit.

'Sir?' Harrit said tentatively, his gaze jerking over the row of commanders, obviously cowed by the seriousness of their expressions. 'Six Auermen are waiting in the court. They say it's important. Should I tell them to come back some other time?'

'Auermen?' Santagithi crinkled his brow, turning to Jakot for input. Due to his forays, few barbarian villages remained in the area. The peoples of the West rarely crossed the southern extension of the Granite Hills that separated the Town of Santagithi from the Western farm villages and the more civilized cities in the central and western areas. A few self-sufficient farm hamlets lay scattered through the area. Lacking armies, they kept to themselves, except for rare trade and gladiator competitions. Since disbanding the pit fights, Santagithi had not heard from any of his neighbors.

'Yes, sir. Auermen,' Harrit confirmed, though surely he realized the question had not been aimed at him. 'They say Northmen razed their village, and they want our help.'

All petty concerns fled Santagithi's mind, and his heart thudded with the calm cadence that came prior to war. *The time has come.* The Northmen's strategy bothered but did not surprise him. There was wisdom in slaughtering the possible allies of enemies, especially when they lived between the warring lands. Perhaps the Northmen hoped to hold Auer, using it as a source of food and battlements. Santagithi saw that as a compliment; it meant that the Vikerians anticipated a protracted battle. 'I'll be back shortly.' Santagithi headed for the door. 'Jakot, try to teach Garn something while I'm gone.' He slammed the door on Bromdun's laughter.

Once outside the strategy chamber, Santagithi paced the corridor with Harrit. 'Did you know any of these Auermen?'

'No, sir.' Harrit trotted to keep up.

Santagithi frowned. The Northmen's lack of response to his message made him suspicious, and weeks planning strategy only fueled that paranoia. Still, Harrit's unfamiliarity with the men meant little. Years had passed since the town had any communications with Auer's hamlet, and the council elder had probably chosen his speakers from availability and need.

'How do they look?' From habit, Santagithi broke pace at the room that Rache and Nantel had occupied.

Harrit accelerated into the lead. He paused a step to get back into stride with his leader. 'Hard-pressed and travel-stained. Dressed for battle, such as a poor village can afford. They do all have swords, at least, though I'd venture to guess they can't use them.'

Harrit opened the door from the guard quarters.

Santagithi exited into sunlight so bright that it made him squint. Harrit's casual mention of a sword for each Auerman bothered the general. It meant that the hamlet had given a third or half of its weapons to these messengers, shorting their defenses. Santagithi frowned. It was a strategy he would never consider, yet he could see how Auer's elder might. *When the only chance for survival lies in gathering allies, there's a certain, warped logic in using strong, well-armed messengers.* Still, Santagithi remained cautious. 'Find Colbey and send him to the court.' Though he knew Colbey hated court affairs nearly as much as having a training session interrupted, Santagithi saw the need for both. Though different and bolder, Colbey's strategies for war and diplomacy often complimented his own. He wanted the old Renshai's input on this matter and his presence if it became necessary. 'Tell him I sent you, and it's important. Get him here as quickly as you can.'

'Yes, sir.' Harrit headed toward the town at a run. Despite the crisp efficiency of Harrit's words and his motion, Santigithi sensed reluctance. He did not envy any man's need to disturb Colbey.

Santagithi forced himself to slow his pace, walking the fine line between delaying long enough for Colbey to arrive and upsetting his guests by not handling their problems with the expediency they deserved. He ambled across the meadows between the guard quarters and his home, pleased by the trampled patches of grass that indicated an increase in the soldiers' spars and practices. Over the years, he had come to know every step of the route he had traced tens of thousands of times, on horseback and on foot. Today, it seemed to gain a special significance.

Santagithi looked out over the village, watching children run and tumble between the neat array of cottages, seeing men and women traveling the dirt roads. Sheep dotted the grassy areas between the houses, and the metallic clang of the blacksmith's hammer sounded reassuringly familiar. Santigithi memorized the scene. Soon enough, that peace might be shattered, and he dared not guess for how long or even how much of his city or his people would remain in the end. He drew some solace from the fact that the Northmen's allegiance to the forces of good meant that his men would die with honor; their women and children would come to little harm. Had the West lost the Great War, the Easterners would have tortured his people, glorying in the screaming agony of rape and slaughter. The worst the Northmen would inflict upon survivors was the gladiator pit, and they might take a few of the women as house slaves. It was a scant comfort that only made Santagithi more determined to solve the problem peacefully, if possible, and successfully if his efforts at negotiation failed.

Santagithi entered his citadel, the hallway to his court seeming shorter than usual. Though he would have liked Colbey's presence from the start, he considered it politically reckless and unfair to make the Auerman wait too long. And the glimpse of his own city made him sensitive to their plight. His delay could cost them their village.

Alert, Santagithi loosened his sword in its scabbard and opened the door. Before his dais stood six men covered so thickly in trail dust that he could not distinguish the color of their garments. Each wore a crude leather hauberk and a flapped helmet that covered most of his head. Their cloaks bore the black silhouette of a dog that was Auer's symbol.

The wary stances and the unwrinkled, black and silver uniforms of Santagithi's six guardsmen who stood at their traditional posts along the walls made the Auermen look demoralized and broken in comparison. The familiarity of his court and the vigilance of his own men at arms relaxed Santagithi as he mounted the raised dais and took his seat.

The Auermen approached and knelt before Santagithi.

Santagithi waved for them to stand. 'There's no formality here. What can I do for you?'

The Auermen rose. The instant they did, all evidence of weariness vanished. They drew swords with gleaming edges, far too well crafted. As one, they sprang at Santagithi.

Despite his suspicions, the swift and coordinated attack of the Auermen caught Santagithi off his guard. He staggered to his feet, his chair tumbling from the dais. His foot came down on air. He plummeted from the platform, his leg jarring on flooring unexpectedly far beneath him. His clumsiness saved him. Three enemy swords rattled against one another. One more bit into the falling chair, jerking it into the path of a fifth soldier. The sixth sword swung true, tearing a gash in Santagithi's arm.

Pain cleared Santagithi's mind. Drawing his sword, he executed broad figure eights, weaving a barrier for his retreat. He could not hope to fight six men at once. He could only delay until his guards joined the fray.

Shouts and the rasp of drawing swords echoed through the court as Santagithi's guards sprang to his defense. A harried series of backsteps slammed Santagithi's heel into the wall behind him. He felt the weave of the paired war tapestries press his tunic into his back. A sea of swords whipped toward him. Two crashed against his blade, aching through his wound. Blood spilled, warm beneath his sleeve. A third sword surged for his face.

Santagithi ducked. The blade sang over his head, tangling in a tapestry. Seeing an opening, Santagithi lunged, his sword burying into the hollow between the wielder's shoulder and neck. The directed maneuver opened Santagithi's defenses. A blade ripped his thigh. Another gashed his forehead.

Blood loss weakened Santagithi, and the Auermen became a blur of steel and leather. Yet their attacks grew less furious as Santagithi's guards fell upon them. A gap appeared, and Santagithi dove through it, rolling from the center of the combat. A guard blocked pursuit with his person, and paid with his life. An Auerman's sword tore open his chest. He fell in silence.

Blood stung Santagithi's eyes, blinding him. He clung to the wall and to his consciousness, unable to find the strength he needed to return to the battle. He willed power into his failing limbs, catching a tighter hold on his sword in time to see an Auerman and a guard collapse together, swords thrust through one another's abdomens. Another of the visitors staggered from the melee, clutching at a geyser of blood from his thigh. An instant later, he toppled.

Three down, three to go. Santagithi raised his sword. Dizziness formed a buzzing curtain in his mind, threatening to overcome awareness. He tensed to charge back into battle, just as a chamber door swung open. For a moment, Colbey, Rache, Episte, and Harrit stood in the doorway. Santagithi followed the old Renshai's gaze to a body on the floor. The leather helmet had fallen away to reveal the blond war braids and pale features of a Northman.

Colbey howled, his swords flashing from sheath to hand to first cut in less time than it took Santagithi to register the Renshai's presence. One Northman fell dead before he realized he was menaced. The other two disengaged from Santagithi's guards and charged Colbey.

The weight of Santagithi's sword overpowered him. It fell, dragging the general to one knee. Blood loss dizzied him, and the battle seemed to spin in tight circles. He scarcely followed the Northmen's strikes, and Colbey looked like a gold-white blur. Blood streaked the gray haze that blurred his vision, and another Northman collapsed. The guards held back, forming a human wall between the battle and their general. Despite his disorientation, Santagithi counted four, hoping the last two were wounded, not casualties, though his visions of the battle told him otherwise.

Santagithi gathered the will to lurch to his feet, vertigo all but buffeting him back to the floor. Fighting the heaving of his stomach and the giant fist that seemed intent on hammering him to oblivion, Santagithi limped toward his dais. Colbey blocked his last opponent's upstroke between his swords. Suddenly, Rache dashed forward, ducking beneath Colbey's arm as he drew his light, short sword. When Colbey disengaged, the child plunged his blade into the Northman's lower back. The enemy stiffened. One of Colbey's swords sent the corpse skidding across the courtroom floor.

As one, the guardsmen spun to tend to their general, only to find that he had moved. As his followers' gazes found him, Santagithi tried to regain control. 'My court isn't a battlefield. Clean this up!' A sudden stab of pain made him catch his breath. 'Harrit, find out who hired these assassins.'

'Yes, sir.' Harrit knelt to examine the mutilated bodies.

'Who did we lose?' Santagithi asked softly.

One of the guardsmen replied. 'Kloras and Monsamer.'

Santagithi tried to gather his wits, holding his gaze on the rivulets of blood twining between his fingers. He feared that any movement of his head might steal his consciousness. 'Don't mention this incident to anyone until I've had a chance to talk to their families.' *Both married, one with children.* Santagithi cursed himself. *Had I waited for Colbey, none of ours would have died.*

The guards glanced at one another, torn between assisting their general and awaiting his commands. Until he either collapsed or asked for help, they dared not touch him.

Less impressed by rank, Colbey placed a steadying arm around Santagithi's waist. 'Come on, old friend. Let me see to those wounds.'

Everyone in the room relaxed tangibly. Weak from blood loss, Santagithi allowed Colbey to lead him out, without protest. Rache followed, gazing in fascination at his bloodied sword. Episte remained behind, more interested in or horrified by the corpses.

Colbey opened the door to the next room, revealing the smaller of Santagithi's two libraries. Shelves lined the walls, holding the handful of texts the general had managed to acquire, surrounded by curios: war trinkets and souvenirs. A single desk sat in the center of the room, along with a matching, wooden chair. Entering, Colbey escorted Santagithi to the seat. Santagithi sat, while the Renshai closed the door. Rache slid to the floor, his back wedged in a corner. The child sat in silence, mesmerized by the scarlet runnels trickling along his blade.

Colbey removed a pouch from his pocket, dumping the contents on the desktop. Bandages, vials, and packets bounced across the surface, one container rolling to the edge. Colbey snatched it before it went over the side. The movement drew his attention to the boy, and his eyes went cold. 'Rache! Show that sword some respect!' Grabbing a bandage, he tossed it to the child. It landed on Rache's sandal.

Rache started. Sheepishly, he collected the rag and set to work on his blade.

Sitting helped Santagithi to overcome his dizziness, but Colbey's quick movements made him queasy. He lowered his head to the table while Colbey tended the tears in his arm and thigh. Though sure and gentle, the Renshai's hands made Santagithi's wounds ache.

Harrit opened the door a crack. 'Sir?'

Santagithi looked up. Revived by pain and the staunching of his wounds, he felt more in control. He waved the guardsman into the room.

Harrit entered, offering a rolled piece of parchment.

Colbey bound Santagithi's leg, and pain made the general wince. 'What's this?'

Harrit shook his head. 'I don't know sir, I found it on one of the Northmen.' He flushed, as if he did not tell the whole story. 'I . . . um . . . I thought you should read it first.'

Santagithi's expression did not change, though he studied the guard's hesitation. The general placed great emphasis on literacy, and only those men who could read were considered for positions as officers. Clearly, Harrit could not. Perhaps embarrassed by his lack, Harrit had chosen to bring the note to his commander rather than his peers. 'Thank you, Harrit.' Santagithi unrolled the parchment, careful to angle it so that he alone could read it:

Surrender the Renshai!

Santagithi muttered a harsh oath, wadding the crude parchment between his fingers until it crumbled into pieces. Surely the six Northmen in his court had known they would die. Likely, they had believed their cause worth the sacrifice, their mission to kill Colbey first and himself second. The haze covering Santagithi's mind seemed to lift, driven away by the necessity for strategy. He would have to act quickly. Probably, the Northmen would stay their next offensive, at least until they discovered the outcome of the battle in Santagithi's court. If Tenja's men had slain Colbey, the king had no reason to attack again. And if they had killed Santagithi, the Vikerians would not expect retaliation until a new leader took command. Probably, they would even try to renegotiate with his replacement.

Colbey pulled the bandage around Santagithi's leg tight. 'So what is it?'

Santagithi spoke slowly, his thoughts distant. 'It's a declaration of war.'

Two days later, Santagithi and Garn led a hundred mounted soldiers through the Granite Hills. In the lead, Santagithi remained alert, senses no longer even slightly dulled from the incident in his court, though his wounds still throbbed. The sun gleamed from his breastplate and helmet; and, as he moved, highlights spun from the hedge of jagged cliffs on either side of the pass. His followers snaked in a double chain behind him, dressed in their leather uniforms and the bits and pieces of armor they had captured during forays, mostly bucklers, helmets, and shields. Garn rode the flank position, proudly garbed in the mail that Santagithi granted his officers.

So far, things had gone well. Santagithi's sharp eyes had spotted no movement but that of animals, nothing to indicate that Vikerian spies had seen them. His scouts reported an open way ahead. He had found his own officers the more pressing problem. Jakot and Bromdun had agreed to keep their troops behind to guard the town. They had followed their general's command without question, though their disappointment had shown through clearly. Mitrian had grumbled about her separation from Garn, challenging her father with a teenager's rebelliousness and a Renshai's exuberance. Yet Colbey had proven the most difficult.

Santagithi shivered, recalling the way the Renshai's cruel blue eyes had seemed to pierce him, as if to penetrate through his words to the intentions behind them. Though he knew it was impossible, he had felt as if the older man read his thoughts as well as his voice and expression. Yet Santagithi had found an argument that worked. Again, he could hear himself speaking words he never believed he would say: 'Colbey, our women and children may be the last bastion this town has. No one else has the time or experience to train them, and no one else could do so as quickly or competently as you. For now, and not for the only time, my town is in your hands.'

The scene carved another from the depths of memory, and the familiarity of war helped bring thoughts of his previous captain, Rache, to the forefront. Santagithi recalled a spring day years ago and words he had hurled in anger at a man more son than captain: 'You've been teaching my daughter to use a sword?! You stupid, pigheaded, overly aggressive, Northie bastard! How dare you! Are you insane?' Then, the idea of training a woman to war had outraged him. Now, it had become necessity.

Santagithi's ranks plodded silently through barren valleys, up the smaller slopes, and along narrow mountain ledges that made the general grit his teeth until every man reached secure ground. He kept his attention ahead, not wishing to miss any changes or movements from Vikerians or his own scouts. Snow-capped mountains passed into barren crests, then merged into the tree-covered ranges that sandwiched the Granite Hills, their distant peaks disappearing into the heavens for the gods' pleasures.

Again, Santagithi found himself on a shelf so narrow that his horse snorted with every step, its head bowed nearly to the ground. To his right, cliffs towered. To his left, the Hills opened into a canyon that seemed bottomless, crags protruding along its length from the mountains on either side. Attentive to his path, Santagithi kept his gaze lowered to the treacherous footing. By his scout's report, it was a long stretch, though fully passable.

Suddenly, a rumble touched the wariest edge of Santagithi's hearing. Before he could shout a warning, a boulder careened down the mountainside, dragging a horse and its rider into the canyon. A mass of rubble followed it down the slope. *Avalanche?* Santagithi's mind dismissed the possibility at once. His scouts had reported a solidity to the rock face that precluded the possibility, which was why he had chosen this route.

More boulders crashed down the hillside, every one clearly beginning its course from the summit. *Ambush!* Fury exploded across Santagithi's thoughts as he realized the gravity of his mistake. *There're Northmen on that crest.*

The ranks broke. Guardsmen fled in panic while Santagithi screamed for order. A stone slammed toward the general. Diverted by a jutting outcrop, it swept the horse behind him from the ledge. Its rider pinwheeled over the side. Santagithi made a desperate grab, managing only to touch his guard's fingers before momentum carried the man to his death.

Anguish clotted Santagithi's anger, and strategy came to him as naturally as breathing. *The ledge extends too far, We can't outrun them. We'll be helpless if we try.* He studied the cliff face, calculating instantly. 'Take the hill!' Santagithi drew his sword, jabbing it toward the tumbling boulders. He wheeled his horse, charging along the path to relay his order himself, even as stones swept his men from the ledge.

Garn hesitated. Then, to Santagithi's relief, the ex-gladiator kicked his horse toward the crags. The animal plunged up the granite slope, floundering but making definite progress. 'Come on!' Garn spurred his men with insults instead of commands. 'Move, you cowardly bastards!'

'Fastin! Marly!' Santagithi remained below, prodding horses with the flat of his sword and men with his tone. 'Draw those weapons, or you'll face worse than stones.'

Santagithi's horse thundered across the farthest edge of the path, a finger's breadth from a fall. Trusting the surefooted mount he had used for years, Santagithi goaded his men without heed to his own danger.

Gradually, the soldiers fell back under his control. Though it seemed like certain suicide, they trusted and obeyed, charging up the cliffs and dodging the falling rubble as best they could. Below, Santagithi heaved a sigh of relief, hoping for the best. Under Garn's supervision, the first wave of Santagithi's soldiers met an incredulous band of Northmen clutching boulders instead of swords. Though outnumbered, Santagithi's men, chosen for stealth and skill, had many advantages over Northern marksmen. Hooves and slashing swords found their mark. Unable to mount their horses fast enough, the Vikerians discovered that a galloping steed slays as quickly as a boulder. When Santagithi gained the crest, he discovered his men embroiled in a slaughter.

The film of trampled bodies on the slope belied the true tally of the dead. Many times more warriors had plummeted to their demise in the jagged valley below. A few of the Vikerians mounted horses and fled. But Santagithi estimated that eight dozen of their companions found death. His own army fared better. Fifty-seven bedraggled swordsmen sorted themselves out from the corpses. A hurried search uncovered eleven more, injured more critically. Santagithi waited while his guardsmen supported their injured companions across the withers or behind the saddles of their mounts. With many Northern horses in tow, Santagithi and Garn led the ranks back to town.

Santagithi said little, his mind spinning from self-directed anger to outrage against the king he had once trusted as an ally. Then another portion of his thoughts kicked in, assessing the wisdom of the Northmen's strategy. Santagithi had lost more than thirty men, yet the outcome could have proven far worse. His mind sifted ideas, seeing the flaws in the Vikerians' plan and finding ways to plug those gaps and reuse the strategy to his own advantage.

Straw covered the floor of the loft bedroom nestled amid the eaves of Emerald's cottage. A pair of filled mattresses and pillows stood side by side, pressed against opposite walls. Episte Rachesson balanced on the top rung of the ladder, the light from candles in the main room casting the barest edge of his shadow into the dark loft. Rache sat on the leftmost mattress, his thick legs crossed and his sword lying, unsheathed, in his lap.

Episte liked the rare times when his younger friend stayed overnight. Though they spent much of the day together, they found no time to talk or play during Colbey's lessons. Afterward, Episte had little energy for anything more than talk, and the childish chases of his peers through the streets of the town held scant appeal. Like brothers, he and Rache shared a language and experiences few could understand, and none of those others were children.

Episte tucked his knees to his chin. He spoke Renshai to keep the conversation private, though they were alone. 'So what's it like to really stab someone?'

Rache looked up, his sandy hair sliding into his eyes. Having learned both tongues at once, he could switch back and forth more fluently than Episte. 'Hard,' Rache said, his young voice scarcely sounding the consonants. He ran a hand along the flat of his blade with gentle reverence, well trained. 'Like stabbing . . . ' His face screwed into a twisted parody of consideration. '. . . rocks almost.' His green eyes met Episte's blue, darkness blurring them both to gray.

Episte nodded, at once proud and jealous of his 'brother.' 'You should have seen those Northmen. All hacked up and bloody and stuff.' He imitated vomiting, using the trade common, child's euphemism for a nauseating spectacle. 'It was bleffy.'

Rache turned Episte a reverent look. 'They tried to kill my grandpa.'

Episte nodded agreement, the conversation at an end. 'I'm going to ask my momma for a drink of water.' He started down the rungs.

Gently, Rache lay his sword on the mattress, then leapt to his feet. 'Wait. I want water, too.' He trotted after his brother.

Episte waited at the bottom of the ladder. Already, Rache stood as tall as he did, and the younger child out-weighed him. But the girth of Rache's limbs made them seem stubby, and it would take him years to master the coordination that came naturally to Episte.

Episte glanced around the living room while Rache descended. He had expected to find his mother here. Candles in metal holders flickered from shelves higher than Episte's reach. No one sat on the chest that served for storage and as a piece of furniture. Beneath his mother's winter clothing lay the last remembrances of Episte's father: a leather jerkin speckled with the ancient stains of dirt and blood, a wheel, a hilt from a broken sword, and a poignard and buckler stripped from a dead enemy. Across from the chest, his mother's cushioned rocker sat empty. Above it, a thick leather flap closed off the room's only window.

'Momma?' Episte said tentatively. Once she had tucked him into bed, Emerald did not allow him to go further than this room. Two exits left the area. He walked to the one into the hearth room, peeking around the corner with a caution that kept his hands and feet in the living room. He found the hearth room dark and empty. Crossing the room, he glanced through the other exit. The blanket still covered his mother's mattress, undisturbed. A lantern burned on the bedside crate.

Episte turned to find Rache standing on the cushion of the rocker, brushing aside the flap. Moonlight spilled through the crack, and a muffled conversation entered with it. Recognizing his mother's voice, Episte clambered up beside his blood brother.

'. . . so the old bastard calls Rache a man now. Can you imagine a child scarcely out of diapers forced to be an adult?'

The voice that followed belonged to one of the female villagers, a close friend of Emerald's with two daughters a few years older than Episte. 'Is he calling Episte a man, too?'

Rache fidgeted, sending the chair into a bucking lurch that nearly threw the children. Episte reversed his equilibrium, clutching his 'brother' to help the youngster keep his balance.'

Emerald was speaking. '. . . can't be good for his self-confidence to have a baby half his age considered a man while he's still just a child.'

Episte kept a firm grip on Rache. He knew his mother was talking about Colbey, Rache, and himself. In general terms, he understood that it bothered her that Rache had become blooded first. He wanted to comfort her, to tell her that his time would come soon, too; but he did not want to get in trouble for being downstairs after bedtime.

Emerald's tone went bitter. 'Leave it to Colbey to teach that killing someone makes a boy into a man. Pah!' She spit. 'Killing someone only makes a boy a killer.'

These words Episte comprehended. He glanced quickly at Rache, but his little brother seemed more intent on his balance than the conversation.

The neighbor rushed to the child's defense. 'Now, Emerald. Rache's a sweet little boy. You've said yourself you love him like a second son.'

'Well, I'm sorry.' Emerald's tone contradicted her words. 'But the last thing that boy needs is a violent crazyman turning him more savage than his bloodline already does. After what happened with Garn, you'd think Santagithi would be more careful. That boy has his father's eyes and his father's size. Do you doubt that he'll get his father's temper as well?'

Now Rache cocked his head, listening. 'They's talking about us?' It was more question than statement, though to Episte it went without saying.

'Yes.' Episte made a quieting gesture. Their brief conversation had already lost him the neighbor's reply. But Emerald's words came clearly to Episte. 'That's because you didn't see what Rache was like after Garn broke his back. You didn't have to watch the most beautiful hero in the world struggle to remain a shadow of what he had been.' Emerald's voice quivered as she lapsed into tears. 'Colbey's training hammered into him since infancy the need to die in glorious combat, and my Rache never learned to find any of the simple pleasures in life. Everything he did, he did in the grandest fashion possible, until a wild, vicious animal of a slave turned him into a cripple. Then, just because that slave marries our leader's daughter, suddenly we're supposed to trust his temper.'

Stunned, Episte remained still, sorting the story as his mind grasped it.

'Now, Emerald . . . ' the woman started, but Emerald could not quit.

'Damn it, I was there after Garn killed his playmate. What happens when little Rache flies into one of his father's rages and hurts Episte?'

'Emerald, you're being ridiculous. Rache isn't three years old yet.'

'And he's already helped kill a man.' Emerald drove her point home. 'Garn was only ten when he slaughtered Mukesh, and he hadn't had any combat training from that senile old Northman.'

Episte had heard enough. He pressed the flap tightly to the window, clamping the conversation into an indecipherable buzz. 'Come on.' He squeezed Rache protectively, dragging the child from the chair. He tried to thrust his mother's words from his mind, but they returned again and again: 'What happens when little Rache . . . hurts Episte.'

Episte knew that his mother had to be wrong. He thought of all the times that Emerald and Colbey had contradicted one another. His mother always claimed that it came of Colbey's strange background, that Episte should learn swordplay from the old Renshai but nothing more. Colbey said that Emerald sometimes put being a good mother ahead of the truth. He claimed that she meant well, but that Episte should not believe everything she said. Their differences confused Episte, but Renshai and mother had raised him. He had no choice except to trust both and to hope he would one day get big enough to understand.

At the bottom of the ladder, Rache turned. 'My daddy made your daddy not walk?'

The question startled Episte. Having grasped only part of the conversation himself, he had not expected Rache to get even that much. 'I think so. Let's get back upstairs.'

Rache climbed. At the third rung, he stopped, arching his head backward to look at Episte upside down. His baby fine hair covered his shoulders like a cloak. 'What's a slave?'

'I don't know.' Episte nudged Rache. 'Come on. Go up. You're blocking.'

Rache scurried to the top of the ladder, then whirled, meeting Episte partway up. 'I wouldn't ever hurt you.'

Episte accepted the words as a challenge. 'You couldn't if you wanted to. I could beat you with a sword in my butt.' He trotted up the ladder, shoving Rache aside, surprised by the amount of strength it took.

Rache giggled, moving aside. 'What if I had a sword in both . . . each . . . every hand?' He waved his arms excitedly. 'And in my feet?' He stuck his toes in Episte's face as he crawled through the loft opening. '*And* in my butt?'

'I'd still beat you, turd toes.' Episte kicked Rache's feet out of his way, then crossed the room and lay on his pallet.

Rache followed, hesitantly glancing between the beds before ignoring his own pallet and crawling in beside Episte instead.

Rache's body cramped Episte against the wall; but, for now, he felt better for the boy's presence. 'Neither one of us will ever hurt each other. Right?'

'Yup.' Rache snuggled closer.

'Promise?'

'Pwomiss.'

'We're brothers, like Colbey says.'

'*Blood* brothers,' Rache said.

Episte knew the relationship had more significance to Colbey than true brotherhood.

'Forever and ever and ever and ever.'

14 Talus Fan

Santagithi paced the lane between his strategy table and the map-covered wall, oblivious to the stares of his commanders that followed his course to and fro. Jakot and Bromdun sat sideways in their chairs to keep from turning their backs on their general. Across the table, Mitrian, Garn, and Colbey remained in silence.

Thirty-two men dead and eleven more out of combat. Thirty-four if I consider the two killed in my court. The needless destruction enraged Santagithi. *And all because I've walked into two Vikerian ambushes.* Mentally, he cursed himself and the incaution that had cost nearly a tenth of his able-bodied fighting men. *This can't go on. We have to turn the tables before we lose anyone else.* He considered King Tenja and the Northmen's ranks, his mind gnawing at the problem. At the start of the Great War, Tenja had commanded two hundred fifty soldiers to Santagithi's six hundred. The war had whittled his army to four hundred fifty and Tenja's to just under two hundred.

Santagithi reached the far wall and pivoted back to face the door. 'Competent, eager soldiers, brave to the point of recklessness.' Santagithi assessed the Vikerians. Then, realizing he had spoken aloud, he explained. 'The Northmen, I mean. Dedicated to their leaders like priests to gods and impressed by a skilled warrior to the point of following him to their graves.' Santagithi stopped, spinning to face the map of the Granite Hills. Finger-traced a million times, the familiar passes seemed to leap to bold relief. Only three routes led from Santagithi's Town to the Northlands, and they all overlapped at some points. 'Put Northmen in a straight line, and they'll hack their way through any wall. But they're not strategists.'

Santagithi's brow furrowed as he worried the information he had just spoken aloud. 'Usually,' he added carefully. Suddenly, all of his mistakes came back to the same misinformation. He whirled toward the table. 'Damn it, those Northmen aren't acting like Northmen.' He pounded a fist on the table between Jakot and Bromdun. 'Who taught those Northie bastards to think!' Usually, strong emotion in the strategy room inspired creative thought. Realizing he might have just offended one of his own, Santagithi regretted his outburst. He planted both hands on the table, turning his attention to Colbey.

The old Renshai returned Santagithi's gaze mildly, a slight smile on his face. He looked more amused than insulted. 'Valr Kirin,' he said.

The reply to his mostly rhetorical question caught Santagithi by surprise. 'What?'

'Valr Kirin,' Colbey repeated. 'That's who taught the Vikerians to think. Actually, he's probably doing their thinking for them.'

Santagithi returned to his seat at the head of the table. He remembered Tenja's lieutenant, a bold, masterful warrior borrowed from the high king in Nordmir. Forced to tend strategy for the combined armies, Santagithi had had few dealings with Kirin Raskogsson who had led Tenja's cavalry, a man the Northmen called 'Valr' which meant 'Slayer.' However, charged with the Pudarian cavalry, Colbey had spent a great deal of time with Kirin. Then, Colbey's heroics had stolen the loyalty of Kirin's followers, and the two had developed an enmity. Now, Santagithi wondered whether this hatred might not have driven Kirin to explore Colbey's background and, ultimately, led to the current war. 'Colbey, I'd like you to stay for a while after the meeting to discuss some details about this lieutenant. In the meantime, I'd appreciate it if you'd keep him in mind while we're planning strategy.'

Everyone glanced at Colbey, who nodded once.

Santagithi rarely placed so much trust in any single man. Always, he insisted on personally having every shred of information in order to form the intricate plots that had made his tiny army as competent as those of the massive cities westward. 'Currently, we have the advantage of numbers. That may change quickly, especially after this morning's defeat.' He glanced at Colbey, who nodded again.

'Kirin knows the difference between vanity and honor. He'll send them for help sooner, especially since he's not a Vikerian himself.'

'I think it's time to call in our allies as well. Jakot, I want messages sent to King Sterrane in Béarn as well as to Prince . . . ' He corrected himself. '. . . *King* Verrall in Pudar.'

Colbey smiled.

Santagithi tapped his fingers on the table, bothered by the knowledge that months would pass before a messenger could reach Pudar and many more months before Verrall could send an army. The trips to and from Béarn would take still longer. 'Colbey, you said Shadimar has a falcon who carries notes. Do you think he'd let us borrow it?' Santagithi considered the possibility of using other animal messengers. Any land creature would take as long to travel as a man on horseback, and it could only deliver, not speak, its news. He doubted any of the many songbirds that flitted about the Westlands could make the journey safely, even if he had the time to teach it and it had the intelligence to understand its mission.

'We can only ask Shadimar.' Colbey sounded doubtful. 'So far, my two experiences with Swiftwing make me think he only carries notes from Wizard to Wizard. You know how Shadimar can be about sharing things, even a simple explanation, with mere mortals.'

Santagithi thought he caught a tinge of bitterness in Colbey's voice and made a mental note to question the Renshai later. 'It's worth trying.' Instantly, Santagithi saw a way to handle two situations at once. 'Mitrian, you've been to Shadimar's ruins before?' Still uncomfortable with the idea of his daughter at war, Santagithi grasped at the chance to send her elsewhere.

'Yes.' Mitrian fidgeted, obviously uncomfortable. 'Well, no, actually. I went there once in a really vivid dream that became real and . . . ' Realizing she was babbling, Mitrian fell silent, flushing. 'I'm sure I could find him.'

'Good. Jakot, I still want the messengers dispatched as soon as possible. Send a group of three each way. Pick good horses and good horsemen. Stealth wouldn't hurt, and at least one in each group should know how to fight reasonably well.'

'Yes, sir,' Jakot said.

Santagithi followed up with the plan that had trickled into his mind just after the Vikerians' ambush and had only now come to fruition. 'When we were out there on the ledge and the first boulders fell, what was your earliest thought?' Santagithi looked at Garn, the only other officer present at the time.

Though Santagithi's gaze clearly fell on him, Garn looked to the left and right, as if to make certain. 'That more might be coming?' When Santagithi continued to stare, Garn tried the bowmen's scattershot approach, throwing out as many answers as possible in the hope of a single bull's-eye. 'That the Northmen were too cowardly to come down to us and fight like men. That we needed to be ready to dodge. That we needed to get off that ledge as fast as possible.' He added one more, apparently to appease Santagithi. 'That we were damn lucky to have the West's prime strategist leading us, because otherwise we would have all been killed.'

Santagithi made another mental note, to keep Garn's title honorary and to make certain his son-in-law always remained under his or Jakot's direct command. *At least he does seem good at inspiring the men, and he doesn't panic.* 'My first thought was that it was a natural rock slide.'

'That, too,' Garn added lamely.

Santagithi continued as if no one had interrupted. He rose, walking to the map. 'But I knew the terrain too well. Here, those boulders could not have fallen by accident.' He indicated the area of the encounter with a finger. 'But here . . . ' He traced three triangular areas on the slope of the most direct route between Vikerin and home. '. . . at the base of these mountains . . . ' He swept a hand over a series of ridges above and beside the trail. '. . . are a series of talus fans.' He looked up to ascertain that his officers had followed.

'Talus fans?' Mitrian said, as if on cue.

Jakot answered first. 'Natural, loose collections of stone and debris.'

Santagithi turned back to the map. 'Up here . . . ' Again, he indicated the higher slopes above the trail. '. . . we could set up a trap similar to the one the Vikerians sprang on us, but using the steepest slopes and the talus fans. We might be able to destroy the remainder of their army before they can gather allies. *Gentlemen, if this is successful, we might end the war in days.*' The idea made Santagithi smile, though briefly. 'But it's not going to be easy. First, we have to give them a reason to take this particular path. Second, we need them closely bunched, not with scouts and formations spread beyond the region of the fans.'

Jakot rose, studying the map. 'It is the shortest route. Maybe if we could anger them enough, they might choose speed over caution.'

Garn yawned, clearly bored with the talk of strategy. 'Maybe if we ambushed their king in his own court. That might anger them to reckless stupidity.'

The comment struck too close to home. As always, Santagithi reined his temper. 'Effective, Garn, but it's already been done.' He glanced at Colbey.

The Renshai rose, his expression even more stern than usual. Apparently, he had wrestled his conscience for the suggestion he was about to speak aloud. 'Do you still have the bodies of the Northmen killed in court?'

'We could dig them up.' Santagithi said nothing more, curious about Colbey's plan.

'I believe I can enrage even Kirin. If you can set the trap, I can bait it. All I ask is that you let me be there to see the results.'

Santagithi frowned. The idea of Colbey's presence at the talus fans did not bother him. Stationed high above sheer mountainsides covered with shifting debris, his men should not become embroiled in hand-to-hand combat. At worst, the Northmen would escape the trap, and the plans would come to nothing. His concerns stemmed from what Colbey might mean by 'bait.' 'Fine,' he said, at length. 'But first, we'll discuss this plan of yours when we talk about Valr Kirin. If I think it's too dangerous, we'll find another.'

Colbey smiled knowingly. 'General, I wouldn't have it any other way.'

*

Familiar with the magical tempest that warded Shadimar's ruins, Mitrian had the foresight to wear a heavy, hooded cloak and to pack a well-protected change of clothes; but that did not fully spare her from the rain. She led her mare past the two headless statues that stood sentinel before the long-dead city of Myrcidë. Dripping trails from her clothing and wet hoofprints betrayed their route. Lightning spidered the sky behind her, and thunder echoed between the granite walls and arches of the inner streets. Shattered stonework littered a courtyard that Mitrian remembered from her dream. Blueberries dotted the vine-choked walls and bushes filling the stretches between crumbling, ancient pillars and monuments. Mitrian smiled at the darting songbirds gorging on the berries, their beaks and talons purple-smeared. Their skimming flight from bushes to statues to walls unnerved Mitrian's horse, so she hurried through the open area and down the streets and alleyways.

The horse whinnied nervously, head low as it picked its way over and around the fragments. Each blast of thunder sent it into a rigid standstill. Gentle coaxing and movement away from the lash of the storm convinced it to continue; but, each time, its first steps became short, stiff jumps. Its antics worried Mitrian. The last time she had visited, her mare had calmed the instant it entered the ruins. The closer they had come to Shadimar, and the longer they remained, the more secure the horse had become. *Of course, that was a dream*, Mitrian reminded herself, though every feature of the ruins seemed exactly as she remembered it.

Mitrian came, at last, to the vast, roofed hall that formed the entrance to Shadimar's home. There, she found a heavy stone door blocking her way. A curl of parchment balanced on the grisly brass face that held the door's ring.

Mitrian stopped, uncertain where to go. At the time of her other visit, Shadimar had met her here; and he had left the door open. Looping the horse's reins around a pillar, she approached the door. She knocked, the stone chafing her knuckles. The sound scarcely reached to her own ears. Certain the Eastern Wizard could never hear her through a door this heavy, she pounded as hard as she could with the side of her fist. The breeze of her motion sent the parchment fluttering to the ground at her feet.

Stooping, Mitrian picked up the note. She had no intention of reading it, certain it concerned private matters between Wizards. But she glimpsed her own name at the top. The writer had used the common trading tongue in a fine, easily legible hand. Curious, she read:

My dear Mitrian:
  I apologize for the soaking and for the wasted trip. I find myself

engaged in matters of grave importance, and it may take years before I return. Rest assured, I could not have helped you in the matter of your visit. The messenger falcon, Swiftwing, is not mine to lend.

Please pass my regards and my sympathy to Colbey and your father. I will keep abreast of the events in your town. If and when Santagithi truly needs me, I will be here.

Shadimar

Mitrian pocketed the note, a shiver of supernatural discomfort fluttering through her. She had spent nearly two years in the Eastern Wizard's company while they researched, plotted, and carried out Sterrane's return to his throne as well as the journeys to and from Béarn. In all that time, he had performed only one feat she considered magic, the sky pictures he had summoned to accompany Mar Lon's music. Yet a gift for illusion did not explain the strangeness she always felt in his presence nor his foreknowledge of events he should have no way of predicting.

Turning from the Eastern Wizard's door, Mitrian headed back to her mount.

Valr Kirin Raskogsson stood before the Vikerian throne, his war braids hissing against his jerkin with every movement. He studied King Tenja from a face hardened by age and war. His hawklike nose and piercing blue eyes heightened the predatory look of his features. 'Sire, there's a matter we need to discuss.' Kirin plucked at the hilt of his sword, hoping the words that he needed would come to him in time. When he had requested an audience that morning, he had felt certain that they would. Now, standing before King Tenja, the king's adviser, and his bodyguard, Kirin found himself nearly speechless, glad for the lack of spectators.

King Tenja perched on his throne, a gaudy trinket adorned with lesser stones that were buffed and polished to appear like gems. His gray-tinged braids swung about his muscled neck. He wore a shirt and matching cloak of fur-trimmed silk that defined a physique trained to war. To his left, his pale, frail adviser watched Kirin expectantly. Named Alvis, the aging, balding Northman seemed lost in a wolfskin wrap. To the king's right, the massive, ugly bodyguard stood with his hands crossed over his chest. From beneath his horned helmet, Eldir regarded The Slayer with the same dead-eyed indifference he grudgingly granted every man. His ax-bladed pole arm rested against the wall, within easy reach.

When Valr Kirin did not go on, King Tenja encouraged. 'Speak freely, Kirin Raskogsson of Nordmir. We have fought side by side and at one another's backs.'

Valr Kirin knew that the king's words meant that he was trusted not only as a subordinate, but as an ally. It only made his pronouncement more difficult to speak. 'Sire, you know that I spent some time recently on the Northern shore of Asci.'

'Summoned by one who claimed to be the Northern Sorceress. Yes, I know that. Did something happen there?'

Kirin glanced about the room, from its rough-hewn, empty rows of chairs, to the wooden doors painted to look like metal and the awkward carvings that mimicked the wealth of the Western Kingdoms. 'Something of a sort, yes, Sire. Lady Trilless alerted me to a danger far more extensive than even you and I had guessed.' He glanced up suddenly, hoping he had not become too presumptuous by placing a limit on the king's speculation. He did not want to offend. 'Sire, she claimed that, if not destroyed, Colbey is destined to annihilate all goodness, all Northmen, and, possibly, the gods themselves.' Kirin swallowed hard.

King Tenja sat in silence for a moment. Alvis became even paler. Eldir remained stony-faced, revealing no emotion at all by his features, though his hand caressed the bulbous hilt of his sword.

'Sire, she believes that the Southern Wizard will try to see to it that Colbey fulfills this prophecy. And also that Colbey will pursue it viciously and with malice, even at the cost of those he loves.'

The king's hands balled into fists, and the veins swelled beneath sun-damaged skin. 'As if a Renshai could love anything, except the destruction he reaps. We're doing what we can to kill the Renshai. Did you tell her that?'

'Yes, Sire.' Valr Kirin nodded. He looked at his feet.

'There's more?' King Tenja prodded, though surely he had heard enough.

'Yes, Sire, there is more.' Valr Kirin forced himself to meet the king's gaze, having come to the part that he knew would make the king most uncomfortable. 'She asked me to become her champion. Her cause is goodness and morality. How could I refuse such an honor?'

'So you accepted her offer.'

'Gladly.'

'What does that mean?'

Valr Kirin plucked at the sword at his belt, recalling when Trilless had handed Ristoril to him. The simple scabbard hid a blade that shone like the midday sun, its purity a constant, reassuring presence at his side. 'Sire, it means I have to place the cause of right and principle above all else.'

King Tenja's eyes narrowed as he interpreted the meaning of Kirin's pronouncement, as it pertained to Vikerin. 'You mean that you serve her first and us second.'

'In a manner of speaking, yes, Sire.' Valr Kirin measured the king's mood, and he found it discomfited. 'But, for now, Vikerin's cause and hers are the same. There's no reason to think that would change.'

Eldir and Alvis watched their king closely. The bodyguard rocked from foot to foot. The adviser rubbed his hands together in a habitual gesture.

The king clarified further, gaze still locked on that of his lieutenant. 'But if our causes separated, you would follow hers.'

Valr Kirin knew the answer that the king wanted, but he would not lie. 'Yes, Sire.'

Tenja heaved a great sigh that shuddered through his muscled body. 'My men's safety means too much to place them in the hands of a leader not wholly committed to them.'

Kirin lowered his head. 'I understand, Sire.'

'No, you don't understand!' King Tenja's fists clamped over the armrests of his chair like huge, white boulders. 'Damn it, Kirin, you're the best warrior I've ever had and the finest leader. We're in the middle of a war, by Thor's beard! Why now?'

'I'm sorry, Sire. I didn't choose the time.'

Tenja opened his mouth, his face purpling as if filled with all the blood his gripping hands had lost. Before he could speak, the doors rattled open, and a soldier named Thorfin stood in the entryway. A lumpy, brown-stained parcel swung from his hand, held at arm's length.

All turned at the interruption. Valr Kirin stepped aside to make room for King Tenja's soldier, glad to be free of the massive king's attention for a time.

The warrior walked toward the throne hesitantly, his gaze straying repeatedly to the package he carried, then shying away as quickly. It appeared as if Thorfin did not wish even to look at the parcel; yet he feared that if he glanced away, it might harm him. His shuffling approach seemed to span an eternity.

King Tenja's patience evaporated before the soldier reached a polite distance for conversation. 'What do you have there?'

Thorfin continued his journey as he answered. 'It's a package, Sire. It came strapped to the back of a horse. One of ours, I believe, that we lost in the battle.' The effort of speaking and moving at once seemed too much for Thorfin. The bundle slipped from his fingers, plummeting to the floor. It landed with an almost liquid slap, and its contents settled to the shape of the floor. Mouth wide in horror, Thorfin looked up. He made no move to reclaim the package nor to move around it.

'What is it?' Tenja demanded.

Thorfin shook his head, sending his gold braids into a whipping dance. 'I'm not exactly certain, Sire.'

'Asps or some such,' Alvis said sourly. 'Destroy it and have done.'

Valr Kirin studied the pack from a distance, certain that the dark stains came from blood. He saw no movement to make him agree with the adviser's guess.

'Open it,' Tenja said.

All the color drained from Thorfin's face. He edged toward the parcel obediently.

Sympathetic to Thorfin's fear, Valr Kirin took a step forward to handle the matter for the soldier. Before he could move any closer, Eldir shoved through, clutching his ax. He glared at Thorfin. 'Warriors don't shrink from the unknown; they destroy doubts with bloodshed.' Using his gigantic frame to shield the king, Eldir cleaved the pack. Twelve severed hands spilled to the floor. They lay paler in death than life, streaked brown, their fingers stiffly bent in rigor.

Grief and outrage clutched Valr Kirin at once. Even Eldir recoiled so suddenly that his horned helm slid askew. No note or explanation accompanied the package, but the Northmen needed none. Without a doubt, these were Vikerian hands that should wield weapons in Valhalla. Now the souls of those brave soldiers would rot in Hel, barred from the reward they'd earned by the malicious swordsman who had dismembered them. History and precedent dictated who that man must be. *Colbey did this, still every bit a Renshai.*

Silence hovered, while all five men stood like carved ivory. The king's face went nearly black. 'Infidel! Beast! Child of Demons! Go. Kill him now. Kill him yesterday.' Tenja's eyes flashed with rage-inspired madness.

'Sire, no.' Valr Kirin spoke softly.

Tenja's attention whipped suddenly to his lieutenant. 'Don't ever try to command me, Slayer. I've killed men for less.'

'Sire, please. I'm not trying – '

The king sprang from his chair, jabbing a finger at Valr Kirin. 'Quiet. You and I still need to talk.' He spun to face Eldir. 'Swiftly, lead B ranks through the hills. Leave no enemy alive. Slay as Northmen were meant, like wild wolves berserk with blood hunger!'

Eldir howled a war call that reverberated through the chamber. Still clutching his poleax, he charged through the doorways. Soon his cries echoed down the corridors as soldiers became caught up in the battle frenzy he inspired.

Alvis slumped with his head in his hands. King Tenja faced the wall, his fist striking the gaudy tiles repeatedly. Sorrow filled Kirin Raskogsson, for the men disembered as well as those rushing to certain death. *If only I had held my news a few moments longer, he might have listened. I could have saved those lives.* Kirin cursed his timing once again. Calmly, he lowered his head, offering prayers to Odin and waiting for the king's acknowledgment.

Though no lower on the crags than any of his men, Colbey saw the Vikerians first. They milled and wove without regimentation, and Colbey knew that they frothed and howled like rabid beasts. Their lust for slaughtering enemies would overcome all caution. Surely some had partaken of the berserker mushrooms that inspired men to fearless insanity. Others whipped themselves into blood frenzy with focused outrage and promises of vengeance. Like Colbey, they all welcomed death. Yet they would not find it in the cold passion of steel. If Santagithi's strategy went as planned, there would be no swordplay.

'Northmen coming!' A sentry steered his mount cautiously around the huge natural triangle of loose rock to the warriors clustered above it.

Colbey raised his arm as the Northmen came into full view on the ledge beneath the talus fan. Their war cries bounced from the cliffs, loosing bits of shale, which tumbled harmlessly down the slope. Colbey examined them, finding nearly fifty braided reavers led by a muscle-bound warrior in mail. The sight stirred a primitive hatred in the depths of his soul. Still he waited, with his hand raised, as the Northmen passed beneath him. The plan called for him to drop the fan not on, but after the Vikerians, blocking escape. A quarter mile farther along, Garn would drop another collection of talus just before them, trapping the Northmen in place before Santagithi's central pile of stone shattered them.

Colbey's men on the mountaintop trembled in anticipation, but their leader waited until the trailing Northmen passed the outer edge of the fan. Then the Renshai dropped his arm, and his followers raced to their task. Boulders bounced through the precariously balanced talus. The mountain shuddered, then it shook beneath an explosion of dirt, slate, and boulders.

What little remained of the Northmen's formation broke into confusion. The narrow ledge did not give them room to turn their horses, so they plunged forward, heedless of those directly before them, to escape the stones thundering down upon them. Nevertheless, when the avalanche trickled to dust, nearly all of the troop remained intact. An unstable pile of rubble blocked their retreat. The wolf howls faded to a relative silence, punctuated by whispered questions.

Colbey listened for the sound of Garn's talus fan falling ahead, and the hush nagged at him. *Come on, Garn. Get that thing moving.*

The Northmen had little reason to believe the rock slide was anything but a natural result of their shouts, but Eldir scanned the cliffs.

Colbey froze, glancing over his men. The horses snorted and danced, tied well above and beyond sight of the Northmen. His men dotted the mountainside, dressed in gray that blended into the stone. Eldir's need to stare into the sun only made the hiding easier. After a time, the Vikerian gestured his followers forward, making a brisk motion to keep them quieter.

Still, Colbey heard nothing ahead. The leading fan had not yet fallen. *Something's wrong.* Rage trickled through Colbey. The trap had taken too much planning to fail now. He made a cutting motion that ordered his men to remain in place, then ran to his horse. Mounting, he spurred the animal through a rift along the higher ledge. His ride took him past Santagithi's dark-clothed soldiers, waiting with massed piles of bolders, then he drew up even with Garn's pile of shale. Harried guardsmen swore, rolling boulders that rattled through the talus fan and flew over the slope but did not set the talus in motion.

Below, the Vikerians rode toward them. Colbey pulled up his horse as the Northmen drew even with the fan above them.

Garn's men had begun to tire, and the hail of boulders ceased. Colbey's obvious frustration sent his horse into a sideways prance. Unmounted and unarmored on the cliffs, Garn's men would need time to prepare before they could catch up to the Northmen and engage them in battle. Meanwhile, the enemy might reach Santagithi's Town, in all their wild fury, with only an abbreviated force to meet them.

Inflamed, Colbey kicked his horse toward the edge of the cliff above the mountain. The beast hesitated briefly. Then momentum carried it over the side. A boulder shifted beneath the impact of horse and rider. The horse skidded into talus, shrilling as it lost its footing. Stones jostled down the mountainside. For a moment, nothing happened. Then silence broke under a deafening roar.

Colbey's horse dragged its hooves, scrambling desperately for a hold. Northmen dived recklessly from the path of the falling talus. Eldir spurred his mount, and it responded with a burst of speed even as the thundering torrent of stone buried the rider at his heels. The leader alone escaped in front of the avalanche. Most of his troop lay, shredded corpses beneath layers of rock. Others had fallen from the ledge into the canyons below. The survivors milled, trapped between rock slides and at the mercy of Santagithi's men.

Colbey fought the wild surges of his horse as it slid toward the pile of rock. Though no longer in motion and piled on the ledge, the talus would surely shift under the weight of Colbey's animal, carrying man and beast over the edge. He struggled for control of his panicked steed. As they stumbled toward the talus, the stone grew less steady. Another rock shifted beneath the animal's hooves, sending it into an uncontrolled slide. Then its hooves bunched on a solid crag. At Colbey's urging, it sprang to the ledge below, on the far side of the fallen stones.

With a howl of triumph, Colbey dug his heels into the horse's side. It leapt forward, galloping after the single retreating Northman. As he closed, Colbey hunkered over its neck, sword drawn.

Apparently hearing the hoofbeats, Eldir swiveled. Seeing Colbey, he cursed and freed his sword. Yet the narrow pathway left no room for him to turn safely. He faced forward, jabbing his horse into a run as Colbey slowly closed the gap between them.

Eldir kept his mount flush with the mountain wall so that Colbey could not draw up beside him. But bloodsickness was on the Renshai like physical pain. Again risking his life on a horse's footing, he tore his reins to the right, drawing his horse to the far side of the fleeing Vikerian. The gelding pulled up effortlessly, its rapidly moving hooves the length of a dagger blade from a fall.

Eldir's eyes became blue blazes of hatred. His thick neck and shoulders threatened tremendous power.

Colbey raised his sword for a death stroke, but Eldir swerved toward him. Slammed by the Vikerian horse's shoulder, Colbey's steed lurched aside. Its right forehoof came down on empty air, and it tumbled over the side. Colbey sprang. He landed hard on the neck of Eldir's mount. His sword crashed against the Vikerian's mail.

Impact threw Eldir from his horse. He staggered to his feet on the ledge behind as Colbey rode off on his mount. Nor could Colbey find the space to turn the horse on the narrow ledge. Instead, he reined to a stop and slid from the matted flank. Sword in hand, Colbey smiled as he stalked Eldir.

The Vikerian officer crouched with his back to the cliffs. The fall had dented his horned helmet, but he wore it with pride. He gripped his massive sword in both hands. His face remained frozen in an expression of abhorrence. He stood half again Colbey's height and twice the older man's weight. 'Renshai!' he screamed. 'Join your tribe in Hel.'

Colbey lowered his sword, waiting.

'The loser of this battle will never reach Valhalla.' Eldir's threat came through clearly. Should he best Colbey, he would take special care to dismember him.

Colbey shouted as he sprang. 'Then rot in Hel, you bastard.' His sword flashed twice before Eldir thought to move. The first stroke smacked harmlessly against armor. The second pierced the lightly mailed armpit.

Eldir staggered. His sword made a wild arc, cutting a gash in the stone. The strength of the maneuver threw him further off balance.

Colbey's blade fell against his mail, hurling the wounded Vikerian over the side of the mountain.

Colbey watched as the Vikerian clawed vainly at the air as he fell. Blood ran from the Renshai's blade, striping his hand. He stood, unmoving, until nothing remained but the echoes of Eldir's dying scream.

Colbey cleaned his sword and sheathed it, realizing as he did that the one blow he landed had severed no body part. His lips twitched into a grim smile. 'You were wrong, Northman. We may still both make Valhalla.'

And the Vikerian's death in honor did not bother Colbey at all.

The forest north of Santagithi's Town sparkled with summer dew, and sunlight speckled the leafy floor in patches defined by the leaves and branches overhead. Garn led Rache and Episte from clearing to clearing, their tiny fists warm in his grip, their palms already adult-rough from forming calluses. It had taken years for Garn to understand the solace and natural beauty that attracted Arduwyn, Sterrane, and Mitrian to the woodlands. Now the aroma of greenery, evergreen, and damp seemed headier than any perfume. Birdsong and warmth buoyed his mood, so light, free, and pleasant after days spent cooped up in Santagithi's strategy room. Later, Garn knew, the general and his officers would rehash terrain they had learned by heart; and Colbey would train his youngest charges. But, until then, Garn had finally found some time alone with the boys.

Releasing Rache's and Episte's hands, Garn stepped over a fallen trunk that animals and the elements had stripped of its bark. The pale brown wood had turned soft, riddled with insect holes, burrows, and scrapes. He turned to assist the boys.

Episte sprang to the surface of the deadfall. 'Look! I'm a squirrel.' Though the ancient trunk rocked beneath his weight, he scurried along its length, the ever-present sword wobbling at his side. When he reached the end, he pirouetted. Perching like a king among the twisted roots, he watched Rache attempt to clamber after him. The younger Renshai used his hands, digging his nails into the wood, trying to fling a short, pudgy leg over the trunk. His light, short-bladed sword hampered his movement..

Though Garn had seized the chance to supervise the children's play, irritation gripped him for reasons he could not fathom. 'Up you go,' he said, taking Rache's arm and assisting his son's scramble to the surface. Garn searched for the source of his ruined disposition, but the need to focus on Rache precluded careful consideration.

The instant Rache's feet touched the deadfall, he tried to run. The log rolled, stealing his balance, nearly dumping him. Rocked in his seat, Episte laughed, catching his equilibrium effortlessly. Garn tightened his grip on Rache's arm, steadying. Rache's face grew somber. His features screwed in concentration, as if his life depended on his ability to negotiate the log. He placed each foot with a serious caution he had not previously displayed. Garn assisted, pacing a course on solid ground that paralleled Rache's on the log.

Episte called out encouragements. 'Hey! Rache's a squirrel, too.'

Rache smiled. Garn glanced at his other charge, studying the short, but disheveled, yellow hair and bright blue eyes as if for the first time. A youthful, golden attractiveness and grace completed the picture. Though Episte had inherited his mother's oval face and the patterns of her speech, in all other ways he resembled the man who sired him.

Rache Kallmirsson. The bitterness that had driven Garn for most of his life flashed to the surface instantly, stifled as quickly by guilt. It seemed evil to revile the son for the cruelty of the father, no matter how deeply that hatred had burned. Garn's feud with Captain Rache had become a thing of the past, worked through fully, or so he thought, in the days and moments prior to the Renshai's death. It surprised Garn how easily a random thought had reawakened malice long-buried, and he tried again to find the joy that had suffused him in the forest. Shame accompanied the effort. Whatever enmity he had harbored for Episte's father had nothing to do with the boy. With his dying breath, Rache had asked Garn to raise Episte well, and Garn knew he had to take that responsibility seriously, no matter the resentment he had not quite managed to crush.

As Rache nearly reached Episte, Garn hefted the younger boy and set him down on the path. Episte skipped back along the deadfall, then hopped to the ground beside Rache and Garn. 'I like playing to be squirrel when . . . '

Garn let the child's voice flow around him, mostly unheard. Episte had reached the age where it took him eight hundred words to say what he could have gotten across in six. Almost two years younger, Rache remained mostly quiet, though he occasionally added a qualifier to Episte's rambling that usually only made things more confusing.

Garn continued walking, each hand clasping a child's. He kept his gaze on the stirring greenery and the carpeting of leaf pulp and needles, avoiding looking at Episte. When he did not see the boy's likeness to his father, Garn could keep the idea of raising Rache's son as a distant construct. His own deep-seated prejudice shocked and upset him. Once he had accepted that his own son would bear Rache's name, the step to attending the man's child seemed simple. Yet, the similarity of features had tripped Garn up, and the natural grace that made Rache seem clumsy in comparison only worsened the problem. Repeatedly,

Garn told himself that the two years difference in age accounted for most of the disparity. In youth, even a few months could mean a great deal when it came to maturation, both physical and emotional.

Even engaged in thoughtful turmoil, Garn remained alert. As they passed a dense copse of vines that lined the looping trail, he heard movement on the opposite side. Instinctively, he crouched.

Cued by Garn's sudden wariness, Episte went silent. Rache pulled at his father's wrist. 'What's wrong?'

'Quiet. I heard something,' Garn whispered back. He strained for the sound again. The rustle and rattle of needled vines filled his hearing. 'Stay here.' He extracted his fingers from the boys' grips.

Accustomed to obedience, the children remained still. Episte took Rache's hand though whether to comfort and protect or out of fear, Garn did not know. Cautiously, he circled the copse, drawing his knife from the pocket of his leathers. With the town at war, he had taken to wearing a sword at all times; but he would not free it until he found the need. It would hamper quiet, careful movement in the forest.

As Garn completed his creep around the brambles, another wild flurry of movement seized his attention. A doe lay on its side in the clearing, its thrashing tangling its hind legs deeper in the brush. Its body lay twisted from injury or pain, and one foreleg hung limp while the others kicked. As the ex-gladiator approached, the crazed struggle resumed. The animal lashed and wriggled. Though it freed itself from the copse, it clearly could not stand.

'Papa?' Rache called.

'It's all right,' Garn said. 'Come here. Slowly and carefully.'

Leaves crunched as the boys worked their way around the clearing. In the moments before their arrival, the deer went still, head flopping to the dirt, flanks heaving. The jagged edge of a broken shaft poked from the shoulder of its flaccid leg. A flake of silver paint from the crest revealed it as the arrow of one of Santagithi's archers. The dried blood around the entry hole looked old.

'Deer.' Rache clapped his hands to his cheeks, excited.

'What's it doing here?' Episte approached Garn, looping an arm around the man's leg.

The sudden closeness shocked Garn, and he felt torn between joy and revulsion. His own mother had hit as often as cuddled him. He had never known his father as anything but stories told to him by Rache and Santagithi's other guards. In his childhood, only Rache Kallmirsson had ever given Garn reassuring pats, hugs, or squeezes. After Rache's betrayal, when Garn had lived with no contact but blade slashes, fist blows, and whip cuts, the physical contact they had shared as children seemed tainted and ugly. It was Mitrian who finally taught Garn to again see touching as a display of affection rather than an attack.

Apparently sensing Garn's discomfort, Episte released him. 'How come it's just lying there?'

'Some hunter hurt it and didn't finish his job.' Seeing an opportunity to teach and pleased by the boys' interest, Garn relied on tenets that Arduwyn had emphasized repeatedly. More than once, the red-haired hunter had delayed travel to track a deer that his arrow had wounded instead of killed outright. At first, Garn believed the hunter's motive was pride, that not delivering a first killing shot bruised Arduwyn's dignity. Later, he had watched the hunter ignore other game while in pursuit of his quarry. Garn's questioning had induced a reply he quoted now for his own son's benefit. 'When you wound something, you have the obligation to hunt it down and kill it, no matter how long it takes or how inconvenient it seems.'

Garn approached the deer. Exhausted, it trembled but did not lurch or thrash again. Shielding the sight from the boys with his body, Garn drove his knife through the neck, tearing to sever the artery. The animal gave one last kick, then stiffened and stilled, bright red blood leaking from the wound.

'Why?' Rache asked, edging forward to stand beside Episte.

It took Garn a moment to realize that Rache had questioned his words not his actions. He cleaned blood from the knife and returned it to his sheath. Turning, he faced the children, steeling himself to carry the carcass back to town. 'Because there're too many people hungry to waste food, and it's not fair to the deer to leave it suffering.'

'Uncle Garn,' Episte said, using the title the adults had chosen. Initially, the boy had referred to him as 'papa' or 'papa-Garn,' but that carried false and embarrassing implications about Garn's and Emerald's relationship. 'Uncle Garn,' Episte repeated, apparently not feeling as if he had captured Garn's attention fully.

Realizing he was still not meeting Episte's gaze, Garn forced himself to do so. With time and familiarity, he felt certain he could overcome his prejudices. For all the time he had spent plotting Rache's downfall, they had ended their relationship at peace. Proud of recognizing his bias and putting it to rest, Garn crouched to Episte's level and clutched the boy's hands with genuine warmth. 'What is it, Episte?'

Episte stared into Garn's eyes with a child's innocence and ignorance of tact. 'When you made my papa's legs not work, how come you didn't kill *him*?'

Garn froze. A million thoughts converged on him at once. He fought for the controlled, rational part of his mind that would have the answer to Episte's question, that could make a child understand the differences between an animal and a man, that could explain hatred, bitterness, and an adult's need for vengeance. Then, emotion swept logic away, stripping Garn of coherent speech. Compassion, terror, revulsion, and desperation grappled him at once. His memory sparked images of the crippled sword master whom he had loved, then despised, then learned to respect.

Trapped, Garn surrendered to emotion, and rage rescued him from the need to consider strategy. 'That's not a subject for children. Don't bring it up again. Ever.'

The boys withdrew from the ferocity of Garn's reply, shocked into frightened silence.

The heavy-handed cruelty of his own method grated on Garn even as the dismissal of the topic brought relief. He knew a more competent parent might have found the words to defuse the situation and the problem, but he had never learned the skill. For now, and he hoped forever, the matter was settled.

15 War's End

The war raged for ten years, and even then showed no sign of ending. Colbey could not recall four consecutive months of peace since the first attack a decade ago. Regularly, men rode to battle the way they once did to their jobs and shops. Those who returned did so in days or weeks, in triumph or defeat, or when food ran low for both armies. Often, Colbey joined the skirmishes and, equally often, he remained behind to train Renshai, women, and children.

Santagithi aged rapidly in the warring years. His hair went white, and Colbey's keen eye for physical detail told him that the old general's reflexes had slowed while his own only seemed to sharpen. But Santagithi's mind remained quick, evidenced, if by nothing else, by the fact that the war continued. For, while the ranks of the Vikerians had swelled with neighboring Northmen eager to kill Renshai, Santagithi's allies sent no aid at all. By the time Santagithi's message arrived, Béarn had been set upon by a small but cunning band of traitors led by Morhane's bastard son. Pirates had also hit the coast, cued or instigated by Rathelon's men. Sterrane had enlisted the aid of Pudar and discovered that the diverse and ever-changing populace of the trading city shared and traded diseases as well as goods. When the Pudarian soldiers left Béarn, with the pirates dispatched but Rathelon still at large, an epidemic of the consumption remained behind. The disease galloped through the royal city, leaving many Béarnides as pale skeletons. By report, Sterrane had lost his wife. Arduwyn and Bel buried two children, and the archer himself had begun to shake with chills.

Yet while plagues in the southwest killed indiscriminately, widows and orphans abounded in the Town of Santagithi. Trade ground to a halt. Men hunted for food in groups. Though it obviously grieved Santagithi, teenagers became warriors overnight to replace casualties of the ceaseless war. Still, Santagithi adamantly insisted that no child join the war before the age of thirteen. So, though Rache was the first blooded, Episte joined Colbey's troop nearly two years before him.

Now, halfway down the line of formation, Colbey watched the two youngest Renshai among the troop of seventy men he and Santagithi led between the Granite Hills' barren crags. Episte had inherited the Renshai's tendency to appear younger than their ages. He stood no talled than a ten-year-old, with wide, innocent eyes and a hairless face. Though small, his hands gripped his father's longsword with confidence. In battle, he moved with the skill of the ages, and his sword danced like a live thing.

Thirteen years old to the day, Rache stood only inches shorter than his sire and nearly as broad. His face was becomingly angular, and his hair hung in a tawny cascade of tangles. His chin sported a few coiled tufts of beard. He raised his head proudly as he rode toward his first battle at Episte's side. He had not landed a single blow since the incident in Santagithi's courtroom a decade ago.

Scraggly grasses and ferns peeked through cracks in the cold, gray stone. Streams wound through passes and the lusher valleys, but the creek bed Santagithi's army rode through lay parched. Obviously wearied by the unvarying continuity of war, many of the men stared at the dust clouds raised by the hooves of their horses. But, to Colbey, every contest became a new endeavor. Whether he rode to his first war or his millionth, his blood warmed, and his sword could never take enough lives to sate its hunger. He felt the wary prickle that signaled an unseen peril, an uneasiness that went far beyond the inevitability of combat. Colbey left his position in line. 'Santagithi.' He drew up his horse directly beside the general's.

Santagithi nodded ever so slightly, a gesture that acknowledged Colbey's presence but gave a clear warning the general did not wish to be drawn from his thoughts.

Colbey continued, undaunted. 'When was the last rain?'

Santagithi frowned, obviously annoyed by what appeared to be small talk pulling him from his strategies. 'Four days. Why?'

Colbey scanned the horizon. The mountains rose, sheer, from the path. A bend ahead hid the winding continuation of the trail. 'This creek is dry. I didn't think it was the right time of the year for that.' Colbey gave the facts, without speculation. Santagithi could draw a conclusion far better than he could.

Santagithi drew up his steed with a broad gesture that arrested the entire army as one. He signaled for Jakot at the rear. 'Good one of us has some sense. Men can drain a stream as well as nature, and it is of the gravest importance that we discover which is responsible in this case.'

Jakot pulled up beside them and Santagithi turned from Colbey to address his captain softly. 'Turn the men around and lead them back to the caves. We need to talk.'

Jakot's expression went as serious as his general's. 'Yes, sir.' Without question, he quietly herded the men around. Colbey and

Santagithi followed the troop from the pass, up a wide slope, to the caves. There, the men dismounted, waiting, as Santagithi conferred with the officers he had brought with him: Colbey, Garn, Mitrian, and Jakot.

Santagithi explained his fears. 'Someone quiet, preferably someone the Northmen will not view as a threat needs to sneak up that mountain.' With a careful gesture, he singled out one of the slopes that formed the valley they had just exited. 'And find out what's going on.' He fell into an uncomfortable silence.

Colbey knew that the general wrestled with his decision. The only reasonable choices for the mission were Mitrian and Episte, either of whom would need to be sent without a sword. If the Vikerians spotted the spy, they would be less likely to act against a woman or one they believed to be a child, especially if they discovered him or her unarmed. Yet Colbey knew, without the need to read a thought, that Santagithi did not wish to send his daughter or Rache's son alone and weaponless into the territory of the enemy.

The Renshai spared Santagithi the decision. 'I'll go. I know stealth best. I can achieve your purposes as quietly as anyone and in less time.'

Santagithi frowned, the same wall of discomfort and guilt radiating from him that Colbey met whenever he placed himself in danger or Santagithi suggested a course of action for the oldest Renshai that did not quite seem to fit with his usual strategies. It appeared to Colbey as if Santagithi had been purposefully hiding some piece of information even from his thoughts, as if he knew the old Renshai could read them. Several times, Colbey had tried to relax the general enough to let that idea slip from him, but without success. Whatever bothered Santagithi was a thing he wanted to keep not only from his people and from his friend, but from himself. Still, though the concept bothering Santagithi for more than a decade did not surface, his strategy did.

Colbey seized upon the knowledge to make his argument. 'If we can't sneak one man to a vantage above the Northmen you and I both know are there, how can you expect to station an army there?'

Santagithi stiffened, apparently still surprised by Colbey's ability, though he had experienced its effects for nearly a decade and a half. 'All right,' he said at length, though with obvious reluctance. 'But be careful. And don't do anything except look.'

Colbey slipped from the cave mouth. Santagithi turned to his other officers and began to detail his strategy.

Colbey clambered up the cliff face as lithe as a cat and as silent as a cat's shadow. Finding an intermittently broken ledge the height of three men above the ground, he flowed along it, easing across the gaps. After a quarter mile, he stopped at a bend in the riverbed. Crouched against a crevice, he wedged his feet against rock, clinging to a twisted root for support. Arranging a curtain of brush over his hiding place, he gathered his mind into a firm, controlled knot.

Eyes tightly closed in concentration. Colbey probed before him with a tendril of thought, just as he had with the sentries before the tent of Prince Verrall of Pudar. He had not actively attempted to read men's minds since that time; his blood brother's insistence made him cautious with his gift to the point of paranoia. Yet Shadimar had only deemed such a violation an act of war, not a blasphemy. Clearly, then, battle was a legitimate use for the talent. Colbey let his consciousness meander forward, connected to his thoughts by a thready, mental umbilical cord.

Gradually, the tendril tapped lightly against another man's thoughts. *Bored. Bored and hungry.* Colbey thrust deeper. *Tired of the wait and anxious for combat. Clashing steel and death screams.* Colbey drew a long breath, feeling strength seem to ebb from him. Having never before used his mind powers so actively, it never occurred to him that the effort might drain him as fully as physical war. Sweat beaded his brow as his consciousness bounced from one Vikerian mind to the next, counting, no longer focusing on content. Every one seemed nearly the same, ruthless barbarians as eager for death as to deal it. They were all warriors who would abandon strategy for a chance to fight like wolves, who would rather think with their swords than their heads. And Colbey understood them all. Except one.

Again, Colbey gathered his thoughts to him. After his previous efforts, the attempt seemed ponderously difficult. Uncertain of the best way to enter the leader's mind swiftly and deeply, he drew his mental strength into a dense ball, then thrust it for the lieutenant with the abrupt and deadly speed of a striking cobra.

Colbey received a brilliant flash of light, surrounded by pain. The Northman recoiled in sudden agony, thoughts scattering. Then, as he grew accustomed to Colbey's presence, the attack dulled to a throbbing headache. The other wasted a few moments wondering about the source of the pain. Seeing the futility in such an exercise, he abandoned this line of thought for the more pressing matter of his plan and his charges. *By the scouts' report, Santagithi's army should arrive any moment.*

Even as Colbey identified the leader as Valr Kirin, the strength of his own mind and body drained away. Colbey's grip failed, and he plummeted from the mountain ledge.

Colbey tried to twist, but found himself unable to gather enough power even to tense. Fully paralyzed, he knew fear for the first time in his life. He tried to prepare his mind for the coming impact, but his efforts had drained the power of directed thought as well as of his body. He landed on the stones in complete relaxation, without pain. Habit goaded him to mentally explore his body for injury, but experience told him that the simple task of trying would steal consciousness as well as strength. Instead, he lay still, granting himself neither thought nor movement until he felt strength ebb back into his limbs and his mind. Only then did he allow his mind to touch his body.

Colbey lay in a sparse growth of brush near the creek bed. Bruises racked his left hip and shoulder. Stones had torn the skin the length of his left calf, and blood oozed from a gash across the back of his head. Finding nothing worse, Colbey considered himself lucky to the point of gods' protection, though logic told him it was the limpness of his body that had spared him. Had he landed stiffened, he would have broken at least a few bones.

Colbey clambered to his feet and clamped a rag to the back of his head to staunch the bleeding. He limped back to the cave.

Santagithi met Colbey at the mouth. The general's gaze followed the dirty tatters of the Renshai's jerkin, then locked on the blood-plastered clump of hair at the nape of his neck.

Colbey did not explain. 'Seventy-four Northmen are lying in wait at a dam they built. And there may be still more waiting in reserve. If we had continued further, they would have unleashed the stream upon us.'

'Did they see you.'

'No.' Colbey felt dizziness sweep through his head in a wash of black and white spots, and a ringing noise filled his ears, so loud that he scarcely heard Santagithi's question.

'What happened to you?'

'I fell.' Colbey explained, his voice sounding distant, as if someone else was speaking.

'How?' Santagithi pressed.

Colbey understood the general's need to understand. Santagithi had too much faith in Colbey's agility to believe he had fallen accidentally. Often the general found foul play in situations others perceived as coincidence. Still, Colbey wished the grilling could wait until his vertigo passed. 'I lost my hold. No one's fault but my own. I have absolutely no doubt about that.'

Concern scored Santagithi's gray eyes. 'Colbey, go home and help Bromdun guard the town.'

Colbey made no move to obey. 'You need me here.' He did not dare probe for Santagithi's motivation. He had never guessed how much energy his mental exploration would claim from him, and a long time would pass before he dared to use his powers again.

Santagithi scowled. 'We don't need a staggering, injured officer.'

The spots before Colbey's eyes faded, taking the ringing with it. 'I'll be all right shortly.'

'Good,' Santagithi granted no quarter. 'Then you should be well by the time you reach town.'

'I'm staying with you,' Colbey said.

Santagithi's gaze went cold, and he squinted with rage. 'Colbey, damn it, you'll do as I tell you. I'm not asking, I'm commanding it. I've never tolerated insubordination, and I won't start now. Not from *anyone*. Now, you get your butt on your horse and head toward town, or I'll kill you where you stand.'

A spark of anger flashed through Colbey, then died instantly. As much as he wanted to remain with Santagithi and the other three Renshai, he trusted the general's judgment too much to question it now. 'Fine,' he said, then louder. 'Fine, *sir*.' Whirling, he headed deeper into the cave to find his horse.

Seated on a rock beside the constructed dam, Valr Kirin studied his unit. Two months of building and a week of waiting had made the mixed group of Northmen impatient nearly to the point of mutiny. They milled and fidgeted like children, sparked to violence by the tiniest argument. Again and again, Kirin had stepped between their drawn swords and axes, reminding them to forget the differences between tribes and concentrate on their real enemy.

'They're coming!' someone called, and the cry echoed through the ranks. Nervous energy seemed to quadruple in an instant as Northmen scurried to their positions with an efficiency that laid some of Kirin's fears to rest. Soon, the Northmen would split the dam, its waters would drown Colbey among Santagithi's dwindling forces, and the war would finally end.

Valr Kirin smiled, assessing the positions of his men from habit, though his thoughts ranged farther. There had been a time, when he had been the age of these men, that the chance to kill enemies and die in glory took precedence over all. He understood their exuberance, but he also saw beyond it. He had been barely thirty when his older brother lost a hand in battle and, with it, the chance to ever enter Valhalla. Yet Peusen Raskogsson had continued to fight, embracing the same ideals and tenets that he had sacrificed his personal glory to attain. Peusen's courage had given Kirin strength as well. He had learned to place the goals of morality and preservation of the Northland tribes above his own.

As the last men slid into place behind the dam, Valr Kirin took his own position on a crag, slightly above and removed from the troop. There, his gestures could be more easily seen and his orders heard. Despite their eager savagery, he knew that the Northmen meant the best. In a land of bleak summers and food-sparse winters, constant skirmishes kept numbers whittled. Young men died in honor so that their women and children could live and so that elders and their wisdom could exist. The infirm nearly always crawled from their sickbeds into the battles. And when the time came for Northern tribes to band together in a cause, they became like brothers.

Santagithi's men rounded the bend and became clearly visible. Kirin kept his back flat to the crags, and his Northmen remained low and unseen. A proud figure in mail led a rank of Santagithi's soldiers in three rows of four. Kirin recognized the captain, Jakot, and the trifling group he led set the Slayer's nerves jangling. The Northmen grumbled in frustration. They had not toiled so long to ambush only a dozen men. Weapons rasped from sheaths. Before Kirin could shout a warning, several of his men sprang to their feet. Others followed, like an audience joining a standing ovation.

'No!' Valr Kirin screamed. 'Men, hold your places!' Howls of frustration and battle madness drowned out his command. Northern soldiers scrabbled onto horses, sending them leaping over the dam, unwilling to waste two months work on a handful of men. They galloped along the creek bed toward the approaching force.

Jakot pulled up his tiny unit and whirled in retreat.

'Stop! Back! Now!' Though he screamed his commands, Valr Kirin could scarcely hear himself over the varied war calls of his men. Scrambling down the slope, he vaulted to the back of his own mount, but he did not follow his men to the wrong side of the dam. Instead, he remained behind it with those few warriors who had kept their heads and obeyed their lieutenant.

Suddenly, Jakot swerved from the path, forcing his horse up the side of the mountain, his men at his heels. The Northmen gave chase, the horses on both sides floundering up the rocky slopes. Once on the crest, Jakot waited only until his men reached safety. 'Now!'

Men rose from positions on the summit, rolling boulders on the trailing Northmen. *No.* Valr Kirin cringed, sick with understanding but helpless to protect the men who had disobeyed his command. Yet he did not have long to ponder. An army with Garn and Mitrian at the head galloped over the crags toward those Northmen still behind the dam. Kirin studied the enemy troop pouring down upon them and the few remaining Northmen. 'Retreat!' he commanded. 'This way. Quickly.' He made a broad gesture designed to direct the Northmen in the creek bed as well as those behind the dam to safety. Less than two dozen soldiers rushed to their lieutenant's command, nearly all of them Vikerians far more accustomed to following him. The others charged into battle with a ferocity that transcended numbers, eager to die in glory.

Valr Kirin paused, allowing his men to catch up. On the far side of the river, he scanned Santagithi's ranks in relative safety. He watched with sadness as Santagithi's army dispatched the few remaining Northmen at the dam. From there, they removed key logs and sprang the Northmen's trap upon those warriors still in the creek bed. A foaming snake of water crashed through the ruins of the dam, swallowing the Northmen. A quick count and a glance at the leaders confirmed that Santagithi had brought about two thirds of his remaining manpower and that Colbey was not among them. 'Come on.' Charged with a mission, Kirin retreated with dignity, taking his most loyal charges with him, racing to link up with his reserves. Though seventy-three Northmen had lost their lives, Valr Kirin knew that his men had to have won the larger battle. And maybe, just maybe, Colbey Calistinsson was already dead.

The miles passed swiftly beneath the hooves of Colbey's horse. Gradually, the wary prickle returned to the edges of his thoughts, sweeping the fog of fatigue into a shrinking, central knot. Early, he thanked gods that he met no opposition on the roadway; he had not dived into the thickest part of every battle for longer than seventy years only to die enfeebled by his own mind. Exhaustion made him careless, and he made little effort to disguise his person or his presence from Northern scouts. Surely, had anyone seen him, they would have attacked.

Colbey drew deeper into the Granite Hills. With the incremental return of strength to his body and mind, he became suspicious. He had not expected to meet armies, but he had anticipated attacks by single Northmen and small groups along the way. Whatever his title or level of skill, almost any Northman would have to test his courage against a Renshai's, even if it meant death. *Unless they fear I would dismember them.* The thought bothered Colbey. Enemies or not, the Northmen were kin of a sort, and he hated to think that they had become cowards afraid to face a man approaching eighty.

The Granite Hills disappeared swiftly behind Colbey, and he glanced back to memorize the positions of caves before entering the pine forest just south of the mountains. His last chain of thought bothered him. His age had become an obsession that rode him without mercy. He had lived the span of three Renshai, yet death of any kind seemed unable to find him. His hair remained full, free from the recession that gave Santagithi an aura of dignity, many strands still gold among the white. His vision remained as crisp and clear as always, his cold blue gaze unmarred by cataracts or the watery film that seemed to haunt most elders. Somehow, beyond all possibility, his sword skill and agility seemed only to improve with practice and time.

When oak and elm began to appear among the evergreens, an acrid odor pinched Colbey's nostrils. *Fire?* He glanced above, seeing nothing in the near vicinity. He kept his gaze trained ahead, in the direction of Santagithi's Town, alert for the first signs of a blaze. For some time, he saw nothing. Then a braid of smoke twined over the forest, and the wind hurled the odor of burning thatch into his face. *The town.* Colbey dug his heels into his horse's ribs, hoping Santagithi's women had not forgotten the tricks he had taught. The horse surged forward, charging through a clumped interweave of branches. Colbey ducked flat to its neck, protecting his face, and the leaves slashed harmlessly across his tunic.

As Colbey raced toward the town, the reek of burning timbers intensified. The pine gave way to oak, hickory, and maple. He kept as close and quiet as possible, avoiding the whipping branches and the huddled groups of soldiers slinking between the trees. Most had Northmen's golden braids, though others were too far to identify. At length, he reached a clearing near the one where he trained the Renshai. Brambles outlined two sides, dotted with green berries that would darken as spring turned to summer. Alerted more by instinct than sound or movement, Colbey pulled his mount to a walk.

Shortly, Bromdun's voice hissed through the thistle, speaking the Western trading tongue. 'Sir, come here. It's safe.'

The promise of security only made Colbey more cautious. He circled the brambles with all of his senses alert. At length, he came to one of the unprotected sides. There, a dozen bowmen sat or lay in various stages of alertness or repose. Four pikemen protected the two open sides. Recognizing every man, though not all by name, Colbey relaxed. 'What's happened?'

The archer's captain rose. His miserable expression and massive form gave him the air of a carved gargoyle perched defensively on a bastion. 'Northmen descended upon the town in hordes like I've never seen. They took the town.' Tears of rage filled the captain's eyes. 'They've got some of the women and other women's children holed up in the citadel. This is the last of the guards.' He gestured at the scraggly looking band around him. 'The Northies know we're here, but they're leaving us alone for now.'

Colbey studied the men with Bromdun. He had found little cause to get to know the archers well. Still, in a town so small, he had become at least vaguely familiar with all of them. All four of the pikemen he knew as competent soldiers.

Having finished his report, Bromdun moved on to another matter. 'Emerald made it known that she needed to see you. She said it was urgent.'

Colbey frowned, finding the summons curious. Probably, Emerald would beg him to keep her son safe and away from the town and the Northmen. Still, she was the mother of Renshai, if not one herself, and he had little choice but to attend her, if possible. 'Where is Emerald?'

'Probably at her cottage.' Bromdun straightened his mail. 'Mostly, the Northmen are letting the women, children, and elders go about their business, except for the hostages.' His dark gaze found Colbey's; and, though it was not proper for him to request information from a superior unsolicited, he did so anyway. 'How is Santagithi?'

'Well, last I knew.' Colbey appreciated the distraction, certain that fatigue must still be dampening his mind, if not his body. He dismounted, addressing one of the archers he did know by name. 'Galan.'

The archer approached, a tall, wiry soldier with bright hazel eyes. 'Yes, sir?'

'Take my horse. Santagithi and the others are on trail three, about a quarter of the way north. I want you to tell Santagithi what happened here.'

'Yes, sir.' Galan mounted quickly, arm threaded through his bow.

Bromdun frowned, but he did not contradict. 'Where are you going?' His words were clearly meant for Colbey.

The Renshai looked toward the village, seeing only distant glimpses of cottages between the trunks and trailers of smoke. Apparently, the fires had been small and scattered, meant mostly to scare the civilians into obedience. Emerald's cottage lay on the eastern side of the town in line with many others. 'I'm going to speak with Emerald.'

'Sir!' Bromdun said, the word an exclamation of disapproval and surprise. He shied slightly. Years of training with Santagithi had taught him never to question authority. He would not have probed Santagithi's motives, but he did challenge Colbey. 'Forgive me, sir. But you don't know what it's like there. There're Northmen everywhere. If you wait for Santagithi – '

Colbey frowned, his loyalities never in question. A Renshai's mother needed to see him. No matter their personal differences, he would not fail her. 'Did Emerald say her concern could wait?'

'No, sir,' Bromdun admitted. 'She said it was urgent.'

'Galan, be on your way.' Colbey gestured toward the Hills, then slipped around the brambles and headed for the town.

Stems brushed Colbey's tunic, then bounced back into place, their young leaves rattling in his wake. Accustomed to quiet movement through forest, Colbey ducked low, placing his feet cautiously to avoid twigs scattered through the mush of dead leaves that formed the forest carpet. He moved like an animal, lithe and sinuous despite his age, though he made less noise. The woodlands seemed eerily silent; apparently even the final, desperate skirmishes had ended. Colbey caught glimpses of Santagithi's Town between the trunks as he walked. A few, selected dwellings lay as litter-strewn ash, smoke still dribbling from the rubble. Most of the cottages stood intact, looking like proud sentinels beside the ruins of their neighbors.

Colbey continued to creep through the forest, remaining low, his footfalls making little sound. As he circled eastward, spiraling toward the town, he could distinguish figures in the streets. Women openly wept over sprawled bodies. A child toddled around the homes, hoarsely screaming, 'Mama! Mama?' Colbey used the call to mask the sounds of his progress, reaching the border of the town. Even his experience did not make him callous to their plight, though it had become familiar enough to keep him from dropping his guard to tend to the lamenting widows and orphans. For now, this seemed as good a time as any for them to grieve; the Northmen would not harm them.

Tucked behind an ancient oak, Colbey studied the scene for some time, seeking war braids, helms, armor, or movement that did not bear the slumping quality of sorrow. He saw no Northmen, and that bothered rather than pleased him. Apparently, the Northmen had already taken what they had come for and left. Yet Colbey found himself unable to relax. He had accepted it as luck or divine intervention that he had come upon no enemies while tired and injured, with his wits dulled. But his luck seemed to be holding too well. The lack of forest creatures suggested that battles or soldiers had filled these woods not so long ago.

Colbey dashed from the forest to the cottage closest to the border. Back pressed to the wall, he waited for an attack or a shout of recognition. No new sounds touched his ears. Keening wound through the streets, punctuated by crying, and he could hear distant, muffled conversation in Western voices. Still, Colbey did not drop his guard. He edged around the building, gaze probing the streets, hearing attuned to catch any sound out of place for battle aftermath. Discovering nothing, he slipped to the next cottage.

Time and cautious effort brought Colbey, apparently unseen, toward Emerald's dwelling. As he crept around the nearby butcher's shop, he discovered that the home between it and Emerald's lay in charcoal ruin. He studied the blackened beams, the ashes scattered with sparkles of brass and tin that had once served as utensils and hinges. Heat haze glimmered around the site, blurring Emerald's cottage, and the last tiny plumes of smoke curled from the wreckage. Seeing no movement, Colbey sprinted for Emerald's home. He flattened to the stone. An elder's sobs covered the quieter noises of the gutted village, including Colbey's passage.

A flap of leather stirred in the light spring breeze. Colbey inched along the wall to it. Waiting until a gust flipped the covering, he peeked through the opening. He caught a glimpse of Emerald, rocking quietly in her chair. He saw no one else. She seemed tense to the point of pain; but, under the circumstances, her discomfort seemed normal. Quickly, Colbey moved to the front of the house and checked the latch. Finding it tripped, he pushed open the cottage door.

Even as Colbey pressed his weight against the panel, a feeling of peril assailed him. A sound, a movement, or instinct, he did not know which alerted him. Naturally, his hands fell to his hilts. His swords skimmed free before he thought to draw them. Three Northmen in mail met him in the doorway, another three behind them. A massive broadsword smashed against his lighter blade, easily blocked. He whipped his opposite sword across its wielder's throat. The man collapsed, as Colbey caught the other two Northmen's blades on each of his. He reversed the direction of both swords, stabbing one through the links and into a Northman's gut. He slashed the other a long deep cut across the face, twisting to dodge the attacks of the second rank and draw his blade free at once. Seeing movement from outside now, he kicked closed the door and spun farther into the main room of Emerald's cottage.

The three remaining Northmen charged without hesitation. The first hacked for Colbey's head with a powerful downstroke, closing his defenses with a battered steel shield. Colbey planted a kick on the man's shield, sending him stumbling to the floor near the door to Emerald's sitting chamber. From the corner of his eye, Colbey saw Emerald moving toward the fallen man. He hoped she remembered some of the war tricks he had taught her and the other women, that she could handle the fallen soldier. Already he heard footsteps at the door, and a low thrust from one of the two Northmen before him stole his attention.

Colbey blocked with an outside sweep, cutting his other sword across the gap between the Northman's mail and chin. As the Northman collapsed, the last charged in with a high stroke that gashed the ceiling. Colbey diverted with a fast parry, driving his sword into the Northman's eyes.

The door crashed open. 'Renshai!' someone screamed. A mailed Northman sprang through the opening, four more at his heels.

Sword still embedded, Colbey whirled to meet the charge, jabbing his other sword defensively before him. Momentum carried the Northman onto Colbey's blade, burying the longsword nearly to the hilt in his abdomen. The force of the attack drove Colbey to his knees. A Northman impaled on each sword, Colbey felt the wild, hot rush of battle joy, and he laughed. Already, six Northmen lay dead. Colbey counted four before him, still acutely aware of the one he had dropped but not killed. That one lay on the floor at his back, near Emerald, and he hoped but did not count on her having the courage to finish him. Three of his opponents carried swords and shields, the last a short-hafted war ax that looked heavy as an anvil.

Even as Colbey tensed, two Northmen attacked as one. The Renshai sprang backward, freeing his swords and gaining his feet. One broadsword embedded into a wooden chest. The other gashed open Colbey's collar, tearing the sleeve of his tunic. *Too close.* Colbey surged upright, one blade opening a Northman's abdomen. The other missed cleanly. The Northman leapt backward, leaving his sword stuck in the trunk. With a lunge, Colbey impaled him, flipping his blades into a defensive position to face his last two opponents. The swordsman kept his shield up, backing carefully from Colbey. The axman advanced, arm muscles knotted, face ugly with directed rage. Suddenly, he lunged.

Colbey threw up a block. The ax smashed down on his blade, the impact aching through his arm. He back-stepped toward Emerald and the fallen guard. The last swordsman ducked through the door and into the daylight, presumably for reinforcements.

The axman gritted his teeth beneath wide, bloodless lips. Again, the ax drove for Colbey's side, and the Renshai caught the stroke on his sword. The force of the blow plunged Colbey another step backward. His arms throbbed, and pain howled in his muscles. Quietly seeking an opening, he took another backward step.

Suddenly, a hand seized Colbey's ankle and yanked. Balance lost, Colbey scarcely met the next mighty pound of the ax, and its power grounded him. He fell to his knees, twisting toward the guard he had kicked, who still lay on Emerald's floor and now held Colbey's foot. The ax slammed down toward Colbey's head. He ducked, dodging behind one blade. Steel met steel with a power that all but broke his grip. More from will than strength, he kept hold of his hilt, circling his sword with an abruptness that tore the ax from the Northman's hand. It fell, shaking the floor with its weight.

The Northman on the floor made a sweep for Colbey's side, but the length of the blade and the closeness of the target stole all power from the blow. It slammed against Colbey's bruised hip, shocking pain through him, though the blade barely scratched him. Not wanting to fall prey to the same mistake, Colbey slid his hand from his own hilt to his blade, shortening the length. The sharpened steel slit his hand painlessly. He drove the blade into the Northman's groin. A shriek echoed through the confines. The Northman's hand fell from Colbey's ankle, and the Renshai surged to his feet.

Having recovered his ax, the last Northman charged Colbey again. Pain screamed through the Renshai. His head pounded, fatigue returning in a whistling, spinning rush. His arms felt on fire, and the bruises he had gotten from his fall ached. Enraged by his own exhaustion, Colbey met the charge with a parry that redirected the ax to the floor. Colbey stabbed through the Northman's defenses. His blade cut through mail and flesh, and the soldier joined his companions on the cottage floor.

A flash of steel at the corner of Colbey's vision was his only warning. A sword blade bit into the back of his knee, carving flesh down his calf nearly to the ankle. An abrupt whirl was all that saved Colbey's foot. One sword battered the enemy's blade aside. The other bit through its wielder's gut and buried into the spine. Only then, Colbey realized that his target was not the injured Northman he expected but Emerald. Every muscle in the woman's body went rigid, then fell suddenly limp. She collapsed, the sword tumbling from her grip. Her gaze fell to the blade thrust through her, and she screamed in realization and terror.

Horrified, Colbey levered his blade free, unable to comprehend the deceit. Emerald's attack made no sense, and he could only feel the anger and guilt of having murdered Episte's mother.

Emerald lay still, except for the wide-eyed expression that seemed permanently locked on her face. Clearly, she was in spinal shock, and Colbey knew from feel alone that she would die in seconds, no matter what he did. At least, he felt certain that she knew no pain.

Emerald's dark eyes were clear, flashing with a hatred so raw Colbey could mistake it for nothing else. 'All your fault,' she whispered, though her words made no more sense to him than her betrayal. A glaze obscured her eyes, taking the emotion with it. 'They wanted you. They only ever wanted you.'

Colbey remained unmoving, waiting for her to make a request that he could fulfill. Some part of his mind hoped that he *had* killed her without cause, so that she could, at least, die with honor.

'One savage old Renshai cost us the town and the lives of so many innocent men and women.' Her lids fell shut. The words that came next held the peaceful, haunting quality that comes just before giving up the battle to death. 'And mine now.' She said nothing more.

The news struck Colbey a blow as heavy as the Northman's ax. He had always known that the Northmen attacked him with far more exuberance than any other, but he had expected nothing less once they knew his heritage. Yet the idea that the war had started and raged over him for ten years sent a shock of self-directed anger and guilt through him. Santagithi's loyalty prided and pained him. Never had a friendship been so sorely tested. At any time, the general could have betrayed Colbey in much the same way as Emerald had, and Colbey would not have begrudged him choosing the lesser of evils. Now, he believed, he had found the information that had heavily plagued Santagithi throughout the warring years. And it pained him.

Colbey shook blood from his swords, drawing a rag to clean the steel. In moments, he knew reinforcements would arrive. He would fight Northmen in even greater numbers, then kill many more before they overpowered him. Finally, his time had come. Yet had he known that he, alone, was the object of dispute, he would have attacked the entirety of the Northlands at once and long ago died in glory.

The shattered door swung open on broken hinges. Colbey crouched into a defensive position, one sword high, the other low. Mitrian and Episte stood framed in the doorway, their postures military, though they carried no weapons. Mitrian wore a black mourning scarf that covered her features. Although she had remained in town for most of the battles, word of a woman in Santagithi's ranks had probably spread. Episte's gaze roved from the scarlet-streaked blades in Colbey's hands to the Northmen's bodies scattered across the floor of his home. His attention fell on his mother's corpse and froze there.

Episte's professional stance disappeared. 'No,' he whispered. Tears welled in his eyes, blurring them to puddles of blue. Suddenly, he was no longer a Renshai man ensconced in a golden whirlwind of combat. In an instant, he went rigid, a four-year-old confused by the demands of an unyielding *torke*. 'Mother!' He ran to Emerald. Heedless of the other corpses, he tripped over one, sprawling to his face on another. The tears came faster, rolling down his face in a ceaseless trail. He scrabbled over the dead Northmen, not bothering to stand, and hugged his mother to his chest. He rocked the body like a child.

Mitrian's face echoed Colbey's concern. She spoke softly. 'We were ambushed on the other side of town. The Northmen made it look as if they had left. When our army came in to help the bereaved, the Northmen attacked. Those of us remaining need to retreat, and fast.' She glanced at Episte. 'Bromdun thought we'd find you here, so we took a chance. I didn't think they'd question a woman and a child. What happened here?' She changed tacks so quickly, it took Colbey a moment to realize that she had.

Colbey's grip had gone slippery from the blood trickling from his palm. More soaked the edges of a hole in his breeks, trailing down his leg to the floor. His bruised side ached nearly as badly as his arms. 'Ambush.' He did not explain further. Still ignoring his own injuries, he walked to Episte and knelt beside the teen.

Episte still hugged his mother's body to his chest, his face buried in her dress. Warrior's sinews shifted through childishly thin arms, making the tiny hairs sparkle.

Episte's behaviour did not suit Renshai, yet Colbey knew that this was no time for a lecture. Cleaning and sheathing his swords, he placed a firm hand on the youth's heaving shoulder. He smoothed the fine, gold locks with his other hand, though the gesture streaked the teen's hair with blood. 'She died fighting an opponent too strong for her. If her beliefs allow it, she found Valhalla.' Colbey used the most comforting words he knew. He saw no need to supply details that would only hurt. Unless Mitrian and Episte had peeked through the windows before entering, no one living could have witnessed the truth.

'Mother.' Episte sobbed, his word lost in the folds of her shift.

Mitrian spoke softly, but with inviolate authority. 'We have to go. Now.'

Colbey twisted to face her, but Episte remained in place. 'We have to go now,' the elder Renshai echoed.

Still Episte did not move.

Colbey waved for Mitrian to start without them.

Mitrian frowned. 'I'll get horses, but that'll draw attention. I'll expect you both to be ready to ride the instant I get back.' She added emphatically. 'Which won't take but a moment.' She disappeared through the door.

Colbey shook his young charge. 'Come on. There's nothing more we can do here. Let's go.'

Episte's grip cinched tighter, then loosened. Suddenly, he whirled and lunged toward Colbey.

Instinctively, Colbey recoiled. The teen's arms looped around the elder, clutching him in an embrace as rigid as the one he had used to cling to his mother's body. Warm tears seeped through Colbey's tattered tunic. Griefmad, Episte spoke in an infant's voice that Colbey scarcely recognized. 'She's dead. Gods, no. She's dead.'

Colbey stiffened, uncertain what to do. He understood that he had been more of a father to Episte than any other man. He knew that the youngster needed to share his grief, that Episte had come to him for the comforting he craved. But Colbey had no experience with such matters. The necessary words and gestures would not come, and he could only seize the opportunity. Catching Episte to him, he hefted the younger Renshai and headed for the door.

Mitrian met him there on the back of a prancing chestnut. She had armed herself with a sword from the streets. She held the reins of a thick-rumped bay. 'This was all I could get. Hurry! The Northmen are on us.'

For the first time, Episte looked up, face red and smeared with tears. Colbey half-dragged the teen to the doorway. 'We'll ride together.' He hefted Episte directly behind the bay's saddle, then leapt into the seat. Mitrian dropped the bay's reins, sending her horse into a gallop. Colbey's horse lurched after it, even before he found his seat or the reins. He caught both at a dead run, pleased to find that Episte kept his balance as well.

Shouts echoed through Santagithi's streets. Northmen mounted and on foot converged on them from every direction. Colbey drew his swords, seeing Mitrian raise hers as well. He slashed at the wild froth of Northmen, his swords a blur; and the enemy scattered in a wild retreat. Mitrian's steed did not slow. She pounded through the press, her horse or sword claiming those Northmen who did not move from her path fast enough. Colbey could hear hooves galloping over cobblestones from the center of town. Toward the woods, he found fewer horsemen, though a line of soldiers blocked Mitrian's route from the town.

Still, Mitrian did not slow. Colbey kicked his mount harder, and it skidded into a rear that required Episte to grab the back of the saddle for balance. As his horse drew up beside Mitrian's, they hacked through the wall together. The Northmen ahead broke, even as those behind narrowed the gap between them. Mitrian and Colbey surged through the hole and into the forest, a cluster of Northmen riding at their heels.

'They're this way!' Mitrian managed to shout over the war howls and curses of the Northmen. Though few Northmen spoke Western trade and fewer Westerners spoke Northern, some words crossed from Renshai to Northern. For the sake of decency, he hoped Mitrian and Episte did not understand many of the swear words.

Apparently, Mitrian had selected her steeds well. Well-rested, the animals plunged into the forest, dodging through gaps between trees and leaping deadfalls with an exuberance that most of the Northmen's tired horses could not match. All but a couple dozen fell behind, but those few remaining seemed to be narrowing the gap, and Colbey knew that running through brush was terribly dangerous. He kept tight to the horse's neck, and Episte flattened against Colbey.

Hearing voices ahead, Colbey shouted a warning. 'Danger before!'

'It's all right!' Mitrian hollered back. 'They're ours.'

A moment later, Colbey veered through a copse of pine and saw the group of retreating horsemen. A quick count left Colbey with an impression of thirty, most wearing the black and silver uniforms of Santagithi's guardsmen. He saw at least one woman among them, and he picked Rache, Santagithi, Garn, Bromdun, and Galan from the others. Northmen rode hard on their heels. The general shouted something that Colbey could not hear, but apparently Mitrian did. She diverted her course, angling to keep from sandwiching Northmen between Santagithi's men and herself.

Like the two sides of an arrow, they sped to a point, meeting just shy of a wide, dead trunk. Mitrian and Colbey veered in among the others, near the lead.

'Where to?' Colbey shouted. He knew they would need to stand and fight soon. Their current course would trap them against the Granite

Hills to be killed by Northmen coming from both directions.

Santagithi hesitated.

Apparently thinking the question was meant for her, Mitrian replied in his stead. 'There's a cave this way.' She waved northeast-ward, to a position far east of the passes that had become so familiar to the man. 'I explored it a few times when you made excuses for me to stay behind. There's a small back exit.'

Santagithi frowned in consideration. Then, apparently finding no better alternative, he nodded. 'Let's go.'

The mountains drew closer with every step. Mitrian took the lead, knowing the location of the sanctuary they sought. Colbey dared to look back, seeing one of their trailing men go down, a victim of the Northmen's fastest steed. Others turned on the Northman. Colbey glanced back, just in time to follow Mitrian into the dark mouth of the cave. 'Down!' Colbey skittered from his saddle, clinging to the side of his horse's neck to give Episte more room. He pulled his mount to a halt, sliding to the ground as it slowed. On a moving horse, a man could have his head torn off by low projections from the roof, and Colbey would rather face blood-hungry Northmen than lose his life or Episte's to foolishness.

Once in the cave, the others stopped and dismounted as well. Santagithi gathered the horses' reins. Colbey crouched near the mouth, glad to see the Northmen pull up outside the cave.

Santagithi made a sweeping gesture, nearly lost in the shadows. 'Mitrian, get everyone out that back exit you mentioned. Quietly. Colbey and I will hold off the Northmen.'

Colbey nodded, watching the Northmen dismount and ready weapons. He counted enemies, not bothering to turn.

If Mitrian protested, Colbey did not hear it. He followed the soft shuffle of footsteps as Santagithi's men disappeared deeper into the cave mouth, leaving only the two elders to hold the entrance.

Santagithi called after the retreating men. 'Go to Shadimar. He'll know what to do.' He did not bother to suggest that he would meet them there. Clearly, the general did not question his own death, nor even Colbey's. He approached the old Renshai. 'The horses . . . ' he started, the remainder of his plan wafting plainly through his thoughts.

Colbey waved Santagithi silent. 'I know what you're thinking. Good idea.'

Santagithi did not question Colbey's knowledge. 'Back here. Come on.'

Colbey moved around behind the clustered horses. Taking bandages from his pack, he bound the wounds on his hand and calf, while Santagithi set the trap. 'There're thirty-one of them,' Colbey said, his blood warming to the imminent combat. He listened to the conversations outside the cave. 'They're coming in after us.'

Swords rasped from sheaths, the sound echoing through the caverns. The Renshai could scarcely hear the Northmen's approaching footsteps beneath the stomping of their own horses, but their brief verbal exchanges gave away their positions.

'Now,' Santagithi said. His sword came free, flat slapping horses' flanks. Colbey drew both of his blades, spooking the beasts. Panicked, the horses raced for daylight, heedless of the Northmen they trampled. Screams replaced conversation and the sounds of readied weapons. Yet as the horses thundered away, fifteen Northerners remained on their feet. These threw themselves upon Santagithi and Colbey.

Steel chimed a reverberating chorus, like a carillon. Backs tight to the wall, Santagithi and Colbey fought side by side, as one. The Northmen struck in anger and with certain triumph, but the two men fought for their lives. Five Northmen died before a single one of their blows landed.

Colbey's blade opened a sixth man's throat, but his block fell short. Pain seared his chest and side. Ribs snapped, and Colbey's mind told him the wound would be fatal. Joy thrilled through him, bringing a battle madness he could never quench. Finally, he had found the death in combat he had sought, yet it would not find him an easy victim. Glorious combat was not enough. To die in honor, he had to take every Northman with him. Otherwise, they would surely dismember him, and he would lose all the purpose and direction his life had held.

'MODI!' The cry came naturally, trained through nearly a century. His charge became the rush of a whirlwind, and he left a line of dying men in his wake. No longer needing to concern himself with defense, he slashed like a crazed thing. Control snapped, plunging his brain into a darkness deeper than hovering death. He was a spinning flicker of lightning, yet far more deadly. The gashes their swords tore in his abdomen and sides meant nothing to him, and his thrusts sent every Northman in his path to Valhalla.

Santagithi continued to fight as well, though he found himself slightly less pressed. He dodged a Northman's stroke with ease. His foot twisted on an irregularity in the stone, and he fell to one knee. He threw up a hand in defense, but a Northman's sword sliced through his face. A second sword buried in his spine.

With a roar of rage, Colbey sprang upon the remaining pair of Northmen as they extinguished all life from Santagithi. One lost his head before he could free his sword from Santagithi's back.

The last Northman shrank from the icy glare of the grim-eyed demon who faced him.

16 Storm Before the Calm

To Mitrian and the twenty-eight survivors of the war with the North, dawn seemed a welcome change from the confining darkness of the caverns. Homeless and horseless, they stared at the layered pink horizon in sorrow. A pair of brothers in guardsman's uniforms clung to one another, unabashed. Aside from Mitrian, Garn, Rache, and Episte, who had one another, every other man and both of the women were alone. Mitrian resisted the urge to clutch her child and husband. Such an action would be cruel to the rest of the scraggly band that was all that remained of Santagithi's people. And still they were not safe. Too many soldiers, wearied by war and running, depended on the guidance of their three remaining leaders; Bromdun, Garn, and Mitrian had little choice but to follow their general's last command.

Thoughts of Santagithi sank Mitrian into the same grieving quagmire as her charges. She knew her father and Colbey had chosen to sacrifice their lives for these townspeople who quivered on the stones awaiting their leaders' orders. She felt guilty mourning the lives of heroes when she still had so much. Yet, for all the relief she felt over the presence of three loved ones, it did not ease the ache of losing her father and the man who had trained her. These pained first, peaking crescendos of agony surrounded by the duller throb of too many friends dead to sort individuals from her mind.

'Quickly.' Turning her back on the Granite Hills, Mitrian hopped down a series of crags like stairs, and slipped into the forest between the mountains and the Town of Santagithi. Many horses grazed singly, or in clusters, still saddled and bridled for the fighting men stricken from their backs. Mitrian chose a hardy chestnut, watching her husband and their followers scramble for mounts as well. They moved with a despairing slowness, lost in the memory of friends, family, and the only reality they knew, stolen from them after ten years of war. Most of the women and children still lived, Mitrian knew, yet they could wait. First, she needed to get the men and women with her to safety. Only then could they worry about collecting survivors and rebuilding the town.

Mitrian set the pace at a trot, certain the Northmen would soon come upon them and renew the chase. She dared not look back as they traveled west, then south along the southern extension of the Granite Hills. Color faded from the sky that turned a uniform blue as the sun crept across the horizon. Mitrian's thoughts slipped again and obsessively to Santagithi and Colbey. She imagined them plunging into battle with an exuberance that never seemed to fail. She saw Colbey as a blur of gold and silver. After watching him plunge into certain death repeatedly, to see age mark him so little, she had come to believe the Golden Prince of Demons invincible. But logic told her otherwise. The single factor that had kept him alive was skill. Numbers and luck would overpower even his abilities, and he had already been injured and exhausted in Emerald's cottage. Nevertheless, she let herself hope. *If anyone can survive an army of Northmen, it's Colbey and my father.*

As her nearly spent group crossed from woodlands to fire-cleared plains, Mitrian veered southward, toward Shadimar's ruins. A wind rose, cold as steel, biting beneath Mitrian's cloak. The sky dimmed to a neutral slate, and icy rain fell without warning. That was when the fog covering Mitrian's mind lifted enough for her to recall the magical tempest that warded the Eastern Wizard's home. She whirled on her horse, screaming a command meant to bunch her followers. But black clouds surged over them like tide, swallowing the sun, and the day grew as dark as a moonless night. Wind slapped Mitrian's face, drowning her command in its howl. Rain pelted her, no longer stinging droplets but a frenzied wave of water that soaked through all the layers of her clothing. Her horse trembled. Mitrian considered turning, but she knew from experience that that would only rob her of all sense of direction. Instead, she hunched against the horse's neck, urging it onward.

Guilt rode Mitrian, its surges as wild as the storm; and she cursed the grief that had allowed her to grow incautious. She had dragged her sorrow-stricken, exhausted followers into a threat familiar only to herself, a rain that sorrow had caused her to forget. She did not know for certain whether Shadimar had even returned from his mission; she could only trust his promise to be home if and when Santagithi needed him. She consoled herself with the realization that the ruins of Myrcidë would offer the surviving soldiers some shelter, and Shadimar's gale would deter the Northmen. At least, her followers knew they headed toward the home of the Wizard. The sorceries might not catch them wholly off their guard.

Something unseen thudded onto the rump of Mitrian's horse. The chestnut reared with a thunder-masked scream. Mitrian twisted numbing fingers in its mane. The horse reared upward again, and Mitrian fought its panic along with her own. She could not recall the storm seeming nearly so malignant in the past. This time, she feared that the slightest diversion might send her and her followers in the wrong direction. Without a horse, she could never hope to battle through the tempest. The chestnut reared again, forelegs clawing through fog, then dropped, rocking into a crazed buck.

Mitrian clung to the mane with one hand. With the other, she drew her sword and swung blindly over her horse's hindquarters. Her blade cut air, then met slight resistance. Lightning split the heavens to reveal a tawny shadow bounding from her horse and racing into the darkness. The horse planted its hooves in the muddy ground.

Mitrian urged the animal forward, sheathing her sword, confused as well as concerned. She dared not believe a predator had smelled her horse through the storm, even had one chosen to hunt in a magical rain; but if it killed her mount she could never reach Shadimar. Even now, the wild surges of the horse had made her lose her bearings, and she feared she might ride the wrong way, right into the swords of waiting Northmen. The wind rushed, agony through her ears. Then another blast of lightning colored the sky, briefly revealing another horseman. Mitrian reined toward the figure. Her horse's leap forward threw them into a wall of wind and rain. Afraid to lose the only person she had seen in the darkness, she flailed for the place where she had seen him. One sweep met a human arm, and she clutched it. A small, damp hand found hers and closed comfortingly. They became two lost souls, locked together and no longer alone.

'Who are you?' Mitrian asked. It was a wasted effort. Only one sound penetrated the thrum of wind, a distant piercing wolf howl. Idly, Mitrian wondered why she could hear this noise but not the frantic whinnies of her mount. Wolves reminded her of Secodon and Shadimar, so she reined toward the sound, hauling her companion with her.

Suddenly, stone scraped cloth and skin from Mitrian's calf. She recoiled with a sharp intake of breath. Her horse reared. Its hooves came down hard on a shattered statue, and it staggered. Tossed abruptly sideways, Mitrian plummeted, scrabbling for a hold on her floundering mount. Gentle hands caught her shoulders, steadying, then guided her to the front of his own saddle. Pinched against the horn, Mitrian pressed to her benefactor, exploring his knee for some clue to his identity.

The other placed his mouth to her ear and spoke loud enough to be heard. 'It's Episte. Hang on.'

Mitrian clung to the horse's mane, relief bringing tears to her eyes. At least one of the young Renshai had survived the storm, though she could not help wishing she had found Rache. Guilty for the thought, she found that it again opened the floodgate of shame and remorse.

Without a warning, she had led survivors into a magical storm that might claim most of their lives. Yet she had never remembered the Wizard's storm being lethal; before it had seemed more of a mild deterrent than a weapon. Another thought hit her. If she had skinned her leg on a statue, it could only mean they had entered the old city.

As if on cue, another flash displayed the ruins of Myrcidë. Knowing the way, Mitrian seized the reins at a point nearer to the horse than Episte's hands and steered for the remembered location of Shadimar's hall. Soon the door loomed before them, closing off an opening that Mitrian had entered without challenge once before, in dream, and had taken a note from on her second visit. The portal whisked open as they approached. The horse rushed for shelter.

Once inside, Mitrian found herself in a massive chamber that had changed little in the years since Shadimar had traded her the two topaz gems that still graced the wolf's head hilt of her sword. She found the Eastern Wizard himself standing like a doorman. Thirteen horses feasted on blueberries, carefully picking around the branches with an unhorselike meticulousness. Their sodden saddles, blankets, and bridles lay in a disorganized heap nearby. Mitrian dismounted, surprised to find that Episte had leapt down first. He stripped off the animal's saddle while Mitrian removed the bridle. Dropping the tack onto the pile, they released the horse. It wandered off to join its companions.

'This way,' Shadimar said. Without awaiting a reply, he headed deeper into the ruins. They passed through a long hall in silence, then the Wizard ushered them into a room. Two steaming bowls sat on a wooden table surrounded by chairs. A pot hung over a blazing fire in the hearth. The wolf sprawled by one of the chairs.

Shadimar gestured them into the room.

Mitrian stepped inside. Episte slipped past, taking a seat at the table. She turned back to face the Eastern Wizard. 'Others are here?' she asked hopefully.

'Yes. And they were famished. Sit. Eat.'

Episte sat.

Mitrian moved toward one of the bowls, still too nervous to eat. 'Were Garn and Rache with them?'

'Rache has come, but not Garn.' Shadimar ran through a list that included Galan and one of the two women. He did not mention Bromdun, and Mitrian guessed the other two commanders had hung back to help as many of the stragglers as possible. Since she knew the route, it made sense for her to stay in front and the other leaders to take up the rear.

'Can I see Rache?'

Episte lowered his head. He stirred a spoon through the mixture in the bowl, but he did not speak or eat.

'Soon enough,' Shadimar said. 'He's fine, but he's sleeping. There are others who may or may not make it through the storm.'

'Hello, Secodon.' Mitrian gave the wolf a feeble greeting and deliberately took the seat nearest him, though her food sat one place further along. She reached to pet him.

Secodon stood stiffly, avoiding her touch. He limped closer to the fire.

Mitrian frowned, surprised by the animal's behavior. He had always seemed friendly before. But, for now, more pressing matters needed attention. 'Garn? Will he make it?'

Shadimar shrugged. 'I don't know. There's no way to tell till he gets here.'

'You knew I was coming to ask about the falcon.'

'I didn't predict that. I was watching when Santagithi sent you.'

Shadimar's revelation did not surprise Mitrian. Sterrane had claimed that he and Shadimar directly spied on Béarn's castle using magic.

Episte continued to stir, as if entranced.

Despite the Eastern Wizard's hospitality, Mitrian could not help feeling betrayed. 'This is your storm.'

'In a strange and simplistic manner of speaking.' In spite of the possible implications of his words, the Wizard's tone made it clear he meant no offense.

'Were you trying to kill us all?'

'Certainly not.' Shadimar paused for a long time, as if he would let the matter rest half settled. At length, he finished. 'I've told you magic is unpredictable. I only wanted to know when visitors approached. The storm came as a side effect. True, I do have some control over its intensity, and I did strengthen it when Northmen fell within its influence.'

'Northmen?' Mitrian repeated.

Episte looked up, his blue eyes deeply haunted and his yellow hair plastered in wet ringlets. To Mitrian, he appeared more childlike than usual, and she wondered where he had found the strength to help her to his horse. Though she knew he had Renshai training and age, he seemed so small and fragile.

'Yes, Northmen. Did you think Renshai would escape them without pursuit?'

'I didn't think the Northmen knew we were Renshai. Except for Colbey.' Sorrow touched her again, but this time hunger accompanied it. The nutty aroma of the mixture in the bowls made her stomach rumble. She pulled the bowl and spoon to the space before her, leaving a wet impression on the wood in the shape of her sleeve.

'I'd be surprised if some hadn't figured it out. Some of your own, too.' Shadimar returned to his original point. 'I won't have your battles at my doorstep. I saw to it that no Northman would make it here. If it costs you some of your own, I'm sorry. That's the price of sanctuary.'

As cold as the Wizard's comments seemed, they ceased to bother Mitrian. Among so many deaths, a few more scarcely seemed significant, a drop of sorrow and guilt lost in an endless torrent. Though Garn's absence stabbed at her with a separate pain, she managed to eat. Starving herself would not help him, but she did vow not to sleep until he arrived safely at the Wizard's home.

Episte stared, still not touching his food. Water dripped from his hair and clothing like tears.

Shadimar continued to talk while Mitrian ate. 'If it makes you feel any better, I did send a guide. Unfortunately, he approached someone with less caution than the situation demanded.' He did not explain further, but Secodon's whine told Mitrian the story.

In a flash of insight, she recalled the creature that had jumped on her horse. She looked at the wolf. Secodon met her gaze, then lowered his head to the floor.

The last bite of stew dispelled Mitrian's hunger. She clambered from the chair to kneel beside the wolf. 'I'm sorry, Secodon. I didn't recognize you.'

The wolf heaved a deep sigh, and his plumed tail struck the floor twice.

Shadimar turned his attention to Episte. 'You should eat.'

'Thank you, for the food and the shelter. But I'm just too tired to eat.'

'We'll talk later,' Shadimar said, obviously seeing a need that Mitrian had missed, enmeshed in her own sorrow, fatigue, and responsibilities. 'For now, come with me.' Shadimar returned to the hall.

Secodon rose awkwardly, following his master and favoring his right hind paw. Mitrian winced, then followed, and Episte accompanied her.

Shadimar led his charges to the next chamber, where the men and women he had named slept in sprawling disarray. Episte curled into a quiet corner. Finding Rache, Mitrian chose a spot beside him. Though she did not want to wake him, her mothering instincts overwhelmed her. First, she placed a hand on his chest. The deep rhythm of his breathing sent a joy through her that she had not known for days. With a finger, she brushed tawny strands of hair from his face. Then, exhaustion crushed her to the floor. She curled up beside him, resting her eyes while she waited for Garn. Her thoughts fragmented, mixed with picture-concepts from the deeper, uncontrollable part of her mind. Sleep came, unbidden.

Mitrian awakened pinned beneath Garn's heavy arm. She sat up suddenly. Garn lay still, eyes closed, though surely her movement had awakened her wary husband as well. Years of living among savage killers had trained him to read the subtlest patterns of breathing, to awaken with the slightest movement, and to hide his own alertness from those around him. Mitrian counted the others. She discovered twenty-one people of the original twenty-eight, and that did not include Episte and Rache whom she knew to be among the survivors, though they were not currently in the room. Bromdun slept deeply, sprawled in the corner where Episte had lain.

Mitrian wiggled free of the restraining arm, patting Garn to indicate that he should sleep. Tiptoeing around the sleeping forms, she crept to the hallway and toward the dining room.

Within a few steps, Episte's voice floated to her from a cross corridor. '. . . said Rache's father and mine hated each other. She said Garn broke my father's back and bragged about it afterward.'

The words froze Mitrian. She had always known this moment would come, yet the constant threat or presence of war had allowed Garn to delay his heart-to-heart with his son. Though Santagithi had kept the guards quiet, Mitrian knew snippets of rumors would slip past. Guilt came in a rush for leaving Shadimar to handle this delicate history, yet she had promised Garn not to do so herself. And, though she hated to admit it, she wondered how the ancient Wizard would reply.

Shadimar cleared his throat, speaking with the annoying indirectness that had become too familiar. 'Chance is man's cruelest mistress. She acts without logic or motive, and you must never attribute her works to gods or mortals.'

In the silence that followed, Mitrian crept closer. She knew eavesdropping was wrong, but to announce her presence meant dealing with an issue she had promised to avoid. She considered waking Garn, but interest held her spellbound. For the sake of her son and Episte, she could not miss any of the conversation. Though he had, as yet, said nothing, Mitrian guessed Rache was with them.

Impatience tinged Episte's voice. 'Are you saying chance crippled my father?'

Shadimar's placid baritone wafted clearly to Mitrian. 'Chance placed your fathers against one another when other circumstances might have made them friends. Episte, your father begged Garn to raise you as he lay dying. And Garn named his only son for your father. Does that sound like an exchange between enemies?'

'No,' Episte admitted.

Mitrian came forward, pleased by Shadimar's approach.

Episte's next statement stopped her cold. 'If he hadn't been a cripple, would my father still be alive?'

'That is not a question with an answer.'

Finally, Rache joined the conversation. 'It doesn't matter, Episte. Our fathers were stupid to hate each other. We're brothers. What our fathers did means nothing to me.'

Mitrian hugged the wall, feeling its cold seep through her. She knew she should make her presence known, yet her feet and her tongue seemed tacked in place.

Episte's next words made it clear that Rache had missed the point. 'Of course, it doesn't matter. Because crippled or not, my father never knew his limits. My mother said he was a battle seeker who craved death more than he did her or me. Colbey taught him, and, when it came to war and death, he was just like Colbey.'

Shadimar hesitated only a moment. 'Your mother should not have said those things.'

'Are they lies?' Episte shouted. When he did not receive an immediate answer, he repeated the question more quietly but with more force. 'Are . . . they . . . lies?'

'There are ways,' Shadimar said, 'to say the same things with kinder words. Any Northman, especially any Renshai, might seem so to one who doesn't understand the philosophy.'

Rache piped in. 'Your father was a hero who died in glory and went to Valhalla. I'm proud to have him as my guardian. Have you ever heard anyone call him anything but the greatest captain and the greatest hero the town ever had? Without him, the guards would never have lived as long as they did.'

'If the guards had been a little less competent, maybe we wouldn't have fought this war at all.' Bitterness tainted Episte's voice, and Mitrian thought she heard fatigue as well. 'And my mother might be alive. Better a slave who returns to his son than a dead hero. What good is it to have a hero for a father, or any father at all, if he never *never* comes home?'

The conversation had gone too far for Mitrian. She walked to the doorway with long, sweeping strides so that no one would guess that she had stood so long listening. 'Good morning.' She smiled, but the reference to Garn as a slave in front of his son dampened the cheerfulness of her greeting.

Shadimar sat across the table from the two young Renshai. Steam rose from their mugs, swirling in wisps toward the ceiling. All three appeared well-rested, though the teens still wore leather tunics and breeks spotted darkly with sweat and grime. A fire danced on a pile of orange bricks in the hearth, the flames licking around a hanging pot. Shadimar rose, returning Mitrian's smile. Blue robes hung loosely from his narrow frame. His beard and hair looked neatly combed, as always, and his gray eyes seemed heavy with knowledge. 'Good morning, Mitrian. Join us for tea.'

Secodon's head appeared from under the table. He stood, tail waving, limped to Mitrian, and pushed his nose against her hand. Laughing, she patted the wolf's head, her fingers tracing one triangular ear.

A knock echoed through the horses' room, reverberating from the net of blueberry bushes and the stumps of crumpled statues. The noise sounded feeble; had the chamber contained furniture, Mitrian would never have heard the tap at all. The Eastern Wizard stiffened as if affronted, and his gray eyes widened with surprise. The wolf crouched, stalking the outer door.

Remembering that the wolf mirrored its master's mood, Mitrian became wary. Her chest seemed to constrict with a mixture of warning and anticipation. Recalling that Shadimar had known of her presence, and that of the Northmen, before she arrived, she questioned. 'Who is it?'

Shadimar followed Secodon, and Mitrian kept pace with the Wizard. 'I don't know,' he said. And, though his voice remained as placid as usual, his words told all. Someone or thing had violated his wards. Clearly that had never happened before.

Mitrian glanced back to check the positions of Rache and Episte and discovered they had followed her. In her moment's pause, Shadimar moved ahead, stopping directly before the heavy, stone panel. Mitrian doubted any sound could penetrate the door, yet the Wizard shouted. 'Who seeks entrance to my home!'

Silence followed. Shadimar must have thrown some magic, because now Mitrian could hear the storm pounding the ruins. Beneath the hammer of the rain came a weak whisper, words borne on a dying breath. Despite the frailness of the voice, it still managed to carry a hint of sarcasm. 'You're such a damned good Wizard . . . ' A shuddering breath broke the stream. '. . . *you* tell *me*.'

Shadimar jerked open the door. Colbey took one staggering step inside, then collapsed on the floor. Shredded strips of cloth were wound about a body gashed and striped with wounds, stained scarlet. She saw the white gleam of shattered ribs poking through the flesh and a dark hint of exposed organs beyond. A muddy pool of water dripped from his hair.

Mitrian froze in shock and horror, uncertain whether to hope for Colbey's life or his death. She hovered between joy and grief. Already, she had accepted his death. As much as she wanted to celebrate his life, she knew his ephemeral grasp on it had probably just disappeared on Shadimar's floor. Having his body only meant that she could give him the proper pyre, the need for which had probably driven him here, through storm and enemies, though he should have died long ago. And she took solace from the fact that all his limbs remained intact. Finally, Colbey would find Valhalla.

Shadimar bent over Colbey, studying him from every angle before rolling the Renshai on his back. Colbey's eyes were closed, his features lax but no less stern. The Wizard shoveled his hands under the Renshai's shoulders. 'Rache, gather some herbs. There's a field to the south. Look for anything with pink flowers.' The Wizard mumbled something unintelligible, and the rain lessened to a trickle. Rache stepped carefully over Colbey and outside. 'Mitrian, Episte, help me carry him.'

Mitrian knelt, catching one leg, and Episte gripped the other. Through the chill of Colbey's sodden breeks, she felt an intense heat. His fever and the steady trickle of blood onto the bandages told her that he still lived. But if his wounds did not take him, infection surely would. Balancing Colbey's weight among the three of them, Mitrian and Episte followed Shadimar down the corridor, past the room in which the survivors slept, and into the next chamber. A straw pallet filled one corner, a closed chest at its foot. Beside it, a round table rested on four boulders, an unlit candle melted to its center. Cloud-muted sunlight spilled through a high hole with jagged edges. Clearly, some heavy weapon had smashed the stone, and it had not always been a window.

Shadimar carried Colbey to the bed, and they set him gently on the straw. Episte sat, cross-legged, on the floor, clutching one of the elder's limp hands. Shadimar knelt, placing both of his palms on Colbey's forehead. Mitrian waited in silence. She had some healing knowledge, learned from Colbey, yet her teacher required far more than she could give him. Uncertain what else to do, she set to work mechanically, removing bandages and bits of clothing. Blood stained her arms, still a bright red.

Shadimar spoke in a language Mitrian did not understand. Holding pressure against the tear in Colbey's chest, she glanced to the head of the pallet. To her amazement the Renshai's eyes opened to slits. His hand trembled momentarily in Episte's grip, and she saw hope flicker in the youth's eyes. Then the lids fell closed again, and every muscle in Colbey's body relaxed. Mitrian still felt a steady heartbeat beneath her grip. Uncertain how hard to work, Mitrian let Shadimar make the judgments. As much as she wanted Colbey to live, she kept her hopes in check. If he was certain to die, she did not wish to prolong his suffering. And, there was no doubt in her mind that he was in pain.

'Can you help him?'

'I don't know,' Shadimar replied, rocking back to his haunches.

Mitrian needed something more definite. 'What do you think?'

Shadimar stood. 'What I think is of little consequence. What Colbey thinks is all that matters now.' Unnervingly calm, the Eastern Wizard turned from his guests and left the room.

King Sterrane of Béarn paced the castle corridors alone, his massive feet clomping echoes along the hallways. The hollow sounds made him lonely, hungry for the playful screams and running footfalls of the children who had once filled these halls. Illness had taken too many. He had buried his cousin, along with three of his own children, and two of Bel's. Yet Miyaga's death seemed not to deter Rathelon's bid for Béarn's throne at all. Individually and in bands, his followers had fallen prey to imprisonment or to battle, and Sterrane had lost many of his own guards to Rathelon's evil. Though the skirmishes had diminished greatly, they never seemed to end. And what Rathelon missed, the Pudar-borne illness ravaged, thwarting Sterrane's need to assist allies he loved, some of whom had helped him regain his own kingdom and had probably already succumbed themselves.

The finery of the palace walls had never held meaning for Sterrane; since childhood, strings of gems and imported carvings had filled his gaze in all directions. He had not missed any of it during his years with Shadimar nor, later, as a hermit in the Granite Hills. Now, the animal-shaped torch brackets seemed to mock him, wealth that had translated to nothing when it came to saving Béarn's allies and citizens. And its children.

Tears washed Sterrane's eyes. He would have cried unabashedly, even had the corridors been filled with courtiers. Apparently sensing the bearlike king's need to be alone, even Mar Lon and Baran had discreetly disappeared. Sterrane appreciated their attempt to read his sorrow. Yet he had always preferred the company of people, even when burdened with responsibilities they could not understand and he would never think to share.

Sterrane shuffled toward the nobles' quarters, mind filled with the Eastern Wizard's words, spoken so long ago he did not understand how or why they had remained with him so vividly: 'The King of Béarn is an anchor, a center for all forces working upon mortals and the world, at times the passive balance that even the Eastern and Western Wizards cannot be, at others an active force of stabilization. When your times comes, Sterrane, you will always make decisions. No matter their content or reason, their seeming grandeur or insignificance, the effects will radiate further than you can guess. Still, you must make those choices with the same simple logic you use to rule your life.

When the time comes, you will make the ideal high king.'

Sterrane kicked at a familiar scuff mark on the stone, feeling like anything but the ideal king. Surely, the gods had had reason for plaguing his lands with traitors and disease, for stealing all of his attention at a time when true allies needed his aid. He could only believe that, when Santagithi's Town fell, it would do so with honor and dignity. For all of the Renshai, he wished for life or, at least, a death in the heated glory of battle. For the women, children, and soldiers he wished long lives, health, and happiness. Still, his decisions ached within him.

Sterrane pressed his back to the wall and sank to the floor, burying his face in his arm. Had he sent his men to Santagithi, so many more at home would have died. Surely, King Verrall of Pudar could have spared some troops, and his reasons for not aiding Santagithi's people sounded like thinly-veiled prejudice. Sterrane knew that had probably worked for the best. Had Pudar sent men to Santagithi as they had to Béarn, the consumption might have taken down Santagithi's soldiers and civilians as well.

A presence settled beside Sterrane, and a gentle hand smoothed his hair. 'Here you are.' Sterrane recognized Arduwyn's voice. 'I've been looking for you.'

'Why?' Sterrane's arm muffled his question.

'Because you needed me.'

The king looked up into Arduwyn's deep brown eye and smiled. Of all his people, the flame-haired archer knew him best.

17 The Survivors

Colbey lay in a quiet slumber that had grown too familiar to Mitrian in the last three days. She sat in vigil by his bedside, her back pressed to the wall and her thoughts distant. Her mind conjured images of the citadel on the hilltop that had once been her home, of the view from its crest that had made the town unfurl like a map below her. Years of memory traced the picture in vivid detail: the straight rows of cottages, the roads dotted with the men and women she had loved, and the yards filled with the white, bushlike forms of sheep. For so many years, the play screams of children had sounded through the streets; at one time, these had called her to her own games.

But the world she had known had crumbled, a war spoil of Northmen. Probably, they had left now; geographical barriers would make it nearly impossible for Northmen to hold the territory. The survivors could return to their loved ones and, over many years, rebuild the city that had once stood, cradled between the mountain ranges. For Mitrian, nothing remained. No matter their condition, the buildings she had lived in since birth were haunted by her parents. Santagithi's strong presence permeated even her mental images of the town.

The men in the next room would need to select a new leader as well, and Mitrian meant to make their choice easy. She knew it would need to be a man. To other societies, like the Renshai, gender mattered little, but the West had a narrower image of female and male roles. Santagithi's remaining citizens had undergone too much to have the foundations of their religion and society disrupted also. Garn's zeal and lack of strategic competence would make him a poor choice. And, having lived most of her life in Santagithi's citadel, Mitrian doubted she could adjust to a cottage. All of her childhood playmates lay dead, casualties of Garn's wrath, the Great War, and the war she had just survived. Those members of her family who were not dead were with her, and Mitrian had no reason to return to a city of ghosts that would spark her memories and grief at every turn.

Mitrian placed her hand on Colbey's, as usual receiving no movement or response. Occasionally, he did stir into consciousness, at times enough to swallow a few spoonfuls of Shadimar's herb concoction. But Colbey never became coherent. No life looked out from his eyes, even when he opened them. Still, Mitrian hoped, fearing the responsibilities his death would force upon her. She still practiced her sword maneuvers daily, and Rache always joined her. Since their arrival in the Eastern Wizard's ruins, Episte had done little more than sleep and keep his vigils at Colbey's bedside.

A tap sounded on the door, then it swung open. Rache stood in the entryway. 'My turn, Mama.'

Mitrian rose, yawning.

Rache stepped across the threshold, studying Colbey in the candlelight. 'Anything?' he asked, mostly from politeness, Mitrian guessed.

Mitrian shook her head. She took one last look at Colbey. Shadimar's robes covered the ugly gashes and bruises that mottled the Renshai's form. Mitrian cringed at the thought. Though her ministrations, and Shadimar's, had caused the wounds to heal far more quickly than she would have believed possible, it seemed like an obscenity and a tragedy that anyone would deface a god's creation of such grace. Her memory could not quite recreate the perfection of his sword katas, his movements more agile, confident, and precise than any dancer. Once, she had believed Episte's father was the epitome of male beauty. But, though the elder Rache had had youth, Colbey's speed and skill put even him to shame.

Mitrian caught her son into a powerful embrace. Rache returned his mother's grip, his tawny mane soft against her face, his shoulders as thick as his father's. Not only had he inherited his father's muscled physique, honed by the intensity of his Renshai training, but he sported the gigantic bone structure that Mitrian had inherited from her father. Mitrian found it difficult to remember that her huge son was barely thirteen.

'I'll take care of things here.' Rache pulled free of his mother's arms. 'They're talking about the future in there.' He jerked a thumb toward the general sleeping room. 'Papa's asleep, and I think one of you should be there.'

Mitrian cast one last look at Colbey. He stirred restlessly but did not open his eyes. Turning, she headed from the room. Soon, she suspected, Episte would join Rache. Although the boys took separate watches, they frequently overlapped their time, blurring it into one long double vigil during which they chatted or played cards or chess.

Though narrow and unadorned, the hallway seemed comfortable after hours in Colbey's sickroom. Shadimar's herbs obscured the odors of infection and old blood, but she did not realize how overpowering the plant smells were until she stepped into the windswept coolness of the corridor. Quietly, she traversed the familiar path to the survivors' sleeping room. Her concerns remained heavy within her, and the nightmare of death and disease followed her to the doorway.

Inside, twenty men and two women discussed the future over bowls of Shadimar's stew. Garn lay in the farthest corner, sleeping lightly. The highest ranking officer, archer Captain Bromdun stood listening, one foot propped against the wall and a steaming bowl in his hand. Episte paced, a fragile child threading amid the others in silence. A stout soldier Mitrian knew as Tobhiyah stood in the center of the room, his stew at his feet.

Seated with the others on the floor, Galan was speaking as Mitrian entered. '. . . can't continue. Shadimar's going to run short of food or patience. Twenty-four house guests become a bother eventually, no matter how much they sleep.'

One of the women kicked a heavyset warrior sitting next to her. 'He'll run out of food tomorrow if Daegga stays.'

Daegga continued to shovel stew into his mouth, ignoring the taunt.

A soldier near Garn raised a more practical issue. 'There're still four of us that never made it through the storm. They could still be coming. And what about Santagithi?'

A man next to the speaker grunted. 'Santagithi's dead.'

The soldier spun around to face the other man directly. 'How do you know? Colbey made it.'

'What's left of him.'

Episte whirled, glaring at the speaker. 'When Colbey wakes up, he can tell us what happened to Santagithi.'

Tobhiyah snorted. 'When Colbey wakes up? What nonsense, child. In three days, we've gotten nothing into him but water and a few herbs and only babbling out. The man is dead.'

Episte's face went purple. Before Mitrian could think to stop him, the teenager sprang in a wild fury. 'He'll outlive you, scum! I'll see to that!' His sword was a blur that seemed barely to flicker in its course from Episte's sheath to Tobhiyah's throat.

Tobhiyah staggered backward, his foot slamming into his bowl. Gravy splashed across stone. The bowl rolled beneath the soldier's foot, and he fell awkwardly to the floor. The bowl clattered over granite, trailing stew.

Tobhiyah's clumsiness gained Mitrian the time she needed to step between the youth and the fallen man. Though red-faced, Episte did not press. His sword hovered, clearly meant to intimidate, not to kill.

The woman who had not yet spoken clambered to her feet, avoiding the spilled stew. 'Quit it! We can't be fighting amongst ourselves. Not now. I was a girl when we built our town and chose our most wise and skilled warrior as our leader. Santagithi was young, but he proved his ability well enough in the battles we fought to arrive at and claim our land. He treated us all with respect. He loved us enough to die for us.' Her words echoed in the growing silence, and she seemed tiny amid so many warriors. 'We owe it to him to wait.'

The others met her pronouncement with nods and grunts of agreement. Episte sheathed his sword. Tobhiyah backed cautiously away. The woman who had playfully insulted Daegga pulled a rag from the bedding and began to clean the mess with Daegga's help.

'I have a suggestion.' Galan kept his gaze locked on Episte, as if he feared resistance to his idea. 'We can decide what to do based on Colbey. If, gods willing, he survives, we can ask him about Santagithi. If he dies, we will accept our leader's death as well.'

Rache appeared in the doorway. 'Then, maybe you should talk with Colbey instead of about him.'

Joy sparked in Mitrian. Doubt did not allow her to become too excited by the news. 'Is he . . . ?' She did not bother to finish.

Rache grinned broadly. 'Awake and aware.' Turning, he headed back toward the sickroom. Mitrian followed. As one, the others scrambled after her, trailing down the hallway in a noisy cloud of speculation. Without knocking, they burst into Shadimar's bedroom, discovering the Renshai propped on the ticking, the Wizard sitting on the floor beside him. A grimy piece of leather filled the Eastern Wizard's lap.

Shadimar frowned at the interruption, but Colbey grinned tolerantly. His face looked pale, even for his Northern coloring, and blankets covered his torso. 'I would be flattering myself to believe all your concern is for me.' He winced with every word; apparently speaking caused him pain. His gaze trailed over the crowd, and Mitrian noticed that the fever had driven some of the coldness from his eyes. 'You want to know about your general.' It was a logical guess.

Episte shoved through to the front; his smile seemed to encompass his entire face.

Colbey coughed, and sympathetic pain stabbed through Mitrian. 'The news is good and bad. Santagithi was killed. We lost a fine warrior, but take solace.'

Tobhiyah interrupted, voice harsh with bitterness and sorrow. 'He died in battle. Yes, we know. Spare us the Valhalla speech. I heard it from Rache. Fifty times was enough. All that matters is he's dead.'

A hush grew, though whether in horror at Tobhiyah's disrespect or in honor of Santagithi, Mitrian did not know. Forced to accept her father's death for certain, Mitrian felt grief crush down upon her again. She dabbed at her moistening eyes, no longer able to deny the truth she had known for days.

Garn broke the silence. 'How did you escape?'

Colbey's gaze plucked Garn from the group. 'After Santagithi and I killed the Northmen who had followed us all, and the general lost his life in valiant combat . . . ' Rerouted by the need to mention the glory of Santagithi's death, Colbey lost the thread of his sentence. '. . . I was sure hundreds of Northmen would soon be upon us. Since I didn't know the cave, I dragged Santagithi's body to a random passage. To my dismay, it ended blind. Before I could choose another direction, I heard voices. Trapped and injured, I bandaged my wounds from habit. I never expected to survive them.' He glanced at Shadimar, as if for explanation, but he did not give the Wizard an opening for reply. 'The Northmen's words echoed through the caverns, and I sifted out their plans. Most had circled the cave to wait at the back exit you had already cleared. The others formed a wall, sweeping the passage from front to back. It would have worked, too, except for one detail. I didn't know how to find the back exit. So I sealed off Santagithi's body with what rubble I could gather, lacking supplies for a pyre. With no other place to go, I went back to the entrance. Unwittingly, the Northmen had left me a herd of horses from which to choose my steed. As agreed, I rode here. And here I am.'

The old Renshai looked directly at Shadimar. 'I could have received a kinder welcome. Your storm nearly finished me.'

Having already defended his tempest to Mitrian, the Eastern Wizard only shrugged. 'I'm afraid, Colbey Calistinsson, magic is not as predictable as your sword.'

Bromdun restored command to his superior. 'So what now, sir. Do you think it's safe to return home?'

The crowd pressed forward, eager for Colbey's reply. Nearly all had left loved ones as captives of the Northmen. Most had left the plight of their kin an unanswered question.

'I think it's safe for you to return home.' Colbey's response seemed noticeably odd. By avoiding the term 'us,' he had excluded himself, at least. 'You'll need to replace your food stores and anything with monetary value, but I don't believe the Northmen would harm anyone who didn't fight back. They may have taken a few children as slaves or gladiators . . . '

Mitrian's eyes strayed naturally to Garn for his reaction. Discovering most of the others looking in the same direction, she cursed her insensitivity. Garn seemed to handle the attention well, his attention completely on Colbey.

'. . . If you deal with it gently and keep your heads, you may barter those children back. Be patient. The Northmen are strict, but not cruel. They shouldn't suffer.' Colbey looked out over the survivors. 'You don't have men to spare for fool's missions or attacks in anger.'

'You're not coming with us, sir?' Bromdun asked the obvious question. You're not going to help us set things right?'

'No.' Colbey lowered himself to the bed, his voice softening. 'The rumors that I'm Renshai have always been true. So long as I'm with you, the Northmen will continue to attack. You have enough to do without worrying about going back, unprepared, to a war once lost.' He shook his head. 'I would never ask anyone to lie. It would, however, be best if the Northmen believed I was dead.'

Order erupted into a clamor of conversation. Apparently sympathetic to Colbey's need for rest, Bromdun raised a hand. 'Quiet! Everyone out.' As the survivors filed back into the hallway, Bromdun addressed Shadimar. 'If we may intrude one more night, we'll leave at sunrise.'

Shadimar remained in place. 'As you wish.'

Colbey waved Mitrian to him. 'Stay behind. I need to talk to the other Renshai.'

Mitrian nodded. She caught Garn's arm, then gestured to Rache and Episte to remain.

The last of the survivors filed through the door, and Bromdun closed the door behind himself and his charges. Shadimar stayed as well. Neither his presence nor Garn's seemed to bother Colbey.

'You have my tunic?' Colbey swiveled his gaze to Shadimar.

Shadimar raised the tattered, bloodstained rag. 'Such as it is.' He shook it gently, and a medallion slid to the floor on a silver chain. 'What's this?' He hefted it.

Colbey's gaze followed the jewelry. 'I found that around Santagithi's neck. That close to his heart, a warrior wears only something he treasures. Rache, Santagithi was your grandfather. I thought you should have it.'

Shadimar handed it to Rache, who stared at the medallion on his palm, the chain dangling through his fingers. Episte fidgeted as if in distress.

Mitrian shifted in closer for a better look. She recognized the piece now. 'My mother used to wear that.' She reached for it, taking it by the chain, and scooting her hands to the medallion. 'It opens. My mother used to keep a lock of Father's hair in it. She believed that if she kept a piece of him with her, he would always come back from his forays.' Mitrian considered a moment, working the clasp. 'And he always did, too.' She opened the medallion. A piece of folded parchment floated to Shadimar's lap.

'Doesn't look like hair to me,' Garn stated the obvious, craning for a peek.

An uneasy feeling settled in the pit of Mitrian's stomach. 'Do you think he left us a message, knowing he would die?' The idea of a note from the grave made her excited and queasy at once.

Colbey shook his head. 'He didn't have time to write anything. At least not since before we left for the final battle.'

Shadimar unfolded the parchment.

'What's it say?' Rache tried to read the words upside down in Shadimar's grip.

'It says . . . ' Shadimar read: 'Why Nantel will let Rache choose his swords from this day forth.'

'What?' The words seemed wildly out of place, nothing distantly approaching anything Mitrian had expected.

Shadimar turned the parchment, orienting the letters in their proper direction for Mitrian. He passed the message to her.

Mitrian read, nodding to confirm Shadimar's recitation. She recognized the handwriting at once. The elder Rache's pen strokes had the same competent precision as his sword strokes. 'Episte's father wrote this. Decades ago, I'm sure.' Her face screwed into a knot of confusion. 'Why would my father carry it?' She waved the page by one corner.

Episte pinched a loose edge, and took it from Mitrian's hand. He studied the parchment, as if to glean some understanding from the handwriting, if not from the words.

Suddenly, Mitrian's question no longer seemed apt. She wanted to describe the man behind the writing, to make Episte know the love and loyalty that would cause a leader to keep an ancient scrap of paper to remember a long dead captain. She wanted to describe the savage courage and beauty that had made Episte's father attract followers and enemies like a flame draws moths. Yet, she knew that Episte had heard the descriptions and stories so many times before. She passed the medallion back to her son.

'How appropriate,' Colbey said softly. 'A memory from both of your grandparents and from your guardian at once.'

Rache tugged at the parchment. Episte released it with obvious reluctance, his gaze rolling to the floor. He said nothing.

Rache refolded the parchment, replaced it into its compartment, then snapped the medallion shut. He studied his older, smaller 'brother.' I have my memories of my grandparents and the knowledge of a guardian hero in Valhalla. That's more than enough.' Taking the medallion, he pressed it into Episte's hand. 'Brother, I think you should have this.'

Episte stared at the offering, palm open and fingers spread. He looked up, meeting Rache's gaze. The two boys exchanged nervous smiles that had meaning only for siblings. 'Thank you,' he said, at last, fingers closing over the medallion. His voice roughened, betraying impending tears. He turned away from the other Renshai.

Mitrian took a step forward to comfort the teen, then thought better of it. At sixteen, Episte would probably resent her intrusion. Alone, he could gain control of his tears more easily. Instead, she turned her attention to another who had also said something that, she felt, needed supporting. 'Colbey, you know that anywhere you go, the Renshai will come with you. And Garn, too, of course.'

Garn stood behind Mitrian, placing his hands on her hips to indicate that he agreed with her decision, though she had not consulted him.

Colbey tucked his hands behind his head, apparently too weak to sit up again. 'Of course.'

Colbey's matter-of-fact pronouncement struck Mitrian momentarily speechless. She had expected him to at least go through the polite motions of pretending the choice was hers, to acknowledge some sacrifice to her giving up what remained of the town in which she had been born and raised.

Colbey seized on Mitrian's silence. 'The Renshai need to find a place where we can live and practice without enemies to interfere. North and east would be best, I think.'

'North and east,' Garn repeated incredulously. 'That's toward the Northmen.'

'Only if we stay on this side of the Great Mountains.' Colbey made a looping gesture to indicate travel to the Western Plains, through the passes of the Great Frenum Mountains and into the Eastlands.

'The Eastlands?' Mitrian shivered, every racial memory coming to the forefront. Legends of the Great War, now over, had long preceded her birth. Since infancy, she had been taught to hate the evil Eastlanders, to understand that they might, one day, destroy the West. 'We can't go there.'

'Why not?'

Mitrian wondered whether Colbey had lost his faculties in the battle. 'Because they're evil. They're the enemy. They'd kill us just for entering their part of the world.'

Colbey chuckled. 'They wouldn't be the first to find Renshai don't die easily. Remember, they just lost a war, too. They've had more time to rebuild, but I can't see them being eager to battle with anyone right now. So long as we put up a strong defense and make it obvious we're not going to start anything. I think they'll leave us alone.' He pulled the blanket nearly to his chin. 'Northmen, on the other hand, the Easterners won't tolerate. I don't think Valr Kirin or his charges would follow us there.'

'You're a Northman,' Garn reminded. He glanced at the other Renshai. 'Episte looks enough like his father to be a Northman, and I think Mitrian managed to give Rache every drop of Northern blood Santagithi had.'

Colbey did not budge. 'Westerners come in a lot of different types. We don't act like Northmen, and I'm the only one with an accent. I think the Easterners will know the difference.'

Garn remained relentlessly practical. 'We don't speak their language.'

'I speak enough to get by. And at least a few of them will know the Western trading tongue.'

Shadimar cleared his throat. 'I speak Eastern. If the Renshai will have me, I'd like to accompany you.' His expression was even more serious than usual. 'Colbey, I think I may take you up on your offer, after all.'

Colbey's brows rose in question. When the Wizard did not clarify, the Renshai addressed the first request. 'We'd be honored to have you.'

Shadimar ignored the compliment. 'I have enemies, too. My presence may place you in grave danger. Any champion of mine will attract my enemies as well.'

Colbey laughed, a deep rumble of wry mirth. 'Are you implying that we're safe without you? Are your enemies worse than hundreds of Northern soldiers hunting Renshai or the warriors of every nation who consider us such a threat that they kill their own for speaking our name?'

Shadimar met Colbey's gaze with a silent glare of fury. 'Yes, they are. Will you still have me?'

Mitrian glanced back and forth, placing a hand on Garn's arm. She felt certain that Colbey and Shadimar were discussing matters that went far beyond what she had heard. No matter Shadimar's enemies, she felt safer with the Wizard.

Colbey did not consider for long. 'The enemies of my brother are my enemies already. We're more powerful together than apart.'

Garn fidgeted. Apparently having regained control of his emotions, Episte returned to Rache, placing a hand protectively on the younger boy's shoulder.

'Very well,' Shadimar said. 'I think we're safe here. We'll leave as soon as you feel well enough to travel.'

Episte placed the chain around his neck, and the medallion disappeared beneath his tunic.

Colbey closed his eyes, clearly worn out by the conversation. Shadimar herded Mitrian, Garn, Episte, and Rache from the room.

Part III
Carcophan's Champion

18 The Journeys Begin

The Northern Sorceress, Trilless, sat cross-legged on the floor of her stone-walled cottage, a tattered, ancient book in her lap. The Northern Sea had splashed against the protective wall for centuries, gradually rounding the contour to the smoothness of a dolphin's head. Waves crashed, roiling the waters of the fjords. Yet Trilless' home had stood for centuries, protected from above by the ragged cliffs and from below by the water animals that were her minions.

Books littered the single table of Trilless' library, many more scattered across the floor. Shelves rose from floor to ceiling along every wall, holding tomes that ranged in age from millennia to months, from the width of a finger to the breadth of all ten. The one in her lap made the next oldest volume seem infantile. It was as old as magic, written by the first Northern Wizard ten thousand years ago. The binding had hardened like stone, and the title had long ago worn away. Trilless scanned each page with an attention that stole meaning from time, place, and person. Sound turned to silence. Her vision ended at the edges of each page. Dry, airless pressure had kept the book intact, and the simple act of turning a page allowed it to crumble to powder. The strongest of her magics could not rescue the ancient leaves any more than she could retrieve a man from death.

Trilless finished scanning, pausing with a sigh. She guessed that the time she had sat reading and, from painful necessity, destroying the artifact could be measured in days. Still, she paused before touching, despising the feel of the first Northern Wizard's written wisdom disintegrating between her fingers. For the thousandth time, Trilless reminded herself that her predecessors had transcribed and updated this information through the millennia. Every word and reference in the ancient tome had become incorporated into another volume. Every word, except the words that Trilless sought, a prophecy spoken by the first Southern Wizard at a time when he was just learning to use his talent. Trilless' discussion with the demon had raised a distant whisper of memory amid her collective consciousness, a glimmer of remembrance that involved the eighteenth Southern Wizard, Carcophan, and a pale champion of near infinite skill.

Trilless turned the page, her long, lean fingers touching lighter than a spider's feet. The parchment sprinkled to oblivion. The uniform glow of her magic struck sparkles from the age-old dust that settled between wisps of hair on her arm. The Northern Sorceress closed her lids. The archaic language strained her eyes and her comprehension. Repeatedly, she called upon the oldest corners of her collective consciousness, finding it nearly as faded and tattered as the book. She had tried to consult the first Northern Wizard for the memory of those written words and the number of the page. Yet the seventeen Wizards who had reigned between them overpowered a granule of remembrance that had become all but obsolete.

Opening her eyes, Trilless found her gaze instantly riveted on a standard symbol in the center of the page, referring her to the bottom. A vague, foreign thought trickled through her, bringing the certainty that the information she sought was in a footnote, though not the one she had just uncovered. Hunger rumbled in her gut, and she set the book aside with a gentleness that saved every remaining page. Starvation could not kill her, but it could weaken her, and she had always thought Shadimar foolish for forgetting food for weeks at a time. *Right now, I can't afford to become frail, even for a moment.* Again, doubts descended upon her, and she wondered whether she had made a mistake by bringing the White Sword of Power back into the world of mortals. For all his skill, Valr Kirin would need the Sword of Tranquillity to kill Colbey. Even that advantage might not prove enough.

Trilless rose. Once Carcophan knew the might of his soon to be champion, he would have to guess that the Northern Sorceress would summon the Sword to oppose him. Surely, he would know that to call the Black Sword would be folly. The Gray Sword bothered her more. Although every predecessor seemed certain that it would take the combined efforts of the Eastern and Western Wizards to create, Trilless could find nothing definite to corroborate the fact. And vivid memories from the fifth Northern Wizard told her that the initial creation of a Sword of Power required only a well-forged blade and a handful of spells. As grueling and costly as those spells were, even Shadimar had enough competence to cast them.

Trilless put that thought from her mind. She had done as she had done. Her seeking magics had tracked Colbey to Shadimar's ruins. There, her spell could not penetrate, nor was she rude enough to try to override another Wizard's wards. Eventually, Colbey would leave; and, eventually, Valr Kirin would kill the Renshai. In the meantime, Trilless needed to find the first prophecy of the first Southern Wizard. Once she had the words and the certainty that came with them, she would warn Shadimar that he was harboring and protecting

Carcophan's champion.

On a weed-covered plain near Shadimar's ruins, Mitrian stood with her legs braced, a hand on her sword. Water drizzled from clouds eternally gray and stagnant, the moisture sending her hair into frizzled curls. She watched as Rache spun, drawing his sword in a sweeping block that reversed into a cut, his blade a whirling halo of steel. Teeth gritted in concentration, he surged into a broad cross sweep. The sword cut a jerky arc.

Mitrian called to her son to halt. 'Keep your shoulder higher and your elbow in.' She caught his arm and demonstrated the motion. 'Keep practicing.'

Rache shook sweat and rain from his hair in a spray of droplets. He launched back into the maneuver with his usual eagerness.

Satisfied that Rache understood, Mitrian turned to confront Episte. She saw only a smashed patch of weeds where the elder teen had been training. Surprise turned to rage. Both gave way to concern. 'Episte?'

The young man appeared from a tall patch of grass, nearly at her feet. He clutched a woven string of daisies.

Startled, Mitrian leapt backward. 'What are you doing?'

Episte tied off the stems with a twist. 'I made this for you.' He handed Mitrian the flowered necklace.

Mitrian stared at the daisy chain that Episte had looped over her hand, incredulous. 'Very pretty, Episte. But you're supposed to be practising.' Her mind raced, trying to guess how Colbey would handle the situation. To him, disrespect for a sword was the ultimate crime. She could picture his face pinched into an angry knot that threatened violence. One glimpse into his cold, blue eyes would be enough to cow her. She never needed actual punishment; her imagination had proven active enough. Experience told her that Colbey would have driven in with a series of attacks on Episte designed to humiliate him. *But Colbey can do that*. Mitrian did not feel secure enough that she could best Episte Rachesson, and she doubted that, in a spar against him with real weapons, either of them would escape fully unscathed. 'Show me *lynstreik*.'

Episte looked stricken. He brushed dirt and seeds from his breeks, hefted his sword, and dropped into a readied crouch.

Mitrian watched, trying not to reveal any emotion. *Lynstreik* was a complicated Renshai maneuver with little practical application. She would have been hard-pressed to perform it herself.

Episte shook back hair the color of the daisies' centers. He gave Mitrian a feeble smile, then began the requested sequence. His legs moved in near-perfect figures, as fast as Mitrian could follow. His sword wove a web of silver about his slight torso. Though his strokes lacked power, that did not detract from the beauty of his *svergelse*. Skill and quickness formed the basis for the Renshai maneuvers, and Episte demonstrated both. Pride welled within Mitrian, and love for the orphaned child who was the son of her hero. *I only wish my Rache had this much skill.* Guilt came, stabbing, with the thought. She could not begrudge Episte his talent, and Rache's persistence would probably make him the better swordsman in the long run. That train of thought bothered her as well. *Episte should be as much a son to me as Rache.* Logic handed her the necessary equality, though she could not quite escape the ties of blood.

Episte held his final pose, legs low and close, the sword a steel extension of his hand in front of him, the other arm spread behind for balance. He broke the position. Flipping the sword to its sheath, he executed a respectful bow.

Mitrian studied the youth in silence, unwilling to spout encouragement after Episte's unacceptable distraction. Nor would Mitrian speak ill of competent technique. 'Good,' she said simply. 'But not perfect. Agility and skill is only half the battle. Without practice, you can't build strength and endurance, nor the necessary battle sense that allows a warrior to choose the right combat maneuver in an instant.'

Episte looked past Mitrian, and his inattentiveness hurt. Her words had pleased her, and she had hoped he would find them profound enough, at least, to listen. She gazed directly into the youth's blue eyes, trying to draw his focus. Only then did she realize that he was not just staring through her. His stare was fixed on something behind her.

Mitrian whirled.

Colbey stood among the weeds, moving with none of the weakness and pain that had seemed so much a part of him for the last three weeks. 'Well spoken, Mitrian.' Suddenly, he lowered his center of gravity, whipping through six sequential performances of *lynstreik* so smooth that they made even Episte look clumsy. Like the boy, Colbey held the final posture for the moment, scarcely winded despite his condition. 'Skill has no limits, Episte. Every time you perform a maneuver, you improve it. If you don't put your all into your practices, any warrior with less skill and more dedication will best you.'

Episte lowered his head, though his eyes told Mitrian he had heard the speech too many times. He shuffled off to practice.

Colbey addressed Mitrian, though his gaze remained on Episte. 'Shadimar tells me that your father's people successfully reclaimed the town.'

Mitrian smiled, pleased by the news, yet nonplussed by Colbey's choice of words. He could have called them Mitrian's people, but he had chosen not to, as if to emphasize that her loyalties and ties now lay elsewhere. She was Renshai. The society that had once been hers could no longer claim her.

'It's officially called "Santagithi" now, and Bromdun was unanimously voted leader. Reconstruction is already underway. And I think it's time for us to leave as well.'

'They couldn't have picked a better leader.' Mitrian felt a joy untainted by bitterness. She had the memories of the town and the people she loved. For her, the village that had once been the Town of Santagithi and was now simply Santagithi could never seem the same. Always, she would feel like a stranger there. The idea of beginning a new life with her family and the Renshai filled her with excitement. 'Good thing Bromdun and his archers were among the survivors. At least no one will starve.'

'Yes,' Colbey repeated, obviously considering a comment Mitrian had meant to toss off casually. 'None of *them* will starve.'

The following morning, Colbey, Episte, Rache, Mitrian, Garn, Shadimar, and the wolf began their eastward journey. The Eastern Wizard seemed reluctant to abandon the crumbling ruins that served as his home, but Colbey found it a pleasure. He had nearly forgotten the thrill of riding amidst the play of summer breezes. Not since the day his fist could close around the hilt of sword had he missed a practice, and his coma had left him twitchy to make up for lost time. Even as they rode, he practiced sword maneuvers between the closing knot of forest branches or worked out intricate routines that took him from the horse to the ground and back in an instant.

While Colbey reveled in the journey, his companions seemed less pleased. Hemmed by endless woodlands, the group found themselves at the mercy of blood-sucking insects; their horses stomped and swished their tails through the night. Scant food remained after Shadimar's guests had departed. Secodon disappeared daily, presumably to hunt. The Wizard seemed content to survive on the handful of berries he gathered en route, but Colbey and the others went hungry. Of them all, only Mitrian could use a bow, and only barely adequately. Her homemade creation made her even more awkward. Tempers flared, particularly Garn's, and Arduwyn's name came to the fore again and again. The flame-haired hunter had never allowed them to go hungry.

Colbey took the brunt of Garn's irritability. His insistence on daily sword sessions forced them to camp well before sundown. Unable to hunt and barred from the teachings of the Renshai, Garn waited with only his rumbling gut and the Wizard for company. Since neither spoke often and they had nothing in common, Colbey guessed each spent most of his time alone. And Garn had far too much time to think.

One morning, a week into their travels, Garn approached Colbey.

He looked thinner. His clothes bore days of dust and slivers of leaves and seed pods. 'Teach me, too. I want to be Renshai.'

Colbey did not bother to meet Garn's gaze. He knew that Garn's strength could add much to the tribe. He could only guess how painful it must be for Garn to watch his wife and child trained to a skill few swordsmen could match. For too long, the ex-gladiator's life had depended on his being the best in might, weapons, and day to day alertness. 'I'm sorry, Garn. You know I can't. The laws are specific about who I can and cannot teach the Renshai maneuvers. I will not break the vows to my people and to my goddess.' Colbey kicked his horse to a trot. For him, the matter was closed.

But Garn persisted. His horse surged forward to keep pace at Colbey's side. 'Surely your goddess will forgive a vow broken in a time of change. The Renshai have many enemies. You've given my wife and son those same enemies. I've fought for your cause, and I'll probably die for it. Wouldn't it serve better to have all of us skilled in the art?'

Colbey dragged on the reins, and his horse dropped back to a walk. He waited until Garn pulled up, then seized a muscled forearm. This time, he met Garn's green gaze. 'I would never call you unskilled. I've seen few who are not Renshai as capable with a sword and none stronger. I'm pleased and honoured to have you with us, and the sire of any Renshai deserves respect.' He released Garn. 'But I won't break an oath to my people, not, at least, without the direct guidance and approval of my goddess.'

Garn bit at his lip with a sour scowl. A life of direct commands, enforced by whips and crossbows had not prepared him for the frustration of fighting disappointment.

Colbey shook his head, not liking his decision, though he knew it was right. 'I'm sorry, Garn.' Many years had passed since fury had driven Garn to attack him for monopolizing too much of Mitrian's time. Then, Colbey had taught Garn a technique he had invented himself, an extension of the Renshai mind control that allowed Garn to focus and channel his strength. That knowledge had satisfied Garn for longer than a decade.

Garn abandoned the struggle, his lip turning white around the indentations of his teeth, and his hands stiffening on the reins. 'Rache is my son. I have things *I* want to teach him.' He added, in reluctant afterthought. 'And Episte, too.'

Garn's reference to Episte carried a discomfort that blunted his anger. Clearly, he had doubts about training the older teen, despite his bold insistence. The concern ran deep, and Colbey guessed it stemmed from Garn's memories of his own weapons training by the boy's father. Throughout his life, Garn had believed his own savagery a product of Rache Kallmirsson's teachings, and he had blamed his killing frenzies on the captain's philosophies. Though Colbey doubted the causality, he did foresee the potential for conflict. At times, Episte's excuses, inattentiveness, and blatant apathy drove even the eldest Renshai to the edge of frustrated violence. *Better Garn's and Episte's relationship remain friendly and unpressured.* Colbey ran a hand through his thick, white hair and made no reply.

Garn continued. 'I have a right to some of the boys' time. They're my – '

Colbey's reply cut Garn short. 'You're right, of course. Why don't you instruct Rache while I work with Episte?' Though Colbey did not know whether Garn's demands stemmed from a sense of duty to his son, boredom, or an argumentative mood, he sincerely believed that Rache would benefit from his father's teachings. 'It'll mean twice as much practice for Rache, because he can't afford to back down from my lessons, but I think he can handle it.'

Garn fell silent, apparently at a loss for words. Clearly, he had not intended to win so easily.

Colbey saw the need to rescue Garn from his other dilemma as well. 'As to Episte, I'm not sure there's much you can teach him. It's difficult enough getting him to concentrate on his swordwork. Besides, he's small. The Renshai maneuvers rely mostly on quickness. He'll never have the bulk to learn to perform your techniques with any competence. If you train him too well, the strokes could become habit; and he might use them in combat.' He looked up, the potential danger of his concern obvious.

'Very well, Rache only.' Garn's tone conveyed cautious uncertainty, but his surrounding emotions betrayed relief.

Garn dropped back to discuss his triumph with his wife and son. Colbey remained at the lead, enjoying a silence broken only by the sweet trills of songbirds and the occasional haunting melody of an *aristiri* hawk. Twice, Colbey's horse sent deer scrambling into the brush, too swiftly for Mitrian to think of readying her bow before they had run out of sight.

As the sun started its downward curve, Colbey searched for a place to camp and practice. The nightly routine had become a chore. He would not compromise when it came to finding a place where he could teach open space maneuvers as well as combat techniques for tightly packed forests where branches disrupted momentum and leaves mired underfoot. He felt nearly as strongly about finding a place where Garn and Shadimar could feel comfortable while the others practiced, and ground on which every member of the group could sleep.

As Colbey's attention shifted from introspection to the specifics of the woodlands, he recognized a gradual progression of the trees. In the past few days, evergreens had become scarce, giving way to twisted *hadonga*, oak, and elm. In the past half day, the trees had become thinner, predominantly poplar and locusts. *First growth*. Colbey realized they were nearing an edge of the forest.

As if to confirm his guess, the woodlands broke before him. Uneven rows of dull green corn rose from the land as far as he could see. Midsummer, the stalks cradled small, tender ears, and yellow-white tassels swung in the breeze.

Garn drew up beside Colbey. At the sight of food, he whooped with delight and rode into the field.

Colbey turned his horse to face the others. 'Mitrian, see if you can't find game birds or rabbits hiding among the corn.' He glanced back to the field. The stalks had closed about Garn, and only the jiggling of leaves and tassels revealed his location. 'Garn,' he shouted. 'Pick enough for everyone, and don't scare away all the rabbits. When you're ready to teach, come find us.' Colbey dismounted. Stripping off the tack, he walked along the crooked boundary between field and forest, waving for the boys to follow. 'Rache. Episte.' He left Shadimar to tend the horses and oversee the camp.

While Colbey instructed Episte in the finest points of swordsmanship, Garn showed his son how to use a stick as a weapon. Later, Garn retired to help Shadimar prepare the evening meal while Mitrian practiced and Colbey instructed Rache. Gradually, the sun seemed to melt into an orange haze. The aroma of roasting pheasant and corn perfumed the air. Colbey ignored the rumbling of his gut until the lesson was finished, then swordplay ceased for a hardy meal of poultry and corn.

Relieved of their packs and tack, the horses grazed the branches and underbush of the forest; Colbey guessed that some magic of Shadimar's kept them from tearing up the farmer's crop. The Renshai had never known horses to choose oak over corn, and the Wizard did seem to have a special rapport with animals. The few times that Shadimar had wandered from the party, Colbey had noticed that the animals seemed more high-strung and restless.

At first, the six people ate in silence, shoveling food into aching stomachs that had gone too long without a true meal. As their bellies filled, Mitrian set aside her third ear of corn to ask. 'Is it common for farmers to burn holes in their fields?'

Accustomed to his role as teacher, Colbey answered the question before asking one of his own. In the civilized Westlands, people have ritual field burnings after the harvest as a sacrifice to the gods for the next year's crops. But that's not until after harvest.' Now, he delved for the source of Mitrian's query. 'Did you see a burned patch?'

Mitrian pointed deeper into the field.

Garn spoke with his mouth full. 'Lightning,' he suggested.

The explanation sounded reasonable to Colbey.

Mitrian seemed more skeptical. 'The rain would have quenched a fire before it spread, or the entire field would have burned. Maybe it was a carelessly placed campfire.'

Colbey rose, yawning. Mitrian's suggestion seemed less likely. 'What fool would set a camp in the middle of a field with a forest so close on the one side and, almost certainly, a town on the other?' He pawed through the packs for his own and drew out a blanket. 'I'm sure the farmer will give us an answer, if we dare admit we stole his corn.' He spread his blanket just close enough to the fire so the smoke would discourage bugs. 'Let's get some sleep.'

Garn eyed the last ear of corn, obviously still more interested in food than sleep. 'I'll take the first watch . . . '

Colbey drifted off before Garn finished speaking.

'Modi.' The cry sounded scarcely louder than a whisper, but it awakened Colbey to full awareness in a way no other could.

The old Renshai leapt to his feet, ready to fight, battle wrath like a fever within him. The camp felt equally hot. He spun into a crouch.

Episte stood, frozen, his eyes fixed on the heavens. Behind him, flames devoured the pile of packs and saddles, and crawled along the underbrush.

'Fire!' Grabbing up his blanket, Colbey sprang for the blaze, slapping the fabric over it. The flames sputtered, shattering to sparks that seared Colbey's bare arms. The horses skittered, rearing, then bolted into the forest. Awakened by Colbey's shout, the others joined him, pounding blankets on the flames. Shadimar disappeared into the woodlands, presumably to find the horses. Mitrian's blanket burst into flames. She dropped it, recoiling with a gasp of pain. Garn and Rache hammered at the fire, stomping smaller grass fires. Episte dumped the remains of the previous night's water onto the worst of the blaze. Water struck with a long hiss that muted the fire. Colbey doused the remaining flames with the charred remnants of his bedding.

'Who was on watch?' Colbey glanced from face to face. Sweat cleared a crooked line through the ash on his arms.

No one replied, though Garn did glance at Rache, who naturally turned his gaze to Episte.

Colbey followed the sequence of the sentries by the nonverbal exchange. Smoke curled from the dying fire, and it faded before the heat of Colbey's anger. That Episte had shirked his duty bothered him, but the teen's silence enraged him. 'Episte!'

The boy lowered his head.

'If you couldn't stay awake for your watch, you should have asked someone else to finish it.'

'I . . . ' Episte started, as if searching for a defense. 'I didn't fall asleep. I . . . It . . . '

Colbey threw down what remained of his blanket. 'You also didn't tend the fire.'

Episte shrank back, his face as pale as a torch in the darkness. 'A winged monster attacked me. It spit fire at me. I tried to fight it, but it flew away and – '

The childish ludicrousness of Episte's excuse snapped Colbey's control. For the first time in his life, he struck a student with his hand, a resounding slap across the face that stunned the youngster into silence. 'You're a man, Episte, not an infant! Renshai don't fear night or the bugbears that babies imagine in it. I can and will forgive your mistakes, but not your lies.' Anger sank into disappointment, and Colbey stared into the dimming glow that remained of the campfire, until his vision hazed to a vast, red darkness. 'Go to sleep. I'll finish this watch.'

Episte turned his back, wandering away from the camp and curling up some distance away. The others returned to their places.

Colbey winced, knowing his blow had stung Episte's pride as well as his flesh and that tears fell from the youngster's eyes. Yet he dared not offer comfort. The boy had grown too old for the wild excuses that the gods forgave from children with active imaginations.

Although Shadimar had not yet returned from his hunt for the horses, Secodon padded softly through the camp. Colbey watched as the old gray wolf chose to lie beside Episte and to lick soothingly at the youth's tear-streaked face.

Colbey and his companions awakened with the sun. Shadimar had rejoined them, along with all the horses. Through the still grayness of dawn, they led the animals between rows of corn, single file so as not to trample the crop. The horses kept their heads low, too weary even to go after the ready food, or perhaps their tractability was attributable to Shadimar's magic. Colbey neither knew nor cared.

They arrived at the edge of the town at midday. Colbey counted thirty dwellings, arranged in a haphazard ring. A larger building stood in the center. Beside it, a mixed herd of cows and goats crowded around a water trough or fountain. Fields like the one they had traveled through surrounded the town, puddles of green and yellow that seemed endless. Distant forest serrated the horizon and, to the east, Colbey could see the towering peaks of the Great Mountains.

More cows, gaunt as shadows, ambled in the streets, not bothering to look up or shuffle away as the strangers approached. Nearby, a stout, middle-aged man in grimy homespun dragged boulders toward a low stone fence that seemed inadequate to keep cows from the crops.

Yet not a single cow had crossed it. As Colbey and the others approached, the farmer turned. Brown eyes riveted on them, soft in a haggard visage. His gaze rolled from faces to weapons. He dropped the stone, twisting toward the town, as if to measure the distance. Then, apparently realizing the strangers would come upon him before he could alert the town, he knelt and picked up a rusty sickle from the grass. He thrust out his chest, stood tall, and waited.

Colbey hailed the farmer, beginning at shouting distance. 'Hello.' He stopped, trying to place the villager at ease with a slow, obvious approach that bordered on ponderous.

The farmer eyed the tattered party suspiciously. 'Hallo.' He returned the greeting with wooden formality. Finally, his gaze found Secodon. 'Wolf!' He brandished the sickle. 'Wolf! Ye'll not maul me cows!' He stalked the wolf, who disappeared behind his master's horse.

Mitrian and Garn came up beside Colbey, and the two younger Renshai moved up to stand at Mitrian's side.

Obviously intimidated, the farmer backed away, ducking behind his sickle, his weathered face pale.

'Secodon won't hurt your animals,' Mitrian said. 'I promise.'

The farmer's gaze jerked to Mitrian.

'And neither will we,' Colbey added, suspecting that the farmer had chosen Secodon as the least dangerous target. 'We've traveled a long way. We're in need of food and supplies, maybe a few days of rest. Do you have an inn?'

The farmer lowered his makeshift weapon. Dark hair mixed with gray fell in a fringe around his head. 'Nawt an inn per say. I'll take ye to the gathrin' house.' Apparently, the party's calmness lent him courage. Yere nawt plannin' any trooble in Greentree?'

'Certainly not.' Colbey reassured the villager. 'We just came for food and a place to rest.'

'Tha toon donna see many strangers.' The farmer escorted Colbey and his companions along an unpaved dirt path toward the center of town. He still clutched the sickle, but he seemed to have forgotten he held it. The blade dragged through dirt and grass, leaving a snaking trail behind him. 'I hight Angus. Those be me fields ye traipsed.'

'Colbey,' the elder Renshai said, uncertain of the proper amenities for farmers. 'Uh . . . the crops seem healthy.'

Angus smiled with pride. 'Aye, the do me well.' He stopped before the door to the central building. Now, Colbey could see that the cows and goats surrounded a basin with a hand pump.

'Let the horses free.' Shadimar remained at the back of the group. 'I don't think they'll stray far from water.'

Angus frowned. He leaned the sickle against the wall. 'Ye can keep yere animals with out'n, but ye mayna want to. Tha blicht be upon them all.'

Colbey let Shadimar answer the farmer's concerns. As much as the old Renshai knew of cures and wound care, he knew little about cows and goats.

'They'll be all right for now.' Shadimar loosed his mount from its lead rope. The fire had damaged several of the saddles as well as most of their rations, so it only took seconds for Rache, Episte, and Garn to strip off the remaining tack.

When they had finished, Angus turned the knob and pushed open the gathering house door. The aromas of fresh bread and mead welcomed them. At the far end of the tavern, a heavyset man and a long-legged, teenaged barmaid stacked wooden bowls on the bar. A ladder connected the barroom to a straw-filled loft that clearly served as alternate sleeping quarters for the villagers as well as for storage. A random cluster of rickety chairs and tables stood scattered around the room. Eight men sat around the largest table, the only patrons. Everyone turned to stare at the strangers in the doorway.

Angus grinned, apparently enjoying the attention of his neighbors. He motioned Colbey and his companions to a table. Secodon squeezed beneath it as the others took seats around him.

Mitrian nudged Colbey with her elbow. 'What do we have for money?'

Colbey searched his pockets, finding only two silver coins. He dropped them on the table, looking expectantly at the others.

Garn shrugged without bothering to check, while the others, at least, went through the ritual. Mitrian added two more silvers and Episte one. Colbey looked at Angus. 'Will that cover a meal for us all?'

'Aye. And a nicht's lodging, if ye donna eat too much.' He signaled the barmaid.

The eight other patrons continued to stare, whispering among themselves. Cautiously, the barmaid sidled to the newcomers' table. She looked about Episte's age, with straight, sable hair that draped her breasts and shoulder blades. She studied the Renshai's group through dark eyes that were huge and framed by long lashes. 'We got bread and cheese. Wi' that do ye?'

Episte gawked at the barmaid, his scrutiny as intense as the villagers'.

'Perfect.' Colbey smiled to put the woman at ease. 'And ale for all of us.'

The barmaid glanced at Episte and Rache. 'The bairns, too?'

Episte's face turned red, and his expression dropped from interest to humiliation. Younger, Rache took the insult in stride.

Colbey scowled. 'Both Rache and Episte have proven themselves men.' He finished with only a nod, believing silence would cause the least embarrassment for all concerned.

The barmaid headed for the kitchen. Colbey turned to the patrons at the other table, who still stared in unabashed wonder. The Renshai addressed Angus. 'Do you know those men?'

'Aye. Ye wish ta meet them?'

Colbey rose. 'I'd like to talk with them.'

Angus stood, wearing the grin of a child displaying new toys to jealous friends. He guided Colbey to the other table, the villagers' gazes following him every step of the way. Angus introduced each one quickly. 'These be Blacki, Carrol, Schaf, Cammie, Loo, Sham, Jackie, and Sturge.'

Colbey acknowledged each introduction with a nod. To a man, they were brown haired and eyed, wearing work clothes that varied little in color or style. Colbey guessed that, if they shifted position, he would never remember any of their names. Taking a chair from a neighboring table, he sat between Jackie and Sturge. 'I'm Colbey.'

The farmers closed around him eagerly. 'Yer North 'uns, arena ye?'

Before Colbey could answer, another asked. 'How far ye come?'

A third chimed in. 'Kin ye use both swords, or be one for spare?'

Another started. 'Do . . . ?'

Colbey interrupted with a wave. 'One question at a time.' He winked at Angus, who still stood. 'Since I made the rule, I get to go first.'

The farmers fell silent.

'Have others like me passed through recently?' Colbey resisted the urge to imitate the townsmen's dialect. 'Northmen, I mean.'

Loo fairly crowed. 'Tol' ye they were North 'uns. Ye owe me a bowl, Cam.'

Scattered laughter followed his pronouncement.

Carrol chose to address the query. 'Nay, sirra. We donna see strangers but oncet ev'ry sev'ral years.'

'Saw Westerkind las' winter,' Blacki said. 'But they dinna enter tha toon.'

Another hush draped the table, and Colbey seized upon it, breaking his own rule about each man asking only one question. 'Angus tells me your animals have been sick.'

Jackie fondled his bowl of mead. 'Aye. Me cows be thin as tha mead.'

Cammie laughed, and no one joined him.

'I have some knowledge of healing. And Shadimar's good with animals.' He indicated the Wizard still at the other table. 'If we can help your herds, would you send us off with a pack of rations?'

'Sirrah,' Jackie drawled. 'If ye bring health t' me heifers, I'll gi' ye me whole harvest.'

Colbey hoped cows responded to the same treatments as people. He relied heavily on Shadimar's knowledge and judgment, and the laws constraining the Cardinal Wizards confused him. Still, as far as he could tell, the Wizards' vows did not extend to animals. Most of the barriers seemed to apply to violence, humans, and the wanton or blatant use of magic. 'I can't promise we'll heal all your animals, but we can try. We'll start this evening.'

The men exchanged glances that alternated between nervous and hopeful. Angus explained. 'Nay, sirrah. Begin tomorrow. Tonicht be Midsummer's Eve.'

Schaf took a huge gulp of ale. 'While we'uns be here, the rest o' tha toon be preparin' fo' tha festival. Tonicht, there be dancin' and feastin' E'ery'un o' tha toon'll be there. Ye should be there, too.'

Colbey smiled. 'That's all very well. My younger companions may want to join you, but Shadimar and I have had our fill of dancing.' Colbey tried to picture the reserved Eastern Wizard twirling farm girls and guzzling mead, and the image turned his grin into a laugh.

'Ye donna understand.' Cammie glanced about the table, as if afraid he was giving away a secret. 'Flanner's bane come curse tha toon. No man gaes safe alone, and noo 't be best if all people stay toge'er.'

'Flanner's bane?' Colbey encouraged.

'Flanner be an evil 'un,' Angus pulled up a chair among his fellows. 'Forced hisself upon a girl richt near Yvesen's temple. Brocht the curse upon us.'

'The blight?' Colbey guessed.

'Noo!' Cammie broke in, shaking his head with a vigor that sent his hair flying. 'Tha bane be a thing, a creature.' He pointed from one side of the common room to the other to indicate size. ' 'ts haid be tha o' a wolf, but 'ts eyes be fire red. 'ts body be tha o' a man with a tail o' a sarpent.'

Colbey willed his expression serious only with effort. He had heard the stories that mothers told their errant children, grim tales of bugbears spiriting away little boys and girls who did not go to bed on time. Colbey had always thought it ludicrous to send toddlers off to bed afraid to sleep.

Blacki finished the description. '. . . 't has wings of leather, talons sharp o' a eagle's, and sets homes afire.'

The final piece struck home, and Colbey's forced somberness became reality. He pictured the wreckage of their camp in the cornfield, and Episte's words returned to haunt him: 'A winged monster attacked me. It spit fire at me.' For a moment, Colbey considered the possibility that Episte had spoken the truth, then immediately discarded the possibility. *I've traveled throughout the world for seventy-six years and never seen any real animal more frightening than a jaguar. Surely, if such a thing as this bane existed, I would have heard stories.* Colbey thought of the strangest circumstances in which he'd ever found himself. In all his time with the Wizards, first Tokar, then Shadimar, he had experienced nothing worse than the illusions that came with Tokar's ceremony of passage.

The turn of his mind brought the early stirrings of pain memory, and Colbey recalled the fiery, manlike creatures that had claimed the Western Wizard, and nearly himself. Yet the pain seemed so much more real than the visual remembrance that Colbey felt certain those creatures had been illusion, that the pain came from another source, perhaps from the dying Wizard himself. When Shadimar had questioned Colbey about the ceremony, he had said that different people see different images, which only confirmed the falseness of the beings Colbey had seen that day and never before or since.

Colbey had seen other grand phenomena, but none without explanation. When Rache had died in the Great War, Colbey had seen a *Valkyrie* come to claim the soul for Valhalla. His sword practice with Sif on the route home from that battle still held a warm corner of his memory. Both of those came from his own mind, nurtured, he hoped, by the gods. But an abomination like the peasants had described made no sense, except to haunt children. Even accounting for exaggeration, physical laws could not allow a creature of its size to fly, nor any creature to spit fire. 'Has this bane hurt you?'

'Noo.' Loo shivered. 'But we found the burnt patches in tha fields.'

Now the tale had returned to a more classical peasants' horror story, and Colbey dismissed his doubts good-naturedly. 'I've yet to meet a creature nastier than me. Shadimar and I will tend the cows.' He rose, excused himself with a wave, and returned to his companions who were gleefully devouring homemade bread topped with cheese.

19 Flanner's Bane

That night, Episte watched flames leap in a wild dance from the last piled hay from the previous harvest. The dark shapes of the citizens of Greentree threaded through moon glow, firelight, and darkness, alternately featureless shadows and vividly detailed individuals. Episte ignored the dancing weave of revelers at the Midsummer's Festival, holding his gaze on the fire. If he kept his attention centered, he could see the grate fires that had warmed him and his mother on winter nights. Deeper, he found his mother's face haloed in the flames, oval as an egg with its familiar snub nose.

Hay shifted, and the fire broke to sparks that sprinkled the image with freckles. Its contour broken by the movement, the illusion became lost to Episte, yet the emotions it inspired remained. Longing filled him, a horrible, haunting need to replace the world that had shattered around him. He closed his eyes against tears, searching deep inside himself. For a moment, he was four years old again, cradled in his mother's lap and arms while she rocked back and forth on her favorite old chair. He relived the raw innocence that had allowed him to believe, without doubt, that he was secure. Nothing could harm him so long as she held him.

The urge to cry receded, and a smile replaced it. Episte opened his eyes. Almost immediately, his gaze riveted on a young woman at the edge of the crowd. She could have fit Emerald's description. Straight, dark hair fell around a rose petal face with a small nose and large eyes. She lacked only the plump curves that came with years. He guessed that she was a year or two younger than himself.

The crowd milled, blocking Episte's view of the girl. Enthralled, he pushed through the throng toward where he had last seen her.

Rache's voice came from behind him. 'Episte!'

Swearing softly, Episte ignored the call. He pressed forward. Finding himself facing a dense crowd of women, he waited for them to pass.

Rache caught Episte's shoulder. 'Take a bowl and join us.'

Episte twisted to look at Rache. The younger Renshai held a bowl of steaming vegetables balanced on one hand. He pointed with the other.

'Mother and – '

'Later.' Episte shook free of Rache's grip and darted into the masses. He found no sign of the girl, and he cursed the delay Rache had caused him. He stood, gaze sweeping the area for some glimpse of the youth he sought.

A female voice came from so close behind Episte, it startled him. 'Hallo.'

Episte whirled to face a young teenager. Her black eyes held a shy twinkle, and her lips were full and pink. She was unattractive by a farmer's standards. Her frame was lean and angular, without the bulges and waves that rewarded affluence. But her small, firm breasts made Episte forget the girl he followed. 'My name is Episte.' He lowered his voice, trying to sound composed and experienced.

'I hight Elanor,' she said in a slurred Greentree dialect that made Episte cringe. 'Hoo's yere bonny friend?'

Episte's stomach lurched. 'My what?'

'Yere friend,' she repeated. 'I ken t' meet him.'

'My friend.' Episte's mood withered. 'My . . . little companion? Rache?' The words sounded foolish, even to him. Though younger, Rache weighed nearly twice as much as Episte.

Elanor giggled. 'Oh, aye, yere *little* friend.'

Elanor's laughter ruptured Episte's fragile pride. 'Come with me,' he said, feeling numb. Turning, Episte hurried Elanor back to where he had last seen Rache, then headed in the direction in which the boy had pointed. They caught up with the youngest Renshai before he reached his parents.

At a touch, Rache whirled.

'Rache, this is Elanor.'

Rache looked confused and embarrassed. Balancing the bowl on his forearm, he made a gesture of greeting that sent the bowl careening off-balance. He caught it before it hit the ground, though vegetables scattered over the grass between them. 'Oh,' Rache said. 'Elanor.' He looked to Episte for guidance.

Ignoring Rache's silent plea, Episte walked away. *It's not fair!* Self-pity dragged at him, and he could feel hot tears of rage building. Suddenly, anger overtook him. He froze, hands opening and closing like the mouth of a gaping fish. He whirled. His sword swept from its sheath as he rushed down upon Rache.

Elanor screamed. Gasping villagers darted from Episte's path. He sprang at Rache with a crazed howl of anger.

Rache met Episte with a parry and a question. 'What's this?'

Episte's reply was a thrust for Rache's chest that the younger Renshai scarcely dodged. He fell silent then, and their swords flickered like sparks in the moonlight, their strokes fast as fire. Episte hissed through gritted teeth. 'You get everything you want! Even when you don't want it!'

Rache said nothing, concentrating on fielding Episte's blows. Fury had granted Episte strength, and he had always been the quicker of the two. He could see Rache tiring visibly, and the need to guide his strokes more cautiously only fueled his anger. He wanted to slash in blind fury, to dispel his rage in a directed flurry of hack and parry.

Suddenly, Rache stepped aside and hurled his blade toward the ground at Episte's feet.

Episte pulled his blow, instinctively catching Rache's hilt. Reversing to hold the blade, he offered the grip.

Rache made no move to accept it.

'Take your sword, Rache, or I swear I'll kill you.'

Rache moved closer, but he did not reach for his weapon. Episte tossed it back in a gentle arc. Rache stepped aside. The sword landed in the grass near his feet.

Incredulous at the disrespect, Episte stared from sword to companion. 'Why did you do that?'

Rache met Episte's gaze. 'Because I don't understand. Because I promised myself long ago I would never try to strike my brother in anger, and I would rather dishonor my sword and myself than you.'

A cold shock of guilt drained Episte's frenzy. 'Damn you, Rache!' He felt the tears returning. As much as Rache's honor touched him, it made his own tantrum seem evil and petty. *Maybe the gods can see that Rache deserves parents and girls and strength and looks and dedication. Maybe Colbey loves him more because he's a better person.* The tears came faster now, hot and painfully violent. He whirled, ignoring the awed press that look as pale and shaken as rescued drowners. For now, Episte needed to be alone. The darkness hid him from the stares of strangers, and he knew he could outmaneuver Rache's attempts to find him. For the moment, Episte needed to find a way to escape from himself as well.

A night spent wrestling and medicating cows and goats left Colbey with a pleasant fatigue that rewarded hard labor. Shadimar and Secodon had already retreated to the loft, leaving Colbey reclining, alone, on the gathering house porch. The thin whine of music from the Midsummer's Festival occasionally broke through the constant shrill of crickets. A red moon glowed faintly through wispy clouds. Colbey gazed at the colored halos the festival smoke formed around the moon. Then, his lids drooped closed, and he relaxed into sleep.

Almost immediately, a subtle shift in the wind awakened Colbey with a premonition of imminent peril. He snapped open his eyes to a sky sprinkled with stars. From the heavens, a dark shape hurtled toward him, obliterating the moon.

Colbey sprang from the porch to the grounds. A wall of flame blasted from the figure, charring the inn porch where he had lain seconds before.

'Modi!' The Renshai drew one sword and swung. His blade cleaved air.

The creature spiraled upward, its form now silhouetted against the moon. The farmers had exaggerated little. It was as large as two cottages, yet it flew with an *aristiri* hawk's grace. At the top of its arc, it spun to face Colbey. The moon flashed from scarlet eyes in a rodent's head, and Colbey could see the white glimmers of fangs as long as his forearm. It plunged for him, a massive shadow etched across the moon.

It's real. For an instant, Colbey knew only remorse for the wrong he had inflicted on Episte. Then, the great head reared back as the creature moved, revealing a cat's body trailing two lizard tails. Jaguar's paws held toenails as long as its teeth.

Colbey dodged aside. A bolt of flame slashed the spot where he had stood. An instant later, he reversed his direction, returning to his previous position. Heat singed the hair from his left arm with a pain that made him shout. 'Modi!' Momentum carried the beast toward him.

The redness of its rat's eyes seemed to swallow Colbey. He hacked, thrust, and swept, his blade slicing into the muscle of its wing and through. Yet, oddly, the sword drew no blood.

The creature soared upward. Its claw tore blistering furrows in Colbey's left hand, driving the hilt from his grasp. Its tails swept for his head. Incapacitated by pain, Colbey barely sprang out of the way. 'Modi! Modi! *Modeee!*' The cry gave him enough clarity of mind to catch his sword in the opposite hand. He tried to draw the other blade in a reverse grip with his injured hand, but his fingers would not function.

Abruptly, Colbey sensed a presence behind him that seemed to disappear as quickly. A bolt of blue light screamed past his ear, slamming into the creature's flank with a force that sent it lurching into a spin. A beastly bellow formed a duet with Colbey's battle cry. The creature plummeted awkwardly, as if injured, though Colbey's blade seemed not to have touched it at all. As it struck the ground, Colbey charged. The beast burst into flames. Heat struck Colbey in a wave, setting his clothes ablaze and stinging his eyes. He rolled, snuffing the flames, and forced his lids open. Through vision blurred by agony, he saw fire flickering as red as the blood from a severed artery. It held the creature's shape, except where its flank had been. There, a smaller blaze flickered sapphire blue.

Colbey rolled to his feet and charged in a motion. He slashed at the shapeless mass of fire. The blue flames strengthened, swirling around and through the red like a separate being. Colbey's sword passed through the figure two hundred times in half as many seconds, yet it met nothing of substance. Blood oozed from his hand, burning like acid.

Gradually, the fire lost all shape, the crimson shrinking before the blue. Suddenly, all redness failed. The blue streaks gathered into a manshape. Then the fire disappeared, but the image it had formed remained. Where it had been, a man knelt in the grass, his shoulders bent and heaving.

Having seen the creature change form before, Colbey did not hesitate. He leapt upon the figure in the grass. At last, his sword met something solid, a wooden staff, and the steel snapped beneath the impact.

Colbey dropped his hilt, pawing for his second sword, and the other met his glance with ancient, gray eyes. Only then, Colbey recognized Shadimar. He recoiled in disbelief, unable to piece together the events of the last several moments. *The blue flames had to be Shadimar. But what kind of abomination was the red?*

Shadimar recovered Colbey's broken blade and hilt. 'Worthless,' he grumbled. 'Worthless despite skill, but I'll change that if it takes every shred of magic I can call.' He stomped off across the charred porch, stopping only when he reached the doorway. He spoke to Colbey without turning, and the booming tone of his voice warned the Renshai not to even try to question. 'I presume this blade was well made?'

'If you ever find one better, you'll have to steal it from *my* sheath.'

Without a reply, Shadimar stormed into the common room, leaving Colbey in a night gone eerily silent. He stared at his mangled left hand, hoping desperately he would find a cure for what remained of it.

Curiosity haunted Colbey, and the ceaseless throbbing of his hand made sleep impossible. When he'd exhausted every herb he could think of and find, the wound settled to a dull ache that still precluded sleep. Eventually, abandoning all hope of dispelling the pain, Colbey chewed some stems that blunted his mind and allowed him to sleep despite it.

Colbey awakened on the piled straw in the gathering house loft, in exactly the place and position in which he had fallen asleep. Sunlight streamed through the windows, trailing square funnels of light on the loft floor. Shadimar sat just outside one of these patches, his back propped against the wall, his head and shoulders sagging over a sword in his lap. Voices reverberated from the common room below, blending into a discordant hubbub that left no individual words to decipher.

Colbey sat up. From the scattered disarray of packs and hay, he knew the others had returned, slept, and already started another day. His head felt heavy, and his thoughts stumbled through fog. His hand ached incessantly. The slightest movement intensified the pain to a pounding, panting agony. Loss of control and concern for his limb drove Colbey into a foul temper. He unwound the bandage from his head, ignoring the flashes this sent through the wound. Four parallel gashes marred the flesh, their edges gaping. The inner skin held an unhealthy pallor that boded poorly for healing, and the outer had gone as red as a sunset. Colbey knew that most men would have sutured each gap, but he knew better. Though it would scar more, the wound would heal better from inside to out. And experience told him that closing dirty injuries made them more prone to infection.

Colbey cleaned the wound meticulously, though every touch sparked more pain. Applying the most potent of the pastes he had created the previous night, he rewrapped it with a clean bandage and hoped for the best.

When Colbey had finished, Shadimar looked up. 'Come here.'

In no mood for power struggles or lectures, Colbey remained in place. 'What do you want?'

'I want you to come here.'

Pain and the aftereffects of the sleeping herb made Colbey sullen, and the Wizard's half-answer increased his annoyance. 'Why?'

Shadimar fixed a stone-hard gaze on Colbey. 'Because I need to talk and to give you something. I don't want to shout, and I won't throw it across the loft.'

Colbey started to grumble something about the Wizard coming to him, then stopped. He saw no reason to antagonize Shadimar, and he could not help becoming interested in the sword in Shadimar's lap. It looked like a twin to the broken blade, except that it was whole. Rising, he walked to the Wizard, mustering mental strength to banish the shreds of fatigue left by the sleeping herb. 'What do you have?'

'I repaired your sword.' Shadimar pointed the weapon at Colbey.

Colbey frowned, reminding himself that Shadimar would know little of weapon etiquette. To a warrior, displayed steel meant a challenge, and anyone who offered anything but a weapon's hilt might just as well have attacked. 'Thank you for your effort, but it's of no use to me now. Even if you could fix it in a way that didn't disrupt the balance, it would always have a weak point.'

Shadimar smiled. 'Try it.' Apparently, recognizing his impropriety, he placed his other hand on the blade. The grasp was awkward, even for one not trained for war, and his excessive caution became his undoing. While guarding his fingers too well, he touched his palm to the blade. It left barely a scratch, a short scarlet line that did not even draw enough blood to bead. Yet Shadimar stared in fascination or horror.

Colbey accepted the sword, more interested in it than in the Eastern Wizard's antics. He had trusted the sword for too many years to dismiss it without at least a glance. It had changed little since he had drawn it to battle the creature that the farmers of Greentree had called Flanner's bane. All its weight seemed bunched just beyond the hilt. If anything, its balance had gone from the best he had ever wielded to perfection. The notches the edges had accumulated through the decades had vanished, and they looked as sharp as the day of their forging. In the shadows, the color seemed ideal. When Colbey carried it to the sunlight, he approved even more. Not so much as a hairline remained to show where the steel had broken.

Lowering his head, Colbey put the sword to its final test. He swept the blade in a long stroke, feigned a block, then reversed the cut. That one maneuver told him all. This was the sword against which all future swords must be measured, one that was everything that Colbey had always imagined the gods would use. Need and longing filled him, followed by the realization that it already belonged to him. Joy swept him then, and he launched into a swirl of grace and movement designed to test the sword and himself to their joint limit. The steel did not disappoint him. It became a willing partner, stabbing and slashing imaginary enemies as if telepathically linked. The balance made it feel weightless. The pain in Colbey's hand seemed to disappear, as his concentration narrowed in on the sword.

Shadimar watched, clutching at the minuscule nick on his palm with the intensity that Colbey had earlier given his damaged hand.

Colbey halted his practice, exhilarated. The fog had lifted from his thoughts, and all irritation had left him. 'It's better than before the break. How?' Colbey broke off, bothered by his own question. The first stirrings of warning rose, and the realization that he might have to refuse Shadimar's gift made him ill.

'Magic,' Shadimar said softly, the precise word Colbey had hoped not to hear, though he knew there could be no other explanation. 'No object currently on man's world has so much power. Use it with care.'

'No.' Colbey flipped the sword with none of Shadimar's caution. He offered the hilt. 'I can't take it.'

Shadimar's face went so blank, it seemed as if even the features had been washed from it. His ancient eyes held no fire of emotion. 'I have paid a high price for it and for you.' He made no motion to take the sword. 'Without it, you can do nothing for me except die.'

Colbey turned away. The idea of losing the weapon he had searched for all his life hurt. 'I think using it would violate the Renshai code of honor. We rely only on personal skill because it has no limits. Like armor, magic would become a crutch. Crutches are too easily lost, and their wielders with them.'

Bitter lines etched across Shadimar's empty features. 'Enchanted or not, a sword is only as good as its wielder. It won't replace skill. It will only help you enhance what you already have.' The Eastern Wizard's mood radiated to Colbey. Many earnest thoughts troubled Shadimar, but they concerned matters beyond Colbey's experience and made little sense to him. He plucked out only vague premonitions of a serious danger and doubts that seemed to pertain as much to Colbey as to the enemies they would need to face.

Shadimar continued, 'That creature we fought last night was a demon. It could only have come from four sources, three if you discount me, and I did not call it. Since the Western Wizard is dead, that leaves two. Either Trilless or Carcophan could have called it. The question is why.'

Colbey lowered the hilt to the ground, balancing the blade against his hand. The Wizard seemed to be speaking more to himself than to Colbey, and the Renshai believed it wrong to interrupt.

'If he or she had called it for information and lost control, it would have slaughtered his or her followers, then left. And if I could best it by myself, either of them could have done so more easily.' Shadimar stared at Colbey, and his tangible emotions receded. Colbey felt certain the Wizard had come to a conclusion. 'That demon was given a task. It was summoned *specifically to kill someone.*'

'Who?' Colbey asked, the possibilities few.

'The one and only person it attacked with intent to kill.' Shadimar rose. 'You, Colbey. It wanted you.' He glanced at the Renshai's bandaged hand. 'And had it inflicted more than a scratch, each claw strike would have aged you a decade.'

If Colbey had sustained a scratch, he dared not envision a significant injury. Still, he did not argue; it was not his way to burden others with complaints about his wounds. Instead, he shook his head, seeing flaws in the Eastern Wizard's conclusion. 'It had me in the cornfield, if it wanted me. Why didn't it just keep shooting fire then?'

Shadimar looked past Colbey, at the ladder leading down from the loft. 'There is only one explanation. Its task was to kill you and no one else. Failing that, it had to wait until it got you alone.'

Colbey's brow furrowed. The noises wafting from the common room below seemed to disappear. 'Why me? I thought these were your enemies.'

'She sees you as a threat.'

'She?' Colbey prodded.

'Trilless.' Shadimar paced. 'I have to guess it's her work. The use of a demon screams Carcophan, but the instructions to hurt no one except you fits Trilless perfectly. And there's precedent. I believe she goaded the Northmen against you.'

Colbey corrected, fishing for the extent of Shadimar's knowledge. 'You mean against Santagithi.'

'I mean exactly what I said. Nothing less.'

Traitor that Emerald was, she was not a liar. Colbey let the knowledge pass. What Emerald had been no longer mattered, except in that she was Episte's mother. Colbey would never disparage her memory in the boy's presence. 'This Trilless is the Northern Sorceress, right?'

Shadimar nodded confirmation as he ambled past Colbey.

'For someone who never met me, she's been a constant source of trouble.'

'It's not personal.' Shadimar turned and headed back the way he had come. 'It never is for Wizards. For reasons I don't yet have the knowledge to fathom, she sees you as a threat to her cause.' One brow arched, apparently in memory of the demon. 'Obviously, a serious threat.' He stopped directly in front of Colbey. 'Like Wizards, demons can't be harmed by anything of Odin's world. Without Harval . . .' He pointed at the sword. '. . . you can't do anything against your enemies, except die.'

Colbey's gaze strayed to the bandage. Had the demon's claws caused much more damage, he would have lost his hand. He had heard rumors of men living nearly a century, then dying as feeble, twisted gnomes as frail as china dolls. A deeper slash would have left him dead of 'age' and handless, barred from Valhalla as the price for a single wound that, without this weapon, he could not defend. Colbey raised the sword again, studying it in the stream of sunlight. It looked no different than before: fire-hardened to Colbey's meticulous specifications, cold silver steel crafted to kill. *Perhaps I will keep you.* He directed the thought at the sword, prepared for a mental battle of control and will. Nothing ensued. The sword had no sentience of its own; it would obey its wielder without question or regard to action. It was a tool, like any weapon, yet with potential for greater harm. *Is it any difference to own a sword whose balance and sharpness come from magic than to find one as well made by more mundane means?*

Colbey internalized the question, seeking Sif's guidance. He received nothing direct, but his thoughts did shift slightly to a statement Shadimar had made indirectly: 'Like Wizards, demons can't be harmed by anything of Odin's world.' *If Harval can kill demons, then it can kill Wizards as well.* Colbey considered the significance of his realization, and it made him smile. *You started this feud, Trilless. You had best hope I don't finish it.* Again, Colbey flipped the weapon, this time catching the hilt. He slid the Gray Blade into the sheath it had occupied before the breaking. Its presence felt good.

Colbey chose a secluded clearing amidst the corn stalks for his practice, a circular burn apparently left by Trilless' demon. Black stubble crunched beneath Colbey's boots, and Harval flickered between the rows of stalks. He concentrated on single-blade patterns and thrusts. Though he hated letting one limb lie dormant, Colbey's herbal studies allowed him to understand the need. First, the injury needed to heal. Sudden, committed movements would hamper his body's restorative powers. Once the wound had closed, rehabilitation could come later.

A feeling of presence touched Colbey first, a distant sensation of another's staring. So soon after the demon's attack, it made him leery; but he continued his practice without a break in stride. The *svergelse* gave him an excuse to have his sword drawn, and he saw no need to alert the other to his vigilance. So far, nothing about the being made it seem overtly malicious. His mind told him that the approaching creature was human. So long as he held a sword, Colbey believed he could handle any warrior in existence.

Colbey performed a dexterous series of blocks, immediately followed by quick-slashes, reveling in the balance of the weapon in his grip. The person came closer. The elder Renshai could follow the unknown's passage by the line of bowing corn tassels and the faint thump of stalk against stalk. As the other came to the edge of the clearing, Colbey lowered his sword. He caught a flashing image of blue cloth among the greenery. Episte shoved aside a pair of stalks in his path and looked in on the clearing. His gaze rolled from the scorched vegetation to the bandage on Colbey's hand, and stopped there.

Colbey sheathed his blade, pleased to see Episte despite the disruption of his practice. The apology he needed to give the youngster held a significance that hounded him, yet comforting, emotion-laden speeches had never come easily to him. He considered his words carefully, certain the right ones could strengthen their relationship regardless of the discomfort on both sides that would invariably hamper the initial proceedings.

While Colbey studied his method, Episte blurted without preamble, whatever approach he had rehearsed en route lost in a sudden boil of emotion. 'Is that the hand you hit me with?'

Colbey followed the youngster's attention to the bandage. Shadimar had given Colbey a poultice, claiming its use once daily would undoubtedly prove enough to heal a scrape. Shadimar's lack of sympathy and insistence on understatement confused Colbey, and the concoction had had no instantaneous effect, though it had deadened the pain. As to Episte's question, Colbey did not need to ponder long. Ever since he had struck his student, the impression of the contact seemed to linger on his flesh, a hot and ugly reminder. 'Yes. Same hand. Poetic justice, isn't it?' He flashed a mild smile, trying to lighten a difficult exchange.

Episte's frown deepened, and his eyes narrowed.

'Everyone makes mistakes, Episte. One's own flaws are the hardest to recognize. The honor comes with admitting and atoning for those mistakes.' Colbey personalized the apology. 'I'm sorry, Episte. You were right about the demon.'

Episte's tone did not change. It remained hurt and resentful. 'You should have believed me.'

'I should have,' Colbey admitted.

'You called me a liar.'

Colbey resisted the urge to defend his action. Surely even Episte had to see how farfetched the story must have seemed. 'There's a virtue to accepting apologies, too, Episte.'

Episte ignored the warning. 'You hit me. I never thought my *torke* would hit me. Especially in the face.'

Colbey could feel the first stirrings of his own anger, nearly lost amid the tide of guilt. Though he reviled what he had done, he could not undo it. Yet the incident could not rest until Episte acknowledged his regret. 'I said I was sorry. I am.'

'I never thought my *torke* would hit me.'

'That's enough. I know what I did.' The repetition fanned Colbey's growing annoyance. 'You're insulting my apology.'

Episte turned away, rubbing at the site on his cheek where the blow had landed. Still, he did not permit the apology.

Frustration drove Colbey to strike back in kind. 'You're not blameless either.'

Episte spun back, hurt instantly replaced by rage. 'So now you're holding me at fault for getting hit by you?'

'No. I'm holding you at fault for attacking your younger brother at the festival.'

Episte avoided Colbey's eyes. His mouth opened, then snapped closed. He spoke in a flat tone indicating building anger. 'Rache told you that?'

Colbey kept his gaze fixed on Episte. He had regained the upper hand, yet that was never what he had sought. 'The farmers told me. And Garn gave me details.'

'It was spar.' Episte defended himself.

'Spar indicates a willingness on both sides. What Garn described didn't sound like that.'

Episte chewed his lower lip, still dodging Colbey's gaze. 'It's none of your business. What happened at the festival is between Rache and me.'

The disrespect further enraged Colbey, and the immediate import-ance of the apology receded. 'First, there's a reason why the Renshai tongue doesn't have a separate word for teacher and sword master. If you learn nothing else, I would have you understand this: Violating the bond of brotherhood is every bit as dishonorable as striking a student. Second, whatever you think of what I did once, I'm still your *torke;* and you will address me with respect.'

This time, Colbey's cold eyes caught and held Episte's, though not for long. The teen glanced away swiftly.

'Do you understand that?'

Episte went perfectly still, gaze on his boots. 'Yes, *torke,*' he said, his tone expressionless and unreadable.

'You will apologize to Rache.'

'Yes, *torke.*' The blandness of the response indicated that Episte was responding without listening to or considering the demands and questions.

Still short of the needed acknowledgement, Colbey pressed one last time. 'Did you understand my apology?'

'Yes, *torke.*'

'Do you have anything to say, Episte?'

Colbey held his breath, hoping his student would take a moment to give the question the consideration it deserved.

But Episte's response came equally quickly. He did not modulate his voice in any way. 'No, *torke.*'

Colbey hesitated, fingers unconsciously massaging Harval's hilt. He could not force his apology upon the boy, yet the absence of acceptance left a hollow in his gut that made him feel incomplete. It was not a need to have things settled so much as a need to reestablish, and to enhance, the bonds beyond blood they had once shared. From this point on, he had no choice but to leave the initiative in the youngster's hands. 'You're dismissed, Episte.'

'Yes, *torke,*' Episte said in the same monotone. Without another word, he spun on his heel and headed from the clearing.

20 The Demon's Mark

Colbey and his students, Garn, Shadimar, and Secodon set out from Greentree that day, their bellies full of festival leftovers and their packs crammed with rations for travel. The farmers knew their herds well enough to recognize the earliest signs of improving health. And, if the lack of a corpse failed to convince them of the demise of Flanner's bane, the charred porch left little doubt that the Renshai and the Wizard had confronted the creature and survived.

Gradually, the fields of the farm town merged into a vista of oak forest. Well-rested and fed, the horses threaded easily between the trunks, choosing deer trails and more open routes whenever possible. Freed from the burden of hunting, Mitrian chatted animatedly with Garn, who seemed thrilled at the companionship. The two younger Renshai rode ahead or halted, exploring every nook and hollow that might catch a teenager's fancy. Even Shadimar seemed uplifted. His features lost some of their craggy solemnity, and he occasionally spoke to the wolf, where it perched on his horse's rump.

Only Colbey seemed alone, a prisoner of the body that had served him unfailingly for seventy-six years. He bore the scars of countless battles, the worst of which still puckered the skin across his chest and side. In the past, Colbey's natural defenses had always repaired the breaks, cuts, and illnesses, with the help of a handful of herbs. But, despite Shadimar's poultice, the claw strikes of the demon did not heal.

Unwilling to alarm his companions, Colbey kept his hand bandaged. When traditional herbs failed, he led the party in wild loops for legendary cures, without explanation. The salivary gland of a black squirrel gained him nothing more than the sap of a maple mixed with river tar. As the wound worsened, Colbey lost the will to unwrap the bandage every day, and pain forced him to wield a single sword, righthanded. Unconsciously, Colbey used his students as an outlet for his frustration. Episte and Mitrian appeared eternally tired, and Rache became haggard due not only to the added violence of the old Renshai's training, but also to Garn's insistence that he learn the use of other weapons as well.

Two weeks outside of the farming town of Greentree, Colbey found himself too troubled to sleep. He took first watch that night. The sky formed a film of gray, tapering to pink at the horizons. The moon hovered like a blood spot, dull compared to the campfire's light and heat. Colbey looked at the withered shadows of the trees. His gaze dropped slowly to the ground, passing over each of his sleeping companions in turn, then flickered across the layers of cloth that enwrapped his left hand.

Colbey looked away. Again, he stared into the distance, but his focus always returned to the same thing, like a fishing line cast outward and always reeled back. The silver disappeared from the sky, replaced by a darkness spoiled only by the dwindling fire and the diffuse glow of the moon. Time passed in a throbbing cycle. The pain of the wound had become too familiar, and deeper with time. From the position of the moon, Colbey knew he should awaken Mitrian for her watch; but he saw no reason to disturb her while he could not sleep. And he knew he had no choice but to look upon his hand.

Once made, the decision allowed him to notice something that had slipped past his gaze before. Swollen red streaks ran along his arm, their edges just beginning to show beneath the bandage. Once discovered, the infection filled his thoughts, and he could not turn away again. Despair threatened to overwhelm him. He had outlived his peers by nearly five decades. He had dedicated his life to his swords and accomplished more than any Renshai before him. Nothing remained except to train his successor and die in glory; but Colbey knew now that he would lose his hand and his arm and, therefore, his chance to enter Valhalla. Moments passed like days while Colbey stared at his inflamed hand, knowing it would soon steal the dignity from life and the honor from death. *The other Renshai deserve better than a ravaged old man condemned to the frozen wastes of Hel.*

Colbey unwrapped the bandage. He could combat a dozen Northmen at once and enjoy the challenge, yet it took all of his courage to look upon his own hand. Once he did, he could not tear his gaze from it. Its back had become a grossly swollen mass of clotted blood and fluid. His fingers had shriveled and purpled, becoming black at the tips. All about it crept the red rash.

'Days.' Only one solution presented itself to Colbey. *I have to die in battle, before the infection claims my hand.* His thoughts raced. *I have to find a town in these dense, forsaken woods, an army to attack and a war in which to die.* Once a threat, death became a mellow promise, and the aching in Colbey's hand gave way before the strength of his mind. Yet guilt rose to spoil the serenity that should have come with the decision. *To kill innocents to preserve my place in Valhalla would undermine all I've tried to do to recreate the Renshai and restore the honor stolen through decades of wanton killing.*

A swishing noise snapped Colbey's attention from his thoughts. Instinctively, he leapt aside, and a dozen arrows fell about the scarlet flicker of the campfire.

'Up!' Colbey screamed. He scattered the coals with a wild kick that plunged them into darkness. 'Scatter,' he whispered gruffly. 'They can't take us all!' He added quickly in Renshai, 'We'll meet back at the damaged tree.' It was a landmark all of his companions would remember, a lightning-struck oak with barkless stripes running down its trunk that they had passed during the day. Hoping Mitrian would interpret for Garn, Colbey headed directly for the bowmen.

The Renshai's feet made no sound on the carpet of greenery that wound beneath the trees. His eyes adjusted to the more complete darkness, and he slowed his pace to think. Without the guidance of the fire, night would foil the archers' aim, and they would need to draw hand weapons to battle. Having lost the advantage of surprise, they would need numbers to fight Renshai. Colbey's mind traced the trajectory of the arrows, and memory told him that the shafts had come from many directions. If so, the enemy would need to regroup.

With the stealth of a predator, Colbey doubled back on his trail. In the distance, he heard some indiscernible calls. A closer movement froze him. An instant later, he heard musical voices using the Northern tongue:

'Aksel, is that you?'

'Quiet. Yes. This way.'

Moonlight glimmered from blond war braids, and the pair passed Colbey, apparently without seeing him. Colbey followed, heart pounding. He touched the cold steel of Harval's hilt with fingers slick with anticipation, scarcely daring to believe his luck. *How generous of the Northmen to come along just when I needed a target.* Blood lust burned like fever, and Colbey went dizzy with hatred. It took a monumental effort to keep from leaping upon these Northmen. *Better to find the other Northmen and fight them all at once.* He tried to clench the fingers of a dying hand he had not had the chance to rebandage, but they would not obey him. He let the arm hang and trailed the Northmen into the woods. At length, he found a gathering of fair-skinned archers.

Colbey sprang with a howl. Two fell before they saw the danger. A third leapt to meet Colbey. The Renshai chopped him down with a single stroke and turned to face the next. Had the Northmen considered their strategy, they would have surrounded Colbey and struck from all sides. But hatred or overconfidence drove them to riot. They bore in on Colbey, a waving wall of steel.

They fought nine to one, but Colbey delivered three blows to each of the most agile Northmen's one. The Renshai let the battle madness take him, without regard to defense. He sought death. He and the sword became a team of slaughter, and two more reavers fell before the Northmen finally closed around him. Three swords swept for Colbey. He knew, with a master's eye, he could block only two.

Colbey loosed a glorious death scream, 'Modi!' One sword glanced from his blade. A second fell against it with an impact that nearly wrenched it from his hands. The third never landed. Its wielder staggered backward, run through by a spear Colbey never saw coming. Suddenly, the Renshai had an ally, a dark stranger who jabbed far more slowly.

Energy rose fresh within Colbey, spurred by his battle cry and frustration. He lunged to meet the last six of his attackers. Even as he did so, other Renshai joined him, drawn by his shout. Three more Northmen came as well. Moonlight danced from a dozen weapons. Screams resounded, thunder to the lightning exchange of swordplay. Blood splashed the trees, and war howls shattered the quiet of the night forest.

When the last of the Northmen fell in red defeat, Colbey found himself without new injury. He glanced at the swordsman at his side. It was Rache. The youngster's sword dripped blood. His gaze locked on Colbey's hand, and his face twisted into a grimace of horror.

Shadimar caught Colbey's sword arm. 'Come with me.'

Though still curious about the spearman who had come to his aid, Colbey followed Shadimar into the forest. As he walked, he cleaned and sheathed his sword. At length, the Eastern Wizard gestured to a tree stump, and Colbey sat in the indicated place. Shadimar reached for Colbey's left hand.

Colbey pulled it away. 'Just a scratch,' he gave the Wizard back his own description by way of explanation. 'Your demon – '

Shadimar placed his hands on his hips. His voice held the hard edge of controlled anger. 'You may attribute the storms at my home to me without insult. But I won't take credit for the work of the Good One or of the Evil One. I took you as my champion. The day I gave you Harval, I put all possible trust into your hands. At the time, I thought them capable. Now I've come to doubt your judgment.'

Colbey lowered his head. 'Without a chance at Valhalla, my life has no meaning. I thought I could kill as many enemies as possible while you escaped.' He looked up, no longer ashamed. 'Once they killed me, they might let the others live. More than enough friends have died for me.'

Shadimar stood, immobile as a mountain. No part of him moved, except for his lips. The explanation seemed lost on him; clearly, Colbey had misinterpreted the Wizard's scolding. 'Why didn't you show me your hand before?'

Colbey blinked, incredulous. 'You knew about it. A scratch, you called it.'

Shadimar frowned, deeply thoughtful. 'And so I believed. Anything more damaging should have aged you decades.'

'Renshai tend to mature slowly.'

Shadimar denied the explanation. 'Even Renshai would show the effect of forty years at once.'

Without a ready answer, Colbey shrugged. 'Then apparently the "scratch" was just dirty and deep enough to fester.'

'Apparently.'

The Eastern Wizard's quiet consideration unnerved Colbey. For now, understanding and explanation had to take a back seat to solution. 'You gave me a poultice. I used it. And a dozen other potential cures. Are you telling me now you could have done more?'

'Indeed.'

Crushed, Colbey stared at his good hand, still smeared with Northmen's blood. 'Can you still?'

Shadimar scowled. 'Maybe. I'll need your help. What would you customarily use for such a wound?'

Colbey balled his good hand to a fist, seeing the other scarcely respond to his command. 'I've seen wounds in this state before. The Renshai knew how to cure them.' He rose. 'We put the injured man at the front of a battle. Then, when the fighting grew most vicious . . . ' Colbey met the Wizard's gaze. '. . . we cut him down from behind.'

For some time, the harsh orchestra of crickets was Colbey's only reply. Shadimar stood in silence, his expression unreadable. At long last, he spoke. 'I meant *herbs*, Colbey!'

'I've tried every herb in this damned forest!'

'Try again.' Shadimar tossed his head. 'Gather what you need. With my help, the result might be better.'

With a surge of desperate hope, Colbey slipped into the forest. He gathered sprigs of *ranweed* and the clear, green stems of touch-me-not. He scored a pine for sap as a thickener and collected the central eyes of *garlet* flowers. By luck, he found a rare red-cupped mushroom. He picked it as well. He returned to find Shadimar sitting on a stump as weathered as himself, writing on a silver piece of bark with a stylus.

Shadimar did not acknowledge Colbey's return. The Renshai sat. Working one-handed made his task difficult, but he tore cloth for a bandage and crushed the herbs for a poultice. When he finished, Shadimar crumbled the bark into the mixture and helped Colbey apply it to his wound.

Colbey stared at his carefully wrapped hand without comment. As a young man, he had never believed in sorcery; and, until Greentree, he had never placed much stock in creatures of myth. But the healing in Shadimar's ruins and the demon battle in the farm town gave Colbey a new perspective. Doubting Shadimar's enchantments would do Colbey no good, so he chose to believe.

'Let's get back,' Shadimar said.

Colbey nodded his agreement.

The two elders brushed through the foliage. Sooner than Colbey expected, he heard voices. Apparently, his companions had shifted their position to escape the Northmen's bodies and the odor of death and blood, choosing the direction the two older men had taken. Colbey adjusted his course to veer directly toward them.

Almost immediately, a man appeared before them, as if created from the shadows of the brush. He stood as large as Sterrane, yet as firm and lean as Garn. Sable hair hung crookedly to his shoulders. He wore only a loincloth of spotted animal hide, and he clutched a stone-tipped spear.

Startled by the other's sudden appearance, Colbey shied into a defensive crouch, hands falling naturally to his hilts.

A moment later, the man disappeared, seeming to fold into the darkness of the greenery. Colbey searched, eyes tracing the position where he had stood, seeking outline where he knew he would find no movement. When the figure eluded him, he turned his attention cautiously to Shadimar.

'I saw him,' Shadimar confirmed. 'He was real.'

Recalling the spear that had saved his life during the battle, Colbey guessed he had discovered his ally. The animal movements, the primitive weapon, and the loincloth identified him as one of the barbarians who roved the southeastern Westlands in tribes. Once, only shortly before Colbey's birth, the exiled Renshai had lived among these barbarians, learning the herbal lore that formed a basis for healing and a stealth that pervaded the Renshai sword maneuvers. Colbey recognized the barbarian's hiding technique as well. The Renshai called it *brunnstil*, which literally meant 'still and brown.'

'*Brunnstil*,' Colbey said softly. He imitated the maneuver, trying to become one with the forest. For all his practice and skill, he knew he could not match the barbarian's thoroughness. Respect blossomed for the wild man.

The barbarian appeared again, this time in front of Colbey and just beyond his reach. Strong hazel eyes trained unwaveringly on the Renshai. '*Brunnstil*,' the barbarian echoed, his voice deep and his gruff dialect emphasizing the consonants. Muscles pulled taut beneath his bronzed skin, and Colbey noted the wiry tension that characterizes one who survives by wile and quickness as well as strength. 'Ranshee?'

Colbey blinked, the second word meaning nothing to him, though he recognized something familiar about it. An instant later, the answer came. *Renshai*. He nearly laughed. 'Renshai.' He restored the vowels and the melodious Northern pronunciation. 'Yes, I am Renshai.'

'Ran-shigh.' The spearman attempted it again, coming closer. He broke into a rapid, guttural patter in a language Colbey did not understand.

Colbey glanced at Shadimar for help.

The Eastern Wizard shrugged to indicate ignorance.

Colbey shook his head.

Apparently recognizing the gap, the spearman fell silent. 'Korgar,' he said. 'Sangrit.'

Colbey took a logical guess. He pointed at the barbarian. 'Korgar Sangrit?'

'Korgar.' The barbarian hammered a fist against his own chest. He pulled free a knife from the waistband of his loincloth, the steel polished and the hilt of Northern design. 'Sangrit.'

Colbey back-stepped. In his culture, waving a weapon was a sure gesture of challenge. But the barbarian kept his spear couched, holding the dagger with its blade pointed at the sky. His expression and voice revealed no malice. Certainly, the barbarian had taken the weapon from a Northman's corpse. If the stranger's people could work steel, Colbey felt certain the spear would not have a stone head.

At Colbey's retreat, the barbarian frowned. 'Korgar.' He tapped his chest. 'Sangrit.' He jabbed the knife upward, then opened his mouth to indicate a missing word. The intensity of his gaze told Colbey that the barbarian expected him to supply it.

'Colbey,' he said. Again, he glanced at Shadimar. 'Does he want me to fight?'

Shadimar made a noncommittal gesture. Clearly, he knew less about barbarians then Colbey.

That surprised the old Renshai, but he saw no reason to make an issue of it now.

'Coolba.' The barbarian mangled the name. He took a stride forward, letting the spear fall to the ground. With his now free hand, he made a lightning grab for Colbey's right arm.

Instinctively, Colbey jerked away. The barbarian's callused fingers scratched across the back of his wrist and fell free. Emotion wafted from the massive figure, its rawness buffeting Colbey: disappointment, frustration, and a waning respect. Colbey tried to grasp thoughts to explain the feelings. He became lost in a maze of superstition and custom, with origins lost to logical understanding. He did read violence in the barbarian's intentions, but it lacked malice or hatred.

The barbarian made a hissing noise of annoyance and reached for

Colbey again.

This time, Colbey allowed his hand to be caught. Meaty fingers engulfed his narrow wrist until it almost seemed to disappear. His flesh looked sallow in the barbarian's dark grip, and the idea of surrendering his only useful hand brought sweat to Colbey's temples.

Apparently drawn by the sound of the exchange, Mitrian, Garn, Rache, and Secodon approached from behind the barbarian. The wild man turned his head to them. Then, apparently deeming them safe, he returned his attention to Colbey. 'Coolba. Korgar.' He raised the knife. Hazel eyes without a hint of animal color or movement bored into Colbey's gray-blue ones. 'Sangrit?'

Colbey nodded, uncertain what his agreement entailed. Before he could ponder the blade flashed in the moonlight. It slashed a shallow line across his wrist. For an instant, he felt nothing. Blood beaded the cut, trickling into his palm. The pain followed, a sharp jab that quickly settled to an ache.

Mitrian gasped. Rache leapt to his *torke's* aid.

'No.' With his bandaged hand, Colbey made a gesture to stay the other Renshai.

Korgar flicked his gaze to Rache and growled. He passed the dagger to Colbey, rested his right wrist on Colbey's bandage, and used his other hand to close the Renshai's fingers around the hilt.

Not wanting to hurt the stranger, Colbey hesitated. He knew enough of barbarians to realize that reticence would be seen as weakness. Taking the knife, he opened a gash on the barbarian's wrist, using care that it fell into the size and shape of the one Korgar had inflicted.

Korgar closed his bleeding hand about Colbey's. Again, he met the Renshai's gaze. 'Korgar. Coolba.' His face wrinkled into deep lines of concentration. His grip tightened. His lips seemed to bend around syllables never meant for his palate. '*Brorin.*' It meant brother in Renshai and the pronunciation was nearly flawless.

Sudden understanding made Colbey smile. 'Northmen exchange vows and share tribes. Apparently, barbarians take the words "blood brother" more literally.' He clapped his still trickling hand to Korgar's shoulder. The words jarred a memory. The elder Rache had become blood brother to Valr Kirin, a bond that had grown into the alliance between Vikerin and Santagithi's Town. The train of thought sobered his mood. 'There are more Northmen out there, I'm sure.' His gaze passed over his assembled companions. Korgar had discovered Secodon and crouched, stroking the wolf. Mitrian and Garn were nodding agreement, and Rache studied Korgar. Shadimar leaned against a sapling, silent. Colbey saw no sign of the remaining Renshai. 'Where's Episte?'

Every eye turned to Rache.

The youngster fidgeted. 'I don't know. I haven't seen him since we all went in different directions. I heard *torke's* shout and came here.'

Thinking back on the battle, Colbey recalled the three Northmen who had joined in later. He tried to remember if they had arrived blooded. He was certain only that they were winded. *Maybe they came upon Episte first. They might have wounded or killed him.*

'He's probably waiting at the burned tree,' Mitrian said, though concern shone through her thin facade of casualness. 'Where we were supposed to meet.'

Mitrian's explanation seemed as likely as his own, yet Colbey could not banish alarm. 'We need to find him. Before the Northmen do.' He glanced into the sky. Dawn grew on the horizon, and they could no longer rely on darkness to shield them. He cursed the time Shadimar's cure and Korgar's ceremony had stolen, wishing he had counted companions before moving on to other things. He plunged into the woods, the others at his heels.

'What about the horses?' Garn asked, always practical.

Colbey frowned. 'There're more Northmen in these woods. The first place they'll look for us is the camp. We can't risk getting the horses or supplies.' He pushed on, need gnawing at him, sparking a guilt that joined the aching burden of concern. Like nothing else, Episte's disappearance translated Colbey's feelings for the boy into love. The possibility that the teenager had died was like a physical pain, and he forced his thoughts to channel into two directions: Episte would return or they would find his corpse intact and surrounded by the bodies of enemies, his soul a treasure of the gods' *Valkyries*. Yet, for once, these thoughts did not sooth. Episte was alive. Until he had proof, his mind could not convince him otherwise.

The deep path widened to a trail. The opening accorded Colbey a distant impression of the lightning-struck oak, and he squinted for a glimpse of Episte in its shadows. He saw no figures, and concern flared, burning him with a doubt that bordered on fear. As the group drew up to the tree, he still saw no sign of Episte, and the silence of his companions became conspicuous beneath the morning trills of birds. Mitrian stared at her feet. Garn continued to glance through the brush long after the others had surrendered to despair. Rache rubbed at his arms, his lip trapped between his teeth and his eyes moist. Shadimar stood, etched like a statue against the dawn. Korgar's hand wandered over Secodon. The wolf lay on its back submissively, its paws in the air. Apparently, the barbarian knew the most satisfying places to scratch a wolf.

Colbey cleared his throat. Instantly, everyone's attention was riveted on him. He saw a pleading in each gaze that begged him to find the solution and the missing child. He knew that it was probably a figment of his imagination, but the burden became a promise, though he did not voice it. Exhaustion rode him, but he could not sleep until he knew for certain and fulfilled that vow he had made to himself and, in his mind, to the others as well. 'Wait here for Episte. Korgar and I will look for him.'

Colbey seized the barbarian's arm and headed into the woods before anyone could protest, yet Shadimar's words followed them. 'Secodon, go with them.'

Paw steps crushed the weeds with a sound no louder than his own passage, then the wolf was with them. Colbey did not mind. When tears blurred his gaze and frustration hardened his muscles to knots, he knew his two companions would never tell.

Colbey wound through the shadows of the foliage, his hood shielding his white thatch of hair and its golden highlights. Korgar faded into the brightly lit forest, then reappeared so often that his skill no longer amazed Colbey. He found himself thinking about the days when his own *torke* had taught him *brunnstil*. Though seventy years had passed, Colbey could still hear himself saying: 'Brown and still?' He made a broad gesture to include the expanse of brush and weeds. 'Wouldn't still and green make more sense?'

The *torke* had smiled with a patience Colbey had long sought to mimic. 'Colbey, think of the wolf, the bear, and the woodland cat. Think of deer and of *wisules*, the worst cowards and best hiders in all the animal world. Think of every animal that has ever eluded man or beast in the woods. And when you have consider them all, I want you to make a list. I want you to consider all of the animals that successfully conceal themselves. Then I want you to name every one that's green.'

Now, in the forests south of the town of Greentree, Colbey smiled at this memory from a time when his only concern was becoming the best swordsman he could. He dwelt on the past and the memories it inspired, glad to release the concern that had wound his nerves to aching coils for the last half day. He knew he should have returned long ago. Already, his companions would be worrying over his own safety as well as Episte's. Yet, his conscience would not allow him to abandon the search.

Korgar emerged from a patch of thistle, without a rustle to betray his passage. '*Anem*,' he said, his voice a guttural growl. He jabbed his hand in the direction from which he had come, then indicated a circular path of avoidance.

Colbey sighed, stopping in his tracks. Over time, he had come to recognize *amen* as the barbarian's word for Northmen. He could not help wondering if he had made a mistake by avoiding the areas that Korgar indicated. Having never seen Episte, Korgar might mistake the young blond for one of the Northmen's own. 'How many?' Colbey held up one finger, adding consecutive digits to the count until he reached five. He used the whole of his bandaged hand for the sixth marker.

Korgar grunted, nodding.

Colbey dropped his count. It made no sense for Episte to be among others, unless the Northmen had captured him. Yet that made less sense. The Northmen would have no reason to keep a Renshai alive, and Colbey could not imagine anyone taking Episte without a lethal fight. He also believed that, despite his communication difficulties, Korgar would mention the oddity of a prisoner. Or so he hoped.

Directly behind Colbey, Secodon sat, whining softly.

Colbey shifted his direction. The turn of his thoughts back to Episte brought with it a feeling as heavy as lead. His mind conjured images of the teenager as a toddler, capering through maneuvers designed for older students. Memories paraded through his thoughts, of Episte at every age, an endless succession of skill and frustration. *So competent, yet so unmotivated*. The idea both pained and brought joy. As much as it hurt to have a student with so much potential and so little desire, it was what made Episte Episte.

Brush rasped from Colbey's jerkin as he worked through a dense copse and into a sparser area of forest. He tried to suppress the rush of memory that hammered at him. The images retreated, replaced by insidious feelings dredged from a depth Colbey had never before discovered. His love for Episte frightened him. The strength of his emotion surpassed anything he could recall from the past, even his ties to his parents. For all that he had tried to leave Episte's nonmartial upbringing to the boy's mother, the temptation to sweep the child away from her had proven strong. Though he had resisted in the physical sense, his mind had betrayed him. Colbey knew without the need to doubt, that he was, in his own mind and in the boy's, Episte's father.

Secodon paused, nostrils twitching in a thin breeze that Colbey scarcely noticed. The wolf plunged ahead, brush crackling in its wake. Colbey continued onward, sticking to the stripes and patches of darkness. The realization opened a deeply buried section of memory, and love seemed to geyser from it with an intensity that again brought tears to Colbey's eyes. They surprised him. He could not remember ever having cried before, not even as a child. Yet he could not have stopped the tears if he tried. Episte meant so much more than just one more student among decades of students. The few remaining Renshai made each one more precious, but none more so than the last that still carried Renshai blood.

The idea rankled. Colbey had spent too long denying the importance of bloodline to place emphasis on it now, but his mind seized the
concept and held it. In his youth, Colbey had fallen in love twice;
neither woman had borne him a child. In turn, each had left him for a
man who could give her a family. From that time, Colbey had never
known any woman as more than a friend, a peer, or a student, and the
idea of settling with one never crossed his mind again. He had no need
nor reason. Of them all, only Episte could carry on the physical traits
that, though secondary to the sword skill, still distinguished Renshai:
the blond or red hair and pale eyes that seemed so natural to Colbey,
the slower aging, and the skill that had come because those with
natural and trained ability survived long enough to procreate.

Secodon returned. The wolf danced an excited circle around
Colbey, then started back the way it had come. After a few steps, it
returned to Colbey.

Colbey followed, curious. As it became obvious that Secodon was
leading him somewhere, guarded hope rose. He could not help but
wonder if the beast would take him to a rabbit's burrow or a fox's den.
Had it been any other trained wolf, he would have expected such a
find. Yet Secodon belonged to Shadimar. Though the wolf seemed
normal, aside from reading the Wizard's moods, Colbey allowed a
shiver of joy to surface.

Episte. Colbey's tears abated, and he smiled. He formed mental
pictures of the teen, imagining the exuberant embrace when the
youngster realized that he was no longer lost in unfamiliar forest.
When the hugs had finished, Colbey promised himself that he would
again apologize for hitting Episte. He would confess that the rage that
had possessed him when he believed Episte was lying had burned
harder because of the love and hopes and plans he had projected on the
last man with Renshai blood. *My son.* Colbey stepped into a clearing.

At his approach, flies rose in a buzzing cloud. Three bodies sprawled
on the ground black with blood. Two lay in familiar positions,
agonizingly twisted and stiffened in rigor. Each bore wounds that
could only have come in battle: one a thrust through the abdomen, the
other a gash across its throat. The third body flopped in the center of
the glade, naked and lying on the tattered remains of a tunic and cloak.
Small and lanky, it obviously belonged to a young teen. The limbs
sprawled as if in sleep, yet their stiffness betrayed death. And it had no
head.

Colbey gasped in a ragged breath. Sadness assailed him first, the
grim knowledge that this youth, whoever he had been, had never
reached Valhalla. The need for the dead to be a stranger kept other
possibilities at bay, and realization seemed to take an eternity to trickle

into Colbey's brain. He stood, frozen and rooted. He did not know for how long; but, when he moved at last, his limbs tingled with a prickling sensation that comes with remaining in one position too long. Korgar had stepped up beside him.

At length, Colbey emerged from his trance enough to approach the body. The neck bore evidence of repeated trauma. No clean stroke had claimed the head, and the lack of wounds on the remainder of the body sickened Colbey. This man had died slowly and in a horrible agony that he could not imagine even the most savage Renshai inflicting on an enemy. Colbey dropped to his haunches beside the corpse, dreading what need told him he must do. Blood did not bother him, nor death. He had claimed both too long and too many times to find them anything but commonplace. But the ugliness at his feet went beyond any mortal honor he could fathom. *Why would anyone do this to anyone else?* The answer came faster than he could suppress it. *Because the Northmen's hatred has grown beyond rational thought or behavior.* The next followed naturally. *Which means this corpse can be no one but Episte.*

The idea evoked a pain that mercifully stole all thought from Colbey. Having conceived the horror, however, he had to know the truth. Catching a cold, bloodless arm, he flipped the body to its back. Though stained with gore, the tatters of cloth matched Episte's cloak and tunic perfectly.

No! Colbey pawed at the clothing in mindless agony. 'No!' he screamed, not caring who heard. 'No! No! No!' And the rest of the call came as naturally as breathing, that which he had learned to shout when cut, though that pain had always before been physical. 'Modi! Modi!' The clothing balled into his lap, some of the blood still wet enough to smear the bandage and gel in the hairs of his arm. Santagithi's locket fell free, the chain snaking across the bloodstained dirt.

Colbey seized the trinket. Though it could be no other, he had to know for certain. He cupped his hand around the piece, fingers quivering on the latch. It opened to reveal the familiar piece of parchment and the words in the elder Rache's hand.

Colbey snapped the locket closed. It pinched the skin on the side of his finger, the sharpness of the pain reviving him from a state of numb shock to a rage that seemed to tear him asunder. He jabbed the jewelry into his pocket so hard that the lining tore. He whipped the sword from his sheath with his unbandaged hand and advanced on the dead Northmen. If they would steal the glory from Episte's death, then he would butcher Valhalla from them as well. From this day forth, no Northman would find the joy of the afterlife. Colbey would see to that. Quickly, he advanced on the dead, intent on hacking them into enough gory pieces so their brothers could never recognize them, could never perform the ceremonies that would assure them the honor of an afterlife.

Yet even as Colbey raised the blade, he knew that he could never let it fall. The two men who lay here had not disgraced Episte. Rather, they had surely fallen at his hand. To dismember them was wrong, and to carry a stark, ugly vengeance against all Northmen equally so. To claim limbs from the dead would require Colbey to abandon all the promises he had made to himself, to his goddess, and to the future of Renshai. It would revive every crime he had vowed to make right, rekindle every hatred against the Renshai that he had dedicated the last decade of his life to undoing. He returned the blade to its sheath.

Colbey's anger continued to flare, the violence that would have dispelled it thwarted by conscience. He channeled it into gathering the largest branches he could handle, slamming them against trees before tossing them into a pile in the clearing. He hauled the corpse onto the bed of logs and kindling, its headlessness a spear that jabbed his heart with every glance. Then he gathered more wood, assisted by Korgar.

Only after Colbey had set the pyre alight did he consider the consequences of his actions. On the surface, he knew the smoke and fire would draw enemies. That did not bother him. For now, he would welcome the chance to send a thousand Northmen to Valhalla. Reward or not, at least they could no longer trouble the Renshai. But Colbey knew he had no right to honor this corpse. To offer the gods this empty shell, its soul already doomed to Hel, was blasphemy. As the red trickle of flame grew into an orange-white fury, Colbey lowered his head, waiting for his goddess' disapproval. Yet Sif gave him nothing.

Grief bunched inside Colbey, still needing an outlet. So many times, he had watched friends, family, and companions collapse in red ruin. So many times, they had died in the glory of battle, and he had known joy instead of sadness, had celebrated instead of mourned. But the means and result of this death allowed Colbey to bear a sorrow and regret like nothing he had ever known. And it still sought an outlet. The fire grew. Its heat became uncomfortable against Colbey's cheek, driving sweat from his brow and threatening damage to his sensitive Northern skin. It created flickering shadows that danced along the trunks of stately oak and hickory.

One more thought nearly stole Colbey's breath. As he had wandered around the clearing, in shock, then rage, then in his search for kindling, he had never found the head. *Why would they take the head?* Only one answer came, and the cruelty of the idea tortured even the Golden Prince of Demons. *We will see that head again.* His hand clutched at the locket through the fabric of his pocket, and he knew how that sight would demoralize Rache, and perhaps the others as well. Even prepared, Colbey doubted he himself could stand the sight, though he felt certain it would enrage rather than paralyze him.

Needing an emotional purge now even more than before, Colbey stepped away from the fire. The howl of grief and agony that escaped his throat surprised him at first. Then he cried out again, and Korgar's mournful note of sympathy forced a sweet and mellow duet, a tribute to the last Renshai who could have passed on the bloodline. And, in the distance, Secodon answered.

By the time Colbey and Korgar returned, dusk smeared the sky gray-pink. The burned tree looked black and skeletal against the lighter colors of the sunset. Its barkless stripes broke the contour, as if holding shadows at bay. Moonlight puddled beneath openings in the foliage, and Colbey could see familiar figures milling in the lighted patches. As Colbey ducked beneath a low hanging bough, his companions closed around him. Mitrian, Garn, and Rache studied him with round, hopeful eyes that begged a happy story he could not give them.

Korgar grunted, fading into the darkness between gaps in the pattern of branches.

Colbey lowered his head. Without explanation, he placed his hand into his pocket, twining his fingers around the chain of Santagithi's locket. Drawing it free, he offered the trinket to Rache.

Rache's jaw sagged open, but no words emerged. He made no move to take the locket.

Mitrian glanced at Garn nervously. The ex-gladiator took the burden upon himself. 'He's dead?'

Colbey lowered his head, finally feeling the weariness that came of two days without sleep. 'Episte is dead.'

'That fire we saw at midday?' Mitrian started and never bothered to finish.

Colbey knew relief. Mitrian's question gave him the opportunity to save the others from the horror without lying. 'His pyre. Yes.'

'Episte's pyre.' Mitrian parroted, as if she could accept the words only with repetition. For the moment, the significance seemed lost, the words only sound without meaning.

Rache remained immobile and silent.

'I'm sorry.' Colbey looped the chain over Rache's head, and the locket settled against the youth's tunic. 'I got there far too late. There was nothing I could do.' When no one said anything more, Colbey turned and headed toward Shadimar, deeper in the forest.

'Wait,' Rache said.

Colbey whirled back to meet innocent green eyes in a child's face above an adult's body. 'Did he die in glory? Did he find Valhalla?'

'I set him to pyre.' Colbey continued to mislead, wanting Episte's memory honored, not mourned, shying from the horror the truth would inflict. His description of action should have proved enough, but Rache remained relentless.

'Did my brother find Valhalla?'

Colbey drew breath, not quite certain what would emerge. His heart told him to spare Rache and honor Episte's memory, to say that setting Episte to pyre should be accepted as answer. But Colbey would not lie. He would not betray his own. 'No.' He said nothing more. He did not clarify or qualify the response. He pushed past.

Behind him, Colbey could hear Rache's sobs, the sound tearing at him over the rising and falling song of insects. He could imagine Garn and Mitrian clutching one another, exchanging consolations. He left them to their grief, letting them handle it in their own way, as he had.

Shadimar hooked Colbey's sleeve. 'Where is Secodon?'

'What?' Colbey had forgotten the wolf in the agony of his sorrow. 'He was with us.'

'He isn't any longer.' Shadimar's craggy features went hard. 'And he is in distress.'

'You think he's in danger?' Colbey found it difficult to raise concern for an animal. He was emotionally empty.

Shadimar squinted in concentration. 'No. It seems more emotional than physical. Frustration, perhaps. Sorrow. Uncertainty.'

Colbey nodded, recalling his grief howl and the wolf's haunting answer, like an echo in the distance. 'I'm afraid that may have come from me.'

Shadimar bobbed his head slowly, but his gaze seemed distant.

'Do you want me to find him?'

'No. I believe whatever he was hunting or seeking has eluded him. He'll come back.'

Shadimar's choice of words set Colbey's mind in motion. *Did Secodon try to track Episte's killer?* The old Renshai knew he had taken a huge leap in logic, yet Shadimar's suggestion that the wolf had lost a quarry intrigued him. Colbey's respect for Secodon trebled in an instant, though it raised concern as well. *A madman capable of the cruelty inflicted on Episte will not quit. Grief blinded me to a necessity that an animal did not forget. That man must be found, and he must be slain. An abomination like that cannot be allowed to live and slaughter.*

The idea came easily, the solution less so. And Colbey knew he had to find it before the other killed again.

21 The Western Renshai

Overnight, Colbey's grief settled into a hollow in his memory. No one had awakened him for a watch. Apparently, each had his own misery to contemplate, and too many could not sleep to bother those who needed rest. Without supplies, they did not trouble to worry about breakfast. Even Garn seemed to realize that complaints of hunger would seem petty to the point of cruelty, and they prepared for the journey ahead in relative silence.

Secodon had returned while Colbey slept. A midsummer shedding had left his coat ragged, and burrs had knotted through the coarse tufts of loosened undercoat. Colbey guessed that the wolf had come back early in the night because he looked well-rested in the morning.

Colbey took the party eastward, knowing they would need to veer south to find the passes through the Southern Weathered Range and onto the Western Plains that had served as the battleground in the Great War. He was only partially familiar with the geography of the Westlands and did not wish to miss the rare passes. So he chose to head for the union between the Great Frenum Mountains and the Southern Weathered Range. From there, he would sweep westward along the base of the mountains. A direct run to the passes would prove shorter, but also more predictable, and Colbey did not trust his direction sense and memory enough to believe he could find the passes on his first try. If he missed, he would have to guess his direction, and the Northmen would surely catch them casting about aimlessly.

Air stagnated between trees thick with summer growth. Discomfort drove the party deeper into an already heavy silence, and hunger added to the burden. Mitrian stared at the ground, showing no inclination to hunt. No one seemed to expect it of her, even as morning brightened into noon, and the rumbles of stomachs broke the self-imposed hush. Gradually, the trunks became sparser, allowing glimpses of the Great Mountains, their caps snow-powdered despite the season. Halfway through the afternoon, the trees gave way to saplings: locusts spotted with thorns and young poplars nearly as tall as the elder pine.

When forest gave way to open plain. Colbey stopped the party.

'There's a town ahead.' He tried to add just a hint of question to his words, hoping to elicit information without frightening the others with his ignorance.

Only Shadimar took the bait. 'A city, actually. Of medium size. It's called Porvada.'

Colbey frowned. *A city one day's journey from where we last camped. It's the first place the Northmen will expect us to go.* 'We'll need to change direction.'

'Change direction?' Garn sounded indignant. 'Didn't you just say the town was ahead?'

'It's too dangerous.' Colbey looked out over a plain obviously cleared by fires to a few distant, peaked rooftops. 'The Northmen will expect us to go for supplies.'

Garn stared back, finding Colbey's conclusion difficult to follow. 'Well, of course, they'll expect us to go for supplies. We'd be stupid to do anything else.'

Shadimar stood aloof, stroking Secodon's head. As usual, Korgar had slipped into the vegetation, unseen. Rache huddled between two trunks, his cheeks dirt-streaked in tear lines and his eyes swollen. Mitrian looked from Garn to Colbey and back.

'They'll be waiting for us,' Colbey explained.

'We'll avoid them.'

'That won't be easy.'

'What choice do we have?' Garn threw up his hands in exasperation. 'I'll go. I'll kill any Northman who dares to show his face.'

'There could be dozens.' Colbey wrestled with the dilemma, knowing Garn was right about the supplies yet seeing the danger in a way no one who had not witnessed the headless corpse could. 'There might be hundreds.'

Garn's gut protested in a loud grumble that traversed its length. 'I'll fight hundreds, then. I'd rather die at the hands of Northmen than of starvation. I've known hunger before. I hated it then. I hate it more now.'

'I'll go,' Mitrian said.

'No,' Colbey said, the idea of losing another Renshai tearing at him.

'No,' Garn repeated.

Mitrian continued as if neither man had spoken. 'It's the only thing that makes sense. If we all go, the Northmen will know us at once. One person might slip in, get supplies, and leave.'

Colbey considered. There was logic to Mitrian's suggestion, and danger as well. 'I don't suppose you know this city. We couldn't have one of our own wandering the streets looking for a place to buy rations. The law would keep Northmen from attacking in a crowd. In an empty side street . . . ' Colbey let the observation dangle.

'I wouldn't have to wander.' Mitrian turned her gaze to the outlying rooftops. 'A medium-sized city will have at least one tavern. I can't get jerked or smoked meat ready for travel, but I should be able to get enough food to keep us until we find a less conspicuous town to – '

'Quit saying "I,"' Garn interrupted. 'It makes more sense for me to go.'

'No one – ' started Colbey, but Mitrian cut in again.

'On the contrary, I'm the only possible choice. Rache needs his training. You and Colbey and Shadimar are too conspicuous. I'm a woman, and I fought mostly at home. Certainly, you and Colbey would be recognized. I might go unnoticed. I'm a Westerner. I look like a Westerner. I talk like a Westerner. I'm the only one born and raised in a Western town in a normal manner, except Rache; and we've already excluded him.'

Colbey dismissed the possibility of sending Korgar. First, Colbey doubted he could communicate the mission in a way the barbarian could understand. Second, Colbey did not yet understand why the barbarian had chosen to follow them, and the Renshai felt certain Korgar might leave as suddenly and unexpectedly as he had come. He saw other advantages to using Mitrian. Surely, the laws of Porvada would preclude violence in its tavern. If the Northmen tried to finger Mitrian as Renshai, they would suffer the consequences. Mitrian's dark hair and Western dialect would protect her from the allegation in a way the Northmen's features would not. And Colbey felt certain the laws and citizens would favor a pretty Western woman over a dirty pack of foreign warriors. 'All right,' he said, still hating the risks and possibilities. 'But go straight to the tavern and come straight back. Don't take *any* chances.'

'I won't,' Mitrian said. Before Colbey could change his mind, she scuttled into the dusk.

Garn glared. 'How could you do that?'

Colbey watched Mitrian go until she blurred to a single dark splotch. 'Because you were right. And she was right, too.'

'Maybe. But her life is worth too much to risk.'

Worth. The word seeped into Colbey's consciousness, raising an issue he had not considered until that moment. Not wishing to face Garn's wrath, Colbey kept the thought to himself. *I just sent Mitrian to buy supplies with nothing but her sword and the clothes on her back.* The idea rankled, yet Colbey forced it to rest. Of them all, Mitrian had the most experience with money and payment. He felt certain that she had considered the problem as well. And he hoped she had a plan.

Mitrian entered the city of Porvada with a caution that bordered on paranoia and with reservations that she had hidden well from Colbey and Garn. As she stared at the neat rows of cottages and shops, so like those of the town in which she had been raised, she let caution usurp the grief that had dampened every thought and movement. The fire-cleared plain brought her to a jumble of rocks that ringed the periphery of the cobbled streets. Stepping over the piles of smaller stones, she headed down the largest roadway.

Dusk colored the sky purple-pink, and buildings of varying shapes and sizes broke the skyline in dark squares, arcs, and triangles. Crude wire fences penned scant herds of sheep and pigs between cottages. Mitrian kept her head low to hide her features, though she let her long, red-brown locks fly freely in the breeze. Pulling her hood over her head in midsummer would draw attention unnecessarily. No one would question the presence of a dark-haired woman on the streets of a Western town. The few Northmen who might recognize her could do so only after a long, studied scrutiny of her face. And she hoped racial features would make all Westerners look as similar to Northmen as Northmen did to her.

As Mitrian continued down the unfamiliar roadway, men and women passed her without a second glance. A misplaced familiarity made her shiver. She might have been traversing the main road of Santagithi's Town, except that her father and his people would have gawked at a woman carrying a sword. Though the women in Porvada carried no weapons, they seemed to take no particular interest in nor insult from Mitrian. For her part, she kept the wolf's head hilt buried beneath a fold of her cloak, concerned that the Northmen might recognize the unusual craftsmanship and the damaged topaz set as eyes.

At length, Mitrian came upon a pair of men in matching brown pants and tucked, yellow shirts. Both had rich chestnut hair, hacked short, and broad Western features. A broadsword hung from each man's belt.

Presuming them to be guards, Mitrian approached. She used the Western trading tongue. 'Hello. Could you tell me where I could find a tavern?'

One man smiled, his teeth a brilliant white in the gathering grayness. He pointed further up the main path. 'Just a few more buildings. On the right.' He twisted, staring in the direction he had indicated. 'You can just see it there. The one past the cooper.'

Mitrian craned her neck toward the indicated landmark. The buildings all looked strange and forbidding, a line of huddling shapes behind which Northmen might lurk. Though she did not see the tavern, she could make out the barrel-shaped sign over the cooper's shop.

The other man turned Mitrian a gap-toothed grin. A grimy hand kneaded his sword hilt, then slid toward his thigh. 'If it's companionship you seek . . . '

His condescending tone coupled with the obscene gesture aroused anger. Anticipating trouble ever since leaving her companions, Mitrian instinctively placed a hand on her own hilt. Then, recognizing the danger of such an action, she forced her grip lax and smiled dryly. 'It's not.' She hurried off, not wishing to antagonize guards. Their response told her what sort of women frequented this tavern, and she did not relish the need to deal with strange men's solicitations. Still, she dared not waste time seeking another tavern when she had found one so close. *No need to upset Garn, Rache, or Colbey. If they come looking for me, we won't escape without a heated battle.*

As she trotted past the cooper's shop, Mitrian found the next building dilapidated, its paint peeling and its door splashed with mud. She paused, wondering whether the guards had steered her in the wrong direction for the fun of harassing a foreigner. She might have believed the shop abandoned if not for a sign swinging from a single nail above the doorway. Dirty and weathered to jagged planks, the sign held lettering that had faded beyond Mitrian's ability to read it; yet its vaulted shape had become symbolic of bar signs throughout the Westlands.

As Mitrian stood staring and considering, the door swung open. Two men stumbled out and onto the street, laughing, their clothing stained and reeking of ale. Seizing the opportunity, Mitrian peered inside. She caught a quick glimpse of crowds, all men, huddled around tables. Candles reflected from polished glass and pewter. No fire lay in the grate; summer heat and hordes of patrons warmed the room well enough. Painted walls of pale blue and white made a cheerful contrast to the unkempt exterior. Mitrian wondered if the look had been created intentionally. The earthy, corroded exterior made the interior seem so much more inviting. The door banged shut, leaving her once again in the darkening street.

Emboldened by her glance, Mitrian pushed the door ajar and slipped inside. She noticed details that her flash of a view had not revealed. Shelves filled one wall, lined with bottles, bowls, and flasks. A doorway had been cut into the center of the shelving. By the chime of pots, she guessed that it led into the kitchen. Before it, two men poured mead from flasks to bowls and mugs, and half a dozen long-legged barmaids carried the drinks to tables.

Those men nearest the door fell silent. From the corners of her vision, Mitrian saw them exchange nudges and whispered comments she could not hear. Ignoring them, she crossed the floor quickly. She tried to look nonchalant, but managed only a self-conscious shuffle across the barroom, where she took a seat at the nearest empty table.

Once settled, Mitrian scanned the patrons. Most were Westerners, dark-haired, muddy-eyed natives in ragged farm dress. Many carried weapons, to her surprise. A few even wore armor of leather, without the studs that her father's officers had worn on duty. Most of the others sported the simple homespun of men who preferred work to war. She saw only one other female patron. A scantily-clad, aging woman wandered from table to table. Her clothes sagged around her thin frame. Surely, she had once made her living seducing men in the tavern, but time had stolen her beauty.

The men seemed far more interested in the drink-touting beauties. Repeatedly, Mitrian watched the girls smile tolerantly at leers, pinches, and propositions. As she studied the crowd, one of the barmaids approached. 'Would the lady have something to eat and drink?'

Mitrian tore her gaze from the others reluctantly, not yet satisfied with her inspection. She looked up into a face nearly a decade younger than her own twenty-nine years. The barmaid wore a haughty smirk that suggested she guessed Mitrian's profession was the same as the other female patron. Though she carried no money, Mitrian's hunger bested her common sense. Recalling the sheep and pigs that she had passed, she ordered accordingly. 'Mutton and wine, please.'

'At once, lady.' The barmaid scurried toward the bar.

Not yet ready to contemplate payment, Mitrian examined the crowd more thoroughly. At the next table, four men spoke the Western tongue in loud tones interspersed with laughter. Beyond them, a press of working men carried on a heated discussion. Mitrian could not understand their words, but they waved their arms wildly as they made their points. Then her gaze riveted on the table of wanderers she had not previously noticed, and the workers were forgotten. In the far corner of the room, three Northmen sat drinking beer.

Mitrian clasped the edge of the table, keeping her face in shadow and cursing the male domination that would make her a center of attention. The Northmen looked conspicuous with their braided yellow hair and savage faces. She wondered why she had not noticed them before, attributing it to their stillness and choice of position. A sword girded each waist, and a pair of long bows leaned against the table. Two of the Northmen sported travel-darkened leather. The third wore a corselet of iron rings. A beaked nose jutted from an otherwise ruggedly handsome face. He was clean-shaven where the others were bearded, and golden clips in the shape of lightning bolts adorned the bands that wound through his braids. Mitrian had seen Valr Kirin only once before, from a distance, but his description had lodged in her memory.

Mitrian's hands fell into her lap as she considered the futility of her predicament. At the time, standing in a secluded forest with the people she loved and the protection of the best swordsman in existence, the decision had made sense to her. She had wanted to be alone for a time, to escape the lead weight of grief that seemed interminable. As much as she had cared for Episte, she found her thoughts straying protectively to Rache. Occasionally, joy had spiked through her pain, inspired by the relief that she had not lost her own son, and this emotion made her feel ugly and evil. She knew it was wrong to place her own bloodline before the orphaned child the gods had so graciously handed to her. And she also knew that, before the Renshai became fully settled, she would almost certainly lose Colbey and possibly others that she loved as well.

The concept shivered through Mitrian. She considered herself wholly Renshai, yet she still clung to some of the moralities and concepts with which Santagithi and her mother had raised her. As many times as she told herself that she could accept the deaths of Colbey, Garn, and Rache, so long as they went down in glorious combat, the reality of the agony she felt for Episte made her question her emotional strength. Though Colbey had given no details, the means of the teen's death did allow her to mourn. But Mitrian had come to realize that far more than the method of Episte's slaying upset her. She missed Episte. She could scarcely imagine life without the natural skill that she had coveted, without the careless grace that had reminded her so much of the boy's father, and without the soft-spoken gentleness, the sensitivity that flared to sullen, bitter rages. She could not help wondering whether her lapse made her a poor excuse for a Renshai. She wished she could be as strong as Colbey. *It might be worth his stony coldness not to hurt so much.*

Recognizing that her thoughts had shifted to the matters she had come to escape, Mitrian forced her mind to a more urgent dilemma. *I'm in a tavern with Northmen, including Valr Kirin. We desperately need supplies, but I can't even pay for the meal I ordered for myself.*

Enmeshed in these concerns, her attention riveted on the Northmen, Mitrian did not notice the man who came up beside her until he spoke in the Western trading tongue. 'Hellooo,' he slurred.

Startled, Mitrian looked at the speaker, a stout, middle-aged Westerner with a crooked smile. The stench of ale on his breath made her cringe. She made a wordless sound of repugnance, then added, 'Go away.'

The man stumbled backward. His smile faded. 'Hozzz-tile wench.' He tottered several steps further, stepping on his own feet as he moved and catching his balance with a hand on the back of a chair.

'Yes. Now go away.' Mitrian sighed, glad that the incident seemed so swiftly finished.

A neatly dressed man at the table beside Mitrian jumped to his feet, his short sword hissing from its sheath.

Mitrian recoiled, her own hand falling to her hilt. She did not draw.

The armed man flicked the tip of his blade to the drunkard's throat, though the other held no weapon and was obviously too intoxicated to defend himself. The drunkard made a garbled noise of defense.

'How dare you insult a lady.' The well-dressed man maintained an air of dignity, but Mitrian guessed that his intentions were no more honorable and far less amusing. He tossed his next line to her. 'I'll take care of this wretch, ma'am.'

The man's antics infuriated Mitrian. She had tried so hard to remain inconspicuous despite her sex, and this stranger professing to defend her honor had destroyed any remaining shred of privacy. Uncertainty exploded to outrage. She sprang to her feet. At this point, she wanted to be left alone. With every eye in the tavern already on her, it no longer mattered how large a scene she created to achieve that goal. 'I can defend my own damned honor!' Her sword whipped from its sheath. Using a basic Renshai disarming maneuver, she wrested the sword from his hand, catching the hilt before it struck the floor.

The drunkard made a hasty retreat that sent him sprawling over a chair. The well-dressed man recoiled in stunned surprise, studying his hand for the damage most disarming maneuvers would have inflicted.

Mitrian sheathed her sword and took her seat in a single motion. She had caught the man's sword out of habit, not from any specific respect. To remedy the lapse that had grown from years of training Renshai, she dropped the other's sword to the floor deliberately. It struck with a clanging thump. With the ball of her sandal, she kicked the weapon back to its owner, turning her back to him to augment her disdain. She suspected that all of the conventional warrior insults were lost on this man, who had probably seen little, if any, combat. Still, they made Mitrian feel better, and her movement did give her a nonchalant position from which to view the Northmen while showing them only a partial profile. She watched the three resume their meal and conversation, like the remainder of the men in the tavern. They had paid her no more heed than the others, yet that was too much for Mitrian. Silently, she cursed her misfortune, knowing that she could only partially blame the drunk solicitor and her false protector. She had not handled the situation as well as she should have.

Gradually, the conversations in the tavern of Porvada returned to normal. The drunkard found his way into the street. The well-dressed man retook his seat amid the laughter of his companions. The bouncers finished glaring and returned to their posts. Apparently, they drew their line of interference at or near bloodshed. Of that Mitrian was glad, and the Northmen's huddled composure lulled her further. *I was lucky.* She considered the other possible outcomes. *The drunkard could have gotten injured. The other man might have felt a need to fight back. Worse, the Northmen could have recognized me.* Now, Mitrian felt better about her strategy. Clearly, her quick and competent action had rescued the drinker, cooled the other's ardor, and handled the matter with minimal time and attention.

The barmaid arrived with Mitrian's dinner, a hearty portion of mutton graced with bread and a glass of wine. The sight of food reawakened hunger. She shoveled meat to her mouth without a pretense of delicacy, hoping her method would discourage amorous patrons as well as satisfying hunger. Occasionally, she tossed a glance at the Northmen. As the crowd changed and grew, Valr Kirin and his men remained for a third round of drinks. Soon, the shifting of Westerners around Mitrian grew familiar, and she paid them no heed. She turned her mind to the gathering of supplies and payment. For now, the best plan she could muster involved remaining until closing, then volunteering to clean in exchange for rations. She did not know how much more than her own meal this would buy, but she hoped the proprietor would have leftovers that would not keep until the following day.

Though deep in consideration, this time Mitrian did not miss the subtle change in the pattern of moving patrons. One man had paused overlong at her right hand.

Mitrian stiffened, trying to gather words to urge him away before annoyance goaded her to violence again. She opened her mouth to speak, prepared to modulate her voice to make her position dangerously clear.

But he spoke first, his voice nearly a whisper. 'Good evening, dear friend.' The accent was Western, the voice unfamiliar, and the phrase fluent Renshai.

Mitrian's blood seemed to ice over in her veins. Her hand tightened on her fork, but she gave no other outward sign of the riot erupting within her. Struggling for a look of confusion, she raised her head to the speaker. 'Excuse me?' She used the Western trading tongue and her best rendition of the local dialect.

The man met her gaze with eyes so pale they looked like the foam through which Mitrian had once glimpsed the faint blue glimmer of the sea. His face was the color of a sun-bleached skull, and his flaxen hair hung in neat braids. She estimated him as a few years older than Episte's chronological age. A sparse beard grew in tufts from his chin. 'My name is Tannin,' he said, still in Renshai. 'We can't talk here. There're Northmen looking for you and the Golden Prince of Demons.'

Mitrian wrestled uncertainty. She knew, with no means nor reason to doubt, that only Colbey and Episte's father had survived the Northmen's attack against Devil's Island. Yet she could not guess how a Northman could have learned so many words of the Renshai tongue. Mitrian drew breath carefully, aware her hesitation would condemn her as much as a direct response to his words. Logic told her this man could not be Renshai, nor a friend. 'I don't understand . . . ' she started and stopped. Pulling a rag from her pocket, she casually wrapped the food remaining on her plate. Despite her hunger, she had left a large piece of mutton and all of the bread. It would not feed every one of her companions, but it would prove better than nothing at all.

Only after Mitrian pocketed the food did she bother to meet the stranger's gaze again. Memory stabbed at her. She recalled catching snatches of Colbey's prayers to Sif on the night that he returned from his search for Episte. She remembered the anguish in his voice, the familiar, pained entreaties of a pious man forced to question as well as revere. Though Mitrian had heard the elder's words through the beckoning fog of approaching sleep, his final line returned to her now: 'Mistress Sif, if my people earned your wrath, if it is your will to see the end of the true Renshai line . . . ' Mitrian cringed at the memory of the agony that had filled his voice, so unlike Colbey's usual impassive fierceness that she wondered if she had dreamed it. '. . . then your will be done.'

Mitrian stared into the blue-white eyes until she felt lost within them. *I shouldn't trust him. I have no reason to do so, and every reason not to.* The expression in those eyes seemed incredibly earnest. *But if this is, somehow, a Renshai, I can't just abandon him. I owe Colbey too much.* She thought of all the elder had done for her, the heritage and skill he had shared, the encouragements he had given, the love and protection he had lavished upon herself and her family in his own passionless way.

Mitrian set aside her fork and took the last swallow of wine. She used the Renshai tongue in a lipless whisper. 'I'll leave first. Don't hurry. I'll meet you at the northern corner of town. Bring food.' She added with a callous tone that could have challenged Colbey's, 'If you are other than you claim, you will die in agony.' Without awaiting a reply, she sprang from her seat, lashing an open hand across Tannin's cheek.

Tannin staggered with surprise.

'A pox on this tavern! A woman can't eat without being harassed!' Mitrian stormed through the barroom and out the door, leaving Tannin to pay her tab.

Although Mitrian's mood appeared as wild as the gales that guarded Shadimar's ruins, it was more like a spring shower. Danger made her cautious, and she entered the dust-choked streets with every sense aware, prepared for an ambush. When she did not immediately skid into the swords of waiting Northmen, her hope rose guardedly. Colbey made rare mistakes, but he had been wrong about Episte's mother. *Maybe he did make a mistake counting survivors. Maybe Tannin is Renshai. Maybe Sif answered Colbey's prayers. Surely, the world's best swordsman could find a war goddess' favor.* Though excited by the possibility of her discovery, Mitrian did not relax her guard. She turned to her left, as much to free her sword arm from the hindering wall as to head toward the camp.

Only a few strides along the road, she heard footsteps behind her. She glanced backward to find the three Northmen leaving the bar, nearly on her heels. Another joined them just outside. *The false Renshai?* Mitrian guessed, though time and distance did not leave her time to identify him for certain. Three carried bows, each with a quiver of arrows at his back. Joy vanished. Mitrian quickened her pace, snarling a curse at Valr Kirin and the Renshai-speaking Northman who had, probably, betrayed her. Mentally, she damned herself as well. *I should have known it was too good, too coincidental to be true.* Battle wrath rose in a welcome rush. She ducked into an alley and sprinted for its end, hoping to run through and out of sight before the Northmen reached the entrance.

The footsteps grew louder behind Mitrian, and a misplaced bird call cut through the darkness. Barrels stood, lined and stacked along the walls of the cottages and shops. Mitrian dodged these effortlessly. As she drew within a few strides of the alley exit, she managed an extra burst of speed. She sprang for freedom.

Suddenly, another four Northmen appeared before her, blocking escape. Each clutched a drawn broadsword.

Mitrian drew up, nearly skidding into the Northmen at the exit. She backed into a stack of barrels, fitting her spine into an irregular niche. For an instant, her heart fluttered in terror. Then, the rhythm dropped to a heavy cadence of war, and killing lust strengthened within her.

A sharp command issued from the opposite end of the alley. The three archers raised their bows, green-fletched arrows nocked.

Mitrian crammed her back deeper into the furrow, hoping but doubting the barrels would give her enough protection to wait out the first round of arrows. Only then would she gain a pause long enough to try to cover the ground between them and attack. The three swordsmen waited, spanning the exit.

As the Northern archers anchored their bow strings, Tannin fell on them from behind. His sword slashed open one's neck. He continued the cut low, severing the muscle behind a second's thigh. It curled into a ball, and the man screamed, collapsing to the cobbles. Tannin lunged for the third, just as Valr Kirin bore in to his defense. The commander's sword crashed against Tannin's, its momentum curtailed by the closeness of his companion. The blow deflected the attack enough to spare the archer's life. Tannin's blade sliced the string, and the bow snapped taut, sending the arrow in a crazed arc.

Mitrian wedged herself tighter between the barrels as the Northmen at the exit advanced. As one, they charged her. Mitrian blocked one stroke. The others thudded against the barrels. One blade bit too deeply. The seconds it took him to wrench it free became the last in its wielder's life. Mitrian buried her blade in his gut, kicking him backward to liberate her sword and regain her opening.

The barrels protected Mitrian, but they also prevented her from executing the sweeping Renshai maneuvers that fed off the power and redirection of previous strokes. Her opponents' jabs fell unnervingly close, but they could only attack as singles. In a zealous attempt to finish Mitrian, one Northman made a wild lunge that she scarcely dodged. When his sword did not meet the anticipated resistance, momentum carried him onto her stop thrust. The Northman stumbled backward, blood boiling from his chest.

Mitrian's last two opponents retreated, winded. Mitrian caught her breath, momentarily lowering the heavy sword. From the corner of her eye, she watched Tannin hammering at Valr Kirin. Though competent, Tannin did not use any maneuver that Mitrian could identify as Renshai. She watched as the Nordmirian lieutenant caught Tannin's blows on his crosspiece. He could not riposte for fear of hitting his archer companion, yet he held his ground before Tannin's assault, each block chiming an echo through the alleyway.

Beside Valr Kirin, the archer fended enough strokes that he had not found time to drop his bow for a more suitable weapon. It blocked many blows, but combat had whittled it, and the Northman was helpless to prevent it. When Tannin's sword snapped the bow, Kirin surged in a frenzied sweep that forced Tannin to block. This gained the archer the opening he needed to escape.

Western shouts wafted into the alleyway, apparently in response to the ring of swordplay. Footsteps pounded toward them.

Town guard? Mitrian hoped. Then, the two Northmen near her leapt back to the attack, and she again found herself ensconced in her own battle. Her two remaining assailants lunged simultaneously, though there was little room for such a maneuver. Disgust momentarily replaced Mitrian's concentration. *If those fools won't use swords in the correct manner, they should limit themselves to stone axes.* While one positioned his broadsword, Mitrian slammed hers against it, driving the blade into his companion's side. The other fell, never knowing whether his enemy's sword or his ally's had cut him down. Mitrian's upstroke finished her last opponent. She scurried to aid Tannin, only to step into his path as he raced toward her.

A voice thundered down the roadway in the Western trading tongue. 'Hey! Drop the weapons. Don't anybody move!'

Tannin avoided a collision with an awkward sidestep. He seized Mitrian's arm. 'Come on!'

Mitrian sheathed her sword, sprinting alongside her new companion. They whipped around the corner, onto a larger street.

An indecipherable hubbub filled the opposite end of the roadway, where Tannin had fought. 'Hey!' The authoritative voice rose over the others.

Mitrian and Tannin did not slow, remaining in the shadows near the walls, their footsteps slapping through the semidarkness. 'Kirin?' she asked, keeping the question short to conserve breath, though it left Tannin to guess at her intentions.

'What?'

'Their leader. What of him?'

'Damn good fighter.' Tannin veered through an alleyway. 'I got lucky. He backed into a barrel, then tripped over one of his own corpses.' Tannin took a jagged course through a series of cobbled roads, then gave the lead to Mitrian. 'He got lucky, too. The town guard got there before I could press.'

Having heard Colbey's impressions of Valr Kirin, Mitrian wondered whether the second part was not Tannin's good fortune as well. She doubted whether the youngster could have bested the Nordmirian, even with such an advantage; but she kept the thought to herself. She headed toward the fire-cleared plain surrounding Porvada. Once outside the city limits, she did not believe the town guard would follow. *The Northmen started this battle. Let them try to explain it to the authorities.*

As they crossed the plain, Tannin continued breathlessly, 'They followed you, and I followed them.'

Mitrian grunted in reply. She dashed into the forest, plunging through a dense overgrowth of grasses near where she recalled the camp. She discovered only a patch of crushed weeds, a pile of ashes ringed with stone, and an oil-stained rag marred by slits that someone had used to clean a sword. Confusion came first, followed by alarm. *The Northmen have been here, too.* She spun, seeking signs of battle. She found none. 'They were here.'

Tannin sifted the ashes. 'Still warm.'

Mitrian trotted past him, seeking tracks into the forest. 'My companions were here.'

A wind wound through the foliage, rustling weeds. Thinking the sound too loud for its source, Mitrian traced it with her gaze. Weeds bobbed and danced in a line, though whether from the breeze or movement, she could not tell. Milkweed floated, ghostlike, from a broken pod. Mitrian's neck tightened with discomfort, as if unseen eyes watched from the darkness. She shivered.

Tannin came up from behind Mitrian and caught her arm. 'Do you see something?'

Mitrian shrugged her ignorance, gaze still playing over the dark blotch of brush.

'You know, you haven't told me your name. Nor how a dark-haired Renshai who knows the maneuvers wound up in a Western city.'

Mitrian chose to address the simpler question. 'Mitrian.' Recalling that Northmen considered sire's name and tribe part of the title, she added. 'Santagithi's daughter.' The 'Renshai' seemed unnecessary.

'Santagithi?' Tannin's grip tightened, yet it felt less secure. 'The strategy general?' He made a noise to indicate a drawn conclusion. 'That explains the choice of *Gullindjemprins*.' He created the title Golden Prince of Demons from the Northern words.

Mitrian did not fully understand the statement. She turned to face Tannin directly. Before she could speak, she saw shadowy figures creeping from the forest beyond Tannin. She shouted a warning. 'Behind you!'

Tannin whirled into a crouch, sword clearing his sheath as he moved.

Mitrian recognized Garn, Rache, and Colbey. 'Wait!' she shouted.

Rache seized Tannin's off-wrist. Tannin twisted, cutting at the youth. Mitrian bore in to protect her son. Before she arrived, Colbey's sword blocked the stroke, metal clanging against metal. Garn's hand closed over Tannin's sword wrist. A slamming blow with his fist dashed the sword from the Northman's grasp. With a yell of frustration and pain, Tannin twisted, then suddenly went still. Though Tannin was pinned between Garn and Rache, Mitrian guessed it was Colbey's sword at Tannin's throat that actually kept him immobile. The elder stood behind the newcomer, his blade hovering into the crevice of Tannin's windpipe.

Fearing for Tannin's life, Mitrian addressed Colbey. 'He's all right. He saved my life. He fought Valr Kirin.'

Colbey circled Tannin, never taking his blade from the younger man's throat. He stared into Tannin's eyes, as if to read the thoughts beyond them. Colbey's grim expression told Mitrian that either he found nothing or the message was contradictory. Experience told her that Colbey read only those thoughts and emotions strong enough to radiate from others. Right now, were she in Tannin's place, she guessed that fear would usurp all other reasoning. She could think of few things more terrifying than the wrong side of Colbey's wrath and his sword.

'You fought Valr Kirin?'

Tannin swallowed cautiously. 'Yes, sir.'

'And you're still alive?'

Tannin answered the self-evident question without hesitation. 'Yes, sir.'

'And he?'

'Is too, sir.' Tannin rolled his eyes past Colbey to Mitrian. They seemed to beg her to tell him how to proceed, how to appease the Golden Prince of Demons.

Though sympathetic, Mitrian gave Tannin no clues. She had passed Colbey the facts. Her loyalty lay with the elder Renshai, and she trusted his assessments before her own.

'Who are you?' Colbey demanded.

Apparently realizing he was on his own, Tannin grew defiant. He raised his head, despite the weapon, and met Colbey's eyes. 'I'm Tannin.' He added the remainder of the introduction slowly, as if measuring the effect of every syllable on Colbey. 'Randilsson. My tribe is Renshai.'

Colbey's fingers blanched. Though his grip tightened, the blade did not move. 'You're lying.' Garn's fingers gouged the flesh of Tannin's arm, leaving bloodless creases. Rache's gaze flitted from Colbey to Mitrian. He clung, less certain of his grip than his more experienced father. Mitrian could see Shadimar standing at the forest's edge with his wolf, not involving himself in Renshai business. She saw no sign of Korgar, nor did she expect to do so. The barbarian came and went as he pleased, usually without a sound, and she only vaguely understood the bonds that held him to Colbey.

Colbey gave Tannin a second chance. 'Speak your name again. Say it correctly this time. Then tell me what you want and why we should spare you.'

Tannin's voice did not falter, although his gaze again rolled to Mitrian. 'My name is Tannin. My father, Randil, is the leader of the Western Renshai. I came seeking the man the Pudarians call the Deathseeker, the rest of the West calls the Golden Prince of Demons, and the Northmen call *Bolboda*. If I am not mistaken, I believe I've found him.'

Colbey's bandaged hand crept to his opposite hilt. 'The Western Renshai.' The malice in his voice deepened.

Shadimar stepped from the forest, interrupting without apology. 'Why do the Northmen call him *Bolboda?* Doesn't that mean Bringer of Evil?'

Tannin seemed glad for the distraction. He glanced from Rache to Garn, then met the Wizard's question. 'Yes, it means what you said. I don't know why they call him that. Until I started looking for *Gullindjemprins*, I had never seen the North or a real Northman. In fact, if I hadn't watched my great-grandfather practice when I was a child, I might not have recognized that maneuver of Mitrian's in the tavern as Renshai.' He kept his attention fixed on Shadimar, apparently more comfortable with the tall, ancient Wizard.

'Sjare or Menglir?' Shadimar asked.

Tannin's eyes widened. 'My great-grandfather was called Menglir. Did you know him?'

'Only by the name in my references.' Shadimar spoke in a conversational manner that took the violence from the confrontation. 'I knew Sjare and Menglir led those Renshai who chose to stay in the West when the rest of the tribe returned to the North at the end of their hundred year exile. You said your father was the tribal leader. I guessed he might have inherited the position.'

His mood spoiled, Colbey sheathed his sword. He plucked Tannin's blade from the ground, examining it methodically. Garn and Rache remained in position.

Shadimar said nothing more. Tannin seemed about to speak. Then his gaze fell to the sword in Colbey's hands, and he returned the initiative to the elder.

Mitrian read anger in Colbey's features. 'Sjare and Menglir were traitors with no right to call themselves or their descendants Renshai. While we were struggling to regain our homeland, they chose to mongrelize the race instead.' He made a looping cut that stopped close enough to Tannin to return the fear to his eyes. 'Had I been more than a child and in command, I would have slain them. Our leader was kinder, but he was wise enough to have them take a vow.' He glared. 'Have you kept it?'

Tannin did not hesitate. 'I swear by my lord, Modi. None of my people have learned the Renshai sword maneuvers.' His tone combined fear, hope, and disappointment.

Colbey frowned, testing the balance of Tannin's sword.

In the ensuing silence, Tannin pleaded his case. 'My ancestors took that vow because they had an obligation to the West. Someday, the North might come against the West, and none of us ever wanted to face one another on opposite sides of a war. But that can't happen anymore. When my people heard about the Renshai massacre, they were grief-stricken. Then word reached us of the Great War and the Golden Prince of Demons.'

'Why weren't you there?' Colbey's question cut through Tannin's explanation.

'What?'

'A warrior tribe should have attended the Great War. It should have been impossible to hold them back.' Colbey glared. 'Why weren't you there?'

'Undoubtedly, some of us were.' Tannin was shouting now, regardless of his nearly helpless position and the sword in Colbey's hand. 'As Pudarians, Western farmers, maybe even among Santagithi's troop.' He glanced briefly at Mitrian. 'Without the sword training to hold us together as a tribe, many left for the larger cities. Others went to the homes of Western wives or husbands. A few, like my father, have clung to the tribal unity. I'm three quarters Renshai, as is my sister. For as long as I can remember, my father always had a dream of returning to the North and the Renshai, but the Renshai were destroyed before my birth so I could never share his dream.'

'You didn't answer my question,' Colbey remained relentless, though Tannin's story had convinced Mitrian. 'Why weren't your father and his followers at the Great War?'

'Because the place where we live, the Fields of Wrath, is officially a part of the country of Erythane. Béarn and Erythane have always been closely linked, but never so completely as when King Morhane ruled. He forbade Erythane and Béarn to take part in the War.' A flush crossed Tannin's face, from the bangs that fringed his forehead to the sparse tufts of his growing beard. 'I'll never forget the battle of conscience my father fought, between his loyalty to his country's laws and his loyalty to the tenets and principles of the West. It was not a decision made lightly or easily.'

Mitrian considered, the choice seeming obvious. Obedience to the law always had to come before personal morality, yet she did not envy Randil's position. Had the Eastlands triumphed, the Béarnides would not have been spared from the Easterners' butchery, torture, and slavery. Their lands would have become as barren as the overtilled fields of the Eastlands.

Grudgingly, Colbey lowered Tannin's sword. 'So what do you want from me?'

'When my father discovered a Renshai still lived, he sent me to find you. I've been to Pudar. I've been to the Northern Weathered Mountains to find the cave of the Western Wizard. I visited the Town of Santagithi, only to find it devastated.'

A jab of sorrow made Mitrian cringe.

Tannin continued. 'I was on my way home when I happened to come upon Mitrian. At first, I doubted my eyes. Why would some Western woman know the maneuvers of the Renshai? Then I overheard the whispered conversations of the one she called Kirin, and knew that she traveled with *Bolboda*. I had run into Northmen near Santagithi's Town. From them, I knew *Bolboda* was Colbey Calistinsson. I remembered hearing stories that the last Renshai could choose to whom he taught the Renshai maneuvers.' Tannin paused, apparently realizing that he had again dodged Colbey's actual question. 'My father hoped you would forgive the crime of our forefathers. We could offer protection, companionship, hope, and the most eager students you ever knew. The knowledge you could give us is priceless.'

Colbey's face twisted into a scowl of consideration. Clearly, only he could answer Tannin's request, so Mitrian and the others remained silent.

Reading Colbey's expression as hostile, Tannin stomped his foot. 'If you won't forgive the feud, at least give me back my sword and let me die with honor.'

Mitrian saw a slight softening of Colbey's expression, though she doubted Tannin knew the face well enough to notice. She could not keep herself from smiling. Tannin could have said nothing that would have pleased Colbey more.

Colbey motioned to Rache and Garn. 'Free him.'

Rache stepped aside. Garn smirked, releasing Tannin with an exaggerated flourish. It had taken volumes of self-control for him to stand so long in silence. 'At your bidding, death-seeking, evil-bringing, golden demon prince, your highness.'

Colbey ignored Garn's sarcasm. He tossed the sword to Tannin.

The young man caught the weapon by the hilt. He looked wildly uncertain.

Colbey let Tannin off the hook. 'No, we don't need to fight to the death. I just want to see how much work I have ahead of me. Show me what you can do.'

Still Tannin hesitated.

Colbey made a wide gesture toward himself with both hands, urging Tannin to attack. 'Come on, you coward. Have at me.'

Eagerly, Tannin squared off with his elder. He charged, sweeping his blade into an upstroke. Colbey drew and parried, trapping Tannin's sword beneath his own. 'Thank you. I've seen all I need to see.'

Tannin reeled as if struck. 'All you need to see?' He shook his yellow braids, annoyed. 'I swung once.'

Colbey wore a blank expression that always infuriated Mitrian. 'That was enough.'

'Enough?' In his rage, Tannin was parroting Colbey's statements into questions. 'No man could judge another's competence by a single stroke taken at night. Not even the master of swordsmen.'

Colbey's half-shadowed face betrayed no emotion. 'How old are you, Tannin Randilsson?'

'Twenty-four.'

Colbey's reply lanced through the thickening night. 'I've trained Renshai for longer than two and half of your lifetimes. You would tell me what a sword master can or can't judge?'

Amused, Mitrian went to Garn's side. Clearly, Colbey had no plans to immediately slaughter Tannin. Though the elder seemed enraged, Mitrian knew that Tannin's spiritedness would please her teacher, even if his sword skill did not.

Tannin was shouting again. 'You only needed to see one stroke because you decided you wouldn't like my abilities before we started. You had no intention of giving me a chance to show you. And you dare call yourself a sword master?'

'Fine!' Colbey screamed back, and his call brought Korgar. The barbarian crouched in the shadows, growling like an animal.

'It's all right, Korgar.' Colbey addressed the barbarian without taking his gaze from Tannin. 'It's spar.'

Korgar seemed to understand. He fell silent, though he remained hunched and wary.

Tannin sprang from Colbey, and the battle began in earnest. Tannin fought admirably, clearly his finest performance, but Colbey still landed three strokes to each of his. After a time, the flat of Colbey's sword crashed against the youngster's knee. Tannin dropped with a howl of pain.

Colbey sheathed his sword. 'If you bested Valr Kirin, then you got lucky. Bloodline has little to do with being Renshai.' Colbey hesitated a moment, as if to consider his own words. 'When you wield a blade as well as Mitrian and Rache or even Garn, then you can call yourself a swordsman.'

Mitrian wrapped her arms around her husband, warmed by Colbey's compliment. Though she had understood her *torke's* obsession with Episte and the Renshai line, she could not help feeling rejected. Now that Colbey had verbalized his pleasure over the mother and son who were Renshai without the heredity, she once again felt like a full member of her adopted family. Strangely, the change in Colbey's position allowed Mitrian to become less defensive herself. She considered her own ties, and she found them at least as strong. Thoughts resurfaced, of her envy for Episte's natural skill, along with her suppressed wish that the agility belonged to Rache. She remembered how Episte's death had driven her to cling to her only child, the flash of relief that she had not lost Rache instead of Episte, and the horror at her own thoughts that had tainted her solace.

What's wrong with Colbey wishing the Renshai could keep at least some of their bloodline? Mitrian clutched Garn tighter, finding reassurance in his answering squeeze. With her father dead, she also had a driving need to keep his line, and her own, alive. Yet Mitrian had

had no more luck in creating a family than her parents: one child, deeply loved, but alone. For now, and perhaps forever, that would have to be enough.

Mitrian glanced at Tannin. Humiliated, he turned away from Colbey, his head low. But his eyes gleamed with excitement. Though he would start his Renshai training older than anyone before him, at least he knew the basics of swordsmanship. Mitrian guessed he would prove an eager and competitive student, a good match as a partner for Rache despite a decade of difference in age.

Mitrian turned her attention to Colbey. He stood in a stony silence that revealed nothing, but his eyes betrayed him. Joy danced in the glaring, blue-gray orbs for the first time since Santagithi's death. Clearly, he had never considered the Western Renshai before. Apparently, he believed that they had married and interbred themselves into oblivion, leaving only splashes of Renshai blood in men and women otherwise wholly Westerners. She recalled how Colbey had once addressed Arduwyn's hatred for Renshai by telling the flame-haired Erythanian archer that Western redheads came from the Erythanian women's obsession with the red-haired Renshai who befriended Béarn, instead of the more common blonds. Mitrian wondered if Colbey had meant the Western Renshai at that time.

Mitrian released Garn, knowing that none of these thoughts mattered. Colbey had found a way to recreate the Renshai before he died. And it pleased her every bit as much as him. She watched him walk away and turn his back to work on something he did not want the others to see. Yet, the loops of bandage that tumbled to the ground gave away his mission. As the end fluttered to the dirt, she saw him stiffen. For some time, he stared at the hand mangled by a demon's claw, the wound that had nearly driven him to take his life, that Shadimar's magics had either healed or, by delaying his suicide, damned him for eternity.

Mitrian waited, breath held. She felt air-starved and dizzied before Colbey's grim stillness broke, and he let out a cry of pure elation. Both swords spun from their sheaths so fast she never saw him draw them. He lashed into a kata then, a capering, lethal devil-dance that required him to invent maneuvers more magnificent than Mitrian believed she could ever perform, even in her dreams. He hacked and slashed for Sif, moonlight reflecting from his blades and filling the trees with glorious, shifting highlights. He displayed his thanks and reverence in a wild flicker of single combat that few would consider prayer. Yet Mitrian knew. She never doubted that it was Sif who brought Tannin and his kin to Colbey nor that Sif had worked her divinity on his injured hand.

Somehow, Mitrian felt certain that Sif appreciated Colbey's exultation. And the goddess heard him.

22 Renshai Swords

Despite the small pack of rations that Tannin had shared, hunger hounded Colbey and his companions as they traveled through the forest on a path they could not have found without the Western Renshai's guidance. Colbey took the advance scout, weaving between the brush and trunks to either side of the path, seeking hidden Northmen. He found nothing to indicate an organized ambush, though occasionally he heard a rustle or snap that indicated another presence in the Western woodlands. Colbey would have attributed the sounds to Korgar; the barbarian twined through trees and copses like an animal, appearing then melting into the forest despite Colbey's familiarity with his technique. But the barbarian made less noise than any animal, and Colbey realized that Korgar could not possibly be the source of the sounds he heard.

For a time, Colbey kept his guard high, doubling and looping to find the intruder. His maneuvers gained him only a distant glimpse of movement. Finally, the sounds disappeared and did not recur. He had little choice but to assume he had tracked a curious deer or wolf. He could not conceive of a Northman so near to a lone Renshai not attacking. Bold, brash, and obsessed with honor, a Northman would have rushed the Golden Prince of Demons at the first opportunity. Yet Colbey could not forget the headless corpse; the brutality inflicted on that body was also not something he could have imagined any Northman doing, no matter how hated the enemy. *A Northman not behaving like a Northman.* Colbey tried to think like the one who had killed Episte, but he found the process so alien and impossible it had no basis in logic. *Surely, Episte's slayer was a madman. How do I anticipate a man without sanity or principle?*

Colbey wrestled with the puzzle, saddened by memories of Episte's death but intrigued by life and its challenges for the first time in months. For the twentieth time in an hour, he looked at his hand. It was paler than he remembered, but flushed a healthy pink. Ugly scars marred the back, four lines that traced the tendons to each finger. Though swollen, the skin had closed over them, warm and dry to the touch. His palm still sported the calluses that he had known for as long as he could remember having hands. The soft, smooth grips of noblemen and the women of most cultures seemed like defects of birth, as abnormal as a face without features. His fingers obeyed his slightest command, clumsy only from disuse. Soon, even that would disappear.

Suddenly, Mitrian's scream shattered the silence behind Colbey. The ground trembled. Instinctively, Colbey caught a trunk to steady himself. As the ground again became stable beneath him, he charged toward his companions. Garn's howl of pained frustration nearly deafened Colbey. The Renshai skidded up beside a deadfall that now spanned the trail, though it had not been there when he had passed this section of pathway moments earlier. Mitrian sprawled on the ground beneath it. She had fallen flat to the ground. Luckily, the tree's branches braced it at a crooked angle that had spared her back. Though shocked, she was alive, and Colbey saw no blood.

Concerned that the branches might shatter beneath the weight of a trunk nature had never made them to support, Colbey mobilized the rest. 'Tannin, Garn, Korgar!' He included the barbarian, though he did not see Korgar. 'Get your hands beneath that tree and lift. Rache, pull her free. But be careful.' The others sprang to obey.

Before the men could find their positions, Mitrian wriggled free on her own. She rose with a slowness that seemed more cautious and dazed than pained. Clearly, she had taken no serious injuries.

Colbey left Mitrian's solace to the others, finding the timing of the tree's falling too convenient for coincidence. He dropped to his knees, searching. At length, he found the slim, dark wire that had triggered the trap and the notched sticks that had held it until Mitrian tripped it. 'Camp,' Colbey snarled. He glanced in Tannin's direction, his eyes narrowing. Tannin had chosen the route, and the self-proclaimed 'Western Renshai' would have answers if Colbey had to rip them from his head. With a sigh of grim annoyance, Colbey went to tend Mitrian's bruises.

That night, Colbey left Rache's earliest session of training to Garn, while the old Renshai sought out Tannin. The shuffle of boots on leaves and twigs wafted clearly to him, interspersed with the swish of a blade cutting air. He followed the familiar music of a *svergelse*, brushing through a line of pine to the edge of a nearby clearing. There, Tannin practised, his sword slashing and jabbing the night air, his face crunched in concentration.

Colbey folded his arms over his chest and watched. He saw a bold commitment that would have pleased him and a simplicity of pattern that would have bothered him, if either of those things mattered now. Colbey knew that he would probably have to kill his newest student, and it enraged him. He had accepted so much ugliness in the Renshai's history and so many changes over the course of his lifetime. But Colbey believed he had finally found one force he might never learn to handle, though it had come gradually. In his youth, a man's word was law. The idea of breaking a promise did not just seem wrong, it had no precedent for consideration. Colbey wondered whether he could ever adjust to judging every man he met, every statement, and every promise. The survival of all Renshai depended on it.

Tannin continued his practice, blithely unaware of his audience.

Colbey considered. He could easily catch Tannin from behind and cut the youth down before he could think to defend. The thought lasted less than a fleeting instant, and it merited no deliberation. Neither the Renshai's code not Colbey's personal honor would allow such a thing. That Tannin may have discarded that same honor was immaterial. Colbey knew that the very substance of honor involved sticking to its tenets despite the nature or methods of the enemy.

Colbey frowned, studying Tannin as he hacked through a wild flurry of attack. Here, following his principles came easy to Colbey. He could confront this problem head-on and without fear, as Renshai were meant to do. Facing Episte's slayer, when it happened, would become another matter, one Colbey tried to cast aside for now. *If I got the opportunity to kill that madman dishonorably, would I take it? Can result ever justify chaotic action or corrupted intent?* Colbey tried to forget questions that had little to do with his current task, but they would not be banished. He considered the dilemma of the Northmen: It is evil to murder, and evil should not exist. So is it evil to murder those who follow evil just because they are evil? Clearly, the Northmen had answered this paradox to their own satisfaction, since they slaughtered that which they considered evil gleefully, without a war of conscience. At times, Colbey wished the world could be as direct and simple for warriors of neutrality.

Colbey forced his thoughts back to the problem at hand. The previous night, he had believed Tannin's story; but the Northmen had no reason to suspect that the Renshai would veer eastward. Whoever had constructed the trap had done so to catch men, and Tannin alone had known the path the Renshai would take. Though circumstantial, the evidence seemed irrefutable. Still hating what he felt a need to do, Colbey stepped into the clearing. A single upstroke stole the weapon from Tannin's hands. Catching the hilt, Colbey jabbed both swords for the youngster, backing him against an oak.

Surprise shocked through Tannin, easily read. It fluttered into confusion. He met Colbey's gaze, then glanced swiftly away. The confusion strengthened and channeled into a fear Colbey could not refute.

Afraid. Is that because he's innocent or guilty? Colbey hated the need to try a man based on radiating emotion, though he knew he would receive more evidence than any judge. 'Why did you lead us into a trap?'

'What?' Tannin flipped up his wrists to indicate surrender. He seemed too startled to answer the question.

Recalling how Tannin had danced around his previous queries, Colbey stuck to the point. 'Why did you lead us into a trap? Reply directly and quickly, if you value your life or your honor at all.'

Emotions flickered and changed. At first, Colbey believed that Tannin intended to comply docilely. A flurry of thought followed, too quick for Colbey to sort. Then came a tiny glimmer of amusement, nearly masked by fear. Finally, Tannin's consciousness settled into a familiar acceptance of death, and all fear disappeared. Despite the threat, Tannin skirted the interrogation. 'The way you phrased the question, I couldn't possibly answer it directly without condemning myself. *Why* did I lead you into a trap? I'm innocent, *Gullindjemprins*. I didn't lead anyone into anything. I chose my route for two reasons only. First, to take you to the Fields of Wrath where my people . . . *our* people eagerly await you. Second, I took us toward the nearest town where I knew we could get rations.' His eyes again rolled to meet Colbey's cold gaze. This time, the youngster did not look away.

Colbey wanted to believe so badly it hurt. He tried not to let hope color his objectivity. 'How did the Northmen know where to put that trap?'

'I don't know.' Tannin glared in defiance. 'Maybe they found us. Maybe they overheard something.'

Colbey considered. He had explored the minds of enemies before, and now he walked the borders of propriety. *If Tannin is untrustworthy, he must die. If he's a friend, I must trust him implicitly. But I have to give him at least the same chance as I gave Valr Kirin and his troop at the dam.* Tentatively, Colbey spread his consciousness, threading into Tannin's mind. Recalling the agony he had caused Valr Kirin, he kept his touch light.

Tannin continued, apparently oblivious, 'Man traps don't fit Northmen's methods anyway. They're more likely to charge into single combat. Maybe the tree just happened to fall then. Or maybe the trap was set by someone else for someone else, and we just came along at the wrong time.'

Colbey heard the words in stereo, once from Tannin's lips and the other as a brash echo in his head. His exploration brought details he would otherwise have missed. The mass of conflicting emotions that assailed Tannin included frustration, the sorrow of loss, and a respect that could pass for awe. Tannin's aggressive bluster covered a fear that stemmed less for his own life than for losing the finest treasure his tribe could find: the Golden Prince of Demons. And Colbey found an eagerness to learn that he searched for in every student, raw and unprotected by normal, outward defenses. He discovered a pocket of comments, the things Tannin would have liked to have shouted, but wisely held back: *If I wanted to kill Renshai, I only had to poison the food I passed around. And I'd be a fool to start with anyone but you.* Colbey's invasion revealed that Tannin was exactly what he claimed to be.

Guilt assailed Colbey. Having established Tannin as an ally, he withdrew instantly, feeling offensive and cruel. Still, though he knew he had used his gift in a manner that Shadimar would not approve, he felt better for having done so. *Had I not found a means to and a comfort in trusting Tannin, I would have had no choice but to kill him.* Colbey lowered his arms, the weapon in each fist feeling inappropriately heavy. He flipped Tannin's sword so that its hilt faced its wielder. Though he had done it tens of thousands of times with hundreds of different swords, this time the maneuver seemed awkward. Only a sudden shift kept him from cutting his hand, and even that movement felt slowed. A new fatigue plagued Colbey, appearing to have no source, and Colbey remembered then how much his mental techniques drained him. He sheathed his own sword cautiously, without wasted motions.

Tannin reached for his hilt, his stance crouched and uncertain.

Colbey revealed his change of heart without explanation. 'Drop *Gullindjemprins*. It's a title of disrespect against the Renshai.'

Tannin paled, hand closing over his hilt. 'I didn't know.'

'It comes from the Westerners' belief that our skill stems from magic and chaos. They called us the Golden-Haired Devils from the North. The Golden Prince of Demons, I believe, is merely their way of naming me a leader of Renshai.'

Tannin sheathed his sword. 'Then what can I call you, sir? It feels wrong to use anything but a title. I'm not partial to Bringer of Evil or to Deathseeker.'

Colbey let the silence build. Despite the simplicity of the question, he knew the response he was about to give would mean more to Tannin than any vow or death threat. He offered more than a means of address. With his answer would come a responsibility without equal, one that went beyond any bonds of blood, as well as a promise. 'Call me your teacher.'

'*Torke*.' Tannin spoke the most important word in the Renshai language without the trace of Western dialect that had pervaded his speech. His lips twisted, then his grin spread to encompass his entire face.

*

The city of Wynix huddled in a steep-walled valley like a fetus in a womb, and sunset struck highlights from its enclosing stone wall. Colbey examined the layout from a broad stretch of forest, with the eye of an invader. Clearly, its citizenry had built the town with the same hopes and specifications as the auspicious trading town of Pudar, though on a smaller scale and with little success. Less accessible and with a more stable population, Wynix could never attract the richer merchant caravans, nor, thankfully, the riffraff and pestilence that seemed to accompany them. Colbey also noticed that the fools had designed the city wholly indefensibly. Archers could annihilate the populace or an infantry siege them without a casualty. Yet Wynix boasted no fertile soil for farming nor mineral wealth, and its low ground would be as difficult to protect for the invaders as the Wynixans. Therefore, Colbey believed, Wynix had almost certainly enjoyed peace in the decades since the Renshai had razed the West.

Colbey turned, heading back to his waiting companions. 'I think it's safe. It's not well-defended, but I doubt the Northmen would assault an entire Western village without exhausting peaceful methods of getting us first. I don't think the Northmen will guess that we've swung eastward.'

'They know.' Mitrian shook a pebble from her sandal, fully recovered. 'Someone set that trap.'

The fading light stole color from vision and made Tannin's hair seem nearly as dark as Mitrian's.

Colbey turned his attention to Tannin, smiling slightly. 'Someone reminded me that traps aren't the Northmen's way. Anyone could have set it. Apparently, this road is well-traveled, so it could have been meant for someone else. Or it might simply have been the work of a highwayman. A cruel trap, but that sort isn't known for chivalry.' Colbey did not voice his deeper concern, that the person or group who had violated the headless corpse was responsible. The memory of movement in the woodlands haunted him, and he wished he had tracked their stealthy follower more persistently.

Always practical, but rarely pensive, Garn fidgeted. 'I don't see it makes much difference. We need food and horses. We can get them there.' He pointed toward the valley.

Rache stared in the direction of Garn's finger, though he could not see Wynix through the foliage. 'If the Northmen can recognize Mama alone, they'd know any of us. I think we're safer together.'

Colbey nodded his agreement. 'We'll need rations, seven horses, and a sword for Korgar.' He caught a glimpse of Rache's notched blade and winced. 'At least one sword.'

'We'll need something else,' Mitrian added. 'We'll need gold. Horses don't come cheap, and I couldn't even pay for my own meal in

Porvada.'

Colbey turned his attention to Tannin hopefully.

The Western Renshai shook his head. 'I have a handful of copper. It'll buy us a modest meal at *The Merchant's Haven*. That's Wynix's inn. One meal. One. It won't cover horses and weapons.'

Colbey frowned. In the past, he had won food and lodging for himself and his companions with his healing arts or by selling his skill. In his youth, the Renshai had swept, slaying, through the West, taking what they wished. Money had no value to him.

Garn glanced from Colbey to Tannin. 'I've been known to . . . um . . . take . . . '

Mitrian silenced her husband with a glare, but not before Colbey recognized his intentions. As a gladiator, Garn had stolen from the guards who kept him prisoner. For the moment, Colbey discarded this option, leaving it as a distant possibility if no better ones appeared.

Tannin kicked at his nearly empty pack. 'In the years I've been traveling looking for you, I've been doing odd jobs for barter or money. That's kept me fed and clothed. If we hang around the tavern at a busy time like . . . ' He studied the sky, assessing the time. '. . . now, we're bound to find someone who can use a group of able-bodied Renshai.' He laughed. 'So long as we don't tell them that's what we are.'

Colbey frowned, disliking the idea of wasting time in a city, yet understanding the need. He could see advantages to remaining in a densely populated area. Though it would raise their profile, it would also hinder open combat. Attacking one stranger in a dark alley in Porvada might have limited complications, but declaring open war on an entire group in a crowded trading city would prove difficult as well as dangerous. So long as the Renshai remained in the inn or on populous streets, the Northmen would not dare to break the laws or risk the lives of bystanders. For their part, the Renshai and their friends could not go much longer without rations. The rest and change promised by Wynix might do them good. 'All right, then we go to the inn.'

Hunger kept contrary arguments at bay. Colbey and his companions spiraled into the valley, following the beaten track that led to Wynix. A cheap copy of Pudar's, Wynix's gate also apparently remained opened until sundown, and no one challenged the group's entrance. They padded down roadways lined with stands and wagons. Most of the tables lay empty in the waning light, as even the more persistent merchants packed the last of their wares until morning. When the Renshai wandered by, some of these looked up, but no one bothered with a sales pitch. Apparently something in the party's manner told the merchants that they had little money or a purpose besides shopping, and Colbey crossed the market square unaccosted.

Tannin took the lead on the narrower streets beyond the market. Colbey tensed, alert to signs or sounds of movement. Occasionally, he heard the shuffle of a foot against cobble, the sound of one man or woman gliding through the alley shadows. This did not bother Colbey. No lone person, whether Northman or footpad, could harm them. Rats scuttled through the alleyway ahead, their nails clicking against stone and their squeaks of protest feeble. Soon, Tannin brought his charges before a stone-fronted building lit by a row of lanterns hanging over its doors. A gaily painted sign proclaimed it as *The Merchant's Haven* in Western trading tongue runes. A dense uproar of inseparable voices filtered through cracks in the doorway.

Colbey entered first. Yellow walls bore murals of farms, carts, and animals from different parts of the world. Dozens of artists had painted the pictures. The styles varied from talentlessly crude to professional, and some of the individual figures had clearly more than one craftsman. A quick search revealed few blonds, and none of those were obviously Northern. The tavern's patrons formed a swarming, boisterous mass around some central entertainment that Colbey could not see. The tables on the periphery stood empty. Serving maids wound through the throng with drinks, returning to a fat, pink-cheeked bartender who clapped his hands with glee.

Colbey steered his charges to one of the empty tables on the fringes, and Secodon slipped beneath it. As they sat, the bartender came personally to their table. He looked over every member of the group interestedly. 'Northmen, eh? Welcome. It's a day for distant travelers.'

Alarmed, Colbey pressed. 'You've seen other Northmen today?'

'Nay. And only once before. Years ago.' The bartender's eyes strayed to the teeming mass of patrons at the center of the bar. 'But I've got an Eastern merchant, the prince of Wynix and Ahktar, and a group from Pudar. Now that you're here, I've got everything.'

Placed at ease by the bartender's denial of Northmen, Colbey considered. He doubted the bartender would mislead. His childlike excitement reminded Colbey of Sterrane, and he could not imagine the Wynixan keeping a secret.

'What can I get for you?'

'Bread and cheese for everyone. And whatever is safe to drink in these parts.'

'I've got the best mead you've ever tasted. It's going well tonight.' Again, the bartender's attention shifted to the crowd.

Colbey had to ask. 'What's going on over there?' He inclined his head in the direction that the bartender was already looking.

The bartender glanced back at Colbey, then returned his attention to the masses. He beamed, taking a skipping step toward Colbey that made his fat bounce like water. His words seemed to tumble over one another. 'Card game. Terrific, isn't it? Brought me a week's crowd in a night.'

'High stakes?' Colbey asked.

Catching a gesture from the crowd, the bartender waved over a serving maid. 'Dayaan the goldsmith and Prince Oswald's playing. Then there's a merchant from the East called Shalan.' He pronounced it '*Shay*-lan,' though Colbey suspected the correct Eastern inflection would be 'Shigh-*layn*.' 'The fourth is Mirkae, a local. Calls himself king of cards and claims he's never lost a game. I seen times when he didn't win neither, but he's certainly winning this one.'

The idea of large sums of money held Colbey's attention neatly. 'This an open game?'

The bartender laughed, and his body shook in rhythmical waves. 'Open to anyone with the twenty gold stake. So far, that ain't been no one.' He leaned uncomfortably close, speaking in a loud whisper, though the noises of the crowd drowned even normal speech. 'Rumor is Mirkae cheats.' With a guffaw that left the odor of garlic breath, the bartender wandered away to fill the order.

Colbey guessed that any rumor the bartender knew would not remain a well-kept secret. Still, if the local was sharking cards, he must be doing so competently enough to fool the other players, despite suspicion. The scam intrigued Colbey.

Rache caught Colbey's arm. 'Are you thinking of playing?'

'We need the money.' Colbey rolled his gaze to Shadimar, knowing the Eastern Wizard would not care for the request Colbey felt obligated to make. 'Shadimar, lend me the sapphire.'

'No!' Shadimar's rage gave volume to his reply, and it cut over the hubbub. As a few eyes swiveled toward them, the Wizard lowered his voice. 'We had an agreement. I keep the Pica Stone so long as we have a vow of brotherhood. I'm not going to let you risk it in some card game.'

A grimace of annoyance replaced Colbey's grin. 'I'm not going to lose it. I'm a damned good card player. And even if I lose it, and I won't, I can get it back.' He patted Harval's hilt.

'No.' Shadimar's face assumed sharp lines. Colbey could feel Secodon's warm breath on his knee. 'The Pica is a magical object, by the gods. One of only two in Odin's world. I won't have people handling it. It's too precious and too dangerous.'

Bothered despite the Wizard's right to deny him, Colbey let his chin droop to his hands, where it remained until the food arrived. While he and his companions ate, Colbey worked on another plan. He took a few bites of cheese-topped bread as he mulled the problem. 'Garn. Go outside and see what you can . . . um . . . find worth twenty gold.'

Mitrian glowered.

'Now?' Garn asked, his mouth full of bread.

'If we wait until the card game is over, I can't win it. But if I do win, we'll have more food than you and twenty like you could ever eat.' Colbey waited while Garn weighed the value of a full plate against the promise of more in the future.

Mitrian's face reddened with rising anger.

Tannin cut a wedge of cheese, balanced it on a slice of bread, and handed it to Garn. The ex-gladiator sighed. He gulped down half his mug of mead, took the proffered food, and left the tavern.

Mitrian opened her mouth to protest, but Colbey caught her arm and dragged her toward the crowd. Just out of earshot of their companions, Mitrian jerked free and turned on him. 'Rache knows his father was a slave. Does he have to think of Garn as a thief as well?' She stormed back toward the table, stumbled over a misplaced floorboard, and caught a chair for balance.

Colbey suppressed an urge to laugh with difficulty. The din swallowed their conversation, but Colbey spoke in Renshai to make certain no one who overheard would understand. 'That's ludicrous, Mitrian. Rache is Renshai. He's dedicated his life to killing. He's slaughtered the sons of mothers and the mothers of innocent sons. Do you suppose he finds it horrible when his father steals so we can eat?'

Mitrian scowled but made no reply.

Colbey took her wrist and again maneuvered her toward the throng. 'Actually, I didn't send Garn away to steal. I got rid of him because he wouldn't approve of what I'm about to do.' Colbey knew no one else would approve of his idea either, including Mitrian, but only Garn would resort to violence. Or so he hoped. 'Do as I say. Please.'

'What about Northmen? You just sent Garn out there to face them alone.'

Colbey denied the possibility. 'Garn's smart enough to be careful and quiet enough to scout. If Northmen had come, I believe the bartender would have known it.' He steered Mitrian into the crowd. Effort, force, and more than a little finesse brought them through the press to a position behind Dayaan, the goldsmith, that gave them a reasonable view of the game.

Colbey scrutinized the players. Shalan sat to Dayaan's right, the standard coarse-featured, swarthy Easterner. He wore tan leather leggings and a red silk shirt. His expression seemed grave, though friendly, haloed by thick eyelashes and a broad, black mustache. A crooked stack of gold lay at his elbow.

To Dayaan's left sat Prince Oswald, a homely youngster with dimples in his cheeks and wrinkles at the corners of his eyes. His teeth jutted at angles when he smiled, which was often, but his dignified manner and rich dress precluded laughter. Colbey studied Mirkae longest. Thin as a rag, the Wynixan moved with the confident ease of a master. His eyes looked dead, dark except for a faint glimmer that Colbey read as avarice. Disliking the card shark, Colbey required no effort to consider the man an enemy and to choose to probe his mind. The Renshai's mental tendril fought through a net of emotion: arrogance, joy, and faint undertones of fear. He recognized no guilt or remorse, and those seemed conspicuously absent. A responding hatred rose within Colbey. He hoped he would find a means to expose the rat-faced card cheat.

'What . . . ?' Mitrian started, but Colbey waved her silent.

The Renshai plunged deeper into Mirkae's thoughts, worming gently into the recesses of the Wynixan's deception. He discovered the answer to Mirkae's success involved the patterns on the card backs, but weariness touched him before he could elicit more than the basics of the technique. Afraid to tap his strength too completely, Colbey withdrew, turning his attention to the cards. Just that short journey made him feel wobbly, but it had given him enough information to begin his own investigation. He watched the game for several hands, occasionally making brief prods into Mirkae's mind for details.

Time ran short. Dayaan lost the last of his coins to Prince Oswald's lucky draw. The goldsmith rose, grumbled something about next year, and forced his way through the crowd.

Though he still had not grasped the complexities of Mirkae's code, Colbey knew Dayaan's opening might be his only chance. 'You seem to have an extra chair. Might I join?' Without waiting for an answer, Colbey sat in the recently vacated seat. He grasped Mitrian's wrist briefly to indicate that she should stay.

Mirkae regarded Colbey coldly, apparently measuring his competence by size and age. 'Any man with gold to lose may join.' His eyes met Colbey's, hovered a moment, and skittered away like insects. 'A Northman.' The thickness of his tone made it sound like an insult. 'You'll have plunder to stake, not coinage, I'd wager. It'll need to have a twenty gold piece value. And someone will have to be willing to cover it.'

Colbey nodded. He laced an arm around Mitrian's waist, and drew her toward the table. 'This is my stake.'

Mitrian stiffened beneath Colbey's grip, and he thought if safer not to meet her gaze.

Mirkae studied Mitrian with the same icy thoroughness, his eyes roving up and down and his mouth leering. At length, he spoke. 'Tempting, old man, but I'm not interested.'

Colbey turned his attention to the other players, maintaining an air of confidence that told the crowd that he knew his offer was worth far more than the requested stake. He hoped his certainty would convince the players.

Shalan examined Mitrian cautiously, with a merchant's eye. The prince's teeth jutted from a lopsided grin. 'I'll play for your stake,' he said before Shalan could offer. 'My father has paid as much for less hardy-looking slaves, and I don't mind losing gold to someone other than Mirkae for a change.'

When Colbey did not meet her glare, Mitrian expressed her dissatisfaction and warning by pinching his arm until it bruised. Colbey released her, trusting her to recognize the importance of playing along. No matter the situation, he would allow no one to take her.

Mirkae passed Colbey the cards. His previous observation told him that the deck had peasant cards numbered one through ten, knights, princes, queens, and kings in each of five colors. It also contained three wild jesters. Colbey took the cards, but he neither glanced through nor shuffled them. Instead, he set them on the table and watched Prince Oswald gather twenty gold to wager against Mitrian.

The click of coins disappeared beneath the whispered speculation of the crowd.

Colbey caught Mitrian's hand and squeezed reassuringly. With her as his stake, he could not drop out of the hand in the event of an unlucky deal. It appeared that he had as much chance to lose as to win, but Colbey found a means to tip those odds as well as to gain the information he needed. 'Since this match is at the whim of the Norns, let's have it swiftly done. We'll each choose a card at random. The highest wins.' With a deft sweep of the hand, Colbey spread the deck, facedown, across the table.

Mirkae's eyes came suddenly to life. Displaying all of the card backs simultaneously trebled the risk of someone recognizing their differences. Surely, the card cheat realized that Colbey could have only one motive for exposing the back of every card, but the Wynixan said nothing. Only the sudden alertness and the tensing of Mirkae's fingers on the table revealed his concern.

Oswald's hand floated uncertainly above the deck. He seized a card and flipped it over. It was the red knight.

The audience applauded their prince's draw politely, but the claps remained scattered. Clearly, many Wynixans wanted to see how a Northman would play.

Colbey paused, knowing how much rested upon his incomplete understanding of Mirkae's code. Though he felt certain he could win Mitrian back by violence, the idea of making more enemies of high exposure and political stature bothered him. Once having made his selection, he saw no reason to delay the inevitable. His hand snaked forward and flipped a card in one motion. The blue queen joined the red knight.

The crowd fell silent. The prince sighed, pushing a pile of gold to Colbey, who had officially joined the game. And now it was a game, where before it had been a killing. Slowly, the gold became rearranged in unequal piles. Circumstances drove the prince from the game, but he remained in his seat to watch. No one tried to take his place. Mirkae kept his lead; but Colbey's winnings continued to grow, mostly at Shalan's expense.

The evening wore on. The spectators grew restless. They wandered off to their own entertainments, and others replaced them as quickly. Mitrian ran between the gaming table and her companions with food, bought by Colbey, and reports of the elder's progress. When Garn returned to the inn, but did not show up to kill him, Colbey guessed that Mitrian had not told her husband the details of how the old Renshai had joined the game.

'I'm out.' Shalan hurled his last hand to the table.

Every eye strayed to the piled gold. Colbey's winnings nearly mirrored Mirkae's. The card shark gathered his coins, but Colbey's cold stare and weathered hand on the deck stopped him. Mirkae met Colbey's gaze like an equal, and that infuriated the Renshai. 'No,' Colbey said sharply. 'Where I come from, there is only one winner.'

Mirkae hesitated. His attention ran from Colbey's stack of gold to his own. Colbey waited patiently while Mirkae wrestled common sense and greed, obviously not convinced by play that his adversary knew the code fully nor that he could match him in skill. The cards and the marks were Mirkae's. At worst, the odds were equal.

Colbey passed the deck to Prince Oswald. 'Shuffle, please.'

The prince complied.

Colbey leaned across the table, and his eyes engaged in a war with Mirkae's. 'We'll cut cards from the deck. Highest takes all.'

Mirkae's mouth twitched like a cut tendon. Since neither man would see his card, front or reverse, until chosen, their chances could only be even.

Mitrian jabbed an elbow in Colbey's ribs. 'What are you doing?' she whispered in Renshai.

Colbey continued to stare at Mirkae, directly and with dignity. 'Exposing a thief,' he replied in the same language. 'All the money in the world isn't worth cheating over. Even in this, there must be honor.'

Prince Oswald set the deck in front of Colbey, and the Renshai made one last excursion into the gutter of Mirkae's mind. He caught the Wynixan's thoughts verbatim: *So what if the old Northie wins. Let's see him enjoy his gold with a dagger in his spine.* The thought amused as much as sickened Colbey.

Angered by Mirkae's depravity, Colbey muttered a brief prayer, then cut the deck randomly and slipped the card free. He pushed the rest of the deck toward Mirkae.

The gamblers stared at one another. Neither dared to look at the card that lay, facedown, beneath Colbey's relaxed fingers. Mirkae broke first. His gaze dropped to the card and remained there. Sweat beaded his forehead, and his breathing quickened. 'I don't want to play. I'm finished.' He gathered gold hurriedly.

Colbey raised his brows questioningly. 'You seemed ready enough to play before. I haven't even turned my card yet. Why would you fear it unless . . . ?' He trailed off with a hiss of suspicion.

Mirkae cleared his throat, his hatred for Colbey tangible. 'I don't want to risk my winnings. Let's quit now, before I touch the deck or you turn your card, while it's still fair.' He half rose. 'There's plenty of gold for both of us.' His tone promised a private settlement.

Colbey examined the back of the card for the first time. 'Why would my draw frighten you?' he asked, his voice modulated to make the whole room curious. 'Unless maybe you can read it from the back.' He studied the pattern. 'Is it a king, Mirkae?'

'How could I possibly know?' Mirkae dismissed the claim as ludicrous, well versed at looking innocent. 'If you'll excuse me . . . '

The prince stood, taking a position at Mirkae's right hand. The crowd closed off his escape. 'Draw!' Oswald said.

Mirkae reached for the deck. The stakes had risen from gold to life, and Mirkae lost his practiced composure.

'Yes,' Colbey said, loud enough for his audience. 'I believe it *is* a king.' He traced an obscure curl in the intricate pattern of the card back.

Mirkae made a pained noise, that would have been lost if not for the throng's sudden silence.

'The black king,' said Colbey definitively. He tossed the card over to display the silhouette of the king.

The crowd erupted in chaos. Mirkae moved like an eel. His hand closed on Oswald's wrists, twisting. Bone snapped, wrenching a scream from Oswald. A dagger in Mirkae's fist sped for the prince's throat.

Colbey sprang forward. His sword sheared free and struck at once, shattering Mirkae's skull. The dagger clattered to the floor. The card shark collapsed, dead before he struck the boards.

Prince Oswald's eyes bulged. A cracked wrist seemed small payment when, without Colbey's interference, he might have been the corpse on the barroom floor.

Colbey and his companions spent a restful night in the inn, though they were the only ones calm enough to sleep. The innkeeper gave them a respect that bordered on servility, and Colbey's negotiations with Oswald had yielded a hundred gold pieces. Though a pittance compared with the winnings that had once sat before him and Mirkae in the card game, the amount more than satisfied Colbey. He could buy whatever the party needed and still have money left for food in the future. He felt far more comfortable restoring an honesty that had, not too long ago, been a certainty for all mankind.

In the morning, Colbey, Mitrian, Garn, Tannin, and Rache headed for the market square. Shadimar remained behind, with Korgar and Secodon, under the pretext of guarding the few valuables they had. As Colbey threaded through the vast sea of noise and people, he guessed that it was simply the Eastern Wizard's excuse for avoiding the crowds. It seemed just as well. A decade at war and weeks of running, constantly looking back, had left the Renshai wearied and in bad humor. Even Colbey recognized the need for some frolic. Apparently, the Northmen had not tracked the group to Wynix. Until the enemy again picked up their trail, a market town seemed like a good place to play.

Though far smaller than the bazaars in Pudar, the Wynixan marketplace was more tastefully decorated, without the gaudy signs and ceaselessly beckoning merchants. It seemed more pleasant for this difference. Garn became a magnet, attracted to all steel. No weapon or shred of armor escaped his scrutiny. Mitrian seemed more interested in the odd shapes and colors of southwestern fruit, having been delegated the job of selecting travel rations and given nearly half of the money. Tannin would select the horses. He guided Rache, showing the youngster the many wonders of a market town.

Crowds made Colbey feel battle-pressed. He remained intent on his purpose, weaponry, noticing only the stands of armorers. Sword after sword fell into Colbey's hand and was rejected. Many failed before they met his grip, merely for the color of their steel. By his seventh stand, frustration plied him. He stared at the merchant, voice loud with scorn. 'Find yourself a blacksmith who can do more than shoe horses. These blades would break in battle, and a rawhide grip will become slippery as a fish when coated in sweat or blood. A fine sword is no more difficult to make than a poor one. These are poor indeed.'

The merchant flushed, not bothering to contradict. Colbey's statements contained too much knowledge to pass for the ramblings of an old man.

Colbey turned away in disgust.

'Over here!' Garn's voice scarcely penetrated the din of the passing crowds, but Colbey managed to follow it. At Garn's side, Mitrian laughed so hard she bent double, nearly incapacitated. Grinning, Garn indicated a sign that spelled out, in the trading runes: *Genuine Renshai Swords*.

Colbey grimaced, anger flashing through him. Then, Mitrian's mirth touched even the Golden Prince of Demons. He smiled, considering a means to vent the harried frustration of what had become constant alertness and paranoia.

Despite Mitrian's laughter, the obvious interest of her companions sparked the mind and tongue of the seller. 'Yes, friends,' he shouted enthusiastically. 'The man who forged these blades . . .' He placed a hand on a row of longswords, slightly shorter and broader than most. '. . . learned his skill from his father. His father took the secret right from the golden-haired devils.' His pause was well-rehearsed and lasted just long enough for the gathering audience to digest his words. 'Before the Renshai were slain, my craftsman's father learned their magic. Anyone who wields these few precious swords will have all the skill of Renshai.'

Colbey scratched his head thoughtfully. Béarn's rule covered a smaller, direct area in the southern part of the Westlands as well as serving as the West's high kingdom. In the years when the Renshai had devastated the West, they had spared Béarn in exchange for hospitality. Apparently, either Wynix fell under Béarn's direct rule or the laws had relaxed. In some towns, it was still a capital offense to speak the tribal name, but this merchant had mentioned them twice. His sign flaunted custom, propriety and, in some places, law. 'I had thought the Renshai gained their skill through practice and war. Because of magic? Bah! I'm an old man if one of those blades can give me the skill of a Renshai.'

Mitrian caught her breath, watching curiously.

Colbey took a sword from the stand and tested the split leather hilt. The balance lay within a hand's breadth of the crosspiece, and the steel appeared the right color. The S-shaped crossguard seemed sturdy, built for stability rather than decoration. A metal finger piece jutted from the wrappings, allowing finer control than the standard grip. Pleased, he picked up a second sword and handed it to Garn. 'Hold this. Flat of the blade up.'

Garn obeyed.

Colbey took a step back. With a brisk snap, he crashed his blade against Garn's.

The sword tumbled from the ex-gladiator's hands, and he rubbed his stinging palms together. 'Why'd you do that?'

The crowd howled with laughter, drawn by the game, but Colbey ignored them. Instead, he examined the edge of the blade. The notch was small but regular, without chips or cracks. The steel seemed hard, yet soft enough that it would not easily break in battle. 'A good sword,' Colbey admitted, wanting to encourage any man who sold quality, no matter his methods. 'But fight like a Renshai?'

Without awaiting a reply or cue, Colbey spun the blade and began a kata as beautiful as life. His dance was a whirl of wind and passion, like the transient flicker of a candle flame. The sword skipped through the air. At times, it moved so swiftly it disappeared. When it came into view again, it never reappeared quite where the crowd expected.

Mitrian tossed a fist-sized fruit toward Colbey, and the elder accepted the challenge. As it fell, his blade darted. The sword halved the fruit, revealing its salmon-colored center. Neither half found the ground unmolested. Four even pieces of scarlet-skinned fruit settled in the dusty street.

When Colbey's last sweep split the air, many men pressed toward the stand to buy their own skill.

Fools who believe any prowess can be bought without pain. Despite his hatred for deception. Colbey knew that the buyers expected merchants to use exaggeration and wild claims to sell their wares. Hawking had become as much entertainment as sales tactics, and assessing the quality of products fell on the patron. *Even if there was a magic powerful enough to make warriors of fat dolts, only the Wizard who cast the spell would benefit, for the blades would wield the men.*

The smile on the merchant's face became a priceless memory. His swords were not priceless, though their cost had tripled in the last few moments. His salesmen busied themselves collecting money, and the merchant did not forget his benefactor. He approached Colbey. 'Sir, keep the swords. No cost.' A broad grin spread across his face. 'I am Kerska.' He bowed.

Colbey returned the smile, not wholly with kindness. Had the swords been less finely crafted or his mood been less benign, he might have met this merchant with violence instead of indulgence. 'Colbey Calistinsson. Of the Renshai tribe.'

The merchant's grin wilted slightly, and he studied Colbey as if trying to guess whether the Northman played him.

The party picked up its *Genuine Renshai Swords* and continued on its way, leaving Kerska to wonder while he wallowed in his newfound riches.

23 The Fields of Wrath

The pleasures of the Renshai's journey westward included the warmth of summer and the green glow it gave the deep forest, full bellies, and more than enough gold to secure provisions in the tiny farm towns they entered. By day, they rode through woodlands, plains and farm fields. Every evening, they stopped to train and practice before settling for the night.

Colbey enjoyed the seemingly endless cycle of travel and teaching. Since Tannin and Mitrian had bested Valr Kirin in a nameless alley in Porvada, Colbey had seen no sign of Northmen, not even another trap like the one Mitrian had triggered. Though unexplained, the change was welcome.

Still, a day did not pass without one of the group trying to understand Valr Kirin's motives. 'Maybe they gave up and went back to the North,' Mitrian suggested one morning.

It seemed plausible. The Northmen's xenophobia had not endeared them to the West, and they had to have encountered hostility in the myriad towns scattered throughout the Westlands. Also, the Northmen had crops and families of their own to tend. Surely most had returned to their homes, but Colbey dared not underestimate Valr Kirin or the Nordmirian's need to slaughter the last Renshai. 'Maybe,' Colbey conceded without enthusiasm. 'But we can't afford to relax our guard.'

Tannin piped in. 'Maybe they got arrested and jailed in Porvada.'

This time, Colbey only nodded. His intuition told him he would see Kirin again, and the frown on Shadimar's face only confirmed the certainty. Still, the summer stretched on without sight or sound of Northmen.

Gradually, the summer became inextricably twined with fall, then surrendered to the autumn gales. Leaves dried and burst into bold colors. Dark, weathered rocks that had earlier borne turtles and salamanders grew cold and barren. Accustomed to the Northland's perennial cold and ice, Colbey enjoyed watching the parade of seasons, his excitement compounded each day the Western Renshai grew closer. Soon, Colbey knew, the Renshai tribe would exist again. Their ranks would swell by eighteen, and one of them, Tannin's sister, was with child. Soon, Renshai blood would again flow among the tribe that had originally come from Renshi. He would find himself surrounded by students eager to learn the sword mastery their ancestors and Northern cousins had known. And Colbey would train them until others could take his place.

Autumn had nearly ended when Tannin led his companions to the Fields of Wrath. And Colbey met his people. He met them as mottled corpses with dull eyes. A stronger enemy had come and gone. The *Valkyries*, too, had come and gone. Wolves, coyotes, and scavenger birds had come, feasted for a time, then they had gone as well. All that remained were rigid, soulless bodies, sword-slashed or riddled with the familiar gold and white crests of Valr Kirin's Northmen's arrows.

Colbey went still, feeling his dreams fragment around him, leaving no emotion at all. The pain had become too familiar to hurt. Tannin froze, his eyes as lifeless as those around him. No one, living or dead, spoke or moved for longer than a minute. Then, Tannin drew his sword and thrust the blade at the sky. 'Sif!' he screamed.

Colbey cringed at the curses that could fly so easily from Tannin's tongue to Gladsheim, cringed that Sif might hear them or Tannin might shout them.

'Sif!' Tannin repeated. 'I left them in your hands.' Tannin struggled to squeeze the words from his throat. 'They died in battle. And I thank you.' After a moment of silence that said so much, he added. 'Allow me to thank you again when Kirin lies dead.' Tannin sheathed his sword, but his eyes still pleaded with the heavens. The agony radiating from Tannin nearly suffocated Colbey, and he recognized that same desperate need for action that had driven him when he found the headless corpse in the grove. He thought Tannin might run, without reason or direction, until something large enough to stop him filled his path.

Instead, Tannin joined Mitrian, who searched desperately for some glimmer of life among the bodies she gathered for pyre. Unintentionally, Colbey shared Tannin's emotions as they collapsed so deeply that their lack felt as tangible as his grief had moments before. Despite the brooding unnaturalness of the feeling, Colbey preferred it. Sapped of strength, Tannin would become more tractable and predictable, more likely to act from logic than emotion, if he could act at all.

Rache and Korgar joined the task, checking and gathering bodies. Shadimar and his wolf perched on a stone the size of Béarn's throne, watching over the woodlands in all directions. Trusting Shadimar to guard them from Northmen, Colbey helped the others, unable to keep tears from his eyes. Eleven of the fifteen bodies bore only wounds that would not bar them from Valhalla, and Colbey could not help appreciating Valr Kirin's honor. Apparently, the Northman who had mutilated Episte was not among those who killed the Western Renshai. Or else Kirin had kept the man under control.

Mitrian started the pyre, and Colbey raised his swollen eyes to the flames consuming all that remained of the earthly Western Renshai. 'An odd group of lasts we are,' he said softly. 'A tribe without tribes: the last Myrcidian, a princess without a kingdom, a freed slave without a history, a lost barbarian, and the last of both Northern and Western Renshai . . . '

Tannin never lifted his gaze from the pyre. 'I'm not the last. I counted the dead. My sister was not among them, nor her husband. There's a third missing, too. Her name is Vashi.'

A blue mirror of the leaping flames grew in Colbey's eyes. *Escaped? Or captured.* He did not know the Western Renshai well enough to speculate. *If they're out in the woods somewhere, we'll need to find them.* 'Tannin. Is there a likely place they'd go?'

Hysteria edged Tannin's voice. 'I don't know. None of them has lived anywhere but here.' His pace quickened, until Colbey could barely make out the words. 'Maybe they're alive? Do you think they're alive? Are they here? Can we find them?'

Colbey chose to address the last question. 'We have little choice but to assume so.' He considered sending Korgar into the forest to search, doubting he could make the barbarian grasp the mission. *Even if he did, how could he make the Western Renshai understand?* Colbey knew any other member of the group would make too much noise to do anything more than scare the others away, and if they searched at random they could wander for months without accomplishing anything. *We need someone who knows these forests, how to track, and how to move through the woodlands in silence.*

A name came instantly to fill the description. *Arduwyn.* Colbey recalled a time just before the Great War when Episte's father had hunted Garn and Mitrian, when Colbey had needed to evade the younger Renshai. Colbey had hired Arduwyn to track Rache from one end of the Westlands to the other, to keep Colbey informed of the other's route, and to keep Rache safe. Arduwyn had done his job admirably. Now, Colbey tried to guess where he might find the archer. He knew that Mitrian and Garn had sent the flame-haired hunter to Béarn, yet he also knew that the Erythanian forests beckoned Arduwyn like a lover. And he would need to pass through Erythane to reach Béarn. 'How far is Erythane?'

'A half day's walk,' Tannin replied. 'Why?'

Colbey answered the question, though surely not in the spirit that Tannin had asked it. 'Because Rache and I are going there in the morning.'

The youngest Renshai glanced up from the pyre, noticeably startled.

Colbey continued, offering enough information to satisfy them all. 'If anyone witnessed this battle, Erythane is a logical place for them to go. It's the largest nearby city. And there may be someone there who can help us.' He did not explain further, skipping instead to stem protests. 'I only need one person with me, and Rache's at a stage where he can't afford to miss a training session.' He glanced sidelong at Garn, realizing he would take the child from the ex-gladiator's lessons.

Either Garn had not yet figured out the implications, or it did not matter. He listened as raptly as the others.

'I want the rest of you to stay here in case the survivors return. If it's a trick, I want most of us here to fight Northmen.' Colbey finished quickly, trying to make it clear that there would be no discussion. He had made the decision, and it would stand. 'Now, it's time for sword work.' He gestured Mitrian, Rache, and Tannin to him. 'Garn, set the camp in the woods. I'm not leaving us out in the open for archer targets.'

Garn began leading horses, and Shadimar came to help him. Colbey gathered his charges and began their practice.

Rache Garnsson rode at Colbey's side, proud to have been chosen to accompany his *torke*, yet intimidated by the honor. Aside from the war and their current journey, Rache had never left Santagithi's Town since he had arrived as an infant. He had heard stories that Erythane dwarfed even Porvada. Its citizens only used the common trading tongue, which was Rache's first language, to communicate with foreigners. For his part, Rache knew just a few words of the Western city language.

Colbey and Rache arrived at the border of the city of Erythane in the early evening, an old man and a young one caked with the dust of their journey. A meticulously lettered wooden sign directed travelers to the major landmarks of the city, including several inns. Colbey tapped a finger on the sign, indicating the closest inn, *The Knight's Rest*. Rache nodded tacit approval. They headed down the main roadway.

Accustomed to hailing every person on Santagithi's streets by name, Rache could not comprehend the vastness of Erythane. He followed Colbey along deeply dug, smooth-paved roads with his head bowed. Occasionally, he looked around the closely spaced stone cottages, with their flower boxes and penned pastures, deluding himself that the city stretched only as far as his vision. Dark-haired men and women passed with lowered eyes and grunted replies to Rache's compulsive greetings.

The Knight's Rest inn rose like a hill above the neat, Erythanian homes. Outside and in, Rache found it clean to a fault, dustless, sterile, and no more amiable than the citizens on the streets. Four work-hardened men sat at a table near the bar, gulping drinks and speaking little. Three others conversed in low tones at the opposite side of the common room. Colbey took a seat at the bar. Tired from the trip, Rache sat beside his sword master, resting his elbows on the counter and his chin in his hands. While Colbey sought the attention of the barkeep, Rache allowed his thoughts to wander.

'Barmaid!' One of the men at the table behind Rache shouted. 'I'd like to buy that child a drink. Bring him milk!' Laughter broke from the men in a strange quartet: two gruff, one sneering, and the last a musical giggle. Rache turned to find the brunt of their joke and discovered that they were looking at him.

Confusion blossomed. *They can't mean me.* Rache knew a simple innocence, much like his father's, that came from inexperience. *I was blooded at two. By Renshai law, I'm a man.* He fought rising anger and glanced at Colbey for direction. The approval of his mentor meant more to Rache than personal pride, though he understood that his love was dangerous. If not to war, he would lose his teacher to age soon enough. *What would Episte have done?* Rache considered, remembering the brother who was just enough older to become a hero and a model in his mind. *Episte hated war; he might have drunk the milk.* Still, Rache could not banish the memory of Episte's attack at the Midsummer's Festival. *Then again, maybe he would have charged them in a bitter frenzy.*

Now that they had gained Rache's attention, one man addressed the Renshai directly. 'Where's your mama, baby?' A stiff black beard and mustache parted as he spoke, filled with beer foam and crumbs. Flies buzzed around the dirty laborers. One perched on the speaker's hand and another on the table beside him. 'Does she know her little *kadlach* stole his father's butter knife?' He used the vulgar term for a disobedient child, indicating Rache's sword with a gesture.

The others howled their laughter, interspersed with wide-mouthed imitations of crying babies. The gruffer voices issued from a bearded redhead and a scar-faced brunet. The giggles peeled from a stout, clean-shaven Erythanian. All four wore battered scabbards at their hips.

Again, Rache looked for Colbey's guidance.

Colbey shrugged, tossing the initiative back to Rache.

The darkly bearded man spoke again. 'Does your mama know your senile, old grandfather takes her *kadlach* into bars?'

The slight against Colbey drove Rache over the edge of impropriety. He sprang from his stool, drawing his sword in an instant. The blade swirled once around his own head, gently caressed the speaker's hair, and bit into the table near his hand. The man hastily withdrew his fingers as Rache's sword returned to its rest.

The redhead staggered to his feet, hand poised on his hilt, but he did not draw. Apparently, memory of Rache's swiftness stayed him. Unfamiliar with taverns and towns, Rache could not know that, at a more popular time of day, *The Knight's Rest* would have had a bouncer who would have evicted Rache. The barmaids avoided the conflict, and the bartender stared at the door of the tavern, finding something that held his attention too fully for him to even notice Rache's confrontation.

Watching all the men around the table at once, Rache pointed at the place where his sword blow had marred the surface. 'There was a fly on your table.' Pinching the mangled insect between his thumb and forefinger, he flipped it into the redhead's mead. Then, with a feigned clumsiness that seemed impossible for a man who had just killed a fly with a sword, he swept the dark-bearded man's drink into his lap.

The speaker jumped to his feet, sputtering. While his companions sat in shocked silence, wits dulled by alcohol, the bearded man whipped a shortsword from his sheath. He lunged for Rache.

Rache struck fast as a heartbeat, seizing the wrist and twisting. The sword clattered to the floor. Rache's eyes blazed like emeralds; all humor left them. 'Do you really want to do that?' A smile eased onto his face, but it could have rivaled Colbey's for coldness. 'I know I want you to.' His fingers tightened around the wrist. Though his forearm remained the same size, it looked chiseled from stone. The power that was an inheritance from Garn made the decision for the bearded man. Hurriedly, he sat down.

Satisfied, Rache returned to the bar as Colbey was ordering mead from the lean, middle-aged barkeeper who wore a stained apron. Dark hair sprinkled with sandy highlights and gray fell around his face, and his eyes trained on Colbey and Rache reluctantly. He seemed more interested in the door at the farther end of the tavern. The abstraction had, apparently, kept him oblivious to Rache's run-in, because he said nothing about it.

'I'll just have milk,' Rache said loudly. 'Those men offered to pay.' He jerked his thumb toward the foursome sitting behind him.

Colbey chuckled softly, and this wordless gesture of approval warmed Rache.

The barkeep dashed off for the drinks, returning shortly with a mug of mead and a tankard of goat's milk. He set the drinks on the counter, so distracted that he gave the milk to Colbey and the mead to Rache. He opened his mouth to speak, still staring at something near the back of his common room. His eyes went cold, the corners of his lips twitched downward, and his words went unspoken.

Rache looked over his shoulder, flashing a warning glance at the foursome, daring them to comment on the mix-up with the drinks. Beyond them, he saw nothing that should inspire a barkeeper's wrath. The three men he had noticed on entering still conversed in hushed tones. The only new patron was a man Tannin's age, dressed in tailored wool and satin, who was flirting with a barmaid no older than Rache.

Colbey took a gold coin from his bulging purse and set it on the bar. The barkeep's gaze snaked toward the coin and rested on it briefly. But even money did not hold his attention long. He could not seem to keep from staring at the far end of the tavern.

Colbey sighed, dropping subtlety. 'I'm used to the attention of men I'm trying to bribe.'

The bartender craned around Rache for a better view. 'I'm sorry. That girl is my daughter.' He gestured toward the young barmaid. 'That rodent comes in here and puts . . . and does . . . ' He sputtered angrily and incoherently, broke off with an enraged toss of his head, and started again. 'He thinks he can paw her because he's the son of one of the king's knights.' The barman's face contorted into a mass of furious wrinkles.

Rache recalled his father's and grandfather's stories about the great and loyal knights of Erythane who served the king in Béarn. Tales of their heroism and pageantry had spread through the Westlands. Many considered their honor the exact opposite of the Renshai's supposed lawlessness; but Rache guessed that, this day, he would see the other side of the glorification.

Colbey rapped a fist on the bar. 'If I can get the knight's son away from your daughter, may I then have your attention?'

The barkeep met Colbey's gaze. 'If you can do it without bringing the king's wrath upon me. Or the boy's father.' He shivered. 'I'm no soldier to risk challenge by a knight.'

Still pleased with his triumph over the four drinkers at his back, Rache volunteered. 'Can I speak to the knight's son?'

Colbey hesitated. Then deciding it was a part of Rache's training, he bobbed his head once toward the knight's son.

Rache grinned, trotting across the common room, aware the barkeep and Colbey watched him expectantly. He would not disappoint his *torke*. He drew up beside the barmaid and the teenager who had his arm around her waist so tightly, he had nearly pulled her into his lap. 'Excuse me,' the Renshai said.

The knight's son rose and bowed, still holding the barmaid's wrist. 'I am Shalfon of Erythane, son of Brignar and apprentice knight to the Erythanian and Béarnian kings: his grace, King Orlis, and his majesty, King Sterrane.'

Rache waited patiently while the other finished his title, so full of other men's names and deeds, then introduced himself. 'Rache. And if you don't remove your hands from that woman, I'll remove them for you. At the wrists.'

'Your pardon?' Shalfon said stiffly.

Rache frowned, not certain they were speaking the same language, though they seemed to understand one another. 'Let's talk outside.'

The knight apprentice bowed. Releasing the young woman, he indicated the door with a broad sweep of his arm. 'Sir.'

Rache hesitated, legitimately concerned about preceding an enemy through a doorway. Colbey had taught that it welcomed daggers in the back. 'You're so damned mannered, you go through first.'

'Fight!' one of the men who had tormented Rache hollered. The tavern emptied. All seven of the other patrons plunged through the doorway. Suddenly, it no longer mattered who left first, so Rache and Shalfon exited together.

Once outside, Rache poked a finger at Shalfon. 'You fancy yourself a nobleman, do you? You treat that young lady without honor.'

Shalfon blinked several times. 'Do you doubt my chivalry, sir?'

'I believe I said that!' Rache shouted, liking the way he had said it better.

'Then I have no choice but to call you out.'

Rache shrugged, his heart pounding. He did not precisely understand the implications, though he knew fighting words when he heard them.

Yet Shalfon did not reach for a weapon. 'An honorable battle. To the death, of course. On the Bellenet Fields by the hill.' He made a grand gesture that told Rache nothing. 'At talvus.'

'Talvus?' Rache repeated, still not wholly certain what was happening.

'Midday,' Colbey explained from the doorway. 'A fine time for a falsely noble fool to lose his life.'

Shalfon glared at Colbey. Then he turned his back on Rache, marching to a dappled gray horse tied to a post outside the tavern. Mounting, he rode away.

Rache watched the other leave. Colbey came to his side, resting a hand between the boy's shoulder blades as the disappointed patrons staggered back into the tavern. 'There are better ways than threat to handle problems. Still, it can't hurt to have a reputation for skill. So long as you choose honorable battles instead of frenzied brawls, you'll do fine.' The elder steered his charge back into the bar. 'Men like Shalfon, who see honor as unwavering rules without exceptions, make people revere the arbitrary and rigid. Honor is situational, Rache. Don't ever forget that. It's making the right decision, without regard to yourself.'

Rache nodded, battle readiness making him too eager to listen carefully. He walked across the common room with Colbey, taking the same seat at the bar. Colbey sat beside him. 'May we talk now?' He slid a gold coin across the bar.

Taking the gold, the barkeeper gave the elder Renshai his full attention. 'How may I be of service?'

'Do you know of anyone who's seen Northmen in the last few days?' Rache sipped his milk, heart still pounding.

'Yes.' The barkeeper studied Colbey, as if for the first time. 'Me. Two days ago.' He took a step backward, and his fingers blanched around the gold piece. 'Are you the one who's supposed to get their message?'

Message? Rache's gaze riveted on Colbey. He supposed that it only made sense for the Northmen to guess that they would eventually visit a tavern in one of the largest cities of the West, but he did not expect them to leave a message. Rache wondered whether the Northmen had slipped from inn to tavern, leaving messages at every one.

'I don't know if I'm the one,' Colbey said carefully. 'But I suppose I could get the message if I asked politely enough.' He pushed another coin to his informant.

'East woods. Wolf Point,' the barkeep whispered. 'Kirin will trade the three he has for the one he calls *Bolboda*.' Though spoken with the harder Western accent, the Northern title was unmistakable.

Rache stared, drink and challenge forgotten. Despite its cryptic nature, the message came clearly through to him. Surely, Valr Kirin held the three missing Western Renshai. And he wanted the party to exchange Colbey for them.

Colbey took a swallow of mead, his nonchalance spoiled by Rache's obvious surprise. 'Did he say anything more? Message or not.'

'No.' The barkeeper continued to stare at Colbey, offering details that could have no significance, apparently to show that he was telling everything. 'They came in a group of five. They ordered mead, and they didn't harass my barmaids. They paid their tab.'

Colbey counted gold coins onto the counter in two neat stacks of five. 'What do you know about this Wolf Point? Is it a place?'

The barkeeper's eyes danced at the sight of this glittering fortune. 'Nothing. It's deep in the East woods. The only people who would go there are hunstmen.' Perhaps afraid his ignorance would lose him the money, the barkeep continued. 'I can name you some guides . . .'

'No need. Thank you.' Colbey left the gold, rising to leave.

But the barkeeper motioned the Renshai back. 'Despite what you are, you did me a favor, and that won't go unpaid. I can't fight for you, but I can give you some advice.'

Colby and Rache leaned closer.

'First, you need to know those Northmen were well-armed. Second, you – ' He broke off, waving a hand at Rache without fathoming a guess at their relationship. ' – may be in more danger than he believes.'

Colby smiled. 'Rache can fight.'

The barman shook his head impatiently, less a fool than he had seemed. 'The Northmen told me who you are.' He glanced about furtively. 'Every Westerner knows Renshai are unbeatable swordsmen. But Shalfon called the challenge, so he chooses the weapon. The Erythanian knights, Prince of Demons, wield pikes.'

The bartender gave Colby and Rache a room for the night, and Colby chose to train his student there rather than in the city streets, where Erythanians might take exception. Despite their cramped quarters, Colby worked Rache brutally, annoyed by the choices that paraded through his mind. Honor required that they stay and let Rache fight, that the Renshai name not became defamed because of one old man's fear for a young student. Yet now was not the time to risk Rache, not with Episte dead and other lives at stake, not on a petty squabble over a barman's daughter.

Rache worked, displaying the same dedication to his sword that he had since childhood, challenged rather than burdened by the harshness of the lesson. Still, even his endurance ebbed, and his movements grew less precise. Colby watched, feeling ire rise as his student became sloppy, then forcing down his anger when he realized its source. *I'm not mad at Rache's performance. It's the decision.* Colby called the practice to a halt.

Rache sheathed his sword with obvious relief, then fell to the straw bedding that covered the floor. He gasped for breath.

Colby paced.

After a long silence, during which Rache gathered enough breath to speak, the youngest Renshai sat up. 'I'm wielding a mountain?'

Colby froze, staring quizzically. Then the answer came. The trading tongue word 'pike' was the same as the Northern term for mountain. 'No, Rache. A pike is a weapon. It's a pole arm, about the length of three swords, with a barb on the end. And you're not wielding it. We're leaving tonight.'

Rache's mouth gaped open, and he stared in speechless astonishment.

Colby winced, understanding the questions that Rache dared not ask, about Renshai honor and running from combat. He took a seat at Rache's side. 'The Renshai can't afford to lose you. This isn't combat; it's a coward's battle.'

Rache stared at his feet. 'If we run, then we're the cowards. That barkeep knows who we are, so it'll make the Renshai look like cowards, too.'

Colbey lowered his head.

'Maybe I could get Shalfon to wield a sword.'

Colbey shook his head. 'The challenger chooses the weapon, place, and time. It's Erythanian tradition.'

Rache stood, cringing almost imperceptibly as he moved. Apparently, the drill had caused him pain, and that bothered Colbey.

Good planning, the elder berated himself. *Make him sore before a battle in which all the odds are already against him.*

'My father taught me to use other weapons and my strength. I can win that contest.' Rache stretched out on the straw. 'And I will.'

Colbey said nothing, but he knew his companion was right. He spread out beside Rache, and both fell into a wary sleep.

The Northern Sorceress, Trilless, sat at the table in her library, staring at a strip of parchment with writing in her own hand. With time, her eyes had become dry from gazing too long, making the letters jump and blur into incomprehensibility, yet Trilless knew that copied footnote as she knew her own name:

The Eyghteenth Dark Lord
Will obtayn in his day
A pale-skinned champyon
To darken the way.
One destined to betray
The West and his clan,
A swordsman unmatched
By another mortal man.

Colbey. Trilless sought another answer, for the thousandth time, but none came. And the old Renshai's thwarting death by age as well as battle only amplified her certainty. *He's under a Wizard's protection, which means he's become a champion.* Her experience did not match her findings. The prophecy stated that Colbey would become Carcophan's hero, yet Shadimar had battled the demon she had called against Colbey.

A chill spiraled through Trilless from an unnamed source that seemed to come from the air or the very fabric of the universe. She closed her eyes, waiting for the presence to pass. She had known its existence for decades, wisps of chaos that seemed stronger than the baseline that traced from pinholes in Odin's wards or the tiny amounts of magic the Wizards dared to perform. She had seen its effects on mankind and their world: crime, lies, oath-breaking, and the loss of nature's strict patterns, gradually replaced by oddities and unpredictability. *Is Shadimar sharing Carcophan's champion a symptom or a cause?* Trilless doubted that it mattered. *How clever of Carcophan. Sit back and let neutrality work his evil for him.*

Despite its danger, Trilless could not help admiring the ingenuity of the plan, although she wondered if it did not border on chaos itself. *Did Carcophan literally trick Shadimar, or did he simply allow Shadimar to fall into a trap of his own making?* Again, Trilless doubted that the answer mattered. She sanctioned goodness; and like all of the Wizards, she also supported 'Law.' Those obligations left her with only two courses of action; and, for that simplicity at least, she was glad. *First, I have to see to it that Colbey dies soon. Second, now that I'm certain, I have to warn Shadimar.*

Trilless rose, cursing the boundaries of Odin's Law that limited her magic. Though she had the power to contact Shadimar more quickly, Odin's system forced her to use the Wizards' messenger. She began the sequence that would summon the falcon, Swiftwing.

24 Frost Reaver

Sunlight glittered from the tended lawn of the Bellenet Fields, sparking from the wood and wire fence surrounding its jousting ring. As Colbey and Rache approached, the elder studied the small crowd of nobles which had gathered to watch one young warrior kill another. It included King Orlis, who perched on a black gelding surrounded by a dozen knights on white chargers with braided and ribboned manes. Each knight wore dress mail and a tabard. The front flap displayed Béarn's blue and tan bear, the back the orange circle and sword of Erythane. Every one clutched a spear-tipped pole arm, and a sword swung at every hip, cocked at the same angle.

Colbey searched for Shalfon Brignarsson and found the knight's apprentice standing aside, in earnest discussion with a knight on foot. The youth wore a mail shirt. He clutched a pike in one hand, its butt resting in the dirt, and the reins of his gray in the other. The knight's white charger grazed, untied, near the fence. A few peasants had gathered. Colbey recognized some of these as patrons who had attended the bar at the time of the challenge. Others, he presumed had seen their king and his entourage and followed out of curiosity.

Colbey frowned, hating the pomp. He viewed war as a normal part of life and death in glory as the ultimate goal, but he saw nothing admirable about two young warriors fighting to the death over the honor of a barmaid only one of them wanted. Killing was a necessity. A competent battle was an honor, not a game to be played in a ring, surrounded by gawking spectators eager for blood, so long as it was not their own.

As Colbey and Rache crossed the fields, looking out of place in their dusty travel garb, a knight approached on horseback. He offered Rache a mail shirt.

Rache frowned, refusing with a gesture of disdain. He spoke loud enough for all the men and women gathered to hear. 'Only cowards hide behind armor. And *I'm* no coward.' He tossed his tousled head defiantly.

Frowns scored the knights' faces. Shalfon took the bait. 'Are you questioning my courage, peasant?'

'No!' Rache shouted back. 'There's no questioning involved. It's clear enough for this peasant. You hide behind armor; I don't. Is that because you're too lazy to dodge? Or are you just afraid I'm quicker than you?'

Colbey watched the knights' faces flush the same shade of red, all a tone lighter than Shalfon's. Colbey placed his hand on Rache's shoulder. 'That's enough,' he whispered. He added good-naturedly, 'Did you inherit that tactless mouth from your father?'

Rache grinned. 'From my *torke* actually. A man crass enough to insult Wizards.'

Now Colbey smiled, too.

Shalfon and the knight exchanged a few words that Colbey could not hear, punctuated by angry gestures. The Renshai guessed that the knight was Shalfon's father, the one the youngster had called Brignar. Apparently, the father lost the argument, because he threw up his arms in a wild gesture of surrender. Shalfon began stripping off his mail, replacing it with a silk shirt and tabard.

While Shalfon dressed, a page appeared from the opposite side of the field, leading a small bay mare and using a pike like a walking stick. He approached Rache. 'Your horse and weapon, sir.' He passed the reins to Colbey and leaned the pole arm against the horse's side.

Colbey studied the horse. It carried more weight than he liked he could neither see nor feel its ribs. It stood shorter than Shalfon's mount, not as well muscled or exercised. Despite its inferiority, its conformation seemed sound, and it did not shy from the touch of the weapon.

Shalfon swung into his saddle, took his pike, and rode onto the field amid the crowd's applause.

Colbey cinched the girth a notch tighter around the bay. 'Patience,' he reminded Rache. 'Dodging blows is never cowardly, and sometimes it's necessary when you're measuring opponents. Parry until you get used to the weapon.'

Rache nodded, twitching with nervous energy as he climbed into the saddle. He lowered his head.

Colbey placed a hand on Rache's thigh, feeling the muscle loosen as Rache used the Renshai's mental techniques to steady his body and mind for battle.

'Quit stalling!' someone yelled. The peasants caught up the sentiment, questioning Rache's hesitation in a wild hubbub of encouragements and name-calling.

Colbey did not react, glad that Rache did not either. After a time, the youngster opened his eyes. Reluctantly, he passed his sword and belt to Colbey.

Colbey accepted the sword, giving Rache his new weapon. The

younger Renshai studied the length of smoothed wooden pole, tipped with its sharpened barb. Then, awkwardly balancing it against the saddle, Rache turned his horse toward the ring.

'May Rache, your namesake, guide your hand from Valhalla.' Colbey gave Rache's booted foot a last pat. 'Use his guidance. He can help more than anyone. He was resourceful and a master of many weapons. You know he taught your father.'

Rache nodded once, curtly. His right fist clutched the pike to his horse's withers, while his left guided the reins. He walked the animal into the ring.

Avoiding the crowd, Colbey found the only position along the rail, directly at Brignar's side. The peasants had given the knight a respectful berth, and his fellow knights perched high enough on their horses to see over the others' heads. In a strange, inexplicable way, Colbey felt a kinship with his enemy's father.

Both men stood in silence as their charges met midfield. Shalfon's voice wafted softly to Colbey.

'I'll teach you that vermin cannot question the nobility of the Knights of Erythane.'

'*Apprentice* knight,' Rache reminded. 'And us vermin do anything we wish.'

Shalfon tugged viciously at his reins. His horse whirled halfway around, then cantered to the opposite side of the ring. Rache rode in the other direction. They turned to face one another, the knight-in-training sitting straight in his saddle, Rache trying clumsily to maneuver his pike into the correct position that he and Colbey had discussed the previous night.

Shalfon waved, but he remained in place.

Rache shifted restlessly. At length, he repositioned his pike and nodded his readiness.

'Let the match begin!' King Orlis shouted.

The horses surged toward one another. The point of Shalfon's pike bounced toward Rache's chest, as if magically guided. As the gap between the horses narrowed, Colbey became fanatically focused on every one of Rache's movements. He could see Garn's son struggling for a more comfortable grip on his oversized weapon, and he willed Rache balance. Unconsciously, his hands clenched on the wooden edge of the fence.

The weapon points came together and overlapped. Rache swung out and over Shalfon's pike, then snapped it into a taut arc. Wood rolled across wood as the shafts slid harmlessly to one side, and the horses passed right shoulder to right shoulder.

Both horses turned for a second pass. Rache wiped his palms on his pants, and his horse's uncommanded lunge nearly unseated him. Yet, somehow, Rache managed to cling to charger and pike. A parry identical to the first took him safely past Shalfon again, and they prepared for the third run.

The audience hissed in annoyance. 'Are you going to fight?' someone yelled. 'Or are you going to dodge and hide?'

'Patience, Rache,' Colbey said, hoping the wind would carry his words to Rache, too far across the field to hear him.

Rache parried the third attack, and the combatants parted and turned for the next rush. Shalfon shook his head indignantly, his neat curls scarcely ruffled. A slight tensing of Rache's demeanor told Colbey that his student had come to a decision. A cold wind snatched a strand of the teen's hair, carrying it like a ghost. Sweat reddened his features. The set of Rache's jaw told Colbey that Rache had a strategy that went beyond gaining control of his monstrous spear.

As Rache, at last, lowered his pike to the level of Shalfon's, the jeering dispersed. The horses galloped toward the final bloody impact. Colbey's fingers tightened on the fence, running splinters beneath his nails.

A gap three times the length of the weapons still separated the two men when Rache made his move. His arm drew back, then snapped forward. He released the pike. It cleaved the air like an arrow from the bow of a giant. Yet Rache had no experience with hurling pikes, and the weapon was not balanced for throwing. It dropped too soon, its barb burying into the chest of Shalfon's gray. The charger managed a single frenzied bleat. It collapsed, and Rache's pike shattered beneath it.

As his mount crumpled, Shalfon sprang free. Rache dismounted, snatching a shard of his broken weapon, choosing one about the size of the staves that Garn had used to train him.

Colbey laughed, pleased by Rache's cleverness, though he heard a chorus of knights behind him calling a foul. He sincerely doubted the rules said anything about a warrior disarming himself, and now the strength Rache had inherited from his father seemed a godsend. 'Hack the fool down, Rache!' From habit, he shouted an encouragement meant for a different weapon, but it spurred the youngster on just the same.

Brignar glared. 'That's my son you called a fool, you scofflaw.'

Colbey did not even grace the speaker with his attention. His eyes remained locked on Rache. 'You only need to look at him.' He pointed at Shalfon, who was staggering, trying to control his pike without the horse's support. 'What do you call a man who wields a pike on foot?'

Rache bore in with his smaller, more manageable weapon. Shalfon retreated, desperately trying to keep the point of his pike between himself and Rache.

Brignar stepped closer, within easy sword reach, and his hand fell to his hilt. 'You speak of fools. Your *kadlach* hid from combat and wielded a pike with a bowman's cowardice.' He spat at Colbey's feet. 'I can see by your smirk that you support his ignobility. What else could I expect from a dirty half-breed with Northie blood? I presume he descends from a long line of cowards?'

Colbey frowned but did not directly answer, not even to correct the obvious misconception that he was Rache's father. Even this close, he did not see the knight as a threat, and he would keep his eyes on the battle until it finished. He watched as Rache slipped past Shalfon's pike, rendering the larger weapon useless.

Colbey smiled at the certain victory. 'Your son challenges a man half his age to battle with a weapon his opponent has never seen. That challenge required no courage. And Rache's accepting that challenge could hardly be considered cowardice.'

Rache delivered a blow that grounded Shalfon, then several more that took him to oblivion. Brignar made a high-pitched noise of horror. Colbey felt a wave of hopelessness radiate from the knight at his side. Then, the emotion exploded to black rage. 'My son is dead, and you would defile his name!'

Colbey felt certain that Rache had only knocked the apprentice unconscious, but he did not waste the words to argue. The events spoke for themselves.

'I shall have to call you out!'

Seeing the danger in letting Brignar choose the weapon, Colbey clung to semantics. 'Don't trouble yourself. I challenge you first. Sword. Now!'

Despite the questionable ethics of who had called the challenge, Brignar drew his sword and sprang. Before the blow fell, Colbey parried. His sword met Brignar's charge and redirected it. He read the knight's skill from that single lunge, and Colbey found it lacking. Either anger had befuddled the knight's style, or he needed a better instructor. 'Higher,' Colbey shouted. 'By Thor, aim for me, not the ground.'

With a cry of rage, Brignar swung again. This time, Colbey dodged, not bothering to take any of his openings. 'Take some weight off your front foot.'

'Stop it!' The knight snapped and howled like a berserk, while the Renshai parried and shortened death strokes with hawklike precision. Colbey felt cruel for the lesson, aware that the knight would see dishonor as worse than death. But Colbey had no wish to slaughter one of Sterrane's knights, no matter how little the nobleman valued his own life.

Brignar executed every lethal trick at his disposal, and Colbey met each with maddening ease. 'Stop playing with me!' Brignar said through gritted teeth. May Zera'im, god of honor, strike you down.' His sword leapt for Colbey's throat.

Colbey met the attack with enough force to drive the knight's arm and weapon nearly to his sheath. With one swift movement, Colbey caught his opponent's sword wrist and held it in his left hand. 'Your god of honor will lose his followers if, in peaceful times, he forces them to call out men who can slay them.' Colbey released the knight and sprang aside. Turning his back in a fearless gesture of scorn, he walked to Rache, who stood just outside the competition ring.

The knight's coiled rage remained tangible at Colbey's back, and he felt it boil into a frenzy. Then, suddenly, the emotion changed. A misplaced sensation trickled through, one that Colbey did not recognize until it strengthened. Even then, he had no name for it, only the realization that it reminded him of the aura of the demon called Flanner's bane. All pride and nobility evaporated from a man the West had trained to chivalry, leaving only a smoldering need for vengeance. Brignar sprang for Colbey's back.

And died on Colbey's sword.

The spectators fell silent, though whether in shock over Brignar's treachery or Colbey's slaying of an Erythanian knight, he did not know. He turned back to Rache. Though Colbey's own blade needed tending, he passed Rache his sword and belt, thinking it ruder to keep a warrior from his weapon. 'You did well.'

Rache said nothing, though he smiled while he fastened on his sword.

Colbey ignored the riot of thoughts and emotions radiating from the crowd, not bothering to focus on individuals. He thought it best to leave Erythane as soon as possible. 'Come on. The others are waiting. We've got a message to deliver and hostages to rescue.'

'Hold!' King Orlis shouted, his voice projecting enough authority to cut over the crowd.

Colbey tensed and spun, sword still unsheathed and trailing blood. Rache's hand went to his own hilt. Both were prepared to fight through all of Orlis' knights, if necessary.

Only one knight approached, riding toward the Renshai without his pike and with his sword sheathed. He drew up a polite distance in front of Colbey and Rache, though his gaze locked on the elder. 'You bested a Knight of Erythane in fair challenge.' He cleared his throat, tensing as if to glance back at the king for encouragement. Instead, he continued. 'By law, you've earned his title and the king's grace. King Orlis wishes to bestow the honor and present you with your steed, Frost Reaver.' He waved in the general direction of the jousting ring, though he seemed concerned about taking his eyes from Colbey.

The gesture fell wide, but Colbey guessed that the knight intended to indicate Brignar's white charger. Its neck arched daintily to a slim, triangular head. Its mane was braided with ribbons of blue and gold, and its pale eyes danced with a deviltry that matched Colbey's own. A broad chest promised endurance, and its short back and powerful hindquarters would make it unmatched for jumps and quick starts. Colbey knew horses well, and the ones the knights rode could not be matched for conformation and training. Colbey disliked only their color. Chosen for beauty and to draw attention, they would not hide well in woodlands, and the sun might burn their delicate skin. Still, Colbey had an eye for horses bested only by his eye for swords. Since childhood, he had daily spent hours on horseback, creating the mounted Renshai maneuvers. He found it almost impossible to refuse a creature so handsome.

The wild look in the knight's eyes completed the decision. To refuse such an honor would cause grave insult. 'Thank you.' Colbey cleaned and sheathed his sword, then headed toward the king, the knight riding at his side.

Rache trotted to catch up, incredulous. You're going to join these enemies?' he whispered. 'You're going to swear fealty to the King of Erythane?'

'They're not enemies, Rache.' Colbey replied at the same volume, continuing toward the clustered knights and their king. 'I see nothing wrong with choosing to ride a good war horse nor in swearing an alliance with a people who have been Renshai allies for the better part of a century. I'm going to vow to work in the best interests of the Westlands, and I'm already locked into that by a promise to Shadimar. If they try to keep me here or make me adhere to a rigid code that regulates means as well as ends, I'll refuse. Remember, too, that ultimate authority of Erythane's knights lies with Sterrane. Him, I trust.'

Colbey's answer seemed to satisfy Rache. And Colbey came forward to accept his charge.

The twelve spires of the castle of Béarn stretched triangular heads toward the clouds. Three days after the joust in Erythane, Colbey led his companions along the irregularly-cobbled streets, looking as gaunt and as gray as the towers he approached, and far more grim. His albino stallion marched with a solemn grace, its mane the color of its master's hair. Behind them plodded six mounted figures and a lightly-provisioned packhorse.

A half dozen Béarnian guards poked plumed heads and the points of crossbow bolts over the ramparts. Two men-at-arms stood behind the gates. 'Who seeks entrance to Béarn's castle?' one demanded coldly.

Colbey reined Frost Reaver up a hand's breadth before the gate, surprised that Sterrane allowed such formality. He had nearly expected the childlike monarch to greet them at the gate. 'One of the king's knights and several of his friends. We want an audience with Sterrane.'

The bolts did not move. The same soldier spoke again. Who are you?'

Colbey gathered breath to shout something sarcastic, but Mitrian cut in. 'I'm Mitrian, Santagithi's daughter, a close companion of your king. This is my family, my teacher, and the Eastern Wizard.' She indicated each in turn.

The sentries exchanged words briefly. Expecting them to be awed by, or at least civil to, the people who had restored Sterrane to his throne, Colbey was caught offguard by the guard's next question. 'What are your intentions?'

'She told you we're friends of Sterrane.' Colbey spoke each word slowly and distinctly, as if to an imbecile. 'Do you think we mustered an army of seven to raze the castle?' As Colbey realized his words were less ridiculous than his tone suggested, amusement replaced ire. 'I think you need one more bowman to fight a fair battle. You're short one to have an arrow for each of us.'

A light pressure in Colbey's mind claimed his attention. Instinctively, he forced the presence from his consciousness, but not before he identified source and motive. Shadimar had chosen this manner to silently protest Colbey's sarcasm. Though gentle and brief, the contact suggested reason for the rigid protocol that bordered on hostility. Accustomed to dealing with pirates, disease, and Rathelon's trickery, the guards had little patience for strangers. Curious about Shadimar's communication, the Renshai returned a mental finger of energy, touching without reading. His probe met scorn, but no resistance. Apparently, Shadimar either did not notice his presence or chose to ignore it.

The soldier tossed his helmed head. 'I'll ask the king if he can see you.' He turned toward the castle. His boots clicked across the moat bridge.

Colbey dismounted, ignoring the sentries on the ramparts as he worked kinks from his legs. Secodon leapt from Shadimar's mount and stood at Colbey's side like a sentinel.

Shortly, the guard returned, mouth pinched in annoyance, though he spoke politely. 'Please leave your horses here. They will be tended.' He addressed the man beside him, presumably making arrangements for the steeds, then again spoke to Colbey and his friends. 'Come with me, please.' He worked open one of the gates. The crossbows withdrew. The speaker forced his lips into a crooked smile of

welcome, though it seemed to pain him. 'You may bring the wolf.'
Stiffly, he turned, heading back toward the castle.

The guard led his charges through a courtyard of flower beds,
around which men, women, and children sat in happy clusters. He
ushered them across the moat to the iron doors of the castle. They
swept through these and into the well-kept hallways that had scarcely
changed in the twelve years since Mitrian, Garn, and Shadimar had
traipsed them. Although finery and wealth meant little to Colbey, who
valued less tangible treasures like ferocity and skill, he instinctively
memorized the corridors to the audience chamber.

The double doors opened abruptly, and a pair of guards led a
merchant from the courtroom. The gruff swordsman who had met
Colbey and his companions at the gate exchanged a few Béarnian
words with his peers, then pointed at the yellow carpet that spanned
the court. 'Come with me.' He started down the walkway, the party at
his heels.

Aside from the men-at-arms, who surrounded the armed party, the
crowd in the main court seemed small. Apparently few took interest in
the trivialities of the king's affairs. Sterrane sat, bare-headed, on his
throne at the end of the carpeting. Colbey studied the king, trying to
read his silence. He looked thinner than Colbey remembered, and his
face seemed less full. A line of wrinkles marred his cheeks, and
crow's-feet sat at the corners of his soft, dark eyes. Gray flecked his
black hair and beard. 'Greetings,' he said in perfect common. 'I hope
you fared well in your travels and that your business with Béarn is
handled to your satisfaction.'

Mitrian went rigid, and her welcoming smile faded. Sterrane's
obviously-rehearsed, ceremonial hospitality caught Colbey by
surprise, as did the king's competence with the Western trading
tongue.

Sterrane addressed a man at his right side, using the tongue of Béarn.
Unfamiliar with the language, Colbey caught only the name, Mar Lon.

The bard glanced from Shadimar to Garn to Mitrian. Then, he
examined the huge barbarian, the two young Renshai, and Colbey
more carefully. He replied to the king.

Sterrane made a broad gesture toward the double doors, saying
something with more authority than Colbey would have thought
possible from the childlike man.

Garn whispered an explanation. 'Sterrane's just sent everyone but
Mar Lon and Baran away.' He pointed out the bard and the captain of
the guard. 'Mar Lon likes us, but I think he's a bit nervous about you.'
He tapped Colbey's foot with his own.

Colbey did not miss a beat. 'Can't blame him. I know I'd worry
about a little, old man when there's a barbarian the size of a horse, a

Wizard, and three young Renshai in the room.' The jest fell short in the wake of Sterrane's unexpected stiltedness.

Mar Lon ushered guards and nobles from the courtroom.

Though he did not laugh, Garn did rise to the occasion. 'Yeah, I guess he really shouldn't worry about the helpless elderly demon prince.'

As the last of the courtiers exited, leaving only the king, their party, Mar Lon, and Baran, Mitrian knelt. Gradually, the others took her cue. Colbey felt like an idiot deferring to one he had so long seen as clownish simpleton, though he had recognized more in Sterrane than the others had.

Sterrane waved his guests to their feet immediately. He descended from his throne with Mar Lon and Baran hovering like anxious parents. Then, the stalwart monarch who had reclaimed the high kingdom of the Western world, who had ruled his country for twelve years, who had bested traitors and weathered two plagues, hurled himself into Mitrian's arms and wept. And she cried with him.

After what seemed like an eternity, Sterrane pulled free. With excitement, his formal correctness degenerated back into his familiar, halting version of the Western trading tongue. 'Me knew you live! Arduwyn owe two stories.'

Apparently, Sterrane's initial clarity had come from tedious rehearsal of the same welcome, not from any new facility with language. It took volumes of self-control for Colbey to keep from laughing at the massive king who was still a child in many ways. 'Ah! So the hunter lives, too. And he's here. We have business with him.'

Mitrian gave Colbey a sharp glare, apparently for raising issues before finishing greetings.

Sterrane seemed nonplussed. 'Baran, call feast. For guests, Arduwyn and family, and you two. No more.'

'Yes, sire,' Baran said, but he seemed reluctant to move. He smiled nervously at Garn and glanced at the Eastern Wizard.

Shadimar must have given a reassuring motion, because the guard seemed to relax. He paused fleetingly to whisper something to Garn, then trotted out through the doors.

Years seemed to melt from Sterrane. His head bobbed with all the eagerness of his youth. 'Good see.' He embraced Garn, then turned back to Mitrian. 'Always happy see you.' He smiled at the Wizard. 'Not always glad to see you. Glad now.' he knelt, catching Secodon into a huge hug. The wolf licked enthusiastically at the king's face. Sterrane laughed happily. Then, apparently realizing he had not finished his hellos, he turned to Colbey. At a loss for words, he greeted the old Renshai lamely. 'You . . . here.'

'Yes,' Colbey gave the only logical answer, then added facetiously and with a flourish, 'Colbey Calistinsson, Knight of Erythane, in your service, Sire.'

Mar Lon stared, obviously stunned. Whether his reaction came from Colbey's title or the recognition of his name, the Renshai did not try to guess.

Deeper concern blunted Sterrane's reaction to the news. '*My* service?' Tears still streamed from his eyes, but now his grin wilted. He looked impossibly grim, an adult expression on his huge-eyed face. 'Me so sorry. So sorry. Me want help Santagithi –'

Colbey cut in, wanting to spare Sterrane, though he knew it was Mitrian's position. 'No need for apologies, Sterrane. Santagithi knew, without a moment's questioning, that if you could have sent troops, you would have. He died in the last battle. A hero. He never doubted your intentions, and neither have we.'

Mitrian nodded vigorous agreement. 'We love you, Sterrane. You know that. I only wish we could have helped you.'

Once again realizing he had not completed amenities, Sterrane pointed at Korgar, Tannin, and Rache. Apparently even more flustered, he did not mince words. 'Who these?'

Garn chuckled, placing an arm across Rache's broad shoulders. 'What's the matter, Sterrane. You don't recognize my baby?'

'Baby?' Sterrane studied Rache with astonishment. 'Baby Rache? Have Garn eyes. Have Garn . . . ' Apparently missing the word, he ran both hands from his own chest to past his sides to indicate musculature. He added good-naturedly, 'Have nothing else Garn's. Lucky. Pretty. Like mama.'

'Thank you,' Mitrian said.

'Yes. Thank you,' Garn said, feigning offense.

Determined to finally finish the introductions, Sterrane pointed at Tannin. 'This *friend* Northman?'

'Tannin Randilsson,' the young man introduced himself. 'I'm a Westlander; not a Northman, Sire.'

'What town?'

'No town, Sire,' Tannin admitted, growing uncomfortable. He glanced at Colbey.

There was no need to hide information from Sterrane. Colbey nodded his encouragement.

'I'm from the Fields of Wrath, Sire.'

'West Renshai.' Sterrane took Mitrian's hand in one of his and Rache's in the other.

Tannin's pale eyes widened. 'You know, Sire . . . but . . . '

'Me king, you know. Not stupid. Know all kingdom. You allies.' Sterrane turned his attention to Korgar.

The barbarian stared back, unblinking. He clutched his spear in one hand and rested his other palm on his 'genuine Renshai sword.'

'Korgar,' Mitrian said. 'He's a barbarian. He only speaks a few words of our language.'

Garn could not resist adding, 'Even worse than you.'

The ex-gladiator earned a stony glare from Shadimar.

A deep, metallic knock rang through the room, and the doors swung open. Arduwyn strode through, flanked by Bel and a young woman Colbey did not recognize. The slight, flame-haired archer seemed not to have changed, except that his eyepatch had been replaced by one of silk; but the years had placed their burden on Bel. Her dark hair was frosted gray, she had put on weight, and her withered breasts sagged.

Arduwyn ran to Mitrian and Garn, while Bel embraced Rache, recognizing him without need for explanation. 'Kinesthe. My little Kinesthe.'

Though her performance touched Colbey, the word 'little' to describe Rache made him smile.

For his part, Rache seemed scarcely to notice Bel's attention. He stared over her shoulder at the third member of the trio. Colbey could see that Tannin's gaze had locked on the girl as well. She was tall and restrained, younger than either of the pair who studied her. Strawberry blonde hair fell to her waist. Long, dark lashes graced a small nose. From the look on the younger Renshai's faces, Colbey guessed that they heard none of the introductions until Arduwyn coaxed the girl forward. 'This is my daughter, Sylva.'

Colbey counted years, guessing this must be the baby in the womb when he and Santagithi had come to Pudar to pick up Rache.

'She's beautiful,' Mitrian said. 'How are the other three?'

Bel replied. 'Jani, the oldest, lives in town with her husband.' Her eyes misted, and she could not go on.

Arduwyn cringed, obviously upset by Bel's suffering. He placed an arm around her. 'I'm afraid we lost Effer and Rusha to illness.'

Mitrian spoke trite sympathies that only made the situation seem more awkward to Colbey. To his relief, the doors opened, and a well-dressed staff carried in a table and enough chairs for everyone present.

'We eat,' Sterrane said.

One arm around his wife, the other on his daughter's arm, Arduwyn led his family to the table. Rache sprinted across the room to claim the seat beside Sylva. One step ahead, Tannin pulled out the chair to seat himself, and Rache crashed to the floor.

Every eye, including Sylva's, turned toward him.

Rache sprang to his feet, desperately trying to salvage his dignity. 'Your floor's wet,' he mumbled, glowering at his companion. Seeing that Bel had already sat in the chair to Sylva's left, and Arduwyn had settled next to his wife, Rache circled the table, taking a seat directly across from the center of his interest.

Sterrane left an empty chair between himself and Arduwyn, that Baran took, and Mar Lon sat at the king's opposite hand. Aware his presence unsettled the bard, Colbey intentionally took a seat beside him. Already, he had tired of amenities, eager to discuss the hostages, and even the boys' antics for Sylva's attention ceased to amuse him. Korgar sat by Colbey, Shadimar beside the barbarian, and Mitrian and Garn took the last two seats, between Tannin and the Eastern Wizard. As usual, Secodon slipped beneath the table.

As a pair of Béarnides set a bowl of soup before each of the diners, Mitrian continued to make polite conversation. 'I thought you had a wife, too, Sterrane. Won't she join us?'

Sterrane swallowed a mouthful of soup and shook his head. 'One come, all want come.'

Mitrian sat, perplexed.

Colbey laughed. 'How many wives do you have?'

The king shrugged. 'Twelve. thirteen. Lots children.' He smiled happily at his last statement. 'Lots wonderful children. What happen you? How you come here?' Sterrane steered his last query to Colbey, 'You really knight?'

'Yes,' Colbey admitted, surprised that Sterrane had not already received a message from Erythane regarding the matter. Surely, King Orlis kept the high king abreast of his knights. 'Due to a truly unusual set of circumstances.' He did not bother to explain further and left the remainder of Sterrane's questions to his companions.

When no one else took the king's offer, Mitrian told their tale as they ate. She spoke with an insight occasionally checked by horrified reluctance, particularly when she talked of Santagithi's and Episte's deaths and the state in which they had discovered Colbey at Shadimar's ruins. When she finished, well into the meal, she seemed calmer for the telling.

A respectful silence followed in the wake of Mitrian's story. Though he knew it was rude, Colbey took this moment to raise their dilemma. 'Arduwyn, we need a guide who knows the forests of Erythane. Are you for hire?'

'I'll do what I can to help friends.' The little archer seemed pleased by Colbey's request. 'I know those forests as well as a man can.'

Abruptly, Bel shoved her chair from the table. 'Excuse me.' She swept down the gold carpet and out the huge portals before anyone thought to stop her.

There was no overt hostility in her words or actions, but Colbey perceived a rage that belied her apparent calm.

Mitrian must have sensed something, too, because she rose. 'Excuse me,' she echoed softly and chased after Bel.

25 Wolf Point

When Mitrian burst through the great doors of Béarn's courtroom, she met a cluster of guards with worried faces milling in the hallway. Some watched her curiously, others started down the corridor that Bel had presumably taken. No one tried to stop Mitrian, and for that she was grateful. She ran in the indicated direction. Turning a corner, she spotted Bel. Slowing to a fast walk, Mitrian pulled up beside her.

'Go away.' Bel continued striding through the grand hallway.

'Let's talk.' Mitrian chose a door at random. Opening it, she ushered Bel into a sparsely-furnished single room. It contained only a bed, a cedar chest, and a desk. Currently, a man sat, writing, at the desk. Dressed in tailored linens with gold trim, he stared at the intruders.

'Get out.' Mitrian jerked a hand toward the door. She glared directly at the Béarnide.

'What?' the man said. The pen fell from his fingers, clattering to the desktop.

'Get out. We need to talk.' Mitrian added in afterthought, 'Please.'

Bel fidgeted, looking around Mitrian toward the open door.

The man rose, studied the women, then perched on the edge of his chair. 'This is my room.'

'Leave!' screamed Mitrian.

Grumbling something unintelligible in Béarnese, the man escaped his room. Mitrian stepped aside to let him leave, then blocked Bel's escape again.

Bel dropped into the vacated chair. 'I hate you.'

Mitrian closed the door. 'I thought we were friends.'

'We're not.' Bel glared sharply. 'Friends wouldn't do what you did to me.'

'I don't understand.' Mitrian tried to think of something she might have said or done to offend Bel. She had introduced all of her companions, complimented Bel's daughter, and told her story with all of the sensitivity she could muster. 'What did I do?'

Bel slammed a fist to the desktop, sending the man's papers wafting. The pen rolled to the floor. 'For twelve years, Arduwyn has stayed by my side and with his child, without you to drag him into danger.'

Bel's accusations raised Mitrian's ire, and she did not consider her words carefully. 'Ardy never needed dragging.'

Bel looked away, tracing the edge of the desk with a finger. 'I know. He still wanders into the woods, but he's always home at night, and he usually takes Sylva with him.' Her gaze met Mitrian's accusingly, then she turned away. 'He's taught her to hunt. Game, not men.' She buried her face in her arms on the desktop.

Mitrian collected the fallen pen and parchments and returned them to the desktop. 'We only want him as a guide for a few days. We'll send him home. We could have used him to help get Sterrane's kingdom back; but we sent him home after the war, didn't we?'

Bel's face flared crimson, and she raised it to confront Mitrian. 'You returned him without an eye. Will he come back blind this time? Crippled? Or maybe you won't return him at all.'

'Bel!' Mitrian tried to cut through the nonsense, but Bel's real concern came through next.

'Did you see how excited he looked? How do I know the forest of his childhood won't offer him more than I can?'

Mitrian planted both hands on the desk, rage stripped from her by the root of Bel's concern. 'If the forest could take him from you, he would have left long ago?'

Bel's dark eyes went ugly with hatred. 'Arduwyn is a hunter, not a soldier. He can't fight Northmen.' She added spitefully, 'And keep your *kadlach* away from my daughter.'

The insult caught Mitrian by surprise. 'I thought you liked Rache.'

'I loved the boy when he was Kinesthe. I won't subject Sylva to the tortures I suffered because my man wandered. Do you know what it's like to love a man who leaves you with nothing, not even the promise of a safe return? Do you know what it's like wondering if he's alive or dead or if he just decided he loves the forest more?' Tears welled in her eyes. 'Have you ever waited alone with three children and no money to feed them, hoping desperately your man will return to save you from starvation, ridicule, and strangers who would beat and rob or rape you?'

There was a long silence.

Mitrian sat on the corner of the desk. 'Sylva could travel with her man, as could you, Bel. My man *is* a wanderer, but I chose to wander with him.'

'And you can.' Bel spat out her words like a bit of sour fruit. 'You're every bit as savage, and you use a sword. My daughter or I would die. Keep your son and that brutish-looking Northman away from Sylva. And I'm not going to let you take Arduwyn, either.'

Mitrian had tired of the insults, her patience gone. 'We need

Arduwyn. And whether he comes or not is his decision.'

'Then I'll have to help him make that decision.' Bel rose daintily, though her tone and words did not match the delicacy of her action. 'And you can go to Hel!' Dodging past Mitrian, she stormed out the door.

After the feast in Béarn's great hall, Garn followed Baran through the castle's gaudy corridors in silence. From the captain's first troubled, knowing glance, Garn had known the Béarnide wished to speak wih him. The whispered promise of a meeting while in Sterrane's court had only confirmed it. Whatever Baran's concern, it unnerved him; and Garn could not fathom a topic better discussed with himself than with Mar Lon, Sterrane, Shadimar, or Colbey.

Baran did not take Garn far. Only a few rooms down from the main courtroom, he halted at a half-opened door, ushering Garn through before him.

Garn stepped into a study, its four walls enveloped by a continuous fresco of two regal, richly-armored men riding white horses and jousting with pikes. A crowd surrounded the combatants. Some shouted or waved their arms encouragingly. Others leaned over a wood and wire fence, enthralled. One young woman kept her eyes closed, her fists cocked and clenched before her, as if horrified by the spectacle. A nearby child crouched, back partially turned, more intrigued by gathering stones than watching the battle. Though bloodless, stylized, and garishly colorful, the scene brought vague reminders of the gladiator pit, and Garn turned his attention to the room's furnishings instead. A padded seat filled the ledge of an arching window; its thick glass magnified his view of the courtyard below. A desk occupied a corner near the door, an unlit lantern on its surface, a matching chair turned askew to face the window seat. On the desk's legs and trim, carved flowers entwined, and a similar pattern decorated the arms and back slats of the chair.

Baran followed Garn inside, pressing the door closed behind him until it clicked fully into place. He waved toward the seats.

Garn chose the window seat. Curiosity kept him perched on its edge.

Baran folded one leg onto the desk chair, but he did not sit. Instead, he pulled a creased piece of parchment from his tunic pocket and tossed it into Garn's lap. 'Look at this.'

Obligingly, Garn opened the parchment. Ink strokes scored the surface in straight, regular lines from top to bottom. Illiterate, Garn stared at the note, saying nothing.

'What do you think?' Baran leaned forward, obviously eager for Garn's opinion.

Lacking a better reply, Garn handed the message back. 'Neat penmanship.'

'Neat penmanship?' Baran's eyes widened, and all of the wrinkles disappeared from his forehead. 'Didn't you . . . ?' Apparently, the significance of Garn's answer dawned on him, and he explained without further questioning. 'It's from the leader of the Erythanian knights. It talks about Brignar's death and Colbey's instatement.'

Garn nodded politely. Colbey had told them the story, and it hardly seemed like a matter to send the Béarnian captain of the guards into a clandestine meeting with a foreign soldier. The overall strangeness of Baran's behavior struck Garn now. From Sterrane's and Mar Lon's reactions to Colbey's teasing, neither had read this message, though Baran must have received it before their arrival in the court. Piqued by the oddity, Garn guessed at the only possible reason. 'There's something else in that note. Isn't there?'

Surprised by Garn's insight, Baran dropped into his chair. He passed the parchment from hand to hand, turning it in circles as he did so, obviously uncomfortable. 'They've got Rathelon in custody. They want to extradite him to Béarn.'

That sounded like wonderful news to Garn, and he could not fathom Baran's problem.' Great! Caught at last.' The most recent rumors had revealed most of Rathelon's supporters imprisoned, dead, or driven away. True to the terms of his banishment, Rathelon had not directly set foot on Béarnese soil for the last twelve years. 'Your troubles with him are finally over.'

Baran seemed not to hear Garn's reply. 'There was a battle. Archers took down all of Rathelon's men. But they captured him alive.'

The seriousness of Baran's tone sobered Garn, and he looked for the flaw in reasoning that had allowed him to miss the captain's concern. 'What happens now?'

'Rathelon's ours to bring to trial in Béarn.'

Garn nodded in understanding, still positive he was overlooking something. 'Isn't that good news?'

Baran slid his leg from beneath his buttocks and sat in the chair properly. Continuously, he refolded and unfolded the parchment. 'Knowing the king of Béarn, how do you think he'll sentence his cousin?'

'Knowing Sterrane . . .' Garn repeated as he considered. ' . . . surely he'd . . .' When the answer did not come at once, his brow furrowed, and he dropped the thread of his sentence.

'I've seen traitors and war criminals paraded before the king's justice for twelve years now. No matter the crime, I've yet to see Sterrane sentence one to death.'

Garn finished the thought. 'And you think that's the sentence

Rathelon should get?'

Baran stiffened suddenly, as if he feared he had chosen his confidant wrongly. 'Don't you?'

'Hel, I told you that the first time. You're the one who didn't want to second-guess the king.'

'Right.' Apparently reminded of the coronation, Baran emitted a short, tight-lipped laugh that seemed more like a grunt.

A horrible idea came to Garn. 'You don't think Sterrane would banish Rathelon again? Do you? Wouldn't that just start this whole mess over again?'

'Imprisonment, more likely.' Baran sighed, saying nothing more.

Garn still did not understand why the captain of Béarn had confided in him. He waited, certain that, given time, Baran would reveal his motives.

Baran returned the note to his pocket. For some time, he fidgeted in silence. His obvious pain made Garn cringe in sympathy, but he did not yet have enough information to make the captain's lot easier.

At length, Baran broke the silence with a question so soft Garn all but missed it. 'I do have to take this note to the king. Don't I?' His gaze jumped guiltily to Garn.

Now Garn paused, fighting the ignorance that made a coherent answer impossible. Surely, Baran was not suggesting leaving Rathelon in Erythane's custody. Stories about social custom gave him no reason to picture Erythane's dungeon as any nastier or more secure than Béarn's own. 'I don't know,' he said carefully. 'What are the other options?'

Baran seemed to be talking to himself, rocking in time to the pattern of his speech. 'If only we could have met in combat. Wartime law would have given us the right to kill him.' Suddenly, Baran's fist crashed to the desktop. 'Why? Why, in Dakoi's deepest pit, did they have to catch him alive?' He pounded the desk again. 'Rathelon practically built this prison. If anyone could escape it, he could; and more people will die in the name of the king's mercy.'

Baran bent his fingers into claws, clapping his head between his hands. 'I love my king, Garn. I can't think of any man in the world I'd rather serve. I especially admire his justice. No matter how cautiously the law is worded, if a kingdom institutes death as punishment, some innocent will eventually die. But, damn it, Garn, Rathelon deserves to die. For the good of the king and his people, the traitor *has* to die.' He looked up, running his fingers across his face, then dropping his hands to his sides. 'What happens when one of my guards tries to feed Rathelon, and Morhane's bastard kills him? That's an innocent life lost, too. That alone is enough to justify the execution, even without the added danger of having Rathelon loose in Béarn. Once we haul him here, we negate his banishment, and he becomes free to terrorize or kill the king, his children, and my men.'

Garn retreated from Baran's tirade. 'You don't have to justify Rathelon's death to me. Given the chance, I'd do it with my own hands.' His lips bent into an evil smile. 'I believe some guard captain said the same thing in a drunken stupor at a king's coronation.'

Baran managed an awkward grin.

'What if you and I went to collect Rathelon and he tried to escape? If he happened to die in the process of regaining control . . . ?' Garn let the possibility hang, excited by the prospect of facing off with Rathelon at last. It had seemed predestined since his first encounter with the sneering Béarnide.

Baran shuffled his feet on the stone floor. 'It would have to be a legitimate attempt. And we'd have to avoid harming him if at all possible.' He sighed. 'The worst part of the whole thing is, if someone else tried to hurt him while he was in our custody, we'd have to protect him.'

Garn clung to his original scenario. 'What if he attacked you? Or someone you brought with you?'

'We'd have the right to defend ourselves. Whatever it took.'

'Then take me with you.'

'What?'

'Take me with you. Don't tell me it's not what you want. You and I can retrieve Rathelon.' Garn recalled Rathelon's final threat at the castle gates, aware that only he and Baran had heard it. 'I don't doubt for a moment that, if I go, Rathelon will give us trouble. And we'll need to defend against him.'

'Don't you and your friends have another problem to deal with?'

'Yes,' Garn admitted. 'But they've got everyone they need, I think. Sterrane offered Colbey as many Béarnian soldiers as he wanted.'

'I also heard Colbey refuse that offer. He said he thought stealth would prove more important than numbers.'

Garn believed Colbey more likely turned down the assistance from concern for shorting Sterrane's defenses and from pride. 'I'm just saying that, if Colbey decides he needs someone strong along, I'm easy enough to replace.'

Baran took a deep breath, but the words he gathered never came. Apparently, he still fought an internal battle.

Believing his plan foolproof as well as brilliant, Garn pressed. 'What's wrong?'

'I just can't help feeling dishonorable.'

'Why?'

'It's the king's decision. I shouldn't be out there goading a prisoner to pass sentence on himself.'

'Does the note say you have to tell Sterrane?'

'No.'

'Does it say you can't bring along a man Rathelon hates?'

'Well, no. But I think those things are implied.'

'Look, Baran.' Recalling his first meeting with Mar Lon, Garn drew on the deep-seated religious beliefs that most men held. He knew from experience that even the most logical tended to credit gods with everything unexplained or fortuitous. 'It's out of our hands. It's fate. Think about it. Rathelon gets captured. Within days, I show up in Béarn. Do you think that's coincidence? How can you doubt that some higher power arranged for this to happen?' More probably, Rathelon had gotten word that Garn had returned to the area and the Béarnide had come hunting him. Or, perhaps, the knights had grown more vigilant following the death of one of their own.

Baran's brow furrowed as he considered an argument that seemed indisputable. 'All right,' he said at last. 'You make arrangements to meet back with your friends afterward, and I'll take you to Erythane. We leave in the morning.' He rose.

Garn stood also, clamping a hand to Baran's shoulder. 'You're a good captain, Baran Bardersson.'

Baran thumped Garn's arm in return. 'That, my friend, remains to be seen.'

That night, Arduwyn paced the master bedroom of the three-room castle quarters he shared with Bel and Sylva. His wife lay, curled like a fetus on the coverlet of their bed, her body shuddering in rhythm to her tears. The silver streaks through the long, brown hair he loved only made her more attractive, reminding him of the years of pleasure they had shared. Her plump curves always seemed stalwart and healthy. Her round face and dark, liquid eyes had become so familiar, they defined love. Her every sob cut him like a knife.

'Bel.' Arduwyn stopped his pacing to sit on the edge of the bed. He smoothed strands of hair from her face, revealing a tanned cheek.

Bel turned her head, regarding Arduwyn through the opening he had created in her curtain of hair. 'Please don't go. Please.' One hand closed over his wiry arm, clutching with a desperation that tore through Arduwyn's conscience.

'Bel.' Arduwyn slipped his hands beneath Bel's arms, pulling her into an embrace. Wrenched by her misery, he held her close. 'I'll only be gone a few days. Don't make this into more than it is. You know I love you.'

'No!' Bel sobbed into Arduwyn's chest. 'Don't go! Something bad's going to happen. I just know it.'

Arduwyn shivered, making a religious gesture to ward away evil with a hand looped beneath her armpit. 'Don't say things like that. Everything will be fine. I'll stand behind the swordsman if they come to war, and I'm not too proud to run.' He kissed the top of her head, then her brow. 'Innocent lives depend on my forest knowledge. Garn, Mitrian, and Colbey have kept me safe in the past. And they're friends. How can I not do everything in my power to help them?'

'Because!' Bel pulled away. Her voice went cold, raw from crying. 'You have obligations here. They're your friends? What am I, then? Don't my needs matter?'

Arduwyn reached for Bel again, but she evaded him. Cut to the heart, he let his hands fall to the coverlet. 'Of course your needs matter. More than anything. But Sterrane's here. And a whole host of courtiers and servants. You can spare me for a few days.'

'I can spare you for a few days. I can't spare you forever.' Bel moved further, arms crossed over her ample bosom. 'Garn's not your friend. I remember a day when he all but killed you for no reason.'

Arduwyn cringed, recalling the time that Garn had gone into a wild, uncontrollable rage at the mention of Rache's name, pounding him nearly to oblivion before Sterrane intervened.

Bel continued, 'You rescued Mitrian once already. You owe her nothing. And I don't want you under the command of the Death-seeker. He seemed as crazy as they say he is the first time I met him. Now that I've seen him again, I'm sure he's cruel and violent as well.'

Arduwyn said nothing, knowing that most of Bel's impression stemmed from rumor, though it held some truth. He pulled at his hands, searching for the words he needed. Years behind a merchant's table, selling wares to reluctant patrons, had made him a convincing speaker. Yet the strength of his love for Bel, even after so many years, still flustered him. His heart hammered into him the need to make her happy; but, this time, his devotion felt torn. His loyalty to his friends meant too much to abandon, even for Bel's comfort, but he could not find the argument to make her understand.

'You promised me, Arduwyn. You said you'd never go away again.'

'Yes, I said that.' Arduwyn spoke, barely above a whisper. He placed a hand on Bel's, tracing the loose skin around her fingers. 'And I meant it. But I need you to free me from that vow.' He met her tear-blurred gaze, trying to keep his expression as desperately earnest as her own. 'Whatever you think of Colbey, the Northmen's three hostages are blameless. How can I just leave them?'

'They're strangers,' Bel said, her assessment as cold as anything Arduwyn could remember ever having heard from Colbey.

'That doesn't matter. What if the Northmen had Sylva? What if the only people who could save her refused because they didn't know her?'

Bel looked away. 'That's not the same thing.'

But it was. Arduwyn knew that either Bel realized that and chose to argue anyway or else she refused to see the comparison. In either case, his insistence in that vein would accomplish nothing. 'Bel, innocent lives are at stake, including that of an unborn baby. My friends need me. My vow to you means everything, but so do my vows to my friends and to the Westlands. I'm going. And this discussion is over.'

It was the first time Arduwyn could remember feeling strongly enough about anything to override Bel's protests; but, in his mind, he had no choice.

Bel whirled to face Arduwyn, rage darkening her eyes. 'How long will you be gone?'

Arduwyn guessed. 'Six, maybe seven days.'

'If you don't return by the twelfth day of the month of bright stars . . . ' Bel's voice dropped to a whisper. ' . . . I'll kill myself.'

'What!' Bel's words staggered Arduwyn, and he quickly did the math. She had given him exactly seven days. He caught both of her wrists. 'No! Don't talk insane, and don't torture me. I love you. I'll be home as quickly as I can. Isn't my word enough?'

'Apparently not.' Bel glared, not a hint of triumph or amusement sliding through the seriousness of her expression, no hint of bluff. 'Your promise to stay meant little enough to you.'

'Bel,' Arduwyn started. 'That's not – '

Bel shook free of his hold. 'See that you're home by the twelfth.'

'Things unforeseen could delay us.' Arduwyn felt the contents of his stomach clutch and roll. Surely, Bel would not carry out such a threat. *Or would she?* It was a chance he dared not take. 'You can't do this. You wouldn't . . . '

'Do you love me?' Bel asked. 'And your daughter?'

Finally, Arduwyn had found a question he could answer without need for thought or wars of conscience. 'More than anything. You know that.'

'Then see to it you return in time.'

The forest wonders of the Wolf Point Woods had gladdened Arduwyn since his childhood: crisp air, the crackle and flash of passing animals, leaves orange, red, and ocher splashed on a background of greenery. Daily, his father had shown him the sights and laws of nature, instilling a love and desire that he had pursued long after his father's death. The woodlands beckoned, promising a life without responsibility or judgment, a world where the strongest and cleverest survived, without the need for the emotional games only people could invent or play.

This day, as on the last two, Arduwyn brushed past trees, seeing only the necessary, passing the panoramas, the bird choruses, and the game trails with the fleeting, ephemeral notice of a man in a dream. The hunter had scarcely spoken since joining the party. When he did, he used short phrases and only addressed Mitrian. Bel's threat weighted his soul like an iron wall, barring him from all gladness.

Arduwyn chose to walk, even through the stream, while the others rode. He would not miss a single track or sign, nothing that might cause him to choose even one step wrongly. *Three days gone.* Arduwyn shook water from his boots and stared into the woodlands east of Erythane. *I'll make it home in time.* His gaze fell on Colbey and the white beacon that was his horse. Arduwyn shuddered. Trouble seemed to follow the old Renshai, even when he did not spark it purposely, and Arduwyn could not spare more than a single day at Wolf Point.

Brush crackled at the forest's edge. Arduwyn tensed, then recognized Korgar emerging from the brush, Shadimar's wolf at his side. The barbarian plucked at Colbey's sleeve, obviously agitated. '*Anem.*' He made a brisk gesture at Arduwyn's quiver. 'Stick spears.'

'Northmen,' Colbey explained. 'I think he's saying they're archers.'

Arduwyn froze, alarmed. Of them all, only he truly understood the deadliness of even a lone archer in woodlands.

Apparently, Korgar had not finished. He continued to tug at Colbey's sleeve. 'Trees. Up.' Releasing Colbey, he jabbed the end of the spear toward the interlace of branches overhead. '*Anem.*' He flashed his hands several times to indicate numbers.

Arduwyn guessed that either the barbarian thought the group should hide from the archers in the trees or the archers were waiting in the trees to ambush them.

More accustomed to conversing with Korgar, Colbey apparently chose the latter possibility. In the past, the barbarian had always just informed, never trying to suggest courses of action. The Renshai swore. 'I expected something like this. They want all of us dead.'

Arduwyn bit his lip, saying nothing.

'What do we do?' Mitrian asked.

No answer came. For once, not even the great sword master or the Eastern Wizard could offer a solution, to Arduwyn's surprise. For his own part, he knew precisely what to do, though he dreaded the idea. He knelt, dangling his fingers in the wind-cooled waters of the stream he had just crossed. Finding no solace from within or without, he chose to speak his plan aloud.

Hours later, Arduwyn paced along the stream, his boots crushing the charred remains of the once healthy copse that would now serve as a firebreak. As dark as the destruction around him, his single eye beseeched the fickle wind sprites to continue flowing southward, toward the stream. He dared not call upon the god of hunters, feeling like a traitor. He had lit the fire, his hand shaking. The sudden flare of the flames exploded through his memory repeatedly, each time bringing a deserved pain. He had watched the fire follow the winds, consuming all in its path until it died in the stream. All that remained to haunt his conscience was the barren patch with nothing left to burn, a safety zone from the larger fire that Colbey and Rache were setting.

The acrid reek of smoke drifted to Arduwyn, reminding him of his own role in the slaughter. Soon, smaller fires would become an all-consuming red hell that would leave the Northern archers three choices: to die in the smoke and heat, to run to the burnt copse by the stream where Mitrian and Tannin waited with readied swords, or to hide in the Wolf Point cave, where Valr Kirin surely held his captives. Arduwyn could not imagine the archers choosing any but the last course. He only hoped the denizens of the woodlands would find the stream.

Shadimar watched in silence. At his master's side, Secodon snuffled the breeze, whining.

Arduwyn knelt, wrapped his arms around the wolf, and buried his face in the furry ruff. He tried to console himself by clinging to the one animal he knew he could save. *It's only a small piece of the forest.* That, alone, did not bother Arduwyn. Even nature found ways to destroy masses of ancient trees and matted underbrush to make way for new growth. But Arduwyn knew how swiftly fire could escape control. So he prayed to Weese, the Western god of winds, that his direction would not change; mental apologies twined through Arduwyn's supplications. The imagined death screams of sylvan spirits and animal orphans weighed as heavily on Arduwyn as Bel's threat.

Hoofbeats interrupted Arduwyn's prayer. He stood, releasing the wolf with a nervous pat intended to soothe. Colbey's war-horse galloped toward archer, wolf, and Wizard. A flaming brand still graced the hand of its aged rider. Behind Frost Reaver came a darker steed, bearing Rache. Beyond them, a forest fire raged, a glorious red monstrosity, trailing smoke. The wind continued to blow southward, and Arduwyn whispered his thankfulness a thousand times in an instant.

'I believe the wind will hold,' Colbey addressed Arduwyn directly, snuffing his torch. Although the Renshai obviously meant the words as a reassurance, Arduwyn knew a deep shiver of fear that seemed to penetrate to his marrow. The elder Renshai knew Arduwyn's thoughts too often for coincidence. There were many things about his past and attitudes he would prefer Colbey did not know, including a fear of and deeply-etched bitterness against Renshai that did not extend to

Mitrian and Rache.

'We'll need to wait until dawn,' Colbey continued, as if oblivious to Arduwyn's discomfort. 'We need to let the fire die and the ground cool. I only hope our hunter friend is right about the size and ventilation of that cave, or we may have killed our allies with our enemies.'

In that matter, at least, Arduwyn harbored no doubts, though he saw Tannin shudder. They all stretched out in the burnt copse. No one spoke, but no one slept.

Dawn came with a maddening slowness born of Arduwyn's anxiety. He shaded his eyes from the sun to gaze upon the ruins of the Wolf Point forest. The underbrush had disappeared, leaving only black stubble. Some trees stood, dark and skeletal against the awakening sky, their bark burned and blistered. Others lay, twisted and broken on the dirt, mute testimony to the crime Arduwyn and his friends had inflicted. Night had driven away much of the heat, but smoke still smoldered amid the ruins. The forest stretched before him like some near-barren waste of hell.

All around Arduwyn, the remainder of the party stirred and stared. The little hunter stared into the distance. From between the crippled trees, he could clearly see the line of stone which men called the Wolf Point, its central area molded into the lupine shape that had given the formation its name. The cave mouth seemed to glare at him, a black hole in stone that seemed more alive than the missing plant and animal life around it.

'What do we do now?' Tannin said, his voice thin and strained. He wiped his hands on his breeks repeatedly.

'Parlay.' Colbey's gaze followed Arduwyn's to the Wolf Point. 'You and I.' He turned his attention to the red-haired Erythanian. 'Arduwyn, we'll need you, too. Slip into bow range.'

Arduwyn glanced up quickly. 'I joined only as a guide. I promised Bel. And there's no cover.' He gestured at the charred expanse of forest.

Colbey's two eyes met Arduwyn's one. The Renshai opened his mouth to speak, closed it with a toss of his head, and motioned to Tannin. 'Fine. Forget him. We're on our own.'

Arduwyn lowered his head, guilt stabbing. He dared not look at Mitrian or Shadimar. Torn between concern for his friends and for Bel, he scanned the rubble and rock for a larger copse of burnt vegetation behind which he could hide.

Colbey and Tannin headed across wasteland, their boots smashing the pointed remains of weeds.

Finding a pocket where two deadfalls had crossed, protecting a tiny patch of undergrowth, Arduwyn called after them. 'Wait! I'll do what I can.'

'Thank you.' Colbey said, without turning. While he and Tannin approached in plain sight, Arduwyn crept to his hiding space and slipped between the piled trunks that still trailed smoke. It felt warm, but not uncomfortably so.

Colbey and Tannin moved to a position that kept them central, yet they did not come as close to the cave as Arduwyn. They remained beyond bow shot of the Northern archers. 'Northmen,' Tannin shouted.

A long silence followed.

Arduwyn eased his bow into his hands, resting a blue and gold fletched arrow against its string.

'Northmen!' Tannin repeated, louder.

A high, steady voice issued from the stone. 'Renshai!'

Tannin glanced at Colbey, apparently for guidance. When Colbey continued to stare at the cave, Tannin cleared his throat and shouted again. 'Do you have them?'

'Three.' The voice made the number sound like a challenge. 'Our offer stands. Three for one, Tannin, including your sister. We just want *Bolboda*.'

This time, Colbey replied. 'Then come out and take me, you coward!' Unsettling echoes bounced between the crags.

A different voice issued from the Wolf Point. 'We have more men than you do. Do you really want to pay with the lives of your followers as well?'

Arduwyn could see Tannin licking his lips nervously, and he did not envy the Western Renshai's need to choose between betraying his family or his teacher. For his own part, Arduwyn kept still with difficulty. The bantering of words could continue indefinitely, and he had little time. If something major did not happen soon, he would have no choice but to abandon his friends the following morning.

Colbey laughed. 'Are you so sure you outnumber us? We've brought an army. We even have archers.'

Arduwyn took his cue, glad for a chance to do something. He nocked, drew, and shot. His arrow flew straight, nicking the cave mouth, then plummeted like a wounded goose. Quickly, he prepared another.

A blond head poked from the cave. 'One archer does not make an army.'

Arduwyn aimed and fired. The arrow pierced the Northman. He collapsed to the stone. Prepared for retaliation, Arduwyn ducked beneath the deadfall.

Colbey and Tannin jerked toward Arduwyn, clearly shocked.

Although the hunter had killed men in the Great War, he had always made his aversion to it clear.

A rain of arrows fell about Arduwyn from the cave. Most landed short. A few bit into the charred trunk of his makeshift barricade. Arduwyn cursed his own brashness. Bel's time limit made him impatient, yet his death would assure hers as well. Still, he knew that either those Northmen or his companions would die. If it cost the lives of a few enemies at his own hand to rescue friends, the choice became easy. He would wrestle his conscience later.

Another long pause ensued. This time, the answering voice sounded less certain. 'You're bluffing, Colbey. The Golden-Haired Devils have no allies.'

'Are you willing to take that chance?' Colbey pressed his advantage. 'It's not for no reason that I ride an Erythanian charger, and we came here by way of Béarn's court. If you attack, you'll lose many more than we will.'

A new voice replied this time, one familiar to Arduwyn. Kirin's tone held the same brooding bitterness as when he had talked about Colbey at the Great War. 'I can see how many you have. There's not enough brush to hide you. At most, you have a dozen.'

Arduwyn backed beyond bow range, needing to inform Colbey as well as challenge the Northman. 'Kirin, how many men do you have? Fifteen? Twenty? That hole in the cliffs won't fit more than twenty-five, and I know last year's rock slide sealed off the back exit.'

Colbey laughed. 'Your men are wolves at bay, Kirin. If you harm our friends, we would kill you all with a few flaming brands.'

'And roast your beloved Western Renshai with us,' the Nordmirian shot back. 'And I dare you to come within range of my archers. In fact, I encourage it.'

Colbey ran a callused hand through his hair. With the unusually clear senses peril brings, Arduwyn noticed that the gold-streaked silver locks had grown longer than he had ever seen the old Renshai allow them before. From another man, this would not have impressed Arduwyn. But when Colbey quit caring about his grooming and the hair that might get into his eyes in battle, it could only mean he had ceased to care about other things as well. Still, obviously, not all of the fight had left the elder. His voice rang. 'We don't need to come closer. We only need to wait until you finish whatever food and water you have. Then you'll have to attack with swords, like real warriors, and all your men will fall.'

Valr Kirin's voice deepened to a growl, though it remained readily audible. 'You arrogant spawn of Loki! My men may die, but we'll take our captives and more than one of you with us. How many Renshai do you have to spare?'

Again, Colbey laughed, this time more cruelly. 'Your men are bowmen. They'll be lucky to swing a stroke before we kill them.' Turning on his heels, he rejoined the party, the first round finished in stalemate. Tannin followed.

Arduwyn met them at the camp, shoving his gear randomly into his pack, with far more force than the effort warranted. 'The rest of you can stay until the Northmen starve. Whatever happens, I'm leaving tomorrow. I promised Bel.'

Colbey glared, his pale eyes seeming to penetrate the hunter. Arduwyn shrank from his gaze, afraid that the Renshai might hold him against his will. But though Colbey's disappointment and disdain seemed tangible, his words remained soft. 'We could use you, Arduwyn, but the decision is yours.'

Arduwyn tied his pack, walking away from Colbey. The remains of the forest floor crunched beneath his feet. All around him it was ominously still, except for the fluttering glaze of heat still rising from the coals. Without trees and undergrowth, Arduwyn felt alone and vulnerable.

Colbey addressed the group. 'We'll keep two guards on the rocks above the cave. Preferably, at least one should know how to use a bow.' He hesitated, presumably to include Korgar. 'Or a spear. I don't want Northmen escaping or slipping away for food or reinforcements. We'll take shifts sleeping, day and night.'

The group spread blankets on the barren ground and huddled beneath hooded cloaks to escape autumn winds that seemed godsent to punish their destruction of the forest. Mitrian and Rache took first watch on the rocks, while Arduwyn and Tannin slept and Shadimar struggled to keep a cooking fire alight. Gradually, the day lengthened then faded into night.

26 A Sword of Gray; A Sword of White

The antechamber to Erythane's prison reeked of mold, urine, and unwashed flesh, its walls peeling a petrified slime Garn did not try to identify. He crouched near the outer door while Baran paced to the ceaseless patter of dripping water. It had not rained for at least two days, and Garn's mind worried over the problem of the droplets' source to keep from concentrating on the smallness of the room and its two closed doors, one that led to the stairway to the upper keep and the other of which opened onto the cells. At regular intervals, he checked the latch to the outer door to assure himself that it still tripped easily and that the panel yielded to his touch. The dinginess of the room and the foul, animal odors of caged men brought back memories better left untouched.

After a period of time that seemed interminable, a guardsman wearing Erythane's circle and sword reentered from the prison side of the antechamber. Earlier, he had introduced himself as Nhetorl. 'Pardon me, Captain. We've got the prisoner ready. I'm going to lock this door now until you're sure you have control.' He thrust his hands into the pocket of his jerkin.

Baran ceased his pacing. 'Carry on.'

Nhetorl headed for the exit, keys jangling in his hairy-knuckled hand. The click of the thrown tumblers set Garn's teeth on edge, and he doubted that would help his mood when he saw the exiled Béarnide again. The Erythanian took a position beside Baran. As large as any of his race, the captain dwarfed the guardsman in breadth as well as height. Though the mixture of colors had looked rakish on either side of the knights' tabards, side by side Erythane's orange and black clashed with Béarn's blue and tan. Moisture had dampened Baran's plume of office, and it sagged limply from his helmet. Still, Baran managed to look powerful and in command, his features chiseled and his black hair starkly cut.

Shortly, another Erythanian appeared, leading Rathelon. Morhane's son held his head high, despite the shackles that pinned his wrists behind him and the fetters that hampered his otherwise broad stride. Thick, black curls tumbled to the nape of his neck, barely touched by gray. His eyes were ebony pinpoints in the gloom, as hard as diamond chips. He wore only a loose pair of britches, and muscles defined a chest massive from heredity and training. His presence made even Baran seem small. His dark gaze swept the chamber to settle on Garn. Rathelon's eyes narrowed. 'You, again,' he said, lips drawing into a smirk despite his predicament. 'They said you were near. I knew you'd have to come.' His voice thundered after the long silence.

Garn had a ready answer. 'Did you think I could resist your humiliation?'

'A coward never can,' Rathelon shot back. 'Run when the lion's free, then laugh when he's bound hand and foot. Once, Garn, I had you pleading and groveling at my mercy. Had I killed you where you lay on your belly in the dirt, I would now rule Béarn.'

The words incited rage. For Garn, the world narrowed to Rathelon and himself, and the movements of Baran and the Erythanians became meaningless background. 'Had you tried, *you* would lie dead and Sterrane would still rule Béarn.'

'You think you could best me in battle?'

'It's not a matter that requires thought.'

Rathelon fairly leered. 'Lucky for you, then, isn't it? Clearly, thinking's not a part of your repertoire.'

Garn felt his control slipping, and he reached for the mental restraint that came of Colbey's training. 'And you're lucky you're shackled. In Béarn, you caught me by surprise, weaponless and injured. Had we met on the battlefield, in fair combat, I'd have severed your ugly head from the suffering body forced to carry it.'

'Is that a challenge?' Chain clanked as Rathelon shifted position.

Garn sensed restless movement to his left. Apparently, the Erythanians and Baran found a significance to the question that went beyond two enemies hurling insults. Hedging his bets, Garn gave a noncommittal response. 'It could be.' He looked to Baran for guidance.

The captain met Garn's gaze earnestly, without returning counsel. Whatever his knowledge or opinion, he did not feel in a position to offer it. The Erythanians studied the confrontation in uncomfortable silence.

Rathelon explained what the others had not. 'In Erythane, single combat is considered the best means of solving disputes. As a prisoner, I have no right to call you out. But you're a free man.' He grinned, displaying straight, white teeth. 'If you're not afraid, Garn, prove it. You would even have the right to choose time, place, and weapon. All you have to do is challenge.'

Joy tremored through Garn. He would relish the chance to pit his skill against Rathelon's as well as to see the Béarnide dead, yet he did not forget that the decision was not wholly his to make. Again, he looked at Baran.

This time, the captain rose to the occasion. 'It would be against all custom and propriety for a man in the service of Béarn to fight a prisoner he's escorting for trial.'

Disappointment tainted Garn's elation. He would not compromise a friend's honor. But before he could refuse Rathelon, Baran continued.

'You're not in my command, Garn. You're a civilian. Do as you will.'

Garn smiled, certain that this had been Baran's plan from the start, and he approved. The Béarnian captain could not have forced Garn to battle, nor even suggested such a thing. It had to come directly from Garn. Once he brought Rathelon and Garn face-to-face, the challenge became a foregone conclusion.

Garn turned his attention back to Rathelon. 'Consider yourself called out.'

The Erythanians exchanged horrified glances.

Rathelon grinned. 'Let's make this interesting, shall we? Would the silent, indecisive captain of Béarn's guards be willing to set up a wager?' Rathelon turned his head to face Baran directly, brows arched in question.

Baran remained impassive. 'Don't taunt me, Rathelon. I'm not going to do anything stupid out of anger.'

Intent on the exchange, Garn missed the backhanded insult to his own methods.

Baran met Rathelon stare for stare. 'What do you want?'

Blood fury pounded Garn's ears, and excitement gripped him. The contest could not begin too soon for him.

'Simply this.' Hands bound, Rathelon tossed his head toward Baran, the movement sending a curl sliding into his eye. 'I'll write up a list with the names of every one of my cohorts: from outside the kingdom to Erythane, to Béarn, and even the few inside the castle.'

Baran stiffened, obviously shocked to learn of traitors in the castle proper. The corners of his mouth twitched, betraying an interest he fought to hide. No doubt, he wanted that list, and Garn could scarcely blame him. That handful of names could end the violence in Béarn forever.

Rathelon continued. 'I'll give the list to him.' He indicated the second Erythanian guard with his chain. 'If Garn kills me . . .' He paused to snort at the possibility. 'The names become your property. If I kill Garn, I get that list back, unread, and no mention of its existence leaves this room.' He glanced from guard to guard in turn, receiving a nod of confirmation from each. If Baran agreed to the terms, they would keep their silence. 'And I get my freedom.'

Baran went rigid. Without reply, he turned away, paced the few steps to the exit, then whirled back to face Rathelon. 'Why would you do that? How could you put your loyal followers at risk?'

Rathelon loosed a deep-throated laugh that reverberated disjointedly through the antechamber. 'Because I believe my followers would want to stand or fall with me. Should the guards root them out, my men would probably die. But Sterrane, with his grand and magnificent innocence, will treat them with the same mercy as he has the others.' He laughed again. 'And it's all moot, really, a way to make an agreement that satisfies you. I don't believe for a moment that I might lose to this puny *wisule* who's more brag than brains.' He indicated Garn with a brisk head gesture that also flung the hair from his eye.

Baran rolled his gaze to Garn. Though nearly a hand's length shorter and little more than half Rathelon's weight, Garn did get to choose the weapon. That might even the odds. 'All right,' Baran said, though he still sounded reluctant. 'You have a deal, Rathelon.' He waved at the Erythanians. 'Release him.'

The guards exchanged wary glances. Neither moved to obey. Nhetorl cleared his throat. 'Are you certain, sir? Would you like reinforcements first?'

Baran's gaze swept back to Rathelon's face. 'Do you swear that you will do nothing but make the list and meet Garn's challenge according to the laws of Erythane?'

Rathelon scowled at the need for oaths. 'I do. Until such time as the contest has finished and I'm freed.'

'Or dead,' Garn finished with a growl.

Rathelon's scowl deepened, and he did not bother to look at Garn. 'That goes without saying. And so should my honor. Whatever designs I had on the throne, I never hid or distorted them. I didn't break the terms of banishment, and my men and I worked within our best interpretation of the law.'

'Free him,' Baran said.

This time, the Erythanians reluctantly obeyed. They inserted keys into the shackle locks. The irons slid from Rathelon's wrists, the chains falling in a clanging heap to the floor at his back. Nhetorl pulled the leg fetters free. Without waiting for Rathelon to move or explore his partial freedom, Baran shoved a sheet of parchment, ink, and a stylus into his hands.

Rathelon retired to a corner to write.

The Erythanians slid the chains and shackles to the prison exit, metal scraping and belling against the granite floor.

Garn approached Baran, his voice soft beneath the clamor. 'Do you always carry writing implements on duty?'

'Not usually,' Baran returned. 'But I spent a long time thinking about how to respond to the knight's note. A *long* time. I considered everything, including resigning.' He drew Garn into the farthest corner from Rathelon. 'That's not the issue now. You –'

Garn interrupted. 'Do you trust Rathelon to give you what he promised? What if he writes down the wrong names? Or none at all?'

'He'll do it right.' Baran seemed certain. 'He's a bastard in every sense of the word, but an honest bastard nonetheless. For all his evil, he does live by a code of honor and by his word.'

'Finished,' Rathelon called out. He handed paper, ink, and stylus to Nhetorl. Unburdened, he headed toward the room's center, attention fixed on Garn, a cruel smile playing over his lips. 'It's you and I, rodent. You made the challenge; by Erythanian law, you decide the weapon. Choose one that gives you an advantage if you want to live longer than a heartbeat.'

Garn felt his control sliding again. For an instant, the opponent he faced became a lithe, blond Renshai and the room Santagithi's gladiator training quarters. He pictured the guards, standing nervously aside with crossbows leveled. Rache had always wielded balanced steel to Garn's wooden, practice blade. Always, Garn had believed equal weapons would have assured the sword master's death. Yet in the end, it had been the simplest weapon of all, Garn's bare hands, that had crippled Rache. 'Advantage? I don't need one. In fact, let's fight weaponless, strength to strength. The best man, not the best sword, should win.'

'Garn.' Baran caught the ex-gladiator's arm, but the warning came too late. The declaration was made, though the reasons behind it dispersed back to memory and obscurity.

Garn studied Rathelon's gigantic form without comment. The Béarnide would surely prove his strongest enemy ever. Yet, he had fought men of all sizes in the pit and placed full faith in his own ability. 'Would it even the fight more if I closed my eyes and let you hit me from behind?'

Rathelon did not grace the taunt with a reply. 'You also get to select time and place.'

Garn decided he'd better consult Baran about this. The captain had gone back to pacing, this time in a line so short it seemed more like a circle. 'I'm in no hurry. Take the time you need. As to place, this seems perfect. It's controlled, and we don't have to worry about spectators getting offended or underfoot.'

Rathelon stretched, muscles rippling. The Erythanians backed away.

Garn also preferred the lack of onlookers. He savored the clarity of mind that had eluded him until Colbey's teachings. That control had allowed Rache to best Garn repeatedly on the practice floor. Now that power was his. 'Here seems as good a place as any other. And now as good a time.'

The issue decided, Rathelon did not waste a moment. He sprang with the blood frenzy that Garn had overcome. Garn sidestepped too late. Rathelon crashed against him with a force that sent them both tumbling to the stone. Locked together, they bucked and kicked. They rolled, the guards jumping out of their path, and Garn managed to disentangle himself. Both men surged to their feet.

Rathelon swung with the incaution and fury of a cyclone. His fists thudded repeatedly against Garn's skull, causing flashes of pain that burned like fire. Garn returned fewer blows of better aim. Rathelon clawed for Garn's eyes. Garn offset the attack with an arm, and the Béarnide's nails opened Garn's forehead. Through a veil of blood, Garn jolted a fist into Rathelon's face. Impact staggered the Béarnide.

Gasping for breath, Garn leaned against the wall, not bothering to press his advantage. Rathelon swayed momentarily. Suddenly, he threw himself at Garn. His superior weight bowled Garn over and bore him to the ground, the breath slammed from his lungs. Rathelon's hands latched onto Garn's throat.

Garn's hands jerked instinctively to the thick wrists. He tightened his neck to a solid cord. Still, Rathelon's fingers gouged into the mass of taut musculature, and Garn fought for breath. The imminence of death filled his head, and the significance of the battle with it. *Baran's counting on me*. Panic touched him, but he borrowed the strength from his mind to amplify his body's power. *So much more than my life or death lies in the balance*. Both men held their grips. Suddenly, Garn shoved upward, and Rathelon's wrists gave.

Rathelon sprang back with a howl of pain. His shoulder blades slammed against the slime-coated wall, turning his cry into a broken gasp. Garn gulped a haggard breath, then plunged onto his opponent. His knee crashed into Rathelon's groin, and the Béarnide stumbled. Garn jolted the ball of his hand against Rathelon's nose, driving bone into brain. The Béarn's eyes blazed, then went dull. He plummeted, dead before he hit the ground.

Bruised and battered, Garn swayed dizzily amidst Baran's hazy, unrecognizable words. Then he fell into oblivion.

That night the moon was nearly full, so dawn brought little change to the brooding wasteland on which Colbey and his companions had camped. The change came from elsewhere. A proud, helmeted figure on a chestnut charger descended from the cliffs, with two men riding at his flank. They made no attempt to hide from the Renshai encampment, and none of the three carried a bow or arrows. Colbey supposed that this was the reason that the guards behind the cave, Rache and Tannin, had allowed the Northmen to ride, unhindered, toward the camp.

Colbey checked his own companions. Arduwyn and Shadimar watched the approaching figures carefully. Secodon crouched, soundless. Mitrian had awakened, her blue eyes open, though she made no movement that might reveal her alertness to the newcomers.

Colbey turned his attention back to the approaching Northmen. He recognized the one in the lead as Valr Kirin, knowing him by the solid set of his body and the smooth efficiency of his few movements. The Northmen pulled up their horses a polite distance from the camp that would require strong or loud voices for conversation. There, Valr Kirin slid the metal helm from his head, freeing a mane of silver-tinged, yellow hair. Blue eyes lay widely set above a hawklike nose. His usually broad mouth was set in a grim slit. His gray linen shirt did not rest flat against his chest, and Colbey knew it covered light armor. His woolen britches and cloak bore intricate embroidery. Many emotions wafted from him, yet they came individually, pure and separate, with none of the confusion that usually accompanied such a vibrant mixture. Colbey found a hatred so thick and raw it seemed primal, as sanctioned by nature as a predator's hunt for food. To Colbey, it typified the Northmen's long-standing hatred for Renshai, a feud that had lost meaning generations past. Yet Valr Kirin's hatred seemed far more specifically focused than that of the men flanking him. Clearly, the Renshai as a tribe no longer galled him. It was only Colbey.

Without the need to probe, Colbey read more. He found a calm and ordered fear that seemed more like hopeless necessity. With it came knowledge of impending violence, hemmed and defined by an honor so distinct it could never be circumvented. Colbey understood that Kirin would fight, but not until the rules and circumstances had become clearly defined. If the Northmen planned a trick or a trap, Valr Kirin was not a part of it. His morality would not allow it. Beneath it all, Colbey discovered a grim certainty without so much as a pinhole of doubt. Whatever Kirin's cause, he followed it with a faith stronger than religion. To Colbey, this seemed the man's most extraordinary talent as well as his biggest flaw. The old Renshai could not help admiring a man so willing to fight and die for his convictions, no matter how much they opposed Colbey's.

'I bring a challenge I think you'll accept, *Bolboda*.' Valr Kirin's voice boomed, pitched to carry over the distance between them. 'And I'd like to exchange vows.'

It seemed only fair to meet Valr Kirin partway, and Colbey disliked the need to shout. Holding his reply, he kept his gaze fixed on the Northmen, as he moved to the horses. He did not bother with a saddle, only bridled Frost Reaver and mounted. He glanced at the Wolf Point hilltops, picking Rache's and Tannin's still figures from the shadows. Turning, he studied the rest of the party. Mitrian stood, no longer feigning sleep. Shadimar remained still, the wolf quiet at his side. Arduwyn had slipped into a tangle of charred boughs, and Colbey did not see Korgar.

Finally, Colbey looked back to Kirin and his entourage. Slowly, without threat, he approached, reining the Erythanian charger just beyond sword range. 'Kirin, I'm willing to hear your challenge, though there's one thing I don't understand. Why do you call me Evil Bringer? I'm only trying to keep what's left of my tribe alive in peace. You, however, want to destroy us for some ancient crime of our forefathers, and men and Wizards call you good. There's no justice in that.'

'I *serve* justice.' Valr Kirin stared, features locked in a scowl. 'I know what you are and what you champion. Your lies may fool your followers, but I see through them, because I know the truth. Wizards and their sources cannot lie. Whatever intentions you claim, your future avows evil and destruction for Northmen and Renshai alike. I have no choice but to oppose that.' His gaze traveled to Shadimar, and his brows rose in anxious question.

Colbey could only see the Wizard from the barest edge of peripheral vision, but he could tell that Shadimar's demeanor stiffened. The old Renshai could not help wondering whether Shadimar could also read the suffocatingly intense sincerity radiating from Trilless' champion. Clearly, Kirin believed every word he spoke with an unshakable certainty that nearly convinced Colbey. *Maybe, just maybe, Trilless sees something in my future that even I could never guess.*

Though Valr Kirin continued to probe the Eastern Wizard, his words could only be meant for Colbey. 'My grudge is no longer with your people, it's with you. It is destined in the truest sense of the word, in the oldest text of the Wizards. You will betray and ruin the Renshai as well as us.'

Anger descended on Colbey. When anyone questioned his courage or skill, he simply showed them the error of such thought. But that any man might believe, even for a moment, that he would work against the Renshai seemed an insult too base to contemplate. Still, to deny the accusation would prove nothing. To his followers, his actions through the decades would say more than Kirin's words ever could. As to Kirin's followers, Colbey did not care what they believed.

The rest of Kirin's accusation came carefully. 'I see no reason for more than one Northman's death nor for any skilled swordsmen to freeze in Hel. This feud is ours Colbey, ours and the Wizards we serve, though you claim to deny your master.' He passed his gilded helmet to the man at his left, a nervous, squinty-eyed youth who appeared no older than Rache. 'I serve goodness, and you've sold yourself to evil. I have no choice but to destroy you before your deceit damns your people as well as mine. If I fail, I only hope the Renshai will come to understand what you are before it's too late.' His soft, pleading gaze flitted from Mitrian to Shadimar.

Both looked away.

Valr Kirin's words did little more than confuse Colbey. 'You're crazy, Kirin. Or, at best, sadly misinformed. My loyalties lie with the Renshai and with Shadimar. If you have no feud with them, then you have none with me. We can end this now and both live in peace.' Colbey studied the man before him without blinking. He hoped that his words demonstrated how much the Renshai had changed, how other principles had joined the insatiable love for battle hammered into him since birth.

Kirin lowered his head, breaking the contact. For a moment, Colbey thought the Nordmirian would cry. 'Trilless said you would lie to the end. And convincingly. I should have known that one so long among the exiled Renshai could not escape the same dishonor that drove them to mutilate their cousins.' He again met Colbey's eyes, his own blue orbs blazing. 'From this moment forth, if the gods will allow it, I declare Northmen and Renshai at peace. We will stop hunting you, if you will allow my men to return to the North unhindered.'

The vow pleased as well as startled Colbey. Still, it did not seem to follow naturally from Kirin's prefacing statement. 'That's all that we've ever asked. I have no problem making this promise. Nor my companions, if their word means more to you.' Colbey responded carefully, waiting for the other shoe to fall.

'You and I will fight. Win or lose, we free your hostages unscathed. But, should you refuse my challenge, my men have orders to kill the Western Renshai.' He raised his hand and rolled his eyes heavenward. 'I swear by Thor, my men and I will honor this vow. Our battle is not finished until one of the two of us lies dead.'

Colbey paused to think, seeing no flaws in the bargain. So long as he took Valr Kirin's challenge, the Renshai could not lose. No matter who triumphed, his people would have what they sought: freedom for themselves and for the captives. The Renshai risked only one thing, Colbey's life, and they no longer needed an old man who should have died decades past. Since Colbey claimed full ownership of that life, he consulted no one before making his decision. 'Lady Sif, goddess of Renshai, hear me now. Your people will join this pact as Kirin spoke it. May you cut down anyone who betrays it.'

Valr Kirin continued to study the sky, but he kept his prayers silent. At length, he passed the reins of his stallion to the man at his right and slid from the chestnut's back. Colbey unbuckled and freed the bridle, balancing it across Frost Reaver's withers. He commanded the charger to return to camp. The horse nuzzled Colbey's arm, then obediently turned and headed toward the others. By the time Colbey turned back, Kirin had chosen a likely battleground on the forest turned graveyard, out of range of archers from either side and where horses would not risk injury from a wild stroke.

The young man who had ridden at Valr Kirin's left also dismounted, passing his reins to the other Northman. He approached Kirin, first handing him a pair of brass-studded gauntlets, then the helmet.

'Thank you, Olvaerr.' Kirin lowered his voice nearly to a whisper, yet the depth of the silence around them, unbroken even by the normal sounds of an awakening forest, allowed Colbey to hear. 'If I die, carry on. Keep your sword arm worked and your honor unwavering.'

'May Thor steer your arm, Father,' Olvaerr replied as softly. He clasped Kirin's wrist so tightly both of their hands blanched. Then, rather than turn away, he pulled his father into an embrace that lasted only seconds. The love that radiated from both came strongly to Colbey, tearing at him. It brought memories of Episte and what might have been, and Colbey knew an envy that nearly brought him to tears. For all that he had done and those that he had killed, if he could have lived only one part of his life again, he would have found a way to retract striking Episte and would have shown the boy his love instead. The memory ached within him. Colbey waited until the embrace had finished and Olvaerr had stepped away before heading toward the Nordmirian lieutenant.

Valr Kirin set his helmet in place, then pulled on the gauntlets. Legs braced, stance defensive, he watched Colbey's approach.

Colbey stopped directly before Kirin. 'We can still call this off.'

'We can't,' Kirin replied, without hesitation. 'You know what you are.'

Colbey believed that he did, yet Kirin's impression seemed so alien, he needed to understand it. He tried to grasp answers from the emotion radiating from the Northman, but all he could read was a direct certainty that Colbey would spread Carcophan's evil on a rampage through all parts of the world. Again, Colbey found himself caught and drawn to that unwavering conviction that left not the tiniest shred of doubt. Never in his life had he believed in anything with such sureness, nor would he have guessed it possible for any man. Even his faith in Sif had moments where it grew shaky, and he questioned. Though he knew it was folly to weaken himself before battle, Colbey could not resist probing just a little deeper.

Colbey's journey into Val Kirin's mind gave him an intensified feel for the emotions that had, already, seemed powerful. He followed the raging torrent of certainty to its root: the Northern Sorceress, a source that could not lie. The facts supported Valr Kirin's assertion. The most ancient prophecies of the Wizards named the world's greatest mortal swordsman as the champion of Carcophan's evil, a Northman who would betray his tribe. Colbey froze there, feeling strength drain from him in a steady wash, yet unable to pull away.

Abruptly, a presence severed Colbey's mental tie to Valr Kirin, as quickly and sharply as a sword cut. The suddenness nearly sent Colbey tumbling backward, though he caught his balance with a clumsy step tempered by fatigue. Before him stood the woman who had sparred with him during his prayers on his return from the Great War. A scowl scored her unearthly beautiful features, and her voice reverberated with power. 'Believe in what you are, Colbey. To intentionally drain your strength before a contest is cowardice of the worst kind.' As suddenly she disappeared.

Colbey shook his head, trying to regain his bearings. The efforts of his mental exploration, the hallucination, and the heavy acrid reek of the charred forest made him queasy. Wildly, he glanced at Kirin to see if the Northman had also seen the vision.

But if he did, Kirin gave no sign. His forehead creased, making his look urgent. 'Colbey Calistinsson, I have one last pact to make with you.' He met and held the blue-gray eyes. 'The man who wins this duel will not bar the loser from Valhalla.'

Colbey nodded once, still dizzy. Until the woman's words, he had not realized what he had tried to do. Wrapped up in Valr Kirin's certainty, Colbey had sincerely believed that he would betray the Renshai, that he would serve Carcophan, and that, for the good of the world, he must die. He did not know if that certainty came from Valr Kirin or himself, but it would not fully leave him. *But if Sif told me to believe in myself, how can I do otherwise? I did not war for seventy years to die a coward.* 'I would have it no other way. I would never dismember a noble enemy, and you are the noblest I've faced. Before we start, though, I do have one question in the name of your blood brother in Valhalla, Rache Kallmirsson.'

Now Kirin nodded curtly. Though he did not visibly flinch, Colbey could feel a flurry of radiating emotion. At the time of the pact, Kirin had never guessed that Rache was Renshai. Sometime in the past decade, he had learned this fact. His more obvious thoughts and actions told Colbey that Valr Kirin had worked through his conflicting loyalties on the matter. Colbey guessed that the relationship might have started the spark of peace between Kirin and the Renshai, though it did not apparently extend to the feud between Colbey and Kirin.

'Whoever killed Rache's son, Episte, mutilated him horribly.' Colbey felt his own composure wavering, the vision of the headless body filling his memory with agony. 'Why?' His voice betrayed his pain.

'No,' Kirin said.

Colbey waited. The lieutenant had not directly addressed his question.

'No.' Kirin's hand clenched around his sword hilt. 'It wasn't one of mine.'

'Circumstance says it was. I found him among dead Northmen.'

'It could not have been one of my men.' Kirin did not waver; though, from the edge of his gaze, Colbey could see Olvaerr shuffling nervously. 'There's nothing more to say.'

Colbey glanced at Valr Kirin's son, tangibly touching his nervous energy, keyed nearly to the point of breaking. The need to know goaded him to search the youngster's thoughts, yet Colbey resisted, Sif's words still echoing in his head.

Valr Kirin paced backward a step and drew his sword from its plain scabbard. The blade glowed so brightly that the cloudless sky paled before it. White flames danced along its edge.

Panic touched Colbey from a source behind him, so strong that it tore past Kirin's aura of determination and Olvaerr's confusion. Without understanding why, Colbey knew the sword's name, Ristoril, the Sword of Tranquillity; and he knew the information could only have come from one source. *Shadimar*? The Eastern Wizard's fear, so unfamiliar and uncharacteristic, shattered Colbey's concentration.

Valr Kirin's sword lunged for Colbey, as if sword, not man, was the wielder. Colbey drew Harval and parried. The swords met with a clang that seemed far too loud to Colbey in the dead stillness of the ravaged forest. Sparks erupted from the contact, milk-white pinpoints against misty gray shadow. Colbey twisted, and the Nordmirian's blade scratched along his own, locking on the crossguard.

Secodon emitted a long, tortured howl.

Slowed by the energy wasted in his mental exploration, Colbey did not press quickly enough. Kirin jerked his sword free, then bore in for another cut. This time Colbey dodged, returning a sweep that Kirin scarcely met. Again, the swords chimed together, the sound as clear and precise as music. Immediately, Colbey reversed, and Kirin slashed. Colbey met this new attack with a parry that he continued into a sweep for Kirin's neck. The Nordmirian backpedaled. The tip of Colbey's sword skimmed along his helmet, leaving a scar across the steel.

Colbey surged in. His blade whipped upward in a feint that fooled Kirin. He raised his sword to block, even as Colbey's countercut opened his shirt, mail, and abdomen. The Northman staggered, his face as pale as his sword.

Valr Kirin made no sound, but Olvaerr screamed as if the wound were his own. 'Father, no!' The youth's blood rage hammered Colbey from without, and Kirin's son drew and sprang for the Renshai.

Colbey wrenched his sword upward to meet Olvaerr's unexpected rush. The chest thrust meant to painlessly end Kirin's life became a broad sweep, and the magically sharpened steel claimed his arm at the shoulder. Colbey's blade met Olvaerr's, and the child's wild eyes reflected the crazed grief and desperation that Colbey could read easily. Rage tightened Colbey's grip on his sword. He had broken his last vow to Kirin, his promise to send the noblest of his foes to Valhalla, and he had no intention of claiming the Nordmirian hero's son as well. To kill Olvaerr also meant breaking a vow to the gods, and it would reawaken a feud that had taken more than a century to quiet.

'Korgar, no!' Mitrian screamed.

Before Colbey could interpret the cry, the barbarian ran toward the fray, spear leveled. Olvaerr's sword hacked frenzied, unpredictable arcs, and the youngster seemed oblivious to his defenses. Colbey carefully measured a disarming maneuver. Before he could strike, Korgar charged in from behind him. Colbey dodged, guessing the barbarian's path by sound, but he misjudged. A meaty shoulder grazed him, and the power behind the charge knocked him to one knee. The spear plowed for Olvaerr.

'Korgar, stop!' Colbey managed a desperate upstroke that tipped the point of the spear toward the sky. The barb tore Olvaerr's tunic, scratching across mail. Unable to check his charge, Korgar knocked the youngster sprawling. Then, tripping over the butt of his spear, Korgar pinwheeled over Olvaerr's head. All three men lurched to their feet. Immediately, Olvaerr resumed his assault, hacking at Colbey repeatedly with tireless, powerful strokes that rage made dangerous. Colbey only defended, seeking the opening that would end the onslaught. Patience had won the attention and respect of many students enraged to reckless stupidity. Though he had no time for such thoughts, Colbey could not help seeing Episte in this other youngster's rage-driven violence, and the relationship with his dying father that Colbey respected and envied.

Behind the Nordmirian's son, Korgar made another charge, spear lowered and aimed for Olvaerr's back.

'No! Korgar! Stop!' Colbey's options ran short, and he still saw no opening. He blocked mechanically, aware it was no longer Olvaerr who needed to be halted. Time ran out in a heartbeat, and still Olvaerr left him no opening. 'No!'

The point of Korgar's spear drew within a hand's breadth of Olvaerr's back. Colbey had no choice but to stop Korgar instantly, or momentum would finish the attack for the barbarian. Out of time, Colbey dove through the frenzied slashes. *Korgar or Olvaerr?* Though he hated the decision, Colbey made it instantly. He jabbed his blade through Korgar's throat and deep into his spine. The barbarian crumpled, spear slamming to the ground, point gouging flesh from Olvaerr's thigh.

Olvaerr hesitated an instant, and Colbey snatched the hilt from the youngster's grip with his free hand. There was no need to check Korgar. Colbey's blood brother was clearly dead for a god-witnessed vow that Olvaerr had broken in a fit of grief and anger. The youth had brought dishonor to his people, had freed the Renshai from their vow, and had damned his valiant father's soul to Hel. Colbey turned on the Northman to say as much, but all words failed him. His mind soured with the image of his slapping Episte, the look of wounded betrayal that had formed in the youngster's eyes, a look that Korgar never had a chance to mirror. Olvaerr knew what he had done. If he shared any of his father's honor, the agony of memory would haunt him for eternity. Nothing Colbey could say would come close to its pain, nor did he have any way to soften it.

Again, Colbey glanced at Korgar's corpse. Guilt ground through him, accompanied by an understanding that evoked terror. *Another betrayal. First Episte's mother, then Episte, and now Korgar. Who's next?* Colbey recalled the certainty he had found in Valr Kirin's mind. *Maybe he and the Northern Sorceress are right. Maybe I can't escape this destiny, no matter my intentions.* Colbey shivered, trying to throw off the chains of this speculation. To believe that all life was predestined and all fate inescapable meant denying the control of body and mind that he had striven for for too long. It reduced decision to meaninglessness and took glory and principle out of the hands of mortals. Colbey shifted Harval and Olvaerr's sword into the same hand.

Olvaerr seemed to awaken from a trance. His gaze strayed behind Colbey, and he gasped like a man dying. 'Father.' The youngster hurled himself at the blood-stained battlefield.

Colbey whirled, realizing how distracted he must have become to leave a noble foe bleeding but alive. It was a cruelty no warrior deserved. Decades ago, every Renshai had kept a *nådenal*, the mercy needle of Sif, in a side slit in the sword sheath, and Colbey still carried one. Reserved for ending the life of suffering Renshai too injured to stagger back into battle, each *nådenal* was crafted of silver, used only once, and melted in the pyre of its glorified victim. Never before had Colbey fought an enemy worthy of Sif's mercy needle. Yet, now, he believed he had found one. The tear-shaped haft filled his hand, devoid of a crossguard, and the long, slender blade tapered to a perfect point. He slid the silver dagger from its rest, the religious symbols carved into its side flickering in the sunlight. The crafting of a *nådenal* required the cooperation of a Sif priest and a smith, and any flaw in construction or ceremony meant that the materials must be discarded. Colbey knew that he held the last one.

Scarlet froth bubbled from Kirin's lips, and the glow of the sword he had carried dulled to ordinary steel. Blood stained the charred grass, seeming like far too much to allow the Nordmirian life, yet his chest still fluttered with shallow breaths. His glazed eyes could have seen nothing, and Colbey hoped the lieutenant would never know the role his own son played in this treachery.

'Kirin,' Colbey said. He knelt at the Slayer's side, eyes naturally seeking a site for a mercy stab.

Apparently, Colbey's voice was the cue that Kirin awaited. Blanched lips stirred, forcing words between them. 'I should have known better than to trust you,' he said. And died.

Olvaerr wrapped his arms around the corpse, soiled with his own tears and his father's blood. The other Northman shifted restlessly, clearly uncertain what to do.

Colbey froze, the *nådenal* still unblooded in his hand. Apparently, Sif had denied Kirin its honor, though her reasons baffled Colbey. Perhaps her decision stemmed from the same lost body part that would bar Valr Kirin from Valhalla. Perhaps she still held a grudge from the Nordmirian's role in the Renshai slaughter, or perhaps she had another sacrifice in mind. Colbey did not ponder his goddess' motivations long. Quickly, he sheathed the dagger, then rose to meet the Northman's gaze, still clutching Harval and Olvaerr's sword. 'I did not break my part of the vow, and I forgive Kirin's son his grief madness. Get the prisoners.'

Obviously relieved, the Northman raced toward the Wolf Point.

Colbey turned his head to glance back at Valr Kirin, his vision arrested by a figure standing over the corpse and the sobbing Olvaerr. There, an unearthly woman stood, not Sif, but just as familiar to Colbey. *Valkyrie!* Colbey stared, unable to move, even had he wanted to tear his eyes from the vision. Seamless, silver armor enclosed perfect curves and sinews trained to war. She shimmered, bathed in golden halos, and her yellow hair tumbled from beneath a horned helmet. She clutched a spear, and a jeweled sword girded her hip. Colbey had seen her once before, or one of her eleven sisters, when Episte's father had died in the Great War. Colbey harbored no doubt that she had come for Valr Kirin, to take the Nordmirian lieutenant to his rightful place in Valhalla.

The *Valkyrie* knelt at Valr Kirin's side, placing her spear upon his chest. She balled her gauntleted hands into claws, as if drawing something from the corpse. Blood discolored her fingers, striping her gauntlets in patterns of silver, black, and red. She tossed something unseen onto her shoulders, then faded into the black expanse of infinity, leaving the corpse noticeably different in Colbey's eyes. The last trickle of bleeding ended, and the blue eyes became empty as marbles.

Only then, the significance of the vision penetrated. *Valr Kirin found Valhalla, even missing a major body part*! Colbey's world blurred and spun, the importance of his discovery spanning generations of hatred and slaughter. *Gods!* The conclusion came first, followed by a million details that stormed forward for consideration. *The centuries of persecution for nothing. The heroes mourned. The ugly killer prejudices and hatreds. All for nothing.* The big issues too overwhelming, Colbey's mind glided to the smaller ones, the myriad of individuals who paraded through his mind. So many corpses arose in his memory, haunting him with the ugliness of their deaths. *All wrong.* Colbey set them to rest, one by one, lingering last and longest over Episte. And that reminded him of another suffering soul who would need whatever solace he could offer.

Shadimar approached, claiming Valr Kirin's sword. Olvaerr glanced up, clearly offended by the action.

Colbey stole that moment to quick-clean and sheath Harval. He seized the youth's shoulder.

Olvaerr spun, baring his teeth like a cornered beast. Terror appeared in his moist eyes, but he met Colbey's gaze.

'Olvaerr, listen to me. This is important.' Colbey hoped desperately that he could get Valr Kirin's son to believe him. 'Your father found Valhalla.' Releasing Olvaerr's shoulder, he offered the youngster's hilt.

Olvaerr stared at the weapon. Colbey understood how much the sword had to mean to the young warrior. It had probably been cautiously selected by his father, whose taste, Colbey guessed, would be rivaled only by the Renshai's own. Yet, Olvaerr made no move to take the hilt. Instead he raised his face to the still summer sky and shouted. 'Mighty Thor, my lord, creator and sower of storms, god's champion of law and honor, please forgive my transgression against you. I will atone however you would have me, and I would dare to ask one more thing. Please. Damn this demon to the coldest, deepest part of Hel. See to it that he dies in the same agony and ugliness he has inflicted upon so many. I will have nothing that he has touched, with his hand or with his madness.' The youngster glared briefly at Colbey, then whirled to Shadimar, apparently to claim his father's sword. Yet, though the Wizard had not moved, the weapon that had once graced his hand had disappeared. Olvaerr turned on his heel and stormed back toward the Wolf Point.

There, at the rock formation, Colbey could see shifting figures. He believed he recognized Tannin among them, apparently moving up to meet his sister.

Believing things were progressing properly at the cave, Colbey turned back to his own people. Mitrian watched the cave, apparently trying to pick Rache from the mass of figures. Arduwyn huddled over Korgar's body, trying to restore some dignity to his death. Colbey felt grief radiate from the hunter, and it pained him that a man who had scarcely known Korgar seemed so much more affected than the man who had taken him as a brother. For his own part, Colbey felt emotionally drained.

Colbey looked at his other blood brother, finding Shadimar still and silent among the charred skeletons of the trees. The Eastern Wizard's gaze locked fanatically on Harval. The strange swirl of idea and feeling radiating from the Wizard became too complicated for Colbey to try to decipher, and he left Shadimar to make his own decisions. He knew that the words Valr Kirin had spoken meant more to Shadimar than he could understand. He knew that the sword the Nordmirian had wielded held a significance that the Wizard alone knew. And he knew that Shadimar had just watched a blood brother, who carried the only weapon that could slay Wizards, ruthlessly slaughter his other brother.

This time, as always, Colbey had chosen to place the vow he had taken for the Renshai over one he had taken for himself. For the first time in his life, he questioned this decision.

27 The Next Betrayal

Arduwyn's horse charged along the familiar pathways of the Erythanian forest, its hooves drumming on the hard-packed earth. *Three days to make a journey on horseback that only took that long on foot.* Arduwyn's thoughts comforted, bringing a joy that was immediately tempered by concern. Though he cantered through the forests he loved, caressed by autumn winds carrying the smells that had grown so cherished and important to him as a child, Bel's threat stole all enjoyment from him. Even the memory of Korgar lying dead at Colbey's hand could not hold his thoughts for long. Always, his mind circled back to Bel.

Sunlight stabbed through holes in the interweave of branches, blinding and warming Arduwyn in cycles. Contemplating Bel and her threat had become tedious to the point of agony. He had rehashed the need to return in time so often he had left nothing for consideration. But the pictures and doubts returned to haunt him again and again. He forced his thoughts to Garn and Mitrian. The years had made the man seem even more dangerous, ridding him of the last of his teenage gawkiness yet leaving the squat power that had won so many contests in the gladiator pit. Warfare had toned Mitrian's sinews, enhancing the feminine curves on a sturdy frame that she could only have inherited from Santagithi. Arduwyn had not yet seen a single gray hair on either head. By the look of them, the years had only improved their beauty and their marriage, and Arduwyn longed for a chance to chat with old friends he had missed so much.

Arduwyn considered their child, unable to keep his thoughts from straying to the other man who had borne the same name. Months of tracking Rache Kallmirsson through the Westland forests had brought a deep respect and a closeness that the Renshai did not have the knowledge to share. Crippled and alone, he had fought scores of Eastern assassins sent to slay him, as well as the usual bandits and the disappointment that grew whenever Colbey used the information Arduwyn gathered to evade Rache once again. Then, as now, Colbey's reasons defied Arduwyn's understanding, and the turn of his thoughts to the Golden Prince of Demons made him shudder. The power that

Colbey held over Arduwyn never seemed to lessen, a shocking, supernatural hold that came as much from fear as awe.

The path widened, and the horse's pace quickened. Arduwyn reveled in the easy roll and bump of the beast's canter. His mind felt tortured and overused, and he caught his thoughts drifting back to Bel. Her familiar beauty expanded to fill his brain, then her words echoed through his mind to spoil the image. Arduwyn winced, edging his thoughts back to Rache, the effort a struggle. Instead, he concentrated on Sylva, considering the two together. The idea of his only daughter among Renshai did not soothe, and his thoughts edged back to Bel.

Suddenly, Arduwyn's horse stumbled. A trigger string snapped beneath its hoof, and pain tore through Arduwyn's upper leg. Blood rushed from his head, and the world swirled in tight circles. His hands and eye riveted on the site of the pain, a black-fletched arrow lodged in his thigh.

'Firfan!' Arduwyn reached for the arrow head poking ominously through his inner leg. His movements became clumsy. His leg burned, then numbed. His consciousness fluttered, threatening to disappear. Desperate, he drew free a rope and lashed his injured leg to the saddle. *A mantrap*. Arduwyn put the events together easily, despite his dizziness. *Not set for me. Couldn't have been set for me*. His head grew too heavy to hold. It lolled forward as he attempted to fasten his other leg. His fingers fumbled. The horse seemed to sway beneath him. His hands failed, and oblivion overtook Arduwyn.

Colbey sat on a fallen tree, his elbows pressed to his knees and his chin cupped in his hands. His thighs had gone numb from the pressure of his elbows, and he no longer saw the wind-swirled circle of brown leaves that he had stared at for the last several hours, while his companions slept. He knew only his thoughts, grim and gray, when they should have been exuberant. He studied the new Renshai, assessing their strengths and weaknesses by attitude and the few strokes he had encouraged them to demonstrate the previous evening. Tannin's sister, Tarah, was soft-spoken and petite, yet she had a bitterness and eager cruelty that suited a Renshai. She would require a long sequence of sword training, but she would learn quickly. Her physical weakness seemed more apparent than Episte's ever had, especially since she had none of his skill to compensate. She was also with child.

Tarah's husband, Modrey, would prove a frustrating student. He possessed no natural dexterity and could never learn the more complicated maneuvers of the Renshai. Of the three, Colbey found Vashi the most talented, a militant teenager with all the ancient Renshai savagery and love for swords. Her enthusiasm, Colbey believed, would one day make her the finest sword master of the group, if it did not kill her first.

Colbey raised the sword he had claimed from Korgar's body, and memory of its source made him ill. *Genuine Renshai sword, its wielder's life stolen by a genuine Renshai. A Renshai.* The word that had claimed Colbey's loyalty since birth seemed to have lost all meaning. The cruel practice that had separated the Renshai from their Northern cousins, that had driven them into an exile that had made them the finest swordsmen in existence, was a lie. Through the night, Colbey had plucked a thousand dead friends and relatives from his mind, trying to understand who had found Valhalla and who had not, who he had mourned and who he should have. Other doubts assailed him, shaking the faith he had followed with an allegiance and devotion that denied question. As the first rays of dawn touched the horizon, he wondered what other parts of his religion were a sham.

Colbey met the new day without joy. He felt weary, an ancient living for decades on borrowed time, as if the gods had simply forgotten him. His three new charges seemed more of a bore than a challenge, another generation of swordsmen gleaning knowledge he could share, another generation of Renshai hated for a crime that had never been a crime at all. *New students, old tricks.* Seasons would pass and return, and Colbey hoped that he would not see many more. He had become too old.

As Colbey stared at the pink streaks dawn painted across the gray, a dot of blackness caught his eyes. It spiraled against the backdrop of the horizon, clearly moving toward the party. Curious, he watched as it drew closer, waiting until its shape became identifiable before dismissing it as an inconsequential threat. Gradually, his sharp eyes defined beginning and end, the red, winged silhouette of a falcon. *Swiftwing.* Colbey did not understand how he knew one bird from thousands any more than he could guess how he had known the *Valkyrie.* But the unexplained had become too routine to bother him. Standing, he waved the bird to him.

Swiftwing swooped, calling a raucous greeting, but he did not land. Instead, he looped around Colbey to alight on the grass beside Shadimar. He loosed a deep-throated noise into Shadimar's ear.

Secodon growled, bristling. Then, recognizing the source of the noise, he waved his plumed tail. Shadimar rose, and the falcon flapped to his forearm. Colbey watched as the claws sank into the Wizard's sleeve, drawing no blood.

Shadimar stripped a piece of parchment from the bird's leg, and the red falcon watched him with one keen, golden eye, as if to read with him. But the Eastern Wizard only clutched the parchment for several moments, as if afraid to read the message inscribed. Then, slowly, he unfurled it and studied the words in silence. At length, he wadded the parchment in his fist, crumbling it until not a letter of a word could remain. He dismissed the falcon with a decisive gesture that sent the bird coiling into the heavens. The Wizard stared at his hands.

Colbey approached. As he drew closer, he could feel bitterness trembling through Shadimar, mingled with grief and uncertainty. Through it all wove an undercurrent of rage.

'What did it say?' Colbey asked politely.

Shadimar jumped, obviously startled by Colbey's approach. He turned and headed deeper into the woodlands, beyond sight and sound of the party. The wolf padded after him.

Colbey kicked Tannin awake. 'Keep watch. I'll be back.'

Tannin nodded sleepily.

Colbey plunged after the Eastern Wizard, easily following his movements through the underbrush. At length, he found Shadimar seated on a stump, seemingly unaware of the army of ants and beetles scrambling up and through cracks in the peeling bark. Colbey crouched before the Wizard. 'What did it say?' he asked again.

The Wizard met Colbey's gaze with dignity. 'It's over, Colbey.'

'Over?' The words confused Colbey. 'What's over?'

'I need to explain?'

'Only if you want me to have the vaguest idea what you're talking about. I thought we were done playing games.'

'As had I.' Shadimar glared. 'Yet you're playing the ugliest, dirtiest game any human or Wizard could imagine. And it's over now.'

Colbey struggled to understand, but Shadimar's words seemed like gibberish. 'Make sense, damn it. How can I answer an accusation if I don't understand it? Explain.'

'Not to you, demon.'

The word stung. Colbey knew that Shadimar had used his most offensive insult, akin to the Renshai calling someone coward. 'I thought we were brothers.'

'Not any more. I've seen how you treat brothers.'

That hurt worse than any gibe. Colbey balled his hands to fists, hating what he had done to Korgar. Yet he had seen no other way. Right or wrong, he had made a decision, and the moment had not granted him time for more than instantaneous consideration. A night of thought had left him with the identical conclusion. In the same situation, he would kill Korgar again. His oath to Sif, to Valr Kirin, and to the Northmen had to take precedence over a vow of brotherhood. Had his own life hung in the balance instead of Olvaerr's, his action might have been different. 'We're still friends?'

'I think not.' Shadimar's gaze slipped to the magic sword at Colbey's hip and hung there.

'Even in the tiniest farm village, the accused knows his crime. Are you punishing me for killing Korgar? Or for sending Valr Kirin to Valhalla?'

'Neither.' Shadimar's lids knitted to a squint, though he still stared at the sword. 'Your feigned innocence serves no purpose any longer. I know the truth.'

'Do you?' Colbey rested his hands on his bent knees. 'Then perhaps you'll enlighten me. What have I done that is so evil as to turn a brother against me?'

Shadimar looked away, but not for long. Obsessively drawn, his attention kept sliding back to Harval. 'Are you asking in order to test the extent of my knowledge? Do you think I would add to your advantages against me?'

'I'm asking because I have no idea what you're talking about!' Colbey's patience vanished as the conversation spun in another useless circle. 'Shadimar, you know Wizard's riddles and ambiguities confuse me. I'm trying to be the best brother and champion I can. If you have something to say, just say it.'

Shadimar shivered, his gaze on Harval becoming even more fanatical. Colbey's words only seemed to agitate him more. Suddenly, he slammed a fist on the stump near his thighs. Beetles and ants fled from the blow in crazy patterns. The Eastern Wizard's eyes narrowed in consideration, then widened in response to some conclusion. 'If you are, indeed, innocent of any crime against our cause, then you should have no objection to me reading your thoughts.'

'My thoughts?' Colbey wondered at Shadimar's request. 'Didn't you once say that intruding on the thoughts of a friend constituted a challenge?'

'I said that only about doing so uninvited.' Shadimar stared directly at Colbey now, obviously trying to read his expression and manner as well as his words. 'Colbey, if you have no dealings with evil or chaos, then you should have no reason not to welcome me into your thoughts.'

Colbey frowned, doubting that to be the case. He imagined any man or Wizard had at least one private indulgence or self-doubt that he would not share, even with a blood brother; but Colbey knew nothing good could come of his refusal. Shadimar had trapped him neatly. He could not deny the Wizard's entrance without raising groundless suspicion, yet he could not help feeling grossly insulted. 'I have no objection to you reading any thought or feeling of mine. I don't understand your need, but I can tolerate it. Someday, maybe I'll understand why you would trust the word of a strange Northman over that of a friend.' Colbey tried to equate the Wizard's demand with his own exploration of Tannin's thoughts, but the comparison would not fit. He had measured Tannin without the other's knowledge, leaving none of the emotional scars caused by mistrust. And Tannin had been an outsider, not a longtime ally and advocate.

Shadimar made no reply, offering no consolation or apology. A moment later, Colbey felt a foreign presence glide into his mind like an arrow through a straw-filled target. He winced, his attention naturally zeroing in at the entry site.

Shadimar's exploratory tendril went still. The Wizard spoke between gritted teeth. 'You gave me permission to access freely. Why are you building defenses against me?'

'I'm not doing anything!' Frustrated, Colbey snapped, 'What's the problem?'

Shadimar shouted. 'Drop that barrier!'

Colbey's thoughts spun as he considered the command. He turned his concentration on Shadimar's probe, trying to find the problem, looking for a tangible physical explanation and solution.

Shadimar screamed. Hurriedly, he withdrew, jumping to his feet. 'Demon's bastard! Child of chaos! I told you to take it down, not strangle me with it!'

Still at a crouch, Colbey glanced up, at a loss for what to say or do. 'I don't understand.'

Shadimar glared, gray eyes flashing. 'Why would you do that? What could you hope to gain?' The Wizard spoke with breathless pauses, and Colbey guessed that mental probing taxed the Eastern Wizard as dearly as himself.

'Stop yelling.' Colbey tried to restore order to the situation, even as confusion and frustration gave way to anger. 'Just explain what I'm doing wrong and what I should be doing. I've never had anyone read my mind before. I don't know the conventions.'

Shadimar paused with breath half drawn to shout again. He looked Colbey over even more minutely. 'You don't have to do anything. Just let me do the work.'

'I thought I did that,' Colbey said softly.

'Don't trifle with me!' the Wizard roared. 'Barriers as ruthless as those you created can't exist without exhausting effort.'

Colbey smiled, his own point made for him. 'Do I look tired to you?'

Colbey's words had the opposite of their intended effect. Shadimar grew even more uncomfortable. His fear became strong enough for Colbey to experience it, though he had made no attempt to intrude. 'No,' Shadimar admitted. 'You're strong, and you hide it well.' Though unspoken, a thought radiated clearly behind the words. *Gods, what more proof do I need that I'm facing a demon, or a man warped by one?* On the heels of the thought came a stronger fear, accompanied by a desperate will to fight, and another thought. *Damn it, it's not fair.*

I'm a slave to truth, while he can deceive, cheat, and blaspheme without consequence, with a sincerity I have no experience to see through. And every time I tell him anything, I do nothing but reveal my weaknesses and the gaps in my knowledge.

It took an effort of will for Colbey not to reply to his blood brother's concerns. 'Try again,' he suggested softly. 'I don't know how to convince you that I want to do whatever I can to regain your trust.' He tried for an explanation one more time. 'I could do so more easily if you told me how I lost it.'

Shadimar lowered his head.

Colbey felt a sudden, sharp stab of presence in his mind. From long Renshai training and battle experience, pain inspired wrath. Immediately, Colbey's mind bunched for control, and his own concentration expelled the intruder.

Shadimar cried out in anguish. He staggered backward, hands clenched to his head.

Horror stole over Colbey. He rose, moving toward the Eastern Wizard to help. 'Shadimar, I'm sorry. I'm really sorry. I don't even know what I did.' He offered a hand to steady the Wizard.

Shadimar struck Colbey's hand aside. He drew himself to his full height, towering nearly a head over the Renshai. 'What were you trying to do? What did you hope to gain? You may have found something nonphysical on the world of law, something that can hurt the Cardinal Wizards, but we both know it couldn't kill me.'

'Kill you?' The suggestion sounded ludicrous to Colbey. Assailed by ignorance, vague accusations, and a friend's mistrust, he did not choose his words with care. 'If I wanted to kill you, I could already have done so.' He patted Harval's sheath.

Shadimar paled. He backed away cautiously, gaze fixed on Colbey. 'Secodon!'

The wolf bounded from the direction of the camp, skidding between Colbey and Shadimar.

Colbey studied the wolf only briefly. If he wanted to attack Shadimar, its presence would prove no deterrent and little more than a delay.

He had to understand what had turned the Eastern Wizard against him. He needed to convince the guardian of the West of the truth necessary for the Wizard to make his earth-shattering judgments, and he wanted to regain the trust and brotherhood they had shared. Yet Colbey saw no purpose to driving their conversation into another loop. If his deeds and motivations over the last several months could not convince Shadimar of his allegiance, words could do nothing more. *I can fight a battle unarmed, but not an argument.* Colbey considered requesting Shadimar's permission to enter his mind; but, under the circumstances, he had no doubt the Eastern Wizard would refuse him. *The safety of the Westlands and the Renshai is at stake. Shadimar can't protect them without the truth. And I can't convince him of that truth unless I know the source of this misunderstanding.*

Shadimar spoke so softly that Colbey, lost in thought, nearly missed the command. 'Give me Harval.'

Colbey's hand slipped to the sword, at first believing compliance might convince Shadimar in a way no explanations or questions could. Then he recalled the Wizard's words in the town of Greentree: 'Like Wizards, demons can't be harmed by anything of Odin's world. Without Harval you can't do anything against your enemies, except die.' If he gave the sword to Shadimar, Colbey knew he had no chance to stand against the Northern Sorceress who had sent minions, in man and demon form, against him. Still, Colbey did not wholly deny the weapon from its guardian. 'I will give it to you, though you know that would make me helpless against our enemies.'

Shadimar balked at the word 'our,' his hands clutching into fists. Despite his obvious discomfort, he wore an expression of wary hope.

'I ask only one thing.'

Shadimar nodded carefully.

'You need only say that we are still friends and that you will do nothing to harm me or the Renshai.'

Shadimar opened his mouth, then closed it. He opened it again, glancing at the sky as if for heavenly guidance. 'I . . . ' he started, and stopped. He whirled suddenly, his back to Colbey. His fist slammed against an oak, loosing a shower of acorns that drummed onto the stump and rattled across the forest's carpet of leaves. 'Damn you! You know I can't lie!'

Secodon crouched, but he seemed confused by the strength of the emotions radiating from his master, unaccompanied by a direct command.

Colbey removed his hand from Harval. Justifying his intrusion with need, he eased a mental probe into Shadimar's mind.

The Wizard remained in position, his fingers tensing and loosening. He seemed to take no notice of Colbey's presence.

Immediately, Colbey found his awareness thrust amid a turmoil of frustration, concern, and rage, liberally entwined with constraints born of law and honor. Emotion scrambled the thoughts into an unreadable jumble. Unable to sort anything out, Colbey pushed past to the source of Shadimar's distress. His consciousness snaked through blinds and passages, weaving through ideas that bore little significance to him, mostly unintelligible fragments of magic and legend. Beyond it all, he discovered a poem:

The Eighteenth Dark Lord
Will obtain in his day
A pale-skinned champion
To darken the way.
One destined to betray
The West and his clan,
A swordsman unmatched
By another mortal man.

Colbey's mind froze there, strength draining away from the effort of maintaining the contact. Shadimar's understanding filled in the gaps in Colbey's knowledge. He knew that the poem came from an origin too ancient and honor-bound to lie. He discovered that the Eighteenth Dark Lord was the Southern Wizard, Carcophan. And, like Shadimar and his sources, Colbey saw how the prophecy had to refer to himself.

Colbey discovered other things, too. He found the end of a more familiar lyric, one there could no longer be any doubt described himself: 'He will hold legend and destiny in his hand and wield them like a sword. Too late shall he be known unto you: The Golden Prince of Demons.' *Too late. What does that mean?*

Before he could contemplate this for too long, Colbey found a prediction that distressed Shadimar more, one that promised the *Ragnarok* would occur when three Swords of Power existed on man's world at once. Harval was one and Ristoril another. He understood that Ristoril had already returned to its rightful place, but only time would tell if the last Sword had existed on this world simultaneously.

Colbey's heart quickened. The total destruction of the world made the claim that he would betray Renshai seem minimal. Yet, for reasons he could not explain, his probe kept returning to the original verse: 'A swordsman unmatched by another mortal man.' Desperately, Colbey searched for the loophole. Perhaps, somewhere, there lived a swordsman more skilled than himself, but he did not consider that too probable. A warrior of such ability could not remain secluded long, and Trilless' certainty had convinced Shadimar. Only one other suggestion presented itself. And, in his excitement and rapidly growing fatigue, Colbey spoke his thought aloud. 'If I really am a demon, or part a demon, perhaps I'm not a mortal man.'

Fogged by an effort that had nearly drained him of physical and mental energy, it took Colbey a moment to find the error in his logic. *If I was a demon, the Northmen's swords could not have drawn blood from me. And they did.*

Even as the thought came, understanding of Colbey's presence flared abruptly through Shadimar's mind. The Wizard yelped, panic obscuring his thoughts. Mental barriers dropped like portcullises.

They sealed mental and emotional pathways at random, revealing to Colbey that Shadimar could not detect the specific location of his probe.

Caught, Colbey retreated. His thread of thought crashed against a barrier in his line of escape. His reality wavered, threatening unconscious. Uncertain what the effect of collapsing while ensconced in another's thoughts would be, on himself or on the Wizard, he drew back and thrust hurriedly against the barrier.

The wall shattered like ancient bone. Shadimar screamed in agony, collapsing to his knees on the forest floor, and Colbey jerked free. Dizzied, he forced his body absolutely still, unwilling to spend even a fragment of his failing stamina. His mind staggered through a haze of whirling flashes of color. Shadimar's form went misty, a warped, unidentifiable shadow highlighted by the moon. Secodon whined in terror, standing protectively over his master.

'Why?' Shadimar said, rising to his hands and knees. Then louder, 'Why!' Yet, despite forcefulness and volume, Colbey knew the Eastern Wizard did not expect an answer. And, for the moment, Colbey feared attempting one might drain him of whatever awareness remained. A thought slipped clearly from the Wizard, bathed in an aura of hope. *If I gave Harval to Carcophan's champion, then he has no reason to summon the Dark Sword. The world may yet be safe thanks to my own gullible stupidity.*

Despite the risk, Colbey knew he had to speak. He kept his voice barely above a whisper, still holding his position with grim stoicism. War had made him adept at hiding weakness from enemies. 'Wizard, once-brother, I give you back your own words. You once told me that prophecies do not predict the future, only guide Wizards to their responsibilities. Why would you damn me for a prophecy I have evaded?'

Shadimar climbed gingerly to his feet, the wolf a quiet sentinel in front of him. His movements seemed uncharacteristically clumsy. He spoke equally softly, wincing with each syllable, like a man awakening from a drinking binge who finds every light too bright and every noise thunderous. 'I can believe that a prophecy was thwarted, I cannot believe that a Wizard would have a hand in ruining his own task. Had you told me that Carcophan had come to recruit you and you killed him, then I would believe you had thwarted the prophecy.' Shadimar paused for breath. 'Carcophan would not abandon the champion rightfully his without a struggle, the like of which would be beyond your imagination. Anything less would violate his Wizard's vows. The consequences of that would prove far worse than anything you could do to him.'

After decades of war, Colbey doubted any struggle could be beyond his imagination, but he appreciated the rational exchange of information, so he let this pass. The need for sleep pressed Colbey unmercifully, but he would not drop the conversation just as he had begun to understand Shadimar's concerns. 'Carcophan has not approached me yet. When he does, I'll refuse him. He won't find it easy to take an unwilling champion who wields a sword that can kill him.' He clutched Harval's hilt. 'My friend, I'll do what's best for you and the Westlands.'

A slash of strength returned to Shadimar, born of raw anger. 'You're no friend of mine.' Rage flared, then died without the physical energy it needed as fuel. Still Shadimar curled into his own defensiveness, the entire emotional exchange readable to Colbey. 'A friend would not rape my thoughts. No man could have the mind powers you possess. They could only come of chaos. And since only the Cardinal Wizards can manipulate magic, you can be nothing other than a demon. The Golden Prince of Demons. And nothing an unbound demon says can be trusted.'

The accusation pained and seemed, at the same time, outrageous. 'If I had a year of life for every man who attributed my sword skill to magic instead of practice, I could outlive the gods.' Colbey felt his own vitality returning, though he still felt dizzy. 'Now you attribute the mental control I've driven myself to achieve for seventy years to that same magic.' His eyes narrowed. 'I thought you knew better.'

Secodon crouched, his brown eyes fixed on Colbey and his lips pulled away from his canines. Colbey saw the same violence echoed in the Eastern Wizard's stance. Instinctively, Colbey went on his guard, though the effort sent a wave of vertigo through him. The wolf, Colbey believed, he could handle. He had no experience on which to judge Shadimar's threat. Logic and observation told him that the Wizards practiced only illusion. Shadimar's confidence suggested otherwise. 'You know what you are.'

Colbey had tired of hearing those words from men who believed him other than what he knew. Yet when so many with power felt so sure, he could not help wondering whether he was not the one who was mistaken.

'As did Kirin and Trilless. And so now do I.'

'We're no longer brothers or friends?' Colbey needed to know for certain.

'How could we be?'

'And I am no longer your champion?'

Shadimar went silent.

'Answer me, Shadimar. I have a right to know.'

The Wizard looked up, his gray eyes cold. The certainty of violence became stronger; it now radiated from his manner and thought as well. 'You are still my champion.' The trailing idea came to Colbey as emphatically as the spoken words. *Death alone can sever that tie, once made.*

Colbey had tired of the mistrust. It incensed him that a Wizard he had considered a brother had written off not only his life, but his honor, on the basis of an ancient prophecy that Colbey had had no hand in writing. 'My death or yours, Shadimar?'

The Eastern Wizard made a sharp cry of distress, pierced by Secodon's whine. Shadimar's hand whipped upward, and he enunciated a foreign string of syllables.

Colbey hesitated only an eye blink, not wanting to act on a misunderstanding. But the murder in Shadimar's intentions struck unmistakably and without place for doubt.

I won't die like this. Colbey drew Harval and charged.

Secodon launched for Colbey's sword arm, but the Renshai anticipated and dodged. He lunged beneath the wolf's attack.

The tempo and intensity of Shadimar's chant changed instantly. Colbey's sword jabbed true, but he met no resistance. The Wizard and his wolf had disappeared.

Under ordinary circumstances, Colbey could have recovered instantly. Now, however, fatigue robbed him of all grace, and he did not even try to pull the blow. Momentum carried him into the stump that Shadimar had used as a seat. He toppled over it, not daring to shield his fall. Further deliberate movement would drain the last dregs of his awareness, and he would not let Shadimar return to find him helpless and unconscious. Delicately, Colbey sheathed Harval.

Destined to betray . . . his clan. Colbey lay still, considering the words of the prophecy. *It can't mean me. I would never stand against the Renshai.* Yet the direction of his earlier thoughts, while on watch, bothered him. Before Valr Kirin's death, Colbey had never thought to question the basic tenets and foundation of his theology and the Renshai's place within it. In fact, he had quelled the questions of those who dared to doubt, at times with violence. *Ungrounded superstition. And how much more of my religion is the same?* He thought about the Renshai then, the wild, savage tribe he had known as a child. It bore little comparison to the scraggly band of six that now called themselves by the same name, half of whom had never learned a single of the sword maneuvers that distinguished the Renshai. All lacked the lunatic, frenzied need for battle that stole meaning from all in life except the chance to die in glory. By choice, Colbey had trained the savagery away, replacing it with a morality based on thought rather than arbitrary rules. And now he scarcely recognized the tribe he protected, nurtured, and called his own.

Colbey remained in place, trusting his instincts to warn him of

Shadimar's return, not even wasting the shred of vitality that forced alertness might cost him. His mind returned him to a day among central Westland farm towns and wearied Pudarian soldiers. He had placed the question of the Renshai's future to Sif, and her presence made him certain that he had trained her people as she preferred. Yet among Renshai, Colbey had become the piece that jarred, the last, ruthless remnant of a tribe that had softened its tactics, if not its rigid pursuit of perfection in sword technique. *Mitrian knows the Renshai maneuvers, and she has an imagination that will drive her to create more, even as she masters those she knows. She can teach and lead.*

One by one, Colbey's foundations and trusts had shattered or disappeared. He had done nothing he considered wrong, yet he had betrayed one blood brother and lost the trust of the other. For all he had tried to devote his body and soul to the Renshai, he had gathered his own personal foes even as the tribe shed the ones they had acquired through centuries of brutality.

Colbey banished these concerns for closer matters. He remained in place, considering. Though exhaustion made his thoughts seem fuzzy, simply thinking did not tap his stores of energy like active mental intrusions. *So now I have two enemies among Odin's Wizards.* The challenge intrigued as well as bothered him. Seeking death, he could not fear consequences, so long as he had a hand in them. The prophecy seemed indisputable, particularly when bolstered by the driving, pounding certainty of Shadimar and Valr Kirin. *They believe I will become a servant to Carcophan.*

Colbey considered drawing on his own experience with prophecies and Wizards' interpretations of them. During the years when the madness had assailed him, before his mind had conquered it, glimpses of future actions and consequences had plagued him. Goaded by the certainty that Episte's father would die if he and Colbey were reunited, Colbey had spent months dodging Rache Kallmirsson's pursuit. Later, Colbey had come to Rache, drawn by the younger Renshai's death call. Colbey revived images of the last full-blooded Renshai, other than himself, lying in sands turned scarlet from his own blood. The picture seemed bittersweet. Though the end of an era, Rache had died in the glory of battle, as Renshai were meant. The *Valkyrie* that had claimed Rache's soul left no doubt that, though poison had had as much claim on his life as the sword stroke that had infused it, he had reached Valhalla.

Intact. The thought came instantly, from years of faith, though now it drew Colbey into a current of bitterness. He forced it aside for the point his memory had raised. *It was not our reuniting that killed Rache; his wound would have proved fatal whether or not I answered his call. All the glimpse told me was that Rache would die when we met again, not that our reunion would lead to his death. My fears added the cause to the effect.* The conclusion came naturally. *If I could make such a mistake, why not the Northern and Eastern Wizards.*

Colbey had never considered himself a brilliant thinker, and it seemed nearly sacrilege to place his musings at the level of Wizards directed by Odin. Still, exposure to Shadimar and his assertions told Colbey that, despite their centuries and scholarship, the Cardinal Wizards were fallible. *When Carcophan tried to thwart the prophecy that a Renshai would kill Siderin, he sent his assassins after Rache. Equally wrong, Shadimar believed Mitrian was that Renshai. None of their grandiose magics revealed me.* Colbey's memory added a detail that still annoyed him. *And even I didn't kill Siderin. Arduwyn's arrow stole that victory.* Once again, Colbey saw how vagaries in the Wizard's prophecies could be misinterpreted. The version that he had heard simply called him the hero of the Great War, never directly stating that he would kill Siderin, only that he would receive the awe and credit. *Whether I wanted it or not.*

Still, the wording that Colbey had gleaned from Shadimar left little room for interpretation. It clearly stated that the world's greatest mortal swordsman would become Carcophan's champion. *And unless and until I die, that can only refer to me.* No pride accompanied the thought, only a certainty that came of reality too strong to deny. *Neither Shadimar nor Trilless cares to listen to me. Perhaps Carcophan will.* The idea intrigued Colbey. *I would not turn against the Westlands without just cause, especially to support an absolute. Perhaps I'll find that just cause in the Evil One's explanation. If not, then I will kill him, and the others, too, if necessary.* For reasons he could not explain, the thought pained Colbey, plaguing his conscience in a way no slaying ever had before. Even the realization that he would not kill unprovoked did not ease his mind. *If Carcophan won't come to me, then I have little choice but to find him.*

The night deepened. Shadimar did not return, and Colbey guessed that the mental effort of constructing barriers had drained him as fully as Colbey. Carefully, Colbey rose and dragged his weary body back to the camp.

Demons taunted Arduwyn's delirium, their bodies shimmering and shifting in manlike parodies, their wolf heads slobbering trails of dark blood across the sands of the Western Plains. Arduwyn flailed wildly with a hand crooked into a claw. The demons retreated. Their fang-filled mouths gaped in soundless laughter. They advanced on him again.

Arduwyn screamed. He scrambled backward, his sudden movement bringing a hovering, yellow sphere into view. He willed it closer, knowing without comprehending reasons that it could aid him in his battle against the creatures that tormented him. It held a power and consequence he could not define, the same lethally irresistible allure that a flame holds for a moth and Colbey held for Arduwyn. The globe remained, a round, floating form beyond his grasp, but its relationship to the elder Renshai remained clear, in a way Arduwyn could only understand in dream.

The demons prowled closer, lips peeled from eyeteeth and amber eyes hypnotic in their depth. Arduwyn banished the creatures to peripheral vision, his concentration centered on the sphere. In halting jerks, it glided toward him, dipping and rolling over the heads of the demons with a slowness that maddened Arduwyn to a frenzy of desperation. Life itself rode on that sphere, one with far more significance than his own. The air grew fetid with demon breath, sapping Arduwyn's remaining strength. He reached for the orb, but it swirled just beyond his grasp. He screamed in frustration, shouting repetitive, shrill syllables that held no meaning, even in his own mind. He turned his focus fully to the words, willing understanding.

Gradually, the words grew comprehensible, and Arduwyn's own crazed voice rang through his ears. 'What day is it? What day is it? What day is it?'

'The eleventh morning of the Month of Bright Stars in the eleventh year of King Sterrane's reign.' The not-quite-familiar voice spoke the words in a weary, hopeless tone that implied he had answered the question many times. 'Long live our king.' The platitude followed in a monotone that stole all sincerity from the words.

The significance of the number came gradually. 'Eleventh!' Arduwyn sat up. He lay on a low pallet in a room so small that the walls seemed to close in on him.

A man whirled to face Arduwyn, obviously startled by his reply. The hunter recognized the soulful dark eyes, the gray stubble of hair, and the large-pored face of Béarn's court physician. 'Arduwyn! Ruaidhri's ever eternal mercy, you're well.'

Arduwyn heard the physician's words as if from a distance, his brain still centered on the date. *She gave me until the twelfth. Bel gave me until the twelfth of this month*! 'The eleventh? It's really the eleventh?' Arduwyn held his breath, sanity hinged on the other man's reply.

The physician continued as if Arduwyn had not spoken, apparently believing the hunter was still shaking off the aftereffects of his delirium. 'I thought our king's eyes would swell to the size of pomegranates. First another death, after we thought we were finally rid of the consumption. Then you. Seeing his majesty cry hurts something in me. It's like stealing a bone from a puppy. I had to send him from the room, you know. And your daughter, too. I couldn't work with—'

Arduwyn made a desperate grab for the Béarnide, catching a handful of cloak. The movement shot agony through his leg. 'Please. I have to know. Is it really the eleventh? Are you certain?'

'Yes, of course.' The physician dismissed the question. 'Do you think I would lie?'

'Then I've returned in time!' Arduwyn tried to rise from the bed.

The physician made a pained noise, using both of his huge hands to pin the struggling readhead to the pallet. 'Damn it, Arduwyn! Lie still. I didn't save that leg to have you reinjure it.'

Arduwyn ignored the physician's comments, though he did go still. 'Where's Bel? I need to see her right away.'

The physician hesitated, just long enough to raise Arduwyn's concern to a panic. 'You stay here. I promised his majesty I'd call for him as soon as you could speak.'

'Sterrane can wait!' Worried to a frenzy, Arduwyn did not use the appropriate amenities. 'I have to see Bel immediately.'

The Béarnide dodged the demand. 'You were poisoned as well as injured. Lucky your horse knew the way home. Such a loyal girl. And who would have guessed you'd run into the captain of the guard on the return trip. If he hadn't carried that *brishigsa* weed . . . it's a broad antidote, you know —'

'Bel!' For now, Arduwyn's wounds had to take second place to Bel's safety. And the explanation of the details of his treatment fell to a distant third. 'Where is Bel?'

'Bel?'

'Yes, Bel!' Arduwyn had begun to wonder which of them had just had his thoughts scrambled by fever. He still felt woozy, as if a dark sheet covered his thoughts, yet his simple request seemed to addle the old Béarnide more. 'My wife, Bel. You know her. You treated our children.'

'Of course I know Bel,' the physician spoke with a pat smoothness that enraged Arduwyn. 'Now you just lie still. And I'll get his majesty.'

Arduwyn shouted. 'Have you gone deaf or stupid? I have to see Bel first. If you don't get her, I will.'

'No.' The physician's expression combined uncertainty, pain, and anger. 'Stay still. The orders of my king come first, and he told me that no one speaks with you before him.'

Despite his dizziness, Arduwyn knew Sterrane too well to believe the king would care whether he spoke with Bel first or second. Usually, his bargaining skills would give him the words to sway the physician to his cause. But sapped of strength by the injury and the last remnants of poison, he abandoned negotiation for desperate need. Though he knew it would hurt him more than the Béarnian court physician,

Arduwyn thrashed wildly. Agony shocked and spiraled through his left thigh, lancing pain from his hip to his toes. Unconsciousness swam down on him, threatening, and he felt a deep nausea like nothing he had ever experienced.

The physician made a wordless cry of outrage. He fought to hold the hunter still.

Arduwyn continued to struggle, fighting hovering blackness as well. He lunged from the pallet. His foot met the floor and buckled beneath him with a pain that flashed a white bolt through his vision. He rolled to the floor.

'Stop it!' The physician tried to grab swirling arms and legs.

The effort of talking roiled nausea through Arduwyn. Pain coarsened his voice to a growl. 'I'll stop when you tell me about Bel.'

'All right!' the healer screamed. 'All right. Just let me help you back in bed.'

Arduwyn went still. He allowed the physician to heft him gently and deposit him back onto the pallet. The Béarnide reached for Arduwyn's leg, presumably to examine the damage. Blood stained the bandage, brown framed by fresher red.

Arduwyn scissored away, as much to avoid the pain as to hold the Béarnide to his promise. 'Bel first,' he reminded, uncertain whether physical or emotional pain brought tears to his eye.

'I ought to let you tear that leg apart.' The physician mumbled, his words clearly meant for himself though he addressed Arduwyn. 'I'm sorry,' he said. 'His majesty thought it best if he told you himself.'

Fear spiraled down on Arduwyn, obscuring the pain. He could not even ask the obvious question.

'The consumption took her. I did all I could. I'm sorry.'

'Took her?' Arduwyn did not dare ponder the obvious euphemism. The pain dropped to a tingle.

'She's dead.'

'Dead,' Arduwyn echoed, incapable of voicing an original thought. All hurt disappeared, and the numbness spread across his body like a rash. 'Dead? Bel?'

'I'm sorry,' the healer said again.

'Sorry,' Arduwyn repeated.

'It happened quickly. She didn't suffer.' He touched Arduwyn's arm in sympathetic silence. 'Should I get his majesty now? And your daughter? They've both had a long vigil.'

'Get his majesty now.' Again, Arduwyn parroted the physician, able to comprehend only the first few words before the other's voice muddled to obscurity. His emotions had emptied, and he had no idea whether or not he wanted to see Sterrane. His memory brought images of Bel to mind easily, but the concept of 'dead' would not register. *I'm still dreaming. The demons are still here.*

'Lie still,' the physician instructed for what seemed the thousandth time. 'Rest, if you can. I'll be back.'

'I got back on time.' Finally, Arduwyn managed to speak, other than with the physician's words. This time he had quoted himself. 'I got back on time. She can't be dead. The gods wouldn't do that. *I got back on time!*'

The Béarnian physician fidgeted. Surely, he had dealt with death too many times to count, but never before in direct defiance of his king's order. 'The gods don't always work in ways we understand.' He pulled a vial from his pocket. 'Here. Take this. It'll calm you.' He offered the vial.

Arduwyn took it. It was easier to follow instructions than to think.

'I'll get his majesty now.' The Béarnide spun on his heels and whisked from the room, closing the door behind him.

Arduwyn closed his eye, certain that the death god, Dakoi, could have no cosmic purpose for Bel. 'I got back on time.' Meaning disappeared from the words, and they became as nonsensical as his ravings in his delirium. Restlessness drove through him. He set the vial down. Sitting up, he kicked it. It skittered across the floorboards, struck an uneven edge, and rebounded beneath the mattress. White pinpoints danced and sparked across Arduwyn's vision, coalescing to a white plain that stole all sight and reason. Gritting his teeth, he held the position, afraid to move for fear of losing consciousness. The whiteness broke in pieces, then faded, leaving the normal darkness of closed eyes.

The need to run seized Arduwyn with a violence that sent him surging to his feet. He ached, the hurt of losing Bel reducing his leg's injury to a distant, dull throb that could not stop him. It was an agony too sharp and new to share, and the idea of facing strangers or friends seemed a chore too painful to bear. He surged to his feet. *Have to go. Have to get away. Have to run.* The idea seized control, and no logic could displace it. Solace would come, not from any person, city, or town, but from movement and from the woodlands. Only one regret could penetrate the irresistible, driving necessity of escape. *Sterrane will take care of Sylva, and she couldn't have a better guardian.* Arduwyn limped for the door.

King Sterrane of Béarn shuffled through Arduwyn's quarters, not bothering to knock until he reached the bedroom that belonged to the hunter's daughter. There he raised a hand as thick and nearly as furred as a bear's claw, knuckling it into a fist. The tears had stopped, arrested by the physician's news, but his eyes ached and burned. His grief had dulled from the fire that had seared his gut to a flat emptiness that memory could no longer spark into wild jags of crying. Still, the task he had come to perform gnawed at him. *I should never have left the room, but Sylva needed the time away. She's been through too much*. He tapped on the chamber door.

A moment of silence followed. Then the panel swung partway open, framing Sylva in the crack. Her strawberry blonde hair lay in disarray, her dark eyes red and swollen. She studied Sterrane expectantly, needing his news too much to waste time with amenities or questions.

'Father well,' he said in his broken Western tongue.

A slight smile twitched at the corners of Sylva's mouth, and Sterrane thought he read relief in her eyes, tempered by uncertainty. Obviously, she could tell he had not yet finished.

'Ardy . . . ' Sterrane said. Unable to deal the girl more bad news, he clung to the good. ' . . . well. Get all better.'

'He ran, didn't he?' Though barely thirteen, Sylva spoke with a rare insight. No malice touched her words.

Sterrane placed a fatherly arm around the youngster, gently steering her back into the room. The bed lay against the far wall, the coverlets rumpled. A chest of clothing sat in the space at the foot of the bed. Beside it, a shelf held an assortment of knickknacks, ranging from a smiling horse Sterrane had carved from a block of wood as a present for her third birthday, to an emerald necklace that Arduwyn had bartered on her thirteenth, to the bow and green and pink fletched arrows she and her father had crafted together. Sterrane led her to the bed. He sat, and she sat beside him. Despite the revelation that she had guessed accurately, she did not cry.

'How you know?' Sterrane asked.

'Because Mama . . . ' Sylva's voice broke on the word, but she managed to continue without losing a word, ' . . . always said he was a runner. She said that whenever something bad happened or he had to take too much responsibility, he would go off into the forests looking for "something." She had to make him take vows just to come home each night.'

Sterrane knew he needed to make Sylva understand, to keep the vital bonds between father and daughter alive. Still, though his block to learning languages hampered his ability to soothe with speech, it never occurred to him to use anything but the native language of Sylva and her parents. 'Ardy love you. Not run *from* you.'

Sylva spared Sterrane the need to explain. 'I know. I spent enough time with Papa in the woods to know lots of things Mama couldn't ever understand.' She patted Sterrane's hand, switching into the role of comforter. It wasn't his vow that kept him coming back, it was his love for her. He just needs to work things out for himself, before he can help me. The forest puts him in the right mind-set. When the time comes, he'll return.'

Sterrane stared, shocked by the girl's calm acceptance. He had seen her just after Bel's death, racked by a grief that left no place for logic. Yet, clearly, she understood her father as well as any man or woman could. 'Me love him and you. If need, me *always* here.' He emphasized the important word, hoping she would understand that no affairs of state, kingdom, or family would take precedence over her need. 'Always. You *my* daughter until Ardy comes back.'

Sylva wrapped her arms around Sterrane's huge waist, pressing her cheek into his soft, ample belly. 'I love you, too, Uncle Sterrane the bear.' She addressed him by the play name she and her half-siblings had used for him since childhood, when the high king had romped and growled with them on the floor.

A sudden warmth replaced the emotional void, and Sterrane began to cry again.

28 The Symbol of the Coiled Serpent

Colbey Calistinsson rode at the head of the band of Renshai, his mood setting the tone for the day. Despite their triumph at Wolf Point, his companions remained generally quiet, whispering amongst themselves, and Colbey made no attempt to overhear their comments, especially those concerning Shadimar. He had simply told his companions that the Eastern Wizard had left. Only Mitrian had dared to question the reasons and whether Shadimar would return. Colbey's silence about the first and ignorance of the second had pacified even her. He scarcely noticed when Garn caught up with them on the trail and related his story, Mitrian tending to his scratches and bruises. That Rathelon had died was all Colbey needed to know.

The day seemed attuned to Colbey's somber disinterest. Clouds obscured the sun, scudding across the dark sky, leaving just a hint of coming rain. Although he had attended his practice, as always, Colbey had ignored his own grooming as well as Frost Reaver's. The soiled ribbons and elegant braids had fallen from the charger's mane, and its shaggy hair flew as free as its rider's. Colbey took to riding farther and farther ahead of the party, on the pretext of scouting. Apparently recognizing his need for solitude, or perhaps to escape his disposition, the others did not press.

Near midday, Colbey discovered a town amid the fields, one among many farm villages in the central Westlands. Cottages lined both sides of the main street, which was wide and cobbled, dirty and completely deserted. Its stillness awakened deep, sweet memories of panicked townsfolk cowering behind the walls of fortresses or temples, raining arrows, rocks, and less lethal objects upon the Renshai warriors. Colbey forced this thought aside with a toss of his head and glanced cautiously at the shuttered windows and bolted doors. Frost Reaver's hooves clopped down the thoroughfare, bouncing echoes across otherwise soundless streets.

A dark head poked through a nearby doorway. 'Hey, old man! Come here. Quickly.'

Colbey drew rein.

'Quickly,' the man cried urgently. 'The streets aren't safe.'

Though afraid of nothing, Colbey dismounted, wondering if he would soon face another demon like Flanner's bane. The challenge lifted his mood enough for him to head toward the call, leading Frost Reaver by the bridle.

At the door, a man met Colbey. Behind him, a plump Western woman clutched a baby to her breast. A girl with hollowed eyes and a dripping nose peeked from behind the woman's leg, shying from the white-haired stranger. A mangy dog growled, but it kept its distance.

As Colbey stopped directly in front of the cottage, a soft-eyed youth slipped past his mother and siblings. Pushing the mutt aside with his leg, he slipped into the street, reaching for Frost Reaver. 'Is that an Erythanian charger?' Hope filled his expression.

'It is.' Colbey refused to relinquish his grip on the bridle.

The older man studied Colbey's lean, grizzled figure doubtfully. 'You're a knight, then? We could use your sword arm to defend Sholton-Or. Let my son take your steed to the stable and please come inside.'

Again, the boy reached for Frost Reaver and, again, Colbey refused him. 'No. I've only come for supplies. If I join your battle, it won't be cowering behind locked doors.

The youth dropped his hands to his sides. The elder frowned. 'At least accept our hospitality long enough to hear our story. We can pay you for your help, if not in money, then with the supplies you need.'

Colbey saw no reason to let his own troubles drive him to rudeness. No matter Shadimar's doubts, the Renshai had pledged to aid the Westlands. He removed the bridle, exchanged it for a halter, and tethered the lead rope to a ring post next to the cottage.

The younger man returned to the cottage. The woman and her children retreated, and the father gestured Colbey inside.

Colbey entered a room furnished simply with stools, crates, and chests. A fire burned in the hearth, and doorways led to the pantry and sleeping quarters. Taking the baby, the youth sat on a crate, balancing the infant on his knees. The woman disappeared into the pantry. The girl skittered through one of the other doorways, studying Colbey from around the corner. The father motioned toward the most comfortable-looking stool nearest the fire. 'Sit. Please.'

Colbey obliged, and the man took a perch on a nearby chest. 'A stranger came to Sholton-Or two days before you. A Northman, our chieftain believes.'

Colbey suddenly became fully engrossed in the story. The woman appeared from the pantry offering each of the men a steaming mug of tea. Colbey accepted his, but caution did not allow him to sip it. He set the drink on the floor beside him, untasted.

The man took a small drink, then put his mug aside as well. 'The stranger joined us at the tavern. He seemed a quiet and mysterious man. He called himself Eksilir.' He gave it a reasonably proper Northern pronunciation.

Colbey translated the name silently. *Exiled One.* By Valr Kirin's vow, the Northmen should all have returned home. Curiosity soured to suspicion. He thought of Olvaerr and the loyalty to father that had driven him to break Kirin's promise and nearly send his father's soul to Hel. *Perhaps his attack against Kirin's oath might have earned him exile.* The idea saddened Colbey. *If I could forgive the transgression, his people have no reason not to do the same.* 'Could you describe this Northman?'

'Ach.' The man waved a hand in testy dismissal. 'All Northmen look alike to me. Yellow hair, pasty skin, armed with swords. I – ' He broke off suddenly, as if noticing his guest for the first time. Golden hairs still wound through the white, and Colbey's fair features betrayed his heritage. 'Are you really an Erythanian knight?'

'Pledged in the service of King Sterrane. You needn't fear me.'

The peasant cleared his throat, continuing more carefully. 'He did have one identifying mark: a coiled serpent etched on the back of his hand. It looked scarred, colored, and permanent, though perhaps not fully healed.'

'A serpent.' Colbey considered. He recalled no such symbol on Olvaerr nor on any other Northman. 'I still don't understand. Why do you fear the streets?'

The man glanced around. His gaze fell on the girl peeking from the room, and he dropped his voice too low for her to hear. 'Jake, our tailor, invited the Northman home. The stranger raped his daughter. When Jake tried to intercede, the Northman killed him. He left Sholton-Or a warning that won't leave my memory, even for a moment.' The elder lowered his head. 'He said: "In three days, a small band of Northmen crueler than I will descend upon your city."' He made a gesture that Colbey did not recognize, though the crisp ease of it made him certain it was a well used religious warding. 'Please forgive my language. I am quoting.' He cleared his throat uncomfortably. 'He called them . . . ' He lowered his voice, peeking around as if afraid someone might spy on him in his own home, ' . . . Renshai. Led by the Golden Prince of Demons himself. He said they'd kill everyone. Women. Children. Everyone.'

Colbey nodded solemnly, more in response to his own thoughts than the other's words. Apparently, the Northman who called himself Eksilir, the Exiled One, hated Renshai enough to set the town of Sholton-Or upon them. Obviously, he had hoped the citizenry would fill them with arrows as soon as they approached the town borders. *Had I not been in my present mood and ranging far ahead, we might* have lost one or two, at least, and slaughtered more than a few townsfolk in retaliation. The intricacy of the plan astounded Colbey. *Northmen fight with weapons, not tactics.* Immediately, the exception presented itself to him. *Valr Kirin.* However, he knew without need to ponder too long that, even had the Nordmirian lieutenant been alive, he would never have stooped to evil. Northmen's laws forbade rape and violence against those who offered hospitality.

The man continued, oblivious to the turn of Colbey's thoughts. 'In front of the entire town, the Northman laughed at us. He stole the chieftain's own horse and slaughtered the seven warriors we sent after him. Good fighters, all of them. Veterans of the Great War.'

The townsman's words put the last piece in place. *A Northman destined to betray the West and his clan. A swordsman unmatched by another mortal man.* Colbey harbored little doubt that the Northman with the mark of the coiled serpent was the same one who had dismembered Episte and, most likely, the one who had set the man trap that had injured Mitrian. *Any Northman who dishonors the dead so completely, who would rape and lie, has already betrayed not only his tribe, but the tenets that unite the North, no matter how loosely, as well as his religion and his gods.* That last thought hit home, and Colbey cringed at the questioning he had done since the appearance of the *Valkyrie* at Valr Kirin's death. *It's not the gods and our religion that need questioning, it's some of the arbitrary rules and restrictions placed on it by men. To hold Sif responsible for our own folly would be the most serious of mistakes.*

Still, though Colbey believed he had found Carcophan's champion, one part of the description did not fit. *A swordsman unmatched by another mortal man.* The phrase had circled Colbey's head so many times, the syllables held a rhythm all their own. *Who is this Northman more skilled with a sword than I am?* Despite the danger, Colbey could not help but feel intrigued. The idea of matching blades with one whom the gods and Wizards considered the better swordsman became an irresistible challenge. If he could get the other to fight fairly, he might finally find Valhalla.

Colbey dropped the thought as more urgent concerns came to the forefront. Soon his companions would reach Sholton-Or, probably to be set upon by arrows and spears.

The man cleared his throat, breaking a long silence. 'Will you help us against the coming threat, Lord Knight?'

'Yes,' Colbey said. Then, more thoughtfully, 'But not from here. I have companions waiting for me to get supplies and return.' He did not specify, not intentionally misleading, but not minding if the townsman believed Colbey traveled with other Erythanian knights. He pulled a handful of gold from his pocket. 'If you can escort me to a food seller, I'll buy supplies and go.'

The townsman lowered his head, clearly unsatisfied.

Colbey finished carefully. 'My companions and I will see to it that the Golden-Haired Devils don't attack your town.'

'Thank you. I'll get you what you need.' He accepted Colbey's money, mouth gaping at the quantity the Renshai had pulled from his pocket so casually. He headed for the door, stopped, and turned. 'Thank you,' he repeated. 'Do you have a name, Lord Knight?'

Colbey thought it better not to say. If Sholton-Or had veterans of the Great War, they would surely know him by reputation. 'No,' he said softly. 'No, I don't.'

Loaded with foodstuffs, Colbey met his companions just outside the farm town and led them in a looping arc around it.

'Seven veteran soldiers,' Rache repeated, clearly awed.

Colbey scowled, not liking the youngster making a hero of an evildoer, no matter how competent his sword skill. 'And I'm a demon from the netherworld.' Colbey guessed that some of his irritation stemmed from his own fascination with the vicious Northman he guessed was Carcophan's champion, but finding its source did not alleviate his annoyance. 'You mustn't believe everything told to you by frightened townsfolk. The Northman might actually have fought one drunken sentry and six children.'

'Or one man at a time,' Mitrian suggested practically.

Garn laughed. 'While they slept.'

Colbey swiftly tired of the word games he had started. 'It matters little.' Armed with this new information, he wished Shadimar was still with them. At the least, the old Wizard could interpret the significance of the coiled serpent. Still, thoughts of the Eastern Wizard bludgeoned at his already foul temper. *If I could trace this evil champion so easily, surely Shadimar could have done so as well. No friend or brother accuses another without testing every other possibility first.* 'We have supplies. I see no reason to ride near Sholton-Or.'

Garn nodded in agreement.

Vashi the Rebellious fidgeted restlessly on the back of her mount. Her green-brown eyes, scanned the horizon from a high-cheeked, oval face, and her tawny hair swept into war braids. Youth stole the sharpness that age promised her features. 'Renshai need no reason to slay men but the joy of it!' She stared accusingly at Colbey, as if to deny him the title of Prince of Demons.

Colbey ignored his new student. He saw no need to explain his motives, and he had no patience for an overeager deathseeker, though others often accused him of the same flaw. Despite Vashi's grumbling, he led the Renshai and Garn around Sholton-Or, toward the Western

Plains and the passes to the Eastlands.

Back in the ruins of Myrcidë, Shadimar stood on the straw pallet that had served as Colbey's recovery bed, his elbows propped on the ledge of the jagged window. Wind swept through the opening, whipping his white hair and beard into disarray, and its dampness plastered strands to his cheeks. Rain drummed steady patterns against the stone rooftops. Lightning snaked and forked across the horizon, accompanied by thunderclaps that slammed the Eastern Wizard's ears. He did not bother to consult his books. A decade of study told him he would find no answers there to what troubled him. In a new situation, he had no choice except to set precedent; but all the pieces had not yet come together. And unless and until he made some assumptions, he feared they never would. *For a Cardinal Wizard to act in ignorance, especially so near the prophesied Age of Change, is madness.*

Shadimar lowered his face, grasping the back of his head to stem the last persistent pain from his run-in with Colbey Calistinsson. *Carcophan's champion.* It seemed impossible. Shadimar had befriended and trusted the aging Renshai, and the deceit stung with an intensity he had not known since his mortal years. Nowhere in his reading had he ever seen reference to two Cardinal Wizards taking the same man or woman to advocate their causes, nor did the lack surprise him. In a world filled with humans, it seemed impossible that two Wizards, supporting different causes could find the same human dedicated to what each represented. *Carcophan's champion.* Shadimar clamped his hands tighter. *Of all the possibilities I considered, that one, I missed.*

Secodon circled, then plopped down at Shadimar's feet. He sighed deeply, head heavy on his master's boot.

Shadimar refused to berate his own lapse. It made little sense for the neutral Renshai to league with the Southern Wizard, and becoming Carcophan's champion still did not explain Colbey's mind powers. *There's something else here. Something I'm still overlooking. And Trilless, too.* Shadimar released his head, stretching his arms to encircle as much of the makeshift window as possible. He stared at the sky. Lightning flashed, leaving its branching presence etched against his retinas. His thoughts seemed to pulse with the thunder, gathering data in concentric shells that raised more questions than they answered. One flaw in the pattern intrigued him, and he dredged up the idea that Colbey had pondered while in the Wizard's mind, the foreign thought that had revealed his intrusion: *If I was a demon, the Northmen's swords could not have drawn blood from me. And they did.*

Where the paradox had stumped Colbey, the explanation came

easily to the Eastern Wizard. *At most, he's part demon, and there's enough humanity left to injure. But as the chaos strengthens within him, he may become nearly impossible to kill.* Shadimar knew he had to act quickly, yet he also knew he could not afford to make an error. Odin's laws strictly banned him from attacking another Wizard's champion or any mortal whose death might have significance to the world. Yet if Colbey harbored chaos, none of the Wizards had any choice but to kill him. Shadimar hated the dilemma. If Colbey had become Carcophan's champion as well as his own, then Shadimar and the Evil One would have to band together. Working alone, Odin's laws would bar each from slaying the other's hero.

Still, other facts did not fit the tapestry of truth Shadimar tried to weave, and each plausible guess seemed to contradict another. Since the claw strikes of Trilless' demon had not appreciably aged Colbey, Shadimar had little choice but to believe that the old Renshai had become something other than a mortal man. But to accept that possibility meant that the prophecy concerning Carcophan's champion might not apply to Colbey, despite Trilless' certainty.

Shadimar sighed, his speculation taking him back into the broad circles he had learned to despise over the past decade. Only one thing had finally become undeniable. The Western Wizard was dead, and no one had stepped forward to claim the title. Finally, the time had come for Shadimar to gather his peers. The position had lain idle for longer than twelve years; surely, no one could accuse him of acting in haste. At the least, he would feel better having another to help handle his doubled responsibilities while he continued the necessary research. *I still haven't found an apprentice who comes close to Colbey's potential, but there's no choice any more but to settle for second best.*

Having made the decision, Shadimar's distress eased somewhat. Gently he extracted his foot from beneath the wolf, turned from the window, and prepared to summon Swiftwing.

Arduwyn caught up with the Renshai party before they reached the Western Plains that had once served as a battleground. The little archer entered the camp during Mitrian's and Garn's watch, slipping among the party with no more noise than his shadow. Yet Colbey saw him. The old Renshai rested little these days. Finding it difficult to fall asleep, he nearly always took first watch. Despite being the last to lie down, he always awakened long before sunup, staring at the patterns the stars and moon drew in the sky and suffering his thoughts.

Between the whispered exchange Arduwyn passed with Mitrian and the grief, self-pity, and sense of responsibility wafting from Arduwyn, Colbey read the entire sad story. Still, its significance paled beside the concerns plaguing Colbey, and he offered no solace. He hoped his silent acceptance of the hunter's presence and his companions' appreciation for the redhead's talents would prove enough. Colbey guessed that the trap that had injured Arduwyn was placed by the same Northman who had injured Mitrian and set up the ambush at Sholton-Or. The poisoned arrow did not surprise him; it only added one more concern to a rapidly growing list.

Autumn stretched into a winter that seemed little different to Colbey. The southern Westlands received less snow than the Northlands did in springtime, and he felt comfortable in the same light tunics and breeks he had worn through the year. Mitrian, Garn, and Rache added only linen cloaks to their wardrobe, but the Western Renshai and Arduwyn doubled the weight of their clothing.

Dark-skinned Eastern war parties assailed them twice upon the Western Plains. In these skirmishes, Colbey proved his prowess to the satisfaction of even Vashi. While caught up in battle, he sliced and slashed with his usual sure strokes and near-berserk exuberance. But when the battles were won, he would lapse back into his thoughts, fettered by the only thing that could contain him: his own doubts.

Even with Mitrian's help, Colbey's need to train five students kept travel time to a crawl. Arduwyn's hunting saved them from needing to find towns and supplies, but the time he took to carefully prepare every leftover scrap for travel added more delays. Winter had become long familiar when the party slipped through one of the rare passes through the Great Frenum Mountains and into the Eastlands. Straying from the path, the party found forest so like that of most of the Westlands as to be indistinguishable. A standard sword lesson made the transition seem even less noticeable.

Awakened for the predawn watch, Garn sat with Mitrian, watching the sky stretch, monotonously gray, through the treetops. Clouds diffused the moonlight, hiding the stars beneath a continuous blanket of mist. Garn spoke little, and Mitrian remained silent, too, apparently afraid her voice might disturb her companions. She leaned against Garn, and her warmth comforted. He looped his arm around her waist.

A distant rustle sent Garn into a crouch. He jerked up his head, scanning the wall of trees.

'What?' Mitrian whispered.

Garn rose, waving her down. Again, he heard the rattle of brush, too loud for a curious fox. 'I heard something. Stay and keep guard over the others. I'm going to find out what it is.' Without waiting for confirmation, Garn slid soundlessly between the trees.

Mitrian's uncertainty chased him. 'Garn? Don't you . . . '

But Garn had disappeared too quickly for her to continue. He glided through the woodlands, wishing he had more light. He no longer heard the noise, and, as he crept farther from the safety of the camp, he began to wonder whether it had been a figment of an overactive imagination, sparked by a new and unknown land. Not wanting to separate too far from the others, he turned back. As he moved, a gleam of silver cut the corner of his vision. He whirled, but it disappeared as completely as the sound.

Garn's heart quickened. His muscles tensed, and he stalked a vision he was unsure he had truly seen. His path took him to a gloomy clearing, where the intertwining boughs of spruce blocked sunlight from all foliage beneath them. At its edge, Garn waited until his eyes adjusted to its more expansive darkness, untouched by even the disseminated moonlight. The clearing looked empty. Sword in hand, Garn entered it.

Leaves crunched to Garn's right. He spun to face a short, lean figure that stepped into the clearing. Heavy furs fell back from the other's shoulders to reveal a pointed buckler and a breastplate that caught what little light penetrated the spruce boughs. Lacquered iron greaves and high, doeskin boots covered black, silk breeks. A fur-lined helmet on the stranger's head obscured most of its face; what little Garn could see looked unwrinkled and ghostly pale.

Garn raised his sword defensively. 'Who are you?' He considered shouting, but judged that he had gone too far and through too dense brush for his companions to hear much. He wondered if that had been the other's intention from the start.

The stranger made no verbal reply. The stance revealed him as male, though his size seemed more suited to a woman. He drew a finely crafted longsword and cut for Garn.

Garn leapt back, dodging, then riposted for the stranger's neck. The swords locked. The other's size belied his strength, and his swiftness was awesome. The armored man retreated from the block and lunged before Garn saw the maneuver coming. All Garn's skill scarcely parried the attack.

Enraged, Garn went on the offensive. He sprang for the stranger, driving the point of the longsword to the ground with his broadsword. The stranger's body fell against him. The barb jutting from the buckler dug into Garn's shoulder. The pain seemed insignficant, but the ease of the maneuver embarrassed Garn. As much from anger as desperation, Garn threw his full weight back against the armored man, driving the buckler deeper into his own flesh. A bizarre, licorice odor wafted over him, a smell Garn knew well, a drug used to induce savagery in gladiators.

Garn's rush off-balanced the stranger. He thrust a leg between Garn's. A deft twist worked Garn's power against him, and the ex-gladiator went airborne. He crashed to the ground, swearing as he rolled. Staggering to his feet, he whipped up his sword, wondering why the fatal blow never landed.

Brush snapped and crackled from two sides, one retreating and one approaching. Garn whirled to meet the coming threat and found himself facing Mitrian and Colbey.

Garn spun, darting glances in all directions, but his assailant had disappeared. 'An armored man attacked me,' he explained briefly. Now that the battle had ended, he envied the other's battle garb and the training that enabled him to use armor as a weapon.

Colbey's gaze followed Garn's. 'Northman?'

Garn recalled the pallid skin he had seen through the helmet's eyeholes. He also believed he had caught a glimpse of a yellow lock of hair. 'I think he was.' Garn's lips felt painfully dry, and he licked them repeatedly. 'Anyone got some water?'

Above the chattering of crickets and the whirring calls of foxes, Garn heard another sound.

Apparently, Colbey heard it as well. 'Horse.' The Renshai addressed Garn. 'He's riding northeast. We'll track him in the morning. Are you all right?'

'Fine,' Garn said, though his head buzzed with an exhaustion far out of proportion to the quickness of the fight. 'Just a scratch.'

Vashi and Tannin reached the edge of the clearing.

'Did he have the coiled snake symbol?' Mitrian asked.

Her words seemed jumbled to Garn. His mouth burned, and his need for water became desperate. 'He was wearing gauntlets.' Speaking made his lips crack. 'I . . . couldn't see. Water, please. Give me some water now.'

Tannin passed his waterskin. As Garn drained the contents, Colbey's features became noticeably alarmed. Protectively, Garn glared. Desiccated eyes blurred the Renshai into a warped, vicious parody, a demon hell-bent on stealing the water necessary for life. The voices of his companions transformed to blood-wild cheers; the spruce-rimmed clearing became the gladiator pit. Garn's eyes blazed emerald madness. A dull ache pounded through his body, pulling in all directions, as if to tear him apart. Hands seized him, the grip of an enemy. *Kill or be killed.* Garn drew his sword and sprang with a howl.

Colbey dodged Garn's sudden, wild stroke, flinging Vashi from the path of the blade. 'Garn! What in Hel —' He broke off as Garn rushed him, blade flailing. Surprised Renshai scattered from the nonsensical attack, aside from Colbey who held his position stoically. The ex-gladiator's blade cleft the air beside the elder, then surged toward him, scarcely controlled and totally uncalculated.

Colbey ducked beneath the attack, catching Garn's hot, dry wrists. The larger man collapsed against him. Colbey lowered Garn to the ground, alarmed by the short, sharp wheezes of his breaths. The sword slipped from Garn's awkward grasp, but his arms lashed wildly.

Avoiding the frenzied sweeps of Garn's hands, Mitrian wrapped her arms around his chest. 'Garn?' she said. 'Garn!' She threw a desperate glance at Colbey. 'What's going on? Why's he doing that?'

As Mitrian turned her attention to Colbey, Garn lunged for her. His fingers curled around her throat. The muscles in his arms tightened.

Mitrian started a scream that Garn's grip choked short. She grabbed for his wrists, her strength miniscule in comparison. Garn kept his eyes clamped closed. Despite exertion, no sweat spangled his brow.

Tannin tackled Garn, hauling him backward. Colbey brought his arms under and through Garn's with an abrupt lurch intended to break the hold. But despite superior leverage, his effort met muscled arms like iron. Mitrian's attempts at escape grew frenzied. She bucked and jerked, fingernails raking Colbey as often as Garn.

Apparently drawn by Garn's howl, Arduwyn, Rache, Tarah, and Modrey arrived.

Tannin tugged at Garn, the latter as immobile as any boulder. Vashi drew and swung. The flat of her blade crashed against the side of Garn's head, sending him sprawling. The sword rebounded from Garn's skull, and Vashi naturally curled its momentum for a second strike. Colbey, Tannin, and Mitrian jerked away at once. The sword cleaved through the place where Colbey had been, skimming Tannin and missing Mitrian and Colbey cleanly. Garn jolted to the ground, fingers crooked to claws. Mitrian gasped for breath, rubbing at a neck criss-crossed with red welts.

Colbey knelt at Garn's side, alert for sudden movement. But though the ex-gladiator's eyes were wide and open, he went still. Radiating from him, Colbey read a pain so intense it nearly brought him to tears. Garn knew a mixture of raw rage, paranoia, and hatred so intense that it ached as severely as any physical agony.

In his days among Northmen, Colbey had seen many warriors partake of the berserker mushrooms that sent them into a wild frenzy of attack, sometimes long after a fatal wound should have claimed them. Once, he had seen a Nordmirian take too much, frothing and foaming in a crazed circle, vomiting continuously, his pupils huge and his mind as empty as an insect's. A friend had given him an antidote imported from the Eastlands, an herb with purple flowers and purple-black berries, the stem of which, when pulverized, could counteract the mushroom. Soon after taking the herb, the Nordmirian had demonstrated symptoms similar to Garn's, before he quit breathing and died. Later, in his study of herb lore, Colbey had discovered that the cure was right, but the dose overzealous, the antidote more fatal than the poison in the wrong proportion.

Colbey tested his theory, finding Garn's mouth dry, his pupils like pinpoints, and his brow hot. But, where fever normally induced sweating, Garn's skin felt parched. His heart fluttered, faster than the elder could count the pulses. Colbey's sharp eyes found the rent in Garn's tunic. Drawing his knife, he cut cautiously around the opening, revealing a short but deep puncture wound in Garn's shoulder. He no longer harbored any doubt. And if the herb was the antidote for the mushroom, the mushroom could be an antidote for the herb.

'Why's he doing this?' Hysteria edged Mitrian's voice and manner. 'What happened? What's wrong?'

Colbey looked up, buffeted by the nearly paralyzing concern wafting from Mitrian. Mixed with the agony of Garn's thoughts, the combination sent shivers through him, nearly disabling him. Suddenly, Colbey's mind gift seemed more like a curse. 'Garn's poisoned, Mitrian.'

'Gods!' Mitrian screamed. She fell to her knees at Garn's side. Pawing her waterskin free, she emptied it on the wound that Colbey had exposed, scrubbing as if this could clear Garn's system of the herb.

Arduwyn sat beside her, his expression pinched in pain. He placed a comforting arm around her as she worked.

Colbey continued. 'There is an antidote.'

Mitrian looked up hurriedly, her task forgotten.

'It's a mushroom some Northmen use to cloud all but Valhalla from their worthless minds. It has dead white gills and tiny orange flecks on its hood.' Colbey did not add that, as far as he knew, it grew only in the Northlands. No matter the possibility, they had to try to save Garn.

Mitrian rose. Most of the others turned, prepared to scour the forest for a mushroom Colbey hoped they would find. 'Stay in pairs,' Colbey instructed. 'Avoid anyone who isn't one of us. If you see the Northman, don't try to fight him unless you have no choice. Get back here, and let me know where he is.' He turned his attention directly on Vashi. 'That means you, too.'

Vashi grumbled something unintelligible, but constrained by time, she did not press the point.

Colbey turned his attention to the weakest member of the group. Despite his knowledge of woodlands, Arduwyn would prove useless in combat, except at a distance. 'Arduwyn, you'll stay with me. Help me get Garn back near the horses. We'll all meet there.'

The Renshai galloped into the forest in hopeful pairs: Rache and Mitrian, Tarah and Modrey, Vashi and Tannin. Garn ceased his thrashing to concentrate on breathing. Colbey called strength to his limbs, hefted Garn's shoulders, and waited. Arduwyn took the ex-gladiator's legs, his single eye brimming with tears. In silence, they carried Garn back to the camp and set him down in the shade, away from the fire that would only aggravate his already dry, feverish skin.

For some time, Colbey sat in silence as dawn chased away crickets and slinking creatures that inhabited the night. Garn lay still, but far from peaceful. A swollen tongue protruded from his opened mouth, and he painfully sucked breaths into failing lungs.

Arduwyn paced, needing movement as desperately as Garn needed air. At length, the hunter turned on Colbey, apparently incensed by the Renshai's calm. 'You consider yourself a healer. Do something! Anything.'

Colbey felt a light die in Garn, a part of his mind that he had nurtured and built through a decade. The loss stabbed through the old Renshai. He winced, crouching at Garn's side. He emptied his last waterskin in a gentle stream over Garn's fevered brow and parched tongue. 'Without the cure, there's nothing I can do.'

'I've never seen mushrooms like the ones you described!'

'I didn't make them up.' Colbey had grown tired of friends and companions questioning his integrity, yet the change in Garn hurt too much for him to take offense at anything smaller. He dropped propriety to explore Garn's thoughts, and what he found there made him ill. All the things that Garn had hated, had worked so long and hard to leave behind, had returned. His mind flashed images of pit fights. Blood and gore splashed through the pictures, accompanied by the cold snap of bone and the heavy odor of death. Colbey found a black void that had once harbored Garn's control. Nothing remained to salvage there, and the rot seethed, spreading to the last vestiges of caring, leaving only the constancy of an inescapable life of whips, chains, and bars, the need to kill, and the certainty of a desperate, ugly end. Finally, the memories of friends snapped out, and Colbey knew nothing that was truly Garn remained to salvage. He retreated in revulsion. 'He's beyond cure.'

Arduwyn blinked, voiceless.

Colbey drew Sif's needle, the *nådenal*, believing he had found the one worthy of its final mercy.

'No.' Arduwyn's eye went nearly as hollow as Garn's. 'What are you doing?'

'What must be done.'

'What? No!' Arduwyn stepped between Colbey and Garn. 'You're not going to kill him, you monster! So long as he lives, there's hope.'

Colbey felt Garn's pain as his own. 'He's beyond cure. If our companions returned now with an armload of the berserker drug, we couldn't save him. Even if we would restore life, Garn would be an invalid. We wouldn't know him. He could never again wield a weapon.'

'Whether Garn can wield a weapon is your concern, not mine. So long as he lives, there's a chance. I won't let you take that from him. Not at any price.'

Colbey took another step toward Garn, the silver head of the *nådenal* growing warm in his fist. 'The price,' Colbey said, 'is pain. While we discuss the fate of a quivering creature that is no longer our companion, Garn is dying in the fashion he always feared he would but believed he had escaped.' Colbey paused, weighing Garn's suffering against the pain his words would cost the hunter. 'Garn is in the gladiator pit. Every moment he lives prolongs that agony.' Colbey took one more step.

Arduwyn's hand closed over his scimitar, and he drew with the awkwardness that characterizes a desperate need for quickness that exceeds accuracy. His single eye betrayed no fear, dark and serious. He looked like a mother mouse standing in defense against a lion.

Colbey went still. Arduwyn's loyalty pleased him, though he hated the suffering it would inflict on Garn. The decision tore him apart. In the end, he chose audacity over mercy, as always. Colbey sheathed the *nådenal* and gave the victory to Arduwyn. He moved to the fire, sharing Garn's nightmare until its end.

Colbey sat unmoving on a deadfall, watching crimson fingers of flame stretch toward the sun from Garn's pyre, fire shadows flickering through the roiling cover of clouds. It summoned the mushroom seekers from their fruitless task. All but one returned empty-handed. Mitrian cradled mushrooms of white and gray and amber, as if the mere act of carrying them would convert them into the one she sought. When she reached the others, the mushrooms fell from her like tears, and she launched herself at Garn's pyre.

Tannin reacted first. He grabbed the grief-mad woman's arm.

Mitrian twisted free. She caught Tannin a blow with her fist that sent him staggering away with a cry of pain. Rache and Colbey moved together. Each seized one of Mitrian's arms, pinning her, writhing and screaming, to the ground.

'No, no, no, no, no! Let me go!'

Colbey tightened his grip, his knee clamping her shoulder to the forest floor. 'Mitrian, stop. It's neither a noble nor worthwhile way to die.'

'Death in glory, Mama,' Rache reminded. 'A place in Valhalla.' His own grief made his words ring hollow, and stimulated other thoughts. He studied Colbey, his need tangible. 'Papa fought. Did he find Valhalla?'

Colbey had seen no *Valkyrie* to confirm the possibility, and he doubted it would happen. Garn had been the consummate atheist. The gods had ignored his prayers in his youth, when the guards' whips and the constant battles had nearly broken the little humanity that remained in him. Only after Garn had turned away from gods and to himself had he managed to escape and to overcome his own savagery. In manhood, he had shunned the gods of Northlands, Westlands, and Eastlands. 'I don't know,' Colbey admitted. 'But knowing Garn, he wouldn't have wanted to serve gods in the afterlife, in any capacity. Surely, there's a place for brave nonbelievers. If so, he certainly went there.'

Gradually, Mitrian went limp, and the men released her. She rose without apology, took a seat at Arduwyn's side, and wept in the hunter's arms.

Colbey prowled the boundaries of the camp, protecting the grieving party, still uncomfortable with his decision to let Garn despair through the last moments of his life. Though less than an hour, the time had dragged like days. Holding hands, Tarah and Modrey cast pitying looks at Mitrian. Tannin comforted Rache, who stood before the pyre trembling with sorrow and rage. Vashi glared into the forest, apparently seeing death in a combat as too much reward to mourn. She had not known Garn long.

Suddenly, Mitrian leapt to her feet, her sharp, blue eyes obscured by tears. 'Northeast,' she said. 'We have vengeance to pay.'

Colbey stared off to the east, having his own debts to claim. Somehow, he would find the vicious, moral-lacking Northman he believed was Carcophan's champion, no matter on whose side any Cardinal Wizard stood. And the Renshai, as a tribe, would triumph or die.

Shadimar leaned against a crumbling archway in the ruins of Myrcidë. A line of stone gargoyles, green with moss, adorned the opening that had once served as a doorway, and the beak of one gouged painlessly into Shadimar's hip. Secodon snuffled at the blueberry bushes, springing into surprised retreat whenever his exploration sent songbirds into flight. Swiftwing perched at Shadimar's eye level, on a gargoyle's serrated wing, patiently awaiting some command from the Eastern Wizard.

Shadimar stared through the archway until the rain seemed to coalesce into wires of slanted silver, broken occasionally by the golden flash of lightning. Six times, he had sent the Cardinal Wizards' messenger to locate Carcophan; and six times the red falcon had returned, still bearing Shadimar's dispatch.

Where is Carcophan? Shadimar had asked himself the question too many times to expect an answer to come this time. He had tried every location that seemed possible or plausible, and others besides, even sending Swiftwing on a month-long sweep of the Eastlands that could have ousted a mouse from dense woodlands. There could be only two possibilities for Swiftwing's failure: Carcophan had gone into hiding or he was dead, too.

Shadimar traced the features of one of the grimacing, granite faces with his finger, driven to restlessness by the prospect. His collective consciousness gave him numerous examples of Wizards who, ensconced in intensive research, rescribing texts, or intimate strategies, had passed decades, or even a century, in solitude. One of the Western Wizards had spoken to his colleagues only once over the entire course of his reign. Shadimar knew that, during his own recent years in the Western Wizard's cave, his peers probably could not have found him either. The wards on the cave would have thwarted an undirected search, and they would not have expected him to intrude on another Wizard's person or property.

Still, though Shadimar found precedent, Carcophan had always proven the least patient of the Cardinal Wizards. Quiet solutions and seclusion were not usually his way, and the Western Wizard's unexpected passing trebled Shadimar's concern for the Evil One. One thing seemed certain. Until he discovered Carcophan's fate and initiated the solution, he could not contact Trilless. Unopposed, she would usurp Carcophan's followers, then Shadimar's; she was too powerful for the least of the Wizards to stand against alone. The balance Shadimar had sworn to defend would fall, and good would lose all definition without evil to contrast it.

Swiftwing failed. I have to find Carcophan myself; and, this time, I have the right and the means. Shadimar knew he could not enter the Eastlands, Carcophan's territory, uninvited except in the presence of his own champion. *But Colbey is there.*

The idea raised all of the frustration and confusion that had accompanied speculation about the old Renshai for years. Now, viewed from a different angle, the link that Shadimar had chased came freely to him, bringing a new insight. No single source seemed responsible for the fresh perspective, and no flash of genius heralded its arrival. Simply, the piece Shadimar had sought finally slid into place; and it was nothing new, just a distant theory long ago discarded and forgotten.

For several moments, Shadimar remained motionless, seeking the flaw that would crumble this notion as it had the others. Though it required faith, the certainty remained. If Carcophan had lost his soul to a demon or a Sword of Power, his destruction would inflict complications on the balance of power that made Tokar's disappearance seem trivial, yet Shadimar could not help feeling glad that his message had never reached the Evil One. The fate of the Southern Wizard still concerned him desperately, but that of the Western Wizard no longer did.

Shadimar stripped the parchment from the falcon's scaly leg. 'Nothing more, Swiftwing. Thank you. Fly and beware the arrows of hunters.'

In response, Swiftwing unfurled red wings and sprang from perch to sky without need to gather momentum. It spiraled upward against the ceaseless pound of rain, growing ever smaller until it became a black dot against the murky sky.

Suddenly struck by the irony, Shadimar burst into laughter amid the rhythmic accompaniment of the storm. After so long, the lapse felt good.

29 LaZar

Icy winds tore at the woolen cloaks of Arduwyn and the Western Renshai, but Colbey felt little discomfort in his linen tunic and breeks. At either side, Rache and Mitrian, too, seemed not to notice the winter gale, every line of their bodies sagging, their minds heavy with a grief that Colbey's talent would not allow him to escape. Still, the enveloping cloud of emotion protected Colbey from his own somber thoughts. Within the week, he would turn seventy-seven, a year past the age that the oldest Renshai had lived and forty years older than any Renshai should become. The thought stabbed at Colbey, mingling with his companions' sorrow, the latter so strong that it dwarfed Colbey's own, personal sense of loss that accompanied Garn's death.

Colbey thought of the last Renshai elder, now three decades dead. Episte's namesake had lived in Nordmir, a spy to warn the Renshai of possible attacks against them. He had died of an aged heart, choosing to spend his last months training young Rache Kallmirsson rather than seeking out the battles that would allow him to die in glory and dwell in Valhalla. He had sold his ancient soul so that the one he believed the last Renshai could live and die as Renshai should. And like the Wizards, Siderin, and the demon Carcophan had questioned, old Episte had not realized that Colbey, too, had survived the slaughter that had all but ended the tribe of Renshai.

The forest thinned as the party walked their horses through one of the few remaining patches of Eastland woods. The thready deer path they followed joined a tightly curving trail, pitted with wheel ruts, hoof hollows, and foot tracks. Both directions led northeast, so Colbey chose at random. The others rode beside or behind him, no one bothering to question his route. Mitrian and Rache festered in the depths of their grief, alternating between sadness and vengeful rage. The others whispered softly among themselves, deferring to their companions' need for quiet.

Pondering age and the elder he had outlived, now in years as well as time, Colbey could not keep his thoughts from sliding to the younger Renshai who had borne the same name. Since the ancient Episte had died of illness rather than in the savage exchange of swordplay, his name should have died with him. Yet Emerald had called her child for his father's mentor, ignorant of the conventions. Deeply mired in his religion, as well as its trappings, Colbey had to wonder if this lack of a guardian in Valhalla had doomed young Episte from the start.

Tears welled in Colbey's eyes at the thought of the child who had been as much son as student, quelled even as they rose by another idea. *But I know now that loss of a body part doesn't bar a brave soldier from Valhalla.* Colbey clung to the thought. *No man or group could have taken Episte without a valiant battle. Maybe, just maybe, Episte did find Valhalla.* His mind ached, needing a certainty he could never have, unless Sif chose to give it to him. He shoved aside his own selfish need to grieve for the hope that Episte had found the haven for the best and most audacious of warriors. Colbey banished tears, mourning all the things he might have said as well as the words he had spoken in their stead. *Someday very soon, Episte, we will meet again in Valhalla.*

Gradually, all of the forest disappeared, replaced by sallow fields of churned earth, flat from erosion. Cold hardened the clods into boulders, and the field lacked the wisps of brown stems and crushed stalks that always littered the Westland fields between harvest and planting. Over the centuries, the Eastlanders had stolen the richness and life from their land, sacrificing the forests for sprawling cities and building on farmland so overtaxed that it had become as hard and grainy as wood.

The wide open area kept nothing hidden, and Colbey did not ride ahead of the others, as was his usual wont. He kept to the road, not wishing to add even a hoofprint to the damage that had already been inflicted on the soil. Where the forest just beyond the mountain passes had reminded him of the central Westlands, the long, open stretches of flatland seemed more akin to the Western Plains. His mind kept seeking the ocean at the end of the beach, somewhere on the far horizon. But he found only a huddled mass of distant stone, the first city of the Eastlands, the one to which the road they traveled led.

As the town drew nearer, Colbey studied his companions. Mitrian kept her head low, mindlessly weaving her horse's reins between her fingers. Rache and Tannin talked somberly in low tones. Occasionally, the Western Renshai placed a comforting hand on the younger man's shoulder. Vashi rode just behind Colbey, hand permanently affixed to her hilt. At the back, Modrey and Tarah rode together. Arduwyn changed positions frequently, making little moans and gasps of agony, as if the land's pain hurt him personally. Over time, Colbey's sharp gaze spotted a pair of figures on the wall surrounding the city. He studied them as he rode, his vision gradually outlining the crossbows on their belts and the swords at their hips.

By midday, Colbey and his companions reined up before the Eastern city. Its bastions and gates dripped an oily green, and the cloudy sky suffocated it in a gloom that seemed permanent and fitting. The guards on the wall wore uniforms of alternating triangles of black and lavender that enhanced swarthy, sun-darkened skin. One called down something to the party in a language Colbey did not recognize. The voice sounded hostile, but the man did not reach for a weapon.

Colbey addressed his companions in Renshai. 'Be prepared to retreat if either one goes for his bow.' He switched to a relevant question,' Does anyone speak the Eastern tongue?' Each of the Western Renshai shook his or her head. Colbey waited while Mitrian translated the question for Arduwyn.

Colbey winced. The fact that only one member of the group needed this service struck hard. In a short space of time, they had lost Korgar, Shadimar, and Garn. Non-Renshai among them seemed cursed, and Colbey wondered if Arduwyn's return might have doomed him as well.

In response to Colbey's translated question, Arduwyn shook his head regretfully.

'Westerners.' The guard on the wall snorted, using the trading tongue with a dry, Eastern rasp. 'There was a time when we guarded those passes. The law still encourages us to kill any of your kind who cross the border without the king's permission.'

Vashi snarled, threading her horse up beside Colbey's.

The elder caught her sword hand in warning. 'We've come in peace.'

'Good,' the other said in pidgin Western. His throaty accent did the flowing language no justice. 'We like our enemies to submit without a fight. His gaze roved over Mitrian and Vashi to rest on Tarah's abdomen. 'Though we do prefer it if the women scream.'

Colbey could feel Vashi's entire body go rigid with offense and need.

'Be still,' Colbey whispered. Aloud, he kept his voice calmly modulated. 'I only said we *came* in peace. That's for your safety, not ours. Should you insist on refusing this generous gift, we would be happy to leave your piled corpses to fertilize your land.'

The guards exchanged incredulous glances. 'Is that a threat, O He Who Leads an Army of Six?'

Colbey shrugged. 'Or a challenge. Your pick.'

Tannin's horse snorted pawing the ground. Apparently cued by Vashi's impatience, her horse pranced, nostrils wide. Colbey's white stallion echoed his composure, a statue with its statuesque rider.

The guards were silent, faces harsh. They exchanged words in the Eastern tongue. Colbey could catch only a faint aura of uncertainty. Clearly his calmness and his willingness to fight, six against a city, convinced them that he had some hidden force, talent, or weapon.

The first guard spoke again, 'Why did you come? What do you want from LaZar?' Black bangs fringed a solidly featured face, and his dark eyes seemed to disappear into the shadow of his sockets.

'May we enter?'

'No.'

'Why not?'

'Why?'

'Why not?'

'Why?'

Colbey shook his head, unwilling to continue with the contradiction. '"Why not?" a million times.'

'Huh?' The guard clenched his features in confusion.

Colbey waved his free hand in a gesture of dismissal. 'Just saving us hours of fascinating but tedious conversation. Now, if you can't match a million "why nots," answer the question, please.'

'We don't like your kind,' the other said, though whether in response to Colbey's tactics or his query, the Renshai did not know.

'I'll try to keep that in mind.' Colbey abandoned all hope of a coherent answer. 'We're just looking for information.' Placing his free hand in his pocket, he blindly shuffled coins from one pouch to another, then drew the smaller one from his pocket. Opening the pouch, he poured coins into his palm. For effect, he sorted two gold ducats from the silver, then dumped the lesser coins to the ground carelessly. 'We can pay.'

The guards' eyes followed the plummeting silver, then riveted on the remaining gold. Their demeanors softened noticeably.

Vashi went rigid as iron in Colbey's grip. She spoke in the Renshai tongue. 'You're going to give money to those cowards? Renshai never needed gold!'

'Hush and be still!' Colbey shook Vashi's arm. The word Renshai sounded reasonably the same in all languages, and no good could come of revealing their heritage so soon. 'Our tribe also respects its *torke*. Every word you speak from now until I've settled this will cost you more than you can afford at your next practice. Do you understand?'

Vashi's hazel eyes blazed, but she did go silent.

'Let me see that money,' the guard said with a caution that did not quite hide his excitement.

Releasing Vashi, Colbey edged forward, motioning the others to remain in place. He tossed a gold coin to the ramparts.

The guard leaned forward and snatched the ducat from the air, nearly falling from the parapet in his haste. Catching his balance, he examined the coin from all sides. His companion reached out a hand, but the first guard ignored the obvious solicitation. They spoke in the

Eastern tongue again, their voices growing louder and their gestures more wild, while Colbey waited. At length, the first one addressed Colbey again, still clutching the coin. 'What do you want to know?'

'We're looking for a Northman. He's heavily armored, a competent soldier, and he bears the symbol of a coiled snake on his hand. Have you seen him?'

The corners of the guard's mouth twitched into a strange smile, which quickly faded. His companion nodded, as if in encouragement. 'Yes,' the first man said.

All annoyance fled Colbey as he followed this new lead. 'What can you tell me about him?'

'Nothing,' the guard said, interest flickering in his black eyes. 'Unless you can prove it's worth something to you to know.'

Money meant nothing to Colbey. He emptied the remaining contents of the pouch to his fist, ducats spilling into a neat pile. Again, he shuffled the silver to the ground. Without bothering to count the gold, he divided the stack approximately in half, pushing one part back into the bag. The other coins he threw, one by one, to the guards. 'You get the rest when I get a satisfactory answer.'

'You'll get a satisfactory answer when I get the rest,' the guard insisted. His companion grinned, nodding brisk agreement.

'If I give you the rest, I'll get no answer at all, will I?' Colbey closed the pouch, replacing it in his pocket. 'Nothing, I can get for free.'

'Very well.' The guard gave in quickly. Clearly, he had not expected Colbey to agree to the terms, though he had felt the need to try. 'A few days ago, the only Northman I've ever seen rode to the Tower of Night, the home of our king, Elishtan the Jaded. It's a single black tower a day's journey north of here. On a clear day, with a good vantage point, you can see it from here.' He pointed, but LaZar's walls blocked Colbey's vision.

The other guard sneered. 'He was a friend of yours, perhaps? I've heard that our lord removed the insolent, blond head from his shoulders. That Northmen exist bothers him.' His gaze wandered over Colbey to the more classically Northern-looking Tannin, then found Vashi, Rache, Tarah, and Modrey in turn.

Colbey ignored the implication, concentrating on the Easterner's inflection. Accent made it harder to judge, but the answer still seemed too pat, almost rehearsed. Not wanting to put himself at too much risk, he made a shallow scoop into the other's mind. He found a vague aura of deceit and a strong, racial prejudice, but no obvious attempt to lie. It seemed more as if he was speaking words that another had given him, but he had his own doubts as to their veracity.

'Thank you,' Colbey said. As promised, he tossed the pouch of gold to the guardsmen. Then, leaving Arduwyn to cover the party against parting crossbow shots, Colbey circled them around LaZar. Behind him, Colbey could hear the rattle of the guards clambering down from the wall for the cast-off silver. The Renshai headed north.

Colbey and his companions skirted the filthy crumbling cottages that spread from LaZar like roots, growing sparser as fog obscured the walled city. Pallid fields gave way to scraggly clumps of trees and brush that shamed the term forest. Here, between widely-spaced, twisted trees Colbey called the party to a halt to start their many lessons. Accustomed to the routine, Arduwyn started working on the camp, while the Renshai formed their singles and groups.

Mitrian prepared methodically. She placed a callused hand properly on her wolf's head hilt and drew wih a casual routineness that defied interest.

Though Colbey understood her sorrow, he could not tolerate it without undermining the training he had instilled in her for nearly fifteen years. No matter his mood or even his need to die, Colbey had never entered a practice without giving his all to it. To do otherwise would mean a serious offense, not only against his swords, but against the gods. Leaving the others to practice *svergelse*, he pulled the widow aside.

Late afternoon sun rays sloped through the scant array of trees. Bare branches swayed in a winter breeze, rattling a quiet song. Chaff clung to the trunks, caught after wind threw it, unhindered, across the flat, bleak landscape. Mitrian stared at her feet.

'What's keeping your mind from your sword?' Colbey asked gently.

Mitrian said nothing. Her head sank lower.

'Talk to me. What's bothering you now?'

Mitrian looked up suddenly. Tears welled, obscuring her vision. 'Death doesn't mean anything to you, does it?'

Colbey hesitated, not certain whether Mitrian intended for him to answer the question or not. He deliberately kept his reply vague. 'In some ways, death means everything to me. It depends on whose death it is and when and how that death occurred.' He tried to steer for the crux of the problem. Mitrian's radiating emotions did not make her intention clear. 'These tears are for Garn?'

It was an innocent question, misunderstood. 'Of course they're for Garn! Who else would they be for?' She sheathed her sword.

Rache, perhaps. Yourself. Colbey thought it crass to mention the possibilities, again hoping the question had been rhetorical.

'You can recover from a loved one's death overnight, but I can't. He's gone, Colbey. Garn's gone, and he's never coming back. The world will just go on as if nothing happened, but Garn is dead.' Mitrian buried her face in her palms, a tear winding between her fingers.

Colbey fidgeted, wishing he had brought Arduwyn. Though Colbey believed he felt emotion as strongly as anyone, he had never done well with comforting or putting those feelings into words. 'Mitrian.' He curled an arm around her shoulders. 'In my time, I've seen a lot of friends and loved ones die. Some of them, I had to kill myself.' He studied his own scarred hand, haunted as much by the memory of slaying Korgar as by sparing Garn.

Mitrian's words came muffled. 'If you're going to tell me it gets easier, don't.'

'I wouldn't lie. To you or anyone.' Colbey's own words raised bitterness, and the memory of Shadimar's accusations returned to sour his mood. 'The family we've lost over the last few months has hurt worse than any I can ever remember. Ever. You survived Rache's death and your father's. You know the pain never goes away, but it does neither the dead nor you any good to dwell on it. Life has to take precedence.' Colbey waited, certain he had not said anything she did not already know.

Mitrian's demeanor still clearly radiated vague discomfort, but now Colbey could tell something more than dealing with the death of friends and family bothered her. He could almost feel her search for the words to explain. He waited patiently, allowing her the time and space she needed.

'I guess it just seems that much worse because they died in vain.' Shuddering breaths interrupted Mitrian's explanation. 'Episte and Garn are gone. It's one thing to die for a cause, but we haven't gained anything I can see. We've lost two friends, three if you count the barbarian. We lost my father's town, not to mention my father and more of his guards than I care to think about. Now we're looking for a place for the Renshai, and all we have is a wasteland full of people eager to kill us. And we can't even enter their towns.'

Colbey knew a pang of guilt, wondering how much his own depression had tainted the group's successes. 'You gave the Westlands back the finest, fairest high king they could ever have, as well as finding Sterrane advisers and friends like Mar Lon. We've defused a centuries old feud between the Renshai and their cousins in the North. We've even managed to make allies in the West.' To Colbey these feats seemed nearly incalculable. 'You've given the Renshai new faces and a new style, approved, I believe, by the goddess herself. Don't lose sight of the huge victories for the losses. Few causes worth winning were ever won without bloodshed.

Mitrian rubbed tears from her cheeks. When she spoke, her voice sounded more solid and stronger. 'But why the Eastlands?'

'Why not?' Colbey asked. Then, realizing it made him sound like the LaZarian guard, he added an explanation. 'The war whittled down their population, and there's space. And, as racially intolerant as the Easterners seem, they don't hold any specific hatred against Renshai. For all their open-mindedness to most cultures, the Westerners do. But, if you'd rather, we don't have to stay here. We do, however, have to face the Renshai's last, real enemy.'

'*Last* enemy?' Mitrian denied the description.

'The Renshai will always live with prejudice. But, for now, this Exiled One is the only enemy I know willing to actively hunt us down.'

Mitrian pulled a rag from her pocket and wiped her nose. 'Who is this Exiled One? Why would he hunt us? How can he do all those dishonorable things?'

'I have ideas, but I don't know for certain.' Colbey's speculation had not taken him far. He had no choice but to attribute the Exiled One's actions to madness. No sane man could violate the gods' codes or men's laws. Colbey had seen chaos spark men's actions twice in the recent past: once when Olvaerr had broken his father's vow, the other time when the Erythanian knight had broken his code of chivalry to attack Colbey, outside of a challenge and from behind. But Brignar was dead, and Olvaerr did not seem worthy of the title of 'unmatched swordsman.' 'I do know this. Soon, there will be another battle. One or more of us will almost certainly die. But, no matter the methods of our enemy, the Renshai will live or die with their honor intact.'

'Even if it means the loss of more lives?'

Colbey slipped naturally into teaching mode. 'Nearly always, Mitrian, the choice between life and honor falls into the hands of the one whose life or honor is at stake.' A sudden feeling of presence nearly lost Colbey his train of thought. Impending danger tingled through him, in the strange, random patterns that had accompanied the change in the Erythanian knight's attack. To Colbey, it seemed less as if he had suddenly noticed a spy and more as if the spy had not been there a moment before. He continued his point, not wanting to reveal his alertness to a potential enemy, his gaze sweeping the trees around them. 'Through all the battles, killing, and prejudice, the one thing our people never lost was their code of laws and their honor.' He turned his head to catch a different arc of vision. 'The West called us demons not because we lacked honor, but because it differed from their own –'

Catching sight of Shadimar and Secodon, Colbey broke off. The Wizard stood nearly behind him, leaning casually against a tree, the wolf sitting quietly at his side. Colbey spun to face the Eastern Wizard.

Shadimar spoke as if he had been a member of the conversation throughout. 'If the Renshai hope to survive this battle, they had best not storm the tower without a careful examination of it. I would suggest a message first.'

Mitrian gasped, obviously noticing the Eastern Wizard only when he spoke. 'Shadimar!'

Anger gripped Colbey. He faced the Wizard, deliberately curling his right fist around Harval's hilt. They both knew he could draw it equally quickly, no matter where his hand had started, but Colbey wanted to make a point. He kept his gaze on the Wizard, but he addressed Mitrian. 'Go back to the party and start the lessons, please. I'll be there shortly.'

Mitrian stepped around Colbey until she stood at a vantage where she could see both men. 'What . . . ? ' she started. Her gaze passed from Renshai to Wizard and back. 'What's going on here?'

Colbey kept his voice level, though he had tired of insubordination. 'It's not your concern. The Wizard and I have some words to exchange. Right now, the most important thing you can do is train Renshai. And properly. The better prepared we are to face this enemy, the more of us will survive.'

Mitrian fidgeted, clearly torn. She studied Colbey again, then Shadimar. Finding nothing in either visage that she could influence, she turned and left the area.

Colbey waited until she had passed beyond hearing range, his keen ears tracking her progress easily despite the need to face a potential enemy. He kept his gaze on Shadimar and, at length, he turned his attention there, too. 'What do you want, Wizard?'

'Wizard?' Shadimar's eyes widened. 'Are we no longer on a name basis?'

'You were the one who decided we weren't brothers, not even friends.' Colbey glared, his blue-gray eyes merciless. 'Now, what do you want?'

'I thought the Renshai could use my help.' Shadimar remained perfectly still, as if locked in position.

'The Renshai have no need of companions who mistrust us.' Colbey, too, did not move. Like dogs vying for the same territory, they remained in place, each apparently waiting for the other to move and begin a challenge. Yet, despite the tension, Colbey sensed no imminent violence from the Eastern Wizard.

'I may have made a mistake.'

Shadimar's near apology seemed far from adequate. Colbey's eyes narrowed, and he made a noise of mock horror. 'Is it within the Cardinal Wizards' vows for you to admit such a thing?' He glanced through the treetops hurriedly.

'What are you doing?' Shadimar demanded.

'Watching for Odin to come strike you down for showing too much humility.'

The Wizard's features stiffened. 'I don't care for your sarcasm.'

Colbey broke the standoff with a wide gesture and a side step. 'And I don't care for a brother who calls me a liar and a demon, asks me to disarm myself, then tries to kill me. Forgive me my petty dislikes, Wizard. I don't want you around, and the Renshai don't need you.'

Shadimar took a deep breath, then loosed it. Secodon whined, pawing at his master's leg. The Wizard made a sudden gesture at a patch of ground near his feet. 'Lie down and stay there.' The wolf circled once, then obeyed, whining one last time to indicate his sympathy. Shadimar returned his attention to Colbey. 'I believe you may be right about this exiled Northman. I think he might be Carcophan's champion.'

Colbey did not need a Wizard's confirmation about things that seemed obvious to him. Still, Shadimar's knowledge bothered and intrigued him. 'How do you know about the Northman? Or my thoughts about him?'

'I've been watching you, and I heard you tell the others.'

'Watching me.' The implications went deep, potentially to an extreme, and Colbey found the idea hypocritical as well as insulting. 'You've read my thoughts.'

'No.' Shadimar shook his head. 'You would know if I had done that. You always have in the past.'

'Not necessarily. You didn't notice when I entered your thoughts. At least not at first.'

'I should have. I can't explain that,' Shadimar admitted, and Colbey believed him. Whatever Shadimar's wrongs and shortcomings, he did seem honest to the limits of his knowledge.

Colbey returned to the original point. 'So how have you been watching us?'

'With magic. It's a Wizard's right to follow his champion anywhere, physically or magically. Even into another Wizard's territory.'

'Which this is,' Colbey supplied.

'The instant you crossed the Great Frenum Mountains, you entered Carcophan's territory.' Shadimar crinkled his nose, waving an arm to indicate the entire Eastlands. 'His existence poisons this place.' Though the evidence of Carcophan's presence clearly bothered him, Colbey sensed relief as well. 'Can't you see it? The land is stunted with his evil.'

'Fine.' Colbey saw no reason to engage in incidental discussion. 'You've spied on me. I hope you had the decency to, at least, study our enemies as well.'

Shadimar shook his head sadly. 'I can only look at those parts of the Eastlands that you're in. I can follow my champion here; but, if not for your presence, I couldn't have passed that boundary. Odin's laws allow other glimpses under specific cirucmstances, but none of those apply here. In particular, I can't look anywhere I suspect that another

Wizard's champion might be.'

'And then, only on nights of a quarter moon in odd years of the Western king's reign.' The rules seemed arbitrary to Colbey.

Shadimar's brows shot up. 'This from a man who just argued that Renshai honor is seen as dishonor only because it differs from others'.'

Cornered and clearly wrong, Colbey dropped the argument. 'What sort of help are you offering, then?'

'First, I sense magic on that tower. You'll have no experience or knowledge to handle that. Second, if Carcophan is there, I should be there, too.'

In Colbey's childhood, the Renshai had devastated the so-called mages of Myrcidë; threats of magic did not faze him. He smiled evilly, relishing the discomfort he would cause Shadimar. 'I can handle Carcophan.' Though he made no obvious gestures, they both knew he meant Harval.

Shadimar inched backward so subtly, Colbey wondered if the Wizard even realized he had moved. 'It would be a bad idea for you to kill Carcophan. It would unbalance the forces of the world. That would hurt mortals at least as much as the Wizards. Quite likely, you would start the *Ragnarok*, and the gods would suffer, too.'

No matter his age or sword competence, Colbey could not imagine himself having a hand in gods' affairs, especially not working against the ones he had worshiped since birth. 'Me? Start the *Ragnarok*?' He snorted at the thought.

Shadimar quoted, 'Too late shall he be known unto you: The Golden Prince of Demons. What do you think that means?'

Colbey considered only briefly. 'Nothing. Of the prophecies I've heard, that's the most vague. Mention the words to a thousand people, and you'll get nine hundred ninety-nine interpretations.' He remained in place, his stance appearing casual though he kept his weight evenly balanced. 'It could simply have predicted that Carcophan and you would miss me while looking for the one who would become the so-called "hero of the Great War."' Colbey chuckled. 'I'm starting to wonder if Odin's prophecies aren't just an elaborate joke, a way to get you to work toward some goal or other so the world doesn't go static. In the end, the result defines the prophecy.'

All of the color returned to Shadimar's features, and his rage became tangible. 'Why do I bother to talk to you? Are you really stupid enough to believe Odin would create and nurture a system of balance through centuries as a prank? If you do, you're a fool. And I'm wasting my time.'

Whatever sense of humor the gods have, the Cardinal Wizards don't share it. Colbey saw little reason to soothe an offended enemy, but the Eastern Wizard had once been a friend. Though his sin seemed unpardonable, he did appear genuinely interested in helping the Renshai tribe. *Until his purposes turn against them.* 'Look, Shadimar, we can discuss what you are and Odin's wit later. If you have information I can use, give it to me. If you've come to try to kill me again, let's have at it and be done.'

Shadimar's anger receded, replaced by an expression so sobering, all thoughts of humor fled Colbey. 'As pleasurable as that possibility might seem to me at the moment, I wouldn't kill you.' He added quickly, clearly to pacify Colbey's ego, 'Nor give you reason to kill me. I believe it would prove as dangerous to our world as you killing Carcophan.'

Colbey focused on the more spontaneous compliment. 'You would place me in the same category as a Cardinal Wizard?'

The last of the rage fled. Shadimar smiled, clearly amused. 'Indeed.'

'Why?'

'Because once I finally realized that you weren't the swordsman unmatched by another man, I had to understand why not. Trilless had already confirmed, beyond a doubt, that no mortal swordsman could best you for straight competence with a sword. Which left only one possibility.'

One, Colbey realized, that he had already considered. Certain, to a depth no one else could conceive, that he would never betray the Renshai, Colbey had let his thoughts drift to options the Wizards had dismissed. 'I'm not a mortal man.'

Shadimar nodded.

'I'm not a demon.' Colbey stated the fact with a firmness that challenged Shadimar to doubt.

'I think,' Shadimar said with the caution of a man dancing on hot coals, 'that you're right. Though demon is a nonspecific term, meaning any being influenced by magic, excluding the Wizards, of course.'

'Of course.' Colbey left the obvious question unspoken, certain Shadimar would address it . . . eventually.

'A wise man once said.' Shadimar paused, reconsidering his words. 'Perhaps I should say that a wise *guy* once said: I make my decisions as quickly as an eye blink, and the more important the decision, the faster I have to make it.'

Recognizing his own words, Colbey chuckled. 'Perhaps you do have a sense of humor. But what does that have to do with me being a demon?'

'It means that sometimes even a wise near-immortal can heed the advice of a man who seems neither particularly wise nor near-immortal, but is both. There's something to be said for listening to one's first intuition and not letting too much contemplation skew the point or the answer.'

Colbey sighed, impatient to cut through the Eastern Wizard's vagaries. 'What are you trying to say?'

Shadimar glanced up, shaking his head. Clearly, Colbey's constant need to attack issues directly grated on him as much as Shadimar's need for cautious subtleties did on Colbey. 'When I first heard your story, I believed that Tokar had chosen you to succeed him as the Western Wizard. Your inability to perform magic and lack of influence by predecessors convinced me otherwise. Now, I believe I was right from the start.'

'Me? The Western Wizard. That's nonsense.' Colbey saw too many flaws in the conclusion. 'So now how do you explain my not knowing magic and not having predecessors?'

'Those go together. Since you never learned magic, you would have had to learn it from the predecessors. But when they tried to influence you, you thought they were some type of madness. One by one, you destroyed them.'

Colbey forced his memory back to his conversations with Shadimar shortly after the Great War. 'You said that was impossible.'

Shadimar shrugged. 'I thought it was. I underestimated you. Don't tell me I'm the first to do that.'

Still, many things jarred, concrete realities that went far beyond the fact that Colbey simply did not feel like a Wizard. Nor did he have any wish to become one. Still Shadimar's belief that Colbey was a Wizard seemed far preferable to the one that he was Carcophan's champion or a demon. Tempered by the thought, Colbey questioned cautiously. 'If I'm the Western Wizard, and have been since Tokar's death, then how come your falcon's toenails stabbed holes in my arm but not in yours? How come a pack of Northmen all but killed me?' The return of Colbey's thoughts to that incident brought a sudden rush of horror. 'Gods! Is that why I survived that attack?'

'No,' Shadimar answered the last question first. 'Wizards can and have died before their time. The reason mortal objects and weapons can harm you and not me is because you haven't undergone the Seven Tasks of Wizardry that all the Cardinal Wizards must survive. It's a series of tests the gods use to assess the competence and value of apprentices. To fail any test means death. If the apprentice succeeds, he becomes impervious to objects of law, though he can still die of illness or age until after his predecessor's ceremony of passage.'

Colbey tried to assimilate all the information. 'But I haven't undergone those tests.'

'True.'

'So how could I be the Western Wizard?'

'You would be the first to do these things in reverse order. And the first to have the title inflicted on you.'

The implications of Shadimar's words came slowly. 'In reverse order. So you're suggesting that I eventually do undergo these tasks.'

'You must.'

Colbey raised his brows, hating ultimatums. 'I must?'

Shadimar opened his mouth, apparently to explain the order of the world and of the Wizards. He closed it thoughtfully, choosing another tack instead. 'When I tell you that the Wizards spend centuries choosing their successors and decades training them, yet fewer than half survive the tasks, I believe the challenge will prove too interesting for you to resist.' Shadimar's thought came to Colbey, unbidden: *Though, without the guidance of predecessors nor any magic, you have no chance at all of surviving those tasks.*

The hidden idea intrigued Colbey far more than the open challenge.

'You'll learn all that we can tell you about the tasks before you go. But I can tell you this now. During the course of those tasks, you'll fight an opponent at least as competent as yourself before the tasks make you immune to most sword strokes.'

Now Colbey seriously considered Shadimar's offer, though he still felt certain that he was not a Wizard. He knew his insistence could only instill more doubt in Shadimar, edging him back to the theory of demons or the belief that the renegade Northman was simply a ploy of Carcophan's to lure Colbey to the Eastlands to become his champion.' We'll talk about this later. For now, we need to face the world's greatest mortal swordsman, whoever he is.'

Shadimar detoured easily. 'Once again, I'd suggest a message. As I said, there's magic. As far as I can discern, it's just construction spells and mild wards that shouldn't trouble you, but it tells me Carcophan had a hand in this. Despite what the guards said at the gates of LaZar, I tend to doubt that the Eastern king lives in this tower. Stalmize has always served as the royal city in the past. Still, it would not do to storm a noble's palace for a Northman who may or may not be in his employ.'

Colbey considered, but no words came to him. 'I don't speak, let alone write, the Eastern tongue.'

'I do.'

'I have no idea what to say.'

'I do.'

Colbey studied the Eastern Wizard. 'I guess we'll find you useful after all.'

Now Shadimar grinned broadly. 'If you had confessed that at the beginning of our discussion, we could have finished long ago. What is it about warriors that makes them jabber endlessly without saying anything?'

'Warriors?' Amused by the role reversal, Colbey laughed. He indulged Shadimar's whimsy for the sake of the joke. 'Maybe. Just maybe, I'm practicing to be a Wizard.'

30 The Tower of Night

Arduwyn approached the walls of the Eastern tower alone, riding on Colbey's white charger, Frost Reaver. He had rebraided the horse's mane and surrendered his weapons to his companions, so as to look official rather than threatening. *As if one of my stature could look threatening.* The idea seemed silly, raising doubts that would never have existed, if not for Colbey's obvious discomfort, an uncharacteristic nervousness that puzzled as well as pleased Arduwyn.

The horse wound between sticklike trees and over the scanty remains of brush between them. Sunlight poured through the huge gaps in the foliage from a sky as bright as a sapphire. Despite his wish to approach the tower openly, Arduwyn felt too exposed. The bright light after days of fog turned the white horse into a beacon, and the scraggly bunch of trees that passed for Eastland forest did little to cover a hunter accustomed to slipping like a fox through Western woodlands.

Arduwyn knew he was in less danger than the others. The laws of every culture forbid the harming of messengers. News was too scarce and important to endanger, and even highwaymen usually allowed couriers free passage. Still, Colbey had taken Arduwyn aside after the others had all bid him good luck. He had requested that Arduwyn study the layout of the Tower of Night with all the caution of an army scout and all the detailed interest of a thief. Then, he had told the hunter to be alert and careful with a grim sincerity that had astonished Arduwyn as well as made him wary to the edge of paranoia.

Awed by Colbey, Arduwyn found the elder's concern a rare treat. He had never seen the old Renshai worry about his own life and only rarely over any other. The hunter could not help feeling privileged for the elder's concern, despite the implication that he might be headed toward more danger than he expected. At a time when grief drove him to believe nothing mattered, another's care for his safety felt good, especially when that other held no ties of blood. And that reminded him of something else.

Sylva. Pain flooded Arduwyn at just the thought of her name. Bel's death had driven him to flee; after nearly fifteen years of hearing her talk about that being the way he handled his deepest emotions and problems, to do otherwise would have belittled their love. He had not meant to hurt another that he loved as much. He knew Sylva would understand and that she had the king of Bearn to tend to her every physical and emotional need. Sterrane had more love to give than all the citizens of most villages together. But still Arduwyn hated the pain his need to run had inflicted. He would return as soon as the Renshai had handled their enemy, his obligations to his friends completed. Then, he hoped, he would talk Mitrian into moving near enough to Béarn that he would see her more often than every decade and a half.

Thoughts of Mitrian naturally brought others of Garn, and Arduwyn's eye went moist with tears. He banished them with the realization that he had already abandoned Colbey's advice, forgetting his necessary wariness by losing his mind to thought. He forced his gaze back to the tower, seeing it now as more than a rapidly approaching goal. It seemed out of place against the royal blue of the sky, a tower without a town, each block perfectly shaped and placed so as to make it appear seamless. A curtain wall surrounded it, as carefully constructed as the monument it guarded. The single obsidian tower stretched toward the sky like an ebony arrow.

As Arduwyn approached the portcullis, he discovered a pair of guards with crimson helmets standing on the ramparts, watching him from sentry stands on either side of the closed entryway. Each clutched a spear adorned with crow's feathers, trained on the nearing hunter.

Affected by Colbey's discomfort, Arduwyn's will faltered. He called up hesitantly, 'I'm a messenger from the West. I'm here to see your king.'

The sentries gave no response. The spears remained in place.

Arduwyn searched his mind for the two Eastern sentences Shadimar had taught him before he left, the words now buried beneath other concerns. His heart pounded. '*Al aila . . . lessakit . . . a Vestan orlane . . . rexin.*' His Western accent rendered the phrase nearly incomprehensible, but one of the men disappeared from his post and the other lowered his spear.

Arduwyn dismounted and tethered Frost Reaver to a tree. Shortly, he heard the metallic clicks of the lifting portcullis. The great iron portal lifted to reveal a barren courtyard and a guard in blood red armor. The Easterner snapped a few sounds at Arduwyn.

Arduwyn shrugged and shook his head, responding with Shadimar's other Eastern sentence: 'I don't speak Eastern.' The Wizard had seemed certain that the king would have at least one translator, and the LaZarian sentries' use of the common trade tongue made Arduwyn certain he would find a way to communicate.

With a frown, the sentry waved Arduwyn toward the tower.

The courtyard of King Elishtan the Jaded made Arduwyn jittery. The thick, high walls surrounding it trapped air around the tower. It seemed inappropriately warm and stale. Each breath pained, and Arduwyn felt caged. He memorized the courtyard from habit, noting the few sentries who paced the sand-colored desolation between the tower and its wall. Up close, Arduwyn could see the construction of the tower, its blocks framed by perfect joints that left no crack thicker than an eyelash. A gully circled the base of the tower, hemmed by a ledge of piled sand. Apparently, workers had begun to build a moat, abandoning their efforts for the sturdier, more practical defense of the wall.

Arduwyn had little time to stare. The sentry jerked his head, his dark hair pinned in place beneath the helmet, gesturing his charge through a set of double doors leading into the Tower of Night.

Once through, the guard took the lead again, and Arduwyn trailed the crimson figure up several large obsidian steps, through a door, and into a corridor lit by an occasional smoking brazier in the stretches between the high windows. Guards in the standard red leather or mail ambled the length of the halls or haunted niches, staring at the stranger with dead black eyes. Shuddering, Arduwyn continued to follow his guide.

The passage twisted, wove, and joined others. Arduwyn followed, growing more skittish by the moment. For its shape, the tower seemed to hold too many passages, and it took him longer than it should have to realize that several of these curved and slanted. Over time, they had spiraled upward several floors.

At length, the guard brought Arduwyn through a doorless entryway and into a room palely-illuminated by a single, arched window that, even from a distance, Arduwyn could see overlooked the courtyard. Another sentry stood, rigid, at the opening, a sword at his belt and a spear in his hand. A matching couch and chair faced one another, clean to the point of unwelcoming sterility. The closed stuffiness goaded Arduwyn naturally to the window, despite its guard. Looking out, he discovered that he had ascended higher than he had expected. He looked down from a height of four of Béarn's castle stories. Far below lay the partially excavated moat, ringed by piled sand and puddled with brackish rainwater.

The two Easterners chatted briefly. The one who had escorted Arduwyn turned and trotted back down the corridor.

The other addressed Arduwyn directly in the trading tongue. 'What's your message?' He scratched languidly at his red mail shirt and leaned on the spear.

Arduwyn passed the rolled sheet of parchment, uncertain of its contents. He could not even read the languages he spoke, and

Shadimar's Eastern lettering looked like a random series of dots and slashes. 'It's for King Elishtan.'

'Elishtan,' the guard repeated, then laughed. 'I didn't know your lords were golden-haired. Wait here for the king's reply.' He pointed to the embroidered couch, the piece of furniture nearest Arduwyn and the window.

The guard's words jarred. Arduwyn nodded politely, gritting his teeth as the sentry swept through the door and into the corridor. The Renshai had chosen him as messenger because he did not look Renshai or Northern. He also suspected no one else would enter the tower unarmed. Now he felt like a deer in shifting winds who fleetingly scent hounds. *Why would the king's name bring such an odd reaction from his guard? And what about the name would indicate the sender of the message?* The question seemed all the more germane since the sentry had not even glanced at the parchment. *Something about the use of the king's name told him things it shouldn't have.* Sensing a trap, Arduwyn slipped across the room, glancing to the right and left down the corridor. Seeing only the message-carrier's retreating back, moving in the opposite direction than the one from which Arduwyn had come, he padded silently after this familiar guard, determined to find answers.

Arduwyn's journey did not take him far. The corridor widened and ended abruptly at a bronze door adorned with a gold carving of a rearing cobra. The set jade eyes formed a strange contrast that the flickering braziers turned into movement. The gaze seemed to follow Arduwyn's every step.

Though he knew it was illusion, Arduwyn sucked air through his teeth and cowered against the wall. Only now, it occurred to him that he had wasted his time following the guard. Even if he managed to walk inaudibly through the corridors, he could not become unseen to slip through the portal. And even if he could, he could not understand their Eastern speech.

Yet luck came to Arduwyn. The man who carried his message flicked the door shut carelessly. The bronze panel clanked behind him, but it did not latch. Arduwyn crept nearer, hunching into the shadow of the portal. Through the crack, he saw red leather shifting in random patterns. Finding the man who carried his message by the soft chitter of his armor, Arduwyn tracked him to the far end of the room. To his amazement, the Easterner used the Western trading tongue.

'My lord, the Renshai sent a one-eyed messenger with this.'

Arduwyn heard the dull crackle of parchment. A high-pitched laugh rent the air, falling into a deep silence.

The sentry cleared his throat, obviously unnerved. 'Should we send a reply?'

'A reply? Yes, we will send them a reply.' The voice seemed out of place, thinner and lighter than the Easterners' guttural accent. He spoke the trading tongue with the lilting pattern of a Westerner. 'Send them their messenger's head.'

Arduwyn staggered, and his heart shifted into a fluttering pattern that stole his breath and his ability to think. He did not wait to hear the closing amenities between king and subject. His mind would not function, unable to contemplate an order that transcended laws unbroken since the beginning of time. Arduwyn's legs took over. They carried him recklessly quickly through the widened passage. As he passed the gilded room in which he was to have waited, his frenzied mind leapt to life to warn him of the futility of racing, unarmed, through a tower with guardsmen prowling the hallways.

Footsteps thumped behind Arduwyn. He dodged into the doorless waiting room, gaze racing faster now than his pounding heart. He saw no place to hide. Keeping his eye on the doorway, he backed toward the window. Climbing to the sill, he studied the four-story drop, the distant walls, and the sparse but beckoning forest beyond it. Logic told him he would probably not survive a jump.

The Eastern guardsman entered the room, eyes riveting directly on the red-haired Erythanian. Apparently, Arduwyn's demeanor cued him to the hunter's knowledge, because he smiled without explanation. The guard's hand moved to his hilt as he headed toward Arduwyn, no longer holding the spear. 'You miserable little eavesdropper. Perhaps you do deserve to die.' His sword rasped from its sheath.

Arduwyn whirled to face the guard. All fear disappeared as the fight reflex took over. He crouched, prepared to battle to his death. Once, he had faced down the Golden Prince of Demons. He would not quail before any lesser threat.

The guard closed and latched the door. He pushed aside both chairs, leaving himself a clear, straight path to the window. With a series of deft pushes, he slid the couch directly before the door. He turned, staring up the long, now-empty lane to the hunter.

Arduwyn measured the distance to escape. Even if he could divert the guard, it would take an interminable amount of time to open the door. Delay would not do. To survive, he would first have to incapacitate the guard. Even buoyed by gathered courage, Arduwyn hated his odds. Even if he carried a weapon, he had little hope of winning a battle against a trained soldier working on the orders of his king.

The guard advanced, stance low, gaze fixed on Arduwyn and alert for any movement.

Again, Arduwyn spun, intending to measure the fall to the

courtyard once more, as if time might have changed it.

The guard charged.

Startled by the sudden attack, Arduwyn twisted, misjudged his footing, and fell through the arched window.

Air thundered and surged around Arduwyn. Instinctively, he attempted to twist to meet the threat. Before he managed to rotate halfway, he struck the ground. His right hand and hip sank into the side of the sand pile. His shoulder crashed into a rock, and the fall slammed the breath from his lungs. He half-rolled, half-slid down the piled sand and into the water, gasping for air, the slope breaking his momentum in stages. His lungs would not expand, and the effort shocked pain through snapped ribs. The certainty of death brought a jolt of panic.

Air wheezed into Arduwyn's lungs. He gasped it madly, despite the agony this ran through his ribs. Surging to his feet, he staggered into the courtyard. His right arm hung, limp and useless, and he tasted blood. Wild with panic, he barely felt the pain. He ran.

Angry Eastern shouts erupted from the window above him. A spear cut the air over and behind him, landing near enough that he felt the shaft against his ankle. A daze cloaked thought. Pain ached through his chest. Blood bubbled from his nose and mouth, churning nausea. Arduwyn fixed his gaze on the cut stone steps that gave the sentries access to the ramparts. And ran.

Arduwyn felt as if he had slipped into a dream where his legs moved, but the scenery changed in slowed motion, as if the ground simply scrolled beneath him. Then, he came to the base of the wall and scrambled up the stairs. Abruptly, a thought cut over the dull chaos clouding his mind. *How long will it take the sentries on the wall to discover me? How long before some bowman takes me from the ground?* He climbed, too one-track to even glance back for pursuit until he stood on the ramparts.

Once there, he hesitated, confused. The drop from the wall to the ground was greater than the one he was lucky to have survived. The spindly forest encroached on the wall, welcome despite its sparseness. Finally, Arduwyn spread his attention to peripheral as well as forward vision, and he shifted his head to his blind side. The sentries on the ramparts sped toward him. From below, a spear tore his tunic and a furrow of skin from his back. With a desperate cry, he dove from the parapet.

Arduwyn's right arm did not obey him. He flailed with the other. His hand closed over a hemlock branch, the quills tearing his fingers. The trunk bent, slowing his fall, modestly bearing the hunter's weight to the ground. Pain-wracked and sobbing, Arduwyn crawled into the safety of the forest.

*

Darkness filled the Eastland forest near the Tower of Night. A crescent moon and a spread of stars added a few shades of gray to the otherwise complete blackness. Tight to the ground, Colbey glanced through the skeletal mesh of barren branches, studying the wall surrounding the tower and the gleaming silver of its portcullis. Frost Reaver stood near the gate, head low in sleep, his white hide clearly visible in the hovering night.

To Colbey's right, Mitrian and Rache waited in silence. To his left, Tannin, Shadimar, and Vashi chatted quietly. Modrey and Tarah had remained behind to guard Arduwyn and tend to his wounds, though Colbey suspected those three had little to fear from Carcophan's champion anymore. The Northman had drawn the Renshai to his lair. Now it made sense to make them meet him on his territory and on his terms.

Colbey frowned, studying the pair of moonlit red helmets that peeked over the battlements on either side of the portcullis. Sneak tactics bothered him. Since his first battle at the age of three, the Renshai had attacked in forthright boldness, though the forewarning meant enemy arrows took down several Renshai before they reached the battle. Yet, here, Colbey saw the need for stealth. The Renshai's feud was only with the Northman who called himself Eksilir, the Exiled One. He saw no need for the last few Renshai to die, nor for taking the lives of too many innocent guardsmen. Once they had reached the Northman, the battle could begin in earnest. Sword to sword. Renshai to Northman. Honor to dishonor. *One to one. Anything more would violate the tenets sanctioned by the gods. Worse, it would violate my own sense of fairness, and I won't do that at any cost.*

The decision haunted Colbey, and he knew it would cost dearly. His conscience told him that the payment for that choice would be his own life, but that did not ease his mind. So much could happen, and he dared not underestimate the cruelty, malice, and chaos of his opponent, a swordsman unmatched by another mortal man. 'If we're forced to retreat, I'll mount Frost Reaver and do battle while the rest of you escape. We'll regroup at the camp; or, if they discover that, at the boundary between East and West. Mitrian, when I'm not there, you're in charge. I expect you to obey any last order I might make. After that, carry on like Renshai. With honor.'

Mitrian studied Colbey, her expression somber to the edge of fear. The war in Santagithi's Town had ended too similarly for her to miss the comparison. She looked away, saying nothing, and a concept came from her thoughts to Colbey. It was a vow of unity, a silent promise that the Renshai would live or die together.

The idea bothered Colbey, but he did not chastise. Honor was not an absolute, and circumstance would have to determine the outcome.

'What about the sentries?' Tannin kept his gaze and the conversation on the matter at hand. 'If we come too close, they'll sound the alarm.'

Colbey said nothing, returning his thoughts to the guards. Rache and the Wizard remained in place, unmoving.

In the hushed stillness of winter night, Vashi fingered her sword. 'Renshai thwarted by sentries? Bah! Let's battle their gate and notch our swords upon their helms. Let their black walls run crimson . . . '

Colbey waved her silent. 'I think I can take one of them from here. I'm not sure I can get both, though. The other may scream.' He considered the mental effort such a task would involve. During the war that had killed Santagithi, Colbey had stabbed into the Valr Kirin's mind hard enough to pain the Nordmirian officer. He had no idea whether he had the mind power to kill a man, but Colbey knew he did not need to kill, only to knock the other from the parapet. Still, he hated the cost. *To weaken myself before a battle is folly.* Yet he saw no other way. *If we fight these guards sword to sword, we will fight every other guard in the tower. Too many will die for the cause of a feud only between Renshai and one man. And we may become too engrossed to face our real enemy.*

Logic told Colbey the necessary tactic, yet still he balked. *By Renshai tenet, to creep up on these men unannounced and slay them is wrong. The same is true of using arrows or spears. But there is no precedent for mind attacks.* Colbey considered at length, while his companions fidgeted. He took his memory back to the reasons for those laws, trying to find the logic that formed their basis. Always, the Renshai honor came from pitting skill against skill. Though the tribe had learned stealth from barbarians like Korgar, they had never considered that a proper combat technique, since an opponent could not directly fight it with stealth of his own. Raining arrows down on enemies meant the likelihood of a lucky shot, rather than a skillful one. And neither of those required true, taxing effort.

Colbey knew that his mental skill came from building his concentration through the decades. Like sword skill, it was an ability any man willing to put in the practice could learn; Colbey had proven that when he had taught Garn to channel his mental strength into physical power. *Had they taken the time and effort to train, these men could fight my mental attacks just as they could fight my sword strokes.* He believed that to be the case, though he needed to know for certain. At the price of even more vitality, Colbey sought knowledge and truth. Gently, he tapped a mental probe against Shadimar's thoughts. *I'm here, Shadimar. May I have access?*

Shadimar stiffened, physically and mentally. Just the proximity of their thoughts gave Colbey a glimpse of the Wizard's nervousness and doubt. Apparently, the old Wizard still harbored some uncertainty regarding Colbey's loyalties. *What do you want?*

Just the answer to a question.

Ask.

Do men have mind powers, or only Wizards? If I am a Wizard . . . Colbey clarified quickly, *and I'm not admitting I am. But if I were a Wizard, would that be the only reason I have these powers?*

Shadimar hesitated a long time. Politely, Colbey withdrew, not wanting to waste his energy nor intrude on the Wizard's private contemplation.

Shortly, Shadimar brought his answer to Colbey. *I did not have mind powers as a mortal, but I don't know whether or not it's possible. Yours are unlike any Wizard's. I could find no references to any Wizard who could enter the minds of mortals, nor any who could search another Wizard's thoughts unnoticed. If, indeed, you subdued or destroyed the knowledge of twenty Western Wizards, then you had to have had strong mind powers before Tokar's ceremony.*

And, hypothetically, if I am a Wizard, I was a mortal before Tokar's ceremony.

It would seem certain.

A mortal with mind powers.

Obviously.

Colbey dropped the line of thought, his question answered. If it fell within Renshai law to fight a man skill weapon to skill weapon and it was possible for the man to have learned the skill, then all he had to do was announce his mental presence before killing to give the other the opportunity to fight back, whether with a mental attack or with a spear. Nothing in any battle code forbid warriors from fighting weaker warriors. Then, ideas of law and honor brought another concern to mind. Again he contacted Shadimar. *If I'm a Wizard, does that mean I can't kill mortals without breaking Odin's laws?* The thought pained.

Shadimar hesitated, as if not quite ready to reveal some piece of information. Then something deeper kicked in, a promise to himself regarding trust. *You're not bound by Odin's laws for Wizards until after you learn those laws. During the Seven Tasks of Wizardry.*

Colbey sensed that the Eastern Wizard had more to say, so he waited.

It isn't exactly true that the Cardinal Wizards can't kill any mortals. For example, we can kill our own champions. Shadimar kept a peacefulness around his words that promised a truce, though his obvious revelation might have reawakened the bitterness between them. *The key to killing other mortals is that any ones we directly kill must have absolutely no significance to the major events of the future or the prophecies.*

The explanation seemed too vague to Colbey. *How could you possibly know that? Does Odin give you some sort of feeling or sign?*

Never. An age-old sense of responsibility washed over Shadimar, clearly readable to Colbey. Apparently, he had uncovered a problem that had plagued Cardinal Wizards since their system began. *Our laws are many, old, and complex. With every action a Wizard has to measure and interpret those laws.*

For the moment, Colbey could sympathize. Renshai honor seemed equally binding.

Colbey must have communicated that concept, because Shadimar seized on it. *Yes, cultural honor goes deep as well; but there's no penalty for ignorant misinterpretation, except guilt or a need to beg forgiveness. If a Cardinal Wizard breaks a law, intentionally or not, we could cause the destruction of all gods, Wizards, and men.*

Suddenly, Colbey believed he understood why Shadimar rarely used magic and why he simplified the law by claiming that he could never harm mortals.

Shadimar continued, returning to the question. *That's why we almost never kill mortals. Of course, if we chose to, the odds would be with us for any individual* not *being of dire significance. But the truth is, it's rare that a mortal without significance comes into a position where a Cardinal Wizard would want to slay him.*

Colbey sensed more, as if Shadimar had needed to make such a decision recently. But the Eastern Wizard sent nothing more. Colbey tried to soothe the Wizard, his thoughts on the *Valkyrie* that had shaken the foundations on which he had placed all faith and reason since infancy. *Sometimes, you have to take a chance, no matter the cost. Without risk, there can be no change. And, without change, the world will stagnate into an oblivion every bit as awful as* Ragnarok's *chaos.* The insight surprised even Colbey, and it gave him pause as well.

Although little time had passed while Colbey and Shadimar had carried out this exchange, it was too long for Vashi. 'If we stay here long enough, daylight will come. If need be, I'll fight both of those sentries.'

'No.' Colbey placed a warning hand on Vashi's sword wrist. 'We have more important enemies than to weaken ourselves fighting hordes of guardsmen who have no stake in this matter. I'll handle the sentries one by one. We'll just have to hope I can work fast enough to prevent a scream.'

'You talk as if you can wish men dead,' Vashi said. 'If that were true, we wouldn't need to wield swords.'

Colbey ignored his eager student. Head sagging, he channeled the power of his body into his mind. His too long hair fell into his eyes. His fingers tightened to tense balls, whitening his knuckles. Gingerly, he stood, walking to the edge of the forest, and his thoughts sought those of one of the sentries.

Instantly, Colbey's mind touched another. He found boredom that went deeper than a single night on a quiet watch. Not bothering to delve, the Renshai sent his message. *I am here, and I am your enemy. Fight me or die.*

The thoughts around Colbey blanked as he withdrew his probe. He stood, fully revealed, in the moonlight, giving the other plenty of time to spot him. Then, he gathered strength from his limbs, hardening and sharpening his thoughts into a single, sharp spear of energy. His head felt heavy and full, as if it might explode. He jerked suddenly, driving half of the collected mental energy for the mind he had explored, saving the remainder for the other.

Both sentries plummeted from the ramparts, and, simultaneously, Colbey collapsed to the ground.

Mitrian ran to his side, catching one of his hands. '*Torke*. Are you all right? What happened?'

Colbey felt power trickle back into his body, glad he had saved vitality for the attack against the second sentry. His throat felt raw and dry. A thickness in the center of his head dulled his thoughts like a fever. His arms and legs seemed weighted. 'I'm fine, just tired. Give me time to recover.' He crawled back into the brush, aware he could not wait too long. Eventually, other guards would come to exchange watches with their dead friends, destroying any advantage his ploy might have gained.

Gradually, the fog lifted from Colbey's mind, admitting an alarming thought. *I killed one sentry, but they both fell. What happened to the other?* He understood little about the mind powers. Previous experience told him that mental current was nonphysical. It would not ricochet or draw others into its range. Clearly, someone else had killed the second sentry. Colbey glanced from the guards, who lay like twisted birds in their red metal plumage, to each of his companions. Mitrian remained at his side, a worried expression scoring her features. Rache, Vashi, and Tannin discussed what they had seen in awed tones. And Shadimar stared at the Tower of Night with his usual impassive silence.

Colbey sat up. 'Go,' he signaled Mitrian.

Mitrian dropped to her belly and slithered to the base of the wall. There, she rose, securing a grapple from the back of her belt. She swung and hurled. The thin-toothed cross of steel struck the wall with a metallic clink, bounced, and fell back to Mitrian. Regathering the rope, Mitrian tried again. This time, the tines bit into the ramparts. She tested its position, then clambered up and over the battlements.

All conversation disappeared. A wind rose, rattling through the stark, leafless branches. This sound was soon joined by the click of the rising portcullis. Mitrian poked her head through the opening and made a brisk gesture.

Shadimar and the Renshai scrambled through the opening and into the desolate courtyard. While the others avoided sentries and scanned the inner wall, Rache and Tannin reaffixed the gate. The red armor of the scattered courtyard sentries glowed like fires in the moonlight, rendering them visible enough to avoid. Vashi's overeager blade found an opening in one's armor, and he dropped without a sound.

Colbey swore in a sharp whisper. Shoving the teenager aside with a warning, he paused to drag the dead man into the abandoned diggings near the wall. The corpse rolled down the embankment and into the brackish water with barely a splash. Without brush to hide the body, Colbey wondered how long it would take for the others to discover it.

Colbey glanced up from his task to find Rache clinging to a rope that graced the tower's slick, black wall. Several stories above him, Tannin's booted feet disappeared through the window, revealing the grapple lodged on the sill. Rache skittered upward.

Colbey took a quick survey. Only he, Shadimar, Secodon, and Vashi remained outside. He nudged Vashi toward the rope, gesturing to indicate Shadimar should follow. Colbey stood on the piled sand, placing his body between the main part of the courtyard and the rope, trying to use his dark clothing to hide flashes of steel and movement. He hoped that people's natural inclination to look in any direction but up would shield the climbers higher on the rope. Doubts assailed him. Despite learning stealth to safely slip past archers, the Renshai had never used the technique for raiding. Sneak attacks did not fit the tribe's honor mentality, yet too few remained for any other tactic. Without stealth, the Renshai would not live long enough to face their enemy.

As Vashi crawled through the window, Shadimar began a dignified ascent. Colbey kept his attention sweeping the courtyard, leaving the others to assess the danger in the tower. Ignorance of furtive tactics made him twitchy, and he questioned his strategy repeatedly. It had only made sense to enter the tower at night, yet he wondered how they would find the one they sought in the maze of corridors Arduwyn had described.

When Colbey turned, Shadimar had disappeared from sight. Quickly, Colbey lashed the rope around Secodon, then enmeshed his hand as high above the wolf as he could reach. The rope swung from the wall as he climbed, using what little friction he could form between the tight, black blocks and his feet. He scrambled in through the window, surveying the room while the others moved forward to hoist Secodon inside. This late, Colbey was surprised to find the doorless chamber still dimly lit by candles. Across the room stood a chair that perfectly matched an embroidered couch facing it. A guard sprawled across the couch, obviously unconscious. Tannin hovered over him, as if daring him to move, and Vashi examined the guard stoically.

Colbey sensed her movement just before it happened. As Tannin turned to watch Mitrian, Shadimar, and Rache haul Secodon in, Vashi drew and thrust. Colbey's blade left its sheath before her sword covered half the distance to the guard. A simple loop and upstroke stole the weapon from her hand, close enough to her fingers to serve as a warning. He caught the flying sword, more to prevent the clatter than out of respect.

Rache, Mitrian and Shadimar untied Secodon. The confrontation with Vashi had passed so swiftly, the others had not even noticed it. Tannin looked back hurriedly, but he did not interfere. Colbey trusted the Western Renshai to bind the guard. For now, his lesson took precedence.

Three sharp sword strokes sent Vashi back into a corner. Colbey pinned her there with an angle-block she knew he could turn into any of a thousand deadly strikes in an instant. 'What were you doing?'

Vashi's eyes blazed. Colbey read just a trickle of fear, well suppressed, and it pleased him. A warrior who could overcome fear would become a hero. To know no fear at all was an insanity and an affliction. 'I was killing an enemy.'

'Renshai do not kill the helpless. No matter who they are. Unless your own battle skill took him down, it's not your right to kill him. Every person deserves the chance to fight. Let his own actions decide the kind of death he earns.'

Vashi lowered her head, and her already soft voice fell to a whisper. 'I just didn't want to leave an enemy behind us.'

'Then you keep him unconscious. Or you tie him. Or you challenge him outright, if the circumstances permit it.' Clearly, here, they did not. Colbey eased back as Tannin tied and gagged the guard. The others finished their tasks and tried not to interfere with Colbey's lesson, no matter how ill-timed. 'There's more to being Renshai than killing. You've disgraced your honor and your tribe. You'll have to earn back Sif's favor. And mine. Neither will be easy.'

Vashi assumed a suitably repentant position, and Colbey jabbed her sword back into its sheath. 'Come on.' He turned to follow the others through the doorway and into the corridor.

Tannin came up beside Colbey. 'It's clear,' he hissed. 'Which way?'

Colbey hesitated, groping around them with his mind, careful to avoid his companions' thoughts. He dared not waste more than a dash of vitality on the search, but his senses warned him of presences in the direction that Arduwyn had indicated as Elishtan's court. Apparently, the man that the LaZarian sentry had called the king was still holding an audience. *Or waiting for us.* The idea seemed unlikely, but it obsessed Colbey. He reclaimed his consciousness fully, dismayed to find that even that short search had made him weaker. 'This way.' He steered Tannin toward the court, taking the lead with the Western Renshai.

The group met no more guards as they paced the widening corridor and came to a stop before the gigantic bronze portal and its jade-eyed snake. Light filtered from the crack beneath the door, and occasional muffled voices scarcely penetrated the portal, their words indecipherable. Many bits of fact and speculation began to come together in Colbey's mind as certainties. Doubtless, the coiled snake symbolized the Southern Wizard's property as clearly as Secodon belonged to Shadimar. The cold-blooded creatures shared the same bond with Carcophan as the land beasts did with Shadimar, the airborne with the Western Wizard, and the water denizens with Trilless. Colbey felt equally positive that this so-called king, Elishtan the Jaded, was the exiled Northman. Surely, the LaZarian sentries had been paid or threatened into passing on their well-rehearsed message to the Renshai. Only the motivations of this Northman remained a mystery, and too many possibilities came to mind: vengeance, racial prejudice, curiosity, the challenge of a swordsman even more competent than himself. *Madness.*

The revelation struck hard, but Colbey shifted his thoughts to the necessary task at hand. Whatever his mental state, Carcophan's champion had proven himself as clever as any fox and as cruel as any demon. Colbey did not doubt that the Renshai would, when they entered the court, walk into a well-set trap. Still, he did not balk or shy from the challenge. He took a quick glance over his companions: all Renshai, except Shadimar, and the Wizard could handle himself. 'Be ready,' Colbey warned. 'Let's go.'

Tannin reached for the door handle. The snake's jade eyes seemed to mock them. The bronze door swung open on silent hinges, and the Renshai found themselves facing two dozen arrows in hastily-drawn bows. Each archer's dark Eastern face looked grim. Beyond the semicircle of archers, one man strode back and forth on a raised dais that held a jeweled throne. Another man stood sentinel beside it. Colbey's gaze went naturally to the still one. The more dangerous a man, the calmer he remained under pressure, and this man's presence drew Colbey as irresistibly as a well-crafted sword. Though aged, he looked powerful. Salt and pepper hair fringed eyes the green-yellow of a cat's. A sable cloak hung from his shoulders, and a smile flickered across his solid, though creased, features. His gaze riveted on Shadimar.

Carcophan. Having identified the Southern Wizard, Colbey dismissed him as Shadimar's problem. His gaze trained on the figure that had already claimed the attention of all of the other Renshai.

A smaller man paced the dais, his polished silver breastplate gleaming in the candlelight as if to mock the Renshai's aversion to armor. Beneath it, a mail shirt covered a red silk blouse embroidered with gold leaf. His greaves were lacquered black, polished to a blinding brilliance, and they lay over light breeks. A spired helmet enclosed his head and face, though wisps of yellow hair poked beneath it. His eyes seemed to dance with a strange, laughing madness, and the chaos hung so thick around him it nearly choked Colbey. Still, though they had changed, Colbey instantly recognized the deep blue eyes and the perfect, graceful stance he could never forget. For the first time in his existence, realization paralyzed the Golden Prince of Demons.

The exiled Northman was Episte.

31 A Swordsman Unmatched

The armored apparition spoke with a stranger's voice. 'Enter, golden-haired dogs with your tails between your legs. Enter, or run like the cowards you are.'

Colbey's legs would not budge. It made no sense to run. The archers would shoot them all down from behind, and the Renshai would never choose to die without glory. He watched as the others edged in through the portal, for the moment unable to move himself. Too many emotions crushed down on Colbey at once, none of them his own. The archers' loyalty touched him, though he sensed a stirring of fear beneath it. Mitrian seemed confused, cued by something, though she clearly had not yet recognized Episte. Rache stewed in a vengeful rage against his father's slayer that required fulfillment. He also did not know his brother, and he had claimed the battle for his own. Under the circumstances, Colbey could not help feeling that perhaps Garn's son was right.

Vashi seemed confused, valiantly tempering her need for action with the need to please her goddess and her *torke*. When she fought, it would be with forethought and principle. The Cardinal Wizards stood as still as statues. From Shadimar wafted indignation, from Carcophan wicked joy. Tannin studied the archers, measuring their weaknesses. Intuitively, he knew that the major battle was not his to fight. Over it all, a madness fed by bitterness stagnated, converging on Colbey like a physical entity. Though it lacked the sharpness of an actual wound, it was nearly incapacitating.

Episte laughed, gaze fixed on Colbey. 'Who would have guessed the Golden Prince of the jackals himself would be the one too afraid to approach?'

But it was not fear that held Colbey. Episte's voice, though changed, opened the floodgates of his own emotions. The feelings of those around him disappeared, leaving Colbey to drown in his own grief, tainted only by a flicker of hope. The truth came together, rewriting history that Colbey had clung to as fact, but an understanding of motivations did not accompany his realizations. He remembered finding the young Northman's headless body, the scraps of clothing and the beloved amulet beneath it that had made him certain of the corpse's identity. Now he knew that Episte had performed the grisly murder, taking the head and leaving his own belongings, stealing the dignity from another's death only to mislead. 'Why?' Colbey managed to ask.

And he knew Episte would tell him. Though Colbey had trained the Renshai never to gloat nor to waste time talking while an enemy found openings, he recognized the intensity of a madness and bitterness that had to be shared. Episte had prepared too long for this moment to sacrifice it for caution or strategy. Surely, he would defy Colbey's lessons just as he had abandoned the Renshai's definitions of cowardice and ethics.

Episte removed the helmet from his head and shook back his golden locks, looking enough like his dead father to be a twin, aside from the chaos smoldering in his eyes. Colbey felt realization shock through his companions, felt Rache's need for vengeance flutter into an odd conglomeration of fury, sadness, and confusion. Colbey gave his mental talent free rein, not wanting to waste energy channeling or directing it. The need seized him to penetrate Episte's mind, to break the force that drove or controlled him. But the consciousness he managed to catch radiating from Episte was not a separate force, and it pained Colbey to discover that it was not just goading. It had become Episte. Still, Colbey needed to prove that to himself. He needed not just to hear but also to understand the betrayal. Though he knew it would weaken him, Colbey focused his mental presence directly into Episte's mind.

Chaos pressed Colbey, a wild insanity that nearly sent him, screaming, to the floor. At first, it seemed formless and without direction, upending his reason and stealing his sense of self. Then Episte spoke, opening a direct link to the source of madness, and Colbey was staggered by the impact. Episte's words rang in his mind as well as in his ears. 'You shaped and battered me with your training and your ruthless techniques. Moment to moment, you made me choose between the mother who loved me and the heritage you forced on me.'

The pathway led to a bitterness that gaped and festered like a dirty wound. Around it, Colbey found only fading sparks of the man whom he had once recognized as Episte. 'My father never wanted me to exist. He damned me to Hel with my name, then left me to seek death in some distant war. And you all called him a hero.' Colbey recoiled from the blasting reek of Episte's malice, desperately examining the surviving pieces of the youngster's conscience and devotion. 'Then I gave my love and trust to a Deathseeker so like my father, only to have him betray me.' Colbey's mind scarcely registered the fact that Episte had descended from the dais and now stood on the floor in front of it.

'You killed my mother, Colbey. Didn't you?'

Believing the question rhetorical, Colbey did not answer. He glanced at the last patchy light of Episte's humanity, finding only ancient fragments of shattered hopes and dreams with origins in early childhood. He caught a momentary sensation of something shapeless, more presence than being. Before he could define it further, Colbey's legs went weak. Reluctantly, he drew back his mental probe to shift its direction, channeling its energy back to himself to keep from collapsing. Suddenly, a rush of dizziness stole all focus, and he knew he did not have the strength to face Episte sword to sword. He forced himself to meet Episte's eyes, seeing there a joy that came as a direct result of Colbey's frailty. Episte reveled in a weakness whose source he could not understand, savoring his control, gloating with an obviousness that flaunted his disdain for Colbey's teaching in the same way as his armor did. Clearly, his aim was to demoralize and then destroy. And Colbey felt ill-prepared to stand against those tactics. No matter how many times his mind reassured him that he faced a stranger, Colbey's heart told him this monster was his son.

Episte lowered his voice, a tiny hint of his familiar tone seeping into it now. The jewel-encrusted throne on the dais behind him seemed like a distant background from another world. 'When I stood there in the woods, surrounded by dead Northmen, I remembered again the last image of my home and saw things that blind trust and grief had hidden. When I got there, all the Northmen were dead and my mother dying. Only one sword was blooded, Colbey, coward and demon. That sword was yours.'

Colbey felt certain that a battle in the forest with Northmen could not, by itself, have triggered such intricate details of memory. Something else had happened in the woodlands that day; someone had handed Episte the clues and the answer, then magnified every scrap of ugliness, resentment, and bitterness it found. Colbey steadied his body with his mind, then let it rest. He would need all the strength he could muster just to see that some of the Renshai did not die. He could feel Mitrian's and Rache's eyes upon him, awaiting his explanation with the same horrified interest as Episte. Tannin and Vashi continued to measure the archers. An impatience touched Colbey, though he could not quite divine the source. Someone had come within striking range of violence.

'Tell me that you didn't kill my mother, and I will let you live.'

Colbey remained silent, wanting the extra moments to capture the vitality of mind and body. If that feeling of imminent attack came from Episte, Colbey had to be its target.

'Tell me!' Episte screamed.

Colbey would not lie, especially not to Episte. 'I did kill her. It was —'

But the explanation never came.

With a howl of desperate courage, Vashi launched herself at the wall of archers. 'Modi!' A dozen shafts flew for her. More than a few found their point-blank target, but the damage was done. Half the archers needed time to reload, and Colbey struck faster than thought. Near the center of the semicircle, three of the still armed archers fell dead before they saw him move.

The room erupted into action as the Renshai plunged into the fray en masse. The archers abandoned their bows, unable to fire without hitting friends as well as foes. Some of the survivors drew scimitars. Half chose to run; these fled through the door. Colbey heard the bronze portal crash closed behind him and the bolt slam into place. Apparently, they preferred to lock their crazed leader inside his court with a pack of Renshai so that the tower would not run with Eastern blood.

While Colbey, Tannin, and Mitrian slashed through the archers, Rache found the opening the others missed. Where Colbey's blade reaped the foremost bowman, Rache slipped through, charging toward the dais and the frenzied youngster who paced before it. Though hard pressed by exhaustion to a battle with bowmen that would, under other circumstances, seem scarcely worth fighting, Colbey did not miss the wave of outrage, hatred, and grief wafting from Rache as he passed.

Colbey dispatched the last of the archers in front of him, trying and failing to channel strength to his body. He stumbled, alert, but physically unable to respond to the lightning fast dodges and strikes that usually came so naturally to him. He discovered that only three archers remained standing, one engaged with Tannin and two with Mitrian. Even as he watched, Mitrian cut down one. Regaining his balance, Colbey turned his attention to the battle at the dais.

Nearby, Carcophan and Shadimar stood in animated dispute, the wolf circling their feet. Rache's and Episte's swords swept for one another in slim arches and circles. For each of Rache's power strokes, Episte had a block or a parry, and he returned them with murderous slashes far quicker than those of his younger foe. Entranced, Colbey watched both adolescents engage in the finest battle of their short existences. And he wished them both the best.

Episte was a flame of fury. The tip of his blade bit rents the length of Rache's body. Repeatedly, Rache's sword thrusts clanged against the breastplate, unable to pierce it. The armor did not appear to hinder Episte at all. Even with its weight and bulkiness, he outmaneuvered Rache. Two dozen harmless strokes cut air in both directions. Then Episte caught Rache's sword between his own weapon and one lacquered greave.

Colbey saw the death stroke coming. If Rache wrenched down-ward, he opened his head to Episte. A leaping back-step would give Episte a free stab at Rache's chest. An instant's pause would place the younger completely at the mercy of his frenzied brother. Apparently, Rache saw the same stalemate. 'Modi!' he screamed, lowering his sword and dropping his body together. Episte's blade whistled overhead, so close it tore some of the sandy hairs from Rache's head. Rache sprang backward and to his feet. Colbey could see the sweat flung by the movement, colored red by numerous superficial wounds. Rache's motions had become nearly as awkward as Colbey's own; the intensity of his concentration and the constant need for attack and parry had sapped the young Renshai of strength. With the new vitality that certain death brings, Rache howled and plunged for Episte.

Mitrian ran her sword through the last of her opponents, pulling the blade free without bothering to watch the Easterner fall. Instantly, she spun, eyes riveting on the battle by the dais. With a cry of horrified alarm, she raised her sword and charged.

Colbey swore, stepping clumsily into her path. 'Mitrian, no. It's not your battle.'

Mitrian skidded to a stop. Her feet slipped on the blood-rimed floor, and momentum carried her into Colbey. She caught her balance with wide flailings of her arms. Then, bearings regained, she glared at Colbey. 'What the hell are you doing? Get out of my way!'

'It's not your battle,' Colbey repeated.

Several braziers had been scattered during the fight with the archers, leaving much of the room in darkness. Rache's and Episte's swords became pulsating dazzles of steel in shadow.

'Not my battle!' Mitrian screamed. 'That's my son!' She tried to veer around Colbey, but he shifted to block her path again. 'No!' she shouted. 'No!' A look of horrified understanding crossed her features. 'You bastard! You're so damned interested in their technique, you don't want anyone interrupting your pleasure. Rache's my child. I won't let him die for your amusement.' She lunged, jabbing for Colbey's abdomen with deadly accuracy.

Anger gave Colbey new strength. He drew and cut in one movement. Their swords rang together. Instantly, the elder reversed the direction of his attack. The tip of his sword claimed the wolf's head hilt, and Mitrian's sword spun to the floor. Though he had plenty of opportunity to honor the blade by catching it, Colbey drew his other sword instead. Mitrian's sword crashed, ringing, to the floor.

'Modi!' Mitrian dove for her hilt.

As her hand closed over the familiar haft, Colbey slammed a booted foot down on the blade hard enough to pinch her fingers between sword and floor. 'That's the last time anyone tells me what I am or why

I do what I do! When Renshai lose respect for a *torke*, there is nothing more for him to teach. But this one last lesson you will learn.' Keeping his foot in place, Colbey motioned Mitrian to her feet.

Reluctantly, Mitrian released her sword and obeyed, rage still radiating from her person as well as her expression.

'Rache has the right to live or die by his own hand, with his honor intact. If you fight for him, you turn him into a coward.'

'But—' Mitrian started desperately.

'There are no exceptions.' Colbey met and held Mitrian's gaze. 'You are not a Renshai only when it suits your needs. Law and glory does not change just because it involves your son. The better swordsman will win. And the other will die a man. Don't buy your son's life at the price of his honor.'

Mitrian lowered her head, not quite hiding her tears.

'When their battle is finished, then you can challenge, if you feel the need.' Colbey released Mitrian's sword. Cut to the heart, he considered the potential of the two young Renshai who had once found solace in one another's presence but now thirsted for one another's blood. Together, they could have made the Renshai great. Now, brother against brother, they would die. It was an old, tired, familiar irony. Always, it seemed, those who could form the most undefeatable alliances became the most powerful of enemies. The most capable warriors solved their problems with swords instead of a heated argument over mugs of mead. Colbey watched the battle, regathering the strength that came with rest.

Rache felt as if his sword had quadrupled in weight, and sweat stung every part of his body. He and Episte exchanged strokes as swiftly as when the fight had begun, but the deadly accuracy waned as they both wearied. Rache made another futile stab for an opening in Episte's armor. Again, Episte caught Rache's sword against his greave.

'Modi!' Rache doubted the same maneuver would work twice, so he relied on speed. He leapt backward. For the second time, Episte's sword whistled over Rache's head. Rache knew that stroke should have claimed his neck. Episte could easily have taken his life. If Episte had missed, it was because he wanted it that way. If Rache still lived, it was because Episte had not yet chosen to kill him. The older teenager was toying with him as cruelly as Colbey had played the Erythanian knight.

Humiliation transformed to wild fury. Rache fought his final, desperate battle with dignity, mixing uniquely perfect Renshai techniques with the less directed power attacks that Garn had taught him. No matter Episte's methods, Rache promised himself that he would fight the best battle he could. He would avenge his father's death and Colbey's honor, and damn the cost. Years of love transformed into a hatred heated by Episte's decision to belittle as well as to kill.

'I loved you, damn it. You were my hero.' Rache's own words brought him a second wind. He rained hammer blows on Episte, each relentless surge driving Episte backward. For the first time, Rache was in control, and his mouth twisted in a howl of triumph.

Episte's foot met the obsidian stair of the dais. He parried as he climbed, weaving a wild web of defense. But Rache did not pause until he pressed his opponent against the jeweled wooden chair that served as a throne. A sudden pang of guilt rose then, driving Rache to the very hesitation that Colbey warned against, that had cost many men their lives. 'You killed my father!' Now Rache knew no mercy. He lunged, thrusting with all the power he could put into the blow.

Episte dodged like an eel.

Instead of flesh, Rache's blade cleft nothing, then embedded deeply into the wooden base of the chair. Episte's blade sped for the hilt of Rache's sword and Rache's fingers.

Rache sprang backward to avoid the blow, disarming himself. Episte advanced. Nearly helpless, Rache retreated. His foot came down on empty air, and he tumbled down the dais stairs. His head banged against wood, and the steps stamped bruises across his limbs. He crashed to the floor, prone, aching in every part of his body. Instinctively, he tensed to roll and rise. Episte's booted foot jarred into Rache's back, sprawling him. The sharp nip of a blade at the base of Rache's neck foretold his death. He dared not move. He steeled his mind for death, knowing in his heart that he had given his all.

The sword flicked across the back of Rache's neck. He felt a momentary pressure at his throat, then the medallion he had worn since the battle near Greentree slithered free of his tunic.

Episte gasped and then he gave one wrenching sob and began to speak, his voice cooing and childlike, the soft alto he had used before time and puberty had deepened it. 'No, Episte. You can't kill Rache. He's your brother.' The sword slipped from his shaking hand. He pulled the helmet from his head and tossed it to the ground. Episte sank to the floor, arms wrapped around his legs, his face hidden against his knees. And he wept.

Rache rose hesitantly and stared, with absolutely no idea of what to do next. The certainty of death had stolen the anger and vengeance that had driven him. The sobbing, huddled figure at his feet seemed too pitiful to kill, and it reminded him of the Episte he had known more than a decade ago. Uncertain whether to comfort, ignore, or kill, Rache turned to Colbey for guidance.

Corpses littered the courtroom floor, along with shattered and overturned braziers. Blood painted the floorboards red. Rache spotted Vashi among the bodies, pierced by more arrows than he bothered to count. Tannin kept a hand clamped around the fletching of a single arrow in his chest, unsure how to remove it. Mitrian returned Rache's gaze, a cautious smile on her face. The Wizards still stood in conference, their demeanors solemn. They had taken no direct hand in the conflict.

Colbey gave Rache no answer. His aging features twisted in agony, and a tragic warmth filled his blue-gray eyes. As he passed Rache, he clamped a hand to the younger Renshai's arm. Though silent, the gesture conveyed an approval that, for a time, stole all of the pain from Rache's battle. Colbey rarely gave praise, and its scarcity made it priceless.

Leaving Episte to Colbey, Rache turned to give his mother a hug, then help her tend to Tannin's wound.

Colbey entered Episte's mind, not caring if the search brought him to the very edge of death. He had to know what remained of the child he had loved. Had to know what he could salvage.

Colbey's exploration first touched an empty sorrow, without obvious cause. Beyond it, Colbey found only the aching, boiling bitterness that had grown and spread to destroy Episte. *He's gone. Dead.* Yet, despite the obvious conclusion, loyalty and grief would not allow Colbey to abandon his charge without a thorough search. Desperately, he scoured Episte's thoughts, seeking the source of the mercy he had shown Rache. There, if anywhere, he would find whatever meager sparks of Episte had survived.

Even as the thought emerged, Colbey blundered into a fading glimmer of childhood, a state of being that had come to life in Episte's earliest years. Again and again, the youngster had retreated to this pocket of memory when his suffering had grown greatest: at the sight of his mother's corpse and after the humiliation at the hand of his *torke*. Colbey cringed at the last; but he did not allow his own regret to surface now, clinging to the last of his failing energy in the desperate hope of saving Episte. The effort seemed incalculable and oppressively bleak. He would have to rebuild all that had been Episte from a single, dying slash of remembrance.

Even as Colbey prepared for the task, the dark, formless presence he had glimpsed earlier enfolded the final thought that he recognized as Episte's.

No!' Though shaky from exertion, Colbey drove in to rescue the young Renshai. He struck a blackness deeper than unconsciousness. Then that, too, shattered to a vision that snapped through Colbey's mind in an instant that dragged like forever. Alone, Episte battled three Northmen in the woodlands outside of the village of Greentree. One lay dead at his feet, neck slashed open by Episte's blade. He impaled the second through the abdomen. Colbey experienced the thrust as his own. He knew the strange jolt as the tip slammed bone, followed by the abrupt feeling of wrongness. When Episte jerked back to face the last of his enemies, he held the hilt and a clinging shard of a sword that should have withstood the impact.

Episte whirled. The last Northman stared, fear wild in his eyes. Repeatedly, his gaze strayed to the dead men. Surely one was a father, brother, or uncle who had coaxed him to his first battle and now had abandoned him, in death, when he needed the assistance most. He stood no taller than Episte, clearly several years his junior. Episte flung his hilt to the ground, feeling a kinship with the Northern teen. He, too, was far from home, alone in a war he was fighting for long dead ancestors.

Seeing his opponent disarmed, the Northman screwed up his courage and charged.

Surprised, Episte crouched, prepared to battle barehanded, if necessary. Light flared in front of him and a sword appeared from nowhere, hovering near his hand. It did not shine in the moonglow; light seemed to shy away from its steel. Though shocked by its sudden presence, Episte did not question. The youngster's hands closed over the grip, and warning buzzed through Colbey. Unlike his charge, he knew the danger. *The Black Sword of Power*. The wisp of poetry returned vividly to him: 'The three Blades together shall close the age. The Age of Change, when Chaos shatters Odin's ward.' *Ragnarok*.

The madness came with the touch. Abruptly, agony hammered Episte. Something dark and orderless speared into his mind, and all the knowledge of the universe seemed to accompany it. First, it brought understanding, distorting truth by amplifying every negative emotion, thought, or feeling ever harbored by Episte. Then it compelled him to destroy.

Panic stole all color from the Northman's face. Whirling, he ran in terror.

Enraged by his opponent's cowardice, Episte gave chase, howling and foaming like a rabid wolf. He leapt upon the Northman, grounding him with momentum, pinning him down to hack repeatedly and mercilessly at the neck. The youngster's screams formed a bold and ugly duet with Episte's laughter, and the salt odor of blood only heartened the assault.

Despite the detail, the image flashed through Colbey's mind in less time than it took to blink. Then Episte's last childhood memory winked out, stolen from Colbey before he realized it was menaced.

No! Colbey searched frantically, finding no miniscule trace of the child he had loved. Helplessness drained him. For now, he faced an enemy too vast and formless to fight. He could stir the chaos mentally until the effort emptied the last of his vitality and claimed his life. But, here in Episte's mind, nothing remained to salvage. Colbey thought of the pyre he had built for the headless corpse he had believed was Episte, knowing that that was still truly the moment he had laid his student to rest.

Scooping up the medallion, Colbey replaced it around Episte's neck. He cradled the youngster into his arms, feeling the warmth against him, the heaving shoulders, the warm wetness of the tears. He rocked the boy tenderly, like a father with an infant. All the words he had promised he would have said to Episte, given the chance, rushed back to haunt his mind. But he knew they would do him no good. The creature that Episte had become could never understand. Like Garn, he was suffering. Yet, unlike Garn, the poison would not kill Episte. It would only drive him to butchery and ruin.

Colbey drew the *nådenal*, finally understanding Sif's plan for her last needle. If he could not reclaim Episte, at least he could honor his death with the ultimate symbol of faith and glory. The greatest of swords had stolen Episte's humanity; the tiniest of blades would restore it in the only way it could. Colbey's fingers fumbled around the bulbous, guardless haft, scarcely in his control. His grip tightened, and he pushed the sharpened silver through Episte's spine. The Renshai child went limp in his arms. Withdrawing the *nådenal*, Colbey rested it on Episte's chest beside the medallion.

A wave of grief enveloped the old Renshai then, and others' emotions accompanied it. Only now, he recognized the desperate concern beneath the Cardinal Wizards' outward calm, and the source of their worry accompanied it. Colbey's eyes roved to Episte's sword. Though proficiently forged, even the edge of the blade did not gleam. It seemed to disappear in the shadows formed by irregularities in the braziers' illumination. Surely the Wizards realized, as Colbey did, that the three Swords must have existed on the mortal world together in the instant that it fell into Episte's grip. It was not the Sword itself that had inflicted the damage but the chaos its untimely summoning had brought.

Gently lowering Episte's body, Colbey hefted the Black Sword. The touch tingled, as clear a warning as the rattle of a snake. This blade was not meant for him to wield or even to hold.

Gingerly, Colbey carried the Black Sword several paces, stopping before Shadimar and Carcophan. It was the Wizards' job to see that prophecies were fulfilled, their god-meted task to follow the laws that bound them to Odin. He could see them causing the *Ragnarok*, blindly obedient to an order that had long ago lost its usefulness in Colbey's eyes. *Have the gods, Wizards, and men become too slavishly devoted to their own law? It is one thing to sacrifice one's own life for honor, quite another to let rigid faith destroy the world. There comes a time when every man, and perhaps every god, needs to redefine his honor and his faith.* Colbey's time had come. One thing seemed certain. Whether or not he attempted the Seven Tasks of Wizardry, he would not be bound by all of its laws. *I won't work toward the* Ragnarok. *If that means opposing every other Wizard and every god, so be it. I will not let this world die for ancient laws no longer applicable and a devotion to duty that precludes common sense.* Colbey hurled the Black Sword at the Wizards' feet. It thudded to the floor, scraping granite without a spark. 'Destroy it,' he said. 'Or I'll find a way.'

Without waiting for the Wizards or the wolf to react to his challenge, Colbey hefted Episte. The still warm body curled into his arms like an infant, and he carried it to the huge, bronze portal unchallenged. He tried to open the door; but, bolted from the outside, it would not yield to his touch.

'Open the door!' Carcophan shouted, his voice loud as a thunder-clap in the too-long silence. 'He means you no harm and your leader no disrespect.'

The ensuing stillness was short-lived. The drawing bolt rasped, the door swung open, and Colbey passed through a small cluster of Easterners in red leather armor. He wandered into the flickering blue-black shadows of the corridor.

That night, Mitrian, Rache, Tannin, Tarah, Modrey, and Arduwyn huddled around a campfire in the Eastern woodlands. Excitement, exertion, and a muddle of conflicting emotions had left Rache drained, yet he still felt certain of one thing, a need he had been considering since the party had left Béarn, His gaze found Arduwyn, the flickering fire striking gray through the archer's hair. 'Arduwyn.' Rache flushed, the address seeming too informal for an elder. 'Sir.' The title felt equally uncomfortable. 'I'd like to escort you to Béarn.'

Arduwyn rested his splinted arm on his knee. The single dark eye met Rache's, and it probed questioningly. 'I appreciate the offer, but you needn't feel obligated. So long as I stay in forests, I don't think I'm in any danger.'

Rache shrugged. His body stung with every movement, from scores of tiny cuts. 'You're wounded. How will you hunt without an arm? And you've done so much for us. We can't let you face these wild lands alone.'

'And?' Arduwyn asked.

The query surprised Rache. 'There needs to be more?'

'No,' Arduwyn admitted. 'But I'm sure there is. Your face has turned the color of my hair. What is it you want?'

Suddenly, Rache felt every eye upon him, which only made him flush more deeply. He would have liked to have discussed the matter with the hunter in private, yet, for now, it seemed better to keep all of the Renshai together. 'Well, sir. It's your . . . your daughter.'

The little archer's face seemed to lose all the color that Rache's had gained. He stopped breathing.

'I'll keep her safe,' Rache said quickly. 'If it's all right with the others, my mother and I thought the Renshai could live on the Fields of Wrath.' He threw a quick glance at the Western Renshai, hoping their previous home would not hold too many memories for them to return there.

When no one contradicted or complained, Rache continued. 'That's right near Béarn.'

Arduwyn still did not move, not even to take a breath.

Rache felt a desperate need to defend the Renshai. 'Colbey often told me that there was an order to the world. I believe him. If this world had no Renshai, it would be different. Not better or worse, just different. Some other power would have served the same function.'

Arduwyn closed his eye.

Alarmed, Rache caught the slight hunter's shoulders. 'Breathe, sir. Please.'

Arduwyn gasped in a lungful of air.

Rache prattled on. 'If it's the will of the gods to place your blood among future devils, what harm can it do? The difference between angels and devils is who looks upon them.'

Abruptly, the flame-haired hunter laughed, first hysterically, then with a more natural calm. 'Easy, Rache, or you'll talk yourself out of a father's permission. My attitude toward Renshai has changed much since I first met Colbey. You have much of your father about you, and Garn was a man I liked well. If Sylva will have you, I won't stand in your way. But you must give her time to learn to know you, time to finish growing up.'

Rache loosed a whoop of joy that sounded strangely light and free after the events of the last long months.

Arduwyn laughed again. 'A long time ago, the first day I met him, Colbey said my blood would never become Renshai except under a truly odd set of circumstances. I guess this qualifies.'

Rache could not contain his excitement. 'When Colbey gets here –'

Mitrian interrupted. 'He's not coming back.'

The words squelched Rache's gladness in an instant. 'What do you mean?' Then, realizing he had asked the wrong question, he tried again. 'How do you know?'

Mitrian rubbed her hand along the winter ground, clutching a stone to her palm. 'Honestly, I'm not sure how; but I do know it's true. We'll leave in the morning. Without him.'

'We can't leave him.' Tannin nursed his injured shoulder, glaring jealously at Rache. Clearly, he wished he had thought to ask for Sylva's hand first. 'Colbey still could come back. He's hurt, emotionally, at least. And he may need our help.'

Mitrian tossed the pebble on the fire. 'Colbey never needed anyone's help. Especially now. You've seen the mood he's been in. The look in his eyes when he left was like that of an old dog before it crawls into the woods to die.' She shook her head.

Rache stared, hating the words, yet knowing his mother spoke the truth.

Tarah added quietly, 'If the Golden Prince of Demons chooses to return, I have no doubt he can find us.'

Every Renshai bowed his or her head in unison. And Arduwyn shared their sorrow.

Epilogue

Colbey cast his gaze from the last smoldering ashes of Episte's pyre to a gladder campfire before him. But for this subtle movement, he might have been carved from the same wood as the stump on which he rested, a petrified testament to the last full-blooded Renshai. Nor did Colbey seem to move when another figure stepped within the circle of his light. Surely, even Shadimar missed the instinctive shifting of Colbey's hand to his sword hilt. Nearby, Frost Reaver whickered softly.

The Eastern Wizard took a seat on the fallen trunk that had once graced Colbey's perch. Secodon lay beside the stallion, watching, while the Wizard set a handful of roots to roast upon the fire.

Colbey said nothing, finding nothing worth saying. Sensing no threat from Shadimar, he let his mind lapse back to the formless entity that had stolen Episte from him, letting logic override emotion for the first time since he had entered the Tower of Night. At the time, he had committed himself too fully to rescuing the youngster to consider the enemy carefully. Then, the battle had not mattered; he had already lost the prize. Now, chaos' familiarity touched him, the knowledge that he had defeated it before too strong to deny. When he analyzed the madness that had assailed him after Tokar's death, he realized that it had consisted of more than just an odd perception of others in his head. Insanity had pervaded those others. He recalled their wild feelings of confusion and the grinding pressure of the sensation he had come to equate with magic and with chaos. A different answer came than the one he had sought.

Suddenly, Colbey understood Tokar's decision. Over the millennia, a madness had become incorporated into the Western line of Cardinal Wizards. The fusion of thoughts had driven one Wizard to the brink of chaos, and that flaw had passed from predecessor to apprentice over centuries. *Tokar felt the insanity pressing him, and he knew it would only get stronger. That's why he chose a weak successor like Haim, probably hoping his apprentice would die in the transfer and a new Western Wizard would have to be found, one unaffected by predecessors and their mind rot. Then, he met me.* Colbey could only guess at

Tokar's motives here, though impressions left by the Wizard before Colbey had crushed the foreign presence gave him room to guess. *Tokar knew I would contain that madness or die trying. At the least, since I had not undergone the Tasks of Wizardry, I could be killed by my own hand or by others.*

For several hours, the two men sat in silence, while the roots cooked amid the pop and hiss of flame. Finally, Shadimar rolled the roots from the fire with a stick and offered a share to Colbey before tossing one to Secodon.

Colbey accepted the offering, biting into the thick, sweet root with a new hope and vitality he had not known for a long time. The Tasks of Wizardry gave him a fresh challenge, and the possible need to work against the Cardinal Wizards, maybe against the gods themselves, made him feel reborn. Yet one simple question still plagued him. 'Shadimar, at the castle walls. I only killed one of those sentries. For you to have slain the other would have required a bigger risk than I've ever seen you take. But I can't think of anyone else who could or would have done it.'

Shadimar continued eating without reply.

Realizing he had never actually asked, Colbey rephrased his thoughts into a question. 'Was it you?'

Shadimar's face twisted into a smile of shocked innocence. 'What can one helpless old man do?' The tip of his gnarled staff dipped into the fire, and the flames danced like mad things.

Perhaps there's hope for the Cardinal Wizards yet. Colbey smiled. For the first time in months, he no longer felt alone.

From the campfire, a column of blue flame shot toward the darkened heavens.

Appendix

Northmen

Aksel (AK-sall) – NORDMIRIAN. A soldier.

Alvis (AHL-vee) – VIKERIAN. Adviser to King Tenja.

Calistin the Bold (Ka-LEES-tin) – RENSHAI. Colbey's father.

Colbey Calistinsson (KULL-bay) – RENSHAI. The leader of the Renshai a.k.a. The Deathseeker a.k.a. The Golden Prince of Demons.

Eldir (EL-deer) – VIKERIAN. King Tenja's bodyguard.

Episte (Ep-PISS-teh) – RENSHAI. The oldest Renshai, now dead. Rache Kallmirsson's second teacher.

Ivhar Ingharsson (EEV-har eeng-HAR-son) – VIKERIAN. A messenger/scout.

Kallmir (KAWL-meer) – RENSHAI. Rache's father.

Kelrhyne (Kel-RINN-eh) – RENSHAI. A sword mistress, long dead, believed to be the subject of Sif's prophecy.

Menglir (MEN-gleer) – RENSHAI. One of the two founders of the Western Renshai. See also Sjare.

Olvaerr Kirinsson (OHL-eh-vair) – NORDMIRIAN. Kirin's son.

Peusen Raskogsson (Pyoo-SEN Rass-KOG-son) – NORDMIRIAN. One-handed general of Iaplege. Brother of Valr Kirin.

Rache Kallmirsson (RACK-ee) – RENSHAI. Santagithi's guard captain, now dead. Episte Rachesson's father.

Ranilda Battlemad (Ran-HEEL-da) – RENSHAI. Colbey's mother.

Sjare (See-Yar-eh) – RENSHAI. Founded the Western Renshai with Menglir.

Tenja (TEN-ya) – VIKERIAN. King of Vikerin.

Thorfin (THOR-fin) – VIKERIAN. A soldier.

Valr Kirin (Vawl-KEER-in) – NORDMIRIAN. Lieutenant to the high king in Nordmir. Peusen's brother.

Westerners

Angus (ANG-us) – GREENTREE. A Farmer.

Arduwyn (AR-dwin) – ERYTHANIAN. A hunter.

Bacshas (BOCK-shahz) – PUDARIAN. Nephew to deceased King Gasir. Oldest of four nephews.

Baran (BAYR-in) – BÉARNIDE. A young lieutenant.

Barder (BARR-der) – BÉARNIDE. Baran's father. A loyal court guard of usurped King Valar. Killed in the coup.

Bel (BELL) – PUDARIAN. Arduwyn's wife.

Belzar (BELL-zar) – PUDARIAN. Legendary swordsman.

Blacki (BLACK-ee) – GREENTREE. A farmer.

Brignar (BRIGG-nar) – ERYTHANIAN. A knight. Shalfon's father.

Bromdun (BROMM-dun) – Santagithi's archer captain.

Brugon (BREW-gun) – PUDARIAN. A merchant. Arduwyn's employer.

Buirane (BYOOR-ain) – BÉARNIDE. A previous king. Father to the twins Valar and Morhane.

Cammie (KAM-ee) – GREENTREE. A farmer.

Carad (Ka-ROD) – A competent gladiator; Garn's father.

Carlithel (KAR-lith-ell) – PUDARIAN. Proprietor of *The Hungry Lion*.

Carrol (KAH-rol) – GREENTREE. A farmer.

Daegga (DAY-ga) – One of Santagithi's guards.

Davrin (DAV-vrin) – MIXED WESTERN. A previous bard. Mar Lon's father.

Dayaan (Da-YAWN) – WYNIXAN. The goldsmith.

Dorina (Door-REEN-a) – BÉARNIDE. The royal nursemaid.

Effer (EFF-er) – Bel's middle child. A son.

Elanor (ELL-a-noor) – GREENTREE. A young teenager.

Emerald – Rache Kallmirsson's girlfriend. Episte Rachesson's mother.

Episte Rachesson (Ep-PISS-teh) – HALF RENSHAI. The son of Rache Kallmirsson and Emerald.

Fastin (FAST-in) – One of Santagithi's guards.

Flanner (FLANN-er) – GREENTREE. A farmer and a rapist.

Flent (FLENT) – BÉARNIDE. A guard.

Galan (GAY-lan) – One of Santagithi's archers.

Garn – An escaped gladiator from Santagithi's town. Mitrian's husband and father of Rache Garnsson.

Gasir (GAH-zeer) – PUDARIAN. The previous king of Pudar. Killed in the Great War.

Haim (Haym) – PUDARIAN. Tokar's apprentice.

Harritt (HARR-it) – One of Santagithi's guards.

Hortoren (HOR-ter-en) – CORPA BICKATAN. A merchant.

Jackie (JACK-ee) – GREENTREE. A farmer.

Jake (JAYK) – SHOLTON-ORIN. The tailor.

Jakot (Jah-KOE) – Santagithi's guard captain.

Jani (JAN-ee) – Bel's oldest child. A girl.

Kakkanoch (KACK-a-nock) – ERYTHANIAN. A knight.

Kerska (KUR-ska) – WYNIXAN. A merchant. The seller of 'Genuine Renshai Swords.'

Kinesthe (Kin-ESS-teh) – The *kjaelnabnir* of Rache Garnsson.

Koska (KOSS-ka) – BÉARNIDE. A guard.

Kruger (KROO-ger) – PUDARIAN. A dock foreman.

Kloras (Klow-RASS) – One of Santagithi's guards.

Korgar (KORE-gar) – BARBARIAN. Colbey's blood brother.

Lirtensa (Leer-TEN-sa) – PUDARIAN. A dishonest guard.

Lonriya (Lon-REE-ya) – Mar Lon's great-grandmother. Creator of the *lonriset*.

Loo (LOO) – GREENTREE. A farmer.

Mar Lon (MAR-LONN) – Davrin's son. The current bard.

Marly (MAR-lee) – One of Santagithi's guards.

Martinel (Mar-tin-ELL) – An ancestor of Mar Lon.

Mirkae (Meer-KIE) – WYNIXAN. A card shark.

Mitrian (MIH-tree-in) – Santagithi's daughter, Garn's wife, and mother of Rache Garnsson.

Miyaga (Mee-YAH-ga) – BÉARNIDE. King Morhane's granddaughter.

Modrey (MOE-dray) – WESTERN RENSHAI. Tarah's husband.

Monsamer (MON-sa-mer) One of Santagithi's guards.

Morhane (MORE-hayn) – BÉARNIDE. The king of Béarn. Valar's younger twin.

Mukesh (Myu-KESH) – A merchant's son in Santagithi's Town. Killed by Garn in childhood.

Nantel (Nan-TELL) – Santagithi's previous archer captain, now dead.

Nhetorl (Nee-TORL) – ERYTHANIAN. A guard.

Nifthelan (Niff-THEYL-an) – BÉARNIDE. The master stone mason. An elder.

Orlis (OR-liss) – ERYTHANIAN. The king of Erythane.

Oswald (OZ-wald) – AHKTARIAN. The prince of Ahktar.

Rache Garnsson (RACK-ee) – son of Mitrian and Garn.

Randil (Ran-DEEL) – WESTERN RENSHAI. Leader of the Western Renshai. Tannin's father.

Rathelon (RATH-eh-lon) – BÉARNIDE. The guard captain of Béarn. Morhane's illegitimate son. Sterrane's cousin.

Rusha (RUSH-a) – Bel's youngest child. A girl.

Santagithi (San-TAG-ih-thigh) – The Westland's best strategist. Leader of the Town of Santagithi.

Schaf (SHAFF) – GREENTREE. A farmer.

Shalfon (SHALL-fon) ERYTHANIAN. An apprentice knight. Brignar's son.

Sham (SHAM) – GREENTREE. A farmer.

Sterrane (Stir-RAIN) – BÉARNIDE. Valar's only surviving child. The heir to Béarn's throne.

Sturge (STURJ) – GREENTREE. A farmer.

Sylva (SILL-va) – MIXED WESTERN. Arduwyn's and Bel's daughter.

Tannin Randilsson (TAN-in) – WESTERN RENSHAI. Randil's son and Menglir's great grandson.

Tarah Randilsdatter (TAIR-a) – WESTERN RENSHAI. Randil's daughter. Tannin's sister.

Thein (THAYN) – BÉARNIDE. A Béarnian guard.

Tobhiyah (Toe-BIE-a) – One of Santagithi's guards.

Valar (VAY-lar) – Morhane's twin. Murdered for the throne.

Vashi the Rebellious (VASH-ee) – WESTERN RENSHAI. An eager warrior.

Verrall (VAIR-al) – PUDARIAN. King Gasir's second oldest nephew. The heir to the Pudarian throne.

Yernya (YERN-ya) – BÉARNIDE. A servant.

Easterners

Elishtan the Jaded (Al-AYSH-tin) – Ruler of the Tower of Night.

Shalan (Shigh-LAIN) – A merchant.

Siderin (SID-er-in) – King of the Eastlands.

ANIMALS

Biff – A Béarnian guard dog.

Bonnie (BONN-ee) – A Béarnian guard dog.

Bork – A Béarnian guard dog.

Bosh – A Béarnian guard dog.

Bouncer – A Béarnian guard dog.

Dond – A Béarnian guard dog.

Frost Reaver – Colbey's white stallion.

Krim – A Béarnian guard dog.

Kram – A Béarnian guard dog.

Los – A Béarnian guard dog.

Morst – A Béarnian guard dog.

Rond – A Béarnian guard dog.

Secodon (SEK-o-don) – Shadimar's wolf.
Stubs – Arduwyn's donkey.
Swiftwing – A red falcon. The Cardinal Wizards' messenger.

GODS & WIZARDS

Northern

Aegir (AY-jeer) – Northern god of the sea.
Baldur (BALL-der) – Northern god of beauty and gentleness.
The Fenris Wolf (FEN-ris) – The Great Wolf. The evil son of Loki. Also called Fenrir (FEN-reer).
Frey (FRAY) – Northern god of rain, sunshine, and fortune.
Freya (FRAY-a) – Frey's sister. Northern goddess of battle.
Frigg (FRIGG) – Odin's wife. Northern goddess of fate.
Gladsheim (GLAD-shighm) – 'Place of Joy.' Sanctuary of the gods.
Hati (HAH-tee) – The wolf who swallows the moon at the *Ragnarok*.
Heimdall (HIME-dahl) – Northern god of vigilance and father of mankind.
Hel – Northern goddess of the cold underrealm for those who do not die in valorous combat.
Loki (LOH-kee) – Northern god of fire and guile.
Magni (MAG-nee) – Thor's and Sif's son. Northern god of might.
Mana-garmr (MAH-nah Garm) – Northern wolf destined to extinguish the sun with the blood of men at the *Ragnarok*.
Modi (MOE-dee) – Thor's and Sif's son. Northern god of blood wrath.
Norns – The keepers of past, present, and future.
Odin (OH-din) – Northern leader of the pantheon. Father of the gods.
Sif (SIFF) – Thor's wife. Northern goddess of fertility and fidelity.
Sköll (SKOEWL) – Northern wolf who will swallow the sun at the *Ragnarok*.
Syn (SIN) – Northern goddess of justice and innocence.
Thor (THOR) – Northern god of storms, farmers, and law.
Trilless (Trill-ESS) – Northern Sorceress. Champion of goodness and the Northlands.
Tyr (TEER) – Northern one-handed god of war and faith.
The Wolf Age – The sequence of events immediately preceding the *Ragnarok* during which Sköll swallows the sun, Hati mangles the moon, and the Fenris Wolf runs free.

Western

Aphrikelle (Ah-fri-KELL) – Western goddess of spring.

Ascof (AZ-kov) – The eighteenth Eastern Wizard. Obsessed with demon summonings. Was finally killed by a self-summoned demon in year 9083.

Cathan (KAY-than) – Western goddess of war, specifically hand to hand combat. Twin to Kadrak.

Dakoi (Dah-KOY) – Western god of death.

Drero (DREY-roh) – The twenty-second Eastern Wizard. The builder of the hidden escape route from Béarn's castle.

The Faceless god – Western god of winter.

Firfan (FEER-fan) – Western god of archers and hunters.

Gherhan (GUR-han) – The sixth Eastern Wizard. Killed by a demon in 3319.

Itu (EE-too) – Western goddess of knowledge and truth.

Jalona (Ja-LOHN-a) – The twentieth Eastern Wizard. Talked Odin into making the bards the personal bodyguards of the Béarnian kings.

Kadrak (KAD-drak) – Western god of war. Twin to Cathan.

Niejal the Mad (Nee-EJ-al) – The ninth Western Wizard. Paranoid and suicidal.

Ruaidhri (Roo-AY-dree) – Western leader of the pantheon.

Shadimar (SHAD-ih-mar) – Eastern Wizard. Champion of neutrality and the Westlands.

Sudyar (SOO-dee-yar) – The fourteen Western Wizard. Paranoid and agoraphobic.

Suman (SOO-mon) – Western god of farmers and peasants.

Tokar (TOE-kar) – Western Wizard. Champion of neutrality and the Westlands.

Weese (WEESSS) – Western god of winds.

Yvesen (IV-e-sen) – Western god of steel and women.

Zera'im (ZAIR-a-eem) – Western god of honor.

Eastern

Carcophan (KAR-ka-fan) – Southern Wizard. Champion of evil and the Eastlands.

God – The only name for the bird/man god of the Leukenyans. Created by Siderin.

Havlar (HEV-ih-lar) – The first Southern Wizard.

Sheriva (Sha-REE-vah) – Omnipotent, only god of the Eastlands.

Foreign words

a (ah) – EASTERN. 'From.'

ailar (IGH-lar) – EASTERN. 'To bring.'

al (AIL) – EASTERN. The first person singular pronoun.

anem (ON-um) – BARBARIAN. 'Enemy'; usually used in reference to a specific race or tribe with whom the barbarian's tribe is at war.

aristiri (ah-riss-TEER-ee) – TRADING. A breed of singing hawks.

bein (bayn) – NORTHERN. 'Legs.'

bleffy (BLEFF-ee) – WESTERN/TRADING. A child's euphemism for nauseating.

bolboda (bawl-BOE-da) – NORTHERN. 'Evilbringer.'

brishigsa weed (brih-SHIG-sah) – WESTERN. A specific leafy weed with a translucent, red stem. A universal antidote to several common poisons.

brorin (BROAR-in) – RENSHAI. 'Brother.'

brunstil (BRUNN-steel) – NORTHERN. A stealth maneuver learned from barbarians by the Renshai. Literally: 'brown and still.'

chroams (krohms) – WESTERN. Specific coinage of copper, silver, or gold.

corpa (KOR-pa) – WESTERN. 'Brotherhood, town' lit. 'body.'

demon (DEE-mun) – ANCIENT TONGUE. A creature of magic.

djem (dee-YEM) – NORTHERN. Demon.

Einherjar (INE-herr-yar) – NORTHERN. 'The dead warriors in Valhalla.'

eksil (EHK-seel) – NORTHERN. 'Exile.'

fafra (FAH-fra) – TRADING. 'To eat.'

feflin (FEF-linn) – TRADING. 'To hunt.'

Forsvarir (Fours-var-FER) – RENSHAI. A specific disarming maneuver.

galn (gahln) – NORTHERN. 'Ferociously crazy.'

garlet (GAR-let) – WESTERN. A type of wildflower believed to have healing properties.

garn (garn) – NORTHERN. 'Yarn.'

Gerlinr (Gerr-LEEN) – RENSHAI. A specific aesthetic and difficult sword maneuver.

gullin (GULL-in) – NORTHERN. 'Golden.'

hadonga (hah-DONG-ah) – WESTERN. A twisted, hard wood tree.

Harval (Harr-VALL) – ANCIENT TONGUE. 'The gray blade.'

hastivillr (has-tih-VEEL) – RENSHAI. A sword maneuver.

kadlach (KOD-lok; the ch has a guttural sound) – TRADING. A vulgar term for a disobedient chld; akin to brat.

kenya (KEN-ya) – WESTERN. 'Bird.'

kjaelnavnir (kyahl-NAHV-neer) – RENSHAI. Temporary name for a child until a hero's name becomes available.

kinesthe (Kin-ESS-teh) – NORTHERN. 'Strength.'

kyndig (KAWN-dee) – NORTHERN. 'Skilled one.'

lessakit (LAYS-eh-kight) – EASTERN. 'A message.'

leuk (Luke) – WESTERN. 'White.'

lonriset (LON-ri-set) – WESTERN. A ten-stringed musical instrument.

lynstreik (LEEN-strayk) – RENSHAI. A sword maneuver.

magni (MAG-nee) – NORTHERN. 'Might.'

modi (MOE-dee) – NORTHERN. 'Wrath.'

Morshock (MORE-shock) – ANCIENT TONGUE. 'Sword of darkness.'

mynten (MIN-tin) – NORTHERN. A specific type of coin.

nådenal (naw-deh-NAHL) – RENSHAI. Literally: 'Needle of mercy.' A silver, guardless, needle-shaped dagger constructed during a meticulous religious ceremony and used to end the life of an honored, suffering ally or enemy, then melted in the victim's pyre.

noca (NOE-ka) – BEARNIAN. 'Grandfather.'

odelhurtig (OD-ehl-HEWT-ih) – RENSHAI. A sword maneuver.

oopey (OO-pee) – WESTERN/TRADING. A child's euphemism for an injury.

orlorner (oor-LEERN-ar) – EASTERN. 'To deliver to.'

pike – NORTHERN. 'Mountain.'

prins (PRINS) – NORTHERN. 'Prince.'

Ragnarok (ROW-na-rok) – 'The destruction of the powers.' The prophesied time when nearly all men and gods will die.

ranweed (RAN-weed) – WESTERN. A specific type of wild plant.

rexin (RAX-in) – EASTERN. 'King.'

Ristoril (RIS-tor-il) – ANCIENT TONGUE. 'Sword of tranquillity.'

sangrit (SAN-grit) – BARBARIAN. 'To form a blood bond.'

skjald (SKYAWLD) – NORTHERN. Musician chronicler.

svergelse (swerr-GELL-seh) – RENSHAI. 'Sword figures practiced alone; katas.'

talvus (TAL-vus) – WESTERN. 'Midday.'

torke (TOR-keh) – RENSHAI. 'Teacher, sword instructor.'

ulvstikk (EWLV-steek) – RENSHAI. A sword maneuver.

uvakt (oo-VAKT) – RENSHAI. 'The unguarded.' A term for children whose *kjaelnavnir* becomes a permanent name.

Valhalla (VAWL-holl-a) – NORTHERN. 'Hall of the Slain.' The walled 'heaven' for brave warriors slain in battle.

valr (VAWL) – NORTHERN. 'Slayer.'

Valkyrie (VAWL-kerr-ee) – NORTHERN. 'Chooser of the Slain.'

Vestan (VAYST-inn) – EASTERN. 'The Westlands.'

wisule (WISS-ool) – TRADING. A foul-smelling, disease-carrying breed of rodents which has many offspring because the adults will abandon them when threatened.

PLACES

Northlands

The area north of the Weathered Mountains and west of the Great Frenum Range. The Northmen live in eighteen tribes, each with its own town surrounded by forest and farmland. The boundaries change, and the map is correct for the year 11,240.

Asci (ASS-kee) – Home to the Ascai. Patron god: Aegir.

Blathe (BLAYTHE-eh) – Home to the Blathe. Patron god: Aegir.

Drymir (DRY-meer) – Home to the Drymirians. Patron god: Frey.

Devil's Island – An island in the Amirannak. A home to the Renshai after their exile.

Dvaulir (Dwah-LEER) – home to the Dvaulirians. Patron god: Thor.

Erd (URD) – Home to the Erdai. Patron goddess: Freya.

Farbutiri (Far-byu-TEER-ee) – Home to the Farbui. Patron god: Aegir.

Gilshnir (GEELSH-neer) – Home to the Gilshni. Patron god: Tyr.

Gjar (GYAR) – Home to the Gjar. Patron god: Heimdall.

Kor N'rual (KOR en-ROOL) – Sacred crypts near Nordmir.

Nordmir (NORD-meer) – The Northland's high kingdom. Home to the Nordmirians. Patron god: Odin.

Othkin (OTH-keen) – Home to the Othi. Patron god and goddess: Aegir & Frigg.

Renshi (Ren-SHEE) – Original home of the Renshai, now a part of Thortire. Patron goddess and god: Sif & Modi.

Shamir (Sha-MEER) – Home of the Shamirians. Patron goddess: Freya.

Skrytil (SKRY-teel) – Home of the Skrytila. Patron god: Thor.

Svelbni (SWELL-nee) – Home of the Svelbnai. Patron god: Baldur.

Talmir (TAHL-meer) – Home of the Talmirians. Patron god: Frey.

Thortire (Thor-TEER-eh) – Home of the Thortirians. Patron god: Thor.

Ti (TEE) – The original name for Devil's Island.

Varli (VAR-lee) – Home of the Varlians. Patron god and goddess: Frey & Freya.

Vikerin (Vee-KAIR-in) – Home of the Vikerians. Patron god: Thor.

Westlands

The Westlands are bounded by the Great Frenum Mountains to the east, the Weathered Mountains to the north, and the sea to the west and south. In general, the cities become larger and more civilized as the land sweeps westward. The central area is packed with tiny farm towns dwarfed by lush farm fields that, over time, have nearly coalesced. The easternmost portions of the Westland are forested, with sparse towns and rare barbarian tribes. To the south lies an uninhabited tidal plain.

Ahktar (AHK-tar) – One of the largest central farm towns.

Auer (OUR) – A small town in the eastern section.

Béarn (Bay-ARN) – The high kingdom. A mountain city.

Bellenet Fields (Bell-e-NAY) – A tourney field in Erythane.

Bruen (Broo-EN) – A medium-sized city near Pudar.

Corpa Bickat (KORE-pa Bi-KAY) – A large city.

Corpa Leukenya (KORE-pa Loo-KEN-ya) – Home of the cult of the white bird, created by Siderin.

Corpa Schaull (KORE-pa Shawl) – A medium-sized city; one of the 'Twin Cities' (see Frist).

The Dun Stag – A Pudarian tavern famous for its ale and frequented by travelers and merchants.

Erythane (AIR-eh-thane) – A large city closely allied with Béarn. Famous for its knights.

The Fields of Wrath – Plains near Erythane. Home to the Western Renshai.

Frist (FRIST) – A medium-sized city; one of the 'Twin Cities' (see Corpa Schaull).

Granite Hills – A small, low range of mountains.

Great Frenum Mountains (FREN-um) – Towering, impassable mountains that divide the Eastlands from the Westlands and Northlands.

Greentree – A tiny farm town.

The Hungry Lion – A Pudarian tavern frequented by locals.

Iaplege (EE-a-pleej) – A secret gathering place of cripples, criminals, and outcasts.

The Knight's Rest – An inn in Erythane.

Loven (Low-VENN) – A medium-sized city.

The Merchant's Haven – The inn in Wynix.

Myrcidë (Meer-si-DAY) – A town of legendary wizards, now in ruins.

Porvada (Poor-VAH-da) – A medium-sized city.

Pudar (Poo-DAR) – The largest city of the West; the great trade center.

The Road of Kings – The legendary route by which the Eastern Wizard is believed to have rescued the high king's heir after a bloody coup.

Town of Santagithi – A medium-sized town, relatively young.

Shidrin (SHIH-drin) – A farm town.
Sholton-Or (SHOLE-tin OR) – A Western farm town.
Strinia (STRINN-ee-a) – A small, barbarian settlement.
The Western Plains – A barren salt flat.
Wolf Point – A rock formation in the forest surrounding Erythane.
Wynix (Why-NIX) – A farm town.

Eastlands

The area east of the Great Frenum Mountains. It is a vast, overpopulated wasteland filled with crowded cities and eroded fields. Little forest remains.
LaZar the Decadent (LA-zar) – A poor, dirty city.
Rock of Peace – A stone near the road from Rozmath to Stalmize where the bard, Mar Lon, preached peace.
Rozmath (ROZZ-mith) – A medium-sized city.
Stalmize (STAHL-meez) The Eastern high kingdom.
Tower of Night – A single, black tower originally built by Carcophan's magic, then rebuilt with normal materials

BODIES OF WATER

Amirannak Sea (A-MEER-an-nak) – The Northernmost ocean.
Brunn River (BRUN) – A muddy river in the Northlands.
Conus River (KONE-uss) – A shared river of the Eastlands and Westlands.
Icy River – A cold, Northern river.
Jewel River – One of the rivers that flows to Trader's Lake.
Perionyx River – (Peh-ree-ON-ix) – A Western river.
Southern Sea – The southernmost ocean.
Trader's Lake – A harbor for trading boats in Pudar.
Trader's River – The Main route for overwater trade.

OBJECTS

Cardinal Wizards – A system of balance created by Odin in the beginning of time, consisting of four, near-immortal, opposing guardians of evil, neutrality, and goodness who are tightly constrained by Odin's laws.
Flanner's bane – A demon.
The Pica Stone (PIE-ka) – A clairsentient sapphire. One of the rare

items with magical power.

The Seven Tasks of Wizardry – A series of tasks designed by the gods to test the power and worth of the Cardinal Wizards' chosen successors.

Swords of Power – Three magical swords crafted by the Cardinal Wizards and kept on the plain of Chaos except when in the hands of a Wizard's champion. It is prophesied that the world will end if all three are brought into the world at once. (see Ristoril, Morshock, and Harval.)

LINES OF THE CARDINAL WIZARDS

Western

Reign	Name	Sex	Apprenticeship	Notes
0–747	Rudigar	male	——	
747–1167	Montroy	male	695–747	
1167–1498	Jaela	female	1122–1167	
1498–2013	Melandry	female	1460–1498	
2013–2632	Dorn	male	1977–2013	
2632–2933	Tellyn	male	2599–2632	
2933–3759	Dane	male	2880–2933	
3759–4741	Annika	female	3705–3759	
4741–5085	Niejal	male	4691–4741	*
5085–5633	Bael	male	5020–5085	
5633–6236	Renata	female	5602–5633	
6236–6535	Caulin	male	6178–6236	
6535–7455	Sonjia	female	6500–6535	
7455–7926	Sudyar	male	7406–7455	**
7926–8426	Shelvyan	male	7878–7926	
8426–8814	Natalia	female	8380–8426	
8814–9522	Rebah	female	8771–8814	
9522–10,194	Muir	female	9476–9522	
10,194–10,556	Vikeltrin	male	10,146–10,194	
10,556–11,225	Tokar	male	10,500–10,556	

*Insane
**No contact with other wizards

Eastern

Reign	Name	Sex	Apprenticeship	Notes
0–636	Kadira	female	—	
636–934	Rhynnel	female	601–636	
934–1299	Raf	male	897–934	
1299–2086	Aklir	male	1258–1299	
2086–2988	Trinn	female	2057–2086	
2988–3319	Gherhan	male	2940–2988	*
3319–3768	Benghta	female	3317–3319	
3768–4278	Shorfin	male	3742–3768	
4278–4937	Annber	female	4246–4278	
4937–5439	MiKay	male	4900–4937	
5439–5818	Takian	male	5400–5439	
5818–6298	Seguin	male	5788–5818	
6298–6657	Resa	female	6265–6298	
6657–7221	Elcott	male	6612–6657	
7221–7665	L'effrich	female	7180–7221	
7665–7971	Dandriny	female	7640–7665	
7971–8289	Mylynn	male	7941–7971	
8289–9083	Ascof	male	8243–8289	**
9098–9426	Pinahar	male	—	
9426–9734	Jalona	female	9389–9426	***
9734–10,221	Zibetha	female	9700–9734	
10,221–10,737	Drero	male	10,187–10,221	****
10,737–11,126	Donnell	male	10,700–10,737	
11,126–	Shadimar	male	11,100–11,126	

*killed by demon
**killed by demon
***built the escape route from Béarn's castle
****established the bards as the Béarnian kings' personal bodyguards

Northern

Reign	Name	Sex	Apprenticeship	Notes
0–790	Tertrilla	female	—	
790–1276	Mendir	male	743–790	
1276–1897	Reeguar	male	1217–1276	
1897–2739	Ranulf	male	1848–1897	
2739–3138	Chane	male	2688–2739	
3138–3614	Sigrid	female	3087–3138	
3614–4128	Quisiria	female	3570–3614	
4128–4792	Brill	male	4083–4128	
4792–5289	Xansiki	female	4751–4792	
5289–5854	Johirild	male	5254–5289	
5854–6531	Disa	female	5813–5854	
6531–7249	Tagrin	male	6492–6531	
7249–7747	Elthor	male	7202–7249	
7747–8369	Frina	female	7700–7747	
8369–8954	Yllen	female	8312–8369	
8954–9628	Alengrid	female	8922–8954	
9628–10,244	Sval	male	9590–9628	
10,244–10,803	Giddrin	male	10,210–10,244	
10,803–	Trilless	female	10,762–10,803	

Southern

Reign	Name	Sex	Apprenticeship	Notes
0–810	Havlar	male	—	
810–1306	Kaffrint	male	767—810	
1306–1821	Pelchrin	male	1270–1306	
1821–2798	Schatza	female	1762–1821	
2798–3510	Ocrell	male	2750–2798	
3510–4012	Laurn	male	3461–3510	
4012–4690	Quart	male	3954–4012	*
4690–5189	Ufi	male	4687–4690	
5189–5925	Achorfin	female	5130–5189	
5925–6617	Mir	female	5872–5925	
6617–7217	Nalexia	male	6574–6617	
7217–7793	Buchellin	male	7177–7217	
7793–8508	Amta	male	7747–7793	
8508–8991	Kaleira	female	8450–8508	
8991–9614	Zittich	male	8940–8991	
9614–10,284	Pladnor	male	9565–9614	
10,284–11,002	Bontu	male	10,220–10,284	
11,002–	Carcophan	male	10,968–11,002	

*killed by Ristoril